October the First
Is Too Late

Fawcett Crest Books by Fred Hoyle and John Elliot:

A FOR ANDROMEDA

ANDROMEDA BREAKTHROUGH

October the First
Is Too Late

FRED HOYLE

A FAWCETT CREST BOOK

Fawcett Publications, Inc., Greenwich, Conn.
Member of American Book Publishers Council, Inc.

Library of Congress Catalog Card Number: 66-20764

PRINTING HISTORY
Harper & Row edition published July 6, 1966
First printing, March 1966
Second printing, August 1966

Selection of Doubleday Science Fiction Book Club, November 1966

First Fawcett Crest Printing, July 1968

Published by Fawcett World Library
67 West 44th Street, New York, N. Y. 10036
Printed in the United States of America

To the Reader

The "science" in this book is mostly scaffolding for the story, story-telling in the traditional sense. However, the discussions of the significance of time and of the meaning of consciousness are intended to be quite serious, as also are the contents of chapter fourteen.

Fred Hoyle

I HAD been invited to compose a piece for the Festival of Contemporary Music, Cologne, 1966. My intention was a set of variations in serial form. I chose the serial formula, partly as a technical exercise, partly because I had a fancy to end each variation with the sound of a farmyard animal.

The first three variations went smoothly enough but I got stuck on the fourth. I decided a change of air was needed to get me out of the rut. My decision to go for a week down to Cornwall was the trifling beginning of a sequence of momentous events. It was as if I had crossed a more or less flat watershed that nevertheless separates rivers flowing to quite different oceans.

I was lying on the clifftops in the sunshine trying to puzzle out exactly how one might imitate the whinny of a horse. I must have dozed off to sleep for perhaps ten minutes. I woke with a tremendous tune, the melody of a lifetime, running in my head. It flowed on and on, statement and response, question and answer, seemingly without end. It began with a series of rocking chords in the bass. Then the first phrase came in the treble. From there on it took off with a momentum that never seemed to die, the kind of *perpetuum mobile* you get in the first movement of the sixth Brandenburg concerto. Quickly, I scribbled the cascade of notes on a piece of score paper, for this was not a case in which I dare trust to memory. How inevitable a melody is while you have it running in your head, how difficult to recapture once it has gone.

On the way back to my lodging at a local farmhouse I passed several horses grazing but the thought of my fourth variation was gone now. Late into the night I pondered on the ramifications of that tune. It is rare indeed for a long melody to go well with harmony. To produce striking orchestral effects one normally uses a mixture of several scraps of melody, mere fragments. But this case seemed different. Orchestral ideas grew naturally around it. The instruments thundered in my head, their individual qualities, their distinctive tones, became ever more clear, ever sharper. The people of the farm must have thought me a queer fish, I dare say. I sat all day writing for the fever of creation was on me. By the end of the week the piece was essentially finished. There was still routine work to do but nothing more.

I was already on my way back to London before the problem of the Festival recurred to me. It was obvious the variations would never be finished in time. It wasn't just a week that was lost. In the past few days I had burnt up a couple of months of normal effort. I wondered about using the new piece. Reason told me no, emotion told me yes. I desperately wanted to hear the new sounds from the orchestra. I had given it everything, maximum sonority. Yet this was exactly where I would run into trouble. A considerable quantity of electronic music would quite certainly be played. My piece, coming late in the programme, would unfortunately look like an all-out attack on other composers. When compared with the full blast of the true orchestra, their stuff would inevitably sound thin and wan.

Then there were two points of conscience. I don't have any rooted objection to the *avant garde*. While the new fashions have nothing very great to recommend them, they do at least contribute *something* to music. Classical methods work wonderfully well for the positive emotions, for sentiments of epic proportions. But the less pleasant emotions cannot be described at all in classical terms. It was beyond the resources of even the greatest of the old musicians to display genuine anger for instance. So really I had no quarrel with modern styles as such. My quarrel was with a fashion that claimed those styles to be everything, as if a craftsman were to insist on always working with a single tool.

My second worry was whether my piece could really be described as "contemporary." Of course it was contemporary in the sense that it was recent, not more than a week old, but there is a sense in which the word represents form and technique rather than chronology.

The choice evidently lay between withdrawing and going ahead with the new piece. After something of a struggle with myself I decided to go ahead. There was a lot to be done, parts to be copied, and then mailed away to Germany. The orchestra was to be the Mannheim Symphony.

The journey to Cologne was uneventful. Two rehearsals were scheduled for me. After a few misunderstandings I managed to get the playing into tolerable shape. My time was an evening of the second week. As it came round I was motivated in the following way. My thoughts on the piece had dulled in the intervening weeks but the sound of the orchestra re-awakened something of the fury I had felt in that week in Cornwall. This, and the fact that several people had heard my rehearsals and had already spread critical rumours, put me in a combative state of mind by the time I walked on to the platform to conduct.

All worries disappeared at the first surge of the music. For the next seventeen minutes I was totally committed to the vision I had had on those faraway Cornish cliffs. In rehearsal I deliberately held the orchestra back. When an orchestra becomes excited with a new work it is good policy to wait until the first actual performance before giving them their full head. I not only gave it them now, I drove them with an intensity I had never shown before. In a sense it comes ill of a composer to speak well of his own work; but it is all so far back now that I think I can be reasonably objective. As the melody surged into the final fanfare I knew I had in no way disgraced myself. I also knew I had contributed little to music except a stirring fifteen minutes or so. The musician's problem is stated very simply: how to display the more worthwhile aspects of human nature differently from the old masters. Modern styles have concentrated in part on the meaner side of things, as I have already remarked, in part on the purely abstract. Modern styles are no solution to the problem but neither was my piece. It was an extrapolation of the old methods. It faced the challenge of comparison with the composers of the past—for fifteen minutes. It pointed no way to anybody else.

This criticism I would have been entirely willing to accept if the audience had admitted the straightforward merit of what had been done. They didn't. There was scattered applause mixed with boos and hisses. Momentarily nonplussed I failed to take a quick bow and to make a quick exit. The hissing increased. Suddenly I became coldly angry. With an imperious gesture I turned to the leader and shouted loudly, "Bar one!" Such is the respect of a German orchestra for its conductor that the players all obediently turned back to the beginning. Before anybody in the audience realized what was going to happen the rolling bass chords started again. The shouting behind me held its own for a little while until the orchestra picked up volume. Then as the full chords broke loose the mob amounted to little more than a whisper in a storm. At the end they had their say, or rather their shout. This time it was quite full blooded. I was in no doubt of what to do. I bowed around the hall twice, shook the leader's hand, patted him on the shoulder, and walked out.

As I made my way back to the hostel I fully intended to quit Cologne the following morning. Yet when morning came I saw no reason to run away like a whipped dog. I found it much easier to behave normally, as if nothing had happened, than I would have expected. My fellow musicians were only meeting me in small numbers at a time now. Perhaps for this reason they had lost something of the confidence of the evening before. Several of the critics went out of their way to tell me, more or less out of the back of the hand, how much they had enjoyed my piece. Well, well. I remembered being told, as a youngster, that if universal approbation represented a hundred per cent on a scale of appreciation, then to be universally well known, but disliked, was already worth fifty per cent. To be entirely unknown corresponded to the zero mark.

I did leave the Festival two days before its end, not under any compulsion, but because I got bored. Two weeks of cater-wauling was more than I could take. So midway through the afternoon I found myself at the airport. It chanced that Alex Hamilton had decided to get out too. We travelled back to-gether. Alex is the untypical Scot. He has a remarkable gift for floating through life. His musical style is modern, abstract, technically very good. His great gift, outside music, lies in avoiding doing the things he doesn't want to do. He couldn't understand why I had gone so deliberately out of my way to make trouble for myself. He didn't criticize me directly. We sat together, Alex making lighter conversation than I was able to do myself. Every now and then he would stop talking and begin shaking with silent laughter. I stood it as long as I could and then said, "I'm glad you think it funny." It wasn't a very worthwhile remark but it sent him into still more violent con-tortions. Then he patted me on the shoulder and said, "It was marvellous, just marvellous."

We got into London airport more or less on time. Quickly we were into the reception hall and through immigration. Then came an unconscionably long wait in the customs hall. If the trend towards faster aircraft goes on long enough we shall end up by taking more time to unload the baggage than for the flight, I thought grumpily. A sudden slap on the back caused me to turn sharply, a cross look still on my face. It was a slim dark-haired man in his early thirties. Recognition came in perhaps half a second. "Thank goodness it's you," he said, "for a second I thought I might have slapped the wrong back."

It was John Sinclair. We'd been at school together. We had

won scholarships to Cambridge in the same year, his in mathematics, mine in music. Besides his mathematics Sinclair had a natural liking for music. In our university days I was as much interested in the piano itself as in composition. The larger part of my musical education I got outside the lecture-room, by playing great quantities of music. I developed in those days the habit of riding through a composer's works totally, symphonies, quartets, as well as straight piano music. John Sinclair used to spend many a spare hour in my rooms.

We were both interested in mountains. Already at school we had been out on one or two walking tours together. We kept it going at university. At the end of our third year we made a great trip to Skye. A party of four of us camped in Glen Brittle. We had a magnificent couple of weeks climbing in the Cuillin. The penultimate day was very wet. We spent it in the tents, cooking and talking. Our talk centered on what we were going to do the following year. Sinclair and I came to the tentative conclusion that we'd make a trip to the remarkable sandstone mountains of the extreme northwest. This plan never came to fruition. I won a scholarship to Italy in the following year. By the time I returned Sinclair was away in the United States. Although we had only met twice in the intervening years I had followed his career with more than a passing interest. The Royal Society just managed to scramble him into its Fellow-ship, at the age of twenty-nine, in time to forestall the award of a Nobel Prize. I followed what was going on as best I could in magazines like the *New Scientist* and the *Scientific American*. I knew he had contributed a decisive step in the physics of elementary particles, something of a highly algebraic nature.

I made the introductions.

"Where are you in from?"

"New York. And you?"

"We're just back from Cologne. Music Festival."

Our bags came at last. Alex and I checked them through customs. I said to him, "Let's wait." It was some minutes be-fore Sinclair joined us. "How about a taxi into town, and hav-ing dinner together?" he said. This was fine by me. I'd been a little shy suggesting it. When you haven't seen a man for six years, when he's gone a long way in those six years, you never know exactly where you stand. But it seemed that John hadn't changed much, in spite of his towering success. He was thinner now than he used to be, and I would have said he'd got a slightly worried look about him. We took a taxi to my place, ostensibly for a drink. We had several drinks.

11

Dinner began to seem less important. Alex had developed quite a sway. He sat firmly down in the largest chair, gave a flowing gesture, with the hand that was not holding a glass, and said, "Music."

"What? Any preferences anybody?"

"Anything, anything you like." He turned to John, "We don't have preferences, do we? What we want is music!"

I had not the slightest idea of what was going to come out as my hands came down on the keyboard. It was a Chopin nocturne, one I couldn't recall having played for years. True I used to go quite a lot for Chopin in my late teens. Quite a bit has been written on the techniques of seduction. My not very humble submission is that most of such stuff is plain nonsense. For every girl of eighteen who can be broken down by feats of muscle power on the football field there are ten who will swoon into your arms at the sound of a Chopin waltz or mazurka. I have no doubt the same system works just as well at later ages, but for me at least it had come to seem too cheap and easy. Seducing a girl with your own music is all fair and aboveboard. Doing it with someone else's had come to seem not quite proper, like hooting a sitting bird, or fishing with maggots. Anyway, out came the nocturne, somewhere from my subconscious memory. The alcohol stopped any worries about forgetting the way it went. As the piece glided to its end I had the feeling I had never played Chopin more perfectly. No doubt this was the effect of the alcohol too. Yet it is a mistake to think in terms of absolutes. It's the way you feel, the way your audience feels, that really counts. Alex was getting quite high now, "More Choppy, please. More Choppy."

They kept me at it for two solid hours. Whenever I tried to leave the stool Alex would have none of it. "Keep playing," he yodelled. Where the stuff came from I simply couldn't say. It just seemed to well up in the fingers. There was a great mazurka. I couldn't even remember its number. The notes came unbidden. I began a piece which at first I couldn't place. Then I realized this was the calm beginning of the tremendous polonaise-fantaisie. For a while I had fears I could never remember the magnificent second half. Then I began to listen intently to the music itself. I became lost in it. Not until my fingers came down on the final crashing chord was I aware of any passage of time. They were both on my shoulder now. For a moment I thought Alex was going to weep. I jumped up and said firmly, "Time for food."

There were eggs in the refrigerator. Within twenty minutes we had a big omelette all piping hot on the table. John and I ate while Alex talked, his mouth full the whole while. Somehow it sounded very witty. Wit, like love, evidently lies in the ear of the listener. We had some fresh fruit. Then I went off to make coffee.

When I came back Alex was nowhere to be seen.

"He's gone, apparently."

That was Alex all over. He had the gift of appearing out of nowhere and of disappearing without the slightest explanation. He was the nearest human embodiment of the Cheshire cat I had ever met.

"Has he really gone?" asked John.

"Oh yes. He never goes in any other way."

"What an odd fellow. Well, Dick, how have you been these last few years?"

Perhaps I should explain that I was christened Richard and that my nose, broken in a boyhood accident, somehow dominates my appearance. With this formality out of the way, let me return to my story.

We settled ourselves comfortably as we drank our coffee. The conversation turned naturally on memories and anecdotes of our earlier years. No third person would have been much interested in the talk. By the time we had done it was half past one. I didn't know where John had been intending to stay the night but it was obvious that he should occupy my spare room. I got out towels and bed linen. Half an hour later I was asleep, blissfully unaware of the strange events that even the near future was to reveal.

WE were nearly through breakfast the following morning when John said, "How about it?"

"How about what?"

"The trip we once planned to the north-west. Liathach, An Teallach, Suilven, and the rest of 'em."

"When?"

"As soon as you're ready."

"I'm ready now. What shall we go in?"

"I can borrow a car easily enough."

"That wasn't what I was thinking. This time of year the hotels in the Highlands are certain to be full."

John thought about this for a minute and got up from the table. "I'll see what I can do. Where's the phone?"

It was half an hour before he reappeared. "Well, it's all fixed."

"What?"

"I've got hold of a caravan with a car to pull it."

It wasn't a very great achievement, not for a Nobel laureate, but he seemed quite proud of it.

After breakfast John went out, took a taxi, and disappeared. I set about cleaning up. I telephoned a few people to say I would be away for about ten days. Then I searched for my boots and other items of mountain equipment. The boots looked just about serviceable. I hadn't kept them as carefully as they deserved. Rucksack, a bit of rope, anorak, socks, breeches, I scattered them over the floor. I packed and was ready when John returned. It was nearly one o'clock by the time we headed our outfit through St John's Wood on to the A1.

The journey to the north became an unmitigated bore. It was dark when we reached Scotch Corner. We turned off the fast highway, taking the smaller cross-country road to Penrith. By the time we reached Brough we had both had enough. So we drove away on the moorland road which leads from Brough to Middleton. It was certain there would be patches of open ground on which we could park the caravan for the night. So it proved, after we had climbed up towards the moors for maybe a couple of miles. We ate a simple but ample meal from provisions we had bought on the way. A mug of tea each, with a big dollop of rum in it, was the last manœuvre before getting down into our bags.

There was a good deal of rain in the night, so we had no great hopes for the weather the following morning. But when I put on the kettle at about six o'clock it didn't look too bad. Although there was mist on the high ground it seemed as if the rain might hold off. I woke John with a cup of tea and asked him how he would feel about stretching his legs. He said that would be fine, so I cooked about six slices of bacon. Instead of eating it there and then we wrapped it in a piece of aluminum foil. This, a knife, a loaf of bread, and a hunk of cake, went into a rucksack. By a quarter to seven we were away. We took the car along the road until John, who was studying the map, announced that the point of attack had been reached. We laughed at the thought of an attack on Mickle Fell. Yet we knew, gentle as the hill might be so far as height was concerned, there would be plenty of really hard walking before we reached the top. Hard because the ground was broken by big tussocks and by peat hags. The mist wouldn't make navigating easy.

We made the top of a little ridge. The line ahead didn't look right to John. It was characteristic of him that he wouldn't move on until we had fixed the exact point where we were now standing. It was pretty damp. I began to grow cold as we argued. At last we had the contours on the map fitted correctly to the mile or so of country we could see ahead. It was now clear what the trouble was. We hadn't started at quite the point we intended. We had left the car almost a mile short of the right spot. John grumbled to himself, to the effect that he must be losing his grip. Next we got into an argument about which was the best line to take, not so much from a point of view of arriving at the top, but of avoiding the worst of the broken ground. We decided to move leftward in order to avoid the green soggy depression below us. After about half an hour we came on a wire fence that seemed to lead in the right direction. Looking at the map it occurred to me that it might mark the boundary between Westmorland and Yorkshire. If it did it would lead us to exactly where we wanted to be. The time seemed about right for breakfast. We cut two or three slices of bread, munched up the bacon, and started off again, each with a lump of cake in his hand.

We made good progress along the fence because the ground was somewhat smoother along its line than it was in open country. About eight o'clock the mists lifted. Mickle Fell was dead ahead of us. Now it was only a simple walk to the top. As soon as we were on the limestone, or what seemed to be limestone, there was a delightful change of vegetation. Gone was the acid peat bog. Now we had grass beneath our feet and sheep were grazing on the long back of the fell. We made quick progress to the east down a longish ridge to a mine perched near a lake under the hillside. By eleven o'clock we were on the road again.

We were anxious to continue our journey to the north as soon as possible. It was nearly three miles back to the car, the best part of an hour's walk, so we decided to try to get a lift from a passing motorist. Because there wasn't too much traffic, and because most cars might only have room for one of us, we split up. I went about four hundred yards ahead, climbed up a steep little bank and lay out on its top, leaving John to deal with the motorists. Within ten minutes he had a lift. He gave a triumphant wave as the car passed by. We had been wise for there certainly wasn't room in it for me.

The minutes lengthened to half an hour. Every so often a car came around a corner in the road about two hundred yards ahead of my little bank. I could hear them before they came into view. Each one I expected to be ours. An hour went by and still no sign of John. Obviously our borrowed car had failed to start. There was nothing for it but to walk after all. As I stumped the hard road I wished I had not given John my rucksack, not because it was heavy, but because I could have changed into rubbers and then I could have trotted the distance in twenty minutes or so.

The car was there, exactly as we had left it. John was not to be seen, plainly he had gone for help, probably to a garage in Brough. I sat down to wait and another hour went by. What the hell was going on? Why hadn't John left a note, or left the keys so that at least I could get into the damned car? I began to curse these impractical scientists. Reluctantly I set off to walk the further mile to the caravan. John had the key to that too but we had left a window open and I managed to climb in without much trouble. Thereafter, I washed and tried to soothe my nerves with a big pot of tea and a further chunk of cake.

But this wasn't funny any more. By three o'clock I was striding my way into Brough in a high old temper. I found two garages and drew a blank at both. It was another hour before

16

I could persuade a mechanic to drive me to our car. He somehow opened it and soon had the engine going. I paid him £1 and he drove away plainly thinking I was daft. What to do now? I had heard of motorists in the United States who gave a lift and then beat up and robbed their unsuspecting passenger but I could recall no such case in Britain. Yet something like this must have happened. I drove to the place where we had come down off the ridge of Mickle Fell, then back again the whole six miles to Brough, very slowly. At that stage I reported the whole business to a police sergeant. He took it all down in a grave manner which I suspected to be routine. He asked where I was staying and I told him the position of the caravan up on the moor. The police, he said, would get on to the matter immediately and someone would come up to the caravan as soon as they had any information.

There was nothing to be done now but drive back to the van. It was coming up to six o'clock by the time I got there. I was in two minds about cooking dinner. Underneath I was hungry but the worry of the situation dulled my appetite. I decided to stretch out on a bunk for half an hour or so before starting preparations for a meal. As far as I was aware this was exactly what I did. It wasn't until I had eaten and washed up that I saw from my watch it was already nine o'clock. Shortly after, there came a powerful knock at the van door.

It was an inspector in plain clothes, from which I guessed this had become a CID matter. He asked me a lot of questions about myself. They were not taking John's disappearance lightly now. His reputation as a scientist would in itself have forced them to take it seriously but I suspected there might also be a security aspect to the matter. Hence the questions about myself. I guessed the police wanted to satisfy themselves that I had no part in the business, whatever it was. After about an hour of the questioning the man prepared to leave. I remembered to check my watch with his before he did so. There was nothing wrong with it.

Darkness came on and I settled down for the night. If I had been thoroughly fit I suppose I would quickly have fallen asleep. Now I tossed around uneasily wondering about John Sinclair. Of course I didn't know much about him as he was now, only as he used to be. It certainly seemed as if the intervening years had never existed. We had resumed the old free and easy days of school and university. Yet the intervening years were real enough. John's life must have become more complicated, professionally and socially, than it was when I knew him. To me he might seem the same person but to the world at large this would not be so. These speculations, sensible enough in themselves, got me nowhere.

Suddenly my attention was caught by approaching footsteps. I wriggled out of my bag, found a box of matches and started to light the little gas lamp over the kitchen stove. I was still fumbling when the door opened. Then the light came on and I saw it was John, his face not a foot from mine. The slightly worried look, which I had already remarked the first evening, was more obvious now.

"Where in the hell have you been?" I asked.

He came into the van, slumped on to his bunk, and began to unlace his boots.

"I haven't the slightest idea, Dick. That's the truth."

It was my impulse to press the matter further. But if what John said was indeed true, if he really had no idea what had happened, it was pointless to argue. Probably it was some kind of blackout. I didn't know whether he had become subject to temporary losses of memory but it was at least a possible explanation. Hard exercise, taken suddenly without any previous training, might have brought on some kind of attack. Anyway he was safe, which was the main thing.

"Hungry?"

"Devilishly so."

I had a feeling that what he wanted was silence and food. I wasn't averse to another snack myself. With an impressive display of energy I had the table set. Wild and wonderful smells pervaded the caravan within a few minutes. John ate more or less silently. I had a big mug of tea and a piece of cake. I told John about the police. With his agreement I drove to a phone box about half a mile down the road. I put through a 999 call telling the constable on duty that John had turned up and that he seemed to have suffered a temporary amnesia but was quite recovered now. When I returned to the caravan I found him in a deep sleep.

We were very late up the following morning. Partly for this reason, and partly because we had another visit from the inspector, it was on midday before we resumed our journey to the north. What was said between John and the inspector I do not know. They went off for a walk together, returning after about an hour, an hour which I spent cleaning up the van. At all events the inspector seemed satisfied now, which was all that seemed to matter.

We took the outfit straight through the centre of Glasgow. Because we were slow-moving this was probably the quickest way. We managed to find the road to Loch Lomond without

18

much difficulty. We passed various camping sites intent on reaching Glencoe if we possibly could. It seemed a long pull up to Crianlarich and the distance to Tyndrum was somewhat longer than I remembered it. Then we were out on to the beginning of Rannoch Moor. John who was driving muttered something about the caravan being wrong. The outfit began to weave rather violently. He brought it to a quick halt. Inspection showed a puncture on the nearside back wheel of the car. As we got out the jack and spare wheel clouds of midges descended on us in their thousands. We were back in Scotland. It took less than a quarter of an hour to change that wheel. Yet we were practically eaten alive.

We had been fighting time to get to Glencoe in the light. I knew the exact spot where I wanted to go, on to the old road which crosses the new road about two miles the other side of Kingshouse Inn. By the time we reached the place the last of the light was gone. It was impossible to execute any complicated movement with the caravan. All we could do was simply drive straight ahead on to the old road. This meant the caravan would be the wrong way round for making an exit. We would have to turn it by hand. Worse, the car was wedged in on the wrong side. After uncoupling, there was no possibility, because of the narrowness of the road, the unsurfaced old road, of getting it back on to the highway. We would need the car itself the following morning to drive about four miles down the glen to the beginning of the ordinary route up Bidean nam Bian. Sufficient unto the day is the evil thereof.

We were early astir. After a quick cup of tea, cooking bacon, packing the rucksack, it was still only six a.m. by the time we were ready to be off. The morning was perfect, not a cloud in the sky. But now we had to tackle the problem of the car. The simplest solution seemed to be to continue along the old road, for the best part of a mile, until it joined the surfaced road again. We took it very slowly indeed. Even so it was a wild ride. This was an occasion for a jeep or a Land-Rover. There was a good deal of scraping of the undercarriage but finally we made it without incurring disaster. Ten minutes later we had parked near the rather gloomy Loch Triochtan.

The track up the mountainside appeared unpleasantly steep. Yet once we made a start it turned out to be not as bad as it looked. We followed the bed of a stream for quite a way up a little valley which lay back into the mountain more than we had expected. After maybe a mile we decided to cut out of the stream bed, up to the left. Once again the slope was not too bad. By eight o'clock we reached a little corrie which I guessed to be about a thousand feet below the summit. Ahead of us was a fine rock buttress, presumably the famous Churchdoor Buttress. In the floor of the corrie there were wonderful pools of clear cold water. It was now quite warm and we spent a good half-hour over a leisurely breakfast. For the first time we appreciated the advantages of the caravan. It was much to be preferred to a tent because of the midges. It was to be preferred to an hotel because of the wonderful early start we could make from it. Down in the hotel at Kingshouse, or at Ballachulish, we should only just now be sitting down to breakfast. It was true we *were* having breakfast, but at nearly three thousand feet, with most of the day's climbing already done.

We were off again just before nine o'clock, on to a rather loose slope of scree and broken rocks. It took us up for about five hundred feet. Then we were on the summit ridge in bright sunshine. The rocks here were firm and warm. We mounted quickly to the top. It was going to be hot and a haze was already rising. To the north the Mamores and Ben Nevis looked tremendous. To the south were the ragged peaks of Glen Etive. We had no need of hurry, we spent a good hour on the top. In my capacity as quartermaster I produced my *bonne bouche,* two tins of orange juice. Then we set off along the ridge at a steady easy pace. We went just as we felt like it, down the long shelving ridge towards Glen Etive, then up again to the beginning of the Beinn Fhada ridge. Then down a steepish short slope, up again over a couple of bumps or so, to a little col. Here our route lay down a steep, broken hillside on the left. There was roughly a thousand feet of it and it didn't look inviting, to untrained men. We had a friendly disagreement as to which was the best way down. John chose a gully between rocky walls, a kind of stone shoot. I thought the more open ground to the right would be better. When I had gone down it for perhaps a hundred feet I realized I was mistaken. As I struggled downward I lost contact with John. When I next saw him he was a long way below me, maybe two or three hundred feet. I stuck at it and at last came to where he was lying resting on a boulder. I suggested we keep going down the widish scoop that lay on our right, that it would take us down to the stream in the big corrie into which we were descending. John laughed. He asserted the scoop would take us down to a cliff edge. I couldn't see how he knew this but after my mistake on the slope above I didn't think it wise to argue.

The bottom of the corrie was an amazing affair. It looked as though it was going to be a flat bottom. Then at the last moment the hillside plunged steeply into a little gorge. The gorge ran for more than a mile along what looked like a flat valley. This was the hidden valley I had heard of many times. Whether by luck, instinct, or sheer skill, I don't know, but John led the way to a point where there was an easy breach in the cliffs where we could get down to the stream and to its opposite side on which we could see a good track.

I was hot with the ridge walk and the steep descent. I suggested we have a bathe in the stream. The idea took on. Within five minutes I was down into one of the clear pools. Being cold is a strange experience when you come to think about it. Being really cold is unpleasant but it isn't a sharp agonizing business. Cold is a stealthy, unrelenting enemy. The only pleasurable aspect of it, to my knowledge, is when you come piping hot down a mountainside and jump into a pool of icy water. The pleasure lasts no more than thirty seconds. You stick it for another minute and then out you crawl as fast as you can. This was exactly what we did. It was while we were drying off in the sunshine that the odd thing struck me. Back at school we had often stripped our shorts off after football. I knew perfectly well John had a strawberry birthmark, about the size of a half-crown, in the small of his back. There was now no trace of it.

BIRTHMARKS and suchlike, "marks prodigious" as the old wizard of Stratford had it, aren't quite the stuff of polite conversation. Back at school I would not have had the least inhibition. Now it took some effort.

"Hey, John, didn't you have a birthmark in the middle of your back?"

"Yes, of course. What of it?"

"Well, it isn't there any more."

"Of course it's there."

"I assure you it isn't."

"Must be the strong sunshine. There's no contrast out here."

We made our way to the throat of the valley. There was an amazing tangle of great boulders. Threading our way through them we came to easy slopes of grass that led down into Glencoe itself. When we were back in camp I put the kettle on for the much needed cup of tea.

John said, "You'd better check that mark."

I had been right. There wasn't the least trace of it. Foolishly, I said, "You haven't had it removed or anything?"

"Of course I haven't."

John made no further comment. His face was knit in a tense expression, one I had seen often enough before when he was engaged on some awkward problem. I knew better than to ask him to explain. He scribbled on a big scratch pad as we drank our tea.

I left him at it and drove down the valley to the sea. I took the left fork towards Port Appin. I didn't quite know what to make of John and his troubles so I put them out of my mind as best I could. I began wondering about the possibilities of a sea symphony. It was certainly an idea but perhaps not a very good one. There is of course great beauty and drama in the sea. Yet the subject is unattractively amorphous, far removed from human problems. In a way it seemed just an escape formula, an excuse for a display of flashing orchestral effects. I doubted whether there was much more scope in this direction.

It was half past six when I returned to the van. John was still figuring. I poured both of us a generous woof of a drink. By the time we were through it I said we'd better be off to the hotel at Ballachulish unless he was keen to cook the dinner.

"Let's go then. I want to use the phone."

I hadn't expected the hotel to be so full. With mild apprehension I asked if they could manage dinner for the two of us. A woman said she would see and would we like a drink in the meantime? We had the drink and the woman came back. Yes, they could manage dinner but we'd have to wait until about a quarter past eight.

"I'll do my phoning now," grunted John when she'd gone.

He left me in a milling crowd, apparently talking for the most part about their experiences on the road. There seemed not the slightest appreciation of the magic of a wonderful day spent in one of the most beautiful places on Earth. At half past seven somebody started bashing away at a gong. All but three or four of the company drifted out of the bar. There was an upright piano along one side of the room. I opened the lid and fingered the keys in an idle fashion. "Do you play?" asked a middle-aged woman. For answer I pulled up a chair and settled into a number from one of the latest shows. The piano was of the honky-tonk variety which I never can resist. It was gloriously out of tune. I meandered through two or three numbers and they loved it. The woman's husband, or so I took him to be, said, "Have a drink?" I asked for half a pint of bitter. I was sipping it, making polite conversation, when John returned. I could judge nothing from his face.

At last our turn for dinner came round, none too soon, for I was hungry. We were put at a table by ourselves.

"Any idea of what you want to do tomorrow?" I asked.

"I'm afraid we'll have to call it off, Dick. But don't let me drag you back to London."

"Is there anything I can do?"

"Not explicitly. How are you fixed?"

"In what way?"

"Have you any engagements, ones it would be difficult to break?"

"Not really. Why?"

"I'll have to go back to the States. If you're free I'd like you to come along."

I laughed. My bank manager was just going to love the suggestion. "What would I use for money?"

"There's no problem. You travel on contract."

We closed the subject at this point until we were back in the van. Then John began, "I suppose I'd better tell you a bit of what's going on. It won't make much sense I'm afraid."

I put a pile of clothing under my pillow, to make a backrest as I stretched out on my bunk. My legs were beginning to stiffen up.

"I suppose you've followed the general outline of the things that have been turning up in space research?"

"Yes, more or less, so far as it's possible from newspaper reports."

"One of the aims of the space programme is to take a look at the outside world in unfamiliar parts of the spectrum."

"You mean things like X-rays and gamma rays?"

"That's right. But of course X-rays and gamma rays are at the high frequency end. There's a lot of stuff in the far infrared, stuff that gets absorbed in our own atmosphere just like the X-rays do. I'm talking now about wavelengths roughly a hundred times less than the shortest radio waves."

"What's the point—curiosity?"

"It started that way. The first idea was to pick up radiation from the Sun, to check that it had the intensity everybody expected it to have."

"Did it?"

"Within a reasonable margin of accuracy. It wasn't something to hold a press conference about. Yet interesting, technically. That was all, or nearly all."

"It doesn't sound as if it would make the girls swoon."

"What was odd though was that some of the electronics, not in this experiment itself you understand, but electronics connected with other things that were going on, went badly wrong. It seemed as if they were suffering from pick-up troubles. Naturally there was a hell of an inquest about it. Nothing sensible could be found. All the circumstantial evidence pointed to a modulation in the region of a hundred megacycles, a modulation on the current output from the new infra-red experiment. On the face of it this seemed impossible. Well, to cut it short, the lads just had time to modify the gadgetry before the next shot went up. The circumstantial evidence unfortunately turned out to be right. There *was* a modulation at nearly a hundred megacycles."

"Could it have been a pick-up as well?"

"Everybody felt it had to be. Well, the inquest grew now to major proportions. It was still going on when I left the States. I'm not involved myself very directly with this stuff. It happens the chap in charge of the experiment is a friend of mine. The last thing I heard was that they had a proof it wasn't the Sun itself, at least they thought so. They thought they'd demonstrated it had come from the rocket. Yet nobody had any real idea of why or how."

"You think it might be the Sun after all?"

I knew how John's mind worked, at any rate psychologically. I had a pretty good notion this was his opinion.

"I don't know—yet. Back at the hotel I put a call through to this friend. I couldn't get him personally but I got one of his chaps. They're going to ring back with some information I need tomorrow morning. Then I'll be in a much better position to say."

I lay awake that night for a long time. It astonished me how easily John had been able to fall asleep. I could hear him breathing deeply and quite regularly as if there was nothing in the world to worry about. I had a general idea of what he had told me. Yet for the life of me I couldn't see its relevance to the disturbing incidents of the last three days.

The following morning John went back to the hotel. It was half past ten by the time he came back.

"We'll have lunch at twelve. There's a plane from Glasgow to London at three o'clock. We should have time to catch it."

"How about the car and the caravan?"

"We'll take the car to Glasgow. I've made arrangements for the van to be collected from here."

"What else?"

"Can you manage the midday plane to New York on Friday?"

This would give me three days to put my affairs to rights in London. It wouldn't be easy but I could make it. "I suppose so."

"Good, I'm going to put in an hour's calculation."

John worked quickly and keenly. I could see it was nothing but algebra and arithmetic. As I watched I was struck by the difference between the mathematician and the musician. When I had worked myself with a similar intensity a few weeks ago, back in Cornwall, I had been in a kind of trance. There was nothing trance-like about John. With a swoop like an eagle he came to a stop. I didn't need to ask him if it had turned out successfully. So much was obvious. Nor did I ask him what it meant.

"Satisfied?"

"Yes." He sat for a minute and then added, "Funny."

"How?"

"The conclusion. I have demonstrated the correctness of a

25

hunch—at the expense of an appalling conclusion. Oddly enough it seems more satisfactory this way round, better than being wrong and having a sensible, straightforward answer. It shows the important thing is to know your reasoning powers work properly. *Where* they lead you is really unimportant, which I suppose is why human beings are able to achieve completely new things. Basically, it's why we're no longer swinging by our tails from trees."

That was all I got out of him.

The journey back to London was uneventful. We parted at the air terminal, each to make his own arrangements. We didn't meet again until an hour before the plane to New York was due to depart on the Friday morning.

The intervening days were busy enough for me. Actually I must admit that I was quite glad to get out of London. Frankly, I had got my personal affairs into something of a tangle. I managed to track down Alex Hamilton, not an easy exercise. I asked him to keep an eye on my place, to use it if he wanted. I told him a little of my difficulties, lest in occupying my simple apartments he should find himself assailed by too many girls on too many sides. This sent him into another of his prolonged fits of silent laughter. He asked me if I had any spare unwanted cash to lend him. I said emphatically I had not.

We grew mellow in the transatlantic plane after a couple of cocktails. The hours slipped away and John and I soon found ourselves through American immigration and customs.

We took a taxi from Kennedy airport to an hotel whose name I have forgotten. It was somewhere mid-town. At dinner that night, which we ate in a near-by restaurant, I at last got around to asking John what his plans were. He answered:

"We're going on to California as soon as I'm through the things I must do here. It'll probably take about three days. I think it's simpler if I work it out alone. Do you think you can keep yourself happy for a day or two?"

I said I had no doubt I could find plenty to do. He went on:

"I'm going to turn in pretty early tonight. I find it's a good idea to take the change of clock in at least a couple of bites."

It may seem strange that until then I had no idea of exactly where we were going. It is my practice in life to take as little account of times and schedules as I can. I like to be as little tied down by commitments. Surprises are the spice of life. Surprises rarely come to those busy fellows who are always consulting their engagement book. As I got into bed that night I had no idea what I was going to do in the next two or three days. It turned out they were quite uneventful. For one thing I felt tired, more exactly, drained of energy, I suppose by the five-hour shift in the clock.

If I had known I should never see New York again, I would have made an effort to do much more in the way of sightseeing during those three days. On the evening of the second day I found a note from John saying we were booked to San Diego on an eleven o'clock flight the following morning and that he would see me at the flight-gate half an hour before take-off.

We were met at San Diego airport by a young man, apparently a graduate student at the university. He drove us north about ten miles to an hotel in La Jolla. We were shown up to our rooms. I decided I was in need of sleep, a wise move in view of the party to which we were apparently invited that night.

I got up at about five o'clock, shaved and dressed, and then took a stroll on the beach. This was my first sight of the Pacific. I was to see much more of it in the days to come. The beach stretched to the north for a mile or so. Beyond were cliffs running into the distance as far as I could see.

A car arrived for me at half past six. The driver introduced himself—I am sorry to say I immediately forgot his name. We chatted without the least trace of embarrassment as he drove up through a complex of small roads on to the side of a steepish hill. It occurred to me that one would never have got into such an immediately casual relationship with anybody back home. We pulled up outside a single-storey house.

John had arrived already. There were one or two women there so it seemed this was to be a social occasion rather than a work conference. But the conference developed all right. If I had been more experienced in the American way of life I would have realized how inevitable this was. Work conferences always develop at every dinner party provided the men have some common interest. We started with drinks, which were enlivened by the arrival of a spritely fellow wearing an incredible hat. It was of the trilby variety. It looked as if it had been treated by being first buried in the ground for a year or two, then by being thrown as food to an army of hungry mice. His name was Art Clementi. I did not forget the name this time.

There seemed plenty to talk about. John was apparently well known in these parts, so drinks took quite a while. They dissolved imperceptibly into a buffet supper. When the women learnt I was a musician there were the usual demands that

I should play. Many musicians detest being invited to the piano at times when they feel they should be off duty. I have never developed a hard and fast dividing line between being on and off duty so playing at odd moments never worries me. I rattled off a couple of Scarlatti sonatas. Then a big fellow standing somewhat unsteadily, a glass in one hand, by the piano, said, "How about that Tchaikovsky thing?" He hummed a few notes. Evidently he meant the first piano concerto. I threw off the big opening chords and said, rather unkindly, "Now you do the orchestra." They all laughed, the big man as well, not in the least embarrassed. So I began the incredible Tchaikovsky Opus 1, No. 1, incredible because it was Tchaikovsky's first work. When I came to the storming finish I heard the big man mutter, "Christ!"

A few of the people left. The women seemed to melt away, at maybe half past ten. I noticed the time because I was beginning to feel sleepy again, in fact I was wondering how soon we would get away. Apart from John and me there were six of them. I guessed Clementi must be the friend John had spoken about back in Scotland. He wanted to know what had brought us hot-footed from England.

"Because I know where the modulation is coming from."

"Then just give us a hint," said the big man.

John was almost irritatingly precise. He took three quite simple diagrams out from his briefcase. On each there were just three lines meeting at a point. On each line there was an arrow, two pointing away from the point of intersection, the other towards it. The angles between the lines were marked.

"We've had three cases where vehicles have changed directions. In each of them I've shown the direction of the Sun, at the moment of change."

"As seen from the vehicle?"

"Right. Now you'd better check my facts because a lot depends on them."

Clementi took up the sheets, studied them, then shook his head. "We could do that tomorrow. I'm sure you'll have it right." He turned to the others and grinned, giving them a wink.

John went on, "Everybody believes something in the rocket is at fault, because the frequencies changed when the rocket changed."

"That seems to settle it."

"Then why are the frequencies somewhat different in the three cases?"

John pulled out a fourth sheet. On it were four columns,

28

three numbers in each column. He pointed to the first. "These were the frequencies on the three occasions before the change of direction was made. You see they're not the same. What should cause the difference?"

"I don't know. But for that matter why the hell is there a change whenever the course corrections are made? The mere fact there *are* changes shows there must be a connection with the rocket."

"I'm not doubting it. But the connection is with the direction of the rocket not with the electronics inside it."

Clementi winked again, not I saw by way of derision but to fire John with a little emotion. He didn't succeed. John went on in the same irritatingly precise fashion, "I'm sorry it's so triflingly simple. The whole thing turns on the direction of the rocket relative to the Sun. In the second column I've divided the frequencies in the first column by the sine of the corresponding angles. You see the numbers are still different."

"I'd expect them to be different," grunted one of the men.

"Then I noticed that if I normalized everything to the speed of the rocket something very interesting happened. The speeds were about twenty per cent different in the three cases. I took one of the three as standard and divided this time by the speeds. These are the numbers in the third column here. They're very nearly identical."

I didn't understand what all this was about. But I did see, elementary as it all looked, that it produced a sharp reaction in the local boys.

"I did exactly the same for the frequencies measured after the shifts of direction."

John produced another piece of paper, again with four columns. He pointed to the third and said, "You see they're the same, not only the same among themselves, but the same as before the changes were made."

"What's the fourth column for?" asked Clementi.

"The numbers in the fourth column are just a little more nearly equal than those in the third. The difference is very slight. It was a check, a sort of clinching factor."

"Clinching for what?"

"For the Sun. Those last figures include the Doppler shift correction, the shift due to the rocket motion in the solar direction."

There was a long silence. Then Clementi nodded gravely, "That's what I was afraid of, right from the beginning. You're telling us it's the solar radiation itself that's got this modulation on top of it. Granted you haven't gone crazy and cooked the numbers that's certainly what it looks like."

"What does it look like?" I asked.

Clementi turned on me. "It looks as if the Sun is emitting a sharply directed beam of infra-red radiation. The modulation was due to our rocket cutting across the interference fringes."

"But how the hell can the Sun be emitting a directed beam? It's impossible," burst out one of the men.

"If you'd asked me an hour ago I'd have said it was impossible. But the facts are clear. It's preposterous and outrageous but it must be true."

I could see John too was beginning to feel tired. He yawned and stretched himself and said, "Well, at least there's something to be done."

"There's a hell of a lot to be done."

"I can't see any point in having a directed beam of radiation —and this must be fantastically directional—unless it's used for transmitting information."

"By whom, for God's sake?"

"How the devil should I know. The thing to do next is to look for some intrinsic form of modulation. We've got to filter out this effect of the interference fringes. Then we must look for some genuine source modulation."

Quite spontaneously everybody began to consume strong drinks at a very rapid rate. In spite of their comparative reticence, John's disclosures, simple as they might be, had produced a profound sense of shock. I didn't understand what had been said with any great clarity so I suppose things weren't as sharp to me as they were to the others. Yet I gathered that someone, or something, was using the Sun as a signalling device.

I LAY awake for a little while that night. A remarkable conclusion had obviously been pieced together from the simplest
fragments, like a crushing position in a chess game built by
a master from a series of seemingly trifling moves. It was the
pattern, the sequence, that really counted, not the intrinsic
difficulty of any particular step. The data John had used were
no doubt well known to hundreds of people, if not to thousands,
but the relevant facts had been embedded in a million-and-one
irrelevancies.

No doubt entirely due to chance I had become involved in
a tremendous situation. It hardly needed special knowledge
to understand the implication of what I had heard. Every
single one of the men involved in tonight's discussion had
sought an alibi, either in understatement or in flippancy. They
were trying to avoid the significance of the situation. Not of
course permanently but to get themselves used to it by slow
stages.

The following day I received a cheque for $1,500, paid
on account, through the University of California. I turned
it straightaway into travellers' cheques. I hired a car from a
local agency. The next two days I spent driving along the
coast and into the back country. Possession of the car gave
me a new dimension of freedom. The effects of the journey,
particularly of the time switch, were passing off now. In
short I was beginning to enjoy myself.

On the third day I was asked to present myself at ten thirty
the following morning at such-and-such a building on the
university campus. I was shown to a pleasant office overlooking the sea. It was rather like looking down from the
Cornish cliffs, except the light was stronger here. John came
in with a man of about fifty-five. I was asked to describe
exactly what had happened on our trip to Scotland.

I gave a simple factual account, answered a few questions,
and that was that. John went out with the man. A few minutes
later he returned alone.

"Sorry, Dick, I've been so much occupied. We'll meet for dinner tonight. Not here, in Los Angeles. Let's say half past six. You've got a car?"

I nodded.

He produced a map. "This is the place here, at the intersection of Wilshire and Santa Monica Boulevards."

I drove to Los Angeles during the afternoon. It would have been quicker by the inland freeway but I decided to keep on the coast road through Long Beach. I wanted to see the various coastal places I had read about. They didn't live up to my expectations. I was glad by the time I reached Santa Monica.

I wasn't familiar with the district or with the traffic conditions. Yet it was less bewildering than I would have expected. Without too much trouble I reached the restaurant. John was late but not grossly so. Yet to be late at all was unusual for him.

"We'll get away from science for one night," he said as we sat down at a table, which he had apparently booked beforehand.

"I've been pretty hard at it ever since we got into New York. To be frank I'm damn tired."

"What's the general pitch?"

"Well, it's obvious we need a new vehicle out there with special instrumentation. There's nothing difficult in it at all. Not experimentally I mean. But it's the devil to get anything unusual done. The whole space programme is going ahead like some enormous juggernaut. Only with the highest priority can you get anything changed."

"I suppose if you know exactly what you want to do that's the most efficient way."

"If you know what you want to do, beforehand. Which of course means you're not going to find anything of very much interest."

"Did you get your way?"

"Yes, with Art's help. We've been up at JPL—the Jet Propulsion Lab all day, arguing. Once they were convinced, everything went smoothly, but they took some convincing."

"When's it going to happen?"

"More or less immediately. A new vehicle was practically ready for launching. It was designed to go a long way out so it's got pretty sensitive controls. It'll do our job very easily. The problem is to get the right packages ready in time."

"The right black boxes?"

"Yes. The lads will be working night and day on it. Here's the point as it affects you. We're going to use the big receiving

32

dish out in Hawaii. It's out in the islands because there's not much man-made interference. Would you like a trip?"

I said I'd be delighted to make a trip to Hawaii. Then a waiter bore down on our table with a multitude of dishes.

Conversation was somewhat spasmodic for the next half-hour. The meal, an excellent one, deserved justice.

Over the coffee I asked, "Is this Hawaii trip a joy ride or is it strictly necessary?"

"Not strictly, if by that you mean absolutely essential. But well worthwhile from my point of view. We'll get the data hot off the line. Art's coming with us. The station on Hawaii is his show."

"When do we take off?"

"I was planning to travel the day after tomorrow. But there's no reason why you shouldn't go on earlier if you want to. By the way I've got an invitation for tonight."

"More science?"

"God forbid, I'm in need of a rest. This is a friend of a friend, out in Beverly Hills. We can always leave early if we get bored."

"Where are you staying?"

"I've got a motel back in Pasadena. You might as well stay over here by the sea though, it's quite a bit cooler."

"Then I suppose I'd better find a place before we go to Beverly Hills."

"Oh, I wouldn't bother. The motels are open all night. You can get one any time. Besides you never know where you'll end up."

On this remark John paid the bill. We went out to the parking place.

"You'd better follow me, we might as well take both cars. I'm not exactly sure of where to go but I know the general direction."

I kept faithfully on John's tail through a succession of boulevards and streets. Then we were in a twisting mass of side-roads among large houses. We both came to a halt. John was muttering imprecations. It seemed he was more disturbed by not being able to find the place than he had been by the scientific situation. We started off again. After two more tries we at last drew up outside a prosperous looking domicile. A dozen cars were parked in the roadway outside. Inside, a good-looking woman pressed two large drinks on us, with a welcoming smile, and no questions asked.

We pushed our way into a large room. Perhaps thirty people were in there, talking loudly. I had the impression it would have been possible for almost anybody to have walked in.

In the general bedlam of a cocktail party I am lucky to have something of an advantage over my fellow men. My hearing is abnormally acute so I can still make out what is being said at a stage where the average person is pretty well deafened. I plunged fairly confidently into the morass.

After a quick, not inexpert, survey of the female company a dark-haired girl caught my attention. I thought her face the most interesting of the female element. It was a face of some considerable character. I moved over into her general environment. Because I could just make out what people were trying to say, I soon found a place in the local conversation. The girl I judged to be in her mid-twenties, a few years younger than I was. There came a lull during which a man, who was probably the host, got himself launched into a description of how he had just bought an estate of vast acreage up near Ojai.

I was able to get the dark-haired girl away to myself. Our talk was trivial in the extreme as it was bound to be. I said I was just out from Britain, a simple, not very effective ploy. Her attention became a little warmer, however, when I told her that I was a musician. It seemed I was on the way to Chopin waltzes and mazurkas again.

We were joined by an older, rather handsome woman. The girl drifted away at the first opportunity, perhaps because she was glad to be rescued or because she didn't like the handsome woman. The woman took me on one side, saying confidentially, "Have you met her before, Lena I mean?"

"No, but I've seen her somewhere I'm sure. Who is she?"

"Do you mean you don't know?"

"Cross my heart."

"Helena Summers. She was in the film, *The Passionate*."

"The passionate what?"

The woman laughed, "No wisecracks." Then she became still more confidential. Taking my arm she murmured, "Lena's in bad shape, plenty trouble there."

There was no opportunity to ask what the plenty trouble was because a handsome, virile man of about my own age suddenly held the stage. I had seen him before so I was pretty sure he must be in the acting world too. He not only had the attention of the others, he had mine too. Astonishingly, he was talking about the effect of Chopin waltzes on young women.

There were two open pianos back-to-back at one end of

the big room. The man began to look through a pile of music evidently with the intention of playing himself. I was becoming combative now, rather like a dog whose territory has been infringed. He started on the big Chopin waltz in A flat Major. The interpretation was quite good, the technique somewhat faulty. I found myself appreciably irritated to see the women crowding around the piano.

Then I had the good sense to feel rather ashamed. After all, a lot of practice was needed to play as well as that, which showed my handsome friend must have a very genuine affection for music. Yet I found it difficult not to be jaundiced by the way he switched in a flash to Beethoven's short E Minor sonata. I resisted entering the discussion that followed. But then the girl Lena broke in with the remark that I was a musician. So I was thrown into the pool. I was introduced to the man. His name, Roger Berard, was just about as vaguely familiar as his face. I did my best to pretend to know it well for anything less would have seemed impolite.

"How about playing four hands? Mozart?"

I said that would be excellent. But they couldn't find the right music. Berard picked up the score of Mozart's K488 concerto. "Do you think we could manage this?" he asked.

I said we'd have to use both pianos.

Two experts with an understanding between them could have managed on one piano. We would have got ourselves into a hopeless tangle of hands and feet.

"There's only one copy. You haven't got another?" my partner asked the man I had guessed to be the host. "Why the hell should I keep two. I can't even play one." This brought a chorus of after-dinner laughter.

"We can use both pianos," I said. "If you take the solo part, I think I can manage the orchestration." This was more vicious than it may sound. I knew Berard was in a show-off mood. I suspected he was interested in one of the girls, not apparently the dark one. By choosing the orchestral accompaniment I naturally had the heavier part. Besides, this was the music I cut my teeth on.

It went as I had expected up to a point. I omitted the orchestral introduction, letting him lead off with the solo part. He began aggressively but with the volume of tone I was able to roll out it must soon have become clear that there was no profit at all for him in a competition. About half-way through the first movement he stopped the nonsense. He began to listen to what he was playing. Then the whole thing went off reasonably well. On a concert platform

35

a four-hands performance is never very attractive. Yet under casual circumstances like this it can be quite exciting, especially if it is unrehearsed. Nobody minds the hesitations and misunderstandings between the two players. It all adds to the fun. We were pressed to continue.

Surprisingly, Berard wanted me to play solo. He got out a volume of Beethoven sonatas talking avidly the while about the late ones. His instinct for music was genuine enough. I saw the artificiality of his earlier remarks really came from the society in which he was living. The world is full of frustrated musicians, people who would have liked to be musicians but who by ill chance had been forced into some other profession. I've met scores of them. They have one characteristic in common. By not being musicians they've done far better for themselves in all material respects than they'd have done as musicians.

I played the Opus 111. There wasn't a great deal of applause at the end but the warmth was obvious. They spoke now in quiet voices, not at all like the uproar that had been going on when John and I came in earlier. It was clear they wanted me to go on but it wasn't easy to think of anything to play after the Opus 111. Almost idly I rattled off the waltz theme of the Diabelli variations. Then I was into the variations proper. There was no turning back now. Once again my memory, or perhaps the thought of the dark girl with plenty trouble, served me well. I got through to No. 33 with a sprinkling of wrong notes but without serious mishap. It was more than enough. They were overwhelmed, crushed. Well they might be. Given the slightest musical sense it is impossible not to be staggered emotionally by the greatest works played at close range. This was the way, at close range, in which the old composers intended their solo works to be heard, intimately, not from the platform in a large hall. More and more, I have come to realize just how unsatisfactory public performances on a piano are. Even the most exquisite playing comes over weakly, attenuated, and thin. It is all rather like eating a well cooked dinner with a strong smell of antiseptic in the air.

Emotionally I had had enough now, at any rate on the piano. We got into small talk of no concern. John whispered discreetly in my ear, "Great stuff, Dicky. This is my phone number, give me a call tomorrow morning." Then he was away. At last I got a chance to talk to Lena. Her face was animated and responsive now. Odd the way it goes, I thought, mazurkas at eighteen, Beethoven sonatas at twenty-five. I wondered what the trick would be at fifty—aleatoricism? More or less spontaneously we decided to leave. This was a community in which you arrived when you pleased and left when you pleased. It would have suited Alex Hamilton. The hostess —I still didn't know her name—asked me to call up any time I was free. It was all aboveboard and genuine. She kissed me as I left. I thought of poor John on his solitary way back to Pasadena or to wherever he was going. There was nothing like science for the good clean life.

Outside, I took Lena's arm. She said, "Can I drive you somewhere?"

"Yes, I'm looking for some place to sleep."

"How am I intended to take that?"

"Quite genuinely. I've got to find a motel."

"There are plenty."

She guided the car with a sure hand through the labyrinth of small roads. I was glad I hadn't been left to make my way out at this time of night. It was warm, the car was open, there was a pleasant fragrance in the air. She said, "I'd like to drive by the sea."

We parked at the top of a cliff. Below us the sea spread out in a huge luminous phosphorescent arc. I turned to Lena. She smiled at my inquiring look.

I remember very little of where we went, of slipping out of the car into the house, or of the trivia of the bedroom. But I do remember lying there afterwards listening to the roar of the sea. I remember that enough light came through a long window for me to see Lena's face. There were tears standing on her eyelashes. When I brushed them away she smiled. A moment later she was asleep. I lay awake for a little while more, at peace, still listening to the sea, before I too fell asleep.

It was late the following morning when we woke. The house was built very close by the water. The beach was fairly steeply sloping, the sand was good. A few minutes after getting out of bed I was tumbling in the surf. After a quick dry off I padded into the kitchen for breakfast. I had decided I wasn't going to Hawaii, not unless Lena would come too. There seemed no point in my tagging along with the scientists like a camp follower. Over coffee I asked Lena if she had any wish to go out to the islands. "I'd like to go, but next week I'm working. If you're going to be there for some time I could join you later." This seemed to be the right compromise.

I rang John during the morning to say I'd prefer not to travel with him the following day but rather come on by

37

myself at the end of the week. There seemed no point in my hanging around in Los Angeles once Lena started at the studios.

The next few days passed all too quickly. We drove around, we swam, and made love and made music. Neither of us had any reason to feel there was anything unique about those days. I was not a soldier going to the wars, someone who might never return. After all, we would meet again in a week or two, if not in Hawaii, in Los Angeles. Yet we parted one morning at the airport with sudden sadness.

The mood lasted with me all the way to the islands. Three hours later I saw them standing up boldly out of a blue sea. I took a taxi from the airport into Honolulu. Soon I was booked into an hotel at Waikiki, close to the sea.

From there I put a call through to John who I knew would be on the island of Hawaii itself. I didn't reach him first shot so I had to leave a message to have him call me back. This forced me to hang around the hotel. When John at last came through, quite a while later, he said it would be best if I made the island hop the following morning. Why didn't I hire a car and take a look around Oahu? I said this was fine by me. It was mid-afternoon by the time I had the car which meant there wasn't a great deal of the day left for sightseeing. I asked at the hotel desk which was the most spectacular beach. The girl suggested I might like to go to the north side of the island to Sunset Beach.

It was warm and sticky as I drove over the twisting mountain road. The beach itself was tremendous, yet somehow I couldn't really get interested. I wondered if this was the way you became old, nothing excited you any more. I drove back by the east coast. After checking my car, I had an early dinner and then went straight to bed. I couldn't sleep. I lay wide awake for an hour, then I got up, dressed, and walked out to the sea.

As I strolled along the flat sand I was in the grip of a fit of loneliness such as I had rarely, if ever, experienced before. It came gradually upon me how much loneliness was increasing in our modern society. I realized it had been a dominating factor in almost all the people I had played to the other night.

I wandered back along the beach wondering whether these ideas, which had a deep validity, I was convinced, could somehow be expressed in sound. Anything new, for it to be worthwhile, must come out of my inner feelings. It couldn't be developed as a mere logical plan. The grandeur of Bach's music came out of his religious impulses, not from his technique. He worked to develop the technique because of the inner convictions, not the other way round.

To the west, away from the city, stars filled the sky. As I looked up to them my senses were suddenly acute and overwhelmingly strong. Reason suggests there could be nothing to it. Yet, knowing now what was to happen, I sometimes wonder whether the future at that moment did not touch me like a cold wind across the face.

THE mood was gone the following morning. The trip from Honolulu to the big island of Hawaii was, I suppose, about one hundred and fifty miles. I was met at Waimea by a car. The country hereabouts was surprisingly flat, considering the fourteen-thousand-foot high Mauna Kea was only some fifteen miles to the south. The journey to the field-station was a short one and soon I was dumping my bags into a room in the sleeping quarters. Although the buildings had a prefabricated look about them they were, nevertheless, very well appointed inside. I had barely finished unpacking when John arrived.

"Just in time," he said. "We're beginning to get results. It's already clear the signal is genuinely modulated."

"You mean the beam really is being used for conveying information?"

"That's what it looks like."

About midday a party of five army and navy officers arrived. Over lunch everybody started to talk. For a while it was all much the things I knew already, apart from some technical interpolations which didn't interest me. John explained his ideas. Clementi quickly went over the general experimental set-up. The officers got the drift, more or less as I did. They asked questions about the interference fringes, questions I was too shy to ask. Clementi drew a series of loops, by way of answer, looking somewhat like a bunch of bananas. There was a lot of talk about near-fields and far-fields but this was beyond me.

The essential idea seemed to be one of phase. If you have something that oscillates up and down the precise position where it happens to be at a given moment is the phase. What it came down to was this: if you chose a particular moment of time, and then considered the phases over a very big area, they all had to be the same, in order to explain the observations. When he was asked how big the area had to be, John replied:

"According to my calculations about ten times the radius of the Sun."

"But how can you get a phase correlation over such an enormous area?"

"That's what we all want to know," muttered Clementi.

The big man padded around and stated sententiously, "Control phase, and you control the universe."

"But that's what we do with our radar, isn't it?" asked an elderly, blue-eyed naval officer.

John nodded. "That's exactly the right way to put it. It's just as if there was a big antenna, measuring ten times the radius of the Sun. Apparently it's beaming a message out into space."

There was silence for a while.

"What would be the directivity, with an antenna as large as that?" asked another of the officers.

"At a big distance, quite fantastic. The beam would go out into space as an extremely fine pencil."

Someone had a bright idea.

"What's the chance of our being in the direct beam?"

"Remembering that we are in the near-field, it works out at somewhere between one in ten and one in a hundred, provided the beam is directed more or less along the ecliptic. Less than that if it's directed at random."

"Isn't it a bit surprising that we just happen to lie in it?"

"We're not necessarily lying in the main lobe. I've thought quite a lot about this point. From a climatic point of view, I mean."

John had their attention now.

"There must be something like a ten per cent difference in the solar radiation according to whether we're in the main beam or not. Of course we can't know anything directly about this infra-red stuff down here on the surface of the Earth. The infra-red never gets through the atmosphere. But it would have the effect of increasing the boundary temperature of the Earth."

"By how much?"

"Anything up to ten degrees I would say. What I've been wondering is whether all the mysterious climatic fluctuations the Earth seems to suffer—the ice-ages for instance—could be caused by our relation to this beam. You know, it may not always point in the same direction. Sometimes the Earth could pass through it, during the year I mean. At other times we might miss it entirely."

Clementi made a kind of humming sound. He wasn't wink-

41

ing. "A few degrees up, or a few degrees down, is really all that might be needed to make quite big changes of climate. It could be at that. But look here, John, old chap, old fellow, old scoundrel more like, are you hinting that this deal up there might have been going on for thousands of years?"

"I should have thought it extremely likely. If it was something that had just started up right now, well, wouldn't it be ridiculously improbable?"

"Yeah, I suppose so."

Several of the men were pacing like caged beasts up and down the lounge floor.

There was a silence which everybody seemed reluctant to break. At last, the naval officer with the blue eyes spoke:

"Gentlemen, it's time we came to the real issues. I don't know whether my colleagues and I can be described as having anything more than a watching brief here. But the questions that stand out in my mind are, first, how's it being done, second, what's it for? I must admit I'm personally in a smoke screen but maybe Dr. Sinclair has something he'd like to add."

This was quite a formal speech. I wondered how John would react to it. He shrugged his shoulders and began:

"I think anybody's guesses are as good as anybody else's at this stage. For myself I can't remotely conceive how this phasing trick is being worked. But being worked it surely is, so for the moment we'd better accept it, and go on from there—if we can. We've tested the deduction that the beam is being used to convey information."

"What information? What the hell is there to send, where and to whom?"

One of the army officers grinned and suggested, "Maybe it's a TV relay."

Most of them laughed at this. I noticed John didn't. When the laughter had died down he simply said, "Could be." Everybody looked at him, so he went on:

"It may sound crazy but what else can it be? Oh, I don't mean a TV relay strictly. Think of the colossal amount of information that's probably being sent out, of the order of a hundred million bits a second. In a year, that's several thousand trillion bits. Something like a hundred million textbooks a year. What sort of traffic would you need to fill a channel like that?"

"You mean there'd be no point in sending out such a lot of stuff unless there was really something to send?" Everybody laughed at this.

After a further short pause John went on:

"There are two speculative possibilities. This might be an interstellar, or even an intergalactic, relay station. Granted the enormous directionality of the system, the fineness of the pencil beam, these signals could be received at an enormous distance away from us."

Clementi had obviously been thinking along the same lines. "The details really aren't as fantastic as the thing itself. But as John says, we know the thing exists, so there's no getting away from it. It's easy enough to do an intensity calculation. If this really is a relay station, if some guy at the other end has even a moderately sensitive detecting device, say only a millionth part as sensitive as our big radio telescopes—as this thing out on the hillside here—then these signals can be picked up—where? Come on, freshman physics! Not just in our own galaxy, but anywhere, out and beyond anything we can see with the biggest telescopes."

"You mean this is just about the most . . ." The naval officer broke off whatever it was he was going to say. It was clear to him, as to me, that the wonders of science had gone beyond all reasonable bounds.

I was back in my room that night, jotting down one or two musical ideas, when John tapped on my door. "Would you like to go for a stroll?"

We slipped out of a side door.

"I don't want any of the others to join us just for the moment."

We had walked along for two or three hundred yards before he came to the point:

"I've been thinking it would be a good idea if you were to write everything down. I mean from the beginning. I think it would be a good idea to have an account from a unbiased person."

"You mean a non-scientist?"

"If you like to put it that way, yes."

My story is built from notes as I made them following this incident. Unfortunately my diary wasn't remotely detailed enough as it has turned out. So perforce I have often had to fill in as best I can from memory—this will explain how it comes about that sharp accounts of what took place are sometimes juxtaposed with obvious lapses of memory—my failure to recollect odd names for instance.

I began to see now why John had more or less press-ganged me into coming along with him. I also felt freer to ask questions with a clear conscience.

"It's all very well to avoid the problem of how this incredible thing is being done but do you have any idea at all about what's really happening?"

We walked on for a little way.

"Not with any precision. The obvious inference is that someone is doing it. I suppose the most straightforward explanation would be to say that it's some creature, some intelligence, on one of the other planets."

"A major boost to the space programme—eh?"

"As you say, a major boost to the space programme."

I guessed that John really didn't believe this. When I asked him point blank he replied:

"It's an outrageous explanation fitted to a fantastic situation. Yet anything else seems worse. It's all a question of the way you look at it. When something really new happens most scientists take the line of least resistance. They accept the explanation that involves the least change from their preconceived notions. Which is what I'm doing now."

"But you don't believe it?" I pressed.

"With me, believing or not believing a particular explanation is more a matter of method than of emotion. If I were emotional I'd be almost certain to plump for what I've just told you. The way I always work is like this. If I find things turning out much as I expect them I follow the line of least resistance, exactly the same as everyone else. But if I find my deductions going wildly wrong it's my instinct to explain my shortcomings by saying that I just haven't got hold of the right idea at all. I don't try to do a patchwork job, to choose the explanation that requires the least possible change from my previous position. I throw the net wide, just as wide as I can."

By now my eyes were accommodated to the dark. We were able to pick our way across the open grassland with more precision.

"I suppose it's really not fair to twist your arm any further but what does this wide net look like? My own imagination just boggles at the idea of there being something still more strange and unusual than creatures on another planet."

"I've got nothing definite to go on, except the day on the moor after we came off Mickle Fell."

"You still think that amnesia business might have had something to do with it?"

"I don't know. What I do know is that every explanation I can conceive of for that gap of thirteen hours, and for the mark that used to be on my back, is much more weird than this planet business. It suggests to my mind there's a real danger of our concepts going wildly astray."

"In what sense?"

"Consider the usual science-fiction story. Let me anatomize the situation for you. Science-fiction is a medium that concerns, above all else, life forms other than ourselves. The real life forms of our own planet belong of course to natural history, to zoology, so science-fiction purports to deal with life forms of the imagination. Yet what do we find when we read science-fiction? Nothing really but human beings. The brains of a creature of science-fiction are essentially human. You put such a brain inside a big lizard, and bang-wallop, you have a science-fiction story. Or if you can't be bothered with the lizard-like aspect of the story, you simply put the human brain in a human creature, and call it a humanoid. To make the story go, the humanoid is usually set up as more intelligent than ourselves, with a better technology. Then the story turns on how the dear old magnificent human species manages to deal with the alien threat. It boils down to a new version of Indians and cowboys.

"Let me be a bit more serious. If these rather simple-minded notions stopped at science-fiction it wouldn't be so bad. But as soon as we try to think quite seriously about intelligence outside the Earth that's exactly the way our concepts go."

"So when you talked about a creature on one of the other planets you were really inventing a science-fiction story?"

"That's the way it seems to me."

"Yet what else could there be?"

"Very hard to say, isn't it? If your brain doesn't have the right concepts you can't really force it to develop them. I'm quite willing to agree there may be lots of creatures more or less similar to us distributed up and down the universe, or even among the stars up there. What I doubt is whether there are any such creatures on Mars or Venus. Even if there were, I don't think they could perform this trick with the Sun."

"You think it's too big? The Sun I mean. That a creature stuck down on a planet could hardly do anything to a star?"

"I'm more or less sure of it."

After a short pause, John went off on a new tack. "In physics, we accept a lot of mysterious things."

"Such as what?"

"Well, it's very mysterious that our consciousness enables us to take decisions which turn out to improve our description of the world—in circumstances, mark you, when improvement ought to be impossible according to our basic physics."

"Sounds the sort of thing our religious friends would be glad to hear."

"They can read it in any textbook if they like. Let me give an example. You take a number of radioactive nuclei of a particular kind, the number being chosen so that there's an even chance of one of them going off in a certain period of time, say ten seconds. Then for ten seconds you surround them with counters, or any other detecting device you might like to use. At the end of the time the question is, has one of them decayed or not. To decide this you take a look at your counters. The conventional notion is that the state of the counters decides whether a nucleus has gone off or not."

"What you're saying is that if you did this experiment a lot of times your calculations require that in a half of the cases a nucleus will have decayed and in the other half there will have been no decay?"

"Right. But my problem now concerns an individual case. Has there been a decay or hasn't there? How do you decide?"

"I would suppose by looking, which is what you said a moment ago."

"Of course. But here comes the rub. It is perfectly possible to put your counters, or your bubble chamber, your camera, all your gobbledegook in fact, into your calculations—and we know quite definitely that any attempt to get a definite answer out of calculation will prove completely fruitless. The thing that gives the answer isn't the camera or the counter, it's the actual operation of looking yourself at your equipment. It seems that only when we ourselves take a subjective decision can we improve our description of the world, over and above the uncertainty of our theories. I'm talking about quantum theories now."

"So you've got a real contradiction?"

I waited as John paused again. He lifted his hand in a gesture. "There's one possible loophole. We could be wrong in comparing ourselves as physical systems with a camera or a counter or anything like that. The essential thing about a camera is that it's local. Its operation can be described by a strictly finite number of variables, its activities are restricted to a limited volume of space-time. It could be that when we make subjective judgements we're using connections that are non-local. If this is right the logical ramifications are enormous. It means we can have connections ranging all over the universe."

46

"What's the relation to this business?"

"This affair could have nothing at all to do with our own local planets. It could be on a vastly bigger scale. It needn't have anything to do with human brains in lizard heads."

"You've one or two fairly definite ideas?"

From long experience I knew that John would not have got himself into this conversation unless there was more than general guesswork behind it.

"There's one thing. You remember we talked about the purpose of this phased infra-red stuff. For God's sake don't tell anyone I don't really go along with that relay station idea. There's another more remarkable possibility. I've got a feeling the more remarkable possibility has a better chance of being right. Think of the enormous volume of communication that must be involved here, the incredibly detailed information. What kind of thing do we know about that would need such a capacity? This is the question I keep asking myself. What was it, a hundred million major text-books a year? The sort of physics we study needs nothing like that. If you know how, you can put all our basic physics into one book. I suppose you could put most aspects of our technology into a hundred books. The only things I can see around me needing anything like this volume of information are biological organisms, our brain processes for instance, or the information needed to construct a human being."

The following day I went for a drive round the island. I went to Volcano House and took a look at the active Kilauea crater. I saw sugar plantations, pineapple fields, rain forests, the sea and the mountains. When I got back to the experimental station I found the place in a wild panic. Somebody told me war had started and that Los Angeles had been destroyed.

THE personal crowded out the general. My first thought was
of Lena. I was dry in the throat. I began rushing around
with the others, in the hope of finding John or one of his
friends. I couldn't really believe the news was true but it
didn't need to be true to be frightening. Of course I knew
there was a bad situation in south-eastern Asia. Yet I hadn't
remotely credited it could blow up into a major war, if that
was what this really was. Then I remembered war always
seems to come as a surprise to civilians, at any rate it had in
1914. At last I ran into Art Clementi.

"Is there any truth . . ." I began.

"Can't say yet. But something serious seems to have happened. A few of us are going over to Pearl City. We can
probably manage to tuck you in if you want to come along.
John's going, the Brass want him down there."

I packed my things as quickly as I could. In a sense, rushing over to Pearl City was a form of panic, a desire to do
something to avoid sitting still and waiting. That's the way
terror got you, you just ran aimlessly around in any direction.

It was only when I walked with my bag out to the car
park that I found John. I was glad to see he didn't look too
worried.

"I find this very difficult to believe. Something's happened
all right but it must have become exaggerated. We'd better go
over and find out exactly what it is."

Scarcely a word was spoken on the journey to Hailo airport. Nobody said very much there either. We all got on to
the plane in silence. It put down for a short stop in the
island of Maui and then went on to Honolulu. A big station
wagon was waiting for us. There was very little traffic on the
road as we made our way to the naval base. Then came a
hold-up when it was found that neither John nor I was an
American citizen. After a delay, in which I suppose a number
of phone calls were put through, we were separated from the
others and told that a car would be made available to take

us to a downtown hotel. After the best part of an hour a car did appear and we made away in it. In the car John said, "I told Art we would go to the Waikiki."

We got rooms at the hotel. I tried to ring Los Angeles but found all lines engaged. Then I lay flat out on my bed in a quiet blank state of mind. I had a call from John on the house phone at about six o'clock suggesting we meet downstairs in the bar for a drink. It seemed as good an idea as anything else. After the drink we went to dinner in the hotel restaurant.

"I wonder if I could have a talk with you chaps?" The speaker was an Australian. We told him to pull up a chair. Clearly he had finished dinner. We were only half-way through the main course. We introduced ourselves, and took stock of our new acquaintance. It struck me I had become far more suspicious, far less free and easy, in the last few hours. I felt as if I was on some kind of an assignment. The Australian had an athletic look about him. His manner was pleasant and open.

"I heard you talking and realized you were a couple of Britishers."

The clans were certainly drawing together. Our exclusion at Pearl City and now this.

"How about a walk on the beach when you've finished, I'll be in the bar."

Then he was gone.

Not long afterwards Art Clementi appeared. We naturally wanted to know the news:

"It looks bad, real bad. There's no doubt the west coast has been attacked."

We tried to get more out of him but either he knew nothing more or he wouldn't say. It was all very odd. It was also odd that Clementi went off without eating dinner with us. He excused himself by saying he had already eaten but I knew from the way he looked at the food that this couldn't be so. What the hell did it mean, the contrast between this frigidity and the uproarious welcome we had received only the other day in California?

We got the beginnings of an answer from our Australian acquaintance. He waited until we were well away on the beach before he would talk. The man was a QANTAS pilot. He had been on a regular flight from Honolulu to the United States. As he approached the international airport at Los Angeles a message had come through directing him to return.

"There was something crook about it."

"In what way?"

"It didn't look right. In fact it was all wrong, just as wrong as it bloody well could be."

"Things wouldn't look very pretty after a nuclear attack."

I had told John nothing of Helena Summers. In the poor light I don't suppose they could have seen my distress.

"That's just it. If I could have seen a lot of damage, a lot of smoke, I wouldn't have been surprised."

"There must have been smoke."

"Well, there wasn't. It was a clear day. Of course I was nearly fifty miles out to sea. Yet as far as I could tell there was nothing."

We stopped in astonishment. The surf broke loudly, not far away on our right. We waited for the rippling noise to die away.

"Nothing?"

"Not a bloody thing. I could see the whole Los Angeles basin. And I tell you there wasn't a bloody thing there."

"I tried to ring Los Angeles this afternoon. They told me all the lines were engaged, so there must be something there."

"Do you think they'd tell you if there wasn't?"

"Didn't you get any signals from the control tower?"

"Not a damn thing. Not a peep. I thought the radio must be out of action. We couldn't pick up anything, not from San Francisco either, or from the control stations to the east. I told the wireless operator to keep trying. He did a big search over the whole shortwave band. Do you know what he came up with?"

"If the war's really started all long-range stuff will be off the air. Local TV stations and news stations will be on, probably."

"Well, I'll tell you this. I got the control back there, exactly as usual. And I got some shortwave stuff from Britain. And that was it, nothing anywhere else."

"You got the usual British channels?"

"As far as I could tell. We're a long way off here. So I only got odd snatches. As far as we could judge it was about what was to be expected in a normal way."

We walked on for a while before John said, "Could that be the trouble do you think? It seems incredible but if Britain's really on the air in any normal way she hasn't been attacked."

"It could be."

"Did you get anything from the west, the other way?"

"From Fiji, nothing from Sydney."

It didn't make sense, except perhaps for one ray of light.

"Do you think they imagine we've gone neutral? If Britain

50

is more or less normally on the air that's what it looks like."

"I'd thought of that," answered John. "It would fit. If they think we've ratted on them it would be natural enough for them to treat us pretty distantly. Yet it seems fantastic. British policy and American policy are in it together. I would have thought we couldn't keep out even if we wanted to."

We headed back to the hotel. I asked, "What are you going to do? With your plane? Go back to Australia?"

The pilot paused for a moment. "I've given quite a bit of thought to that. I'm supposed to be on a through flight Los Angeles to London, with a refuelling stop in Canada. I suppose if I insist they'll let me take off as long as I agree to keep over Canadian territory all the way."

"Isn't that the natural thing to do?"

"I suppose so. But I'm leery about it. I can't say exactly why, but I'd prefer it if I could go right through in one hop."

"I thought the new planes could pretty well do that, at any rate from California. Can't you make it with a light load?"

"I've got one of the old jobs."

"Pity, because we ought to be getting back home—at any rate if the atmosphere doesn't get warmer around here."

"Day after tomorrow we have a long-distance plane coming through. It could make the trip. I'll have a word with the captain if you like."

We said we thought it might be a good idea.

By now we were nearing the hotel. After a drink at the bar I decided to turn in. Sick at heart I took one last look out over the sea before I climbed into bed. Unpleasant emotions seemed inseparable from this damned place. I lay there thinking about Lena. I could remember the tears and the smile which followed them.

What the devil did the Australian mean by saying there was nothing? Not even the dead and the dying? I little realized that I had become separated from Helena Summers by much more than death.

I was awakened the following morning by the phone burring in my ears. It was John saying he was going out to Pearl City, that the climate seemed to have changed back just as suddenly as it had shifted yesterday. I asked him why, but he didn't know. When I came down to breakfast in the coffee shop I found the blue-eyed naval officer waiting for me. We sat down together. I ordered a stack of wheatcakes and coffee. He ordered coffee.

"I'm afraid we owe you a very sincere apology. Yesterday

we didn't know where we were, not that we're much better today. But we can see things a bit more clearly now."

Then he went on to tell me, rather haltingly, much the same as John had already guessed, that radio communications from Britain, apparently still covering the normal radio waveband, had convinced them Britain had somehow managed to stay out of the war. This had made for a peculiar situation so far as we were concerned. They had thought the best thing was to do nothing and say nothing. I said both John and I had appreciated what the situation must look like and we quite understood his position. He became less embarrassed but no less worried. I told him I had a close friend in Los Angeles and could he tell me anything of what had happened there. He looked about him, to see whether anybody was listening, and then said, "We can't understand it, we just can't understand it. We've sent planes over and—well, there's nothing there, nothing at all."

I asked if this could be some strange new development in war technique. Yet even as I asked the question I realized it was absurd. The officer shook his head. He looked tired and old and I could see the situation was quite beyond him.

"It may sound horrible. If it had been war, the kind we expected, I would at least have understood what was going on. It looks like a nightmare, as if we were all dreaming. I keep hoping I'll waken up. That sounds kinda silly."

"Don't you think we ought to stop trying to understand it, at any rate for the time being. Perhaps we ought to get back to the way we were when we were kids. We all took the world the way we found it. Only later as we grew up did we try to make sense of it."

"Yes, I suppose so. But at my time of life it isn't easy to learn new tricks. You get set in your ways as the years roll past. You see I had a son and daughter-in-law and two kids in Los Angeles."

We shook hands sadly and he left.

For the next two days I sat in my room writing as hard as I could go. I wanted to get all the old, more normal, stuff down before my standards of judgement became distorted by this strange new world. I knew John and his colleagues would seek me out as soon as the next move was decided. As I say, I was given two days' grace. I emerged from my room only for meals. My fingers grew stiff with writing, always writing, twelve hours a day.

John appeared at last late on the second day. He had not

eaten at lunchtime so I went with him back to the restaurant, although I had already had dinner. I asked for the news.

"Fragmentary in the extreme. The balance of opinion still favours war of some sort. Nobody can fit the facts together. It seems quite certain that Los Angeles really has ceased to exist. We don't know much about the rest of the States. In Britain it seems to be just as normal as it is here. There's some activity in Europe, although it doesn't look normal there either. From Russia there's as big a blackout as there is from the American mainland."

I waited. It was an old trick with John, the dramatic pause.

"Back home they're in just the same mess. We managed to get a message through. They wanted news, saying they're just as much in the dark as we are."

"I had the old naval chap in again this morning. He doesn't like it at all."

"The devil is that everything is so normal here. It's only the outside communications that are crazy."

"Could it be some sort of hoax, some ridiculous psychological experiment, connected with the military programme? To determine the population reaction."

"Well, if it is, we shall soon know. You remember the Australian. He told us a plane was coming in from Fiji, one that might manage to get through to Britain in one hop? It's here now, it came in yesterday evening, and it's the only really long-range plane in the islands. So they've decided to send it over the States. It can get to somewhere in the region of Denver or Chicago and still manage to get back here to the islands. The military people have commandeered it. After a bit of argument I've got the two of us included on the trip. I've given them the idea I might come up with some explanation of what's going on." John ran his hand through his hair and added, "Some hopes."

At breakfast the following morning I realized a strange thing had happened in the preceding days, the days in which I had been shut away in my room. From the beginning, from the moment the war rumours first spread, smiles had disappeared, there had been less talk, less laughter, fewer vehicles on the street. Now there was an almost complete silence. Everybody spoke quietly, as if someone or something was listening to what was being said. In these islands of sunshine it was weird and unnerving.

We got to the airport at about nine o'clock. I would say about forty persons, mostly service officers, were already assembled there. I looked around for Art Clementi, hoping to straighten out the misunderstanding and embarrassment of our last meeting, but he wasn't there.

"Looks as though we're taking a very light load," I said.

"To give as big a range as possible."

A few minutes later we climbed up an old-fashioned ramp into the rear door of the plane. An Australian girl smiled at us as we enplaned. A few minutes later we were in the air.

We settled down in our seats. The hostess brought us quite large glasses of fresh orange juice. It was a welcome change from the inevitable coffee.

"Australian idea," said John. "Genuine stuff, not artificial muck."

"What's been going on the last two days?"

"I got involved in two things. Damn queer, both of them. I was out at the university, at the seismic department. On the face of it not very exciting. Simple equipment and so on. I'm not familiar with the details of that business so I had to accept what they told me."

"And what the devil did they tell you?"

"Well, the general background of seismic disturbances— you know there are always slight earth movements going on all the time—has gone up enormously in the last four days."

"I didn't notice any earthquake."

"Oh, this was below the subjective threshold. But it was much above the usual noise level by several orders of magnitude."

"Maybe there's been a big earthquake somewhere, a long way off."

"It couldn't be just one earthquake, it wouldn't last long enough. More like a succession of them. And even that doesn't fit the pattern properly. From a single earthquake, particularly a big one, you get a pretty clean-cut record. This stuff is all confused, it looked like real random noise."

"What could be doing it?"

"Nobody has the slightest idea. It isn't very dramatic, not like the other things, but I thought I'd mention it. Often it's the non-spectacular things that lead you in the right direction."

"You said there was something else, two things you'd been looking at."

"Right. Signals from the rocket have stopped. Art Clementi's boys are getting a blank record."

"How long did you expect to go on getting a signal before the rocket got too far away from the Earth?"

"Oh, for several weeks more. The natural interpretation is

54

that a small meteorite has hit something in the electronics. It was a rush job so we couldn't take every precaution we would have liked to have done. Yet it's queer to find the signals stopping only a few minutes before the war was announced."

Several officers and the pilot came to talk to John during the flight. It struck me as odd how much status depends on the social situation. War had reduced us to persons of no account. The present situation, with all its weird implications, taking one as far as the shifting frontiers of science or even beyond that, made John a commanding figure. He was the most distinguished scientist available for consultation. On his coat tails, almost literally, I managed to get into the cockpit as the plane approached the American mainland.

There were a lot of us jammed in there. Yet I could see a great deal more than was possible from an ordinary passenger seat. I gathered it was the Los Angeles basin ahead. The air was completely clear. There was nothing of the banks of brown smog I had seen when we came in from New York two weeks ago. Was it only two weeks ago? It needed no more than the most casual glance to see there was no city here.

"Take a look along the Sierra Madre. Look for the Observatory."

We were coming lower now, to an altitude of about ten thousand feet I guessed. There were mountains below us, heavily wooded. I noticed there were no fire-rides. We flew immediately above their crests, sharp and jagged. The trees covered the very topmost point. If this was Mount Wilson, there was no observatory here. We left the mountains and came back to the flatter land by the coast, dropping down still further, to only a few thousand feet. It was then we caught brief glimpses of habitation in the woods. The woods were now covering places where only two weeks before there had been great sprawling boulevards, streaming with traffic, swarming with humanity.

But there were signs of life below us and this lifted our spirits to an astonishing degree. The trouble was we couldn't land the plane. An enormous runway was needed for that and no such thing as a runway was to be seen in the wilderness below us. We came low enough to notice a few cultivated patches of land and this was all. Whoever was down there was keeping out of sight.

The itch to get to the ground was overwhelming, I think, to everybody on the plane. Since we had plenty of fuel we did the obvious thing of heading east, into the American

55

mainland. Sooner or later we all felt it must be possible to find an airstrip. Two weeks ago every town of any appreciable size had its airport, with runways extended for the new jets. The day was so clear that even after we climbed back to forty thousand feet we could still see the ground below quite well.

As we flew on we all kept a sharp lookout for towns and roads. We saw neither in the usual sense. There was an occasional rough track through the mountains. Now and again we thought there were further signs of primitive inhabitations. Whether or not there were houses we couldn't say. Further east, and ever further, we went. The search for a place to land was becoming fruitless. We tried Phoenix, or what used to be Phoenix, then Albuquerque, then at last we were over the central plains. We came down very low over Denver. It wasn't entirely easy to be sure we had located the correct place. There were no radio beacons to guide us. All navigation had to be done with the compasses, and even by the old-fashioned method of simply looking down on to the ground. Denver was a good place to look for. The big sudden rise of the Rockies lies only thirty miles or so to the west. That landmark was quite unmistakable, so all we had to do was to fly on a north-south line until the crew felt convinced they had found the right place. Once again we came low, to a thousand feet or so. Below us there were open grasslands. There were no signs of growing crops. Manifestly, the vegetation was in a natural state, a natural ecology.

With the present light load the plane was expected to have a range of between eight and nine thousand miles. So far, we had done about three thousand. Perhaps it would have been wise to have turned back. Yet the desire to find a landing spot was so strong in all of us that we felt impelled to make one more try, in the direction of Chicago. We wouldn't have a great deal to spare in the matter of range, but by taking a more direct route back to Hawaii the pilot thought he would be all right.

We picked up a powerful tail wind. Quite strong radio signals were coming in now from the east, probably of European origin. We found nothing at Chicago, except endless lakes and woods. Then came the critical discussion, to go on or to go back. The big advantage of going back was we knew exactly where we were going. The disadvantage was that we didn't have a great deal in hand in the way of range. We would have to fight the head wind, although this wouldn't matter too much as long as we found a reasonably direct route. The advantage of going on was that radio-guidance systems seemed to be working more or less normally somewhere to the east. And we still had the tail wind so range would be no problem that way. Besides it was manifestly desirable to establish actual physical communication with whatever it was that lay to the east.

Truth to tell, I think everybody wanted to take a look at New York. It was much the same story as we flew over the Appalachians in the fading light. But there were far more signs of life here, far more primitive shacks, it seemed. It all looked as America might have looked around the year 1800. Darkness came on. We saw little more, except twice there were flickering lights below us, fairly obviously camp fires. Then we were out over the Atlantic.

By now we were back in our seats. The stewardess served us with a meal. There wasn't much conversation, and what there was of it was pretty terse. John and I sat silently, each immersed deeply in his own thoughts. The irrational feeling swept over me that somehow the plane had become a world closed in on itself, that it would go on and on flying for ever. We had frequent reports from the pilot, however, to say that radio communication ahead was entirely normal. But perhaps this was just another monstrous deception? Emotionally, I felt we must go on and on until at last we came to our starting point, back in Hawaii; that we would find everything wiped clean even on the islands, just as it was on the American mainland.

I saw John looking repeatedly at his watch. Like me, like all of us, he was finding the passage of time excruciatingly slow. We had still three hours more to go before the next stage in the drama would unfold itself.

In retrospect I am not sure whether the innocence of my mind was an advantage or not. To build any rational explanation of what had happened, of what I had seen, was utterly beyond me. So I was left only with monstrous images and grotesque explanations.

After an age, in which every ten minutes seemed stretched to an hour, as it does in childhood, the little speakers above our heads crackled. The pilot's voice came over to say we had just passed the west coast of Ireland, that we would be landing at London airport in about three-quarters of an hour. Even the harshness of the speakers failed to conceal the relief, the emotional tones, in his voice.

All the evidence was that London airport was working normally. From the tilt of the fuselage you could see we were coming down now. The moon was shining on banks of clouds below us. Then we were down to the clouds and into them. These were the clouds that hang so frequently over the British Isles, blotting out the sun, giving the grey skies I knew so well. The clouds were astonishingly thin, the layer couldn't have been thicker than a few hundred feet. We broke suddenly below it. There on the ground was a multitude of lights. The sheer normality of it, the roads we could now pick out, set up a sharp reaction. I returned quickly to my seat and lay back feeling I might be sick. It wasn't airsickness, rather that of faintness. Then I saw we were going down to the ground at last. The landing wasn't a good one, there was a big bump as the wheels hit, but at least we were down. Within a few seconds I felt all right again.

As we taxied along the runway I had the odd thought that maybe I had been dreaming. Perhaps I had snoozed away the whole of a perfectly normal flight. It was hard to believe otherwise as the pilot manoeuvred the plane into its final resting spot.

There was an unconscionably long delay before steps appeared and the rear door was opened. We stood up, collected our belongings, and waited in the aisle in precisely the usual fashion. The people ahead began to move slowly. A minute later I was in the open air. We were shepherded by a girl into a waiting bus. There was another delay and then the crew joined us.

I expected to be taken to the usual assembly hall, or waiting hall, or whatever they called it, prior to immigration and customs. But the bus came to a gate that led off the airfield. The gate was opened. While we were halted two policemen got in. Away over on my right, in the distance, I had the impression of an airport crowded with thousands on thousands of people. It was as if they were waiting there, in the hope of seeing planes coming in to land. Soon we were at a traffic light that led out on to the highway. Then we were speeding into London. Here too, as in Honolulu, there was very little traffic. It was a fair guess that we had been brought this way to avoid the crowds, perhaps to avoid reporters and television cameras. Quite evidently, I had not been dreaming.

WE were taken to what was obviously the headquarters of some intelligence unit. Men in uniform, men in civilian clothes, were walking around in a strained, taut way. The American officers were quickly separated from the rest of us. In fact only John and myself and the Australian crew were in civvies. We were shown into rough sleeping quarters. John took this without comment. With a grin he said to me, "They'll soon change their tune."

The following morning, after an unappetizing breakfast, two officers came looking for John. They asked him to follow them, or more politely to go with them. John insisted I should go along too. They were doubtful, but once he had told them I knew as much about the business as he did—a gross exaggeration—they made no further objections. We were taken to a waiting car. In the front, beside the chauffeur, was a fellow whom I took to be a plain-clothes officer of some species or other.

The car headed out into west London. It kept on into the country for an hour or thereabouts. At last we turned in at the gates of a pretty flossy place. The house was vaguely familiar.

"Chequers," grinned John, "I told you they'd change their tune."

We were received courteously by the Prime Minister himself. There were a number of other guests, quite a mob of them. The Prime Minister introduced us round. There was the Foreign Secretary, the Chancellor, the Minister of Defence, the Chief of Staff, and about half a dozen other high-ranking service officers. They were drinking sherry. A glass of the stuff was pressed into our hands.

John explained my presence by saying I had been making a complete record of everything that had happened. This seemed to please everybody, as if a record is equivalent to an explanation. I also noticed how easy it is for a scribe to get himself into even the most intimate conference. It comes I supposed from the laziness to which all flesh is prey. I also noticed the heavy preponderance of the military. It struck me wryly that whenever the unusual happens the stock of the military always seems to rise.

Before lunch John gave an excellent and precise account of what had happened in California, in Hawaii, and on the flight back across America. His narrative was put together so concisely and with such logical consistency that his audience listened without comment or question until it was finished. Then everybody waited for the Prime Minister to comment:

"Obviously you've been thinking of explanations for all this. You've given us the facts. But what do they mean?"

"It's too early to say, sir. It's common dictum I believe among lawyers that one must wait for all the evidence to be in before forming an opinion. I've been waiting for all the facts. You must have an awful lot of things we don't know anything about."

"We've got plenty of facts, but I don't mind telling you we haven't the slightest idea what they mean. You've given us a pretty succinct account of the American situation. Here's what's happened to us. As far as we can make out everything is quite normal in Britain. From the American mainland we've had absolutely nothing, which doesn't surprise me in view of what you've just said. From Europe too there's been a black-out except in the last few hours."

"When did the blackout start?"

"Oh, nearly two days ago."

"At 10.37 p.m."

One of the officers had consulted a notebook. I felt there must be something wrong here. John was looking puzzled:

"That's only about thirty-six hours. It happened four days ago with us."

It was their turn to look surprised.

"You mean you lost contact with the American mainland four days ago?" asked the Chancellor.

We both affirmed that this was so.

"Very strange, very strange."

The Prime Minister was drumming his fingertips on the table.

John went on, "That's another interesting fact. You were talking about Europe, what's going on there?"

"We don't know." This from the Minister of Defence.

"You mean it's just as blank as the American mainland?"

"No, it isn't. We've been getting wireless messages but they're strange in every conceivable respect."

"Why haven't you sent planes over?" I broke in.

The Prime Minister looked at me for a few seconds. I saw his eyes were dark and troubled. "Of course we sent planes over. They never returned."

On this new and sombre note we sat down to lunch. A short menu had been typed. I was engrossed in my own thoughts, hardly listening to the discussion, significant as it might be. Idly I looked at the menu. It was dated September the 19th. Of course it must be a mistake. I waited until there was a lull in the talk and then asked, feeling very foolish, whether the date on the menu was right. The triviality of the question riveted everybody's attention. A few seconds went by in which I had the impression they were all ticking off the days in their minds. Then someone said, "I think it's right." Another added, "Of course it's right." The Prime Minister looked at me and asked, simply, "Why?"

"Because according to my reckoning it should be somewhere in the middle of August. I think the 13th, certainly within a day or two of that. What's your reckoning, John?"

"Somewhere about that, within a day or two. I've been so heavily occupied that I've really lost precise contact. Yet there isn't the slightest doubt we're still in August. At least Dick and I are in August."

At this very dramatic point the girl serving the food whispered something to the Prime Minister. He nodded and she went away. A moment later a young lieutenant in uniform appeared. He went to the Chief of Staff, stood behind his chair as if to serve some dish, saluted and handed him an envelope. The Chief of Staff turned and said, "Thank you. You can wait outside."

Everybody watched the envelope being slit open very precisely with a knife. I would have ripped it open with thumb and finger myself. We watched the Chief of Staff reading with growing astonishment. Then he got up and took the papers to the Prime Minister. He stood behind the Prime Minister's chair, waiting for them to be read through. Then the Prime Minister said:

"It's jibberish. Here's a sample:

My views are known to you. They have always been "defensive" in all theatres but the west. But the difficulty is to prove the wisdom of this now that Russia is out. I confess I stick to it more because my instinct prompts me to stick to it, than because of any good argument by which I can support it.

"Where the devil did this stuff come from?"

The Chief of Staff handed the Prime Minister another sheet. The Prime Minister went on:

"Apparently a man in uniform approached the Dover dock authorities this morning. He was in a distraught frame of mind. He insisted on being provided with transport to take him to London, to the War Office. Police took him in custody and found this letter on him. That all?"

"That's all I have here."

"Why the hell should we be bothered by some lunatic? There must be thousands of them around just at the moment."

This point of view commended itself to me for every crackpot in the country would now be at work. I could see the ranters in Hyde Park predicting the end of the world.

"There's something very familiar about that passage," said the Minister of Defence in a puzzled voice.

"Yes," nodded the Chief of Staff, "and I think I know where it comes from." He turned to the Prime Minister, "If you'll excuse me, sir, I'd like to take a look in the library."

We all followed him to the library. He looked at the shelves, here and there, for a while. Then with a satisfied grunt he pulled out a volume. He flicked through the pages until at last he came to what he wanted.

"Here it is, the exact passage. You can see for yourselves."

He held the book down on the table. It was indeed there, exactly as I remembered the Prime Minister reading out a few moments before. It was part of a letter, the rest of which I supposed the Prime Minister hadn't bothered with. Then I noticed the volume was an official war history.

"It's part of a letter from Sir Douglas Haig to Sir William Robertson, written September 27th, 1917."

Coffee was served in the library. We sipped it silently until John said:

"I wouldn't take this as a hoax."

"How would you take it?" asked the Prime Minister.

"That's another matter. What I mean is our natural impulse is to take it as a hoax because that's the way we'd like to see it."

"You're not suggesting we should take it literally?"

"I think we ought to know more about it. What about the man they got the letter from. You say he was dressed in uniform. What was the uniform? Surely the people in Dover can tell us. And where did he come from? Did he come from the sea? Why not find out before we get into an argument?"

The Chief of Staff went away. He came back half an hour later, his face ashen grey.

"The man was dressed in a sergeant's uniform, exactly as he would be in 1917. He did come from the sea. They found the boat. There were more than a hundred other passengers. They're all dressed in the uniforms of 1917, or rather they were before they were moved *en bloc* to the local mental hospital. Every one of them swears we are in the year 1917."

John banged his hands together for a few seconds, "That's what I expected was going to happen. On a small scale it's the only explanation that makes sense. There's one thing I'd like to find out before coming to the point though."

There was a phone in the library. In a bemused state of mind I heard John's voice—apparently involved in a technical discussion. After the call was finished, he said:

"Yes, there's been a lot of Earth movement here too, not much below subjective threshold. The noise level is much higher than it was in Hawaii. Normally this is one of the quietest parts of the Earth."

"What do you get out of that?"

"Nothing in itself. But that was the way it had to be for consistency. I think I know now *what* has happened, although I haven't the slightest idea of *how* or *why*. In fact it's pretty obvious, isn't it?"

We were leaning forward in our chairs. John went on:

"I'll put it as crudely as I can. We've got ourselves into some kind of time-machine. Remember the old Wells story?"

The Chancellor smiled wryly, "You mean about the fellow who invented a black box in which you could travel either forwards or backwards in time?"

"That's right, a remarkable black box it was. But our time-machine is much more singular. It's not just a case of our being precipitated into other moments of time. And I don't think anybody else has been either. I think everybody, all over the Earth, will have the impression they're living quite normally in the present, as they understand the present. Nobody has noticed any sudden shift of time and nobody will do so, except in the way Dick here did while we were at lunch."

The Prime Minister pulled a face and threw out his arms in a wide gesture, "Let's try to see through a glass a little less darkly. Is there any reality in the discrepancy of a month, or are you under some hallucination, or are we under an hallucination?"

"Neither. We're both right. There is no inconsistency in it's being September 19th here in Britain, and the year being 1966.

And there would have been no inconsistency to us in the time being the middle of August if we had stayed in Hawaii. It was only when we got together that the discrepancy came out."

This touched them all off into animated comment. The Chancellor's voice stood out above the rest, "You mean there are different times in different places on the Earth?"

"That's right. That's the way it must be. In Hawaii it is the middle of August 1966, in Britain it is September 19th, 1966, on the American mainland I would guess it is somewhere before the year 1750, in France it is the end of September 1917."

This was enough for the Prime Minister. "If there's any possibility you're right we've got a lot of things to do, and without delay. I'm going to suggest we meet back here in four hours, shall we say?" There were nods around the room. Without further ado the Chief of Staff got up and went out. He was followed by the other officers. It was clear the Chief of Staff, the Chancellor, and the Minister of Defence also felt the need for action, so John and I went out into the garden. After pacing around for a while we decided to go for a walk.

"I see everything fits together, that way. But every instinct, every emotion I've got, rebels against it," I said with some warmth as we strode out along a country lane.

"Because, like all of us in our daily lives, you're stuck with a grotesque and absurd illusion."

"How's that?"

'The idea of time as an ever-rolling stream. The thing which is supposed to bear all its sons away. There's one thing quite certain in this business: the idea of time as a steady progression from past to future is wrong. I know very well we feel this way about it subjectively. But we're the victims of a confidence trick. If there's one thing we can be sure about in physics it is that all times exist with equal reality. If you consider the motion of the Earth around the Sun, it is a spiral in four dimensional space-time. There's absolutely no question of singling out a special point on the spiral and saying that particular point is the present position of the Earth. Not so far as physics is concerned."

"But there certainly *is* such a thing as the present. Without the ideas of the past, the present, and the future we could make no sense at all out of life. If you were aware of your whole life at once it would be like playing a sonata simply by pushing down all the notes on the keyboard. The essential thing about a sonata is the notes are played in turn, not all at once."

64

"I'm not really trying to say the present is without validity. Rather that it can't have any validity in physics."

"Then physics isn't everything? A big admission for a physicist, isn't it?"

"Remember the night we were out walking, back in Hawaii? I said then there were parts of our experience which simply defied physical law. I can develop those ideas a lot further. In a way I'd sooner get it off my chest now, rather than later. It sounds too crazy to put before a lot of people. Yet I'm sure something along these lines must be right. I'm going to put it in terms of a parable. Suppose you have a lot of pigeon holes, numbered in sequence, one, two, and so on . . . up to thousands and millions, and millions of millions if you like. In fact the sequence can be infinite both ways, if you prefer."

I said that I didn't mind. John went on, "All right, let's come now to the contents of the pigeon holes. Suppose you choose one of them, say the 137th. You find in it a story, as you might find one of those little slips of paper in a Christmas cracker. But you also find statements about the stories you'll find in other pigeon holes. You decide to check up on whether these statements about the stories in the other pigeon holes are right or not. To your surprise you find the statements made about earlier pigeon holes, the 136th, the 135th, and so on, are substantially correct. But when you compare with the pigeon holes on the other side, the 138th, the 139th, . . . you find things aren't so good. You find a lot of contradictions and discrepancies. This turns out to be the same wherever you happen to look, in every pigeon hole. The statements made about pigeon holes on one side are always pretty good, those made about pigeon holes on the other side are at best diffuse and at worst just plain wrong. Now let's translate this parable into the time problem. We'll call the particular pigeon hole, the one you happen to be examining, the present. The earlier pigeon holes, the ones for which you find substantially correct statements, are what we will call the past. The later pigeon holes, the ones for which there isn't too much in the way of correct statements, we call the future. Let me go on a bit further. What I want to suggest is that the actual world is very much like this. Instead of pigeon holes we talk about states."

"I understand what you're saying. You have a division into a number of states. Choice of any one of them constitutes the present. My problem is, who decides which pigeon hole to look in, the one that constitutes the present?"

"If I could answer that question I'd be a good half-way

towards solving everything. Before I say anything about it let me ask *you* a question. Suppose that in each of these states your own consciousness is included. As soon as a particular state is chosen, as soon as an imaginary office worker takes a look at the contents of a particular pigeon hole, you have the subjective consciousness of a particular moment, of what you call the present. Think of the clerk in an office taking a look, first at the contents of one pigeon hole, then at the contents of another. Suppose he does this, not in sequence, but in any old order. What is the effect on your subjective consciousness? So far as the clerk himself is concerned, he's jumping about all over the place among the pigeon holes. So your consciousness jumps all over the place. But the strange thing is that your subjective impression is quite different. You have the impression of time as an ever-rolling stream."

We walked on for a while. I saw that if the contents of a pigeon hole could never be modified then John was right. It would be possible for his clerk to look into a particular pigeon hole a dozen times or more and you'd never know about it. All you could be aware of, on his idea, was the contents of a pigeon hole, not when or how it was sampled. But there was one thing that bothered me:

"Doesn't the idea of a sequence of choices on the part of your clerk itself imply the flow of time? If it does, the argument gets you nowhere."

"I'm sure it does not. A sequence is a logical concept in which time doesn't really enter at all."

I saw in a general sort of way what he meant. Yet I was troubled. "But if you have a rule that requires you to pass from one pigeon hole to the next, like passing from one number to the next, isn't it really exactly the same as a smooth flow of time?"

"If the rule were the one you say, yes certainly. But you could have rules that didn't require the next number to be the succeeding pigeon hole. Look, suppose we do it this way. We could choose number 1, then number 100, then number 2, then number 99, and so on until we've had every pigeon hole from 1 to 100. Then we could do the same thing from 101 to 200. That would be a different kind of rule. In fact there are infinitely many ways in which you can lay down rules, if the sequence itself is infinite. Any particular rule establishes what we call a correspondence between the pigeon holes and the choices. If every pigeon hole is chosen exactly once we have what mathematicians call a one-one correspondence. If every pigeon hole is chosen many times we have a one-many correspondence. The crux of my argument is that you get exactly the same subjective experience whatever the correspondence you choose. It doesn't matter what order you take the pigeon holes, it doesn't matter if you choose some or all of them a million times, you'd never know anything different from the simple sequential order. All you can know is the original contents of the pigeon holes themselves."

"So really the choices could be an incredible hotch-potch. You could have youth and old age interlaced with each other and you'd never know?"

"Not only that, but you could experience your youth a million times over and you'd never know. If the clerk were to put a note in a pigeon hole whenever he used it, then of course you could know you'd had a certain experience before. But as long as he leaves no note you can never know."

"I suppose so. Where have we got to now?"

"Quite a way. We've got our sequence of pigeon holes, that's the physical world. We don't think of one pigeon hole as having any more significance than another, which agrees with what I said before. We don't think of one particular state of the Earth as having any more significance than any other state of the Earth. We've completely eliminated the bogus idea of a steady flow of time. Our consciousness corresponds to just where the light falls, as it dances about among the pigeon holes. It lights up first one, then another, in some sequence that is quite irrelevant.

"Now let's come to the hard part. What is this light? I'm no longer talking in terms of a clerk in an office, because I don't want to get bogged down in human images. All our pigeon holes are in darkness except where the spot of light falls. What that light consists of, where it comes from, we know nothing. It lies outside our present-day physics.

"You remember I told you that it's possible to defy our own present-day physical laws and still to make a clear gain in our assessment of the world. You remember the radioactive nuclei with the counters surrounding them? We wanted to know whether or not in a certain period of time a nucleus had undergone decay. I said there was only one way to find out. By looking. In other words by using the spot of light in our pigeon hole. My strong hunch is that it's the spot of light that permits decisions which lie outside the laws of physics. This is why I'm so sure something else must be involved. It doesn't need to be anything mystical. It may be subject to precise description, to law and order, the same as in our ordinary physics. It may only be mysterious because we don't understand it."

"There's certainly a lot of things I don't understand. This light of yours, or whatever you like to call it, how does it decide that you are you and I am me?"

"That could be another illusion. Look, along one wall of our office we have one complete set of pigeon holes, all in their nice tidy sequence. Along another wall we have another set of pigeon holes. Two completely different sets. But there is only one light. It dances about in both sets of pigeon holes. Wherever it happens to be, there is the phenomenon of consciousness. One set of pigeon holes is what you call *you*, the other is what I call *me*. It would be possible to experience both and never know it. It would be possible to follow the little patch of light wherever it went. There could be only one consciousness, although there must certainly be more than one set of pigeon holes."

I found this a staggering idea. "If you're right it would be possible to be a million people and never know it."

"It would be possible to be much more than that. It would be possible to be every creature on every system of planets, throughout the universe. My point is that for every so-called different creature, for every different person, you need a separate set of pigeon holes. But the consciousness could be the same. There could even be completely different universes. Go back to my decaying nucleus. Hook up a bomb which explodes according to whether you have decay of a nucleus or not. Make the bomb so big that it becomes a doomsday machine. Let it be capable—if exploded—of wiping out all life on the Earth. Let the whole thing go for the critical few seconds, you remember we were considering whether a nucleus would decay in a particular ten seconds? Do we all survive or don't we?

"My guess is that inevitably we appear to survive, because there is a division, the world divides into two, into two completely disparate stacks of pigeon holes. In one, a nucleus undergoes decay, explodes the bomb, and wipes us out. But the pigeon holes in that case never contain anything further about life on the Earth. So although those pigeon holes might be activated, there could never be any awareness that an explosion had taken place. In the other block, the Earth would be safe, our lives would continue—to put it in the usual phrase. Whenever the spotlight of consciousness hit those pigeon holes we should be aware of the Earth and we should decide the bomb had not exploded."

We walked on and on. There were weird implications here.

"You speak about completely different worlds, different universes. Do you think there was a world in which everything

68

went normally? I know I'm not using words perhaps in the way you'd like me to, but I think you can get the idea. Was there a world in which none of these queer things happened?"

"I don't have any doubt about it. There was certainly a world in which, on September 27th, the men in the trenches in Flanders had Lloyd George as their Prime Minister. We know what happened in that world. It remains to be seen what will happen in this one."

I thought about this for a moment and then burst out, "You don't mean to say those men out there are going through the same experiences that men actually went through in 1917? All the mud and the shellfire?"

"Yes, of course. We're not in a pretty world."

"But don't you see what it means? Damn it all I had an uncle killed in those Flanders battles. For all I know he's out there now."

"For all you know he may not be killed this time. For all you know you may see him. It's fifty years on or thereabouts, so I don't suppose there'll be many queer cases. I mean of men being alive twice."

Incredulously, I realized what he meant, someone who had survived the trench battles might still be living. There might be two of them, a young man out there in 1917 and an old man here in 1966.

"But it's fantastic. There can't be two of you."

"You don't seem to take much notice of what I've been talking about. Remember the states of consciousness, remember the subjective impression of consciousness is not the same thing as the pigeon holes of the physical world. The consciousness of the man in the trenches is not the same as the old man living over here. The pigeon holes are different and they can never be lighted up by the same spot of light."

"You mean the spot could dance about between the two of them but so long as the pigeon holes are different there would be the subjective impression of their being totally different individuals."

"Exactly the same as you and I have the impression of being different."

We walked back in silence. I think both of us were overwhelmed, not only by these ideas, but by the situation that was soon to develop.

We got back to the garden. Then an odd detail occurred to me, "What was all that stuff about seismic disturbances?"

"My idea, only a fancy if you like, runs something like this. I've told you we're living in a new physical situation. A new bunch of pigeon holes. The game, as I see it, is that the new pigeon holes are similar in most respects to some of the pigeon holes in the other system. It's as if the present world were built out of copies of bits of the old world. Do you remember the day on the moor below Mickle Fell? Don't you realize it was a copy that came back to the caravan that night. Not quite a perfect copy, the birthmark was missing.

"Well, this whole world is a copy of some of the bits from another, the more normal world. This world may be queer by every standard we're used to but the bits must have a proper relation to each other."

"You mean there's nothing supernatural in it?"

"You might put it that way. Well, look what's involved. Think about the Earth. Things change slowly as the years pass. Landforms are not quite the same now, in 1966, as they were in 1866. So if you copy the part of the Earth that corresponds to the England of 1966, and try to fit it to the Europe of 1917, and to the America of 1700 or 1800, things won't exactly match."

An idea was working itself around in my head. "You'd need a lot of information, wouldn't you, to make copies like that?"

John paused as we entered the house. "Right you are, Dicky my boy. A lot of information. Remember what I said about that infra-red transmission. It was taking an awful lot of traffic."

"Traffic needed for the copying."

John nodded and added in a whisper, almost as if he were afraid of being overheard. "Needed for the copying. We still don't know *how* it was done but at least we know *why*. Different worlds remembered and then all put together to form a strange new world. We shall find out more as we go along. This isn't the end of it."

AS soon as we returned to the house John was collared by one of the service officers. I had spotted a piano earlier in the day. I went to see if there was any chance of my being able to play. Luckily the room with the piano was unoccupied so I shut the door and began to run my fingers over the keyboard. I was horribly out of shape and the first few minutes were pretty bad. I can't remember exactly what I played. Fragments here and there mixed in with a lot of improvisation. I was pretty wound up. For me this was the best way to get any tensions out of my system.

I became aware that someone had entered the room. It was the Prime Minister.

"I hope you don't mind my playing a bit. There didn't seem to be anybody about."

"Not in the least. It's a relief to hear something different from this appalling situation we're in."

"Is it true then? About Europe I mean?"

"There doesn't seem to be any doubt about it. Evidence is coming in from all directions. By radio, and by ships coming into port. The whole thing's a fantastic chaos. Whenever a ship comes in, both sides, those on board and those on shore, think the other is completely mad."

"What are you going to do?"

"That's what we're going to decide. We must put an end to it somehow."

"Sinclair thinks the situation is real. So far as the soldiers in France are concerned it's real, nothing different from what it was."

"I don't know which is the more surprising thing, the facts, the situation, or the whole psychology of my own position. It's all completely changed."

"I can see everything's changed, but what especially worries you?"

"Well, it's not unlike a rather delightful and remarkable

71

story I once heard. About a wagon train crossing the United States during the last century. Two children happened to survive an Indian attack, their parents and friends being killed. One was a boy of twelve, the other a girl of three. The little boy took on the responsibility of getting his sister to California, and somehow succeeded. A complete change from dependence to responsibility. For the last two decades we've been drifting here in Britain in a thoroughly aimless fashion. There was nothing we could do to have any real effect on the world. After the responsibilities of the nineteenth century we'd suddenly become peripheral. Of course we've been pretending, I've been pretending, that we could have influence in other countries, and so influence the course of events. But it was a pretence really designed to keep up our own self-respect. Now everything's suddenly changed, just as it did for those two children. It seems as if what's happening in Europe, and what's going to happen, depends utterly and completely on us."

The Prime Minister paced rapidly up and down the room. There was suddenly a decisive air about him, an attitude far removed from the bumbling policies of the last few years.

The number of visitors at Chequers had increased sharply during the afternoon. In addition to the politicians and the military there were now economists and two professors of history from Oxford. Messages from the outside world were constantly arriving, replies were constantly being sent. A buffet supper had been arranged. We took platefuls of food to a long table, sat down, and the discussion began. The Home Secretary said an immediate policy decision must be made, within the hour.

"We've reached the stage where something really definite must be said to the people. It can't be very long before the truth gets known. The strong westerly winds of the last few days have dropped. People in the south, particularly in Kent, can actually hear the gunfire in Flanders."

The Prime Minister agreed to make an appearance on television, to make a frank statement about the whole position. Messages to the BBC and ITV were instantly dispatched.

Then the meeting got down to the problem in everybody's mind, how to stop the tragedy in France. Not a single person round the table had any thoughts otherwise. At all costs the disastrous attacks of early October, the attacks inevitably leading to the mud of Passchendaele, had to be prevented.

With the superior technology of 1966 it was at first sight easy to force a dictated peace on all the combatants. But how could the deadly weapons of the post-nuclear era be explained

72

to minds still immersed in the second decade of the century? A simple display of force would be almost meaningless. Nor was there any prospect of peace being imposed through conventional weapons. In fact the conventional weapons at the disposal of the Prime Minister and his colleagues were negligible in total weight compared to the weapons possessed by the European armies. Guns and tanks were now vastly more refined, it was true, but their numbers were far too small to have any real effect. Only with planes and bombs could anything be done in this line. The air marshals confidently asserted that with complete mastery of the air it would be possible to destroy railway communications on the German side. In this way it would be possible to cut off all supplies to the German side of the fighting line. It was generally agreed, however, that this would only be done as a last resort, if the Germans were unwilling to take an immediately negotiated peace seriously.

The historians were called in at this point, to assess the German attitude to the war in 1917. There was a lot of talk about German political parties, the Social Democrats, the Centre, about the army and the Junkers. Surprisingly perhaps, the opinion was that negotiation might be easiest with the Junkers. It was said their chief motive in fighting the war, besides maintaining the prestige of the Germany army, was to hold on to their estates in East Germany. The Social Democrats were apparently wrong in the head, expansionist in outlook, and the Centre was worse than impossible.

The French position was plainly tricky. Their country had been violated, their army was passing through a difficult psychological phase, and their only dream was the eventual defeat of Germany. It was open to question whether the French would take kindly to a negotiated peace. The Prime Minister must visit Paris without delay, it was agreed.

At this point the problem of communication with the continent came in for discussion. It was pointed out that the first planes sent from Britain had failed to return. Perhaps the crew members had been taken for madmen, or perhaps the planes had been shot down? I saw the hint of a smile on John's face and knew he had a different explanation. Later he told me those planes had simply flown into—nothingness, before the different zones of the Earth were fully joined.

The opinion was that there would be no difficulty in landing in France provided a strong force of planes was sent. Then the problem of what to do about the British army came up for discussion. This was a matter of some delicacy. Yet even the Chief of Staff agreed that the commanding officers, particularly

Sir Douglas Haig, must be recalled without delay. This would be a matter of difficulty, it was realized. The simplest method might be a letter purporting to come from Lloyd George, which would involve forging the old gaffer's signature. Arrangements were immediately put in hand.

Lastly it was agreed to mount an intense psychological campaign. Scores of heavy transport planes would be sent over the fighting line with thousands of tons of leaflets. There would be leaflets for the British, the French, and the Germans. They would say the same thing, they would tell the common soldier to stop it, not to fire another shot, another shell. This would be on the full authority of the British government.

As I heard these preparations being put in train I wondered to myself what it was that had changed in the British government between 1917 and 1966. Here was the Prime Minister in much the position Lloyd George had been in in 1917. Yet, whereas Lloyd George's thoughts had been wholly on how to prosecute the war more efficiently, we were now discussing it on the basis of an instant ceasefire. Nobody around the table had the slightest doubt of what must be done. I saw the difference came from the condition of our minds. In 1917, 1917 in Britain, nobody had been able to think outside the war situation. No doubt everybody wanted the war to stop. Yet everybody in 1917 had lacked the confidence to take the necessary steps. In 1966 our minds were completely outside that situation.

Everybody now had an inner confidence that the situation could be dealt with, somehow. This confidence, I saw, came from the technology of 1966. If our high-speed planes had been taken away, if there were no nuclear weapons in the background, if our industries were not enormously more efficient than the European ones, then we might have found ourselves thinking differently. Our escape from the mentality of 1917 really came from a lack of the fear that haunted the British government in 1917.

When the economists began to speak I realized that our situation in the long term wasn't any too favourable, however. Our technology depended to a considerable extent on large imports of oil. These would no longer be forthcoming, if the world of 1917 existed also in the Middle East. Here it transpired that absolutely nothing had come from the armies in the East, nothing from Egypt or from Mesopotamia. It was agreed this should be looked into forthwith. There would have to be a large-scale conversion back to coal as an energy source. And our coal reserves in 1966 were not too good. Above all, where would we get food imports? With the

United States and Canada out of the picture, there was no simple answer to this question. Nothing was known yet about Australia. So there was still some hope of food from the Antipodes. But this was only a hope. It was manifest that the only satisfactory policy for the world of the future was to use the manpower of Europe. With the war ended, every available part of Europe must be put to food production. Oil production must be started in the Middle East without further delay.

I wasn't clear where John and I would come into this picture. When the meeting broke up for a short rest, at about nine o'clock, John got me on the side. He told me he had made arrangements, with the Prime Minister's approval, to get a survey of the world started. If it was 1917 in Europe, about 1750 in North America, there was no telling what it was on the rest of the Earth.

We would use one of the big long-distance planes, at any rate in the first instance. We would make a survey for possible landing places. If there were none, then at a later stage we would have to use flying boats, which could quickly be made available for our use. With these we could land on water, more or less as we pleased, provided the weather was fine. All this was clearly an excellent idea and I was not at all disappointed to be in on it. Yet the situation in Europe, its inner psychology, fascinated me. I hoped we would remain fairly close to events as they developed.

The Prime Minister left to make his speech to the nation. Everybody crowded around a television set as the time for the telecast at last came up. It was a good clear account of the situation, gravely delivered. I could not help wondering what the effect would be on the average viewer. Two months ago it would have seemed raving madness. But now the people would be partially prepared for it. I remembered the crowds back at London airport the previous evening. For all I knew, an end to uncertainty would prove more a relief than otherwise.

We also watched the programme which followed the Prime Minister. With their usual pertinacity, the news agencies must already have discovered the truth. A BBC team of commentators had managed to get across to France. Well-known faces appeared. They had lost their usual smooth technical competence. Wild and distraught now, they were with the British army at Ypres.

We learnt that most of their number had been arrested by the army authorities but a film of what they had found there had been smuggled out of France, presumably with the aid of a light aircraft. To me, the First World War has always had the aspect of a nightmare viewed from the comforting light of the day. Here it was displayed in all its nightmare qualities with the urgency of the present about it. The camera spared us neither the mud, nor the shellfire, nor the wounded and the dead. There were interviews with the living, conjuring up visions of hell. Then quite suddenly it was all over. With mature perception, the BBC announced a complete closure of all its services for the night; for nothing in the way of a normal programme could possibly have followed what we had just seen.

The next day there was an outcry from the Press. *The Times* demanded that whatever was going on in France must be stopped, instantly, without delay. The cry was echoed on every hand. It was clear that action must be swift and immediately effective if the government was to survive even for a week. The irony of the change in outlook of the British people over fifty years escaped almost everyone.

For the next month little useful work was done by the population at large. Most people spent a large part of their time within range of a television set. Everybody in any way immediately involved in the crisis itself worked, however, with a furious intensity. The day after our conference at Chequers we were told to proceed on our voyages of exploration. So we were back at London airport, back with our Australian friend and his plane. We took off early on the morning of September 21st, as the date was here in Britain. Our mission was to proceed east, to the battlefront between the German and Russian armies. It occurred to me that the Tsar was still in power in Russia, Lenin and the Bolsheviks had not yet appeared. This would have given great satisfaction to the Americans if they had been there to appreciate it. Of course there was still Hawaii. This was another ironical situation, for the fiftieth state had suddenly become the first.

I wondered whether the pilot would make a deliberate excursion into northern France. I was rather glad he did not. I needed no further convincing about what was going on there. We were soon across the North Sea and over the southern part of Denmark. Then we headed more or less due east. At our height we were quite immune from any primitive anti-aircraft fire. Our immediate objective was Berlin. Although we had no radio guidance, apart from the fixes which we got from stations back in Britain, we found the city without undue difficulty. There, thirty thousand feet below us, was the city of the Kaisers. War stricken now, its people ill-clad and hungry, dreading the approach of winter, the fourth winter of war. Twenty-five years earlier we should have been dropping bombs. Today we dropped some twenty tons of leaflets which had been printed in a high priority rush job the previous day. I was fascinated by the thought of what the people would think when they read:

BRITISH GOVERNMENT DEMANDS CESSATION OF WAR

There followed a precise statement of the numbers of the dead, wounded, and missing. They were given month by month, for the different battlefronts. To the authorities in Germany they would appear quite fantastically accurate, for they had been compiled from the Germans' own postwar records. The leaflets fluttering down through the air below us were likely to prove vastly more effective than a plane load of bombs could ever be. There would also be the fantasy generated by the sight from the ground of our plane, monstrous by the standards of 1917. The shattering effect of all these factors was clear to me.

Clouds gathered as we flew further east. We could see nothing of what lay below. Our mission was to discover the state of things in Russia, if possible to report on the eastern battlefront. To do this it would be necessary to go down to lower altitudes to break through the cloudbank which now obscured our view. There seemed no particular reason to fear anti-aircraft fire.

We must have been somewhere near the Russian border when the pilot set us on a gentle glide. To begin with it was very much the same as it had been coming into London airport on our flight from Hawaii. There we had come down on to a sea of clouds, had gone quite quickly through it, and had at last come out with a clear view of the ground. It had been exactly what we expected and hoped it would be. Now as we came out through the clouds we saw a great flat plain stretching away in all directions, brown and desolate, without the slightest trace of vegetation. It was a wilderness of bare rock.

We flew on towards the east. An hour later we were somewhere over the position of Moscow. The clouds were clearing. To our astonishment what looked like a vast ocean lay ahead. Yet it was an ocean such as none of us had seen before. As we came clear of the clouds we were dazzled by an intense light from below, coming from the direction of the Sun. The ground was evidently a far better reflector than the waters of the oceans. Compared to the intense light towards the south, the north was dark, a dark purple. Once we had learnt to avoid the southern glare we were amazed by the profusion of colours the sunlight was bringing out in the material below us.

We came down low, to about five hundred feet on the altimeter. Still we could see nothing but a smooth plain. There were no familiar landmarks from which we could judge our height, it all looked the same from any height. There were no trees, houses, no rocks or boulders, nothing.

Still we flew on. Two hours later we were over what should have been the Ural mountains. The level plain was unbroken. There was neither hill nor valley. There was always the iridescent plain below us. We discussed the possibility of landing. There was no problem about finding a flat place, it was all flat. What we didn't know was whether the surface was firm or soft. If it were soft we should simply bog in. Take-off would be impossible even if the pilot managed the landing safely. To be marooned in this trackless waste was certain death. We were well into Siberia by now, more than a thousand miles from the nearest inhabitation. We could never cross this great plain on foot. Nor was it easy to see how we could possibly be rescued if we got ourselves into trouble. If a landing was impossible for us, it would be impossible for any plane sent out to our help. Yet we all felt something had to be done. Somehow we had to find out what this thing below us was. We could go back to base, of course, and make plans for tomorrow, or for the following week, but it was hard to see how this would get us any further.

One thing was favourable, there was almost no wind. This meant we could go down in a smooth gentle glide if we wanted to. Our Australian pilot was not to be put off, "I'm going to have a crack at the bastard," he said. "We'll go down until our wheels touch, then I'll bring her up again. We ought to be able to tell from the hydraulic shock on the wheels whether we're dealing with soft or hard ground."

Now we were down to a thousand feet, then quickly down to five hundred. The last seconds seemed interminably long. The jolt was much harder than I expected, really because the pilot didn't quite know where the surface was. As we came up again it needed no examination of the hydraulic system to know that we had hit hard ground.

Our line was to the north so as to avoid the glare of the

Sun. After stabilizing the aircraft and checking the instruments we came down again. This time we made a normal landing. There would be nobody here to wheel a flight of steps out to the plane. We would have to hang a ladder of some sort. The crew got out a lightweight metal job. I was glad of this, because the rigidity of the metal would make the climb back into the plane reasonably easy. We opened the front hatch and let out the ladder. A couple of minutes later I was swinging down it.

I stepped gingerly on to the ground, then away from the ladder, and down on my hands and knees. I ran a hand over the surface. It was completely smooth. I tried to dig into it with a fingernail, but it was quite resistant. The colours were more vivid down here. By turning round in a circle from the direction of the Sun in the south to the antisun in the north, and then back again in the south, it was possible to go through a whole cycle of changes. It was a vivid yellow towards the Sun, then green as one swivelled round towards the west, then a pale blue in the north-west, purple in the north, and back through the same colours in a reverse order as one turned through east to the south again. It was the same wherever one stood.

I walked away from the plane to a distance of about three hundred yards. The difference between looking towards the plane and looking away from it was quite fantastic. Looking away from it one had no impression of scale whatsoever. It was impossible to know whether you were looking ten yards, a hundred yards, or even a hundred miles. The effect was bewildering and distinctly frightening. It was far more weird than the kind of white-out you sometimes get on a snowfield in the mountains. Yet as soon as you turned round, there was the plane—the whole scene jumped instantly into scale.

John came up to me.

"What do you make of it?" I asked.

"It's a kind of glass. We're on a huge glass plain stretching for thousands of miles."

"But how, how the hell did it happen?"

"Heat. Heat from outside. The surface has been melted and fused. It's a kind of glass, rather like a tektite. Except it's much more homogeneous, and far less brittle."

"You said heat from the outside. What could cause that?"

"It's a bit like the glass you get after the explosion of a nuclear weapon. But there doesn't seem to be any radioactivity, from the Geiger counters in the plane."

This explained the equipment I had seen John fiddling with during the flight.

"How far do you think it goes?"

79

"God knows. Perhaps all the way to China."

"That's going to take out a big slice of the land area."

"You know it's very strange. . . ."

John stopped, as he always did, when he was in the middle of some important statement. Now he went on, "How smooth it all is. You'd expect the surface to be scratched, by blown sand or bits of grit. It should have a sort of sand-blasted, matt finish."

"You think that's important?"

"Well, it must mean there's never been any bits of sand or grit, there's no other explanation. The point I think is that everything's been melted, every damn last bit of surface rock. Nothing was left over."

"If we follow up your idea about different parts of the Earth belonging to different ages, do you think this could refer to a time after a disastrous nuclear war?"

"It could, I suppose. If it were a few centuries or more afterwards, I suppose the radioactivity would mostly have died down. We'd better dig up a chunk of the stuff and take it back with us for analysis. That should tell us if there's any long-lived artificial radioactivity in it. Probably it isn't much good speculating until we know the facts."

When we attempted to quarry the material we found the ground quite extraordinarily hard. We laughed at our fears about making a landing. The whole plain, millions of square miles of it, was just one ideal, perfect airstrip.

It began to grow chilly as the Sun fell lower in the west. We decided to eat a meal before taking off. After a short argument it was decided to have it out of doors. The food was handed down the ladder by the crew. Soon we were munching sandwiches and drinking hot coffee. We took a last walk around the plane. A quarter of an hour later we were back in the air. Turned towards the Sun we were on our homeward journey.

We managed just about to hold our own with the rotation of the Earth, so the Sun maintained its position pretty well constant in the sky as we flew westward. Scattered clouds began to appear, then there was a thicker cover below us. An hour and a half later we were back over eastern Germany. I wondered what furious interchange of messages was going on down there, what diplomatic activity.

It was about six o'clock when we landed at London airport. We were almost smothered by reporters and cameramen. A posse of police managed to make a way for us. It occurred to me that not one of the newshounds around us could have suspected, eerie and odd as this new world might seem to them, that we had come back from something still stranger and more remote.

We discovered there was no possibility of getting the plane serviced soon enough for us to be able to make another exploratory voyage the following day. So I returned for the night to my own apartments in London. I found Alex Hamilton glued to the television set. He asked me what I knew about the situation. I told him a little, not too much. Then I asked him for his opinion. He said it was very interesting that, with America out of the way and with Europe back in 1917, we were way ahead of Webern and Schoenberg. All we had to do was to murder all the musicians in Britain, to destroy all the libraries, and we would be made. I said I thought he was completely on the wrong lines. These new events called for an epic style, not for abstractionalism. At this he fell into one of his laughing fits. "So you're thinking of reviving the Cologne piece."

I said I was thinking of much more than that, but along the same lines. In fact I was bursting with ideas and would be glad of the following day to jot a few things down.

I made dinner while Alex went on watching TV. Afterwards we both watched it. The BBC seemed to have moved into France *en bloc*. They reported that the Prime Minister had seen the French Prime Minister, Monsieur Briand. According to the reports the French were proving difficult. They were insisting that honour be satisfied. Then we learnt the Germans were sending their Foreign Minister to London, a man of the name of Kuhlmann. The British commanders in the field had been replaced by modern officers who were preparing a general retreat from the trenches.

At this stage I must put my own experiences aside in order to relate at secondhand how it came about that the war situation in France simply collapsed like a pack of cards. First the men themselves, the ordinary fighting soldiers. In the last months of 1917 they were in a curious psychological state of mind. They had come to see the trenches as the real world, they had come to regard the situation back home as an unreal dream. It was as though they had walked out of the ordinary world into hell and now hell was the place which really counted. If they thought at all of the people back home, then apart from their families it was with a dull sullen hatred. This was true as much on the one side as the other. So when

81

instructions came to cease from the horrible slaughter the men had not the slightest compunction about obeying. It was what they wanted anyway. It had been the *outside* that had been impelling them. Suddenly it seemed as if a miracle had happened somehow on the outside, which was the way it had to be. What they had gone through could only be made good by a miracle. They had paid enough in agony for any miracle. If there was little element of rationality in this point of view it was backed by intense emotion. To the men it was a heaven-sent deliverance. The psychological effect of discovering a hiatus of fifty years seemed more or less in tune with the horrors of the battlefield itself.

On the German side there was little will to continue the fight. Kuhlmann had in any case been on the point of proposing peace terms himself, similar to those which the British government now suggested. And the German High Command was shaken to its roots by the situation in the east and south. Nothing **at** that stage was known in Germany of the existence of the huge Plain of Glass, but all communication with the East had mysteriously ceased. The railway tracks to the east continued normally to Warsaw and somewhat beyond that. Every town, every village, down to the smallest hamlet, seemed to be entirely normal up to a certain point. Then it all simply vanished. The railway tracks ceased. The vegetation ceased. Not a single person could be found. It was just a complete desert. Those who knew these facts, and there were not many at this stage, had the bottom knocked out of their self-confidence. Hindenburg and Ludendorff knew of course, as did most of the High Command. It could only mean that what was being said in the west, in Britain, was true. Added to the already bad state of the war, to the privations in Germany, it was decisive. It was agreed that Hindenburg should travel to London for the proposed conference.

A cease fire was already in effect by the time the conference was held. The biggest card in the hand of the British government was of course the military weapons of 1966. The immediate problem was to bring the strength of those weapons over to the German mind. An actual physical demonstration was to be avoided if at all possible. But in the game of political manœuvre it is known, at least in the world of 1966 it was known, that even the strongest card will have no effect unless you take steps to acquaint your opponents of its existence. There is little point in keeping a card secret and then playing it as a sudden surprise. Almost exactly the reverse. Playing a strong card always alters a situation so it is never the same at the end as it was at the beginning.

The problem was solved in a simple fashion. It was solved by using one of the most remarkable feats of 1966, but one quite unmilitary in character. It was done simply with a high fidelity gramophone. Delegates from the continent were ushered through a room in which an old-fashioned tinny machine, the sort you wind up, with a little horn, was playing. It wheezed out its feeble sounds as the delegates assembled in the conference room. The delegates were at first surprised at this apparent eccentricity. Then they were shattered by a sudden switch to full volume on the 1966 equipment.

All that needed to be done was to draw a simple analogy. The Prime Minister just pointed out that the weapons of his own day, of 1966, bore the same relation to the weapons being used in France, as did this new powerful gramophone to the little whining horn of 1917. He asked the German staff officers to compare their own weapons with those of the year 1860. Then perhaps they would understand how things stood. He wasn't telling them this in order to claim a victory. He wasn't interested in a victory as they would understand it. The important thing was to get down to a discussion of acceptable peace terms. All that was needed was a rational, reasonable approach to the problem. It was rather like a headmaster scolding a group of naughty boys.

Two days after our first flight of exploration we made a second one. Our aim was to discover the state of affairs in the Mediterranean, the Near East, and the Middle East. Our plan was to fly out over the Balkans, then over Turkey, Armenia, into Persia, and back via Palestine, Greece, and Italy. We wanted to find out how far to the south the great Plain of Glass extended. It was the same crew and personnel as before.

As we climbed aboard the plane I was in a divided state of mind. I had a host of musical ideas hammering away in my brain, but I was dead set to make the trip for I was utterly fascinated by the strange new geography of the Earth. Also I was baffled and intrigued by the psychological problems that were going to occur when the men from 1917 came home to the world of 1966. How were the two worlds to collaborate with each other? What would happen when a man, perhaps of thirty, back from the trenches, met his own son in the year 1966, his son at the age of sixty. And how of the strangest cases of all, those in which a man appeared twice, both young and old? Questions such as these seemed so weird and singular that I would have been astonished to learn as I walked up the steps into the aircraft that I was on the verge of a trip which would take me still farther away from the sane, stable world of a month ago. I still had no conception of how deep the waters were to run.

WE flew out across the battlefields. From our height, about twenty-five thousand feet, the devastation had a pitiful aspect about it. After our flight across America, and our recent flight in the East, the scale here seemed very tiny. It was tragic to think so small a fragment of the Earth had cost so many lives.

Within an hour we were over central Germany, then over Austria-Hungary, as I suppose it must now be called. The sharpness of the transition in the Balkans was obscured by the mountainous country. By the time we emerged into the flat lands of Rumania all was changed. Gone were patterns of organized cultivation. Plainly the line of demarcation between 1917 and something quite different occurred somewhere in the Transylvanian Alps.

We came down low. There was no absence of vegetation here. It grew in abundance. It was all utterly out of control, without organization. It looked as though man had never set his hand on the forests and grasslands which lay below us.

We flew over the Black Sea to the Turkish coast. Not a single ship or craft of any kind did we see. It was the same story in Turkey, wild vegetation without any sign of human activity or interference.

By now I was greatly impressed by how vast the Earth really was compared to the limited regions of which I had any knowledge myself. At first the changes in these regions had seemed of enormous significance. Yet Europe had shifted by only fifty years, America by only a couple of hundred years or so. Over most of the Earth the times might well be utterly different.

We flew on over Armenia to the Caspian. Then on the far side of the Caspian we saw one of our objectives, the shining Plain of Glass. Evidently we were again near some line of demarcation. We found the actual line running just south of what used to be the Aral Sea. Of that sea there was not the slightest trace. We turned south in the direction of Tashkent and Samarkand. The glass gave way to sand quite suddenly as if the fusing agent had extended to a particular point and then no further. Here there was straightforward desert, sand.

We must have been somewhere near latitude 40° when we picked up the first traces of humanity. There was not much of it, only an occasional very tiny village. Yet we were enormously encouraged by this modest discovery. We found nothing at all in the place we took to be the site of Tashkent. So we turned west again with the intention of exploring Baghdad and the Tigris-Euphrates valleys. We found more scattered evidence of human habitations, all on a very tiny scale. Even before we reached Baghdad I think we realized we were not looking down on the world of 1917.

On the site of Baghdad—there could be no doubt about the site from the contours of the river below us—there was only a small collection of hovels. Again we found only minute villages on the banks of the great rivers. This was not a part of the world I had been in, or over, before. So I had no real standard of comparison. But there seemed more water than I would have expected. Our pilot was in no doubt of it himself.

"A bloody great swamp down there, almost like the mouth of the Ganges. Completely changed. Pity we don't have a flying boat."

We flew quite low on two or three occasions but could see no people. Perhaps this was not surprising for anybody down there must surely have thrown themselves into hiding at the roar of the plane. Our failure to find anything of interest as we travelled back to the west depressed us more and more. Nothing was to be seen in Mesopotamia of the armies of 1917. We flew on towards Palestine. Our intention was to locate the city of Jerusalem. This we could easily do once we found the Dead Sea, simply by flying on a westerly course from the northern end of the Sea.

We missed the Dead Sea on our first run. Since we were operating on our compasses we could always expect to be a hundred miles off course due to the wind. We did indeed come over a large expanse of water but it was clear we had reached the Mediterranean. So we turned south along the coast of Palestine in the direction of Egypt. We kept on until the coastline turned due west. This we knew must be the neighbourhood of Gaza. From there we found the Dead Sea quite easily. We carried out our plan of flying west from the northern tip. In five minutes or so we were over what should have been Jerusalem. There seemed to be signs of habitation but once again it was just a few hovels. There was no sign of the city of David, captured around the year 1050 B.C. It was plain the

Hebrews had not, and now never would, reach the lands below us. Into this new world Christ would not be born.

We headed out over the Mediterranean. Very soon we were over the wine-dark seas of Greece. My reveries were sharply interrupted by a sudden grip on the arm:

"My god, look down there."

The sea was breaking around a headland twenty thousand feet below us. Standing proudly on the headland was a temple. At once we were all animated. We flew round in circles coming lower and lower.

"Look, it's complete, it's not a ruin."

"Where do you reckon we are?" I asked the pilot.

"I think we're just south of Athens."

John had been looking at the chart. "It fits the Attic peninsula. There's this island here off the east coast. Its shape fits that long one down there, doesn't it?"

There wasn't any doubt about it. We flew lower and lower. Now we could just make out people below us. They were running to the temple. I realized it was the temple of Sounion.

We said nothing as we turned up the coast to the northwest. It took only a few minutes before we were over Athens. Standing complete on the Acropolis was the Parthenon. Close by was an amphitheatre full of people. The city was not very large but at least it was a city. Whatever the time was down there it obviously had little to do with the twentieth century. The time had to be somewhere between the date of construction of the Parthenon, which I remembered to be about 450 B.C., and the date at which the temple at Sounion fell into ruin, which it must have done in the first centuries A.D. There seemed little doubt that we were looking down on the Greece of classical times.

We would have liked to have flown around for a long time, to have come as low as we dared, but we all realized it would be better not to do so. The people down there would see the great bird in the skies as a visitation from the gods. There would be panic and a wailing and gnashing of teeth. The sooner we were away the better. So regretfully we headed west towards Corinth. Naturally there was no canal cutting through the narrow neck of land which separates the Peloponnese from the land to the north. We saw a multitude of small boats as we flew along the Gulf, propelled it seemed by human muscle power, by oarsmen.

A further surprise was in store for us. Very naturally we were heading for Rome. We were doing so in the full expectation of it being classical times everywhere throughout the

Mediterranean. The situation in Rome would allow us to date the epoch more closely. We were due for a sharp disappointment for over the Italian mainland there was nothing but vegetation. We flew on and on and it was the same everywhere. No city of Rome at all. No towns, villages, or hamlets. Only as we came north of the Alps did the wild country change. Quite abruptly we were in a modern society with its towns and streets and its factories. It was probably 1917 down there but we all felt we had suddenly come back to our own times. It was the same all the way from Switzerland across France. Then we were over the English Channel. It was hard to believe as we flew over the neat fields of Kent that the other regions of the Earth were so grotesquely changed.

To say it felt like waking from a dream is an admitted cliché yet there was a dreamlike quality about it all. Even now, I thought as we moved in to land, we have seen only a fraction of the Earth. We don't really know the Glass Plain extends right through China. We had no idea of the situation in Africa, or in South America, or anywhere in the southern hemisphere for that matter.

After the sandy deserts of the Middle and Near East, after the missing city of Jerusalem, Greece had seemed real enough. Now I was back in London it all seemed wildly ridiculous. Could one seriously credit that out there it might still be the third, fourth, or fifth century B.C. Yet the fifth century B.C had been just as real and sharp as 1966.

I had dinner the following night with John. We discussed at length our next moves. It was clear the flights of discovery had to go on without hindrance or delay. It was imperative to get a general idea of the new layout of the whole Earth. One of us at least must continue on those trips. The problem was to decide whether we should both go or whether we should split up, one to continue the general survey, the other to investigate details, perhaps details of the situation in Greece. This would have to be done with the greatest care. The Greeks would not be alarmed by the arrival of strangers, provided they came in a fashion that seemed normal, by boat from the sea. But not in a modern boat with thumping engines. John told me preparations were already being made along these lines. The government had asked the navy to send in an expedition. Did I want to be included in the party? If I did it would be necessary to drop my name in the right quarter, and without delay. I said I would sleep on it. We agreed to meet again at lunch on the morrow.

The decision was an awkward one pretty well evenly

balanced. I was completely fascinated at the prospect of seeing classical Greece at first hand. This would be the real thing, not a cruise organized two thousand years after the event. Yet I had the feeling I would be pushing myself out of the main stream of events. The trip must surely be a leisurely one taking weeks if not months. I would lose contact with John. I would hence lose my entrée to the high-stepping circles in which I had moved of late. This was entirely a matter of unbridled curiosity not at all of snobbery. I wanted to know what was going on. Quite clearly the intricate dealings between Britain and Europe would be utterly intriguing to observe at close quarters.

Ironically these considerations were grossly wide of the mark for the mainstream of events was not at all where I supposed it to be. As it came about my decision made no difference to my arriving at the true mainstream, but in the ultimate outcome it did make a critical difference, that of my arriving independently not by John's much more direct route. No thoughts of this kind were in my mind of course when at last I came down on the side of the Grecian expedition. It was music which swayed the balance. For one thing, here was the chance to settle all the controversy and arguments about ancient music. For another, I was more and more feeling the need of leisure to give expression to my own creative impulses. The flights, the discussions, marvellously intriguing in themselves, were consuming the whole of my time and energies. A reduction of tempo was needed.

When I told John of my decision he was a little doubtful:

"Things have changed a bit in the last twenty-four hours, I'm afraid. The government is getting itself bogged down more and more with the European situation. They're really not in a position to give much priority to the Greek business. It was agreed yesterday to keep things pretty well on ice for the time being."

"You mean the expedition is off?"

"Not entirely but it's only going to be a small show."

I have an obstinate streak in me. When I'm thinking about any issue I like to hear the opinions of other people. I like to collect as much information as possible. But once I've made a decision I like to stick to it. Once I've made up my mind I hate to be "advised." I passed off John's entirely good-tempered warning. I'd made my decision. I told him so and without further ado he regarded the matter as closed.

"They've put the whole thing under an old naval boy, Admiral Cochrane. You'll be hearing from him pretty soon."

Throughout lunch I could see John was bubbling over with something or other. Until my problem was out of the way he wouldn't say what it was. Then he chuckled and let it all out:

"Remember we were talking the other day about what would happen when a man in 1966 came face to face with himself in 1917? Well, it's happened, in a way."

"How d'you mean, in a way?"

"Not a direct confrontation, as of yet."

"Go on."

"A most exalted member of the government. They've managed to hush it up so far, but it's bound to come out."

"Why shouldn't it come out?"

"They're still keeping the identity of the exalted member secret but I don't think I would need more than one guess."

"I wish I could guess what it is you're driving at."

"We were thinking in terms of a man from the trenches coming back and meeting himself. Remember?"

"For heaven's sake, out with it!"

"It's not the man that's come back from France, it's the mother."

"I'm getting in deeper, into a bog."

"The mother was in the VAD. She's come back. So the son has met his mother, aged twenty, thirty years or so younger than he is."

"Very touching I would imagine."

"You're still not with it, I'm afraid. The point is the mother was, more properly *is*, of a kindly disposition. She took pity on a young officer. Natural enough in the circumstances, considering what's been going on in France. In a curious way, death always tends to breed life."

The preposterous implication hit me. "You mean the *alter ego* is still in the womb!"

"Right. You could hardly imagine a confrontation more curious than that, could you? I thought I'd covered most of the possibilities but this one got completely past me."

On this ludicrous note John and I parted, the one of us as it turned out to follow the high road, the other the low road. Not to Scotland, to somewhere very different.

WHILE the events of this narrative were still happening it was difficult to separate the trivial from the important. It was also difficult to perceive any general structure underlying the whole affair. Yet looking backward it is easy to see that the structure was rather like the two acts of a play with each act divided into two scenes. The experiences in Scotland, California, and Hawaii constituted Act 1, Scene 1, the juxtaposition of the Britain of 1966 with the Europe of 1917 constituted Act 1, Scene 2.

The second act remains for me to describe. My point here is that the two acts were connected by occurrences whose very ordinariness quite concealed the inexorable transition which took place from the still more or less normal world of Act 1 to the utterly new and strange world of Act 2.

Outwardly nothing more was involved than the transport by sea of a small party from Britain to Greece. In the spring of 1966 it had been easy to breakfast in London, to lunch in Athens, the flight by air took a mere two hours. By September 28th, the day we left Portsmouth Harbour, there were no flights. The number of planes now existing in the whole world was quite few. There were no airports in Greece any more. There were no rail tracks, no roads even, across the Alps. Every available ship had been diverted to the European crossings. There was no simple way of reaching Greece any more, and those ways which apparently were open, like our sea route, became closed only a few days later. We crossed a barrier on September 30th as we steamed south off the coast of Portugal. The following day, October 1st, would have been too late.

The day after my last talk with John Sinclair I had a call from Admiral Cochrane. I learned the party was to be under the "command" of a Captain Morgan Evans, a one-time classical scholar of Balliol. An anthropologist, also with a knowledge of ancient Greek and also from Oxford, had been chosen. I believed I had heard of Anna Feldman, a formidable battle-axe as I recalled. Two other members from an intelligence unit remained to be assigned to the expedition. The general idea was to take a naval vessel to a point south of Greece and just west of Crete. A small boat would then be launched and would continue to the Greek mainland. The boat would be equipped both with sail and with auxiliary engines. Following a discussion of such details the Admiral suggested the whole party might meet for dinner that night, would I be available?

Outwardly there was nothing about Anna Feldman to suggest the tempestuous virago, inwardly it might be another matter. To the eye she seemed a pleasant-looking woman in the middle thirties. I took immediately to Morgan Evans. I judged him to be about fifty. I also judged him to have a real Welsh temperament underlying the reserve of the naval officer. Of the chaps from intelligence there was still no sign— I presumed they were lying doggo until the last possible moment.

Dinner was over before nine o'clock. It seemed a bit early to break up so I suggested we might all proceed to my apartments after making the usual apologies for untidiness and disarray. We flagged a taxi and drove through the nearly empty streets.

I had been chosen for the expedition because of my presence on the original discovery flight. Only when the Admiral noticed sheets of manuscript scattered over my piano did he realize I was a musician. The old boy turned out to have a regular passion for Schubert. I started with the *Rosamunde* ballet music, then the Opus 90 impromptus. Whenever I play any composer's works I always become increasingly enthusiastic as I go on. More and more Schubert poured forth, the Schubert of the popular image, with wonderful tunes and rustling accompaniments. Then I remembered the other Schubert, the Schubert of fire and grandeur, a Schubert almost unknown to the world at large. I hunted quickly among stacks of music. At last I found what I wanted, the three posthumous sonatas. I started on the F sharp Minor.

What can one say of the Andantino in this sonata? Why call it Andantino, why refer to a shattering achievement as if it were a child's piece? How the devil did the man do it? How did the composer of *Rosamunde* suddenly become the composer of the F sharp Minor? How did extreme subtlety suddenly become combined with a consuming flame of passion and tragedy?

I continued to ponder these questions in the weeks and months ahead. I came at last to understand far more of what I now believe to be the essence of music, more than I ever gleaned from my teachers or from my own endeavours as a pianist and as a composer. Great music has nothing really to do with technique or even with an honest determination. Technique, skill, experience, determination, all these are necessary factors, but they are only peripheral. For every musician who has achieved anything truly great there must have been hundreds with adequate technique and keen determination. The missing component was the inner wellspring of emotion. Unless the inner fires burn with a fierce intensity the rest serves only as a gloss, like an automobile standing there with its paintwork and chrome all polished and shining but without any engine to drive it.

I have always had barely hidden doubts about much of contemporary music. I understand abstract music, I know what composers are trying to do: I have myself written quite a lot of abstract music but always I have had a sense of unease. Now I see why. Abstract music represents an attempt by very highly skilled people to eliminate from music the essential component which they themselves lack, the emotional fires. Abstract music is an attempt to make technique sufficient, an indefensible position I think. For why on this basis should one not be a mathematician? Music is the wrong profession for the purely abstract.

The difficulty of course is that you can't conjure emotion, sexual emotion perhaps, but not the deeper emotions. Schubert wrote those posthumous sonatas because he was impelled to do so. But not by thoughts of box office or of the plaudits of the world. There must indeed have seemed every likelihood that his manuscripts would even be thrown away, that every note would be lost to oblivion. Yet this was of no consequence, for Schubert wrote in his last year, with the figure of Death standing clearly over him. These sonatas were his dialogues with Death. They were his inquiry, a musician's inquiry, into the meaning of life and death. The world, in the sense of "success" or of "recognition," had no part in them.

Perhaps here we have a clue to why the Andantino was so named. Perhaps it did seem like a child's piece when taken in such a grim dialogue. I played the Andantino with very little pedal. At the end the Admiral was so affected that for a moment I thought he had been overcome by a heart attack—in a sense he had, but of a favourable kind.

The evening with Schubert had two consequences. For one, everybody wanted a small piano to be included in the expedition's equipment. Stowing a piano aboard a ten-ton yacht would create problems but the Admiral was keenly determined on their solution.

Two days went by in which we found ourselves hanging around still waiting for the chaps from intelligence. Cochrane at last told me he was having "difficulties." Intelligence was more than fully occupied in Europe. It was now felt impossible to release anybody for our "show." This brought home very sharply the extent to which I had allowed myself to be shunted on to a side-track, very much confirming John's warning. Yet the obstinate streak in me was still dominant. I had no thought of withdrawing. I asked the Admiral if he would come along himself. Regretfully, the answer was the same, European commitments. So rather as an afterthought I asked if there would be any objection to a friend of mine, another musician, being included. This was how it came about that Alex Hamilton was aboard when at last we steamed out of Portsmouth Harbour. The second outcome of the Schubert evening.

Our ship was not very prepossessing, it was a workaday ship. It had to be because of the equipment needed to launch our boat. By the evening of September 30th we were off the coast of Portugal. The days slipped placidly away. Beyond Gibraltar now, we steamed steadily east towards the isles of Greece. We would sit on deck until far into the night. The sea was calm. Surrounded by the darkened waters, stars filling the sky, anything seemed possible. Jason and the Argonaut might have glided by.

During the next days we familiarized ourselves with the gear on the yacht. Launching was a somewhat hectic process. We anchored in as shallow water as the captain dared. Then the men built a good-sized slipway. I had visions of the yacht getting out of control as it went down into the sea but everything passed off quite well. Held on powerful ropes, the boat moved slowly foot by foot down to the water, not at all the swift dramatic launching I had expected. With its auxiliary engines started, the crew quickly had it away from the edge of our ship to a safe distance. The last step before we ourselves embarked was to check with our captain on the rendezvous we had arranged for two months hence. Greece might well be flooded by tourists and newsmen long before two months were up. Yet if this should not happen we intended to make our departure as inconspicuously as possible. We would simply reverse the procedure of our arrival. We had sufficient fuel to return to the neighborhood of Crete where we would be met by our naval escort.

It was early morning when our yacht was launched. By nine

o'clock we were on our way. We waved goodbye and within an hour we were alone in an open sea.

Really all we had to do was to run almost exactly due north. Inevitably this would bring us to the Attic peninsula. From there we could navigate simply by eye. Timing was something of a difficulty. Arriving at a modern port in the evening with modern electrical illumination was one thing. Arriving at an ancient port more or less in darkness was another. We decided it would be better not to rush things, to go slowly and to arrive the following morning. This we could easily do by changing to sail. There was a lot of sense in this because we needed practice with the sails. We were distinctly clumsy in our work. We kept the engines running at low revolutions until we got the hang of it.

By nightfall we had been going nine hours. I reckoned we must have come some fifty miles. We took down the sails and started the engines again. Our course now was somewhat to the east of north. Twelve more hours at five knots should put us just about right, providing the weather held. Luckily it did. I slept very well indeed considering the circumstances and the occasion. In a queer way it had all come to assume the aspect of an everyday experience. Saturated by the new and the strange, I was ready simply to accept whatever chanced to come along.

I woke to the smell of cooking bacon. Anna had a primus stove going. Soon I was washed and dressed and munching happily. Then it was time to stop the engines and to go back to sail. This time we managed with less incident and argument. Except that Alex almost got himself knocked overboard by a swinging boom. In the harassment of the moment I reflected that he might keep away from his sudden exits, at least for the next few hours.

By ten o'clock we could see land all the way ahead of us. The island of Hydra lay on the left. This was as it should be. Throughout the morning we sailed on, coming ever nearer to the coast ahead.

Now occurred the first event to signal our passage to a new world and a new era. We came up on a boat such as I had never seen before. It was of about the same size as our own but undecked. Although it had a single large crude sail the main contribution to its speed came from oarsmen, about ten to each side of the boat. We started the engines as a precaution, for we had no wish to fall foul of a pirate ship. Then we went in to hailing distance. There was an interchange between the men in the boat and Morgan, of which I didn't understand a word. We accelerated away from them. When we were about a quarter of a mile ahead I asked, "What did they say?"

"Only that they're on their way to Athens too. I said we were strangers which must have seemed pretty obvious. I said we'd go in ahead of them."

"I suppose it wasn't the right occasion to find out what's going on?"

"I've been thinking about that, you know. We'll have to be extremely careful in our inquiries. Remember the Greeks date their years from 776 B.C., the year in which they started the Olympic Games. The best thing will be to ask them for an explanation of how they count the years."

Then Morgan and Anna fell into an impassioned discussion about what the men in the boat had been saying. Classical scholars of the twentieth century were going to have their troubles, it seemed. Suddenly Alex gripped my arm and pointed ahead. We were getting quite close in now to what I took to be the port of Piraeus.

"Look, aren't those the Long Walls?"

We were all gazing at the seven or eight miles of unbroken wall, a wall that swept from near the sea away to the northeast. Athens we knew must lie at the northern end.

"The wall is complete," whispered Anna. "It must mean we're somewhere around the time of Pericles."

Now came the worst of our problems, to tie up the boat without using the engines. The harbour lay ahead. We could see more open boats, charmingly and somewhat impractically designed. We took the simple line of taking down sail, throwing out an anchor, and waiting for the people on shore to come to us. This worked out exactly as one might have expected. Soon there was an excited throng at the water edge obviously wondering at the strange lines of the new vessel which had appeared from the sea. Within a few moments half a dozen boats were rowed out to us. Morgan somehow managed to convey the idea that we wanted a tow to a safe spot. A dozen or more men took our rope. With much argument and laughter they hauled us about two hundred and fifty yards to a sheltered spot where there was a draught of about ten feet. Once again we put down anchor. Morgan and Alex rowed ashore in our dinghy. They made fast with a rope. Within a few minutes we were all safely landed. I realized now that our story of being strangers from the north, the land of giants in Greek lore, would seem entirely true. I was a full head taller than any of these people.

IT would be easy to become deeply involved in the very many detailed differences between modern society and the times in which we were now immersed, but an encyclopaedic description of the situation would only obscure the wood by the trees. It was the differences of principle which really counted.

Take the height of the people. I found it hard not to think of them all as children, simply because they were ten inches to a foot shorter than I was, a difference of only some fifteen per cent when you think about it. My reaction came because I was conditioned to think of significantly smaller people as children. Yet these people were just as clever, just as much driven by strong emotion, by the desire for power, love, intellectual achievement, as we ourselves were.

Everything about us was hand-made, every movement—at any rate on the land—was provided by muscle, either animal or human. While most things were meaner, evidence of better taste was to be seen in almost every article. Nothing in our modern society could exceed, or perhaps even equal, the finest women's dresses I was to see here. Yet these dresses demanded enormous effort, a far greater fraction of the productivity of the community, than was the case in modern society. This meant that fine clothing could only be worn by privileged persons and then only on special occasions. The everyday dress of the average citizen was rough and crude by our modern machine standards. It would have been impossible for it to be otherwise in a society of such limited resources.

The same was true of the buildings. On the whole people lived in houses little better than hovels. Only the wealthiest members of the community approached what we would call average middle-class comfort. Yet public buildings, the Parthenon, were of a magnificence our modern society could not equal at all. Indeed the situation was exactly reversed in the world of 1966. Private homes could be spacious and tasteful. Public buildings, public offices, hospitals, the whole gamut of state enterprises, were nearly always painfully sordid.

It took a little time both to notice and to get used to these differences. Immediately after our landing we were concerned to ensure the safety of our boat and to see our few important possessions adequately locked away below deck. No doubt hundreds of pairs of inquisitive hands would work themselves over every exposed inch of the yacht. Yet it seemed doubtful they would actually break in through the closed hatchways. At any rate we decided to take the risk. There was no car or bus to carry us the eight miles to Athens. We simply walked along the great fortified wall of the city.

We were met three miles out by civic dignitaries. I could tell nothing of what was said, for in the beginning I had only the crudest knowledge of the language, picked up from Morgan and Anna on the few days of our voyage from Britain. Morgan took on the task of explaining our position. He spoke clearly and slowly. His inflexion provided the populace at large with a considerable source of amusement. Yet his commanding height, combined with a Welsh flair for erudition, had a disarming effect on his audience. Clearly we were well received.

All I could tell was that we were escorted under favourable circumstances into the city. We arrived at length at an open area where about a thousand people had quickly gathered at the news of our arrival. The place of our congregation was a discussion arena, of the name Agora, I learnt later. There seemed to be nothing for it but that Morgan should give an account of the manner of our journey from the north, through the Pillars of Hercules, the western Mediterranean, and thence to Athens. I was surprised at the length of his speech. Only later did I realize that time was a commodity not in short supply in this community. It would have been taken as an insult, when so many were gathered together, to have spoken tersely. Morgan knew this from his classical studies. Later he told me he addressed the throng something along the following lines:

"At this time of the year the days in the north are short, the Sun lies low in the sky. Our fields and our houses are battered by the strong wind which blows everlastingly from the west. Rain clouds fill the sky with an ever-present threat of violent storms. So you may understand the thoughts of my countrymen turn often to the lands of the south, for it is a belief among our people that southern lands are warmer, winds lighter, that in every way the natural elements are less destructive of human comfort. It was to discover whether this was so that we commenced our journey."

98

I give only this short example of Morgan's discursive style. It would be painful to attempt even a partial repetition of his speech, of the manner and construction of our vessel, of the nature of our rivers and harbours, of the terrors of the open sea. He described our farewell to our native land giving them a Greek version of John Gaunt's speech from *Richard II*. Then the sights we had seen on our journey, the birds and fishes, the Rock of Gibraltar. The words flowed on and on until I wondered if he was intent on talking the whole day away. Not a sound came from the audience. Although, as I say, there was upward of a thousand of them, everyone seemed able to hear. The excellent acoustic properties of Greek theatres, always such a marvel to the modern world, came from the fact that the spoken word, discussion and argument, had absolute top priority. In days before the microphone and loud speaker, acoustics simply had to be good. Soon I was to realize that to be able to speak clearly, with persuasion and reason, was equivalent to power in this city.

Everybody listened in rapt attention. I expected a barrage of questions at the end. Yet there were no questions, only applause. Later I realized that questions were regarded as perfectly proper in any argument or disputation, but questions were not asked at the end of a free speech.

It was not until about two in the afternoon that we left the Agora. We were taken to the house of one of the wealthiest inhabitants. A meal had been prepared. For the first time I was aware of the existence of slaves. Not in any violent way but by the manner in which certain people were addressed, the voice tone is unmistakable in any language. The food was simple but of good quality. The mutton with which we were served was very far from being the everyday diet of the average Greek. The bread likewise was something important and precious. The bread was served by itself as a separate course. We were given a cup of liquid which turned out to be olive oil. Luckily I have a liking for olive oil and so did not suffer the torments which afflicted Alex. The meat was served with wine, which soon cut away the greasy taste of the oil. The oil in its turn prevented any strong intoxication. The meal ended with fresh fruit of a quality I had never tasted before.

Through the meal Morgan and Anna had of necessity to take on themselves the whole interchange of information. I noticed there was no interest at all in what we did. I was never asked what I was, and I think the notion of my being a musician would have baffled them. Everybody here was what they wanted to be, what they were interested in. This was among

99

the leisured classes, for it was taken for granted that we ourselves must be wealthy persons. Only the wealthy could contemplate a voyage such as we had made. Our hosts were concerned with the structure of the seas beyond the Pillars of Hercules, with what we believed about the nature of the world. How was our political life organized?

They didn't like the idea of elected representatives of the people. To them it was important that every free adult member of the community should be permitted to vote on every specific issue. It was impossible to explain that the very size of our population precluded their own democratic system. Morgan pointed out that our people were scattered in many cities, that it was impossible for them to be constantly travelling in order to discuss things together. It was essential for each city to appoint its own representatives and for the representatives of all the cities to confer together. I was surprised and rather alarmed by the serious, chilled manner in which this was received. The idea of a number of cities working together on terms of equality was apparently repugnant to them.

After the meal our party divided up. We were taken separately to the house of some wealthy person. My own host got little out of me, I am afraid, for in the beginning I could do no more than smile and nod. It is true my ears were already picking up the sounds of this new language. I was listening keenly, and watching the manner in which the sounds were made by the mouth, but it would be several months yet before I would be able to converse with any freedom. It came as a surprise to find how soon after sundown everybody retired for the night. I quickly became used to this aspect of life, however. Indeed, a reverse reaction set in, it became difficult to understand why the possession of artificial light persuades modern society to outphase the day. Within a week I came to think of the practice of staying up, out of bed, after the Sun has long since set, and of then staying in bed after the Sun has long since risen, as entirely absurd.

The following day I managed to convey to my host that there were certain things on the ship I would like to fetch. Lots of people wanted to help. Nobody seemed to think anything of a sixteen-mile walk, eight miles there and eight miles back.

What I wanted was the piano. It was a devil of a problem to get it out of the yacht's cabin on to the shore. There were willing hands in plenty. We took it to pieces as far as we could. It was not particularly difficult to get the smaller pieces across, the legs, the keyboard, and so forth. The trouble came with the main iron frame. Yet it is surprising what a sufficient amount of muscle power will do. I was haunted by the fear of the whole thing ending up at the bottom of ten feet of clear water. But these people knew how to lift weights. Their major buildings were an astonishing tribute to their abilities in this respect. The essential thing was not to be in a hurry. So far as possible they never made a move which could not be reversed. The first thing was to distribute the weight over the maximum possible area. The trouble with an iron frame taken by itself is the sheer concentration of its weight. So what was done was to build a kind of wooden raft to which the frame was securely tied with many ropes. Then on to the raft long poles were securely lashed, so the whole thing could be moved more or less like a passenger in a sedan chair. The long poles allowed a dozen men or more to take part in the lifting operation. First they lifted it from the yacht into one of the big open boats. Then they manœuvred the boat close enough to the shore for men wading to reach it. After this the rest was easy. They managed the full eight miles back to the city in less than three hours. I spent the afternoon and the following day carefully reassembling the parts with an apparent infinity of helpers.

Tuning was something I wasn't at all used to. I had taken the precaution of bringing a number of forks, which ensured the fundamentals of the job. Then I simply trusted to my ear. There isn't any difficulty in knowing when a piano is in tune or out of tune. The difficulty is to know exactly what to do if it's out of tune. You have to judge what move you must make next. My advantage over a professional tuner was time. I had plenty of it, I didn't have to rush on to the next job in order to earn my living. In fact I took the whole afternoon of the first day and the following day before I had it to my liking.

At this point I should mention that Alex plays the violin with great competence but like a solitary drinker he would usually only play to himself. Yet I noticed he had brought his fiddle with him. In fact I'd been quite envious of the ease with which he packed it and the ease with which he got it ashore. It struck me how much the shape and size and weight of musical instruments are related to their origin. Violins, easily carried, from itinerant players. Flutes and reed instruments, also easily carried, the possessions of wandering shepherds. Drums, not easily carried, the prerogative of courts, of pomp and circumstance. Double basses and pianofortes, not easily carried, the inventions of later ages when transport had become highly organized. I was acutely aware that, whereas Alex would be able to carry his violin from house to house, city to city, into

101

the country if need be, I would be more or less stuck here in Athens with my piano.

Of course there were compensating advantages. Harmony and counterpoint could both be given full range, or nearly full range, on a piano. On the violin only simple harmonies could be achieved, and then only by superb playing. Counterpoint was hardly to be thought of on a single violin. This wasn't the end of it. I had the whole of musical literature, not merely piano music, but symphonies and quartets, available to me.

I began to play the second afternoon of our arrival. So many people gathered around that it was necessary to move out of doors, into a fairly extensive courtyard. My audience was obviously amazed at the intricacy of the whole thing. I realized, as it turned out correctly, that their ears were not tuned to complex sounds. So I kept to simple lines. It was natural for me to play a selection of operatic arias. I played just what came into my head. There was a considerable proportion of Mozart in it. Naturally I was curious as to how the music would be received by my audience. In a quite strange way, mainly with argument. At the end of a number there would be a crowding round the piano, there would be a lot of gesticulation, and there would be a great deal of talk. I was soon to realize that the two things taken most seriously here were war and speech. Both were far ahead of sex in the estimation of the people. In fact sex was like food, a regular necessity but not to be fussed about. Talk ranged over the whole gamut, from private groups of half a dozen people up to the great oratorical speeches to many thousands. An immense amount of time and care went into the big speeches, for as I have already remarked persuasion was equivalent here to power. You were not permitted to murder a neighbour whom you might detest, but if you could persuade your fellow citizens that your neighbour was a danger to the community then the city itself would turn on him, imprison him, exile him, deprive him of his rights and property, and in extreme cases might even execute him. The gift of gab was a matter of no small importance. It extended even to music.

It wasn't long before two flutes and a lyre appeared. They were very simply but well made. A sturdy, bright-faced young fellow of eighteen or nineteen began to pipe away on one of the flutes. Soon he was joined by a girl at the lyre. She used a small piece of wood to pluck the strings. The music was in a simple 4/4 rhythm. It was highly modal in its melodic structure. That is to say the notes used depended on the pitch of the octave in which the melody happened to lie.

Let me add a word here on different systems of musical composition. They all depend on some kind of restriction. In the modern style, modern in the sense of the twentieth century, there is no restriction at all on the notes you can use. They all have equal weight. The restriction comes on the order in which the notes are to be played, the restrictions being determined in part by the order which the composer himself lays down at the beginning of his composition, and in part by certain standard rules. In tonal music, the music of the eighteenth and nineteenth centuries, the restriction comes on the notes to be used. Only seven out of the twelve notes in the octave have equal weight. The other five appear only occasionally as accidentals. The manner in which the restriction to seven notes is made is also subject to certain rules, your particular choice being called the key in which you elect to operate. Once you have restricted yourself by a choice of key you are free to arrange your seven notes in any order you please. You are free to use the same seven notes in any octave you may please. And at any time you may change your restriction, you may modulate into another key. The style of this Greek music was more akin to the key system than to the modern serialization. It restricted the notes to be used to seven, but you had no freedom over which seven, you couldn't choose your key to suit yourself. The seven notes were decided by the pitch of your octave. I think the practice probably came from the manufacture of the instruments themselves. The instruments produced certain notes better than others, unlike the piano which produces all its notes equally. The general effect was rather plaintive to an ear grown accustomed to the key system.

The young man turned over his flute to someone else, took hold of one of the girls, and began to dance. The motions were simple, rather static, but graceful none the less. When they had finished I went back to the piano and played three or four waltzes. There was much laughter as several of the bolder spirits tried to find the right steps. I stopped the music to give them a short demonstration, first alone, then of the positions of the two partners, with my young friend's girl, then of the real speed of the dance with an imaginary partner. Back at the piano I played the dances at first quite slowly, then with increasing speed. The dancing was more or less a fiasco but everybody enjoyed it for all that.

This was the beginning of a reputation which I soon acquired for myself and of which I shall have more to say later on. It was made clear that I didn't have to go to bed by myself if I didn't want to, but I did want to. To me, it was still not much more than a month since the tragic affair in Los Angeles. The memory of those few whirlwind days was still sharp and clear. In what had started as a more or less casual liaison I had perhaps made the mistake of giving too much of myself. At any rate I was still numb from the sharp catastrophic end of a passionate situation. I saw it would be a good idea to spread the intelligence that I was suffering from a grievous bereavement. I resolved to ask Morgan to put this story around the following day.

Before dropping off to sleep I mused on one small item of information I had gleaned from the talk around me. The young flute player's name had been Xenophon. Was this the Xenophon who was later to rescue a whole Greek army from disaster in Mesopotamia? I had no means of knowing how common the name might be so there was no clear answer. I had also discovered the name of my host, Andocides. I had a feeling the name should mean something to me and I resolved to ask Morgan about it on the morrow.

As it turned out I had no need to seek out the others, they were waiting for me the following morning. Morgan knew now exactly where he was. He knew the year and the time of year. It was 425 B.C.

"Man, we're right in the middle of it."

I was still sleepy and wondered vaguely what it was we were in the middle of.

"The war, the war between Athens and Sparta."

"Then why are there so many men about?"

"Because winter is coming on. These things run more or less on a strict time-table. You know we ought to do something about it, to put an end to it."

He was very excited, understandably so. To the classical scholar the fall of Athens in the Peloponnesian War must seem utterly tragic. Yet this was a different world now. It was inconceivable that a war between two tiny Greek cities, with a population of only a few hundred thousand, would be permitted to drag on year after year. The situation was tragic all right but not in the sense Morgan seemed to think. He had immersed himself so much in classical literature, he was thinking so much in the ancient Greek language, that he seemed to have forgotten the barbarians from the north who would soon be arriving here. Soon this delicate civilization around us would collapse like a house of cards. Financially the people would do all right of course. There were not very many of them, only a million or two, I suppose. With their great tourist attractions, the standard of living would rise sharply, but the civilization and culture would soon be lost. Above all the confidence would be lost. This was the problem, not the problem of Athens and Sparta.

An odd thought occurred to me, what was it Morgan had said? We must do something to stop it. Wasn't that exactly what the Prime Minister had said, about the situation in Europe? In many ways we had the same situation here. A disastrous war knocking the stuffing out of both sides. In one place the year was 1917, in the other 425 b.c., but the pattern was really the same.

Morgan had now drawn up a list of prominent Athenians, men whom sooner or later we could expect to find in the city. Socrates, Euripides, and Aristophanes were the names which meant most to me. At the distance of the twentieth century these men seemed more or less contemporaries. From Morgan's list I realized their respective ages were forty-five, fifty-five and twenty. "Socrates is out of town. With the army in the north."

In the next few days the general picture of what was happening gradually came into focus. This was indeed a city at war. We had been deceived into thinking otherwise because the fighting during the last few months had gone almost uniformly in favour of Athens. Standing out above a number of minor victories, there had been a major success at Pylos, on the far side of the Peloponnesus. A Spartan peace offer had been refused, and the peace offer had been followed by the arrival in Athens of a couple of hundred Spartan prisoners. It was a pathetically minor affair compared to what had been happening in Europe, yet it accounted for the apparently carefree aspect of the city. Nobody had any doubt that the war with Sparta would soon be brought to a victorious conclusion, least of all the commanding officers. Yet we knew that if it were to follow its own course the war would last for another twenty years and would result in the defeat of Athens. But how was one to convince them of this?

Morgan, with the enthusiasm of a Welsh revivalist, made a shot at it. He made more progress than might have been supposed, partly because of his impressive height, partly because he knew from his historical studies more or less what the Spartan envoys had said when they had come to request peace earlier in the year. The coincidence between his arguments, the arguments of a complete foreigner, and the entirely reasonable point of view of the Spartans, made an impression. It accorded with one section of Athenian opinion. But it fell foul of the influential generals. After their recent success at

Pylos, these men, Cleon and his friends, were riding the top of the wave. There was little Morgan could really do except make us thoroughly unpopular. Indeed our respective hosts began to find us something of an embarrassment. With some relief they seized on my suggestion that we acquire a house of our own. Everybody, friends and those not so friendly, made an effort to get us installed in congenial quarters. We were given half a dozen slaves and left to look after ourselves. So much for Morgan's preachings.

I didn't have much enthusiasm myself for this stop-the-war project. I was quite convinced that things would change drastically and catastrophically for the reasons I have already given. What I did have strong feelings about, however, were the slaves. I had no objection to hiring the middle-aged man and woman, the three girls, and the boy, as paid servants. So I conveyed to them that henceforward they were freed, although they could continue to work for a wage if they so pleased. All but the boy decided to stay.

This move increased our unpopularity, as I suppose it was bound to do, since it touched the whole Greek society at a sensitive point. The former owners took the point of view that we had spurned a generous gift. In answer to this there was nothing to be done but to pay for the slaves. I offered seven gold sovereigns for each of them. The money was taken with not very good grace.

There were some who were intellectually curious about our point of view, however. I remember in particular a man of the name of Protagoras. I gathered he was some kind of teacher, so perhaps he had a professional interest. Quite a crowd assembled when we started to argue. What none of them could understand, even the most reasonable ones, was how we got menial tasks performed in our country if we had no slaves. To the answer that we either did such tasks ourselves or paid some poorer but still free person to do them for us, they expressed frank disbelief. There was so much to be done they said, in the fields, the factories, and in the home. Surely we couldn't do it all ourselves? The argument was pressed home quite skilfully and at considerable length. The gist of their point of view was that if you didn't have slaves you'd have no leisure whatsoever. Plainly we were men of leisure. How else could I play the great lyre-in-the-box so skilfully?

There was really nothing for it except to explain that much of the manual work, which they found so necessary, was performed by machine in our society. This they couldn't understand, so I was pressed into giving descriptions and details.

The bog got deeper and ever more sticky. As they took me more and more for a foolish liar I became angry. I asked them if it was possible to propel a boat without sail and without oars. Of course not, they insisted.

So it came about that we made a journey to our yacht still anchored in the harbour at Piraeus. We had been in the habit of going over there two or three times a week, to make sure everything was all right, and gradually to transfer various articles of which we might have need. Lately we had managed to make the journey without too much in the way of an attendant retinue. Now however there was a huge procession as we walked the eight miles of the wall to the harbour. Quite a number of the foremost citizens turned out. There was my former host, Andocides, Cleon, the people's leader, a sculptor of the name of Myron, and an old boy who turned out to be none other than Sophocles. Everybody apparently wanted to give the lie to these boastful strangers.

I said we could manage to take half a dozen of them. Cleon and half his retinue stepped forward, setting themselves immediately above the rest. I left Alex to sort out the job of who was going to go with us. Morgan and I went out to the yacht. We spent some time working at the engine, making sure there was adequate fuel in the tank. When the motor had spluttered a few times, and was clearly on the point of starting, I signalled to the party on shore to come aboard. Nothing ever seemed to put Alex out of humour. As if it was all a big joke he somehow managed to limit the number to the specified six. Somehow he kept the others back as the six climbed aboard, the politicians I noticed.

The engine sprang to life. We soon had the anchor up. Then we were out in the bay. Morgan took the wheel and immediately made the mistake of turning north, into the straits between the island of Salamis and the mainland. As a naval officer he obviously had a fancy to see these straits, where the great Persian fleet had been defeated less than fifty years earlier. The mistake was that we were headed towards the city of Megera, an enemy city, in some ways the cause of the war itself. To those on deck it must have seemed as if we were determined to hand them over to the enemy. Only by locking ourselves in the little cabin could they be prevented from taking over the boat. We put on speed to about ten knots, which astonished the natives. There were ships in the straits. We went quite close to them and swished past with contemptuous ease. The whole trip round the island took I suppose about five hours.

On the way back, when it was realized that we had no unpleasant intentions, the atmosphere thawed a good deal. Everybody seemed in good spirits as we made our way back to port. The crowd on shore had grown even larger. I expected something in the way of a great cheer, such as might greet a troopship coming into harbour. Instead there was a curious silence. We prepared to return to shore. This was not to be, however. The boat was invaded by determined men. They wanted to see exactly how the trick was done. What was it we had up our sleeves? Men swarmed everywhere. There was nothing for it but to show them the engines. We started them up again. We showed one group after another, in a seemingly endless sequence, the rotating propeller shaft. I think they realized how the boat came to be propelled through the water. What they couldn't understand was what was going on inside the engine.

I knew exactly what was going to happen. We should never have control of our boat again. At any rate not until they had taken it entirely to pieces. Perhaps when they couldn't put the engine together again, or if they ran out of fuel, they would call on us for help. Everybody was very pleasant and polite, but now it was they who wanted us back to shore.

We had in the cabin a transistor radio receiver and transmitter. It was obvious we should take them with us, to enable us still to contact our naval friends. Indeed we had agreed to make radio contact, since it was always possible the weather would turn out to be too bad for us to make our agreed rendezvous. So we returned to Athens carrying the radio equipment ourselves. Two days later we were told our boat had been commandeered by the city. I was not surprised. With so much speed its uses in the war would obviously be very great. All along I had realized it would be unreasonable not to expect something like this to happen. I blamed myself for not keeping my big mouth shut. In a way I had been just as foolish as Morgan.

The incident did improve our popularity however. I no longer had the feeling we might be thrown into prison at any moment. This had not been an idle fear. Only seven years earlier the great Phidias, the designer of the Parthenon itself, had died in prison.

Now within the space of a fortnight two remarkable things happened. Messengers arrived from the north. There was great excitement in the city. We thought the long awaited penetration into Greece from the Balkans had occurred. We were wrong. It was the Delphic Oracle. The prophecy was that a continuation of the war would prove the ruination of Athens, a disaster to Sparta, and to the whole of Greece. This was the meaning, it was said, of the great roaring bird which had appeared in the sky at the time of the solstice.

Nobody in Athens had ever referred to the day when we had flown directly over the city. Many tens of thousands of persons must have seen our plane. Yet not a soul had said a word about it. To mention it was to court ill-luck apparently, to tempt providence, to give substance to the portent. Now the meaning was made known. The oracle's words had far more effect than I would have expected. The discussions that went on in the Agora, in the hall of Poikile, had every aspect of rationality about them. Yet not far beneath the surface there was a deep instinctive belief in the supernatural. The old beliefs were not very far away, just as the Middle Ages were not really very far away from twentieth-century Britain.

An important effect for us personally was that our standing was enormously improved. The very reason for our previous unpopularity, Morgan's uncompromising advocacy of peace, was now the word of the oracle. Why I wondered had the oracle spoken in this fashion? None of us could recall any mention of it in classical literature.

With our new-found popularity there was a lot of music making. Alex had suddenly lost his inhibitions about playing in front of people. I guessed it might be the girl with whom he was now living, a Corinthian of great beauty, named Lais. She was taller than most of the Greek girls, fair like many of them. This was something that had surprised me, how much fairer the general population was than I'd expected. It was of course the Dorian strain which had come in from the north a century or two earlier. Anyway Alex had got himself a succulent specimen, and good luck to him, I thought. At about that time he developed a passion for Hungarian gypsy music. It proved surprisingly popular with everybody. We used to bash away at the stuff. Somehow Alex got them all whirling around like dervishes.

I played my part adequately but without real gusto. I was now seriously worried by the fact that we still heard nothing at all from the outside. It scarcely seemed credible. And there was a second queer thing.

Soon after the episode of the yacht we tried out our radio receiver. Not a sound could we get on it. Convinced the electronics had gone wrong we switched on the transmitter. Whereupon we almost blew the receiver. One afternoon I set out on a long walk. About ten miles from Athens I turned on the transmitter which I had managed to bring with me without attracting notice. On my return to Athens I found Morgan had easily picked up my transmission. Of course it was one thing to pick up a transmission from only ten miles away and quite something else to receive signals from stations a thousand miles or more away. But the transmitters back home were vastly more powerful than our little piece of equipment. It could all be explicable in terms of a lowered sensitivity of the receiver. But it could be something quite different.

The others had not been through the strange experiences of August and September in quite the way I had. Probably for this reason I was more sensitive to the situation than they appeared to be. My fear was that another gross shift had taken place. It looked to me as though the juxtaposition of different worlds and different times might have come to an end. Those different worlds might have come together for a brief spell and then separated again. It could be that we had managed to transfer ourselves from the twentieth century to the fifth century B.C., and now there was no simple retreat. It could be our naval friends would never appear off the coast of Crete, not in this world anyway. Otherwise it seemed to me quite impossible to explain our continued isolation from the outside world.

These thoughts filled my mind. I was in a stormy, gloomy mood as the time for our visit drew to an end. As it turned out the weather itself was stormy, the seas rough, and there would have been no possibility of our putting out in the small yacht. We had heard nothing further about it so presumably it was still in the hands of the shipbuilders. I was hardly worried about this aspect of the matter. Our main reason for leaving by sea had been to avoid disturbing the people here too much. If they wanted to take an awkward line that was just too bad. Now we should just have to wait until the external world arrived here, if it ever did. If there was no external world now, then there was little point in our putting to sea.

More and more as the days passed an explosion boiled up inside me. I tried to get it all out of my system, in long fierce sessions at the piano. Our house was not large and these violent sessions soon became wearying to my companions. Increasingly I thought of moving somewhere by myself, to some place where I could play to myself, not always to an audience. Another thing, I was becoming fed up with always being odd-man out. There was Morgan and Anna who made a pair, Alex and his girl friend, and myself, alone. Somehow it didn't fit.

THE others greeted the suggestion that I might go off for a few weeks to get some composition done with an ill-disguised enthusiasm. The question was where to go. I wanted space. In summer when it would be possible to spend much of the day outdoors these small houses would be fine. Now in winter it was altogether too cramping. Yet where was I to get space? The city was obviously overcrowded, everywhere. We started to make inquiries. The solution came in a curious way.

My stormy sessions at the piano had not passed unnoticed. There was the madness of Dionysus in it. And the dances, the gipsy music, the gay music I somehow contrived to play for our numerous visitors, was also the music of Dionysus. I was told of a temple to the god some fifteeen miles down the peninsula. It was said to be in a pleasant spot overlooking the sea. Why did I not go there if I wanted to be alone? I could take two slaves, or rather two servants, to see to my needs. To the Greeks it was a logical solution.

I visited the temple. Space there certainly was. I had no quarrel with the site, only with the winds that blew there. Yet there was plenty of wood, colossal quantities of it, within easy range. It would be easier to build magnificent fires here than it was in the city. All in all the solution seemed a possible one.

The transition from the city to the temple was made smoothly and easily. I was once again amazed by the ease with which the piano was transported. The middle-aged couple came with me. It was from them, during the coming months, that I gradually acquired reasonable proficiency in the language. Isolated down the coast there was nobody else to speak to. Not that I had any overriding desire to talk but the practical matters of every-day life had to be attended to. There were the fires to be built in the right places, tables where I could write, and so on.

For now a great fever of composition was on me. I had always composed before out of a sense of duty, really because it was my job. I had made plans of the kind of music I would write and then more or less carried them out. This time I needed no plans. The sounds simply filled my head of their own accord. What I had to do was to order them and to write them down. Only later did I realize that this was the right way. When you feel compelled to write music you write good music. The compulsion came from the experiences of the previous months. The shock and tragedy of the beginning of the whole affair. The thoughts of men who emerged from the trenches into a clean and decent world again. The landing on the great Plain of Glass with its wonderful shimmering colours. Then this delicate but deadly civilization in which I was now living. The agony, the loneliness, and the grandeur were all there in my head, above all the mystery of it. The emotions were there. Gradually the sounds built themselves to give expression to the emotions.

I worked at an ever-increasing intensity. The Greek couple were quite convinced I was mad, and in a sense I was. Never had I been so entirely gripped by the task in hand. I would go to bed utterly exhausted in the evening. Strangely enough, I had little difficulty in falling asleep. Perhaps even more strangely I wakened early, feeling quite refreshed again. Time passed almost without my realizing it. A whole symphony grew until everything was there, orchestral sketch and all. Only the more or less mechanical details of the final copy remained. While the fever was on me there was no point at all in taking up time in a straightforward job. So I rushed on to other ideas, which were now forming. Two sonatas simply tumbled out, more properly sonata-fantasias. The urge to break the bounds of all the forms proved irresistible. The symphony had structure but it wasn't a structure I could put a name to.

Then I began the work that was to consume me for over two months. It was for orchestra and chorus. I fretted and fumed for a while. I had no literature. I wanted words to give expression to the kind of feeling I now had within me. I had thrashed around for several days before the obvious solution occurred to me, first to conceive the music and its moods, then to write appropriate words myself. It was the species of work all composers want to write, what in the old days would have taken the form of a Mass, set to the standard text. My lack of belief in the text, the usual Credo for instance, would have made a mockery of a formal Mass.

By this new method I was entirely free to build the musical structure as I went along. I was not inhibited by the need to set meaningless words. It was the creation, the meaning, the purpose of the world that had significance. It was the tragedy of man, the tragedy that he can sense such problems but not solve them, which overwhelmed me. The last thing I wanted was easy solutions beginning with the words "I believe." It was the juxtaposition in all of us of the primitive with something better that troubled me.

Early on, my friends and the people of Athens came out to see me quite often. I was so ill-mannered at these interruptions that the visits became less and less frequent. By the time of the first spring flowers I had become almost a hermit. Even Alex hardly came any more. Only in retrospect did I realize this for at the time I was entirely preoccupied. Undoubtedly in the popular mind I was now well-placed, a mad priest in the temple of Dionysus. Gradually the work came to an end, the fires began to damp themselves down. I looked around me and realized where I was. I began to think again about the everyday world. There seemed no doubt now but that my wild prognostication was correct. The different ages of the Earth which had come momentarily together had somehow separated again. Otherwise there would have been evidence long ago of the vibrant, harsh civilization of Europe.

As the spring days lengthened I became more and more fretful. Once again I had the need of human company. I decided the time had come for a return to the city. One day I made the journey alone. After the quietness of the winter the noise of the city startled my ears. I came at last to my friends' house. For a moment I had the irrational fear that they too would be gone leaving me alone in a new existence. But there they were, heartily glad to see me apparently safe and well.

I was all agog to hear the news:

"Have you heard anything at all from our people?"

"Not a thing," answered Morgan.

From his face I could see that at last he too was worried. "What does it mean? Man, they must have been here before now. How is it that nobody comes?"

"We'd better face it I think. Somehow this world, this time, has cut adrift again. I don't know how. I don't know how it happened before, how they ever came together. But we're adrift now, that's the only way it can be."

Alex was the least perturbed of the three of them, he still had his girl friend apparently. Anna began to weep, almost silently. Morgan went over to comfort her as best he could. Then he came back to me:

"What's to be done? We've just got to decide on some course of action."

"How about the boat? Have they said anything about it?"

113

"I gather they've loused it up. The engine I mean. Still we might put it in shape again, if we're lucky."

"Maybe we should go into the prophecy business. We ought to do pretty well in that line."

We chatted on for several hours. I decided I was moving back to the house. It would really have been more sensible to have spent the winter in the city, then to have gone out into the country now in the spring. But this would be to order one's life by rational argument. The period I had just come through was not the sort of thing one could legislate for. We began to discuss details. The best thing would be to move back in two or three weeks' time. There was still quite a bit of work to be done. It was more or less plain sailing now. But I would get through the scoring quicker by myself than in the middle of an uproar. With this settled I returned to the temple.

When I came to the reasonably straightforward parts of my work I became restless. I found it impossible to devote the same long hours, ten hours or more each day. I found it best to put in five or six hours in the morning, to take a long walk in the afternoon, and so early to bed. I came to move more and more about the peninsula. Not that I could yet go very far. I began looking forward to the prospect of longer trips. I decided that in April and May I would make a journey into the Pelopponesus, if circumstances permitted it.

One day I came on a large temple on the slopes of the mountain of Aegaleos. This was the hill from which Xerxes was said to have watched the defeat of his fleet at Salamis. The temple was to Apollo. It stood on a flat grassy knoll covered with a profusion of wild flowers set in a beautiful meadow. After winter in my rougher accommodation down by the sea it seemed just about perfect. The day was almost unaccountably soft up here. I remembered the strange oracle from Delphi. That too came from the temple of Apollo. From the god himself according to the beliefs of these people.

The immediate approaches to the temple were carefully kept. I walked up the steps out of the sun into the darkened interior. At the far end there was a door, or rather an opening, into an enclosed garden. Flowers were to be seen everywhere in the garden. I was looking generally around when I heard a quiet sound behind me. I turned quickly to find a girl looking down at me from the top of a short flight of steps. She was instantly different from any girl I had yet seen. The hair was of the usual light brown, but the eyes were grey. At first I thought she seemed tall because she had the advantage of the steps. Then I realized that indeed she was tall, of almost my own height.

"This is a beautiful day on which to meet a beautiful girl in such a garden as this."

My Greek was still not very fluent, but I hoped it would be good enough.

"Not many come here. You are welcome."

I found this difficult to believe, with such a girl as this. Yet possibly she was too tall to be attractive to the average Greek male.

"I fear I came without any knowledge that you would be here. So I brought nothing to sacrifice to the god, or even a small gift to please you."

"I see from your face you are a stranger."

"It would be a lucky man on whom you would look with favour."

The girl threw back her head and laughed. Then she became serious and said, "You forget where you are. We are not now in the temple of Dionysus."

There was nothing unfavourable in this. By now I knew enough of Greek customs to realize what was meant, or at least I thought so. Two advances, two retreats, then a decision. Enough dalliance to satisfy the human sense of dignity, not so much as to be an undue waste of time. The enormous death rate from disease and war demanded a high birth rate. I felt I knew exactly where I stood. I took the girl's hand in mine, prepared to make a pretty speech, when to my surprise she said:

"What you would have must be worked for. I must remind you again what place this is."

Of course she meant she was a priestess of Apollo. Yet I was unaware of anything inhibiting about such an occupation. Perhaps the time of the year was wrong.

"All worthwhile things must be earned. It will be my pleasure to do whatever you wish."

"Are you not the strange man who for months past has sacrificed himself to Dionysus?"

I was a bit sensitive to this suggestion. Just because I had been forced to use the temple down by the shore, to avoid living in a rabbit hutch, was no reason why I should be thought insane. Yet I had some idea of what the girl meant. I had been puzzled in the beginning by the attitude of the Greeks to their gods. On the face of it religion did not seem to be taken very seriously. But in at least one important respect the gods were still thought of in terms of reality. The gods represented a quintessence of human emotions and abilities. Madness, wild actions, lack of restraint, moderated by genuine spontaneity, those were the qualities of Dionysus, the qualities I appeared to possess. In a way the judgement was fair enough. Here in the temple of Apollo the ideal was of controlled form, aesthetics in general. This was the place where beauty did not need to be sensual.

"You practice your art without license. *This* is the abode of music."

Now I saw what she was driving at. Apollo of course was the god of song and music. By not making obeisances in the temple of the god I had in effect set myself up in opposition to him. I was guilty of sacrilege, at any rate in the eyes of his priestess. If I hoped to make any further progress with her it would plainly be necessary to carry out some act of appeasement. A further assessment of the situation persuaded me appeasement would be worthwhile provided it was not too serious. I was wondering just what to suggest when she said:

"You will remember what happened to the satyr Marsyas?"

I racked my brains as to who this satyr fellow might be. Clearly I was being compared to him, not flatteringly I suspected. Then it flashed through my mind that the fellow was supposed to have engaged Apollo in a musical contest, the one on the lyre, the other on the flute. I had a notion he came to a sticky end.

"I would be ready to engage in any contest that seemed fitting."

"You are haunted by a foolish pride."

I could not help smiling for the thought of a contest between a primitive lyre and a modern piano seemed ludicrous.

"You cannot really mean such a contest is possible?" I asked in frank incredulity.

For answer the girl took me into the temple. She showed me a lyre measuring about a yard across. She played a melody on it. The inference was obvious. The girl, or some other person in the temple, was indeed willing to engage in a musical trial of strength.

"It will be necessary for me to fetch my own instrument."

"That was expected. You will come two days before the next full moon. You may bring what you please and you may bring whom you please. We shall begin half-way through the last third of the day."

We walked amicably out of the front entrance of the temple. We strolled through the field to the beginning of the pathway down the mountain. There were still one or two points to be settled:

"Who is to be the judge?"

"We shall be the judges, you and I."

"And the stake? What is the winner to receive and what the loser?"

"You have already made your request clear. What the penalty might be I will leave you to reflect upon during the coming days."

I started down the path in excellent spirits. My only worry in such a contest would have been the judges. Anything might happen if untrained ears were permitted a vote. This way, with the girl and myself as judges, the worst that could happen would be a stalemate.

I sat down at the piano to recover the melody the girl had played. It was a beautiful thing, a little sad, but a great deal better than anything I had yet heard since coming to Greece. Someone at the temple, if not the girl herself, was very much out of the common run. I supposed they were aware of it. No doubt this was why the challenge had been issued. I began to play variations on the melody. It was certainly a beautiful thing but no better than hundreds of other melodies that could be conjured up. With the whole of European musical literature behind me there could be no question of the outcome of the contest.

I walked into Athens the following morning. My story put Alex Hamilton once again into fits of laughter. "Wonderful, that's quite marvellous."

Of course everybody soon knew about it, Alex saw to that. To him it was the joke of the year. I was not surprised to find the Greeks taking it more seriously. One or two of them, particularly I remember a chap of the name of Diagoras, came and congratulated me. They said it was high time the old superstitions were broken. From the gravity of their manner, I realized the superstitions went deeper than even they themselves supposed.

I suspect I would soon have had an ugly situation on my hands if the people hadn't felt the god to be entirely capable of looking after himself. It was as though I had desecrated a temple, not a trivial offence.

My worry that too many people would flock on to the hill was apparently shared also by the Boule, the council of the city. A decree was quickly passed that nobody outside my personal party was to approach the temple within ten stadia, that is to say within a mile.

Only on the morning of the day itself did the full implication of the situation really become clear to me. The way I had fixed things with the priestess this was to be a private affair. There was no suggestion of a public contest. In fact that had been exactly my worry. I wanted to avoid a contest by popular acclamation. Yet in a sense this was exactly what it had become. Even worse, how could I possibly win? Even if the priestess were to come down on my side she could hardly say so in public. The populace would tear her limb from limb. And the stalemate, which I had fondly imagined would be the worst that could befall me, would become a mockery if those at the temple should declare against me. I saw I was in really serious trouble. I also saw the priestess had probably planned this from the beginning. My crime against the god was probably a serious one in her eyes. I started up the pathway in the middle morning with far less enthusiasm than I had come down it four days before.

My forebodings proved very accurate. Even in the early afternoon a considerable crowd was already gathered on the flat ground in front of the temple. They obeyed the orders of the city fathers up to a point. They were keeping about three hundred yards from the temple. I had no doubt the city fathers themselves would come even closer. I was accosted by a small, ugly-looking man:

"Is it really true you are to engage the god in a contest?"

"Is it really true there is a god?"

"I see it is true."

He looked me over for a long time. Then reflectively he added, "Well, well, it should prove interesting."

I looked him over carefully. "Can I ask you a question? Are you sure of anything?"

"I am sure the summer is hot and the winter cold."

"And you are sure your fellow citizens have too many pre-conceived opinions?"

"Of that I am also sure. They say the last one to challenge the god was flayed alive for his pains. Of that I am *not* sure."

"Thank you for your encouragement."

I left him at the foot of the temple steps. I had reached the top, when as an afterthought I shouted, "By the way, have you paid that cock to Asclepius yet?"

Nuts, I thought, as I walked into the temple. This just can't be true. But the stone pillars were hard enough and the piano was real enough. It was a meeting of two different worlds.

By now I had some experience of the best place to site the

piano in order to get the best resonant effects. The men who carried it up knew nothing of this so it had to be moved. I had to go out again to get the necessary help. Once I was satisfied with the position, my helpers cleared off just as quickly as they could.

I still had a long tuning job. I wanted to make the best possible job for the acoustics in the temple were wonderful.

Already we were in the third part of the day, the third division of the day, so I wouldn't have much longer to wait. I strolled outside and came on Alex, Morgan, Anna, and a few Greek friends who were still willing to stand by me.

Alex was somewhat contrite at the commotion he had caused. "Don't worry, just play," he said. "You can't lose, except by being too ambitious."

I suggested it would be best if they came through the temple to the little inner garden. The piano was placed towards that end and they would hear better from there.

"I think it's going to be a good evening," said Anna. This might well be true. The remarkable carrying power of sound was one of the secrets of the Greek open air theatre. On many evenings the sound travelled horizontally instead of upwards, as it tends to do in northern climates.

The light inside the temple was not very good. It was fortunate I had decided to trust my memory. As the light gradually faded it would have been difficult to read notes inside here. Actually I had no fears upon the musical side, the troubles were political. I guessed the whole thing was a trick organized by the politicians we had offended soon after our arrival.

So far nobody from the other side had shown themselves in the temple. Now at last a priest appeared. He was of a similar colouring to the girl priestess, light brown hair, and he was similarly tall. In the subdued light I could not judge the colour of his eyes.

"Is it your wish to proceed with the contest?"

I suppose in the circumstances it would have been sensible for me to have called it all off. There was no point in running my head into a political noose. Yet this was ostensibly a musical contest. How could I retreat from a trial of strength in my own craft? Perhaps it was pride which impelled me to go on but I think not.

"Yes, I wish to continue."

The priest then withdrew. Some five minutes later the first sounds came. I say came because I had no idea as to their exact source. It had to be from one or other of the three side chambers opening out from the main floor.

The melody was the one the girl had played for me four days earlier. The melody was the same but the instrument was not. It had a far clearer, more penetrating, quality. It was played with much greater decision. If this indeed was the girl then she had been fooling me before. The melody was followed by a complex variation from which it emerged again as a single line. But now the line was changed, in a fashion I couldn't exactly determine. There were three more variations, each rapidly and lightly played. Following each one came the melody, always with changes. It was as if the tune were made to evolve through the intervening sections of complex structure. This was all I could make out in the beginning. It lasted for some six or seven minutes.

Now it was my turn. I decided to match the light rippling music I had just heard. I think it was Liszt who referred to shooting the octaves out of one's shirt-sleeves. I played four Chopin studies. This I felt was a fair return. Even though I had kept things very light and delicate it was clear the piano was more powerful than whatever instrument was being played behind the scenes. Even so I was amazed at the quality of what I had heard. It was really beautiful miniature stuff, enormously superior to anything I had heard in the city. Who the hell was playing it I began to wonder.

The next round was instantly more serious. The texture was fuller and louder. Yet the precision of detail was still there. A casual listener would have judged there to be long and short notes, exactly as in our own music. Yet this was not so. Every note was short. The impression of a long note was given by several short notes played very close together. You can't do this at all on a piano, no matter how quickly you move your finger. It takes the key so long to respond that by the time you press it for a second time the total volume generated by the first note has already fallen so far that the second one stands out as a quite separate pulse of sound. In this case, when a long note was desired the second pulse came before the first one had died more than a little way. There was a slight dying effect of course, otherwise the note would have been long and uniform, exactly the way it can be on a violin. Here you could just about detect the separation of the pulses. This indeed was one of the things which gave the music its quite novel sound. It was as if somebody were plucking a string at an enormously high rate, as if the string were responding instantly. So much could I make out of the individual notes themselves.

It still baffled me as to exactly what restrictions were being placed on the choice of the notes themselves. This was not twelve-tone music, all the tones were not being used. Yet it wasn't tonal in the sense of our system of keys. The structure was more complicated than anything I had heard before. I had the strong impression of rules depending somehow on the form of the work itself. It was as if the rules, the restrictions, depended on the place in the piece. The rules at the beginning and those at the end seemed different, and different again from those in the middle. It was as if the large-scale development of the work influenced its manner of construction.

I mention all this to show why it wasn't in any way easy even for a trained musician to grasp instantly what was going on. Plainly I had to deal with a subtle and complex form. My last thought of the people outside was that they could hardly find the music of the god easier to comprehend than my own. I think it was at this point, as the second of my opponent's sections came to an end, that the first chill of apprehension swept over me.

My response was essentially automatic. I made my choices from *The Art of Fugue*. I made them instinctively, allowing the music to well out of the fingertips. As I came to an end I no longer had any idea of playing to the crowd outside, or even to my friends in the little garden, but to whatever it was that lay out of sight somewhere in the darkening temple.

With the beginning of the third trial all was changed. The music was now full-toned, slow and majestic. Its quality and power was a fitting tribute to the gods. This was no simple priest or priestess, or even a thousand of them. A power was abroad here that could not be denied. It was a power hitting at me, not at the crowd. There was no appeal to popular taste, even the popular taste of the twentieth century. It was exactly what it claimed to be, Apollonian in stature.

Although I was far more concerned to listen now than to analyse, I was overwhelmingly impressed by the tonal ambivalence, by the difficulty of deciding what note or chord would come next. Even before the end was reached I knew there could only be one answer.

I began the Adagio Sostenuto from Beethoven's Opus 106. I took the tempo as slow as I dared. The movement, long as it is, had now to be stretched to the limit. The sonority was wonderful, every note rang out true and clear. The minutes passed and the music flowed everlastingly on. It might be the god himself who was opposing me, yet he should learn something of the depths of human agony. I was already playing the arpeggiated bass chords that bring the movement to an end when the fantastic risk I had taken flashed through my mind. But the memory I had always relied on so heavily in the past had not let me down. Nor could I have ever been reconciled to myself if it had.

There came a long pause. It did not signify the end, I knew. A pause was necessary for aesthetic reasons. I was sitting waiting when a light step caused me to swivel suddenly and apprehensively round. It was the girl, the priestess, dressed in a quite beautiful long gown. It had no relation to the dresses of the women of Athens. It buttoned around the neck in a manner reminding me of the costume of a Chinese woman.

"It is necessary for the last part that you should play only the music you have written yourself."

After this calm command she was gone.

So the ground was swept from under me as the first notes of my opponent's last section rang out loud and triumphantly. It was altogether bigger in its proportion than the previous rounds. It was quite symphonic in scale, although there was no suggestion of orchestral instruments. Everything was built out of plucked notes. It lacked something of the colour of an orchestra but this can be my only criticism. How much of it I failed to appreciate with my ears untrained to the basic style I do not know. Yet enough of the splendour of it was clear to me for the near hopelessness of my position to be obvious. Yet it was only at the end that desperation seized me. While the music played I listened with bowed head.

I knew I could only answer one vision of creation with another. I needed full orchestra and chorus, all I had was a single piano. I sat for a little while, the sweat dripping down my face. Then I began with the slow maestoso section of my last work. A lifetime's discipline of listening to what I was playing steadied my nerves. The ideas came back more and more. Gradually the intense fury of those winter months reasserted itself. How long I played I could not tell. It was quite dark now, apart from shafts of moonlight coming through the entrances to the temple. I came at last to a convenient stopping point. Then I just sat, silently waiting.

The girl came to me. Without seeing any clear-cut gesture I realized she wanted me to follow her. I kept two or three paces behind as we crossed the main floor. We came out of a side entrance into the open moonlight. The scent of flowers seemed overwhelmingly strong.

"You may sit here if you wish," almost in a whisper.

I sat down, not because I was tired, but because it was the easiest way to unwind myself.

"What is your verdict?" she asked.

So they were sticking to the bargain, whoever they were.

"I can say nothing about the end, my last piece. You asked for it to be my own. Nobody can give a fair judgement of his own music. Of the other three parts, I do not think I lost."

"Do you wish to claim victory, even apart from the fourth and last section?"

I thought for a long time. All my instinct told me that nothing could equal Bach or the finest of Beethoven. Yet the mere fact I hesitated showed it would be wrong to claim too much. I knew the works of Bach and Beethoven as I knew the back of my own hand, so I was familiar with their tremendous merits. I had heard this new music but once. It was inconceivable I could have distilled out of a single hearing all that was in it.

"No, I do not wish to claim victory. But you, what is your opinion?" I asked.

In a soft voice, the girl replied, "I am content to take the same view."

The load lifted instantly from my mind. It was the proper verdict. The styles were too different for a judgement of better or worse to be made. Only similar things can be compared in a direct fashion, only when they set out to obey the same rules and restrictions.

"So we end as we began. Except I hope you will no longer think of me as an uncontrolled madman."

"I never did, I simply wanted to hear you play."

The cool effrontery of this reply shattered my growing complacency. The girl went on. "Because you make no claims for your own work, I will give you that which you asked for."

She took me a few steps further into the little side garden, to where I could see a flat couch. I was rather surprised she paid no heed to the crowds outside. I suppose she thought the people would be so frightened at what they had heard that there could be no danger of them entering the temple. She laughed quite openly as I began to kiss her.

The night was a subtle compound of many ingredients. Moments of high passion, of whispered conversation and laughter bubbling along like a stream in the woods, of the scent of the flowers, of snatches of sleep, and of long intervals lying quiet—the girl in my arms—looking up at the sky above our heads. Time was measured not on my watch but by the changing positions of the stars. It was not until the glow of morning was spreading upward from the eastern horizon that at last I fell into a deep sleep.

I awoke with the instant conviction of having slept long and wonderfully well. With languorous disappointment I realized the girl had gone. It was not until I heaved myself into a sitting posture that the first shock came. I was inside some building. It was obviously not the temple. For a flash I thought I had been carried away to prison. Then I saw this could be no prison, it was far too comfortable.

Not only that but I was dressed in a queer garment. It could be said to be a pair of pyjamas, or more accurately pyjamas, because as far as I could see I was completely fastened up in the damn thing. It was all in one piece and there seemed to be no possibility of getting it either on or off. The material too was strange. It was coloured in a multitudinous and expensive manner. It somehow suggested Joseph's coat, yet the colours were delicate rather than garish.

Quickly I jumped out of bed. Then I saw it wasn't a bed. It was simply a flat piece of the floor of the room itself, but raised two or three feet above the rest of the floor. The carpeting, or whatever it was, was extremely soft to the tread. I didn't bother to examine it but moved quickly to the opening out of the room—there was no door. I came into a very large room indeed, a room which was odd in the extreme. To begin with, there wasn't a single chair, not a single item of furniture, in the usual sense. The floor was in the same deep blue material as the bedroom. It was everywhere uneven. It had raised and lowered portions in no particular pattern that I could discern. The walls and the ceiling were coloured in a fashion both gay and restrained. The dominant colours were different on the different walls, one had green and yellows, another was tinged largely with gold, another red. The overall shape was rectangular. Generally speaking the walls were vertical. Like the floor, however, there were few strictly plain surfaces. The effect was pleasing and soothing. One side of the room was open, and I could see sunshine beyond a curtaining material. I tried to get through the curtain but I could find no means of pulling the material aside. It took some minutes before I got the trick of it. I noticed that one could simply put one's hand through it, as if the whole fabric were rotten. Then I walked through it. Instead of the tear being permanent the material closed up behind me.

I was out on a large balcony. The house was built on the side of a hill. A smooth path came towards it from a near-by clump of trees. This was the only sign of a road I could see anywhere. Apart from the hum of insects it was quite silent. Everywhere over the hillside, running for miles in all directions, were banks of flowers and trees. I saw an occasional glimpse of some other house. Below me in the distance lay green fields. In the very far distance the mountains rising high into the sky were snow capped.

THIRTEEN   *ALLEGRETTO E SEMPRE CANTABILE*

MY first thought was that I had awakened at last from a long nightmare, or more likely from some fever. It was in Hawaii everything had started to go wrong. At a first glance here I was back again in Hawaii. The quality of the light, the high mountains, were superficially similar. Could this strange building be some kind of isolation hospital?

The pyjamas I was wearing might also at first glance have been taken for some exotic Hawaiian garment. But the material wasn't right, it was much too expensive in its weave and colouring. Then nobody I had ever known had conceived of a house like this, not even in the wildest dreams. Besides it couldn't be Hawaii. Those mountains must be at least fifty miles away. The visibility was tremendous. At such a range on Hawaii I would have been looking out over the sea but there was no sign of an ocean. There had been many flowers on Hawaii but nothing to compare with this luxuriant profusion.

Step by step I went over recent events. The night at the temple was last night. I was convinced of it. Yet this was quite certainly not Greece. The style of the house, its spaciousness, the countryside, and above all those mountains, were definitely not Grecian.

Although strange and singular things had been happening, up to this point they had not happened to me personally. This was the first big jump in my own personal consciousness. Subjectively I felt quite normal, yet objectively it seemed as if I must be as nutty as a squirrel.

I decided to search the house. I saw a second curtain opening off the balcony. As it was of the same material as before I simply walked through it without experiencing any sensation except a gentle brushing against the cheek. There were further rooms, smaller but designed in much the same fashion as the big room. However in one of them there was a table. It was the only article of furniture to be seen anywhere. On it was a considerable pile of musical manuscripts. The briefest inspection showed they were the works on which I had spent the winter, in the little temple of Dionysus. At least in that respect I was not crazy. I flicked through the pages. My memory was right in every respect, all the details were in place, exactly as they should have been. At least some things were right, inexplicable as the basic facts seemed on the face of it. I went back to the large room. Sitting there on the floor was John Sinclair.

I collapsed by his side and said weakly, "What the hell's going on?"

"I thought you might be getting worried. I've been round twice before but you were asleep. It's incredible you managed to get here."

"Incredible?"

"You'd better tell me exactly what happened, before you woke up to find yourself here I mean."

I started to give a general outline of my experience in Greece. John would have none of it. He demanded I should go through everything in complete detail. I came at last to the night in the temple. At the end of my description of the contest with the god, John began to laugh delightedly.

Remembering the ordeal I said, sourly, "You're not the only one to find it funny. By now the whole of Athens will be laughing hysterically about it."

"Piqued, eh? You know it's ironical. While I would have been quite incapable myself of putting up any sort of musical performance, I could have told you straightaway what it was you were dealing with."

"What the devil d'you mean?"

"Isn't it perfectly obvious? It was the music of the future."

I sat digesting this as best I could. He went on, "Perhaps now you can realize why I was so keen to look everywhere, all over the Earth. Don't think I didn't want to come with you to Greece. I would have loved it, but I was convinced that the Britain of 1966 wasn't the last moment of time to be abroad on the Earth. Remember all the different periods we saw, perhaps five thousand B.C. in the Middle East, four hundred B.C. in Greece, the eighteenth century in America, 1917 in Europe, why stop at 1966 in Britain? There had to be something more."

"So you went on searching?"

"High and low. We drew a complete blank everywhere in the southern hemisphere. I can't be entirely sure about South America because we ran into terrible weather there. You remember the Plain of Glass?"

I nodded and he went on:

"You see that just had to be the distant future, far away in the future."

"Why?"

John made no immediate answer. He took a small box-like device from his pocket and pressed what seemed to be a switch. Instantly the floor became everywhere very soft, as if one had sunk into a feather bed. Because of the rises and hollows it was easy to get oneself into a comfortable position. Then he did something again to the box and the floor went quite hard again, at least hard compared to what it had been a moment before. I found myself sitting in what might have been taken for an extremely comfortable chair.

"So that's why they don't need any chairs?"

"That's right. Would you like some food?"

Now he came to mention it, I was damned hungry. I said so.

"Come on then. I'll show you some other gadgets."

He led the way to one of the subsidiary rooms. He pressed a small button. Instantly a panel slid by and what seemed to be a typewriter keyboard appeared on one of the walls.

"What would you like?"

I said I would like fruit juice and bacon and egg.

"I'll do the best I can."

John tapped the keyboard as if he was writing a message, then gave one final flourish, pressing what seemed to be a master button. About ten seconds later a kind of hatchway opened and out came a metal arm on which were two trays. On each tray was a large glass of yellow juice, which I took to be orange juice. There was also what seemed to be a slice of bread or toast covered in some reddish fluffy stuff.

"What the hell is this?"

"Your bacon and egg. I think I got it right."

He dipped his finger into the froth and tasted it. Then he nodded and said, more seriously:

"Let's go back and talk."

Somewhat bemused, I followed him. We took up our respective positions on the floor.

John explained: "You see these people don't eat animals, so all the food is either vegetable or synthetic. There are literally hundreds of these preparations. I haven't sampled more than a small fraction of them yet."

I tried the orange juice. It was excellent, in fact I couldn't recall tasting any better. Then I addressed myself to the froth. I had no complaint about that either. It wasn't bacon and egg by any means but it fell into the right kind of savoury class. "Where the devil does the taste come from?"

"Well of course it's artificial in the sense the chemicals are produced synthetically, but they're the right chemicals, the ones you really get in the sort of food we're used to. Incidentally, you'll find the caloric value is quite low. You can eat bags of this stuff without growing fat."

And then we were back to more gadgets. John had a piece of his bread and froth left. He smeared the froth on to the carpet material and chucked the piece of bread to the far side of the room. "Time to get the sweeper out," he remarked cheerfully. "Better come over to the doorway."

He took out his little box and fiddled again with it. There was a sort of blowing noise from the sides of the room, from what would be the wainscoting in a normal house. A white strip started at one side. It moved slowly across to the other side, where it finally disappeared. In its wake there was nothing but clean carpet. The whole process took about thirty seconds. John was like a small boy with a toy. "Not much trouble about housekeeping, is there?"

He stopped clowning and we went on to the balcony. He produced what looked rather like two deck chairs. Thank god for a touch of normality, I thought.

"You were talking about the Plain of Glass. Why does it belong so obviously to the future?"

"Because it's been melted, everywhere, smoothly. You know the Sun is going to get hotter and hotter as time goes on. There'll be a stage when the whole surface of the Earth melts. After that the Sun will cool. Everywhere over the Earth there'll be smooth glass. You remember what I said about it's not being etched by blown grit or sand. There couldn't be any sand with everything fused. Besides at that stage there would be no atmosphere, no wind. The Plain of Glass is the ultimate fate of the Earth."

I sat for some time sipping my orange juice, letting all this sink in.

John went on. "You see, it was a fair bet that if the distant future were represented here, there ought to be something in between, between 1966 and the far-off future. That's why I was so convinced it was worth going on searching."

"Didn't you expect these people of the future would show themselves?"

"Not necessarily. Remember your own point of view about the Greeks. You were worried at the mere idea of mobs of our own people streaming into Greece. You wanted to leave it as much the way it was as you could. The future could be quite shy of appearing amongst us for exactly the same reason. They couldn't simply declare themselves as strangers, in the way you could when you arrived at Athens. The same thing in London would be impossible."

"Yet they must have appeared in Greece."

"For exactly the reason I've just given you. One thing I don't quite understand is how they've managed to keep Europeans out of Greece. You must have been lucky enough to get through their barrier before they closed it."

"You think that's why our own people never arrived?"

"Fairly obvious, isn't it? Somehow the communication lines must have been cut. I can't quite see how, but we must realize these people are at least as far ahead of us technologically as we are ahead of the Greeks. I don't think there's much profit in worrying too much about practical details. If the Britain of 1966 could put an instant stop to the war in Europe, with only a technological lead of fifty years, a society with a lead of thousands of years wouldn't have too much trouble in hiving off a bit of the Earth. In any case that's exactly what they've done with their own country."

I looked away towards the mountains. "Where are we? I was trying to puzzle it out before you came. The nearest I could get was Hawaii, but that didn't seem right."

John looked at his watch. "It not very far from midday. If you were to sit here for several hours you'd see the Sun move from left to right. Now work it out for yourself."

The Sun moved from left to right, did it? I thought for a few minutes. This must mean we were in the northern hemisphere, because the Sun had to be south of the zenith. As far as I could judge, there was an angle of about twenty degrees between the direction of the Sun and the vertical. So far so good. Then it was early spring, at least it had been only the beginning of April in Greece. If it was the same here it meant the angle between the Sun and the vertical was pretty well the geographical latitude, evidently twenty degrees north or thereabouts. My next thought was of the Himalayas. Could these mountains be the Himalayas? Then I remembered the Himalayan range is much further north than one usually supposes. In fact the equator goes south of the whole of India, the mountains come at thirty degrees north. I looked up again towards the Sun, the angle couldn't be as much as thirty degrees. Mentally I ran along a parallel of latitude, first into Burma. Obviously Burma wasn't right either, unless the vegetation was completely changed. Then I thought about Arabia

130

and Africa. None of it fitted. The solution came to me last of all. The twentieth parallel must cut through America somewhere about Mexico City. The clarity of the air, the feeling I had of altitude, the mountains, were right.

"Mexico, of course."

"Very good."

"How did you get here yourself?"

"A good question, considering the way *you* got here. Damn it, I know what I'm looking for and I have to comb the whole Earth before I find it. All you have to do is to walk up a hill to a temple and what happens, you run slap bang into these people of the future."

I had a clear memory of the priestess standing on the steps looking down at me in the little garden. So that was the explanation of why she seemed so different, why she was so tall. Melea, she had told me her name was last night, if it was last night.

"You know, John, my manuscripts. When I came up to the temple I didn't bring them with me. I left them back at the place where I was working. Somehow they must have been retrieved."

"Oh, I'm sure you're definitely *persona grata*. After your musical performance. You see it's very likely they've lost all of our music. It must have come as quite a shock to them to hear it. I'm all right myself now, but it wasn't easy in the beginning. We got here during a storm. Otherwise I'm sure they would have misled us through the radio. We found a place to land and come down."

"What happened to the rest of the crew?"

"I'll tell you about them in a moment. Of course the people here wanted to know who we were, all manner of detail."

"How about language difficulties?"

"You'll see how they cope with that, all in good time."

"So you got to the place where you wanted to be?"

"I was agog to find out what they knew. I was curious about a lot of technical problems in physics, obviously. It was like doing a puzzle in a newspaper. You're told the solution is on page eight, column four. If you find you can't do the puzzle, the natural thing is to look at the answer, which was the way I felt about a lot of things. I asked a lot of questions in return, which was lucky for me, otherwise they'd have dealt with me the same way they did with the rest of the crew.

"We had to go back in their textbooks quite a fair way before we reached the things I know about. One of my own discoveries I found under somebody else's name. Naturally I didn't take at all kindly to this. When I pointed it out, they instantly changed their tune and became very friendly. All doors were opened to me as it were. Well, two or three days after our landing, I learnt the plane was being sent away. I didn't want to go myself for obvious reasons but I did want to send a message. So I sought out the crew."

John stopped at this point, his usual habit, just when he had reached the decisive point.

"Well," I grunted.

"They didn't know me, they damned well didn't know me from Adam. There was nothing wrong with them physically. Of course when they made no move to recognize me it was clear the people here didn't want any message sent. I saw it wasn't a good idea to press the point. So I simply let the plane go."

"Why didn't they recognize you?"

"Well, it's perhaps not really so surprising. What we can do with drugs, anaesthetics and so on, would seem astonishing to the Greeks, wouldn't it? I don't think they had been harmed in any way, except they would lose their memory of the whole incident. It would be a kind of artificially induced amnesia."

"You think that's why I remember absolutely nothing between the temple and here?"

"I would say so. Probably they didn't want you making a fuss."

I decided I would have another glass of orange juice. For some reason I was extremely thirsty. John gave me a description of which button to press and I went to the kitchen alone. With a bit of fiddling I got what I wanted, but I got plenty of other stuff as well. I took the whole lot back to the balcony, for I was getting hungry again. I had in fact lost weight during the winter. For the most part I had lived on fish and on a kind of cake made out of honey and flour. After such a pleasant but monotonous diet, the profusion of tastes coming from the machines in the kitchen had quite a fascination.

"How advanced are these people, technologically I mean?" I asked as I munched the odd concoctions.

"Considering they're something like six thousand years beyond us, not as much as I would have expected. At the development pace of the nineteenth and twentieth centuries, I'd say they're about five hundred years on. Of course that's impressive enough. It's about the gap which separated us from the fifteenth century. They've apparently been able to put into practice things we could only just conceive of. For instance they can produce enormous captive magnetic fields,

132

You do this with a superconducting material, which prevents you from having ridiculous heating problems. Our trouble was that we couldn't get sufficiently rigid materials, and we had to fuss with very low temperatures. Somehow they've got rigid serviceable materials. Very strong magnetic fields have become a standard part of their technology, like the electric motor and dynamo are with us. You'll find their vehicles look at first sight like a hovercraft. They float over the ground. But they don't do it by blowing air. They simply ride on a magnetic field. The logistics of it work just like a railway system. They've got tracks laid out all over the country. But the tracks are magnetic, nothing at all like railway lines. The great thing about it is that it's all silent, and it's all computer controlled. Apparently you ring up for a vehicle in the same way as we might ring up for a taxi."

"But with travelling as individual as that, like taxis, I'd have thought there'd be an almost impossible crush."

"I think the secret of it is that there just aren't many people. We think in terms of tens or hundreds of millions. I haven't found out yet exactly how many of them there are, but it can't be anything like a twentieth-century population."

It was all very intriguing. Already I had a fancy to do a bit of travelling around myself.

"How did you know to come up here?"

"I had information you were here."

"You realize what that means?"

"I don't think it's as bad as you think. Look, who were your special friends in Greece? You give me an answer because I've asked an entirely reasonable question, not because I force an answer out of you. That's probably what you did. There may be nothing more to it."

"And I've since forgotten all about it?"

"I thought we agreed about that. Anyway they told me you would be here. Something more, they're going to put on a special film show for us. To give us an idea of the things that have happened in the span of time between our day and theirs. I gather it'll last for quite a time, although they apologized for the sparsity of some of the material. They said we would realize why when we'd seen it."

We went back inside to the main room. John hunted around until he found a master switch. When he pressed it the same thing happened as in the kitchen, a panel slid back and a kind of typewriter keyboard appeared. Only this time there were many more keys on it. John took out a piece of paper:

"I've got the code here, as least I've got instructions about

133

which buttons to press. Until we get used to it we'd better do what they tell us. Otherwise we may find ourselves inside the washing machine."

He pressed I suppose about half a dozen keys. On one of the flat pieces of the wall there appeared a picture. It was a pleasant country scene in colour, no more. "That must be the call signal."

We made ourselves a couple of comfortable armchairs in the floor and sat down to wait. There was a sudden commotion outside. Then in streamed my priestess, Melea, followed by another girl. I kissed Melea, and for good measure the other girl too. They were strikingly similar. Noticing the picture on the wall Melea said something in a strange language. She went to the keyboard on the wall and punched a few buttons. The picture disappeared. Something else must have happened, for there were a few small clicks, but I didn't notice anything by eye. Then Melea made quite a little speech, again in the strange language. A second or two after she had finished I was astonished to hear her voice again in the room. I say in the room because it didn't come from any particular place. I suppose there must have been a lot of small speakers distributed everywhere over the walls. The astonishing thing was that the language was English, with a very curious pronunciation, but English nevertheless.

"This is my friend Neria. She too was in Greece, at the temple of Delphi. That also was a temple of Apollo. It was she who made the prophecy about the war between Athens and Sparta. Will you not introduce your friend?"

I began to speak in my not very good Greek. She interrupted me:

"It will be much better if you speak in your own language."

So I made the introduction. Immediately I had finished there came my own voice, I would have sworn it was mine, in a language of which I didn't know a single word. Naturally I was pretty dumbfounded. The girls stepped forward and kissed John, one after the other, which must have surprised him as much as the language business did me. Off his guard, he turned to me and said:

"Did they behave in Greece like this?" Immediately after he had finished, his voice was heard everywhere throughout the room in the new language. The girls made the incident into a joke which helped break the ice. I've noticed before that when you've been close and intimate with a girl you haven't known for more than a short time the second meeting is always a slight embarrassment. One can never be sure whether the situation is

134

still the same as it had been. So I was glad this moment of embarrassment was out of the way.

Melea turned to me and smiled. "We have brought you a present. In fact we've brought you two, one from each of us, but we are only going to let you see one at a time."

The translation system made for very accurate understanding but I could see it was going to be a bit stilted. It wouldn't be right over breakfast.

Now it was Neria who went to the keyboard. With a deliberate flourish of the hand she tapped away at two or three of the buttons. I was quite unprepared for what followed. I suppose I expected some kind of picture to appear on the wall. But no, in through the doorway from the direction of the kitchen an object glided into the room. It made no sound as it moved. Neria pressed a button and it stopped not far from the exit on to the balcony. I realized they must have the magnetic tracks John was talking about even under the damned floor itself.

We all turned our attention to the object. At the touch of a switch on its side the top folded back. There underneath was a keyboard, a piano keyboard, with the usual eighty-eight keys. At the right-hand end there was a small metal lever, and nothing else.

The two girls stood waiting like expectant children at a party, just after the conjurer had arrived. For me, some conjuring would be necessary it seemed. There was no piano stool, no pedals, and the box itself just wasn't big enough to contain any appreciable length of string.

"Where do I sit?"

"Haven't you got an adjuster?"

"No," said John, before I could reply.

The girls laughed. "Then he is going to be very uncomfortable unless we fetch one from the storage room."

We all made quite a business of adjusting the shape of the floor to fit the position of the box. It was every bit as impressive as the usual adjustment of the piano stool. At last I decided I was comfortable enough and that my hands were in the right relation to the keyboard.

The three of them were sprawling on the floor, Melea actually at a height above me, so contoured was the room. I felt as if I was in a kind of arena. I began to play a Handel chaconne. The effect was indescribable, indescribably good and indescribably bad. Sometimes the music came through with a really wonderful tone. Then an instant later there would be the most

135

horrible overload effect, the volume would become enormous. I stopped for a moment.

"You'd better either adjust the control or play more lightly," said Neria.

I tried moving the lever. As I did so, the pressure needed on the keys to give the same volume of tone changed. I began to experiment with single notes. It was the pressure on the key that decided the volume. Any increase of pressure after a key reached its bed, any key-bedding, produced a grotesque increase of output. The mechanics of striking a single note were completely different from a piano. On the piano you get maximum output at the moment the hammer hits the strings. From that moment on, the volume of tone sags badly. A long-sustained note is impossible if you judge by an objective criterion. The thing which makes piano music possible is the curious subjective effect by which you continue to think you hear the tone after it has really sagged. Of course the manner of striking the strings makes some difference but the appalling fall-off of tonal quality is always there. Here the situation was quite different. The volume could be held steady, for seconds if necessary, simply by keeping a constant downward pressure on the key. In fact by increasing the pressure you could increase the output, exactly as a violinist can.

It took a lot of experimenting before I had the feel of it. Indeed it would be weeks or months before I would be able to get maximum effects out of this new system. In a sense it was a little like switching from piano to organ, in that the sound stopped as soon as you took your finger off the key. Unlike the organ, however, you could get a surge of tone in the middle of a note, like the thrill a violinist can produce.

When I had got the hang of individual notes I found the general tonal structure had interesting differences and interesting possibilities. It was sharper, less vague than a piano. This seemed to come from control over high harmonics particularly in the treble. The general effect was a greater clarity and a more legato quality. The harsh percussive effects of the piano could not be reproduced, they were quite lost. I found by adjusting the general output control that I could either play with the usual kind of heavy pressure the strong finger effect I was normally used to, or I could go over to quite light fingering as one does on a harpsichord. Either way I could get the same big volume of tone. This made it possible, using light fingering, to play passages both very fast and very loud.

I had to be almost literally pulled away from this new box of tricks. Apparently a meal was ready. Incredibly it was set on the floor. The girls had made all kinds of indentations to hold the various articles and dishes. The colours of the food stood out sharply against the dark blue flooring material. It looked exactly as if a bed of flowers had been laid out. The effect was so remarkable that I felt it could not be due to chance.

It was all entirely vegetarian food. They didn't eat animals John had said. Yet you wouldn't have known it. The tastes were there. In fact my only problem was there seemed to be too many tastes, almost as if you were getting the whole of a large menu all at once. The wine was very good. Apparently a span of ten thousand years made little difference so far as wine was concerned.

"How do you like your little present? You haven't thanked us for it yet."

"He is exactly like a child with it," said John with a tinge of jealousy.

I pressed my advantage. "You said you had two presents."

"None for me," muttered John. At this the girl Neria stroked his face:

"There are better presents for you than a little black box," Neria smiled.

I saw John was going to have his troubles, and especially because of the way the translation system operated. It suddenly struck me how much the pronunciation of English by the girls had changed. It was now very much more like normal everyday English. My curiosity flowed over and I had to ask how it was all done, although I realized we were pretending that nothing seemed unusual to us.

"Oh, it is really very simple," said Melea.

"I would not have thought you would have had any difficulty with that," grinned the other girl.

John took up the challenge. "Let me make a guess. First you have a system of language translation set up in a computer. As well as grammatical rules, synonyms, and so forth, you have a library of mouth sounds. When a word is spoken it is analysed for its sounds, taken to pieces. Then it is put through the translation procedure. The same is done for the translated word, in reverse. It's a matter really of having sounds as well as a dictionary. But how did you manage to change the pronunciation as you went along?"

The same thing was puzzling me.

The girls laughed: "Your own pronunciation was analysed, of course. As you spoke each word, the sound formation was taken to pieces. After that, when the same word was used in the translation of something that we said, it was put together in the way you had used. Now do you understand?"

John nodded, and I think I got a pretty good idea myself. But there was still one thing that worried me. "How do you get the voices to sound so right?"

"Because each of us has a library in our computer of the way our voice sounds. Not just in our own language, but of all the sounds that can be made with the human voice. By doing this our voice could be translated into any language whatever, even though we ourselves could not understand a word of it."

"You haven't a library of our voices?"

"No, we are not really using your voices at all. We've used the voice of one of our own people, not anybody we happen to know well personally. Otherwise it would be very strange."

By now we had finished the meal. I was again astonished by the speed with which it was all cleared away. Just the same carpet-sweeping procedure that John had used. The really striking thing was when the white strip reached the position of the piano, or rather the piano-like box of tricks, the whole thing lifted up off the floor, and the white strip went underneath it. Thirty seconds and the room was clear. Dinner was finished.

Both girls went out. Several minutes later they came back carrying two large parcels which they put on top of the piano. With smiles they bowed at me and said: "They're yours."

They were the most normal articles I had yet seen, apparently straightforward parcels, wrapped in what looked uncommonly like paper. I undid the first one. It was just a large metal disc about two feet in diameter and an inch thick.

"Handle it very carefully, please."

John came over: "It must be hollow, or layers of metal. Otherwise it would be much heavier."

It had seemed heavy enough to me. I undid the other parcel. Here there were three discs of the same diameter but less thick. The girls were watching us with amusement. John and I talked about it for some time. It was obviously connected with some sort of electronic device. But what? They were like huge, weighty gramophone records, the sort of thing a stone-age man might have produced, only they were made of bright metal not stone. We gave it up.

Melea took the biggest of the discs, while her friend went to the keyboard on the wall. I was beginning to wonder what these people would do without their walls and floors, when a metallic arm moved smoothly and slowly out of the wall. Melea fitted the disc into it and the whole thing retreated completely from view.

There was a lot to be said for not cluttering up the room with chairs and tables and a hundred and one other articles. The room might have been expected to look bare but it didn't. This was due to the shape and the colours which somehow conveyed the impression of being out-of-doors. I realized what it was that had struck me as being so queer in the first place. Normally when you go into a building you change your sense of scale. Rooms that would seem ridiculously small if they were out-of-doors become tolerably large. What happened here was that you didn't make any change of scale, you had the same sense of size as you have in the open air.

I just had time for these reflections before the music started. I was transfixed at the first chords. It was the beginning of the Mass I had taken three months of the winter to write. It was all there, the whole orchestra. At least it was very nearly the orchestra as I knew it. Very nearly, but not quite, the harmonic balance of the individual instruments was a little different. The music flowed on and I lost all sense of calm judgement. Listening to one's own music is a little like listening to one's own voice, you do it with a sense of wonder, fascination, and horror. You can't believe it really sounds like that. The wonder now was that the instruments were all there, the notes all correct. I could detect no mistake of pitch or of timing. Indeed the timing was if anything too accurate. When the chorus came in the words were English. They were my own words.

Now we were at the section I had played in the temple, the section I had conceived of in an agony of mind. It held me now, playing on my emotions as if I, its creator, were no more than a keyboard. The pain and tragedy dissolved at last into sunlight and the work came to an end, after what seemed like a vast span of time. It was I suppose about two hours.

I knew of course what was on the other discs, the symphony and the piano pieces. I had no thought to hear them now, I wanted no more music that day. I took hold of Melea and we went out onto the balcony. There were no lights anywhere on the ground but the sky was incredibly full of stars. It was even clearer, more remote, than the Grecian sky had been.

It was like the night we had passed at the temple, last night so far as my memory was concerned. Even so there were a thousand and one questions I wanted to ask which still perturbed me, but this was not the occasion for them. The morning would come soon enough.

I woke first. Melea was still there, her face close to mine, her long hair entangling her shoulders. I lay without moving for some time, not wishing to waken her. The feeling was in part selfish for I wanted to study her face. There was natural beauty in it but not a trace of glamour. It was a face that could not have existed in the year 1966.

The eyes opened at last. There was the usual fleeting fraction of a second while the eyes come into focus and the brain comes to life.

"Today will be a happy day," she said, a little sleepily. There was an emphasis on the word today which I could not understand.

It was indeed a good day. We started early, not long after sunrise. It turned out there was some reasonably shaped clothing in the house, a kind of shirt and trousers. Fashions can't change too much simply because of the shape of the human body. The odd thing about these clothes, however, was they had no buttons or fastenings of any kind. You put them on after the style of a boiler suit, except they were very well cut and there was no zip-fastener. There was a special kind of cloth along the fastening which simply pressed against the cloth on the other side of the seam. It was like scotch-tape, except you could use it time and time again. You simply pulled it apart with a good stout tug.

After the usual frothy breakfast we called up a taxi. Unlike the taxis I was used to, it wouldn't come to the house itself, only to the nearest taxi rank, a good mile away. There had been a heavy dew during the night which was still covering the trees, bushes, and flower beds as we walked down the hillside. The vehicle was already waiting for us. I can best describe it as a squashed sphere. The lower third of it was opaque, the rest was made of some translucent material. There was a little kiosk near by. Melea beckoned me to follow her. I watched while she tapped out what I took to be our destination on one of the inevitable keyboards. A slip of material, translucent, about six inches long by one inch wide appeared. Set within the material were about a dozen characters, apparently in metal. We got into the vehicle. Melea pulled out a rectangular sheet about two feet long. Into this she inserted the smaller slip and then replaced the sheet. Neria touched a button and instantly we began to move.

I could see now as we moved away the reason for the squashed appearance of the sphere. The vehicle itself was about fifteen feet across. The walls were rather like the kind of shop window that doesn't seem to have any glass in it. You had the impression you were looking straight out. There was no rattle or rumble as we picked up speed. Very soon we were whistling along at what I guessed to be about eighty miles an hour. It took about two hours to our destination. We went towards the south. I could see the big mountains I had glimpsed from the balcony. They were volcanic cones, not unlike the mountains of Hawaii in fact.

"One of them will be Popocatepetl, I suppose," said John.

"They must have cleared the whole of the jungle that used to occupy these parts," he added.

We passed mainly through green fields. Every now and then I could see little valleys filled with flowers, like the one we had come from. I thought I could glimpse houses. Also in the distance I caught flashes of vehicles similar to the one we were travelling in. At an intersection of the pathways, or magnetic tracks, or whatever they were, we came quite close to another vehicle. The occupants waved and we waved back.

As we approached the mountains it was obvious the jungle had indeed been cleared. We went quite smoothly and silently up the mountainside. Eventually we passed from fields to grassland. It was for all the world like an alp, except there were no animals.

"What has happened to all the animals?"

I asked this in Greek, for Greek was now our only means of communication—strange we had to work through a language that lay two thousand years in the past for me, eight thousand years in the past for the girls.

"The situation is very sad. All the major animals were wiped out and became extinct long ago."

"How about the domestic animals?"

"We no longer have any need of them. They are not here, not in our country anyway. We turned them loose in places suited to them. Many exist in a wild form like cattle and sheep, but the animal population of the Earth has become very poor. At least it was so until these new events occurred. Now we have collected them again."

We reached our destination high on the grasslands. I could feel the altitude quite appreciably, which meant we were probably above eleven thousand feet. Grass still grew at this elevation because of the sub-tropical climate. For about three hours we climbed along a pleasant track. At last we came to rougher ground. There was a hut where we had lunch. We took exactly what we needed. I was now keenly aware that nobody ever paid for anything.

When I remarked on this to John he said, "Obviously this

141

is a high-powered civilization with very few people. I imagine they could make far more than they need, so why worry about paying."

"To make sure people work."

"It's obvious they have so many machines, so much automation, there isn't any need for anybody to work, not in our sense. I imagine their problem must be leisure not work."

Another party arrived, a party of six. They looked at us curiously and I thought a little sadly. I couldn't make out why for I didn't feel sad myself. The newcomers had a remarkable family resemblance to the two girls. These people must all look pretty much alike. The man who had appeared for a brief moment back in the temple on the mountain, he also had been remarkably like Melea. I saw now why the girls didn't bother to glamorize themselves. If everybody looked more or less the same, there really wouldn't be any point in it.

I asked Melea how many people there were in total. She told me about five million.

"Over the whole Earth, only five million?" I asked in astonishment.

"We don't live over the whole Earth, only in this country here."

"You mean the rest of the Earth is empty?"

"Not empty but wild, in its natural state. Why should we want to live everywhere? Five millions is quite enough people to know. How many people do you know in your country, more than five million?"

"Of course not. We make a choice of those we wish to know."

"There is no point in us making such a choice. Why should we want to know one person and ignore another?"

The view away to the north was tremendous as we walked back again downhill by a different path.

"I think we must hurry," said Neria.

This was translated to us, with the explanation that there would be a thunderstorm about four o'clock in the afternoon. We got back to our taxi barely in time. It was a wonderful ride down the mountainside through the driving rain and the flickering lightning. Several times the lightning struck at points not far removed from us. Neither of the girls seemed at all worried about being hit ourselves. John noticed this and whispered, "They must have some protective field, lowering the potential a bit, near the track."

It was amazing there was so little noise inside our sphere. Once we quitted the vehicle back at our own valley we soon got thoroughly wet. The girls didn't seem to mind in the least and strode along, uncaring. We followed them to a house which wasn't ours. Quite a few people were already here. One of them showed us to what seemed to be a changing-room. There was a strong hot-air blower that dried you off completely in a couple of minutes. Then we picked ourselves a selection of garments and sealed ourselves up inside them. We took less than ten minutes but it could have been done in under three or four.

About twenty people came in that evening to what was evidently a party. It was not quite as free and easy as a party can be where everybody speaks the same language, because quite often we had to go through the translation system. Yet it was all far, far easier than attending any sort of function in a foreign country in the world of 1966. I had been right about the preparation of meals. They all made a big thing about the arrangement of the colours, into patterns like flower beds, and about the shape of the floor. They divided into two halves and had a kind of race. From the gun it took about ten minutes.

During the meal a sly game went on, of softening up the floor under one or another of us. It may sound ridiculous but it certainly looked funny, especially after a modicum of alcohol. Although everybody talked twenty to the dozen there was no appalling volume of sound. The floor, the ceiling, and the walls, were evidently sound absorbing. Yet when I had played the previous night I hadn't had the impression of playing into a sink. It seemed as if the reflecting qualities of the room must be changeable.

After dinner the little piano suddenly appeared. It came in by itself through a doorway. There was nothing for it but that I should sing for my supper. There was a very good reason why everybody wanted to hear me. What I had already begun to suspect, that nobody in this society played any musical instrument, was confirmed. Music could be put together so readily using electronic techniques that incentive was quite lacking for anyone to go through the long years of drudgery so necessary for proficient performance.

The evening reminded me in a curiously vivid way of the party back so long ago in Los Angeles. I found myself beginning the waltz theme of the Diabelli variations. I had not played them since the night in Los Angeles. Until now I had associated Beethoven's great masterpiece with a different time, a different age. But now the variations emerged with as much freshness as ever, and with more power than I had been able to produce on the instruments of that apparently far-off epoch.

143

THE following morning the party had quite dissolved. When Melea and I appeared for breakfast we found John talking to a white-haired man of about sixty. Melea instantly became serious. She said:

"This morning it has to be different. It is about the film we stopped you from seeing the other afternoon. You will soon understand why it was better left until the end."

This made me uneasy.

"What do you mean, by there being an end?"

"I think you must see first. After that you must hear what we have to say. Then you can decide."

The two girls and the man left us. The beginning of the film appeared. Evidently the others didn't want to watch it.

The showing took upward of four hours. It was the longest documentary film I had ever seen, naturally enough for it dealt with a time span of six thousand years. We covered time at an average rate of a century to each four minutes. There was no place here for intricate involvements, or for the niceties of politics. Yet it was all too easy to follow. The black record of the human species swept remorselessly on as the minutes and hours ticked away.

It was a shock at the beginning to be very quickly out of both the twentieth and the twenty-first centuries. The first quick point was a transition from poverty to affluence in the undeveloped continents of the twentieth century, Africa and Asia. A homogeneous civilization swept with incredible speed over the whole Earth. There were brief flashes of the people, of their machines, their customs, their political leaders. It was all done visually. We sat in silence watching, our ears free of the cacophonous uproar of the usual sound track. It was easy to comment to each other on what we saw, not that we had much to say beyond the occasional exclamation.

Earth teemed with people. Cities spread out farther and farther until they became joined to each other. Urban populations covered an increasing fraction of the land surface. At first it was only one per cent, then five per cent, then twenty-five percent. The technological drive went irresistibly on. Land became of more and more value. There was no room any longer for any animal save man. So we watched the gradual extinction of the whole animal world. Even the bird population declined and withered away.

We saw something of domestic life. We saw the standardized little boxes in which almost everybody was now living. The insistent question formed in your mind, what was it all good for? What conceivable reason could there be to prefer a thousand little boxes to one dignified house? The same of course for the people. What was the advantage of this appalling fecundity of the human species?

Soon we were in the twenty-fifth century. Angry voices began to be heard. The pressures were mounting, competing with the technology. The technology itself was kept going by the most rigorous demands on individual freedom. It was indeed a veritable ant-heap. The average person became restricted to a life that lay somewhere between the freedom of the twentieth century and the lack of freedom of a man serving a life sentence in prison. Nobody travelled now, except on official business—I mean travelled to distant parts. Everything was provided in one's own locality, food, amusements, work. The work itself demanded little initiative. The people were leading what can only be described as a punched-card life.

The technology wasn't working too well any more. Food was mostly of poor quality, mostly factory produced. At that stage, in the twenty-fifth century, the seas were essentially swept clean of fish. The land animals had been the first to go, then the birds, now last the fish.

The first disaster happened with amazing suddenness. What had seemed a more or less homogeneous civilization split into two, like the division of an amoeba.

"It's a point of instability," whispered John. "Look, the whole thing's going to grow exponentially."

Whatever he meant, this vast gargantuan, sprawling, tasteless, in every way appalling, civilization exploded in a flash. It started with bombs and rockets, with fire. The film, so far silent, now came alive, not with any synthetic sound track, but with the crackling of the actual fire, with the shriek, instantly cut short, of a woman enveloped in a cloud of burning petrol. Then it was all over. It was quiet everywhere. Death and decay swept at an incredible speed, like some monstrous fungus, everywhere over the Earth. There was no movement, no transport, no food distribution. The intricate organization which had itself fed on the efforts of a large fraction of the whole population was dead. Everything which had depended on it, including the lives of the people, now died too. We could hear the whine of infants, the despairing cries of children. The abomination came at last to an end. It seemed as if the human species, having wiped everything else from the face of the planet, had now itself become extinct.

Miraculously this did not happen. A dozen or more specially favoured, especially lucky, small centres of population managed to survive. They were already beginning their recovery by the time we saw them. I suppose because no camera had been there to record the worst moments. Indeed the technique of photography suddenly became very crude, almost the way it had been when photography was first invented.

We saw the slow steady expansion of one centre after another. The population increased, the technology improved. We saw the people happy and smiling again. We heard them talking in a new language. We saw them attempting to recover the relics and treasures of the past, particularly books and manuscripts. We saw how they made every effort as they improved to absorb the culture of the past. Amazingly, a great deal survived.

By now we were almost a thousand years on. The new civilization was becoming exuberant. There was nothing of the deathly, machine-like quality of the situation before the first upheaval, the Great Disaster as it came to be known. People were individuals again. There was hope for the future once more.

The different centres were by now overlapping each other. They were in argument. There was a period of war, astonishingly short it seemed to us on this kaleidoscopic record. The war turned out to be no more than a kind of lubricant that allowed the hitherto separate regions to join up with each other into a coherent whole. With a growing sense of horror I realized it was all going to happen again. There was going to be a second disaster. It became so completely inevitable as one watched. Century after century went by. Each brought its contribution to the elephantine growth. Gone was the zip and zest of the first pioneers of this new civilization. We were back again in a punched-card era. It all happened with horrible predictability. The first and second catastrophes might have been interchanged and you couldn't have told the difference.

So it was with the reconstruction. We saw it all beginning again. There was a longish sequence belonging to North

146

America, in what used to be the United States. It had a vaguely familiar look about it. John burst out loudly, in contrast to our previous whispers:

"That's it, look, that's it! That's what we saw, when we flew across America from Hawaii!"

So it was. What we had seen was not the America of the eighteenth century. It was the America of the fourth millennium.

The record was relentless. I could see now why the girls and the white-haired man had not wanted to stay. Added to horror of intimate detail, I had the feeling of a whole species in some monstrous, unclean cycle from which it could never escape. Each cycle was occupying a little less than a thousand years. Always during the reconstruction phase we could see the same bland confidence that this time it would be different. Because these phases were reasonably long drawn out, over three centuries or so, it always seemed as if the disease had been cured. Then quite suddenly, almost in a flash, the monstrous expansion started again. It was a kind of shocking social cancer. Then came the major surgery of flame and death, and so back to endeavour, to a temporary happiness, and to unrequited hope.

Yet at last something different did happen. At last, when it seemed as if extinction had finally come, just two centres managed to survive. They grew to a reasonable and moderate size, and at that they stopped, or almost stopped, for nearly a thousand years. The film became quite detailed. An important point had evidently been reached.

Always when a centre of population expanded from a small beginning the people were far less heterogeneous than the kind of human population we were used to. Now we had a rather uniform situation. Yet there were still the two population centres.

There was no suggestion of war, however. The people, looking much like the people of the future, were restrained and reasonable, they had learnt the lesson of the past. The two centres maintained a quite friendly rivalry, with the aspects of a favourable situation about it. The rivalry seemed to prevent complacency, it seemed to provide an incentive to achievement. Yet as time went by I could detect a slow steady growth in both population groups, caused apparently by the friendly competition between them.

Both groups were quite well aware of what was happening. They noted the growth, yet they decided after considerable thought that the situation could be kept within bounds. So it was for a long time. Quite suddenly, however, control seemed to be lost. There was a stage beyond which expansion simply could not be prevented. This stage was reached before anybody expected it. From then on we watched a wretched society being forced along a road down which it did not wish to travel. It seemed as if everybody knew what was going to happen, yet nobody could prevent it.

"They've got beyond a point of instability. It's inherent in the organization. They can't get back."

John's prognostication was right. The controlled rivalry disappeared. In its place came an unrestrained rivalry. The groups grew, merged together, after the usual momentary outburst, and so the disease spread to its inevitable conclusion.

At the next re-expansion phase there were three groups. When they reached a very moderate size, about a million people each, discussions took place between them. The outcome was that all three groups merged voluntarily, not to cover the whole Earth, but to contain themselves in a small portion of it. So the people of the future at last appeared. I saw clearly now why they lived in only one place.

How long had they been in their present state? It turned out, upward of a thousand years. In that time strikingly little change had taken place. They believed a genuine stability had at last been achieved, and their belief had more substance to it than the facile, arrogant claims we had seen so often in the earlier parts of the film.

We sat for a long time in silence. There did not seem very much to say. Maybe an hour later, the girls and the white-haired man returned.

"I think the time has come for us to speak seriously," said the man.

I could see something of the appalling predicament that he and his people were in. It was clear the Earth, with its different centres of population, might already be beyond all control. John was evidently thinking along the same lines, for he asked:

"What plans have you made, about how you're going to organize the Earth?"

The white-haired man answered simply: "We have no such plans, because none are possible."

The horror of the situation was at last becoming clear to me. It wasn't so much that we, the remnants of the twentieth-century world, were inevitably condemned to a catastrophic future, with its rhythmic disasters, but that these people, the

148

people of the future, were condemned to return to the agony of the past.

I could see the hopelessness of trying to impose any kind of control. It might last for a few years, even for a few generations, but from what we had seen there could be no permanent stability. Sooner or later the same grotesque swings, from arrogant expansion to pitiful collapse, would occur. It could only be prevented through the gross annihilation of the whole of the past. I had no doubt the technology of these people would enable them to carry through such an annihilation. Yet this was just as impossible as any attempt at control. It would destroy, psychologically, the annihilators. It would be a complete negation of all that these people stood for.

John had been silent for a while, evidently in perturbed thought. Now he asked, surprisingly, "Have you seen the situation in Africa and in the southern hemisphere?"

"Yes, we have made a survey."

"What did you find?"

"Nothing, the same as you."

"Isn't that a bit odd? I know you have elected to live here in this part of the world. But surely some of your people, if only small expeditions, must have explored other parts of the world fairly frequently?"

"You are wondering why neither you nor we have run into any of our expeditions. The point has not escaped us."

"What's your explanation?"

"We know of nothing definite."

John was pacing about restlessly. He was evidently much agitated. Dramatically he turned. "You know what I think, I think both Africa and the southern hemisphere belong to the future, like the great Plain of Glass. I don't think they're your contemporary world at all. Otherwise there would be unmistakable traces of your people somewhere."

The white-haired man smiled a little sadly.

"You are very intelligent, Dr. Sinclair. There seems to be little that has escaped you. Yes, it is possible that those regions may represent the future, the future even to us."

"You realize the implication?"

"Naturally."

I could contain myself no longer. "For heaven's sake what does it mean?"

John turned on me. "It means that in the future, in the time belonging to those lands, the human race has become extinct. It has all come to nothing, the great experiment of animal life on this planet. Nothing has survived except a few insects."

149

"I do not see why you should be so perturbed, Dr. Sinclair."

"It is a confession of failure."

"I cannot see why. In that sense, failure must come in any case, quite inevitably. You yourself have stood on the great Plain of Glass. You know what the whole Earth will come to in the end. The only question is whether it comes later, or sooner."

I turned incredulously. "Extinction! It doesn't worry you?"

"In the sense of a serious critical problem, no. It will be hard for you to understand our point of view. In your time, everything of importance always lay in the future. You worked for the future, you were dominated by a sense of progress. The path along which you walked was always less important than the view around the next corner. Our philosophy is quite different. We have strong ideas of how life should be lived. If the conditions we believe to be necessary can no longer be met we would prefer there to be no future. You see, we do not believe in time as an ever-rolling stream. We believe all times are equally important, the past is not lost."

I looked quizzically at John, for this was much what he himself had said one afternoon back in England. I remembered his argument about consciousness and about rows of pigeon holes, except I couldn't remember the details. Whether because he actually agreed with the white-haired man, or because he thought I had detected him in some inconsistency, John now took a different line.

"I could sympathize with your point of view if you could be sure extinction will come quickly. Do you think that will be the way of it? Surely there will be a long slow downward trend, at any rate to begin with. The degeneration will occur by slow creeping degrees. Things will go just a little wrong at first, then more wrong, then catastrophically wrong. We have seen enough today to be sure our species will not die easily. Extinction will be a long-drawn-out, agonizing affair. Surely you can't maintain that living through such an experience would be in any way pleasant? Surely it is to be avoided, if it possibly can be?"

The white-haired man fell silent. I could see John's point had great force with him. The girl Neria took up the argument:

"These are exactly the questions we have been occupied with during the past months. We have only come to a decision after much discussion."

The white-haired man continued. "It is only fair to tell you that what we are now saying is being heard by all our people." He pointed to the walls of the room as if to signify their qualities as receiving and transmission systems, qualities that were really obvious from the translations we were receiving.

He went on, "I tell you this to make it clear that I am not giving just a personal opinion. These are the considered views of our whole community."

"So what it comes down to," said John, "is that you're not going to do anything definite. You're going to continue in the same way as before?"

"You are correct. We have weighed the likelihood of extinction against all the other factors. We see that a general mixing of ourselves with the people of Europe might be said to give the human species another chance. But it would only be a blind chance."

"It may be better to take even a blind chance."

"With the certainty of a repetition of what you have just seen?"

We were back at the dilemma.

"Is there no way of proceeding slowly, of making experiments as you go?" I asked. For answer, the white-haired man went on:

"It is necessary for me to tell you something further, which I do not think you have yet appreciated. This strange world, this world with different ages living side by side, is not going to last permanently. Soon we shall revert to where we were before, or very nearly to where we were before."

John nodded. "Yes, I've been having suspicions in that direction. The question is, whose world is it going to be?"

"There can be no doubt at all about that. It will be ours. The play is already complete so far as you are concerned. There is no possibility of changing your society. It is we who are balanced on the knife edge."

Deep within me I had the concept of there being some sort of plan.

When I said so, the white-haired man answered, "The concept of a plan involves the idea of working to a specified end. You have in mind an ultimate El Dorado, which some day you may attain. Yet there can be no such El Dorado for the Earth. You have seen the final state of the Earth, out there in the great Plain of Glass. Perhaps you may think we could escape to some other planet moving around some other star. Yet that star too will die. So it will be for our whole galaxy. Ultimate continuity, in a physical, material respect is impossible.

"It is possible that gradually, inevitably, a huge intellect is being built from the creatures evolving on trillions of planets, everywhere throughout the universe. What in these circum-

151

stances you wonder would be our personal contribution? Perhaps if we were lucky we might contribute some small fragment to the sum total. More likely, we should contribute nothing. In all respects duplication occurs on an enormous scale, galaxies, stars, planets, living creatures, all in vast numbers. Stars like each other, living creatures like each other, all doing more or less the same thing, many indeed following almost exactly the same course of evolution. Yet, like the occasional mutation, something a little different may happen in exceptional cases. Perhaps in one case in a thousand a new facet may emerge. The question we have asked ourselves is whether this small chance is worth all the agony. Is it worth even the few thousand years you have observed this morning? Was the long process of evolution, lasting hundreds of millions of years, perhaps still to go on for hundreds of millions of years, worth the eventual small chance of life here on the Earth making a fragmentary contribution to some higher level of attainment, of which we can barely conceive? To an imaginary planner, the answer would of course be yes, because the planner would be interested only in the higher levels being built from the lower, just as we ourselves are pleased to have evolved from more primitive creatures. Yet to the creatures themselves the answer may be no."

I saw now where the argument was leading. "Your answer I take it is no?"

"Our answer is no. If we hold firmly with the utmost determination to our present point of balance we may hope to deny what we believe to be the normal course of evolution."

John was walking up and down. "Can we come back now to the how and the why of it?"

"There are several interpretations. It could be an opportunity to repair some biological defect in our heredity. We may have lost some essential component which your population has still within it. It could be a punishment, by showing us our own extinction, to cause us distress. It could even be an experiment to see how we react in the face of both these things."

"Surely we're faced now with a situation that doesn't concern you alone? Your technology is naturally better than ours, but there are now at least twenty times as many people in our world as there are in yours."

"That is quite incorrect I am afraid. Your people exist only in a ghost world. For a little while your world may have a vivid reality, but very soon now, now that we have made our decision, it will be gone. It will go in a brief flash, just as it arrived."

152

I found it difficult to conceive of myself as a ghost. "I would not have said there was anything ghostlike about the two of us."

"Not in the least, you are real enough."

Melea spoke for the first time. "The different zones of the Earth will change back to what they were before. The Greece in which we met, the temple, will be gone. It will be gone far more completely than even the ruined remains of your own time. It will be gone almost without trace. It will be gone, except for the records in our libraries. Europe too will be gone, so will the great Plain of Glass. It will only be this zone here that will remain."

The man nodded and went on. "So you must decide. For the people of your country there is no decision to make. For us, we have made our decision. But for you it will be difficult. If you leave here you will disappear, into oblivion. If you stay, you will continue to live out your lives among us. The decision you will take must depend on your own thoughts and emotions. We cannot guide you further. Between you there is both reason and emotion. You must find where *your* balance lies."

Before they left, Melea came to me and said, "I will not stay with you tonight, because I do not want to influence the way you will decide."

The three of them, the two girls and the white-haired man, looking almost infinitely sad, left us to our thoughts and deliberations.

My first reaction was to question what had been said. "Is there any possibility of it not turning out the way they think? I mean about Britain and Europe simply disappearing. It seems preposterous."

"Well, it's only the inverse of what happened before. If it was possible to go one way, it must be possible to go the other."

"But everything back home, John, it was real enough. Those weren't ghost people, they were people with real feelings."

"Of course they had real feelings, but they were apparitions nevertheless. For us it's different. We shall live out a perfectly real life if we stay here, but only if we stay here."

"Well, there can't be any doubt about it. Going back—to oblivion I mean."

"That was the way I felt until I began to think about it. What you must realize is, you really wouldn't be going back to oblivion, you'd be going back to one life not two."

"I don't understand, even faintly."

"Surely you could see from the film we've just watched that we've already lived our proper lives. Our lives exist— you remember the pigeon hole business—lives in which we quitted Los Angeles for Hawaii. Somewhere in Hawaii there was a forking point. Instead of a single set of pigeon holes, suddenly there became two sets. One of them went along perfectly normal lines."

"You mean the lines we expected, a life in which we returned to the Los Angeles of the twentieth century?"

"Yes, of course."

"Why don't we know anything about it?"

"Because the two have separated, they've forked apart. There's no connection between them. You're either in the one or the other. It's the sequence all over again. Whichever you're in you never know of the other. In this sequence you can never know what happened when you returned to Los Angeles. In that other sequence you can never know even a single thing about this one. The two are utterly separated. In the other sequence, neither you nor I will know about the future, about the film we saw this morning."

"Then what does it come down to? What's the decision?"

"The decision is whether we want this particular sequence to end in a kind of cul-de-sac. We can either prolong it out into the usual lifetime or we can simply chop it off."

"What would be the sense of chopping it off!"

"Because we might find this sequence intensely painful. Let me put it to you this way. You know you've got two lives to live. One life is perfectly normal and pleasant, but in the other you commit some serious offence, an offence which carries either the death penalty or a penalty of life imprisonment. You have the choice of which it shall be. If you only had one single life you might well choose imprisonment, in order to be able to go on. But with two lives do you really make that choice? There would be a lot to be said for avoiding the continual agony of being cooped up in prison, without any possibility of escape, year after year for several decades. You might well say to yourself—remembering you know about the more or less pleasant life—let's make an end of this one, let's make it into a cul-de-sac. You see my point?"

"Except I don't see any parallel between being in prison and being here."

"That's exactly the thing we've got to decide. That's exactly what our friend meant by saying we've got a difficult decision. I'm going to argue in favour of us both leaving. You take the other line. Then we must sleep on it and each make up his own mind about it."

So we started. It was a long talk, very long, so I will give only a condensed version of what John said.

154

"Try to see what we're in," began John. "We're in a fossilized society. They've decided, completely as a matter of policy, that they're not going to change. They're not going to seek after progress. They're satisfied with the way life is. For them this may be fine but to us it would be a living death. We have a drive that forces us towards further achievement. Of course it may be quite illusory, probably it is. But being the way we are I think we would find it very much an imprisonment."

"I don't see there's anything to stop us from going on doing the things we want to do."

"I see plenty. I've got several thousand years of scientific development to learn before I could possibly get down to any really useful work. Of course it would be interesting enough to begin with. There'd be the solution to the problems that I know about. In a way it would be marvellous to read about it all. But just think of the years of grind and drudgery that would be needed before I could do anything at all creative. It's likely I'd never succeed. You've got to begin as a child, with a child's ability to learn, if you're to break through the wall of an entirely new civilization. I'm afraid I should be reduced to a useless potterer.

"You yourself may be a little better off. The kind of music you know of has some validity. In fact you've got more or less a complete open field. Yet even your position wouldn't be too good. These people may have a liking for music, they may be able to compose it, but none of them can actually play. You can see for yourself that everything is done electronically. Perhaps you would get them to sing but that would be about all. You would never hear a real orchestra again.

"These are the bigger issues but think of the smaller ones. There are a million and one simple things these people take for granted. Yet they'd all be strange to us. It's fine enough for a few days, but think how it'd be for a whole lifetime. We'd never really belong. We'd never again hear our own language spoken, except through an artificial electronic device. Remember Art Clementi and his boys. Remember the night you were first in La Jolla. It was all very wild and woolly maybe compared to these people. But wouldn't you come to ache for some of the zip and zest of that old life? In a way it was very squalid, but it had a vigour we should miss terribly. Remember we're not just walking out into nothingness. We're simply saying that this is a life we don't want to live, just as these people themselves have refused to follow

155

a life of what we are pleased to call progress. Logically I can go along with them, but emotionally I'm not conditioned to their sort of existence."

This is the main substance of what he said. I lay awake a long time that night. Even when I did get to sleep it was a troubled sleep. It was clear to me that John had already made up his mind to leave. If I stayed I'd be entirely alone. The point about never again hearing my own language hit me heavily, more than some of the logical arguments. It was true that within a few months or a year I would learn the language of these people, just as I had learnt to get along in Greek. But obviously there would always be a hankering back to the language of my youth.

I saw I would make pilgrimages back to my old home. There would be nothing but wild country. The glens of the Highlands would be much the same as I had known them. The shape of the hills would be the same. There would still be the hidden valley down which John and I had walked, apparently only a few months ago. But there would be no people, anywhere. I would make one or two such pilgrimages. Then I would go no longer, for the sadness of it all, the knowledge of what had happened, would be borne in on me too heavily. If I stayed here I would be in a kind of psychological no man's land. On the one side there would be a civilization which I liked but which I was not really a part of, on the other side there would be the vivid memories of my own people, and the knowledge of what they had come to suffer.

The following morning Melea and her friend were there. John told them we had decided to leave. Melea said that transportation arrangements had already been made. It was a sad little breakfast we had together. The time for departure came. We all agreed that delay would be bad. I took one last look around. There was the electronic box, the thing I had come to think of as a piano, looking now strangely pathetic. I had a strong urge to play on it for one last time. I told the others, saying I would prefer to be alone, that I would follow in a few minutes. Melea answered:

"Don't be too long. There isn't much time."

I began to play. I realized that only in music could I find the answer I was seeking to the questions of the previous evening. Argument I could follow, it weighed with me, yet I could decide nothing from it. I did not know exactly what the music was, it was an improvisation not so much on a

156

musical theme as on the agony of the destiny of man. I continued to play on and on, aware at last that I had made my commitment. I was playing the Schubert Andantino when Melea returned.

THE prognostications were correct. Within a few hours of the departure of John Sinclair the world reverted to "normal." The England of 1966, the Europe of 1917, the Greece of 425 B.C., all vanished just as remarkably as they had appeared. I have not seen John again, nor do I think there is the smallest possibility I will ever do so.

Although much more science is known here than was known in the world of 1966, the detailed operation of the singular mixing of epochs is not well understood. As I make it out, issues involving time-reversal were involved, but the physics of the matter is not within my competence. What *is* quite certain is that the affair was brought about from a higher level of perception than our own. That such levels exist seems reasonable. That we ourselves are unable to comprehend the thoughts, the actions, the technology perhaps, of an intelligence of a higher order also seems reasonable. Disturb a stone and watch ants scurrying hither and thither underneath it. Can those ants comprehend what it is that has suddenly turned their tight little world upside down? I think not. It emerges very clearly that humanity can also be stirred up at any time, just like ants under a stone.

Two years have passed since these events. I have learned the new language. I no longer speak any English. For the most part this causes no distress. Yet occasionally a pang sears through me, an overriding desire to hear the old sounds again. I began this present narrative while in such a mood, feeling that if I couldn't speak my native language with any purpose I might at least write it.

In these two years I have composed a great deal of music. I do not compose nowadays for plaudits, for box office, or to please critics. I compose simply to please myself and my friends. I have returned to Europe, to England and even to Glencoe. I have climbed Bidean nam Bian again, followed the same ridge and come down into the same hidden valley. There is no village of Glencoe, no Macdonalds and Campbells to feud with each other, no motorists touring the glen. The country is entirely wild and still more beautiful.

More and more the old life has become vague and remote, like the memories of distant childhood. This gradual evaporation of a life which at one time was so intensely vibrant has come upon me with profound sadness. In these pages I have been able in some measure to give a sense of reality to what are now mere outlines in a gathering mist. Yet one detail stands out harsh and stark.

The day John Sinclair was missing from the caravan on the moors below Mickle Fell, I myself had the impression of a time gap of about two hours, between six and nine in the evening. I bitterly regret that I did not mention this impression to John. Of course I couldn't be at all sure I hadn't simply nodded off to sleep. I didn't want to appear to be dramatizing myself. Then subsequent events soon swept the incident out of my mind. Yet I suspect this small detail—reconsidered in the light of all that followed—assumes a deep significance. Accepting a bifurcation of worlds, accepting the copying process which John himself believed in so strongly, accepting his view that it was an apparition, a copy of himself, who returned to the caravan after the gap of nine hours, could it have been a copy of myself who was waiting there to receive him, another apparition who cooked the meal when he said he was so devilishly hungry?

After the bifurcation there were two worlds, the straightforward world of 1966 in which nothing particularly unusual happened, and this strange new world belonging to the people of the future. Which of these worlds got our copies, which got the "originals"? We both took it for granted that the copies went to the new world, copies of everything, of the Prime Minister, of our Australian pilot. This presumption may well have been correct except for the two of us. For us it may well have been the world of 1966 which had the apparitions.

Why the two of us? Why should just the two of us be different? Because we were just the two who managed to penetrate into the territory of the people of the future. John always thought of this penetration as accidental. He laughed about my getting through to Greece, about my encounter with Melea in the temple on the hill. But was it really an accident? Hardly, I think, for it fits too smoothly into a pattern, a pattern that would have been completed if John had elected to stay here, a pattern in which "copies" vanished and "originals" remained.

After the bifurcation in Hawaii, I was in the company of

John Sinclair for a mere ten days. If at any time during those ten days I had looked for it I strongly suspect I would have found John's old birthmark. The birthmark was a telltale clue giving away the whole story. An opportunity did indeed fall our way, perhaps was even deliberately put in our way, the day of our trip to Popocatepetl, the day when we all got so very wet on the return journey. But for the sexual distraction of the two girls being there as we dried off, the mark would very probably have been noticed. I have no doubt now it was the real John Sinclair who was sent out from here—into oblivion. The irony and tragedy is that to the two of us it was the world of 1966 that was the real cul-de-sac.

NATHANIEL HAWTHORNE was born on July 4, 1804, in Salem, Massachusetts, the son and grandson of proud New England seafarers. He lived in genteel poverty with his widowed mother and two young sisters in a house filled with Puritan ideals and family pride in a prosperous past. His boyhood was, in most respects, pleasant and normal. In 1825 he was graduated from Bowdoin College, Brunswick, Maine, and he returned to Salem determined to become a writer of short stories. For the next twelve years he was plagued with unhappiness and self-doubts as he struggled to master his craft. He finally secured some small measure of success with the publication of his *Twice-Told Tales* (1837). His marriage to Sophia Peabody in 1842 was a happy one. *The Scarlet Letter* (1850), which brought him immediate recognition, was followed by *The House of the Seven Gables* (1851). After serving four years as the American Consul in Liverpool, England, he traveled in Italy; he returned home to Massachusetts in 1860. Depressed, weary of writing, and failing in health, he died on May 19, 1864, at Plymouth, New Hampshire.

JAMES R. MELLOW is the author of *Charmed Circle: Gertrude Stein & Company* and of the acclaimed *Nathaniel Hawthorne in His Times*.

The Scarlet Letter

and

*The House of the
Seven Gables*

A ROMANCE

by
NATHANIEL HAWTHORNE

WITH AN INTRODUCTION BY JAMES R. MELLOW

A SIGNET CLASSIC

SIGNET CLASSIC
Published by the Penguin Group
Penguin Books USA Inc., 375 Hudson Street,
New York, New York 10014, U.S.A.
Penguin Books Ltd, 27 Wrights Lane,
London W8 5TZ, England
Penguin Books Australia Ltd, Ringwood,
Victoria, Australia
Penguin Books Canada Ltd, 2801 John Street,
Markham, Ontario, Canada L3R 1B4
Penguin Books (N.Z.) Ltd, 182–190 Wairau Road,
Auckland 10, New Zealand

Penguin Books Ltd, Registered Offices:
Harmondsworth, Middlesex, England

Published by Signet Classic, an imprint of New American Library,
a division of Penguin Books USA Inc.

First Printing (Double Signet Classic Edition), October 1981
12 11 10 9 8 7 6 5 4

Introduction Copyright © 1981 by James R. Mellow
Bibliography Copyright © 1980 by The New American Library, Inc.
All rights reserved

The Scarlet Letter and *The House of the Seven Gables* are also available as separate
volumes in Signet Classic editions.

 REGISTERED TRADEMARK—MARCA REGISTRADA

Library of Congress Catalog Card Number: 81-81591

Printed in the United States of America

INTRODUCTION
Hawthorne's Divided Genius
by James R. Mellow

IN one of those perfect antitheses that seem more natural to
literary criticism than to literary history, Hawthorne's earliest major novels, *The Scarlet Letter* and *The House of the
Seven Gables*, represent the opposing poles of his divided
genius. The first, published in 1850, is a gloomy allegory of
sin and redemption set in Puritan Boston, a book that
Hawthorne himself characterized as "positively a hell-fired
story" into which he had found it impossible to introduce
even a ray of cheering light. The second, published a year
later, was Hawthorne's depiction of contemporary Salem
life (with flashbacks into the past of his fictional Pyncheon
and Maule families)—a picture that Hawthorne had hoped to
finish with all the minute detail of a Dutch genre painting.
As he acknowledged in a letter to a friendly critic, *The House
of the Seven Gables* was "a more natural and healthy product
of my mind and [I] felt less reluctance in publishing it."

Hawthorne's reluctance over the earlier publication of
The Scarlet Letter had not been feigned; but strangely, he
had been more concerned about the stark mood of the story
than the possible scandal of its subject—the adulterous relationship between a sensitive and weak-willed Puritan minister, the Reverend Arthur Dimmesdale, and his beautiful
parishioner, Hester Prynne, whose husband is mistakenly
believed to have died at sea. Originally Hawthorne had
planned for *The Scarlet Letter* to be a long short-story, one
of a series of historical tales to be published in a single
volume by his newly acquired publishers, Ticknor, Reed
and Fields. But James T. Fields had encouraged him to

expand the tale and publish it as a novel by itself. Writing to Fields on January 20, 1850, Hawthorne had explored his misgivings, maintaining that the story stuck too closely to its point, that it kept turning over "the same dark idea" and would very likely weary or disgust his hard-earned readership. Hawthorne's concern was natural enough; he had never been a popular or a well-paid author and he was, at that moment, in the middle of a financial crisis. "Is it safe, then," he asked Fields, "to stake the fate of the book entirely on this one chance?"

The question was rhetorical; it was clear from his letter that Hawthorne was ready to accede to Fields's suggestion. The fate of the book is a fact of literary history; it was a resounding critical success. For many critics, then and now, *The Scarlet Letter* established itself as the first indisputable classic in American fiction.

Considering the genteel taste of the mid-nineteenth-century American readership, with its preference for stories of sentimental love and characters of exemplary moral behavior—a literature written by what Hawthorne testily described as "a damned mob of scribbling women"—a novel about adultery was a daring choice of subject. But Hawthorne, the anatomist of guilt rather than the historian of sin, completely avoided any suggestion of the sexual pleasures in which his loving couple might have indulged. He concentrated instead on the penitential burden they were forced to bear (one publicly, the other in private remorse) in their strict New England community. Hawthorne opened his narrative at the moment when Hester Prynne, carrying her infant daughter Pearl, and bearing the embroidered scarlet letter on her breast, stands on the scaffold, enduring her public penance and refusing to name her fellow-sinner. At that point—the first of three highly dramatic tableaux centering around the scaffold, which provides the novel's structure—Hester catches sight of her husband, Roger Chillingworth, the deformed physician who becomes the catalytic agent for the Reverend Dimmesdale's psychological fall from grace. Hawthorne's lovers may reflect upon or endlessly discuss their moral transgression, but they never look back upon the Eden of their passion. Only once does Hester suggest—with a boldness more characteristic of later feminist heroines than the usual insipid nineteenth-century female protagonist—that their love affair had its own justification, whatever the world's view. "What we did had a consecration of its own," she tells the minister during their meeting in the woods. "We felt it so! We said so to each other!"

But if *The Scarlet Letter* was the most licit of novels on an illicit theme, Hawthorne did not altogether escape criticism from some of his more morally minded reviewers. An Episcopalian bishop, Arthur Cleveland Coxe, writing in the *Church Review*, characterized the story as "the nauseous amour of a Puritan pastor, with a frail creature of his charge, whose mind is represented as far more debauched than her body." (The latter stricture refers to Hester's somewhat emancipated views on the position of women in a male-dominated society.) The clergyman also complained of Hawthorne's introduction of French realism into the purer streams of American fiction; he asked if "a running undertide of filth" would now become a prerequisite for a popular romance. In the highly principled *North American Review*, another critic, Anne W. Abbott, questioned how Hawthorne, a writer with "a wizard power over language," could have chosen such a revolting subject as adultery—a subject "to which fine writing seems as inappropriate as fine embroidery." Subliminally, perhaps, she had caught Hawthorne's analogy between works of literature and the sinful condition of human nature. For Hawthorne clearly intended to establish the parallel: it is one of the obsessive themes of his stories and novels. The scarlet "A," so artfully embroidered by Hester's hand, is intended to signify Art as well as Adultery. For Hawthorne, writing—like Hester's embroidery—was an art that was something of a luxury "in a land that afforded comparatively little scope for its exercise."

The fact that he had created a masterpiece on the theme of one of the capital sins exposed Hawthorne to a sharp attack from the influential social critic and labor reformer Orestes Brownson, who declared: "There is an unsound state of public morals when the novelist is permitted, without a scorching rebuke, to select such crimes, and invest them with all the fascinations of genius, and all the charms of a highly polished style." Brownson, writing in his own *Brownson's Quarterly Review*, obviously intended to administer that rebuke.

The success of *The Scarlet Letter*, however—by September, 1850, it had gone through two editions, amounting to five thousand copies, and a new stereotyped edition had been called for—had less to do with the daring subject matter than to the notoriety of the author's recent ouster from his political post as Surveyor of the Salem Custom House. On June 8, 1849, by way of the newly instituted telegraphic service, Hawthorne was informed of his dismissal. He had been led to believe, by the local Whigs, that his position was secure, since the new administration under Zachary Taylor did not intend to remove qualified men for partisan political reasons, Hawthorne, an appointed Democrat, maintained an air of aggrieved innocence throughout the resulting scandal, which was a subject of nationwide editorial comment. A number of eminent Whigs—including Daniel Webster, William Hickling Prescott, the historian, and Horace Mann, Hawthorne's brother-in-law and a Massachusetts congressman at the time—tried to have him reinstated without success. The publicity, however, proved beneficial when his novel was published seven months later. Hawthorne's wonderfully sardonic account of his tenure of office and his political "decapitation," written as "The Custom-House," the introductory chapter to his novel, only served to revive the controversy. Moreover, Hawthorne's publisher, James Fields, was an energetic publicist, prodding editors and critics with advance copies, courting favorable reviews, introducing stepped-up advertising campaigns, and plastering New York and Boston with show cards of his new publications. "We intend to publish your books à-la-Steam Engine," he told Hawthorne, by way of indicating his up-to-date approach to the trade. In certain respects, *The Scarlet Letter* was one of the first American novels to benefit from modern promotional methods.

The customary image of Hawthorne as a shy, unworldly man, the reclusive author of dreamy tales and fantasies that had little relation to the life of his time, has become entrenched in our literary history. But it stands in the way of a fuller understanding of the complexity of his work and the complexity of his life. It is true that following his graduation from Bowdoin College in 1825, Hawthorne had returned to Salem to spend a decade living in seclusion on Herbert

Street with his reclusive mother and sisters. (Hawthorne's father, a sea captain, had died in Surinam when Hawthorne was four.) There, writing in his "dismal and squalid chamber" under the eaves, he served his lengthy apprenticeship as a writer, producing an unsatisfactory novel, *Fanshawe* (which he later disowned), and the series of tales and sketches he began sending around to the ephemeral literary magazines and gift annuals of the period. But Hawthorne was scarcely the hermit he liked to present himself as in his later prefaces to his novels and volumes of stories. During his summers he took notable journeys: to Connecticut, Martha's Vineyard, the Shaker community at Canterbury, New Hampshire, and, once, during the cholera-ridden summer of 1832, as far west as Niagara Falls and perhaps to Detroit. His travels, as his letters and notebooks indicate, were meant to provide him with material for his stories and sketches. Sometimes during these excursions, according to his sister Elizabeth, Hawthorne engaged in mild flirtations with young women, but neither he nor his family seems to have taken these affairs seriously.

Even the briefest review of Hawthorne's political or professional careers gives the lie to the now-outmoded image of him as a literary recluse. In 1836, he served as the editor of the Boston-based publication, *The American Magazine of Useful and Entertaining Knowledge.* In 1837, with the help of his friends Senator Franklin Pierce and Congressman Jonathan Cilley (both former Bowdoin colleagues), he unsuccessfully tried to get a position as historian of the Wilkes Expedition, which circled the globe in 1838-1842. In 1838, he pressed another friend, John Louis O'Sullivan, editor of the *Democratic Review,* to use his influence in obtaining for him the job of Postmaster in Salem. In 1839, his future sister-in-law Elizabeth Peabody pressured the wily politician and historian George Bancroft into appointing Hawthorne a Measurer in the Boston Custom House. He kept the post until 1841, when he quit to become the unlikeliest member of the new utopian community, Brook Farm, in West Roxbury, Massachusetts. (Hawthorne had hoped to establish a residence for himself and his bride-to-be, Sophia Peabody, but he soon found the work thoroughly unconducive to his literary ambitions.) For three years, following his marriage in 1842, Hawthorne actively campaigned for a political appointment in Salem and, after much wheeling and dealing, was rewarded with the Surveyorship in 1846. In 1852, with characteristic diffidence, he offered his services as campaign biographer to Franklin Pierce, who was running for the presidency. Although Hawthorne maintained he had no political intentions in making such a gesture, he promptly reconsidered and accepted the lucrative post of American consul in Liverpool when Pierce was elected. After a profitable post-inaugural trip to Washington, Hawthorne even managed to add to his consular salary the "emoluments" from the then-vacant consulship at Manchester. He was scarcely the apolitical figure that literary critics and literary biographers have sketched for us in the past.

In one of those unpredictable mergers of art with some of the less-promising aspects of the personal life, Hawthorne's political embarrassment during his ouster from the Salem surveyorship had its relationship to the thematic circumstances of *The Scarlet Letter*. The poignancy of Hester Prynne's public penance, her ordeal on the scaffold where she is pilloried for her sins, is directly related to the shame and bitterness Hawthorne experienced when his name was unexpectedly "careering through the public prints." Throughout the controversy Hawthorne had publicly maintained that he was merely an innocent man of letters who had been offered a political post, that he had been, at best, an indifferent politician who had never taken an active part in party politics. His protestations of innocence were somewhat disingenuous. He had, in fact, deliberately campaigned to get the office. Prior to his dismissal, he had allowed himself to be used as a shield behind which his Democratic cronies held on to their posts in the Custom House. Finally, and with some justice, the Salem Whigs decided that the only way they could take over the Custom House patronage was to remove Hawthorne himself. Hawthorne had not been the passive politician he claimed to be; one of his first acts of office was the dismissal of two elderly inspectors whom he had found it his duty "to report as incompetent," and whom he replaced with "firm friends of the administration." Nor is it altogether certain that Hawthorne was completely free of taint in the case of pressuring—or allowing his name to be used in pressuring—two of his subordinates into paying large assessments for the benefit of the local Democratic party newspaper under threat of being dismissed.

Hawthorne, whose obsessive sense of guilt motivates many of his finest stories, had brought to his account of Hester Prynne's ordeal on the scaffold the burden of his own uneasy compromises during his recent political tenure. The reader of *The Scarlet Letter* who attempts to unravel the "inextricable knot" that ties together the fates of Hester Prynne, Arthur Dimmesdale, and Roger Chillingworth will find no innocent party. The only innocence in *The Scarlet Letter* is the cruel innocence of little Pearl, whose unnerving questions about the scarlet A only add to her mother's sense of guilt and shame.

The Scarlet Letter, however, is not important for its autobiographical hints. Aside from the emblematic figure of Hester (one of the most vivid female characters in American fiction), the real significance of Hawthorne's classic novel is its psychological force. In the Reverend Dimmesdale's fall from pedestal and pulpit, Hawthorne traces with uncanny intuition the hidden connection between physical suffering and repressed guilt. And in the dark relationship between Dimmesdale and the physician Roger Chillingworth, Hawthorne proves himself a premature Freudian, exploring—years before their actual discovery—the manipulative techniques of psychoanalysis. His account of the process by which Chillingworth establishes his unwary victim's guilt is masterly:

> A man burdened with a secret should especially avoid the intimacy of his physician. If the latter possess native sagacity, and a nameless something more—let us call it intuition; if he show no intrusive egotism, nor disagreeably prominent characteristics of his own; if he have the power, which must be born with him, to bring his mind into such affinity with his patient's, that this last shall unawares have spoken what he imagines himself only to have thought; if such revelations be received without tumult, and acknowledged not so often by an uttered sympathy, as by silence . . . then, at some inevitable moment, will the soul of the sufferer be dissolved, and flow forth in a dark, but transparent stream, bringing all its mysteries into the daylight.

Hawthorne was an explorer of the interior self. The above passage from *The Scarlet Letter* illustrates what Hawthorne's most perceptive admirer, Herman Melville, called the "power of blackness" in his prose—the ability to trace the darker emotions, the submerged torments of the mind. It was a quality that set Hawthorne's writing apart from the more popular but shallower fiction of his time.

Hawthorne made ambivalence a method. It was not simply a question of indecision or indifference or a means of escape from the hard social issues of the period—as some of his severest critics claimed. It was Hawthorne's attempt to hold in precise and delicate balance contradictory assumptions, a way of presenting a view of the world that was more complex than could be accommodated by the jingoism either of reactionaries or reformers. In his life, that ambivalence was to cost him uneasy relationships with his Concord neighbors and result in sharp criticisms from the New England abolitionists. Early in the Civil War, for example, writing about a group of Confederate prisoners he had seen at Harpers Ferry, he could not bring himself to repeat the usual bloodthirsty prejudices of the hour. And when Franklin Pierce, because of his outspoken anti-war, anti-Lincoln opinions, was being publicly branded a traitor, Hawthorne—against the advice of his publisher—dedicated his book of English reminiscences, *Our Old Home,* to Pierce. "I find that it would be a piece of poltroonery in me to withdraw either the dedication or the dedicatory letter . . ." Hawthorne wrote Fields. "I should never look at the volume again without remorse or shame." In his writing, Hawthorne's ambivalence provided the opposing symbols, the seemingly antagonistic viewpoints that sustained the tension of his best stories and novels. In *The Scarlet Letter,* the primitive forest, the haunt of the Devil, and the still-raw community of Boston mark the symbolic antipodes of man's moral experience. The harsh justice of the Puritan colony and the private sexual consecration of Hester and the Reverend Dimmesdale appear to be irreconcilable. But in Hawthorne's moral universe, time—and the penitential exile of Hester from the community—bring about a change in public opinion.

II

In his introductory chapter to *The Scarlet Letter,* Hawthorne had bravely announced his intended self-imposed exile from Salem. "Henceforth . . ." he claimed, "I am a citizen of somewhere else." His native town—the Salem of his igno-minious political defeat—would be remembered only as "an overgrown village in cloud-land, with only imaginary inhabi-tants to people its wooden houses and walk its homely lanes." But Hawthorne was not able to dismiss it so easily. In the Berkshires, where he had moved his family in the summer of 1850, he came down with a "tolerable nervous fever," which was finally cured by doses of belladonna. "Mr. Hawthorne thinks it is *Salem* which he is dragging at his ankles still," Sophia Hawthorne wrote her family.

In his next novel, *The House of the Seven Gables,* Haw-thorne re-created his native town, situating it not in "cloud-land" but in the everyday present: a village of (albeit fictional) shabby-genteel families and small tradesmen, elm-lined streets and paltry gardens with scratching hens, parochial ambi-tions, and former crimes (such as the notorious witchcraft trials and, quite possibly, Hawthorne's shameful political ouster) inescapably haunting its present.

Stylistically, the book represents another of the essential dichotomies in Hawthorne's work. Unlike the stark alle-gorical drama of *The Scarlet Letter,* the new novel was full of rambling descriptions and homely details—the kind of details that Hawthorne ordinarily committed to his note-books and letters and indicative of his sharp observational powers rather than his brooding imagination. The Salem of *The House of the Seven Gables* has its history, of course: the ancient history of the Pyncheon house (modeled after the weathered old home of one of Hawthorne's family connec-tions) symbolizes the heavy burden of the past upon its present occupants. But the Salem in which the principal action takes place is an American town in the mid-nineteenth century, with its technological improvements—the railroad, the telegraph, store-bought clothes; a rising merchant class outstripping the declining aristocracy; a breed of new men—like the Honorable Judge Pyncheon—who have dispensed with the old republican virtues and are eager to take on the management of American politics and American society.

As an instance of the contemporaneity that Hawthorne now sought as a writer, the profession he chose for his young hero, Holgrave, was that of "an artist in the daguerreotype line," a practitioner of the new science of photography, which had been introduced into the United States late in 1839 and, by the mid-1840s, was in high vogue. (Hawthorne, interestingly, in 1841 had been one of the early visitors to the "rooms" of the pioneering Boston daguerreotypist, Albert Sands Southworth. Unfortunately, the "miniature" that Hawthorne had sat for then seems to have been lost.)

The House of the Seven Gables has its balance of opposites: Holgrave, a representative of radical youth (like Hawthorne's former Concord neighbor, Henry Thoreau), makes speeches "full of wild and disorganizing matter." He is an apostle of individualism and self-reliance, a severe critic of the past, who complains "Shall we never, never get rid of this Past! It lies upon the Present like a giant's dead body." Phoebe Pyncheon, the symbol of conservative values and rural virtue, is at first put off by the young man because of his "lack of reverence for what was fixed"; but she soon tames him into love and marriage. Clifford Pyncheon is the ineffectual dilettante and lover of the beautiful, a man out of step with the new American success ethic. Released from prison where he has served time for a crime he did not commit, he lives in a world of childish appetites and small secrets, petulantly whining "I want my happiness . . . Many, many years have I waited for it! It is late! It is late!" Even Clifford, with his aristocratic tastes, has his compulsion for the Hawthornean opposite. He experiences a mad urge to throw himself into a banal political procession wending its way along Pyncheon Street, the marchers all "perspiration and weary self-importance" (how many small-town parades are summed up in that accurate phrase!)—his way of identifying with something larger than himself, the plodding mass of ordinary humanity. (Ironically, one of the defenses Hawthorne had mounted against his political enemies in Salem was his contention that he had never in his life taken part in such processions. "I am almost tempted to say [I] would hardly have done anything so little in accordance with my tastes and character," Hawthorne explained with a fastidiousness that would have been thoroughly appropriate for Clifford.)

Although Hawthorne's long narrative account of the death of Judge Pyncheon, reviewing in masterly prose the hypocrisy and opportunism of the American public servant circa 1850, is one of the great set pieces in American literature, his chapter, "The Flight of Two Owls," better illustrates his modernity and his use of ambivalence. In it, he sends his two principals, Clifford and his equally timorous and reclusive sister Hepzibah, in a tragi-comic flight to freedom, escaping from the prison of the old house and the dead Judge, only to find themselves prisoners in the new symbol of progress—a railroad coach whose destination they do not know. In their fear and flight, the two pathetic holdovers from an earlier generation have simply embarked on a journey to nowhere in particular.

In the course of the journey, Clifford becomes a somewhat dotty exponent of modern technology, praising, for the benefit of the bewildered and uncomfortable passengers, the railroad that will bring about a new "nomadic" life for mankind, releasing it from its moneygrubbing ways and its adherence to property and real estate. "A man will commit almost any wrong—" Clifford maintains, "he will heap up an immense pile of wickedness, as hard as granite . . . only to build a great, gloomy, dark-chambered mansion, for himself to die in, and for his posterity to be miserable in." At the same time, Hawthorne introduces an elderly passenger, who enters into a discussion with Clifford and ends by pronouncing his views "All a humbug!" Yet the passenger, too, has his contradictory opinions on the subject of progress. He is wary of the telegraph—which Clifford has also praised—because he suspects it will become merely a tool for "speculators in cotton and politics," but regards it as "a great thing" for the speedy detection of bank-robbers and murderers. Clifford, who was unjustly accused of murder and now fears that he will be charged with the death of Judge Pyncheon, finds his newfound faith shaken. He immediately begins to argue against the telegraph as "an infringement" upon a man's "natural rights." Here Hawthorne, in contradictory fashion, appears to be both endorsing and satirizing some of his own views, for his book was intended as a

criticism of American materialism, an attempt—as he described it in his preface—to "convince mankind (or, indeed,
any one man) of the folly of tumbling down an avalanche of
ill-gotten gold, or real estate, on the heads of an unfortunate
posterity."

No admirer of philosophy or the cloudy metaphysics of
his transcendentalist friends and neighbors, Hawthorne was
usually ill at ease with general arguments of the kind he
produced in his preface. But as a writer, through his ambivalence and in the deployment of his fictional characters, he
was able to turn a given idea in several directions at once.
One of his great gifts as a novelist, and one that he exposes
in his strangely oblique conversation between Clifford and
the elderly passenger, is the realization of the irreducible
personal bias of all our opinions, even our cloudiest metaphysical speculations. We think what we are, Hawthorne is
saying, and what we allow ourselves to become.

The Scarlet Letter

Contents

CONTENTS

PREFACE
to the Second Edition of
The Scarlet Letter

MUCH to the author's surprise, and (if he may say so with-out additional offence) considerably to his amusement, he finds that his sketch of official life, introductory to *The Scarlet Letter*, has created an unprecedented excitement in the respectable community immediately around him. It could hardly have been more violent, indeed, had he burned down the Custom House, and quenched its last smoking ember in the blood of a certain venerable personage, against whom he is supposed to cherish a peculiar malevolence. As the public disapprobation would weigh very heavily on him, were he conscious of deserving it, the author begs leave to say that he has carefully read over the introductory pages with a purpose to alter or expunge whatever might be found amiss, and to make the best reparation in his power for the atrocities of which he has been adjudged guilty. But it appears to him, that the only remarkable features of the sketch are its frank and genuine good humor, and the general accuracy with which he has conveyed his sincere impressions of the characters therein described. As to enmity, or ill feeling of any kind, personal or political, he utterly disclaims such motives. The sketch might, perhaps, have been wholly omitted, without loss to the public or detriment to the book; but, having undertaken to write it, he conceives that it could not have been done in a better or a kindlier spirit, nor, so far as his abilities availed, with a livelier effect of truth.

The author is constrained, therefore, to republish his introductory sketch without the change of a word.

Salem,
March 30, 1850

NOTE: Originally, as he explains in his footnote (p. 57), Hawthorne had intended to publish several other tales and sketches along with the main narrative, which he felt to be too short to stand alone. But the first edition included only "The Custom House." Certain political figures in Salem protested that Hawthorne was making an unfair attack on them. Hence this preface. Most editors have followed Hawthorne's lead in treating "The Custom House" as an introduction to the romance itself.

—L.M.

The Custom House

INTRODUCTORY TO THE
SCARLET LETTER

IT is a little remarkable that—though disinclined to talk overmuch of myself and my affairs at the fireside, and to my personal friends—an autobiographical impulse should twice in my life have taken possession of me, in addressing the public. The first time was three or four years since, when I favored the reader—inexcusably, and for no earthly reason that either the indulgent reader or the intrusive author could imagine—with a description of my way of life in the deep quietude of an Old Manse. And now—because, beyond my deserts, I was happy enough to find a listener or two on the former occasion—I again seize the public by the button, and talk of my three years' experience in a Custom House. The example of the famous "P.P., Clerk of this Parish," was never more faithfully followed. The truth seems to be, however, that, when he casts his leaves forth upon the wind, the author addresses, not the many who will fling aside his volume, or never take it up, but the few who will understand him, better than most of his schoolmates or lifemates. Some authors, indeed, do far more than this, and indulge themselves in such confidential depths of revelation as could fittingly be addressed, only and exclusively, to the one heart and mind of perfect sympathy; as if the printed book, thrown at large on the wide world, were certain to find out the divided segment of the writer's own nature, and complete his circle of existence by bringing him into communion with it. It is scarcely decorous, however, to speak all, even where we speak impersonally. But, as thoughts are frozen and utterance benumbed unless the speaker stand in some true relation with his audience, it may be pardonable to imagine that a friend, a kind and apprehensive, though not the closest friend, is listening to our talk; and then, a native reserve being thawed by this genial consciousness, we may prate of the circumstances that lie around us, and even of ourself, but still keep the inmost Me behind its veil. To this extent, and within these limits, an author, methinks, may be autobiographical, without violating either the reader's rights or his own.

It will be seen, likewise, that this Custom House sketch has a certain propriety, of a kind always recognized in literature, as explaining how a large portion of the following pages came into my possession, and as offering proofs of the authenticity of a narrative therein contained. This, in fact—a desire to put myself in my true position as editor, or very little more, of the most prolix among the tales that make up my volume—this, and no other, is my true reason for assuming a personal relation with the public. In accomplishing the main purpose, it has appeared allowable, by a few extra touches, to give a faint representation of a mode of life not heretofore described, together with some of the characters that move in it, among whom the author happened to make one.

In my native town of Salem, at the head of what, half a century ago, in the days of old King Derby, was a bustling wharf—but which is now burdened with decayed wooden warehouses, and exhibits few or no symptoms of commercial life; except, perhaps, a bark or brig, halfway down its melancholy length, discharging hides; or, nearer at hand, a Nova Scotia schooner, pitching out her cargo of fire-wood—at the head, I say, of this dilapidated wharf, which the tide often overflows, and along which, at the base and in the rear of the row of buildings, the track of many languid years is seen in a border of unthrifty grass—here, with a view from its front windows adown this not very enlivening prospect, and thence across the harbor, stands a spacious edifice of brick. From the loftiest point of its roof, during precisely three and a half hours of each forenoon, floats or droops, in breeze or calm, the banner of the republic; but with the thirteen stripes turned vertically, instead of horizontally, and thus indicating that a civil, and not a military, post of Uncle Sam's government, is here established. Its front is ornamented with a portico of half a dozen wooden pillars supporting a balcony, beneath which a flight of wide granite steps descends towards the street. Over the entrance hovers an enormous specimen of the American eagle, with outspread wings, a shield before her breast, and, if I recollect aright, a bunch of intermingled thunderbolts and barbed arrows in each claw. With the customary infirmity of temper that characterizes this unhappy fowl, she appears, by the fierceness of her beak and eye, and the general truculency of her attitude, to threaten mischief to the inoffensive community; and especially to warn all citizens, careful of their safety, against intruding on the premises which she overshadows with her wings. Nevertheless, vixenly as she looks, many people are seeking, at this very moment, to shelter themselves under the wing of the federal eagle; imagining, I presume, that her bosom has all the softness and snugness of an eiderdown pillow. But she has no great tenderness, even in her best of moods, and, sooner or later—oftener soon than late—is apt to fling off her nestlings, with a scratch of her claw, a dab of her beak, or a rankling wound from her barbed arrows.

The pavement round about the above-described edifice —which we may as well name at once as the Custom House of the port—has grass enough growing in its chinks to show that it has not, of late days, been worn by any multitudinous resort of business. In some months of the year, however, there often chances a forenoon when affairs move onward with a livelier tread. Such occasions might remind the elderly citizen of that period before the last war with England, when Salem was a port by itself; not scorned, as she is now, by her own merchants and ship-owners, who permit her wharves to crumble to ruin, while their ventures go to swell, needlessly and imperceptibly, the mighty flood of commerce at New York or Boston. On some such morning, when three or four vessels happen to have arrived at once—usually from Africa or South America—or to be on the verge of their departure thitherward, there is a sound of frequent feet, passing briskly up and down the granite steps. Here, before his own wife has greeted him, you may greet the sea-flushed shipmaster, just in port, with his vessel's papers under his arm, in a tarnished tin box. Here, too, comes his owner, cheerful or sombre, gracious or in the sulks, accordingly as his scheme of the now accomplished voyage has been realized in merchandise that will readily be turned to gold, or has buried him under a bulk of incommodities such as nobody will care to rid him of. Here, likewise—the germ of the wrinkle-browed, grizzly-bearded, careworn merchant —we have the smart young clerk, who gets the taste of traffic as a wolf cub does of blood, and already sends adventures in his master's ships, when he had better be sailing mimic boats upon a millpond. Another figure in the scene is the outward-bound sailor, in quest of a protection; or the recently arrived one, pale and feeble, seeking a passport to the hospital. Nor must we forget the captains of the rusty little schooners that bring firewood from the British provinces; a rough-looking set of tarpaulins, without the alertness of the Yankee aspect, but contributing an item of no slight importance to our decaying trade.

Cluster all these individuals together, as they sometimes were, with other miscellaneous ones to diversify the group, and, for the time being, it made the Custom House a stirring scene. More frequently, however, on ascending the steps, you would discern—in the entry, if it were summer time, or in their appropriate rooms, if wintry or inclement weather—a row of venerable figures, sitting in old-fashioned chairs, which were tipped on their hind legs back against the wall. Oftentimes they were asleep, but occasionally might be heard talking together, in voices between speech and a snore, and with that lack of energy that distinguishes the occupants of alms-houses, and all other human beings who depend for subsistence on charity, on monopolized labor, or anything else but their own independent exertions. These old gentlemen—seated, like Matthew, at the receipt of custom, but not very liable to be summoned thence, like him, for apostolic errands—were Custom House officers.

Furthermore, on the left hand as you enter the front door, is a certain room or office about fifteen feet square and of a lofty height, with two of its arched windows commanding a view of the aforesaid dilapidated wharf, and the third looking across a narrow lane, and along a portion of Derby Street. All three give glimpses of the shops of grocers, block-makers, slop-sellers, and ship-chandlers; around the doors of which are generally to be seen, laughing and gossiping, clusters of old salts, and such other wharf-rats as

haunt the Wapping of a seaport. The room itself is cobwebbed and dingy with old paint; its floor is strewn with
gray sand in a fashion that has elsewhere fallen into long
disuse; and it is easy to conclude, from the general slovenli-
ness of the place, that this is a sanctuary into which womankind, with her tools of magic, the broom and mop, has very
infrequent access. In the way of furniture, there is a stove
with a voluminous funnel; an old pine desk with a three-
legged stool beside it; two or three wooden-bottom chairs,
exceedingly decrepit and infirm; and—not to forget the
library—on some shelves, a score or two of volumes of the
Acts of Congress, and a bulky Digest of the Revenue Laws.
A tin pipe ascends through the ceiling, and forms a medium
of vocal communication with other parts of the edifice. And
here, some six months ago—pacing from corner to corner,
or lounging on the long-legged stool, with his elbow on the
desk, and his eyes wandering up and down the columns of
the morning newspaper—you might have recognized, honored reader, the same individual who welcomed you into
this cheery little study, where the sunshine glimmered so
pleasantly through the willow branches, on the western side
of the Old Manse. But now, should you go thither to seek
him, you would inquire in vain for the Locofoco Surveyor.
The besom of reform has swept him out of office; and a
worthier successor wears his dignity, and pockets his
emoluments.

This old town of Salem—my native place, though I have
dwelt much away from it, both in boyhood and maturer
years—possesses, or did possess, a hold on my affections,
the force of which I have never realized during my seasons
of actual residence here. Indeed, so far as its physical aspect
is concerned, with its flat, unvaried surface, covered chiefly
with wooden houses, few or none of which pretend to archi-
tectural beauty—its irregularity, which is neither picturesque
nor quaint, but only tame—its long and lazy street, lounging wearisomely through the whole extent of the peninsula,
with Gallows Hill and New Guinea at one end, and a view
of the alms-house at the other—such being the features of
my native town, it would be quite as reasonable to form a
sentimental attachment to a disarranged checkerboard. And
yet, though invariably happiest elsewhere, there is within
me a feeling for old Salem, which, in lack of a better phrase,

I must be content to call affection. The sentiment is probably assignable to the deep and aged roots which my family has struck into the soil. It is now nearly two centuries and a quarter since the original Briton, the earliest emigrant of my name, made his appearance in the wild and forest-bordered settlement, which has since become a city. And here his descendants have been born and died, and have mingled their earthy substance with the soil; until no small portion of it must necessarily be akin to the mortal frame wherewith, for a little while, I walk the streets. In part, therefore, the attachment which I speak of is the mere sensuous sympathy of dust for dust. Few of my countrymen can know what it is; nor, as frequent transplantation is perhaps better for the stock, need they consider it desirable to know.

But the sentiment has likewise its moral quality. The figure of that first ancestor, invested by family tradition with a dim and dusky grandeur, was present to my boyish imagination as far back as I can remember. It still haunts me, and induces a sort of home-feeling with the past, which I scarcely claim in reference to the present phase of the town. I seem to have a stronger claim to a residence here on account of this grave, bearded, sable-cloaked and steeple-crowned progenitor—who came so early, with his Bible and his sword, and trode the unworn street with such a stately port, and made so large a figure, as a man of war and peace—a stronger claim than for myself, whose name is seldom heard and my face hardly known. He was a soldier, legislator, judge; he was a ruler in the Church; he had all the Puritanic traits, both good and evil. He was likewise a better persecutor; as witness the Quakers, who have remembered him in their histories, and relate an incident of his hard severity toward a woman of their sect, which will last longer, it is to be feared, than any record of his better deeds, although these were many. His son, too, inherited the persecuting spirit, and made himself so conspicuous in the martyrdom of the witches, that their blood may fairly be said to have left a stain upon him. So deep a stain, indeed, that his old dry bones, in the Charter Street burial ground, must still retain it, if they have not crumbled utterly to dust! I know not whether these ancestors of mine bethought themselves to repent, and ask pardon of heaven for their cruelties; or

whether they are now groaning under the heavy consequences of them, in another state of being. At all events, I,
the present writer, as their representative, hereby take shame
upon myself for their sakes, and pray that any curse incurred by them—as I have heard, and as the dreary and
unprosperous condition of the race, for many a long year
back, would argue to exist—may be now and henceforth
removed.

Doubtless, however, either of these stern and black-browed
Puritans would have thought it quite a sufficient retribution
for his sins, that, after so long a lapse of years, the old trunk
of the family tree, with so much venerable moss upon it,
should have borne, as its topmost bough, an idler like myself. No aim that I have ever cherished would they recognize
as laudable; no success of mine—if my life, beyond its
domestic scope, had ever been brightened by success—would
they deem otherwise than worthless, if not positively dis-
graceful. "What is he?" murmurs one gray shadow of my
forefathers to the other. "A writer of storybooks! What
kind of a business in life—what mode of glorifying God, or
being serviceable to mankind in his day and generation—
may that be? Why, the degenerate fellow might as well have
been a fiddler!" Such are the compliments bandied between
my great-grandsires and myself, across the gulf of time! And
yet, let them scorn me as they will, strong traits of their
nature have intertwined themselves with mine.

Planted deep in the town's earliest infancy and childhood
by these two earnest and energetic men, the race has ever
since subsisted here; always, too, in respectability; never, so
far as I have known, disgraced by a single unworthy member! but seldom or never, on the other hand, after the first
two generations, performing any memorable deed, or so
much as putting forward a claim to public notice. Gradually,
they have sunk almost out of sight; as old houses, here and
there about the streets, get covered halfway to the eaves by
the accumulation of new soil. From father to son, for above
a hundred years, they followed the sea; a gray-headed shipmaster, in each generation, retiring from the quarter-deck
to the homestead, while a boy of fourteen took the hereditary place before the mast, confronting the salt spray and
the gale, which had blustered against his sire and grandsire.
The boy, also, in due time, passed from the forecastle to the

cabin, spent a tempestuous manhood, and returned from his world wanderings, to grow old, and die, and mingle his dust with the natal earth. This long connection of a family with one spot, as its place of birth and burial, creates a kindred between the human being and the locality, quite independent of any charm in the scenery or moral circumstances that surround him. It is not love, but instinct. The new inhabitant—who came himself from a foreign land, or whose father or grandfather came—has little claim to be called a Salemite; he has no conception of the oysterlike tenacity with which an old settler, over whom his third century is creeping, clings to the spot where his successive generations have been imbedded. It is no matter that the place is joyless for him; that he is weary of the old wooden houses, the mud and dust, the dead level of site and sentiment, the chill east wind, and the chillest of social atmospheres—all these, and whatever faults besides he may see or imagine, are nothing to the purpose. The spell survives, and just as powerfully as if the natal spot were an earthly paradise. So has it been in my case. I felt it almost as a destiny to make Salem my home; so that the mould of features and cast of character which had all along been familiar here—ever, as one representative of the race lay down in his grave, another assuming, as it were, his sentry-march along the main street—might still in my little day be seen and recognized in the old town. Nevertheless, this very sentiment is an evidence that the connection, which has become an unhealthy one, should at last be severed. Human nature will not flourish, any more than a potato, if it be planted and replanted for too long a series of generations in the same worn-out soil. My children have had other birthplaces, and, so far as their fortunes may be within my control, shall strike their roots into unaccustomed earth.

On emerging from the Old Manse, it was chiefly this strange, indolent, unjoyous attachment for my native town, that brought me to fill a place in Uncle Sam's brick edifice, when I might as well, or better, have gone somewhere else. My doom was on me. It was not the first time, nor the second, that I had gone away—as it seemed, permanently—but yet returned, like the bad halfpenny; or as if Salem were for me the inevitable centre of the universe. So, one fine morning, I ascended the flight of granite steps, with the President's commission in my pocket, and was introduced to the corps of gentlemen who were to aid me in my weighty responsibility, as chief executive officer of the Custom House.

I doubt greatly—or, rather, I do not doubt at all—whether any public functionary of the United States, either in the civil or military line, has ever had such a patriarchal body of veterans under his orders as myself. The whereabouts of the Oldest Inhabitant was at once settled when I looked at them. For upwards of twenty years before this epoch, the independent position of the Collector had kept the Salem Custom House out of the whirlpool of political vicissitude, which makes the tenure of office generally so fragile. A soldier—New England's most distinguished soldier—he stood firmly on the pedestal of his gallant services; and, himself secure in the wise liberality of the successive administrations through which he had held office, he had been the safety of his subordinates in many an hour of danger and heartquake. General Miller was radically conservative; a man over whose kindly nature habit had no slight influence; attaching himself strongly to familiar faces, and with difficulty moved to change, even when change might have brought unquestionable improvement. Thus, on taking charge of my department, I found few but aged men. They were ancient sea captains, for the most part, who, after being tossed on every sea, and standing up sturdily against life's tempestuous blast, had finally drifted into this quiet nook, where, with little to disturb them, except the periodical terrors of a Presidential election, they one and all acquired a new lease of existence. Though by no means less liable than their fellow-men to age and infirmity, they had evidently some talisman or other that kept death at bay. Two or three of their number, as I was assured, being gouty and rheumatic, or perhaps bedridden, never dreamed of making their appearance at the Custom House during a large part of the year; but, after a torpid winter, would creep out into the warm sunshine of May or June, go lazily about what they termed duty, and, at their own leisure and convenience, betake themselves to bed again. I must plead guilty to the charge of abbreviating the official breath of more than one of these venerable servants of the republic. They were allowed, on my representation, to rest from their arduous labors, and soon

afterwards—as if their sole principle of life had been zeal for
their country's service, as I verily believe it was—withdrew
to a better world. It is a pious consolation to me, that,
through my interference, a sufficient space was allowed
them for repentance of the evil and corrupt practices into
which, as a matter of course, every Custom House officer
must be supposed to fall. Neither the front nor the back
entrance of the Custom House opens on the road to Paradise.

The greater part of my officers were Whigs. It was well
for their venerable brotherhood that the new Surveyor was
not a politician, and though a faithful Democrat in principle, neither received nor held his office with any reference
to political services. Had it been otherwise—had an active
politician been put into this influential post, to assume the
easy task of making head against a Whig Collector, whose
infirmities withheld him from the personal administration of
his office—hardly a man of the old corps would have drawn
the breath of official life within a month after the extermi-
nating angel had come up the Custom House steps. According to the received code in such matters, it would have been
nothing short of duty, in a politician, to bring every one of
those white heads under the axe of the guillotine. It was
plain enough to discern, that the old fellows dreaded some
such discourtesy at my hands. It pained, and at the same
time amused me, to behold the terrors that attended my
advent; to see a furrowed cheek, weather-beaten by half a
century of storm, turn ashy pale at the glance of so harmless
an individual as myself; to detect, as one or another addressed me, the tremor of a voice, which, in long-past days,
had been wont to bellow through a speaking-trumpet, hoarsely
enough to frighten Boreas himself to silence. They knew,
these excellent old persons, that, by all established rule—
and, as regarded some of them, weighed by their own lack
of efficiency for business—they ought to have given place
to younger men, more orthodox in politics, and altogether
fitter than themselves to serve our common Uncle. I knew it
too, but could never quite find in my heart to act upon the
knowledge. Much and deservedly to my own discredit, therefore, and considerably to the detriment of my official conscience, they continued, during my incumbency, to creep
about the wharves, and loiter up and down the Custom
House steps. They spent a good deal of time, also, asleep in

their accustomed corners, with their chairs tilted back against the wall; awaking, however, once or twice in a forenoon, to bore one another with the several thousandth repetition of old sea stories, and mouldy jokes, that had grown to be passwords and countersigns among them.

The discovery was soon made, I imagine, that the new Surveyor had no great harm in him. So, with lightsome hearts, and the happy consciousness of being usefully employed—in their own behalf, at least, if not for our beloved country—these good old gentlemen went through the various formalities of office. Sagaciously, under their spectacles, did they peep into the holds of vessels! Mighty was their fuss about little matters, and marvellous, sometimes, the obtuseness that allowed greater ones to slip between their fingers! Whenever such a mischance occurred—when a wagonload of valuable merchandise had been smuggled ashore, at noonday, perhaps, and directly beneath their unsuspicious noses—nothing could exceed the vigilance and alacrity with which they proceeded to lock, and double-lock, and secure with tape and sealing-wax, all the avenues of the delinquent vessel. Instead of a reprimand for their previous negligence, the case seemed rather to require an eulogium on their praiseworthy caution, after the mischief had happened; a grateful recognition of the promptitude of their zeal, the moment that there was no longer any remedy.

Unless people are more than commonly disagreeable, it is my foolish habit to contract a kindness for them. The better part of my companion's character, if it have a better part, is that which usually comes uppermost in my regard, and forms the type whereby I recognize the man. As most of these old Custom House officers had good traits, and as my position in reference to them, being paternal and protective, was favorable to the growth of friendly sentiments, I soon grew to like them all. It was pleasant in the summer forenoons—when the fervent heat, that almost liquefied the rest of the human family, merely communicated a genial warmth to their half-torpid systems—it was pleasant to hear them chatting in the back entry, a row of them all tipped against the wall, as usual; while the frozen witticisms of past generations were thawed out, and came bubbling with laughter from their lips. Externally, the jollity of aged men has much in common with the mirth of children; the intellect, any more than a deep sense of humor, has little to do with the matter; it is, with both, a gleam that plays upon the surface, and imparts a sunny and cheery aspect alike to the green branch, and gray, mouldering trunk. In one case, however, it is real sunshine; in the other, it more resembles the phosphorescent glow of decaying wood.

It would be sad injustice, the reader must understand, to represent all my excellent old friends as in their dotage. In the first place, my coadjutors were not invariably old; there were men among them in their strength and prime, of marked ability and energy, and altogether superior to the sluggish and dependent mode of life on which their evil stars had cast them. Then, moreover, the white locks of age were sometimes found to be the thatch of an intellectual tenement in good repair. But, as respects the majority of my corps of veterans, there will be no wrong done if I characterize them generally as a set of wearisome old souls, who had gathered nothing worth preservation from their varied experience of life. They seemed to have flung away all the golden grain of practical wisdom, which they had enjoyed so many opportunities of harvesting, and most carefully to have stored their memories with the husks. They spoke with far more interest and unction of their morning's breakfast, or yesterday's, today's, or tomorrow's dinner than of the shipwreck of forty or fifty years ago, and all the world's wonders which they had witnessed with their youthful eyes.

The father of the Custom House—the patriarch, not only of this little squad of officials, but, I am bold to say, of the respectable body of tide-waiters all over the United States— was a certain permanent Inspector. He might truly be termed a legitimate son of the revenue system, dyed in the wool, or, rather, born in the purple; since his sire, a Revolutionary colonel, and formerly collector of the port, had created an office for him, and appointed him to fill it, at a period of the early ages which few living men can now remember. This Inspector, when I first knew him, was a man of fourscore years, or thereabouts, and certainly one of the most wonderful specimens of winter-green that you would be likely to discover in a lifetime's search. With his florid cheek, his compact figure, smartly arrayed in a bright-buttoned blue coat, his brisk and vigorous step and his hale and hearty aspect, altogether he seemed—not young, indeed—but a kind of new contrivance of Mother Nature in the man, whom age and infirmity had no business to to voice and laugh, which perpetually reëchoed through the Custom House, had nothing of the tremulous quaver and cackle of an old man's utterance; they came strutting out of his lungs like the crow of a cock or the blast of a clarion. Looking at him merely as an animal—and there was very little else to look at—he was a most satisfactory object, from the thorough healthfulness and wholesomeness of his system, and his capacity, at that extreme age, to enjoy all, or nearly all, the delights which he had ever aimed at, or conceived of. The careless security of his life in the Custom House, on a regular income, and with but slight and infrequent apprehensions of removal, had no doubt contributed to make time pass lightly over him. The original and more potent causes, however, lay in the rare perfection of his animal nature, the moderate proportion of intellect, and the very trifling admixture of moral and spiritual ingredients; these latter qualities, indeed, being in barely enough measure to keep the old gentleman from walking on all fours. He possessed no power of thought, no depth of feeling, no troublesome sensibilities; nothing, in short, but a few commonplace instincts, which, aided by the cheerful temper that grew inevitably out of his physical well-being, did duty very respectably, and to general acceptance, in lieu of a heart. He had been the husband of three wives, all long since dead; the father of twenty children, most of whom, at every age of childhood or maturity, had likewise returned to dust. Here, one would suppose, might have been sorrow enough to imbue the sunniest disposition, through and through, with a sable tinge. Not so with our old Inspector! One brief sigh sufficed to carry off the entire burden of these dismal reminiscences. The next moment, he was as ready for sport as any unbreeched infant; far readier than the Collector's junior clerk, who, at nineteen years, was much the elder and graver man of the two.

I used to watch and study this patriarchal personage with, I think, livelier curiosity, than any other form of humanity there presented to my notice. He was, in truth, a rare phenomenon; so perfect, in one point of view; so shallow, so delusive, so impalpable, such an absolute nonentity, in every other. My conclusion was that he had no soul, no heart, no mind; nothing, as I have already said, but instincts; and yet, withal, so cunningly had the few materials of his character been put together, that there was no painful perception of deficiency, but, on my part, an entire contentment with what I found in him. It might be difficult—and it was so—to conceive how he should exist hereafter, so earthy and sensuous did he seem; but surely his existence here, admitting that it was to terminate with his last breath, had been not unkindly given; with no higher moral responsibilities than the beasts of the field, but with a larger scope of enjoyment than theirs, and with all their blessed immunity from the dreariness and duskiness of age.

One point, in which he had vastly the advantage over his four-footed brethren, was his ability to recollect the good dinners which it had made no small portion of the happiness of his life to eat. His gourmandism was a highly agreeable trait; and to hear him talk of roast meat was as appetizing as a pickle or an oyster. As he possessed no higher attribute, and neither sacrificed nor vitiated any spiritual endowment by devoting all his energies and ingenuities to subserve the delight and profit of his maw, it always pleased and satisfied me to hear him expatiate on fish, poultry, and butcher's meat, and the most eligible methods of preparing them for the table. His reminiscences of good cheer, however ancient the date of the actual banquet, seemed to bring the savor of pig or turkey under one's very nostrils. There were flavors on his palate, that had lingered there not less than sixty or seventy years, and were still apparently as fresh as that of the mutton chop which he had just devoured for his breakfast. I have heard him smack his lips over dinners, every guest at which, except himself, had long been food for worms. It was marvellous to observe how the ghosts of bygone meals were continually rising up before him; not in anger or retribution, but as if grateful for his former appreciation, and seeking to repudiate an endless series of enjoyment, at once shadowy and sensual. A tenderloin of beef, a hind-quarter of veal, a sparerib of pork, a particular chicken, or a remarkably praiseworthy turkey, which had perhaps adorned his board in the days of the elder Adams, would be remembered; while all the subsequent experience of our race, and all the events that brightened or darkened his

individual career, had gone over him with as little permanent effect as the passing breeze. The chief tragic event of
the old man's life, so far as I could judge, was his mishap
with a certain goose, which lived and died some twenty or
forty years ago; a goose of most promising figure, but which,
at table, proved so inveterately tough that the carving knife
would make no impression on its carcass, and it could only
be divided with an axe and handsaw.

But it is time to quit this sketch; on which, however, I
should be glad to dwell at considerably more length, because, of all men whom I have ever known, this individual
was fittest to be a Custom House officer. Most persons,
owing to causes which I may not have space to hint at,
suffer moral detriment from this peculiar mode of life. The
old Inspector was incapable of it; and, were he to continue
in office to the end of time, would be as good as he was
then, and sit down to dinner with just as good an appetite.

There is one likeness, without which my gallery of Custom House portraits would be strangely incomplete, but
which my comparatively few opportunities for observation
enable me to sketch only in the merest outline. It is that of
the Collector, our gallant old General, who, after his brilliant military service, subsequently to which he had ruled
over a wild Western territory, had come hither, twenty
years before, to spend the decline of his varied and honorable life. The brave soldier had already numbered, nearly or
quite, his three-score years and ten, and was pursuing the
remainder of his earthly march, burdened with infirmities
which even the martial music of his own spirit-stirring recollections could do little towards lightening. The step was
palsied now, that had been foremost in the charge. It was
only with the assistance of a servant, and by leaning his
hand heavily on the iron balustrade, that he could slowly
and painfully ascend the Custom House steps, and, with a
toilsome progress across the floor, attain his customary chair
beside the fireplace. There he used to sit, gazing with a
somewhat dim serenity of aspect at the figures that came
and went; amid the rustle of papers, the administering of
oaths, the discussion of business, and the casual talk of the
office; all which sounds and circumstances seemed but indistinctly to impress his senses, and hardly to make their way

into his inner sphere of contemplation. His countenance, in this repose, was mild and kindly. If his notice was sought, an expression of courtesy and interest gleamed out upon his features; proving that there was light within him, and that it was only the outward medium of the intellectual lamp that obstructed the rays in their passage. The closer you penetrated to the substance of his mind, the sounder it appeared. When no longer called upon to speak, or listen, either of which operations cost him an evident effort, his face would briefly subside into its former not uncheerful quietude. It was not painful to behold this look; for, though dim, it had not the imbecility of decaying age. The framework of his nature, originally strong and massive, was not yet crumbled into ruin.

To observe and define his character, however, under such disadvantages, was as difficult a task as to trace out and build up anew, in imagination, an old fortress like Ticonderoga, from a view of its gray and broken ruins. Here and there, perchance, the walls may remain almost complete; but elsewhere may be only a shapeless mound, cumbrous with its very strength, and overgrown, through long years of peace and neglect, with grass and alien weeds.

Nevertheless, looking at the old warrior with affection—for, slight as was the communication between us, my feeling towards him, like that of all bipeds and quadrupeds who knew him, might not improperly be termed so—I could discern the main points of his portrait. It was marked with the noble and heroic qualities which showed it to be not by a mere accident, but of good right, that he had won a distinguished name. His spirit could never, I conceive, have been characterized by an uneasy activity; it must, at any period of his life, have required an impulse to set him in motion; but, once stirred up, with obstacles to overcome, and an adequate object to be attained, it was not in the man to give out or fail. The heat that had formerly pervaded his nature, and which was not yet extinct, was never of the kind that flashes and flickers in a blaze; but, rather, a deep, red glow, as of iron in a furnace. Weight, solidity, firmness; this was the expression of his repose, even in such decay as had crept untimely over him, at the period of which I speak. But I could imagine, even then, that, under some excitement which should go deeply into his consciousness—roused by a trumpet peal loud enough to awaken all of his energies that were not dead, but only slumbering—he was yet capable of flinging off his infirmities like a sick man's gown, dropping the staff of age to seize a battle sword, and starting up once more a warrior. And, in so intense a moment, his demeanor would have still been calm. Such an exhibition, however, was but to be pictured in fancy; not to be anticipated, nor desired. What I saw in him—as evidently as the indestructible ramparts of Old Ticonderoga, already cited as the most appropriate simile—were the features of stubborn and ponderous endurance, which might well have amounted to obstinacy in his earlier days; of integrity, that, like most of his other endowments, lay in a somewhat heavy mass, and was just as unmalleable and unmanageable as a ton of iron ore; and of benevolence, which, fiercely as he led the bayonets on at Chippewa or Fort Erie, I take to be of quite as genuine a stamp as what actuates any or all of the polemical philanthropists of the age. He had slain men with his own hand, for aught I know—certainly, they had fallen, like blades of grass at the sweep of the scythe, before the charge to which his spirit imparted its triumphant energy—but, be that as it might, there was never in his heart so much cruelty as would have brushed the down off a butterfly's wing. I have not known the man to whose innate kindliness I would more confidently make an appeal.

Many characteristics—and those, too, which contribute not the least forcibly to impart resemblance in a sketch —must have vanished, or been obscured, before I met the General. All merely graceful attributes are usually the most evanescent; nor does Nature adorn the human ruin with blossoms of new beauty, that have their roots and proper nutriment only in the chinks and crevices of decay, as she sows wall-flowers over the ruined fortress of Ticonderoga. Still, even in respect of grace and beauty, there were points well worth noting. A ray of humor, now and then, would make its way through the veil of dim obstruction, and glimmer pleasantly upon our faces. A trait of native elegance, seldom seen in the masculine character after childhood or early youth, was shown in the General's fondness for the sight and fragrance of flowers. An old soldier might be supposed to prize only the bloody laurel on his brow; but

here was one, who seemed to have a young girl's appreciation of the floral tribe.

There, beside the fireplace, the brave old General used to
sit; while the Surveyor—though seldom, when it could be
avoided, taking upon himself the difficult task of engaging
him in conversation—was fond of standing at a distance,
and watching his quiet and almost slumberous countenance.
He seemed away from us, although we saw him but a few
yards off; remote, though we passed close beside his chair;
unattainable, though we might have stretched forth our
hands and touched his own. It might be that he lived a more
real life within his thoughts than amid the unappropriate
environment of the Collector's office. The evolutions of the
parade; the tumult of the battle; the flourish of old, heroic
music, heard thirty years before—such scenes and sounds,
perhaps, were all alive before his intellectual sense. Meanwhile, the merchants and shipmasters, the spruce clerks and
uncouth sailors, entered and departed; the bustle of this
commercial and Custom House life kept up its little murmur
round about him; and neither with the men nor their affairs
did the General appear to sustain the most distant relation.
He was as much out of place as an old sword—now rusty,
but which had flashed once in the battle's front, and showed
still a bright gleam along its blade—would have been, among
the inkstands, paper folders, and mahogany rulers on the
Deputy Collector's desk.

There was one thing that much aided me in renewing and
re-creating the stalwart soldier of the Niagara frontier—the
man of true and simple energy. It was the recollection of
those memorable words of his—"I'll try, Sir!"—spoken on
the very verge of a desperate and heroic enterprise, and
breathing the soul and spirit of New England hardihood,
comprehending all perils, and encountering all. If, in our
country, valor were rewarded by heraldic honor, this phrase—
which it seems so easy to speak, but which only he, with
such a task of danger and glory before him, has ever spoken—
would be the best and fittest of all mottoes for the General's
shield of arms.

It contributes greatly towards a man's moral and intellectual health, to be brought into habits of companionship with
individuals unlike himself, who care little for his pursuits,
and whose sphere and abilities he must go out of himself to

appreciate. The accidents of my life have often afforded me this advantage, but never with more fulness and variety than during my continuance in office. There was one man, especially, the observation of whose character gave me a new idea of talent. His gifts were emphatically those of a man of business; prompt, acute, clear-minded; with an eye that saw through all perplexities, and a faculty of arrangement that made them vanish, as by the waving of an enchanter's wand. Bred up from boyhood in the Custom House, it was his proper field of activity; and the many intricacies of business, so harassing to the interloper, presented themselves before him with the regularity of a perfectly comprehended system. In my contemplation, he stood as the ideal of his class. He was, indeed, the Custom House in himself, or, at all events, the mainspring that kept its variously revolving wheels in motion; for, in an institution like this, where its officers are appointed to subserve their own profit and convenience and seldom with a leading reference to their fitness for the duty to be performed, they must perforce seek elsewhere the dexterity which is not in them. Thus, by an inevitable necessity, as a magnet attracts steel filings, so did our man of business draw to himself the difficulties which everybody met with. With an easy condescension, and kind forbearance towards our stupidity—which, to his order of mind, must have seemed little short of crime—would he forthwith, by the merest touch of his finger, make the incomprehensible as clear as daylight. The merchants valued him not less than we, his esoteric friends. His integrity was perfect; it was a law of nature with him, rather than a choice or a principle; nor can it be otherwise than the main condition of an intellect so remarkably clear and accurate as his, to be honest and regular in the administration of affairs. A stain on his conscience, as to anything that came within the range of his vocation, would trouble such a man very much in the same way, though to a far greater degree, than an error in the balance of an account, or an ink-blot on the fair page of a book of record. Here, in a word—and it is a rare instance in my life—I had met with a person thoroughly adapted to the situation which he held.

Such were some of the people with whom I now found myself connected. I took it in good part, at the hands of Providence, that I was thrown into a position so little akin to my past habits, and set myself seriously to gather from it whatever profit was to be had. After my fellowship of toil and impracticable schemes with the dreamy brethren of Brook Farm; after living for three years within the subtile influence of an intellect like Emerson's; after those wild, free days on the Assabeth, indulging fantastic speculations beside our fire of fallen boughs with Ellery Channing; after talking with Thoreau about pine trees and Indian relics in his hermitage at Walden; after growing fastidious by sympathy with the classic refinement of Hillard's culture; after becoming imbued with poetic sentiment at Longfellow's hearthstone—it was time, at length, that I should exercise other faculties of my nature, and nourish myself with food for which I had hitherto had little appetite. Even the old Inspector was desirable, as a change of diet, to a man who had known Alcott. I looked upon it as an evidence, in some measure, of a system naturally well balanced, and lacking no essential part of a thorough organization, that, with such associates to remember, I could mingle at once with men of altogether different qualities and never murmur at the change.

Literature, its exertions and objects, were now of little moment in my regard. I cared not, at this period, for books; they were apart from me. Nature—except it were human nature—the nature that is developed in earth and sky, was, in one sense, hidden from me; and all the imaginative delight, wherewith it had been spiritualized, passed away out of my mind. A gift, a faculty, if it had not departed, was suspended and inanimate within me. There would have been something sad, unutterably dreary, in all this, had I not been conscious that it lay at my own option to recall whatever was valuable in the past. It might be true, indeed, that this was a life which could not, with impunity, be lived too long, else it might make me permanently other than I had been, without transforming me into any shape which it would be worth my while to take. But I never considered it as other than a transitory life. There was always a prophetic instinct, a low whisper in my ear, that within no long period, and whenever a new change of custom should be essential to my good, a change would come.

Meanwhile, there I was, a Surveyor of the Revenue, and, so far as I have been able to understand, as good a Surveyor as need be. A man of thought, fancy, and sensibility (had he ten times the Surveyor's proportion of those qualities) may, at any time, be a man of affairs, if he will only choose to give himself the trouble. My fellow-officers, and the merchants and sea captains with whom my official duties brought me into any manner of connection, viewed me in no other light, and probably knew me in no other character. None of them, I presume, had ever read a page of my inditing, or would have cared a fig the more for me, if they had read them all; nor would it have mended the matter, in the least, had those same unprofitable pages been written with a pen like that of Burns or of Chaucer, each of whom was a Custom House officer in his day, as well as I. It is a good lesson—though it may often be a hard one—for a man who has dreamed of literary fame, and of making for himself a rank among the world's dignitaries by such means, to step aside out of the narrow circle in which his claims are recognized, and to find how utterly devoid of significance, beyond that circle, is all that he achieves and all that he aims at. I know not that I especially needed the lesson, either in the way of warning or rebuke; but, at any rate, I learned it thoroughly; nor, it gives me pleasure to reflect, did the truth, as it came home to my perception, ever cost me a pang, or require to be thrown off in a sigh. In the way of literary talk, it is true, the Naval Officer—an excellent fellow, who came into office with me and went out only a little later—would often engage me in a discussion about one or the other of his favorite topics, Napoleon or Shakespeare. The Collector's junior clerk, too—a young gentleman who, it was whispered, occasionally covered a sheet of Uncle Sam's letter paper with what (at the distance of a few yards) looked very much like poetry—used now and then to speak to me of books, as matters with which I might possibly be conversant. This was my all of lettered intercourse; and it was quite sufficient for my necessities.

No longer seeking nor caring that my name should be blazoned abroad on title pages, I smiled to think that it had now another kind of vogue. The Custom House marker imprinted it with a stencil and black paint, on pepper-bags, and baskets of anatto, and cigar boxes, and bales of all kinds of dutiable merchandise, in testimony that these commodities had paid the impost, and gone regularly through the office. Borne on such queer vehicle of fame, a knowledge of my existence, so far as a name conveys it, was carried where it had never been before, and, I hope, will never go again.

But the past was not dead. Once in a great while, the thoughts, that had seemed so vital and so active, yet had been put to rest so quietly, revived again. One of the most remarkable occasions, when the habit of bygone days awoke in me, was that which brings it within the law of literary propriety to offer the public the sketch which I am now writing.

In the second story of the Custom House, there is a large room, in which the brick-work and naked rafters have never been covered with panelling and plaster. The edifice— originally projected on a scale adapted to the old commercial enterprise of the port, and with an idea of subsequent prosperity destined never to be realized—contains far more space than its occupants know what to do with. This airy hall, therefore, over the Collector's apartments, remains unfinished to this day, and, in spite of the aged cobwebs that festoon its dusky beams, appears still to await the labor of the carpenter and mason. At one end of the room, in a recess, were a number of barrels, piled one upon another, containing bundles of official documents. Large quantities of similar rubbish lay lumbering the floor. It was sorrowful to think how many days, and weeks, and months, and years of toil, had been wasted on these musty papers, which were now only an encumbrance on earth, and were hidden away in this forgotten corner, never more to be glanced at by human eyes. But, then, what reams of other manuscripts— filled not with the dulness of official formalities, but with the thought of inventive brains and the rich effusion of deep hearts—had gone equally to oblivion; and that, moreover, without serving a purpose in their day, as these heaped-up papers had, and—saddest of all—without purchasing for their writers the comfortable livelihood which the clerks of the Custom House had gained by these worthless scratchings of the pen! Yet not altogether worthless, perhaps, as materials of local history. Here, no doubt, statistics of the former commerce of Salem might be discovered, and memorials of her princely merchants—old King Derby, old Billy Gray, old Simon Forrester, and many another magnate in his day, whose powdered head, however, was scarcely in the tomb before his mountain-pile of wealth began to dwindle. The founders of the greater part of the families which now compose the aristocracy of Salem might here be traced, from the petty and obscure beginnings of their traffic, at periods generally much posterior to the Revolution, upward to what their children look upon as long-established rank.

Prior to the Revolution, there is a dearth of records; the earlier documents and archives of the Custom House having, probably, been carried off to Halifax when all the King's officials accompanied the British army in its flight from Boston. It has often been a matter of regret with me; for, going back, perhaps, to the days of the Protectorate, those papers must have contained many references to forgotten or remembered men, and to antique customs, which would have affected me with the same pleasure as when I used to pick up Indian arrowheads in the field near the Old Manse.

But, one idle and rainy day, it was my fortune to make a discovery of some little interest. Poking and burrowing into the heaped-up rubbish in the corner, unfolding one and another document, and reading the names of vessels that had long ago foundered at sea or rotted at the wharves, and those of merchants, never heard of now on 'Change, nor very readily decipherable on their mossy tombstones; glancing at such matters with the saddened, weary, half-reluctant interest which we bestow on the corpse of dead activity—and exerting my fancy, sluggish with little use, to raise up from these dry bones an image of the old town's brighter aspect, when India was a new region, and only Salem knew the way thither—I chanced to lay my hand on a small package, carefully done up in a piece of ancient yellow parchment. This envelope had the air of an official record of some period long past, when clerks engrossed their stiff and formal chirography on more substantial materials than at present. There was something about it that quickened an instinctive curiosity, and made me undo the faded red tape that tied up the package with the sense that a treasure would here be brought to light. Unbending the rigid folds of the parchment cover, I found it to be a commission, under the hand and seal of Governor Shirley, in favor of one Jonathan Pue, as Surveyor of his Majesty's Customs for the port of Salem, in the Province of Massachusetts Bay. I remembered to have read (probably in Felt's Annals) a notice of the decease of Mr. Surveyor Pue about fourscore years ago; and likewise, in a newspaper of recent times, an account of the digging up of his remains in the little grave-yard of St. Peter's Church during the renewal of that edi-fice. Nothing, if I rightly call to mind, was left of my respected predecessor, save an imperfect skeleton, and some fragments of apparel, and a wig of majestic frizzle; which, unlike the head that it once adorned, was in very satisfac-tory preservation. But, on examining the papers which the parchment commission served to envelop, I found more traces of Mr. Pue's mental part, and the internal operations of his head, than the frizzled wig had contained of the venerable skull itself.

They were documents, in short, not official, but of a private nature, or at least written in his private capacity, and apparently with his own hand. I could account for their being included in the heap of Custom House lumber only by the fact that Mr. Pue's death had happened suddenly; and that these papers, which he probably kept in his official desk, had never come to the knowledge of his heirs, or were supposed to relate to the business of the revenue. On the transfer of the archives to Halifax, this package, proving to be of no public concern, was left behind, and had remained ever since unopened.

The ancient Surveyor—being little molested, I suppose, at that early day, with business pertaining to his office—seems to have devoted some of his many leisure hours to researches as a local antiquarian, and other inquisitions of a similar nature. These supplied material for petty activity to a mind that would otherwise have been eaten up with rust. A portion of his facts, by the by, did me good service in the preparation of the article entitled "Main Street," included in the present volume.* The remainder may perhaps be applied to purposes equally valuable, hereafter; or not im-possibly may be worked up, so far as they go, into a regular history of Salem, should my veneration for the natal soil ever impel me to so pious a task. Meanwhile, they shall be at the command of any gentleman, inclined, and competent,

*See note p. 57

to take the unprofitable labor off my hands. As a final disposition, I contemplate depositing them with the Essex Historical Society.

But the object that most drew my attention in the mysterious package was a certain affair of fine red cloth, much worn and faded. There were traces about it of gold embroidery, which, however, was greatly frayed and defaced; so that none, or very little, of the glitter was left. It had been wrought, as was easy to perceive, with wonderful skill of needlework; and the stitch (as I am assured by ladies conversant with such mysteries) gives evidence of a now forgotten art, not to be recovered even by the process of picking out the threads. This rag of scarlet cloth—for time, and wear, and a sacrilegious moth, had reduced it to little other than a rag—on careful examination, assumed the shape of a letter. It was the capital letter "A." By an accurate measurement, each limb proved to be precisely three inches and a quarter in length. It had been intended, there could be no doubt, as an ornamental article of dress; but how it was to be worn, or what rank, honor, and dignity, in by-past times, were signified by it, was a riddle which (so evanescent are the fashions of the world in these particulars) I saw little hope of solving. And yet it strangely interested me. My eyes fastened themselves upon the old scarlet letter, and would not be turned aside. Certainly, there was some deep meaning in it, most worthy of interpretation, and which, as it were, streamed forth from the mystic symbol, subtly communicating itself to my sensibilities, but evading the analysis of my mind.

While thus perplexed—and cogitating, among other hypotheses, whether the letter might not have been one of those decorations which the white men used to contrive, in order to take the eyes of Indians—I happened to place it on my breast. It seemed to me—the reader may smile, but must not doubt my word—it seemed to me then that I experienced a sensation not altogether physical, yet almost so, as of burning heat; and as if the letter were not of red cloth, but red-hot iron. I shuddered, and involuntarily let it fall upon the floor.

In the absorbing contemplation of the scarlet letter, I had hitherto neglected to examine a small roll of dingy paper, around which it had been twisted. This I now opened and had the satisfaction to find, recorded by the old Surveyor's pen, a reasonably complete explanation of the whole affair. There were several foolscap sheets, containing many particulars respecting the life and conversation of one Hester Prynne, who appeared to have been rather a noteworthy personage in the view of our ancestors. She had flourished during the period between the early days of Massachusetts and the close of the seventeenth century. Aged persons, alive in the time of Mr. Surveyor Pue, and from whose oral testimony he had made up his narrative, remembered her in their youth as a very old, but not decrepit woman, of a stately and solemn aspect. It had been her habit from an almost immemorial date to go about the country as a kind of voluntary nurse, and doing whatever miscellaneous good she might; taking upon herself, likewise, to give advice in all matters, especially those of the heart; by which means, as a person of such propensities inevitably must, she gained from many people the reverence due to an angel, but, I should imagine, was looked upon by others as an intruder and a nuisance. Prying further into the manuscript, I found the record of other doings and sufferings of this singular woman, for most of which the reader is referred to the story entitled *The Scarlet Letter*; and it should be borne carefully in mind, that the main facts of that story are authorized and authenticated by the document of Mr. Surveyor Pue. The original papers, together with the scarlet letter itself—a most curious relic—are still in my possession, and shall be freely exhibited to whomsoever, induced by the great interest of the narrative, may desire a sight of them. I must not be understood as affirming that, in the dressing up of the tale, and imagining the motives and modes of passion that influenced the characters who figure in it, I have invariably confined myself within the limits of the old Surveyor's half a dozen sheets of foolscap. On the contrary, I have allowed myself, as to such points, nearly or altogether as much license as if the facts had been entirely of my own invention. What I contend for is the authenticity of the outline.

This incident recalled my mind, in some degree, to its old track. There seemed to be here the groundwork of a tale. It impressed me as if the ancient Surveyor, in his garb of a hundred years gone by, and wearing his immortal wig—which was buried with him, but did not perish in the grave—had

met me in the deserted chamber of the Custom House. In
his port was the dignity of one who had borne his Majesty's
commission, and who was therefore illuminated by a ray of
the splendor that shone so dazzlingly about the throne. How
unlike, alas! the hangdog look of a republican official, who,
as the servant of the people, feels himself less than the least,
and below the lowest, of his masters. With his own ghostly
hand, the obscurely seen but majestic figure had imparted
to me the scarlet symbol, and the little roll of explanatory
manuscript. With his own ghostly voice, he had exhorted
me, on the sacred consideration of my filial duty and reverence towards him—who might reasonably regard himself as
my official ancestor—to bring his mouldy and moth-eaten
lucubrations before the public. "Do this," said the ghost of
Mr. Surveyor Pue, emphatically nodding the head that looked
so imposing within its memorable wig, "do this and the
profit shall be all your own! You will shortly need it; for it is
not in your days as it was in mine, when a man's office was a
life-lease, and oftentimes an heirloom. But, I charge you, in
this matter of old Mistress Prynne, give to your predecessor's memory the credit which will be rightfully its due!"
And I said to the ghost of Mr. Surveyor Pue, "I will!"

On Hester Prynne's story, therefore, I bestowed much
thought. It was the subject of my meditations for many an
hour while pacing to and fro across my room; or traversing,
with a hundredfold repetition, the long extent from the
front door of the Custom House to the side entrance, and
back again. Great were the weariness and annoyance of the
old Inspector and the Weighers and Gaugers, whose slum-
bers were disturbed by the unmercifully lengthened tramp
of my passing and returning footsteps. Remembering their
own former habits, they used to say that the Surveyor was
walking the quarter-deck. They probably fancied that my
sole object—and, indeed, the sole object for which a sane
man could ever put himself into voluntary motion—was to
get an appetite for dinner. And to say the truth, an appetite,
sharpened by the east wind that generally blew along the
passage, was the only valuable result of so much indefatigable exercise. So little adapted is the atmosphere of a Custom
House to the delicate harvest of fancy and sensibility, that,
had I remained there through ten Presidencies yet to come,
I doubt whether the tale of *The Scarlet Letter* would ever

have been brought before the public eye. My imagination
was a tarnished mirror. It would not reflect, or only with
miserable dimness, the figures with which I did my best to
people it. The characters of the narrative would not be
warmed and rendered malleable by any heat that I could
kindle at my intellectual forge. They would take neither the
glow of passion nor the tenderness of sentiment, but retained all the rigidity of dead corpses, and stared me in the
face with a fixed and ghastly grin of contemptuous defiance.
"What have you to do with us?" that expression seemed to
say. "The little power you might once have possessed over
the tribe of unrealities is gone! You have bartered it for a
pittance of the public gold. Go, then, and earn your wages!"
In short, the almost torpid creatures of my own fancy twitted
me with imbecility, and not without fair occasion.

It was not merely during the three hours and a half which
Uncle Sam claimed as his share of my daily life this wretched
numbness held possession of me. It went with me on my
seashore walks and rambles into the country, whenever—
which was seldom and reluctantly—I bestirred myself to
seek that invigorating charm of Nature, which used to give
me such freshness and activity of thought the moment that I
stepped across the threshold of the Old Manse. The same
torpor, as regarded the capacity for intellectual effort, accompanied me home, and weighed upon me in the chamber
which I most absurdly termed my study. Nor did it quit me,
when, late at night, I sat in the deserted parlor, lighted only
by the glimmering coal fire and the moon, striving to picture
forth imaginary scenes, which, the next day, might flow out
on the brightening page in many-hued description.

If the imaginative faculty refused to act at such an hour, it
might well be deemed a hopeless case. Moonlight, in a
familiar room, falling so white upon the carpet, and showing
all its figures so distinctly—making every object so minutely
visible, yet so unlike a morning or noontide visibility—is a
medium the most suitable for a romance writer to get acquainted with his illusive guests. There is the little domestic
scenery of the well-known apartment; the chairs, with each
its separate individuality; the centre-table, sustaining a workbasket, a volume or two, and an extinguished lamp; the
sofa; the bookcase: the picture on the wall—all these de-

tails, so completely seen, are so spiritualized by the unusual light, that they seem to lose their actual substance, and become things of intellect. Nothing is too small or too trifling to undergo this change, and acquire dignity thereby. A child's shoe; the doll, seated in her little wicker carriage; the hobby-horse—whatever, in a word, has been used or played with during the day is now invested with a quality of strangeness and remoteness, though still almost as vividly present as by daylight. Thus, therefore, the floor of our familiar room has become a neutral territory, somewhere between the real world and fairyland, where the Actual and the Imaginary may meet, and each imbue itself with the nature of the other. Ghosts might enter here without affrighting us. It would be too much in keeping with the scene to excite surprise, were we to look about us and discover a form, beloved, but gone hence, now sitting quietly in a streak of this magic moonshine, with an aspect that would make us doubt whether it had returned from afar, or had never once stirred from our fireside.

The somewhat dim coal fire has an essential influence in producing the effect which I would describe. It throws its unobtrusive tinge throughout the room, with a faint ruddiness upon the walls and ceiling and a reflected gleam from the polish of the furniture. This warmer light mingles itself with the cold spirituality of the moonbeams, and communicates, as it were, a heart and sensibilities of human tenderness to the forms which fancy summons up. It converts them from snow-images into men and women. Glancing at the looking glass, we behold—deep within its haunted verge—the smoldering glow of the half-extinguished anthracite, the white moonbeams on the floor, and a repetition of all the gleam and shadow of the picture, with one remove further from the actual, and nearer to the imaginative. Then, at such an hour, and with this scene before him, if a man sitting all alone cannot dream strange things and make them look like truth, he need never try to write romances.

But, for myself, during the whole of my Custom House experience, moonlight and sunshine and the glow of firelight were just alike in my regard; and neither of them was of one whit more avail than the twinkle of a tallow candle. An entire class of susceptibilities, and a gift connected with

them—of no great richness or value, but the best I had—
was gone from me.

It is my belief, however, that, had I attempted a different
order of composition, my faculties would not have been
found so pointless and inefficacious. I might, for instance,
have contented myself with writing out the narratives of a
veteran shipmaster, one of the Inspectors, whom I should be
most ungrateful not to mention, since scarcely a day passed
that he did not stir me to laughter and admiration by his
marvellous gifts as a story-teller. Could I have preserved the
picturesque force of his style and the humorous coloring
which nature taught him how to throw over his descriptions,
the result, I honestly believe, would have been something
new in literature. Or I might readily have found a more
serious task. It was a folly, with the materiality of this daily
life pressing so intrusively upon me, to attempt to fling
myself back into another age; or to insist on creating the
semblance of a world out of airy matter, when, at every
moment, the impalpable beauty of my soap-bubble was
broken by the rude contact of some actual circumstance.
The wiser effort would have been to diffuse thought and
imagination through the opaque substance of today, and
thus to make it a bright transparency; to spiritualize the
burden that began to weigh so heavily; to seek, resolutely,
the true and indestructible value that lay hidden in the petty
and wearisome incidents and ordinary characters with which
I was now conversant. The fault was mine. The page of life
that was spread out before me seemed dull and commonplace, only because I had not fathomed its deeper import. A
better book than I shall ever write was there; leaf after leaf
presenting itself to me, just as it was written out by the
reality of the flitting hour, and vanishing as fast as written,
only because my brain wanted the insight and my hand the
cunning to transcribe it. At some future day, it may be, I
shall remember a few scattered fragments and broken para-
graphs, and write them down, and find the letters turn to
gold upon the page.

These perceptions have come too late. At the instant, I
was only conscious that what would have been a pleasure
once was now a hopeless toil. There was no occasion to
make much moan about this state of affairs. I had ceased to
be a writer of tolerably poor tales and essays, and had

become a tolerably good Surveyor of the Customs. That was all. But, nevertheless, it is anything but agreeable to be haunted by a suspicion that one's intellect is dwindling away, or exhaling, without your consciousness, like ether out of a phial, so that, at every glance, you find a smaller and less volatile residuum. Of the fact, there could be no doubt; and, examining myself and others, I was led to conclusions, in reference to the effect of public office on the character, not very favorable to the mode of life in question. In some other form, perhaps, I may hereafter develop these effects. Suffice it here to say that a Custom House officer of long continuance can hardly be a very praiseworthy or respectable personage, for many reasons; one of them, the tenure by which he holds his situation, and another, the very nature of his business, which—though, I trust, an honest one—is of such a sort that he does not share in the united effort of mankind.

An effect—which I believe to be observable, more or less, in every individual who has occupied the position—is, that, while he leans on the mighty arm of the Republic, his own proper strength departs from him. He loses, in an extent proportioned to the weakness or force of his original nature, the capability of self-support. If he possess an unusual share of native energy, or the enervating magic of place do not operate too long upon him, his forfeited powers may be redeemable. The ejected officer—fortunate in the unkindly shove that sends him forth betimes to struggle amid a struggling world—may return to himself and become all that he has ever been. But this seldom happens. He usually keeps his ground just long enough for his own ruin, and is then thrust out, with sinews all unstrung, to totter along the difficult footpath of life as he best may. Conscious of his own infirmity—that his tempered steel and elasticity are lost—he forever afterwards looks wistfully about him in quest of support external to himself. His pervading and continual hope—a hallucination, which in the face of all discouragement, and making light of impossibilities, haunts him while he lives, and, I fancy, like the convulsive throes of the cholera, torments him for a brief space after death—is, that finally, and in no long time, by some happy coincidence of circumstances, he shall be restored to office. This faith, more than anything else, steals the pith and availability out of whatever enterprise he may dream of undertaking. Why should he toil and moil, and be at so much trouble to pick himself up out of the mud, when, in a little while hence, the strong arm of his Uncle will raise and support him? Why should he work for his living here, or go to dig gold in California, when he is so soon to be made happy, at monthly intervals, with a little pile of glittering coin out of his Uncle's pocket? It is sadly curious to observe how slight a taste of office suffices to infect a poor fellow with this singular disease. Uncle Sam's gold—meaning no disrespect to the worthy old gentleman—has, in this respect, a quality of enchantment like that of the Devil's wages. Whoever touches it should look well to himself, or he may find the bargain to go hard against him, involving, if not his soul, yet many of its better attributes; its sturdy force, its courage and constancy, its truth, its self-reliance, and all that gives the emphasis to manly character.

Here was a fine prospect in the distance! Not that the Surveyor brought the lesson home to himself, or admitted that he could be so utterly undone, either by continuance in office, or ejectment. Yet my reflections were not the most comfortable. I began to grow melancholy and restless; continually prying into my mind, to discover which of its poor properties were gone and what degree of detriment had already accrued to the remainder. I endeavored to calculate how much longer I could stay in the Custom House, and yet go forth a man. To confess the truth, it was my greatest apprehension—as it would never be a measure of policy to turn out so quiet an individual as myself, and it being hardly in the nature of a public officer to resign—it was my chief trouble, therefore, that I was likely to grow gray and decrepit in the Surveyorship, and become much such another animal as the old Inspector. Might it not, in the tedious lapse of official life that lay before me, finally be with me as it was with this venerable friend—to make the dinner hour the nucleus of the day, and to spend the rest of it as an old dog spends it, asleep in the sunshine or in the shade? A dreary look-forward this, for a man who felt it to be the best definition of happiness to live throughout the whole range of his faculties and sensibilities! But, all this while, I was giving myself very unnecessary alarm. Providence had meditated better things for me than I could possibly imagine for myself.

A remarkable event of the third year of my Surveyorship—to adopt the tone of "P. P."—was the election of General Taylor to the Presidency. It is essential, in order to gain a complete estimate of the advantages of official life, to view the incumbent at the in-coming of a hostile administration. His position is then one of the most singularly irksome, and, in every contingency, disagreeable, that a wretched mortal can possibly occupy; with seldom an alternative of good, on either hand, although what presents itself to him as the worst event may very probably be the best. But it is a strange experience, to a man of pride and sensibility, to know that his interests are within the control of individuals who neither love nor understand him, and by whom, since one or the other must needs happen, he would rather be injured than obliged. Strange, too, for one who has kept his calmness throughout the contest, to observe the bloodthirstiness that is developed in the hour of triumph, and to be conscious that he is himself among its objects! There are few uglier traits of human nature than this tendency—which I now witnessed in men no worse than their neighbors—to grow cruel, merely because they possessed the power of inflicting harm. If the guillotine, as applied to office holders, were a literal fact instead of one of the most apt of metaphors, it is my sincere belief that the active members of the victorious party were sufficiently excited to have chopped off all our heads, and have thanked Heaven for the opportunity! It appears to me—who have been a calm and curious observer, as well in victory as defeat—that this fierce and bitter spirit of malice and revenge has never distinguished the many triumphs of my own party as it now did that of the Whigs. The Democrats take the offices, as a general rule, because they need them, and because the practice of many years has made it the law of political warfare, which, unless a different system be proclaimed, it were weakness and cowardice to murmur at. But the long habit of victory has made them generous. They know how to spare, when they see occasion; and when they strike, the axe may be sharp, indeed, but its edge is seldom poisoned with ill will; nor is it their custom ignominiously to kick the head which they have just struck off.

In short, unpleasant as was my predicament at best, I saw much reason to congratulate myself that I was on the losing side, rather than the triumphant one. If, heretofore, I had been none of the warmest of partisans, I began now, at this season of peril and adversity, to be pretty acutely sensible with which party my predilections lay; nor was it without something like regret and shame, that, according to a reasonable calculation of chances, I saw my own prospect of retaining office to be better than those of my Democratic brethren. But who can see an inch into futurity, beyond his nose? My own head was the first that fell!

The moment when a man's head drops off is seldom or never, I am inclined to think, precisely the most agreeable of his life. Nevertheless, like the greater part of our misfortunes, even so serious a contingency brings its remedy and consolation with it, if the sufferer will but make the best, rather than the worst, of the accident which has befallen him. In my particular case, the consolatory topics were close at hand, and, indeed, had suggested themselves to my meditations a considerable time before it was requisite to use them. In view of my previous weariness of office and vague thoughts of resignation, my fortune somewhat resembled that of a person who should entertain an idea of committing suicide, and, altogether beyond his hopes, meet with the good hap to be murdered. In the Custom House, as before in the Old Manse, I had spent three years; a term long enough to rest a weary brain; long enough to break off old intellectual habits, and make room for new ones; long enough, and too long, to have lived in an unnatural state, doing what was really of no advantage nor delight to any human being, and withholding myself from toil that would, at least, have stilled an unquiet impulse in me. Then, moreover, as regarded his unceremonious ejectment, the late Surveyor was not altogether ill-pleased to be recognized by the Whigs as an enemy; since his inactivity in political affairs—his tendency to roam, at will, in that broad and quiet field where all mankind may meet, rather than confine himself to those narrow paths where brethren of the same household must diverge from one another—had sometimes made it questionable with his brother Democrats whether he was a friend. Now, after he had won the crown of martyrdom (though with no longer a head to wear it on), the point might be looked upon as settled. Finally, little heroic as he was, it seemed more decorous to be overthrown in the downfall of the party with which he had been content to stand, than to remain a forlorn survivor, when so many worthier men were falling; and, at last, after subsisting for four years on the mercy of a hostile administration, to be compelled then to define his position anew, and claim the yet more humiliating mercy of a friendly one.

Meanwhile the press had taken up my affair, and kept me, for a week or two, careering through the public prints, in my decapitated state, like Irving's Headless Horseman; ghastly and grim, and longing to be buried, as a politically dead man ought. So much for my figurative self. The real human being, all this time, with his head safely on his shoulders, had brought himself to the comfortable conclusion that everything was for the best; and, making an investment in ink, paper, and steel pens, had opened his long-disused writing desk, and was again a literary man.

Now it was, that the lucubrations of my ancient predecessor, Mr. Surveyor Pue, came into play. Rusty through long idleness, some little space was requisite before my intellectual machinery could be brought to work upon the tale, with an effect in any degree satisfactory. Even yet, though my thoughts were ultimately much absorbed in the task, it wears, to my eye, a stern and sombre aspect; too much ungladdened by genial sunshine; too little relieved by the tender and familiar influences which soften almost every scene of nature and real life, and, undoubtedly, should soften every picture of them. This uncaptivating effect is perhaps due to the period of hardly accomplished revolution, and still seething turmoil, in which the story shaped itself. It is no indication, however, of a lack of cheerfulness in the writer's mind; for he was happier while straying through the gloom of these sunless fantasies than at any time since he had quitted the Old Manse. Some of the briefer articles, which contribute to make up the volume, have likewise been written since my involuntary withdrawal from the toils and honors of public life, and the remainder are gleaned from annuals and magazines, of such antique date that they have gone round the circle, and come back to novelty again.* Keeping up the

---

*At the time of writing this article, the author intended to publish, along with *The Scarlet Letter*, several shorter tales and sketches. These it has been thought advisable to defer.

metaphor of the political guillotine, the whole may be considered as the *Posthumous Papers of a Decapitated Surveyor*; and the sketch which I am now bringing to a close, if too autobiographical for a modest person to publish in his lifetime, will readily be excused in a gentleman who writes from beyond the grave. Peace be with all the world! My blessing on my friends! My forgiveness to my enemies! For I am in the realm of quiet!

The life of the Custom House lies like a dream behind me. The old Inspector—who, by the by, I regret to say, was overthrown and killed by a horse, some time ago; else he would certainly have lived forever—he, and all those other venerable personages who sat with him at the receipt of custom, are but shadows in my view; white-headed and wrinkled images which my fancy used to sport with and has now flung aside forever. The merchants—Pingree, Phillips, Shepard, Upton, Kimball, Bertram, Hunt—these, and many other names, which had such a classic familiarity for my ear six months ago—these men of traffic, who seemed to occupy so important a position in the world—how little time has it required to disconnect me from them all, not merely in act, but recollection! It is with an effort that I recall the figures and appellations of these few. Soon, likewise, my old native town will loom upon me through the haze of memory, a mist brooding over and around it; as if it were no portion of the real earth, but an overgrown village in cloudland, with only imaginary inhabitants to people its wooden houses, and walk its homely lanes, and the unpicturesque prolixity of its main street. Henceforth, it ceases to be a reality of my life. I am a citizen of somewhere else. My good townspeople will not much regret me; for—though it has been as dear an object as any, in my literary efforts, to be of some importance in their eyes, and to win myself a pleasant memory in this abode and burial place of so many of my forefathers—there has never been, for me, the genial atmosphere which a literary man requires in order to ripen the best harvest of his mind. I shall do better amongst other faces; and these familiar ones, it need hardly be said, will do just as well without me.

It may be, however—O, transporting and triumphant thought!—that the great-grandchildren of the present race may sometimes think kindly of the scribbler of bygone days, when the antiquary of days to come, among the sites memorable in the town's history, shall point out the locality of the town pump!

I

The Prison Door

A THRONG of bearded men, in sad-colored garments and gray, steeple-crowned hats, intermixed with women, some wearing hoods, and others bareheaded, was assembled in front of a wooden edifice, the door of which was heavily timbered with oak and studded with iron spikes.

The founders of a new colony, whatever Utopia of human virtue and happiness they might originally project, have invariably recognized it among their earliest practical necessities to allot a portion of the virgin soil as a cemetery, and another portion as the site of a prison. In accordance with this rule, it may safely be assumed that the forefathers of Boston had built the first prison house somewhere in the vicinity of Cornhill almost as seasonably as they marked out the first burial ground, on Isaac Johnson's lot and round about his grave, which subsequently became the nucleus of all the congregated sepulchres in the old churchyard of King's Chapel. Certain it is that, some fifteen or twenty years after the settlement of the town, the wooden jail was already marked with weather-stains and other indications of age which gave a yet darker aspect to its beetle-browed and gloomy front. The rust on the ponderous iron-work of its oaken door looked more antique than anything else in the New World. Like all that pertains to crime, it seemed never to have known a youthful era. Before this ugly edifice, and between it and the wheel-track of the street, was a grass plot, much overgrown with burdock, pigweed, apple peru, and such unsightly vegetation, which evidently found something congenial in the soil that had so early borne the black flower of civilized society, a prison. But on one side of the portal, and rooted almost at the threshold, was a wild rose-bush, covered, in this month of June, with its delicate gems, which might be imagined to offer their fragrance and fragile beauty to the prisoner as he went in, and to the condemned criminal as he came forth to his doom, in token that the deep heart of Nature could pity and be kind to him.

This rosebush, by a strange chance, has been kept alive in history; but whether it had merely survived out of the stern old wilderness, so long after the fall of the gigantic pines and oaks that originally overshadowed it—or whether, as there is fair authority for believing, it had sprung up under the footsteps of the sainted Ann Hutchinson, as she entered the prison door—we shall not take upon us to determine. Finding it so directly on the threshold of our narrative, which is now about to issue from that inauspicious portal, we could hardly do otherwise than pluck one of its flowers, and present it to the reader. It may serve, let us hope, to symbolize some sweet moral blossom that may be found along the track, or relieve the darkening close of a tale of human frailty and sorrow.

II

The Market Place

THE grass plot before the jail, in Prison Lane, on a certain summer morning not less than two centuries ago, was occupied by a pretty large number of the inhabitants of Boston, all with their eyes intently fastened on the iron-clamped oaken door. Amongst any other population, or at a later period in the history of New England, the grim rigidity that petrified the bearded physiognomies of these good people would have augured some awful business in hand. It could have betokened nothing short of the anticipated execution of some noted culprit, on whom the sentence of a legal tribunal had but confirmed the verdict of public sentiment. But in that early severity of the Puritan character, an inference of this kind could not so indubitably be drawn. It might be that a sluggish bond-servant, or an undutiful child, whom his parents had given over to the civil authority, was to be corrected at the whipping-post. It might be that an Antinomian, a Quaker, or other heterodox religionist, was to be scourged out of the town, or an idle and vagrant Indian, whom the white man's firewater had made riotous about the streets, was to be driven with stripes into the shadow of the forest. It might be, too, that a witch, like old Mistress Hibbins, the bitter-tempered widow of the magistrate, was to die upon the gallows. In either case, there was very much the same solemnity of demeanor on the part of the spectators; as befitted a people amongst whom religion and law were almost identical, and in whose character both were so thoroughly interfused, that the mildest and the severest acts of public discipline were alike made venerable and awful.

Meagre, indeed, and cold, was the sympathy that a transgressor might look for from such bystanders at the scaffold. On the other hand, a penalty which in our days would infer a degree of mocking infamy and ridicule might then be invested with almost as stern a dignity as the punishment of death itself.

It was a circumstance to be noted, on the summer morning when our story begins its course, that the women, of whom there were several in the crowd, appeared to take a peculiar interest in whatever penal infliction might be expected to ensue. The age had not so much refinement that any sense of impropriety restrained the wearers of petticoat and farthingale from stepping forth into the public ways and wedging their not unsubstantial persons, if occasion were, into the throng nearest to the scaffold at an execution. Morally, as well as materially, there was a coarser fibre in those wives and maidens of old English birth and breeding than in their fair descendants, separated from them by a series of six or seven generations; for, throughout that chain of ancestry, every successive mother has transmitted to her child a fainter bloom, a more delicate and briefer beauty, and a slighter physical frame, if not a character of less force and solidity, than her own. The women who were now standing about the prison door stood within less than half a century of the period when the manlike Elizabeth had been the not altogether unsuitable representative of the sex. They were her countrywomen; and the beef and ale of their native land, with a moral diet not a whit more refined, entered largely into their composition. The bright morning sun, therefore, shone on broad shoulders and well-developed busts and on round and ruddy cheeks that had ripened in the far-off island, and had hardly yet grown paler or thinner in the atmosphere of New England. There was, moreover, a boldness and rotundity of speech among these matrons, as most of them seemed to be, that would startle us at the present day, whether in respect to its purport or its volume of tone.

"Goodwives," said a hard-featured dame of fifty, "I'll tell ye a piece of my mind. It would be greatly for the public behoof, if we women, being of mature age and church members in good repute, should have the handling of such malefactresses as this Hester Prynne. What think ye, gossips? If the hussy stood up for judgment before us five, that are now here in a knot together, would she come off with such a sentence as the worshipful magistrates have awarded? Marry, I trow not!"

"People say," said another, "that the Reverend Master Dimmesdale, her godly pastor, takes it very grievously to heart that such a scandal should have come upon his congregation."

"The magistrates are God-fearing gentlemen, but merciful overmuch—that is a truth," added a third autumnal matron. "At the very least, they should have put the brand of a hot iron on Hester Prynne's forehead. Madam Hester would have winced at that, I warrant me. But she—the naughty baggage—little will she care what they put upon the bodice of her gown! Why, look you, she may cover it with a brooch, or suchlike heathenish adornment, and so walk the streets as brave as ever!"

"Ah, but," interposed, more softly, a young wife, holding a child by the hand, "let her cover the mark as she will, the pang of it will be always in her heart."

"What do we talk of marks and brands, whether on the bodice of her gown, or the flesh of her forehead?" cried another female, the ugliest as well as the most pitiless of these self-constituted judges. "This woman has brought shame upon us all, and ought to die. Is there not law for it? Truly there is, both in the Scripture and the statute-book. Then let the magistrates, who have made it of no effect, thank themselves if their own wives and daughters go astray!"

"Mercy on us, goodwife," exclaimed a man in the crowd, "is there no virtue in woman, save what springs from a wholesome fear of the gallows? That is the hardest word yet! Hush, now, gossips! for the lock is turning in the prison door, and here comes Mistress Prynne herself."

The door of the jail being flung open from within, there appeared, in the first place, like a black shadow emerging into the sunshine, the grim and grisly presence of the town beadle, with a sword by his side and his staff of office in his hand. This personage prefigured and represented in his aspect the whole dismal severity of the Puritanic code of law, which it was his business to administer in its final and closest application to the offender. Stretching forth the official staff in his left hand, he laid his right upon the shoulder of a

young woman, whom he thus drew forward; until, on the
threshold of the prison door, she repelled him, by an action
marked with natural dignity and force of character, and
stepped into the open air, as if by her own free will. She
bore in her arms a child, a baby of some three months old,
who winked and turned aside its little face from the too
vivid light of day; because its existence, heretofore, had
brought it acquainted only with the gray twilight of a dungeon, or other darksome apartment of the prison.

When the young woman—the mother of this child—stood
fully revealed before the crowd, it seemed to be her first
impulse to clasp the infant closely to her bosom; not so
much by an impulse of motherly affection, as that she might
thereby conceal a certain token, which was wrought or
fastened into her dress. In a moment, however, wisely judging that one token of her shame would but poorly serve to
hide another, she took the baby on her arm, and, with a
burning blush, and yet a haughty smile, and a glance that
would not be abashed, looked around at her townspeople
and neighbors. On the breast of her gown, in fine red cloth
surrounded with an elaborate embroidery and fantastic flourishes of gold thread, appeared the letter "A." It was so
artistically done, and with so much fertility and gorgeous
luxuriance of fancy, that it had all the effect of a last and
fitting decoration to the apparel which she wore; and which
was of a splendor in accordance with the taste of the age,
but greatly beyond what was allowed by the sumptuary
regulations of the colony.

The young woman was tall, with a figure of perfect elegance on a large scale. She had dark and abundant hair, so
glossy that it threw off the sunshine with a gleam, and a face
which, besides being beautiful from regularity of feature
and richness of complexion, had the impressiveness belonging to a marked brow and deep black eyes. She was ladylike, too, after the manner of the feminine gentility of those
days; characterized by a certain state and dignity, rather
than by the delicate, evanescent, and indescribable grace,
which is now recognized as its indication. And never had
Hester Prynne appeared more ladylike, in the antique interpretation of the term, than as she issued from the prison.
Those who had before known her and had expected to
behold her dimmed and obscured by a disastrous cloud,

were astonished, and even startled, to perceive how her beauty shone out and made a halo of the misfortune and ignominy in which she was enveloped. It may be true that, to a sensitive observer, there was something exquisitely painful in it. Her attire, which, indeed, she had wrought for the occasion, in prison, and had modelled much after her own fancy, seemed to express the attitude of her spirit, the desperate recklessness of her mood, by its wild and pictur-esque peculiarity. But the point which drew all eyes and, as it were, transfigured the wearer—so that both men and women, who had been familiarly acquainted with Hester Prynne, were now impressed as if they beheld her for the first time—was that *Scarlet Letter*, so fantastically embroi-dered and illuminated upon her bosom. It had the effect of a spell, taking her out of the ordinary relations with human-ity and enclosing her in a sphere by herself.

"She hath good skill at her needle, that's certain," re-marked one of her female spectators; "but did ever a woman, before this brazen hussy, contrive such a way of showing it! Why, gossips, what is it but to laugh in the faces of our godly magistrates, and make a pride out of what they, worthy gentlemen, meant for a punishment?"

"It were well," muttered the most iron-visaged of the old dames, "if we stripped Madam Hester's rich gown off her dainty shoulders; and as for the red letter, which she hath stitched so curiously, I'll bestow a rag of mine own rheu-matic flannel, to make a fitter one!"

"O, peace, neighbors, peace!" whispered their youngest companion; "do not let her hear you! Not a stitch in that embroidered letter, but she has felt it in her heart."

The grim beadle now made a gesture with his staff.

"Make way, good people, make way, in the King's name!" cried he. "Open a passage; and, I promise ye, Mistress Prynne shall be set where man, woman and child may have a fair sight of her brave apparel, from this time till an hour past meridian. A blessing on the righteous Colony of the Massachusetts, where iniquity is dragged out into the sun-shine! Come along, Madam Hester, and show your scarlet letter in the market place!"

A lane was forthwith opened through the crowd of specta-tors. Preceded by the beadle, and attended by an irregular procession of stern-browed men and unkindly visaged women,

Hester Prynne set forth towards the place appointed for her punishment. A crowd of eager and curious schoolboys, understanding little of the matter in hand except that it gave them a half-holiday, ran before her progress, turning their heads continually to stare into her face, and at the winking baby in her arms, and at the ignominious letter on her breast. It was no great distance, in those days, from the prison door to the market place. Measured by the prisoner's experience, however, it might be reckoned a journey of some length; for, haughty as her demeanor was, she perchance underwent an agony from every footstep of those that thronged to see her, as if her heart had been flung into the street for them all to spurn and trample upon. In our nature, however, there is a provision, alike marvellous and merciful, that the sufferer should never know the intensity of what he endures by its present torture, but chiefly by the pang that rankles after it. With almost a serene deportment, therefore, Hester Prynne passed through this portion of her ordeal, and came to a sort of scaffold, at the western extremity of the market place. It stood nearly beneath the eaves of Boston's earliest church, and appeared to be a fixture there.

In fact, this scaffold constituted a portion of a penal machine, which now, for two or three generations past, has been merely historical and traditionary among us, but was held, in the old time, to be as effectual an agent in the promotion of good citizenship as ever was the guillotine among the terrorists of France. It was, in short, the platform of the pillory; and above it rose the framework of that instrument of discipline, so fashioned as to confine the human head in its tight grasp, and thus hold it up to the public gaze. The very ideal of ignominy was embodied and made manifest in this contrivance of wood and iron. There can be no outrage, methinks, against our common nature—whatever be the delinquencies of the individual—no outrage more flagrant than to forbid the culprit to hide his face for shame; as it was the essence of this punishment to do. In Hester Prynne's instance, however, as not unfrequently in other cases, her sentence bore, that she should stand a certain time upon the platform but without undergoing that gripe about the neck and confinement of the head, the proneness to which was the most devilish characteristic of this ugly engine. Knowing well her part, she ascended a flight of wooden steps, and was thus displayed to the surrounding multitude, at about the height of a man's shoulders above the street.

Had there been a Papist among the crowd of Puritans, he might have seen in this beautiful woman, so picturesque in her attire and mien, and with the infant at her bosom, an object to remind him of the image of Divine Maternity, which so many illustrious painters have vied with one another to represent; something which should remind him, indeed, but only by contrast, of that sacred image of sinless motherhood, whose infant was to redeem the world. Here, there was the taint of deepest sin in the most sacred quality of human life, working such effect that the world was only the darker for this woman's beauty, and the more lost for the infant that she had borne.

The scene was not without a mixture of awe, such as must always invest the spectacle of guilt and shame in a fellow-creature, before society shall have grown corrupt enough to smile, instead of shuddering, at it. The witnesses of Hester Prynne's disgrace had not yet passed beyond their simplicity. They were stern enough to look upon her death, had that been the sentence, without a murmur at its severity, but had none of the heartlessness of another social state, which would find only a theme for jest in an exhibition like the present. Even had there been a disposition to turn the matter into ridicule, it must have been repressed and over-powered by the solemn presence of men no less dignified than the Governor and several of his counsellors, a judge, a general, and the ministers of the town; all of whom sat or stood in a balcony of the meeting house, looking down upon the platform. When such personages could constitute a part of the spectacle without risking the majesty or reverence of rank and office, it was safely to be inferred that the inflic-tion of a legal sentence would have an earnest and effectual meaning. Accordingly, the crowd was sombre and grave. The unhappy culprit sustained herself as best a woman might, under the heavy weight of a thousand unrelenting eyes, all fastened upon her and concentred at her bosom. It was almost intolerable to be borne. Of an impulsive and passionate nature, she had fortified herself to encounter the stings and venomous stabs of public contumely, wreaking itself in every variety of insult; but there was a quality so much more terrible in the solemn mood of the popular mind, that she longed rather to behold all those rigid countenances contorted with scornful merriment, and herself the object. Had a roar of laughter burst from the multitude—each man, each woman, each little shrill-voiced child, contributing their individual parts—Hester Prynne might have repaid them all with a bitter and disdainful smile. But under the leaden infliction which it was her doom to endure, she felt, at moments, as if she must needs shriek out with the full power of her lungs and cast herself from the scaffold down upon the ground, or else go mad at once.

Yet there were intervals when the whole scene, in which she was the most conspicuous object, seemed to vanish from her eyes, or, at least, glimmered indistinctly before them, like a mass of imperfectly shaped and spectral images. Her mind, and especially her memory, was preternaturally active, and kept bringing up other scenes than this roughly hewn street of a little town on the edge of the Western wilderness; other faces than were lowering upon her from beneath the brims of those steeple-crowned hats. Reminiscences, the most trifling and immaterial, passages of infancy and school-days, sports, childish quarrels, and the little domestic traits of her maiden years, came swarming back upon her, intermingled with recollections of whatever was gravest in her subsequent life; one picture precisely as vivid as another; as if all were of similar importance, or all alike a play. Possibly it was an instinctive device of her spirit to relieve itself, by the exhibition of these phantasmagoric forms, from the cruel weight and hardness of the reality.

Be that as it might, the scaffold of the pillory was a point of view that revealed to Hester Prynne the entire track along which she had been treading since her happy infancy. Standing on that miserable eminence, she saw again her native village, in Old England, and her paternal home; a decayed house of gray stone, with a poverty-stricken aspect, but retaining a half-obliterated shield of arms over the portal, in token of antique gentility. She saw her father's face, with its bald brow and reverend white beard that flowed over the old-fashioned Elizabethan ruff; her mother's, too, with the look of heedful and anxious love which it always wore in her remembrance, and which, even since her death, had so often laid the impediment of a gentle remonstrance in her daughter's pathway. She saw her own face, glowing with girlish beauty, and illuminating all the interior of the dusky mirror in which she had been wont to gaze at it. There she beheld another countenance, of a man well stricken in years, a pale, thin, scholar-like visage, with eyes dim and bleared by the lamplight that had served them to pore over many ponderous books. Yet those same bleared optics had a strange, penetrating power, when it was their owner's purpose to read the human soul. This figure of the study and the cloister, as Hester Prynne's womanly fancy failed not to recall, was slightly deformed, with the left shoulder a trifle higher than the right. Next rose before her, in memory's picture gallery, the intricate and narrow thoroughfares, the tall, gray houses, the huge cathedrals, and the public edifices, ancient in date and quaint in architecture, of a Continental city, where a new life had awaited her, still in connection with the misshapen scholar; a new life, but feeding itself on time-worn materials, like a tuft of green moss on a crumbling wall. Lastly, in lieu of these shifting scenes, came back the rude market place of the Puritan settlement, with all the townspeople assembled and levelling their stern regards at Hester Prynne—yes, at herself—who stood on the scaffold of the pillory, an infant on her arm, and the letter "A" in scarlet, fantastically embroidered with gold thread, upon her bosom!

Could it be true? She clutched the child so fiercely to her breast that it sent forth a cry; she turned her eyes downward at the scarlet letter, and even touched it with her finger, to assure herself that the infant and the shame were real. Yes!—these were her realities—all else had vanished!

III

The Recognition

FROM this intense consciousness of being the object of severe and universal observation, the wearer of the scarlet letter was at length relieved, by discerning on the outskirts of the crowd a figure which irresistibly took possession of her thoughts. An Indian in his native garb was standing there; but the red men were not so infrequent visitors of the English settlements, that one of them would have attracted any notice from Hester Prynne at such a time; much less would he have excluded all other objects and ideas from her mind. By the Indian's side, and evidently sustaining a companionship with him, stood a white man, clad in a strange disarray of civilized and savage costume.

He was small in stature, with a furrowed visage which, as yet, could hardly be termed aged. There was a remarkable intelligence in his features, as of a person who had so cultivated his mental part that it could not fail to mould the physical to itself, and become manifest by unmistakable tokens. Although, by a seemingly careless arrangement of his heterogeneous garb, he had endeavored to conceal or abate the peculiarity, it was sufficiently evident to Hester Prynne that one of this man's shoulders rose higher than the other. Again, at the first instant of perceiving that thin visage and the slight deformity of the figure, she pressed her infant to her bosom with so convulsive a force that the poor babe uttered another cry of pain. But the mother did not seem to hear it.

At his arrival in the market place, and some time before she saw him, the stranger had bent his eyes on Hester

Prynne. It was carelessly, at first, like a man chiefly accustomed to look inward, and to whom external matters are of little value and import unless they bear relation to something within his mind. Very soon, however, his look became keen and penetrative. A writhing horror twisted itself across his features, like a snake gliding swiftly over them, and making one little pause, with all its wreathed intervolutions in open sight. His face darkened with some powerful emotion, which, nevertheless, he so instantaneously controlled by an effort of his will, that, save at a single moment, its expression might have passed for calmness. After a brief space, the convulsion grew almost imperceptible, and finally subsided into the depths of his nature. When he found the eyes of Hester Prynne fastened on his own, and saw that she appeared to recognize him, he slowly and calmly raised his finger, made a gesture with it in the air, and laid it on his lips.

Then, touching the shoulder of a townsman who stood next to him, he addressed him in a formal and courteous manner.

"I pray you, good Sir," said he, "who is this woman? —and wherefore is she here set up to public shame?"

"You must needs be a stranger in this region, friend," answered the townsman, looking curiously at the questioner and his savage companion, "else you would surely have heard of Mistress Hester Prynne, and her evil doings. She hath raised a great scandal, I promise you, in godly Master Dimmesdale's church."

"You say truly," replied the other. "I am a stranger, and have been a wanderer, sorely against my will. I have met with grievous mishaps by sea and land, and have been long held in bonds among the heathen folk, to the southward; and am now brought hither by this Indian, to be redeemed out of my captivity. Will it please you, therefore, to tell me of Hester Prynne's—have I her name rightly?—of this woman's offences, and what has brought her to yonder scaffold?"

"Truly, friend; and methinks it must gladden your heart, after your troubles and sojourn in the wilderness," said the townsman, "to find yourself, at length, in a land where iniquity is searched out, and punished in the sight of rulers and people; as here in our godly New England. Yonder woman, Sir, you must know, was the wife of a certain learned man, English by birth, but who had long dwelt in Amsterdam, whence, some good time agone, he was minded to cross over and cast in his lot with us of the Massachusetts. To this purpose, he sent his wife before him, remaining himself to look after some necessary affairs. Marry, good Sir, in some two years, or less, that the woman has been a dweller here in Boston, no tidings have come of this learned gentleman, Master Prynne; and his young wife, look you, being left to her own misguidance—"

"Ah!—aha!—I conceive you," said the stranger, with a bitter smile. "So learned a man as you speak of should have learned this too in his books. And who, by your favor, Sir, may be the father of yonder babe—it is some three or four months old, I should judge—which Mistress Prynne is holding in her arms?"

"Of a truth, friend, that matter remaineth a riddle; and the Daniel who shall expound it is yet a-wanting," answered the townsman. "Madam Hester absolutely refuseth to speak, and the magistrates have laid their heads together in vain. Peradventure the guilty one stands looking on at this sad spectacle, unknown of man, and forgetting that God sees him."

"The learned man," observed the stranger, with another smile, "should come himself, to look into the mystery."

"It behooves him well, if he be still in life," responded the townsman. "Now, good Sir, our Massachusetts magistracy, bethinking themselves that this woman is youthful and fair, and doubtless was strongly tempted to her fall— and that, moreover, as is most likely, her husband may be at the bottom of the sea—they have not been bold to put in force the extremity of our righteous law against her. The penalty thereof is death. But in their great mercy and tenderness of heart, they have doomed Mistress Prynne to stand only a space of three hours on the platform of the pillory, and then and thereafter, for the remainder of her natural life, to wear a mark of shame upon her bosom."

"A wise sentence!" remarked the stranger, gravely bowing his head. "Thus she will be a living sermon against sin, until the ignominious letter be engraved upon her tombstone. It irks me, nevertheless, that the partner of her iniquity should not, at least, stand on the scaffold by her side. But he will be known!—he will be known!—he will be known!"

He bowed courteously to the communicative townsman, and, whispering a few words to his Indian attendant, they both made their way through the crowd.

While this passed, Hester Prynne had been standing on her pedestal, still with a fixed gaze towards the stranger; so fixed a gaze, that, at moments of intense absorption, all other objects in the visible world seemed to vanish, leaving only him and her. Such an interview, perhaps, would have been more terrible than even to meet him as she now did, with the hot, midday sun burning down upon her face and lighting up its shame; with the scarlet token of infamy on her breast; with the sin-born infant in her arms; with a whole people, drawn forth as to a festival, staring at the features that should have been seen only in the quiet gleam of the fireside, in the happy shadow of a home, or beneath a matronly veil, at church. Dreadful as it was, she was conscious of a shelter in the presence of these thousand witnesses. It was better to stand thus, with so many betwixt him and her, than to greet him, face to face, they two alone. She fled for refuge, as it were, to the public exposure, and dreaded the moment when its protection should be withdrawn from her. Involved in these thoughts, she scarcely heard a voice behind her, until it had repeated her name more than once, in a loud and solemn tone, audible to the whole multitude.

"Hearken unto me, Hester Prynne!" said the voice.

It has already been noticed that directly over the platform on which Hester Prynne stood was a kind of balcony, or open gallery, appended to the meeting house. It was the place whence proclamations were wont to be made, amidst an assemblage of the magistracy, with all the ceremonial that attended such public observances in those days. Here, to witness the scene which we are describing, sat Governor Bellingham himself, with four sergeants about his chair, bearing halberds, as a guard of honor. He wore a dark feather in his hat, a border of embroidery on his cloak, and a black velvet tunic beneath; a gentleman advanced in years, with a hard experience written in his wrinkles. He was not ill fitted to be the head and representative of a community which owed its origin and progress and its present state of development, not to the impulses of youth, but to the stern and tempered energies of manhood and the sombre sagacity of age; accomplishing so much, precisely because it imagined and hoped so little. The other eminent characters by whom the chief ruler was surrounded were distinguished by a dignity of mien belonging to a period when the forms of authority were felt to possess the sacredness of Divine institutions. They were, doubtless, good men, just, and sage. But, out of the whole human family, it would not have been easy to select the same number of wise and virtuous persons who should be less capable of sitting in judgment on an erring woman's heart, and disentangling its mesh of good and evil, than the sages of rigid aspect towards whom Hester Prynne now turned her face. She seemed conscious, indeed, that whatever sympathy she might expect lay in the larger and warmer heart of the multitude; for, as she lifted her eyes towards the balcony, the unhappy woman grew pale and trembled.

The voice which had called her attention was that of the reverend and famous John Wilson, the eldest clergyman of Boston, a great scholar like most of his contemporaries in the profession, and withal a man of kind and genial spirit. This last attribute, however, had been less carefully developed than his intellectual gifts, and was, in truth, rather a matter of shame than self-congratulation with him. There he stood, with a border of grizzled locks beneath his skullcap, while his gray eyes, accustomed to the shaded light of his study, were winking, like those of Hester's infant, in the unadulterated sunshine. He looked like the darkly engraved portraits which we see prefixed to old volumes of sermons; and had no more right than one of those portraits would have, to step forth, as he now did, and meddle with a question of human guilt, passion and anguish.

"Hester Prynne," said the clergyman, "I have striven with my young brother here, under whose preaching of the word you have been privileged to sit"—here Mr. Wilson laid his hand on the shoulder of a pale young man beside him—"I have sought, I say, to persuade this godly youth that he should deal with you, here in the face of Heaven, and before these wise and upright rulers, and in hearing of all the people as touching the vileness and blackness of your sin. Knowing your natural temper better than I, he could the better judge what arguments to use, whether of tenderness or terror, such as might prevail over your hardness and obstinacy; insomuch that you should no longer hide the name of him who tempted you to this grievous fall. But he opposes to me (with a young man's oversoftness, albeit wise beyond his years) that it were wronging the very nature of woman to force her to lay open her heart's secrets in such broad daylight, and in presence of so great a multitude. Truly, as I sought to convince him, the shame lay in the commission of the sin, and not in the showing of it forth. What say you to it, once again, Brother Dimmesdale? Must it be thou, or I, that shall deal with this poor sinner's soul?"

There was a murmur among the dignified and reverend occupants of the balcony; and Governor Bellingham gave expression to its purport, speaking in an authoritative voice, although tempered with respect towards the youthful clergyman whom he addressed.

"Good Master Dimmesdale," said he, "the responsibility of this woman's soul lies greatly with you. It behooves you, therefore, to exhort her to repentance and to confession, as a proof and consequence thereof."

The directness of this appeal drew the eyes of the whole crowd upon the Reverend Mr. Dimmesdale; a young clergyman who had come from one of the great English universities, bringing all the learning of the age into our wild forestland. His eloquence and religious fervor had already given the earnest of high eminence in his profession. He was a person of very striking aspect, with a white, lofty, and impending brow, large, brown, melancholy eyes, and a mouth which, unless when he forcibly compressed it, was apt to be tremulous, expressing both nervous sensibility and a vast power of self-restraint. Notwithstanding his high native gifts and scholarlike attainments, there was an air about this young minister—an apprehensive, a startled, a half-frightened look—as of a being who felt himself quite astray and at a loss in the pathway of human existence, and could only be at ease in some seclusion of his own. Therefore, so far as his duties would permit, he trod in the shadowy bypaths, and thus kept himself simple and childlike, coming forth, when occasion was, with a freshness, and fragrance, and dewy purity of thought, which, as many people said, affected them like the speech of an angel.

Such was the young man whom the Reverend Mr. Wilson

and the Governor had introduced so openly to the public
notice, bidding him speak, in the hearing of all men, to that
mystery of a woman's soul, so sacred even in its pollution.
The trying nature of his position drove the blood from his
cheek, and made his lips tremulous.

"Speak to the woman, my brother," said Mr. Wilson. "It
is of moment to her soul, and therefore, as the worshipful
Governor says, momentous to thine own, in whose charge
hers is. Exhort her to confess the truth!"

The Reverend Mr. Dimmesdale bent his head, in silent
prayer, as it seemed, and then came forward.

"Hester Prynne," said he, leaning over the balcony, and
looking down steadfastly into her eyes, "thou hearest what
this good man says, and seest the accountability under which
I labor. If thou feelest it to be for thy soul's peace, and that
thy earthly punishment will thereby be made more effectual
to salvation, I charge thee to speak out the name of thy
fellow-sinner and fellow-sufferer! Be not silent from any
mistaken pity and tenderness for him; for, believe me, Hester, though he were to step down from a high place, and
stand there beside thee on thy pedestal of shame, yet better
were it so, than to hide a guilty heart through life. What can
thy silence do for him, except it tempt him—yea, compel
him, as it were—to add hypocrisy to sin? Heaven hath
granted thee an open ignominy, that thereby thou mayest
work out an open triumph over the evil within thee, and the
sorrow without. Take heed how thou deniest to him—who,
perchance, hath not the courage to grasp it for himself—the
bitter, but wholesome, cup that is now presented to thy lips!"

The young pastor's voice was tremulously sweet, rich,
deep, and broken. The feeling that it so evidently manifested, rather than the direct purport of the words, caused it
to vibrate within all hearts, and brought the listeners into
one accord of sympathy. Even the poor baby at Hester's
bosom was affected by the same influence, for it directed its
hitherto vacant gaze towards Mr. Dimmesdale, and held up
its little arms, with a half pleased, half plaintive murmur. So
powerful seemed the minister's appeal, that the people could
not believe but that Hester Prynne would speak out the
guilty name; or else that the guilty one himself, in whatever
high or lowly place he stood, would be drawn forth by an

inward and inevitable necessity, and compelled to ascend the scaffold.

Hester shook her head.

"Woman, transgress not beyond the limits of Heaven's mercy!" cried the Reverend Mr. Wilson, more harshly than before. "That little babe hath been gifted with a voice to second and confirm the counsel which thou hast heard. Speak out the name! That, and thy repentance, may avail to take the scarlet letter off thy breast."

"Never!" replied Hester Prynne, looking, not at Mr. Wilson, but into the deep and troubled eyes of the younger clergyman. "It is too deeply branded. Ye cannot take it off. And would that I might endure his agony, as well as mine!"

"Speak, woman!" said another voice, coldly and sternly, proceeding from the crowd about the scaffold. "Speak; and give your child a father!"

"I will not speak!" answered Hester, turning pale as death, but responding to this voice, which she too surely recognized. "And my child must seek a heavenly Father; she shall never know an earthly one!"

"She will not speak!" murmured Mr. Dimmesdale, who, leaning over the balcony, with his hand upon his heart, had awaited the result of his appeal. He now drew back, with a long respiration. "Wondrous strength and generosity of a woman's heart! She will not speak!"

Discerning the impracticable state of the poor culprit's mind, the elder clergyman, who had carefully prepared himself for the occasion, addressed to the multitude a discourse on sin, in all its branches, but with continual reference to the ignominious letter. So forcibly did he dwell upon this symbol, for the hour or more during which his periods were rolling over the people's heads, that it assumed new terrors in their imagination, and seemed to derive its scarlet hue from the flames of the infernal pit. Hester Prynne, meanwhile, kept her place upon the pedestal of shame, with glazed eyes, and an air of weary indifference. She had borne, that morning, all that nature could endure; and as her temperament was not of the order that escapes from too intense suffering by a swoon, her spirit could only shelter itself beneath a stony crust of insensibility, while the faculties of animal life remained entire. In this state, the voice of the preacher thundered remorselessly, but unavailingly, upon her ears. The infant, during the latter portion of her ordeal, pierced the air with its wailings and screams; she strove to hush it, mechanically, but seemed scarcely to sympathize with its trouble. With the same hard demeanor, she was led back to prison, and vanished from the public gaze within its iron-clamped portal. It was whispered, by those who peered after her, that the scarlet letter threw a lurid gleam along the dark passageway of the interior.

IV

The Interview

AFTER her return to the prison, Hester Prynne was found to be in a state of nervous excitement that demanded constant watchfulness, lest she should perpetrate violence on herself, or do some half-frenzied mischief to the poor babe. As night approached, it proving impossible to quell her insubordination by rebuke or threats of punishment, Master Brackett, the jailer, thought fit to introduce a physician. He described him as a man of skill in all Christian modes of physical science, and likewise familiar with whatever the savage people could teach, in respect to medicinal herbs and roots that grew in the forest. To say the truth, there was much need of professional assistance, not merely for Hester herself, but still more urgently for the child, who, drawing its sustenance from the maternal bosom, seemed to have drunk in with it all the turmoil, the anguish and despair, which pervaded the mother's system. It now writhed in convulsions of pain, and was a forcible type, in its little frame, of the moral agony which Hester Prynne had borne throughout the day.

Closely following the jailer into the dismal apartment appeared that individual of singular aspect, whose presence in the crowd had been of such deep interest to the wearer of the scarlet letter. He was lodged in the prison, not as suspected of any offence, but as the most convenient and suitable mode of disposing of him until the magistrates should have conferred with the Indian sagamores respecting his ransom. His name was announced as Roger Chillingworth. The jailer, after ushering him into the room, remained a moment, marvelling at the comparative quiet that followed his entrance; for Hester Prynne had immediately become as still as death, although the child continued to moan.

"Prithee, friend, leave me alone with my patient," said the practitioner. "Trust me, good jailer, you shall briefly have peace in your house; and, I promise you, Mistress Prynne shall hereafter be more amenable to just authority than you may have found her heretofore."

"Nay, if your worship can accomplish that," answered Master Brackett, "I shall own you for a man of skill indeed! Verily, the woman hath been like a possessed one; and there lacks little, that I should take in hand to drive Satan out of her with stripes."

The stranger had entered the room with the characteristic quietude of the profession to which he announced himself as belonging. Nor did his demeanor change when the withdrawal of the prison-keeper left him face to face with the woman, whose absorbed notice of him in the crowd had intimated so close a relation between himself and her. His first care was given to the child, whose cries, indeed, as she lay writhing on the trundle bed, made it of peremptory necessity to postpone all other business to the task of soothing her. He examined the infant carefully, and then proceeded to unclasp a leathern case, which he took from beneath his dress. It appeared to contain certain medical preparations, one of which he mingled with a cup of water.

"My old studies in alchemy," observed he, "and my sojourn, for above a year past among a people well versed in the kindly properties of simples, have made a better physician of me than many that claim the medical degree. Here, woman! The child is yours—she is none of mine—neither will she recognize my voice or aspect as a father's. Administer this draught, therefore, with thine own hand."

Hester repelled the offered medicine, at the same time gazing with strongly marked apprehension into his face.

"Wouldst thou avenge thyself on the innocent babe?" whispered she.

"Foolish woman!" responded the physician, half coldly, half soothingly. "What should ail me, to harm this misbegotten and miserable babe? The medicine is potent for good; and were it my child—yea, mine own, as well as thine!—I could do no better for it."

As she still hesitated, being, in fact, in no reasonable state

of mind, he took the infant in his arms, and himself administered the draught. It soon proved its efficacy, and redeemed
the leech's pledge. The moans of the little patient subsided;
its convulsive tossings gradually ceased; and, in a few moments, as is the custom of young children after relief from
pain, it sank into a profound and dewy slumber. The physician, as he had a fair right to be termed, next bestowed his
attention on the mother. With calm and intent scrutiny, he
felt her pulse, looked into her eyes—a gaze that made her
heart shrink and shudder, because so familiar, and yet so
strange and cold—and, finally, satisfied with his investigation, proceeded to mingle another draught.

"I know not Lethe nor Nepenthe," remarked he, "but I
have learned many new secrets in the wilderness, and here
is one of them—a recipe that an Indian taught me, in
requital of some lessons of my own, that were as old as
Paracelsus. Drink it! It may be less soothing than a sinless
conscience. That I cannot give thee. But it will calm the
swell and heaving of thy passion, like oil thrown on the
waves of a tempestuous sea."

He presented the cup to Hester, who received it with a
slow, earnest look into his face; not precisely a look of fear,
yet full of doubt and questioning, as to what his purposes
might be. She looked also at her slumbering child.

"I have thought of death," said she, "have wished for it,
would even have prayed for it were it fit that such as I
should pray for anything. Yet, if death be in this cup, I bid
thee think again, ere thou beholdest me quaff it. See! It is
even now at my lips."

"Drink, then," replied he, still with the same cold composure. "Dost thou know me so little, Hester Prynne? Are my
purposes wont to be so shallow? Even if I imagine a scheme
of vengeance, what could I do better for my object than to
let thee live—than to give thee medicines against all harm
and peril of life—so that this burning shame may still blaze
upon thy bosom?" As he spoke, he laid his long forefinger
on the scarlet letter, which forthwith seemed to scorch into
Hester's breast as if it had been red-hot. He noticed her involuntary gesture, and smiled. "Live, therefore, and bear about
thy doom with thee, in the eyes of men and women—in the eyes
of him whom thou didst call thy husband—in the eyes of yonder
child! And, that thou mayest live, take off this draught."

Without further expostulation or delay, Hester Prynne drained the cup, and, at the motion of the man of skill, seated herself on the bed where the child was sleeping; while he drew the only chair which the room afforded, and took his own seat beside her. She could not but tremble at these preparations; for she felt that—having now done all that humanity, or principle, or, if so it were, a refined cruelty, impelled him to do, for the relief of physical suffering—he was next to treat with her as the man whom she had most deeply and irreparably injured.

"Hester," said he, "I ask not wherefore, nor how, thou hast fallen into the pit or say, rather, thou hast ascended to the pedestal of infamy on which I found thee. The reason is not far to seek. It was my folly, and thy weakness. I—a man of thought, the bookworm of great libraries—a man already in decay, having given my best years to feed the hungry dream of knowledge—what had I to do with youth and beauty like thine own! Misshapen from my birth-hour, how could I delude myself with the idea that intellectual gifts might veil physical deformity in a young girl's fantasy! Men call me wise. If sages were ever wise in their own behoof, I might have foreseen all this. I might have known that, as I came out of the vast and dismal forest and entered this settlement of Christian men, the very first object to meet my eyes would be thyself, Hester Prynne, standing up, a statue of ignominy, before the people. Nay, from the moment when we came down the old church steps together, a married pair, I might have beheld the bale-fire of that scarlet letter blazing at the end of our path!"

"Thou knowest," said Hester—for, depressed as she was, she could not endure this last quiet stab at the token of her shame—"thou knowest that I was frank with thee. I felt no love, nor feigned any."

"True," replied he. "It was my folly! I have said it. But up to that epoch of my life, I had lived in vain. The world had been so cheerless! My heart was a habitation large enough for many guests, but lonely and chill, and without a household fire. I longed to kindle one! It seemed not so wild a dream—old as I was, and sombre as I was, and misshapen as I was—that the simple bliss, which is scattered far and wide for all mankind to gather up, might yet be mine. And so, Hester, I drew thee into my heart, into its innermost chamber, and sought to warm thee by the warmth which thy presence made there!"

"I have greatly wronged thee," murmured Hester.

"We have wronged each other," answered he. "Mine was the first wrong, when I betrayed thy budding youth into a false and unnatural relation with my decay. Therefore, as a man who has not thought and philosophized in vain, I seek no vengeance, plot no evils against thee. Between thee and me, the scale hangs fairly balanced. But Hester, the man lives who has wronged us both! Who is he?"

"Ask me not!" replied Hester Prynne, looking firmly into his face. "That thou shalt never know!"

"Never, sayest thou?" rejoined he, with a smile of dark and self-relying intelligence. "Never know him! Believe me, Hester, there are few things—whether in the outward world, or, to a certain depth, in the invisible sphere of thought— few things hidden from the man who devotes himself earnestly and unreservedly to the solution of a mystery. Thou mayest cover up thy secret from the prying multitude. Thou mayest conceal it, too, from the ministers and magistrates, even as thou didst this day, when they sought to wrench the name out of thy heart and give thee a partner on thy pedestal. But, as for me, I come to the inquest with other senses than they possess. I shall seek this man as I have sought truth in books, as I have sought gold in alchemy. There is a sympathy that will make me conscious of him. I shall see him tremble. I shall feel myself shudder, suddenly and unawares. Sooner or later, he must needs be mine!"

The eyes of the wrinkled scholar glowed so intensely upon her that Hester Prynne clasped her hands over her heart, dreading lest he should read the secret there at once.

"Thou wilt not reveal his name? Not the less he is mine," resumed he, with a look of confidence, as if destiny were at one with him. "He bears no letter of infamy wrought into his garment, as thou dost; but I shall read it on his heart. Yet fear not for him! Think not that I shall interfere with Heaven's own method of retribution, or, to my own loss, betray him to the gripe of human law. Neither do thou imagine that I shall contrive aught against his life; no, nor against his fame, if, as I judge, he be a man of fair repute. Let him live! Let him hide himself in outward honor, if he may! Not the less he shall be mine!"

"Thy acts are like mercy," said Hester, bewildered and appalled. "But thy words interpret thee as a terror!"

"One thing, thou that wast my wife, I would enjoin upon thee," continued the scholar. "Thou hast kept the secret of thy paramour. Keep, likewise, mine! There are none in this land that know me. Breathe not, to any human soul, that thou didst ever call me husband! Here, on this wild outskirt of the earth, I shall pitch my tent; for, elsewhere a wanderer, and isolated from human interests, I find here a woman, a man, a child, amongst whom and myself there exist the closest ligaments. No matter whether of love or hate; no matter whether of right or wrong! Thou and thine, Hester Prynne, belong to me. My home is where thou art, and where he is. But betray me not!"

"Wherefore dost thou desire it?" inquired Hester, shrinking, she hardly knew why, from this secret bond. "Why not announce thyself openly, and cast me off at once?"

"It may be," he replied, "because I will not encounter the dishonor that besmirches the husband of a faithless woman. It may be for other reasons. Enough, it is my purpose to live and die unknown. Let, therefore, thy husband be to the world as one already dead, and of whom no tidings shall ever come. Recognize me not, by word, by sign, by look! Breathe not the secret, above all, to the man thou wottest of. Shouldst thou fail me in this, beware! His fame, his position, his life, will be in my hands. Beware!"

"I will keep thy secret as I have his," said Hester.

"Swear it!" rejoined he.

And she took the oath.

"And now, Mistress Prynne," said old Roger Chillingworth, as he was hereafter to be named, "I leave thee alone; alone with thy infant, and the scarlet letter! How is it, Hester? Doth thy sentence bind thee to wear the token in thy sleep? Art thou not afraid of nightmares and hideous dreams?"

"Why dost thou smile so at me?" inquired Hester, troubled at the expression of his eyes. "Art thou like the Black Man that haunts the forest round about us? Hast thou enticed me into a bond that will prove the ruin of my soul?"

"Not thy soul," he answered, with another smile. "No, not thine!"

V

Hester at Her Needle

HESTER Prynne's term of confinement was now at an end. Her prison door was thrown open and she came forth into the sunshine, which, falling on all alike, seemed, to her sick and morbid heart, as if meant for no other purpose than to reveal the scarlet letter on her breast. Perhaps there was a more real torture in her first unattended footsteps from the threshold of the prison than even in the procession and spectacle that have been described, where she was made the common infamy at which all mankind was summoned to point its finger. Then, she was supported by an unnatural tension of the nerves and by all the combative energy of her character, which enabled her to convert the scene into a kind of lurid triumph. It was, moreover, a separate and insulated event, to occur but once in her lifetime, and to meet which, therefore, reckless of economy, she might call up the vital strength that would have sufficed for many quiet years. The very law that condemned her—a giant of stern features, but with vigor to support, as well as to annihilate, in his iron arm—had held her up through the terrible ordeal of her ignominy. But now, with this unattended walk from her prison door began the daily custom; and she must either sustain and carry it forward by the ordinary resources of her nature, or sink beneath it. She could no longer borrow from the future to help her through the present grief. Tomorrow would bring its own trial with it; so would the next day, and so would the next; each its own trial, and yet the very same that was now so unutterably grievous to be borne. The days of the faroff future would toil onward; still with the same burden for her to take up and bear along with her, but never to fling down; for the accumulating days and added years would pile up their misery upon the heap of shame. Throughout them all, giving up her individuality, she would become the general symbol at which the preacher and moralist might point, and in which they might vivify and embody their images of woman's frailty and sinful passion. Thus the young and pure would be taught to look at her, with the scarlet letter flaming on her breast—at her, the child of honorable parents, at her, the mother of a babe, that would hereafter be a woman, at her, who had once been innocent—as the figure, the body, the reality of sin. And over her grave, the infamy that she must carry thither would be her only monument.

It may seem marvellous, that, with the world before her— kept by no restrictive clause of her condemnation within the limits of the Puritan settlement, so remote and so obscure, free to return to her birthplace, or to any other European land, and there hide her character and identity under a new exterior, as completely as if emerging into another state of being, and having also the passes of the dark, inscrutable forest open to her, where the wildness of her nature might assimilate itself with a people whose customs and life were alien from the law that had condemned her—it may seem marvellous, that this woman should still call that place her home, where, and where only, she must needs be the type of shame. But there is a fatality, a feeling so irresistible and inevitable that it has the force of doom, which almost invariably compels human beings to linger around and haunt, ghostlike, the spot where some great and marked event has given the color to their lifetime; and still the more irresistibly, the darker the tinge that saddens it. Her sin, her ignominy, were the roots which she had struck into the soil. It was as if a new birth, with stronger assimilations than the first, had converted the forestland, still so uncongenial to every other pilgrim and wanderer, into Hester Prynne's wild and dreary but lifelong home. All other scenes of earth —even that village of rural England, where happy infancy and stainless maidenhood seemed yet to be in her mother's keeping, like garments put off long ago—were foreign to her, in comparison. The chain that bound her here was of iron links, and galling to her inmost soul, but could never be broken.

It might be, too—doubtless it was so, although she hid the secret from herself, and grew pale whenever it struggled out of her heart, like a serpent from its hole—it might be that another feeling kept her within the scene and pathway that had been so fatal. There dwelt, there trod the feet of one with whom she deemed herself connected in a union, that, unrecognized on earth, would bring them together before the bar of final judgment and make that their marriage altar, for a joint futurity of endless retribution. Over and over again, the tempter of souls had thrust this idea upon Hester's contemplation, and laughed at the passionate and desperate joy with which she seized, and then strove to cast it from her. She barely looked the idea in the face, and hastened to bar it in its dungeon. What she compelled herself to believe—what, finally, she reasoned upon as her motive for continuing a resident of New England—was half a truth, and half a self-delusion. Here, she said to herself, had been the scene of her guilt, and here should be the scene of her earthly punishment; and so, perchance, the torture of her daily shame would at length purge her soul and work out another purity than that which she had lost; more saintlike, because the result of martyrdom.

Hester Prynne, therefore, did not flee. On the outskirts of town, within the verge of the peninsula, but not in close vicinity to any other habitation, there was a small thatched cottage. It had been built by an earlier settler, and abandoned because the soil about it was too sterile for cultivation, while its comparative remoteness put it out of the sphere of that social activity which already marked the habits of the emigrants. It stood on the shore, looking across a basin of the sea at the forest-covered hills toward the west. A clump of scrubby trees, such as alone grew on the peninsula, did not so much conceal the cottage from view, as seem to denote that there was some object which would fain have been, or at least ought to be, concealed. In this little, lonesome dwelling, with some slender means that she possessed, and by the license of the magistrates, who still kept an inquisitorial watch over her, Hester established herself, with her infant child. A mystic shadow of suspicion immediately attached itself to the spot. Children, too young to comprehend wherefore this woman should be shut out from the sphere of human charities, would creep nigh enough to behold her plying her needle at the cottage window, or standing in the doorway, or laboring in her little garden, or coming forth along the pathway that led townward; and, discerning the scarlet letter on her breast would scamper off with a strange, contagious fear.

Lonely as was Hester's situation, and without a friend on earth who dared to show himself, she, however, incurred even no risk of want. She possessed an art that sufficed, even in a land that afforded comparatively little scope for its exercise, to supply food for her thriving infant and herself. It was the art—then, as now, almost the only one within a woman's grasp—of needlework. She bore on her breast, in the curiously embroidered letter, a specimen of her delicate and imaginative skill of which the dames of a court might gladly have availed themselves, to add the richer and more spiritual adornment of human ingenuity to their fabrics of silk and gold. Here, indeed, in the sable simplicity that generally characterized the Puritanic modes of dress, there might be an infrequent call for the finer productions of her handiwork. Yet the taste of the age, demanding whatever was elaborate in compositions of this kind, did not fail to extend its influence over our stern progenitors, who had cast behind them so many fashions which it might seem harder to dispense with. Public ceremonies, such as ordinations, the installation of magistrates, and all that could give majesty to the forms in which a new government manifested itself to the people, were, as a matter of policy, marked by a stately and well-conducted ceremonial and a sombre, but yet a studied magnificence. Deep ruffs, painfully wrought bands and gorgeously embroidered gloves were all deemed necessary to the official state of men assuming the reins of power; and were readily allowed to individuals dignified by rank or wealth, even while sumptuary laws forbade these and similar extravagances to the plebeian order. In the array of funerals, too—whether for the apparel of the dead body, or to typify, by manifold emblematic devices of sable cloth and snowy lawn, the sorrow of the survivors—there was a frequent and characteristic demand for such labor as Hester Prynne could supply. Baby linen—for babies then wore robes of state—afforded still another possibility of toil and emolument.

By degrees, nor very slowly, her handiwork became what would now be termed the fashion. Whether from commiseration for a woman of so miserable a destiny; or from the morbid curiosity that gives a fictitious value even to common or worthless things; or by whatever other intangible circumstance was then, as now, sufficient to bestow on some persons what others might seek in vain; or because Hester really filled a gap which must otherwise have remained vacant; it is certain that she had ready and fairly requited employment for as many hours as she saw fit to occupy with her needle. Vanity, it may be, chose to mortify itself by putting on, for ceremonials of pomp and state, the garments that had been wrought by her sinful hands. Her needlework was seen on the ruff of the Governor; military men wore it on their scarfs, and the minister on his band; it decked the baby's little cap; it was shut up, to be mildewed and moulder away, in the coffins of the dead. But it is not recorded that, in a single instance, her skill was called in aid to embroider the white veil which was to cover the pure blushes of a bride. The exception indicated the ever relentless vigor with which society frowned upon her sin.

Hester sought not to acquire anything beyond a subsistence, of the plainest and most ascetic description, for herself, and a simple abundance for her child. Her own dress was of the coarsest materials and the most sombre hue; with only that one ornament—the scarlet letter—which it was her doom to wear. The child's attire, on the other hand, was distinguished by a fanciful, or, we might rather say, a fantastic ingenuity, which served, indeed, to heighten the airy charm that early began to develop itself in the little girl, but which appeared to have also a deeper meaning. We may speak further of it hereafter. Except for that small expenditure in the decoration of her infant, Hester bestowed all her superfluous means in charity, on wretches less miserable than herself, and who not unfrequently insulted the hand that fed them. Much of the time which she might readily have applied to the better efforts of her art, she employed in making coarse garments for the poor. It is probable that there was an idea of penance in this mode of occupation, and that she offered up a real sacrifice of enjoyment in devoting so many hours to such rude handiwork. She had in her nature a rich, voluptuous, Oriental characteristic—a taste for the gorgeously beautiful, which, save in the exquisite productions of her needle, found nothing else in all the possibilities of her life to exercise itself upon. Women derive a pleasure, incomprehensible to the other sex, from the delicate toil of the needle. To Hester Prynne it might have been a mode of expressing, and therefore soothing, the passion of her life. Like all other joys, she rejected it as a sin. This morbid meddling of conscience with an immaterial matter betokened, it is to be feared, no genuine and steadfast penitence, but something doubtful, something that might be deeply wrong, beneath.

In this manner, Hester Prynne came to have a part to perform in the world. With her native energy of character and rare capacity, it could not entirely cast her off, although it had set a mark upon her more intolerable to a woman's heart than that which branded the brow of Cain. In all her intercourse with society, however, there was nothing that made her feel as if she belonged to it. Every gesture, every word, and even the silence of those with whom she came in contact, implied, and often expressed, that she was banished, and as much alone as if she inhabited another sphere, or communicated with the common nature by other organs and senses than the rest of humankind. She stood apart from moral interests, yet close beside them, like a ghost that revisits the familiar fireside and can no longer make itself seen or felt, no more smile with the household joy, nor mourn with the kindred sorrow; or, should it succeed in manifesting its forbidden sympathy, awakening only terror and horrible repugnance. These emotions, in fact, and its bitterest scorn besides, seemed to be the sole portion that she retained in the universal heart. It was not an age of delicacy; and her position, although she understood it well and was in little danger of forgetting it, was often brought before her vivid self-perception, like a new anguish, by the rudest touch upon the tenderest spot. The poor, as we have already said, whom she sought out to be the objects of her bounty, often reviled the hand that was stretched forth to succor them. Dames of elevated rank, likewise, whose doors she entered in the way of her occupation, were accustomed to distil drops of bitterness into her heart, sometimes through that alchemy of quiet malice, by which women can concoct a subtile poison from ordinary trifles, and sometimes, also, by a coarser expression, that fell upon the sufferer's defenceless breast like a rough blow upon an ulcerated wound. Hester had schooled herself long and well; she never responded to these attacks, save by a flush of crimson that rose irrepressibly over the pale cheek, and again subsided into the depths of her bosom. She was patient—a martyr, indeed—but she forebore to pray for her enemies, lest, in spite of her forgiving aspirations, the words of the blessing should stubbornly twist themselves into a curse.

Continually, and in a thousand other ways, did she feel the innumerable throbs of anguish that had been so cunningly contrived for her by the undying, the everactive sentence of the Puritan tribunal. Clergymen paused in the street to address words of exhortation that brought a crowd, with its mingled grin and frown, around the poor, sinful woman. If she entered a church, trusting to share the Sabbath smile of the Universal Father, it was often her mishap to find herself the text of the discourse. She grew to have a dread of children; for they had imbibed from their parents a vague idea of something horrible in this dreary woman, gliding silently through the town, with never any companion but one only child. Therefore, first allowing her to pass, they pursued her at a distance with shrill cries, and the utterance of a word that had no distinct purport to their own minds, but was none the less terrible to her, as proceeding from lips that babbled it unconsciously. It seemed to argue so wide a diffusion of her shame that all nature knew of it; it could have caused her no deeper pang had the leaves of the trees whispered the dark story among themselves, had the summer breeze murmured about it—had the wintry blast shrieked it aloud! Another peculiar torture was felt in the gaze of a new eye. When strangers looked curiously at the scarlet letter—and none ever failed to do so—they branded it afresh into Hester's soul; so that oftentimes, she could scarcely refrain, yet always did refrain, from covering the symbol with her hand. But then, again, an accustomed eye had likewise its own anguish to inflict. Its cool stare of familiarity was intolerable. From first to last, in short, Hester Prynne had always this dreadful agony in feeling a human eye upon the token; the spot never grew callous; it seemed, on the contrary, to grow more sensitive with daily torture.

But sometimes, once in many days, or perchance in many months, she felt an eye—a human eye—upon the ignominious brand, that seemed to give a momentary relief, as if half of her agony were shared. The next instant, back it all rushed again, with still a deeper throb of pain; for, in that brief interval, she had sinned anew. Had Hester sinned alone?

Her imagination was somehow affected, and, had she been of a softer moral and intellectual fibre, would have been still more so, by the strange and solitary anguish of her life. Walking to and fro with those lonely footsteps in the little world with which she was outwardly connected, it now and then appeared to Hester—if altogether fancy, it was nevertheless too potent to be resisted—she felt or fancied, then, that the scarlet letter had endowed her with a new sense. She shuddered to believe, yet could not help believing, that it gave her a sympathetic knowledge of the hidden sin in other hearts. She was terror-stricken by the revelations that were thus made. What were they? Could they be other than the insidious whispers of the bad angel, who would fain have persuaded the struggling woman, as yet only half his victim, that the outward guise of purity was but a lie, and that, if truth were everywhere to be shown, a scarlet letter would blaze forth on many a bosom besides Hester Prynne's? Or, must she receive those intimations—so obscure, yet so distinct—as truth? In all her miserable experience, there was nothing else so awful and so loathsome as this sense. It perplexed as well as shocked her by the irreverent inopportuneness of the occasions that brought it into vivid action. Sometimes the red infamy upon her breast would give a sympathetic throb, as she passed near a venerable minister or magistrate, the model of piety and justice, to whom that age of antique reverence looked up as to a mortal man in fellowship with angels. "What evil thing is at hand?" would Hester say to herself. Lifting her reluctant eyes, there would be nothing human within the scope of view, save the form of this earthly saint! Again, a mystic sisterhood would contumaciously assert itself as she met the sanctified frown of some matron, who, according to the rumor of all tongues, had kept cold snow within her bosom throughout life. That unsunned snow in the matron's bosom, and the burning shame on Hester Prynne's—what had the two in common? Or, once more, the electric thrill would give her warning—"Behold, Hester, here is a companion!" —and, looking up, she would detect the eyes of a young maiden glancing at the scarlet letter, shyly and aside, and quickly averted, with a faint, chill crimson in her cheeks as if her purity were somewhat sullied by that momentary glance. O Fiend, whose talisman was that fatal symbol, wouldst thou leave nothing, whether in youth or age, for this poor sinner to revere?—such loss of faith is ever one of the saddest results of sin. Be it accepted as a proof that all was not corrupt in this poor victim of her own frailty, and man's hard law, that Hester Prynne yet struggled to believe that no fellow-mortal was guilty like herself.

The vulgar, who, in those dreary old times, were always contributing a grotesque horror to what interested their imaginations, had a story about the scarlet letter which we might readily work up into a terrific legend. They averred that the symbol was not mere scarlet cloth tinged in an earthly dyepot, but was redhot with infernal fire, and could be seen glowing all alight whenever Hester Prynne walked abroad in the nighttime. And we must needs say it seared Hester's bosom so deeply, that perhaps there was more truth in the rumor than our modern incredulity may be inclined to admit.

VI

Pearl

WE have as yet hardly spoken of the infant; that little creature, whose innocent life had sprung, by the inscrutable decree of Providence, a lovely and immortal flower, out of the rank luxuriance of a guilty passion. How strange it seemed to the sad woman as she watched the growth, and the beauty that became every day more brilliant, and the intelligence that threw its quivering sunshine over the tiny features of this child! Her Pearl!—For so had Hester called her; not as a name expressive of her aspect, which had nothing of the calm, white, unimpassioned lustre that would be indicated by the comparison. But she named the infant "Pearl," as being of great price—purchased with all she had—her mother's only treasure! How strange, indeed! Man had marked this woman's sin by a scarlet letter, which had such potent and disastrous efficacy that no human sympathy could reach her, save it were sinful like herself. God, as a direct consequence of the sin which man thus punished, had given her a lovely child, whose place was on that same dishonored bosom, to connect her parent forever with the race and descent of mortals, and to be finally a blessed soul in heaven! Yet these thoughts affected Hester Prynne less with hope than apprehension. She knew that her deed had been evil; she could have no faith, therefore, that its result would be for good. Day after day, she looked fearfully into the child's expanding nature; ever dreading to detect some dark and wild peculiarity, that should correspond with the guiltiness to which she owed her being.

Certainly, there was no physical defect. By its perfect

shape, its vigor, and its natural dexterity in the use of all its
untried limbs, the infant was worthy to have been brought
forth in Eden; worthy to have been left there, to be the
plaything of the angels, after the world's first parents were
driven out. The child had a native grace which does not
invariably coexist with faultless beauty; its attire, however
simple, always impressed the beholder as if it were the very
garb that precisely became it best. But little Pearl was not
clad in rustic weeds. Her mother, with a morbid purpose
that may be better understood hereafter, had bought the
richest tissues that could be procured, and allowed her imaginative faculty its full play in the arrangement and decoration
of the dresses which the child wore before the public eye. So
magnificent was the small figure when thus arrayed, and
such was the splendor of Pearl's own proper beauty, shining
through the gorgeous robes which might have extinguished a
paler loveliness, that there was an absolute circle of radiance around her on the darksome cottage floor. And yet a
russet gown, torn and soiled with the child's rude play,
made a picture of her just as perfect. Pearl's aspect was
imbued with a spell of infinite variety; in this one child there
were many children, comprehending the full scope between
the wild-flower prettiness of a peasant baby, and the pomp,
in little, of an infant princess. Throughout all, however,
there was a trait of passion, a certain depth of hue, which
she never lost; and if, in any of her changes, she had grown
fainter or paler, she would have ceased to be herself—it
would have been no longer Pearl!

This outward mutability indicated, and did not more than
fairly express, the various properties of her inner life. Her
nature appeared to possess depth, too, as well as variety;
but—or else Hester's fears deceived her—it lacked reference and adaptation to the world into which she was born.
The child could not be made amenable to rules. In giving
her existence, a great law had been broken, and the result
was a being whose elements were perhaps beautiful and
brilliant, but all in disorder; or with an order peculiar to
themselves, amidst which the point of variety and arrangement was difficult or impossible to be discovered. Hester
could only account for the child's character—and even then
most vaguely and imperfectly—by recalling what she herself
had been, during that momentous period while Pearl was

imbibing her soul from the spiritual world, and her bodily frame from its material of earth. The mother's impassioned state had been the medium through which were transmitted to the unborn infant the rays of its moral life; and, however white and clear originally, they had taken the deep stains of crimson and gold, the fiery lustre, the black shadow, and the untempered light, of the intervening substance. Above all, the warfare of Hester's spirit, at that epoch, was perpetuated in Pearl. She could recognize her wild, desperate, defiant mood, the flightiness of her temper, and even some of the very cloud-shapes of gloom and despondency that had brooded in her heart. They were now illuminated by the morning radiance of a young child's disposition, but, later in the day of earthly existence, might be prolific of the storm and whirlwind.

The discipline of the family, in those days, was of a far more rigid kind than now. The frown, the harsh rebuke, the frequent application of the rod, enjoined by Scriptural authority, were used, not merely in the way of punishment for actual offences, but as a wholesome regimen for the growth and promotion of all childish virtues. Hester Prynne, nevertheless, the lonely mother of this one child, ran little risk of erring on the side of undue severity. Mindful, however, of her own errors and misfortunes, she early sought to impose a tender but strict control over the infant immortality that was committed to her charge. But the task was beyond her skill. After testing both smiles and frowns, and proving that neither mode of treatment possessed any calculable influence, Hester was ultimately compelled to stand aside, and permit the child to be swayed by her own impulses. Physical compulsion or restraint was effectual, of course, while it lasted. As to any other kind of discipline, whether addressed to her mind or heart, little Pearl might or might not be within its reach, in accordance with the caprice that ruled the moment. Her mother, while Pearl was yet an infant, grew acquainted with a certain peculiar look that warned her when it would be labor thrown away to insist, persuade, or plead. It was a look so intelligent, yet inexplicable, so perverse, sometimes so malicious, but generally accompanied by a wild flow of spirits, that Hester could not help questioning, at such moments, whether Pearl was a human child. She seemed rather an airy sprite, which, after playing

its fantastic sports for a little while upon the cottage floor,
would flit away with a mocking smile. Whenever that look
appeared in her wild, bright, deeply black eyes, it invested
her with a strange remoteness and intangibility; it was as if
she were hovering in the air and might vanish, like a glimmering light that comes we know not whence and goes we
know not whither. Beholding it, Hester was constrained to
rush towards the child to pursue the little elf in the flight
which she invariably began, to snatch her to her bosom,
with a close pressure and earnest kisses—not so much from
overflowing love, as to assure herself that Pearl was flesh
and blood, and not utterly delusive. But Pearl's laugh, when
she was caught, though full of merriment and music, made
her mother more doubtful than before.

Heart-smitten at this bewildering and baffling spell that so
often came between herself and her sole treasure, whom she
had bought so dear and who was all her world, Hester
sometimes burst into passionate tears. Then, perhaps—for
there was no foreseeing how it might affect her—Pearl would
frown, and clench her little fist and harden her small features into a stern, unsympathizing look of discontent. Not
seldom, she would laugh anew, and louder than before, like
a thing incapable and unintelligent of human sorrow. Or—
but this more rarely happened—she would be convulsed
with a rage of grief, and sob out her love for her mother in
broken words, and seem intent on proving that she had a
heart, by breaking it. Yet Hester was hardly safe in confid-
ing herself to that gusty tenderness; it passed as suddenly as
it came. Brooding over all these matters, the mother felt
like *one* who has evoked a spirit, but, by some irregularity
in the process of conjuration, has failed to win the master-
word that should control this new and incomprehensible
intelligence. Her only real comfort was when the child lay in
the placidity of sleep. Then she was sure of her, and tasted
hours of quiet, sad, delicious happiness; until—perhaps with
that perverse expression glimmering from beneath her opening lids—little Pearl awoke!

How soon—with what strange rapidity, indeed!—did Pearl
arrive at an age that was capable of social intercourse,
beyond the mother's ever-ready smile and nonsense words!
And then what a happiness would it have been, could Hester Prynne have heard her clear, birdlike voice mingling

with the uproar of other childish voices, and have distinguished and unravelled her own darling's tones, amid all the entangled outcry of a group of sportive children! But this could never be. Pearl was a born outcast of the infantile world. An imp of evil, emblem and product of sin, she had no right among christened infants. Nothing was more remarkable than the instinct, as it seemed, with which the child comprehended her loneliness; the destiny that had drawn an inviolable circle round about her; the whole peculiarity, in short, of her position in respect to other children. Never, since her release from prison, had Hester met the public gaze without her. In all her walks about the town, Pearl, too, was there; first as the babe in arms, and afterwards as the little girl, small companion of her mother, holding a forefinger with her whole grasp, and tripping along at the rate of three or four footsteps to one of Hester's. She saw the children of the settlement on the grassy margin of the street, or at the domestic thresholds, disporting themselves in such grim fashions as the Puritanic nurture would permit; playing at going to church, perchance; or at scourging Quakers; or taking scalps in a sham-fight with the Indians; or scaring one another with freaks of imitative witchcraft. Pearl saw, and gazed intently; but never sought to make acquaintance. If spoken to, she would not speak again. If the children gathered about her, as they sometimes did, Pearl would grow positively terrible in her puny wrath, snatching up stones to fling at them, with shrill, incoherent exclamations that made her mother tremble because they had so much the sound of a witch's anathemas in some unknown tongue.

The truth was that the little Puritans, being of the most intolerant brood that ever lived, had got a vague idea of something outlandish, unearthly, or at variance with ordinary fashions, in the mother of the child; and therefore scorned them in their hearts, and not unfrequently reviled them with their tongues. Pearl felt the sentiment, and requited it with the bitterest hatred that can be supposed to rankle in a childish bosom. These outbreaks of a fierce temper had a kind of value, and even comfort, for her mother, because there was at least an intelligible earnestness in the mood, instead of the fitful caprice that so often thwarted her in the child's manifestations. It appalled her, nevertheless, to discern here, again, a shadowy reflection of the evil that had existed in herself. All this enmity and passion had Pearl inherited, by inalienable right, out of Hester's heart. Mother and daughter stood together in the same circle of seclusion from human society; and in the nature of the child seemed to be perpetuated those unquiet elements that had distracted Hester Prynne before Pearl's birth, but had since begun to be soothed away by the softening influences of maternity.

At home, within and around her mother's cottage, Pearl wanted not a wide and various circle of acquaintance. The spell of life went forth from her ever creative spirit and communicated itself to a thousand objects, as a torch kindles a flame wherever it may be applied. The unlikeliest materials—a stick, a bunch of rags, a flower—were the puppets of Pearl's witchcraft, and, without undergoing any outward change, became spiritually adapted to whatever drama occupied the stage of her inner world. Her one baby-voice served a multitude of imaginary personages, old and young, to talk withal. The pine trees, aged, black and solemn, and flinging groans and other melancholy utterances on the breeze, needed little transformation to figure as Puritan elders; the ugliest weeds of the garden were their children, whom Pearl smote down and uprooted, most unmercifully. It was wonderful, the vast variety of forms into which she threw her intellect, with no continuity, indeed, but darting up and dancing, always in a state of preternatural activity, soon sinking down as if exhausted by so rapid and feverish a tide of life, and succeeded by other shapes of a similar wild energy. It was like nothing so much as the phantasmagoric play of the northern lights. In the mere exercise of the fancy, however, and the sportiveness of a growing mind, there might be little more than was observable in other children of bright faculties; except as Pearl, in the dearth of human playmates, was thrown more upon the visionary throng which she created. The singularity lay in the hostile feelings with which the child regarded all these offspring of her own heart and mind. She never created a friend, but seemed always to be sowing broadcast the dragon's teeth, whence sprung a harvest of armed enemies against whom she rushed to battle. It was inexpressibly sad—then what depth of sorrow to a mother, who felt in her own heart

the cause!—to observe, in one so young, this constant recognition of an adverse world, and so fierce a training of the
energies that were to make good her cause in the contest
that must ensue.

Gazing at Pearl, Hester Prynne often dropped her work
upon her knees, and cried out with an agony which she
would fain have hidden, but which made utterance for itself,
betwixt speech and a groan, "O Father in Heaven—if Thou
art still my Father—what is this being which I have brought
into the world!" And Pearl, overhearing the ejaculation, or
aware through some more subtile channel of those throbs of
anguish, would turn her vivid and beautiful little face upon
her mother, smile with spritelike intelligence, and resume
her play.

One peculiarity of the child's deportment remains yet to
be told. The very first thing which she had noticed in her
life, was—what?—not the mother's smile, responding to it,
as other babies do, by that faint, embryo smile of the little
mouth, remembered so doubtfully afterwards, and with such
fond discussion whether it were indeed a smile. By no
means! But that first object of which Pearl seemed to become aware was—shall we say it?—the scarlet letter on
Hester's bosom! One day, as her mother stooped over the
cradle, the infant's eyes had been caught by the glimmering
of the gold embroidery about the letter; and, putting up her
little hand, she grasped at it, smiling, not doubtfully, but
with a decided gleam, that gave her face the look of a much
older child. Then, gasping for breath, did Hester Prynne
clutch the fatal token, instinctively endeavoring to tear it
away; so infinite was the torture inflicted by the intelligent
touch of Pearl's baby hand. Again, as if her mother's ago-
nized gesture were meant only to make sport for her, did
little Pearl look into her eyes, and smile! From that epoch,
except when the child was asleep, Hester had never felt a
moment's safety; not a moment's calm enjoyment of her.
Weeks, it is true, would sometimes elapse, during which
Pearl's gaze might never once be fixed upon the scarlet
letter; but then, again, it would come at unawares, like the
stroke of sudden death, and always with that peculiar smile
and odd expression of the eyes.

Once this freakish, elvish cast came into the child's eyes
while Hester was looking at her own image in them, as

mothers are fond of doing; and, suddenly—for women in solitude, and with troubled hearts, are pestered with unaccountable delusions—she fancied that she beheld, not her own miniature portrait, but another face, in the small black mirror of Pearl's eye. It was a face, fiendlike, full of smiling malice, yet bearing the semblance of features that she had known full well, though seldom with a smile, and never with malice in them. It was as if an evil spirit possessed the child, and had just then peeped forth in mockery. Many a time afterwards had Hester been tortured, though less vividly, by the same illusion.

In the afternoon of a certain summer's day, after Pearl grew big enough to run about, she amused herself with gathering handfuls of wild-flowers and flinging them, one by one, at her mother's bosom, dancing up and down like a little elf whenever she hit the scarlet letter. Hester's first motion had been to cover her bosom with her clasped hands. But, whether from pride or resignation or a feeling that her penance might best be wrought out by this unutterable pain, she resisted the impulse, and sat erect, pale as death, looking sadly into little Pearl's wild eyes. Still came the battery of flowers, almost invariably hitting the mark, and covering the mother's breast with hurts for which she could find no balm in this world, nor knew how to seek it in another. At last, her shot being all expended, the child stood still and gazed at Hester with that little, laughing image of a fiend peeping out—or, whether it peeped or no, her mother so imagined it—from the unsearchable abyss of her black eyes.

"Child, what art thou?" cried the mother.

"O, I am your little Pearl!" answered the child.

But, while she said it, Pearl laughed, and began to dance up and down, with the humorsome gesticulation of a little imp whose next freak might be to fly up the chimney.

"Art thou my child, in very truth?" asked Hester.

Nor did she put the question altogether idly, but, for the moment with a portion of genuine earnestness; for such was Pearl's wonderful intelligence that her mother half doubted whether she were not acquainted with the secret spell of her existence, and might not now reveal herself.

"Yes; I am little Pearl!" repeated the child, continuing her antics.

"Thou art not my child! Thou art no Pearl of mine!" said

the mother, half playfully; for it was often the case that a sportive impulse came over her, in the midst of her deepest suffering. "Tell me, then, what thou art and who sent thee hither?"

"Tell me, Mother!" said the child seriously, coming up to Hester, and pressing herself close to her knees. "Do thou tell me!"

"Thy Heavenly Father sent thee!" answered Hester Prynne

But she said it with a hesitation that did not escape the acuteness of the child. Whether moved only by her ordinary freakishness, or because an evil spirit prompted her, she put up her small forefinger, and touched the scarlet letter.

"He did not send me!" cried she, positively. "' have no Heavenly Father!"

"Hush, Pearl, hush! Thou must not talk so!' answered the mother, suppressing a groan. "He sent us all into this world. He sent even me, thy mother. Then, much more, thee! Or, if not, thou strange and elfish child, whence didst thou come?"

"Tell me! Tell me!" repeated Pearl, no longer seriously, but laughing, and capering about the floor. "It is thou that must tell me!"

But Hester could not resolve the query, being herself in a dismal labyrinth of doubt. She remembered—betwixt a smile and a shudder—the talk of the neighboring townspeople, who, seeking vainly elsewhere for the child's paternity, and observing some of her odd attributes, had given out that poor little Pearl was a demon offspring; such as, ever since old Catholic times, had occasionally been seen on earth, through the agency of their mother's sin, and to promote some foul and wicked purpose. Luther, according to the scandal of his monkish enemies, was a brat of that hellish breed; nor was Pearl the only child to whom this inauspicious origin was assigned, among the New England Puritans.

VII

The Governor's Hall

HESTER Prynne went one day to the mansion of Governor Bellingham with a pair of gloves, which she had fringed and embroidered to his order, and which were to be worn on some great occasion of state; for, though the chances of a popular election had caused this former ruler to descend a step or two from the highest rank, he still held an honorable and influential place among the colonial magistracy.

Another and far more important reason than the delivery of a pair of embroidered gloves impelled Hester, at this time, to seek an interview with a personage of so much power and activity in the affairs of the settlement. It had reached her ears that there was a design on the part of some of the leading inhabitants, cherishing the more rigid order of principles in religion and government, to deprive her of her child. On the supposition that Pearl, as already hinted, was of demon origin, these good people not unreasonably argued that a Christian interest in the mother's soul required them to remove such a stumbling block from her path. If the child, on the other hand, were really capable of moral and religious growth and possessed the elements of ultimate salvation, then, surely, it would enjoy all the fairer prospect of these advantages by being transferred to wiser and better guardianship than Hester Prynne's. Among those who promoted the design, Governor Bellingham was said to be one of the most busy. It may appear singular, and, indeed, not a little ludicrous, that an affair of this kind, which in later days would have been referred to no higher jurisdiction than that of the selectmen of the town, should then have been a question publicly discussed, and on which statesmen of eminence took sides. At that epoch of pristine simplicity, however, matters of even slighter public interest, and of far less intrinsic weight, than the welfare of Hester and her child were strangely mixed up with the deliberations of legislators and acts of state. The period was hardly, if at all, earlier than that of our story, when a dispute concerning the right of property in a pig not only caused a fierce and bitter contest in the legislative body of the colony, but resulted in an important modification of the framework itself of the legislature.

Full of concern, therefore—but so conscious of her own right that it seemed scarcely an unequal match between the public, on the one side, and a lonely woman, backed by the sympathies of nature, on the other—Hester Prynne set forth from her solitary cottage. Little Pearl, of course, was her companion. She was now of an age to run lightly along by her mother's side, and, constantly in motion from morn till sunset, could have accomplished a much longer journey than that before her. Often, nevertheless, more from caprice than necessity, she demanded to be taken up in arms; but was soon as imperious to be set down again, and frisked onward before Hester on the grassy pathway, with many a harmless trip and tumble. We have spoken of Pearl's rich and luxuriant beauty; a beauty that shone with deep and vivid tints; a bright complexion, eyes possessing intensity both of depth and glow, and hair already of a deep, glossy brown, and which, in after years, would be nearly akin to black. There was fire in her and throughout her; she seemed the unpremeditated offshoot of a passionate moment. Her mother, in contriving the child's garb, had allowed the gorgeous tendencies of her imagination their full play; arraying her in a crimson velvet tunic of a peculiar cut, abundantly embroidered with fantasies and flourishes of gold thread. So much strength of coloring, which must have given a wan and pallid aspect to cheeks of a fainter bloom, was admirably adapted to Pearl's beauty and made her the very brightest little jet of flame that ever danced upon the earth.

But it was a remarkable attribute of this garb, and, indeed, of the child's whole appearance, that it irresistibly and inevitably reminded the beholder of the token which Hester Prynne was doomed to wear upon her bosom. It was the scarlet letter in another form; the scarlet letter endowed with life! The mother herself—as if the red ignominy were so deeply scorched into her brain that all her conceptions assumed its form—had carefully wrought out the similitude; lavishing many hours of morbid ingenuity to create an analogy between the object of her affection and the emblem of her guilt and torture. But, in truth, Pearl was the one as well as the other; and only in consequence of that identity had Hester contrived so perfectly to represent the scarlet letter in her appearance.

As the two wayfarers came within the precincts of the town, the children of the Puritans looked up from their play—or what passed for play with those sombre little urchins—and spoke gravely one to another:

"Behold, verily, there is the woman of the scarlet letter, and, of a truth, moreover, there is the likeness of the scarlet letter running along by her side! Come, therefore, and let us fling mud at them!"

But Pearl, who was a dauntless child, after frowning, stamping her foot, and shaking her little hand with a variety of threatening gestures, suddenly made a rush at the knot of her enemies, and put them all to flight. She resembled, in her fierce pursuit of them, an infant pestilence—the scarlet fever, or some such half-fledged angel of judgment—whose mission was to punish the sins of the rising generation. She screamed and shouted, too, with a terrific volume of sound which, doubtless, caused the hearts of the fugitives to quake within them. The victory accomplished, Pearl returned quietly to her mother, and looked up, smiling, into her face.

Without further adventure, they reached the dwelling of Governor Bellingham. This was a large wooden house, built in a fashion of which there are specimens still extant in the streets of our elder towns; now mossgrown, crumbling to decay, and melancholy at heart with the many sorrowful or joyful occurrences, remembered or forgotten, that have happened and passed away within their dusky chambers. Then, however, there was the freshness of the passing year on its exterior, and the cheerfulness, gleaming forth from the sunny windows, of a human habitation into which death had never entered. It had, indeed, a very cheery aspect; the walls being overspread with a kind of stucco, in which fragments of broken glass were plentifully intermixed; so that, when the sunshine fell aslant-wise over the front of the edifice, it glittered and sparkled as if diamonds had been flung against it by the double handful. The brilliancy might have befitted Aladdin's palace rather than the mansion of a grave old Puritan ruler. It was further decorated with strange and seemingly cabalistic figures and diagrams, suitable to the quaint taste of the age, which had been drawn in the stucco when newly laid on, and had now grown hard and durable, for admiration of after times.

Pearl, looking at this bright wonder of a house, began to caper and dance, and imperatively required that the whole breadth of sunshine should be stripped off its front, and given her to play with.

"No, my little Pearl!" said her mother. "Thou must gather thine own sunshine. I have none to give thee!"

They approached the door, which was of an arched form, and flanked on each side by a narrow tower or projection of the edifice, in both of which were lattice windows, with wooden shutters to close over them at need. Lifting the iron hammer that hung at the portal, Hester Prynne gave a summons, which was answered by one of the Governor's bond-servants; a free-born Englishman, but now a seven years' slave. During that term he was to be the property of his master, and as much a commodity of bargain and sale as an ox, or a joint-stool. The serf wore the blue coat, which was the customary garb of serving-men at that period, and long before, in the old hereditary halls of England.

"Is the worshipful Governor Bellingham within?" inquired Hester.

"Yea, forsooth," replied the bond-servant, staring with wide-open eyes at the scarlet letter, which, being a new-comer in the country, he had never before seen. "Yea, his honorable worship is within. But he hath a godly minister or two with him, and likewise a leech. Ye may not see his worship now."

"Nevertheless, I will enter," answered Hester Prynne; and the bond-servant, perhaps judging from the decision of her air and the glittering symbols in her bosom that she was a great lady in the land, offered no opposition.

So the mother and little Pearl were admitted into the hall of entrance. With many variations suggested by the nature of his building-materials, diversity of climate, and a differ-

ent mode of social life, Governor Bellingham had planned
his new habitation after the residences of gentlemen of fair
estate in his native land. Here, then, was a wide and reasonably lofty hall, extending through the whole depth of the
house and forming a medium of general communication,
more or less directly, with all the other apartments. At one
extremity, this spacious room was lighted by the windows of
the two towers, which formed a small recess on either side
of the portal. At the other end, though partly muffled by a
curtain, it was more powerfully illuminated by one of those
embowed hall windows which we read of in old books, and
which was provided with a deep and cushioned seat. Here,
on the cushion, lay a folio tome, probably of the Chronicles
of England or other such substantial literature; even as, in
our own days, we scatter gilded volumes on the centre-
table, to be turned over by the casual guest. The furniture
of the hall consisted of some ponderous chairs, the backs of
which were elaborately carved with wreaths of oaken flowers; and likewise a table in the same taste; the whole being
of the Elizabethan age, or perhaps earlier, and heirlooms,
transferred hither from the Governor's paternal home. On
the table—in token that the sentiment of old English hospitality had not been left behind—stood a large pewter tan-
kard, at the bottom of which, had Hester or Pearl peeped
into it, they might have seen the frothy remnant of a recent
draught of ale.

On the wall hung a row of portraits, representing the
forefathers of the Bellingham lineage, some with armor on
their breasts, and others with stately ruffs and robes of
peace. All were characterized by the sternness and severity
which old portraits so invariably put on; as if they were the
ghosts, rather than the pictures, of departed worthies, and
were gazing with harsh and intolerant criticism at the pursuits and enjoyments of living men.

At about the centre of the oaken panels that lined the hall
was suspended a suit of mail, not, like the pictures, an
ancestral relic, but of the most modern date; for it had been
manufactured by a skilful armorer in London the same year
in which Governor Bellingham came over to New England.
There was a steel headpiece, a cuirass, a gorget, and greaves,
with a pair of gauntlets and a sword hanging beneath; all,
and especially the helmet and breastplate, so highly bur-

nished as to glow with white radiance and scatter an illumination everywhere about upon the floor. This bright panoply was not meant for mere idle show, but had been worn by the Governor on many a solemn muster and training field, and had glittered, moreover, at the head of a regiment in the Pequod war. For, though bred a lawyer and accustomed to speak of Bacon, Coke, Noye, and Finch as his professional associates, the exigencies of this new country had transformed Governor Bellingham into a soldier, as well as a statesman and ruler.

Little Pearl—who was as greatly pleased with the gleaming armor as she had been with the glittering frontispiece of the house—spent some time looking into the polished mirror of the breastplate.

"Mother," cried she, "I see you here. Look! Look!"

Hester looked, by way of humoring the child; and she saw that, owing to the peculiar effect of this convex mirror, the scarlet letter was represented in exaggerated and gigantic proportions, so as to be greatly the most prominent feature of her appearance. In truth, she seemed absolutely hidden behind it. Pearl pointed upward, also, at a similar picture in the headpiece, smiling at her mother, with the elfish intelligence that was so familiar an expression on her small physiognomy. That look of naughty merriment was likewise reflected in the mirror, with so much breadth and intensity of effect, that it made Hester Prynne feel as if it could not be the image of her own child, but of an imp who was seeking to mould itself into Pearl's shape.

"Come along, Pearl," said she, drawing her away. "Come and look into this fair garden. It may be we shall see flowers there; more beautiful ones than we find in the woods."

Pearl, accordingly, ran to the bow window at the further end of the hall and looked along the vista of a garden walk, carpeted with closely shaven grass and bordered with some rude and immature attempt at shrubbery. But the proprietor appeared already to have relinquished as hopeless the effort to perpetuate on this side of the Atlantic, in a hard soil and amid the close struggle for subsistence, the native English taste for ornamental gardening. Cabbages grew in plain sight; and a pumpkin vine, rooted at some distance, had run across the intervening space and deposited one of its gigantic products directly beneath the hall window; as if to warn the Governor that this great lump of vegetable gold was as rich an ornament as New England earth would offer him. There were a few rosebushes, however, and a number of apple trees, probably the descendants of those planted by the Reverend Mr. Blackstone, the first settler of the peninsula, that half-mythological personage, who rides through our early annals seated on the back of a bull.

Pearl, seeing the rosebushes, began to cry for a red rose, and would not be pacified.

"Hush, child, hush!" said her mother, earnestly. "Do not cry, dear little Pearl! I hear voices in the garden. The Governor is coming, and gentlemen along with him!"

In fact, adown the vista of the garden avenue a number of persons were seen approaching towards the house. Pearl, in utter scorn of her mother's attempt to quiet her, gave an eldritch scream and then became silent; not from any notion of obedience, but because the quick and mobile curiosity of her disposition was excited by the appearance of these new personages.

VIII

The Elf-Child and the Minister

GOVERNOR Bellingham, in a loose gown and easy cap—such as elderly gentlemen loved to endue themselves with, in their domestic privacy—walked foremost, and appeared to be showing off his estate and expatiating on his projected improvements. The wide circumference of an elaborate ruff beneath his gray beard, in the antiquated fashion of King James' reign, caused his head to look not a little like that of John the Baptist in a charger. The impression made by his aspect, so rigid and severe, and frostbitten with more than autumnal age, was hardly in keeping with the appliances of worldly enjoyment wherewith he had evidently done his utmost to surround himself. But it is an error to suppose that our grave forefathers—though accustomed to speak and think of human existence as a state merely of trial and warfare, and though unfeignedly prepared to sacrifice goods and life at the behest of duty—made it a matter of conscience to reject such means of comfort, or even luxury, as lay fairly within their grasp. This creed was never taught, for instance, by the venerable pastor, John Wilson, whose beard, white as a snowdrift, was seen over Governor Bellingham's shoulder; while its wearer suggested that pears and peaches might yet be naturalized in the New England climate, and that purple grapes might possibly be compelled to flourish against the sunny garden wall. The old clergyman, nurtured at the rich bosom of the English Church, had a long-established and legitimate taste for all good and comfortable things; and however stern he might show himself in the pulpit or in his public reproof of such transgressions as that of Hester Prynne, still, the genial benevolence of his private life had won him warmer affection than was accorded to any of his professional contemporaries.

Behind the Governor and Mr. Wilson came two other guests; one, the Reverend Arthur Dimmesdale, whom the reader may remember, as having taken a brief and reluctant part in the scene of Hester Prynne's disgrace; and, in close companionship with him, old Roger Chillingworth, a person of great skill in physic, who, for two or three years past, had been settled in the town. It was understood that this learned man was the physician as well as friend of the young minister, whose health had severely suffered, of late, by his too unreserved self-sacrifice to the labors and duties of the pastoral relation.

The Governor, in advance of his visitors, ascended one or two steps, and, throwing open the leaves of the great hall window, found himself close to little Pearl. The shadow of the curtain fell on Hester Prynne, and partially concealed her.

"What have we here?" said Governor Bellingham, looking with surprise at the scarlet little figure before him. "I profess, I have never seen the like, since my days of vanity, in old King James' time, when I was wont to esteem it a high favor to be admitted to a court mask! There used to be a swarm of these small apparitions, in holiday time; and we called them children of the Lord of Misrule. But how gat such a guest into my hall?"

"Ay, indeed!" cried good old Mr. Wilson. "What little bird of scarlet plumage may this be? Methinks I have seen just such figures when the sun has been shining through a richly painted window and tracing out the golden and crimson images across the floor. But that was in the old land. Prithee, young one, who art thou, and what has ailed thy mother to bedizen thee in this strange fashion? Art thou a Christian child—ha? Dost know thy catechism? Or art thou one of those naughty elfs or fairies whom we thought to have left behind us, with other relics of Papistry, in merry old England?"

"I am Mother's child," answered the scarlet vision, "and my name is Pearl!"

"Pearl?—Ruby, rather!—or Coral!—or Red Rose, at the very least, judging from thy hue!" responded the old minister, putting forth his hand in a vain attempt to pat little Pearl on the cheek. "But where is this mother of thine? Ah! I see," he added; and, turning to Governor Bellingham, whispered, "This is the selfsame child of whom we have held speech together; and behold here the unhappy woman, Hester Prynne, her mother!"

"Sayest thou so?" cried the Governor. "Nay, we might have judged that such a child's mother must needs be a scarlet woman, and a worthy type of her of Babylon! But she comes at a good time; and we will look into this matter forthwith."

Governor Bellingham stepped through the window into the hall, followed by his three guests.

"Hester Prynne," said he, fixing his naturally stern regard on the wearer of the scarlet letter, "there hath been much question concerning thee, of late. The point hath been weightily discussed, whether we, that are of authority and influence, do well discharge our consciences by trusting an immortal soul, such as there is in yonder child, to the guidance of one who hath stumbled and fallen amid the pitfalls of this world. Speak thou, the child's own mother! Were it not, thinkest thou, for thy little one's temporal and eternal welfare, that she be taken out of thy charge, and clad soberly, and disciplined strictly, and instructed in the truths of heaven and earth? What canst thou do for the child, in this kind?"

"I can teach my little Pearl what I have learned from this!" answered Hester Prynne, laying her finger on the red token.

"Woman, it is thy badge of shame!" replied the stern magistrate. "It is because of the stain which that letter indicates, that we would transfer thy child to other hands."

"Nevertheless," said the mother calmly, though growing more pale, "this badge hath taught me—it daily teaches me—it is teaching me at this moment—lessons whereof my child may be the wiser and better, albeit they can profit nothing to myself."

"We will judge warily," said Bellingham, "and look well what we are about to do. Good Master Wilson, I pray you, examine this Pearl—since that is her name—and see whether she hath had such Christian nurture as befits a child of her age."

The old minister seated himself in an armchair, and made an effort to draw Pearl betwixt his knees. But the child, unaccustomed to the touch or familiarity of any but her mother, escaped through the open window, and stood on the upper step, looking like a wild tropical bird of rich plumage ready to take flight into the upper air. Mr. Wilson, not a little astonished at this outbreak—for he was a grandfather sort of personage, and usually a vast favorite with children—essayed, however, to proceed with the examination.

"Pearl," said he, with great solemnity, "thou must take heed to instruction, that so, in due season, thou mayest wear in thy bosom the pearl of great price. Canst thou tell me, my child, who made thee?"

Now Pearl knew well enough who made her; for Hester Prynne, the daughter of a pious home, very soon after her talk with the child about her Heavenly Father, had begun to inform her of those truths which the human spirit, at whatever stage of immaturity, imbibes with such eager interest. Pearl, therefore, so large were the attainments of her three years' lifetime, could have borne a fair examination in the New England primer, or the first column of the Westminster Catechism, although unacquainted with the outward form of either of those celebrated works. But that perversity, which all children have more or less of, and of which little Pearl had a tenfold portion, now, at the most inopportune moment, took thorough possession of her and closed her lips, or impelled her to speak words amiss. After putting her fingers in her mouth, with many ungracious refusals to answer good Mr. Wilson's question, the child finally announced that she had not been made at all, but had been plucked by her mother off the bush of wild roses that grew by the prison door.

This fantasy was probably suggested by the near proximity of the Governor's red roses, as Pearl stood outside of the window; together with her recollection of the prison rosebush, which she had passed in coming hither.

Old Roger Chillingworth, with a smile on his face, whispered something in the young clergyman's ear. Hester Prynne looked at the man of skill, and even then, with her fate hanging in the balance, was startled to perceive what a change had come over his features—how much uglier they were—how his dark complexion seemed to have grown dusk-

ier, and his figure more misshapen—since the days when she
had familiarly known him. She met his eyes for an instant,
but was immediately constrained to give all her attention to
the scene now going forward.

"This is awful!" cried the Governor, slowly recovering
from the astonishment into which Pearl's response had thrown
him. "Here is a child of three years old, and she cannot tell
who made her! Without question, she is equally in the dark
as to her soul, its present depravity, and future destiny!
Methinks, gentlemen, we need inquire no further."

Hester caught hold of Pearl, and drew her forcibly into
her arms, confronting the old Puritan magistrate with almost
a fierce expression. Alone in the world, cast off by it, and
with this sole treasure to keep her heart alive, she felt that
she possessed indefeasible rights against the world, and was
ready to defend them to the death.

"God gave me the child!" cried she. "He gave her in
requital of all things else, which ye had taken from me. She
is my happiness!—she is my torture, none the less! Pearl
keeps me here in life! Pearl punishes me too! See ye not,
she is the scarlet letter, only capable of being loved, and so
endowed with a millionfold the power of retribution for my
sin? Ye shall not take her! I will die first!"

"My poor woman," said the not unkind old minister, "the
child shall be well cared for!—far better than thou canst do it."

"God gave her into my keeping," repeated Hester Prynne,
raising her voice almost to a shriek. "I will not give her
up!"—And here, by a sudden impulse, she turned to the
young clergyman, Mr. Dimmesdale, at whom, up to this
moment, she had seemed hardly so much as once to direct
her eyes. "Speak thou for me!" cried she. "Thou wast my
pastor, and hadst charge of my soul, and knowest me better
than these men can. I will not lose the child! Speak for me!
Thou knowest—for thou hast sympathies which these men
lack—thou knowest what is in my heart, and what are a
mother's rights, and how much the stronger they are when
that mother has but her child and the scarlet letter! Look
thou to it! I will not lose the child! Look to it!"

At this wild and singular appeal, which indicated that
Hester Prynne's situation had provoked her to little less
than madness, the young minister at once came forward,
pale, and holding his hand over his heart, as was his custom

whenever his peculiarly nervous temperament was thrown into agitation. He looked now more careworn and emaciated than as we described him at the scene of Hester's public ignominy; and whether it were his failing health, or whatever the cause might be, his large dark eyes had a world of pain in their troubled and melancholy depth.

"There is truth in what she says," began the minister, with a voice sweet, tremulous, but powerful, insomuch that the hall reëchoed, and the hollow armor rang with it—"truth in what Hester says, and in the feeling which inspires her! God gave her the child, and gave her, too, an instinctive knowledge of its nature and requirements—both seemingly so peculiar—which no other mortal being can possess. And, moreover, is there not a quality of awful sacredness in the relation between this mother and this child?"

"Ay!—how is that, good Master Dimmesdale?" interrupted the Governor. "Make that plain, I pray you!"

"It must be even so," resumed the minister. "For, if we deem it otherwise, do we not thereby say that the Heavenly Father, the Creator of all flesh, hath lightly recognized a deed of sin and made of no account the distinction between unhallowed lust and holy love? This child of its father's guilt and its mother's shame hath come from the hand of God, to work in many ways upon her heart, who pleads so earnestly, and with such bitterness of spirit, the right to keep her. It was meant for a blessing; for the one blessing of her life! It was meant, doubtless, as the mother herself hath told us, for a retribution too; a torture to be felt at many an un-thought-of moment; a pang, a sting, an ever-recurring agony, in the midst of a troubled joy! Hath she not expressed this thought in the garb of the poor child, so forcibly reminding us of that red symbol which sears her bosom?"

"Well said, again!" cried good Mr. Wilson. "I feared the woman had no better thought than to make a mountebank of her child!"

"O, not so!—not so!" continued Mr. Dimmesdale. "She recognizes, believe me, the solemn miracle which God hath wrought, in the existence of that child. And may she feel, too—what, methinks, is the very truth—that this boon was meant above all things else, to keep the mother's soul alive, and to preserve her from blacker depths of sin into which Satan might else have sought to plunge her! Therefore 'it is good for this poor, sinful woman that she hath an infant immortality, a being capable of eternal joy or sorrow, confided to her care—to be trained up by her to righteousness —to remind her, at every moment, of her fall—but yet to teach her, as it were by the Creator's sacred pledge, that, if she bring the child to heaven, the child also will bring its parent thither! Herein is the sinful mother happier than the sinful father. For Hester Prynne's sake, then, and no less for the poor child's sake, let us leave them as Providence hath seen fit to place them!"

"You speak, my friend, with a strange earnestness," said old Roger Chillingworth, smiling at him.

"And there is a weighty import in what my young brother hath spoken," added the Reverend Mr. Wilson. "What say you, worshipful Master Bellingham? Hath he not pleaded well for the poor woman?"

"Indeed hath he," answered the magistrate, "and hath adduced such arguments that we will even leave the matter as it now stands, so long, at least, as there shall be no further scandal in the woman. Care must be had, nevertheless, to put the child to due and stated examination in the catechism, at thy hands or Master Dimmesdale's. Moreover, at a proper season, the tithing-men must take heed that she go both to school and to meeting."

The young minister, on ceasing to speak, had withdrawn a few steps from the group and stood with his face partially concealed in the heavy folds of the window curtain, while the shadow of his figure, which the sunlight cast upon the floor, was tremulous with the vehemence of his appeal. Pearl, that wild and flighty little elf, stole softly towards him, and taking his hand in the grasp of both of her own, laid her cheek against it; a caress so tender, and withal so unobtrusive, that her mother, who was looking on, asked herself, "Is that my Pearl?" Yet she knew that there was love in the child's heart, although it mostly revealed itself in passion, and hardly twice in her lifetime had been softened by such gentleness as now. The minister—for, save the longsought regards of woman, nothing is sweeter than these marks of childish preference, accorded spontaneously by a spiritual instinct, and therefore seeming to imply in us something truly worthy to be loved—the minister looked round, laid his hand on the child's head, hesitated an instant, and then kissed her brow. Little Pearl's unwonted mood of sentiment lasted no longer; she laughed, and went capering down the hall, so airily, that old Mr. Wilson raised a question whether even her tiptoes touched the floor.

"The little baggage hath witchcraft in her, I profess," said he to Mr. Dimmesdale. "She needs no old woman's broomstick to fly withal!"

"A strange child!" remarked old Roger Chillingworth. "It is easy to see the mother's part in her. Would it be beyond a philosopher's research, think ye, gentlemen, to analyze that child's nature, and, from its make and mould, to give a shrewd guess at the father?"

"Nay; it would be sinful, in such a question, to follow the clew of profane philosophy," said Mr. Wilson. "Better to fast and pray upon it; and still better, it may be, to leave the mystery as we find it, unless Providence reveal it of its own accord. Thereby, every good Christian man hath a title to show a father's kindness towards the poor, deserted babe."

The affair being so satisfactorily concluded, Hester Prynne, with Pearl, departed from the house. As they descended the steps, it is averred that the lattice of a chamber window was thrown open, and forth into the sunny day was thrust the face of Mistress Hibbins, Governor Bellingham's bitter-tempered sister, and the same who, a few years later, was executed as a witch.

"Hist, hist!" said she, while her ill-omened physiognomy seemed to cast a shadow over the cheerful newness of the house. "Wilt thou go with us tonight? There will be a merry company in the forest; and I well-nigh promised the Black Man that comely Hester Prynne should make one."

"Make my excuse to him, so please you!" answered Hester, with a triumphant smile. "I must tarry at home, and keep watch over my little Pearl. Had they taken her from me, I would willingly have gone with thee into the forest, and signed my name in the Black Man's book too, and that with mine own blood!"

"We shall have thee there anon!" said the witch-lady, frowning, as she drew back her head.

But here—if we suppose this interview betwixt Mistress Hibbins and Hester Prynne to be authentic, and not a parable—was already an illustration of the young minister's argument against sundering the relation of a fallen mother to the offspring of her frailty. Even thus early had the child saved her from Satan's snare.

IX

The Leech

UNDER the appellation of Roger Chillingworth, the reader will remember, was hidden another name, which its former wearer had resolved should never more be spoken. It has been related, how, in the crowd that witnessed Hester Prynne's ignominious exposure, stood a man, elderly, travel-worn, who, just emerging from the perilous wilderness, beheld the woman, in whom he hoped to find embodied the warmth and cheerfulness of home, set up as a type of sin before the people. Her matronly fame was trodden under all men's feet. Infamy was babbling around her in the public market place. For her kindred, should the tidings ever reach them, and for the companions of her unspotted life, there remained nothing but the contagion of her dishonor, which would not fail to be distributed in strict accordance and proportion with the intimacy and sacredness of their previous relationship. Then why—since the choice was with himself—should the individual, whose connection with the fallen woman had been the most intimate and sacred of them all, come forward to vindicate his claim to an inheritance so little desirable? He resolved not to be pilloried beside her on her pedestal of shame. Unknown to all but Hester Prynne, and possessing the lock and key of her silence, he chose to withdraw his name from the roll of mankind, and, as regarded his former ties and interests, to vanish out of life as completely as if he indeed lay at the bottom of the ocean, whither rumor had long ago consigned him. This purpose once effected, new interests would immediately spring up, and likewise a new purpose; dark, it is true, if not guilty, but of force enough to engage the full strength of his faculties.

In pursuance of this resolve, he took up his residence in the Puritan town as Roger Chillingworth, without other introduction than the learning and intelligence of which he possessed more than a common measure. As his studies at a previous period of his life had made him extensively acquainted with the medical science of the day, it was as a physician that he presented himself, and as such was cordially received. Skilful men of the medical and chirurgical profession were of rare occurrence in the colony. They seldom, it would appear, partook of the religious zeal that brought other emigrants across the Atlantic. In their researches into the human frame, it may be that the higher and more subtle faculties of such men were materialized, and that they lost the spiritual view of existence amid the intricacies of that wondrous mechanism, which seemed to involve art enough to comprise all of life within itself. At all events, the health of the good town of Boston, so far as medicine had aught to do with it, had hitherto lain in the guardianship of an aged deacon and apothecary, whose piety and godly deportment were stronger testimonials in his favor than any that he could have produced in the shape of a diploma. The only surgeon was one who combined the occasional exercise of that noble art with the daily and habitual flourish of a razor. To such a professional body Roger Chillingworth was a brilliant acquisition. He soon manifested his familiarity with the ponderous and imposing machinery of antique physic, in which every remedy contained a multitude of far-fetched and heterogeneous ingredients as elaborately compounded as if the proposed result had been the Elixir of Life. In his Indian captivity, moreover, he had gained much knowledge of the properties of native herbs and roots; nor did he conceal from his patients, that these simple medicines, Nature's boon to the untutored savage, had quite as large a share of his own confidence as the European pharmacopœia, which so many learned doctors had spent centuries in elaborating.

This learned stranger was exemplary, as regarded, at least, the outward forms of a religious life, and, early after his arrival, had chosen for his spiritual guide the Reverend Mr. Dimmesdale. The young divine, whose scholar-like renown

still lived in Oxford, was considered by his more fervent
admirers as little less than a heavenly-ordained apostle, destined, should he live and labor for the ordinary term of life,
to do as great deeds for the now feeble New England
Church, as the early Fathers had achieved for the infancy of
the Christian faith. About this period, however, the health
of Mr. Dimmesdale had evidently begun to fail. By those
best acquainted with his habits, the paleness of the young
minister's cheek was accounted for by his too earnest devotion to study, his scrupulous fulfilment of parochial duty,
and, more than all, by the fasts and vigils of which he made
a frequent practice, in order to keep the grossness of this
earthly state from clogging and obscuring his spiritual lamp.
Some declared, that, if Mr. Dimmesdale were really going
to die, it was cause enough that the world was not worthy to
be any longer trodden by his feet. He himself, on the other
hand, with characteristic humility, avowed his belief that if
Providence should see fit to remove him, it would be because of his own unworthiness to perform its humblest mission here on earth. With all this difference of opinion as to
the cause of his decline, there could be no question of the
fact. His form grew emaciated; his voice, though still rich
and sweet had a certain melancholy prophecy of decay in it;
he was often observed, on any slight alarm or other sudden
accident, to put his hand over his heart with first a flush and
then a paleness, indicative of pain.

Such was the young clergyman's condition, and so imminent the prospect that his dawning light would be extinguished, all untimely, when Roger Chillingworth made
his advent to the town. His first entry on the scene, few
people could tell whence, dropping down, as it were, out of
the sky, or starting from the nether earth, had an aspect of
mystery which was easily heightened to the miraculous. He
was now known to be a man of skill; it was observed that he
gathered herbs, and the blossoms of wild-flowers, and dug
up roots, and plucked off twigs from the forest trees, like
one acquainted with hidden virtues in what was valueless to
common eyes. He was heard to speak of Sir Kenelm Digby,
and other famous men—whose scientific attainments were
esteemed hardly less than supernatural—as having been his
correspondents or associates. Why, with such rank in the
learned world, had he come hither? What could he, whose

sphere was in great cities, be seeking in the wilderness? In answer to this query, a rumor gained ground—and, however absurd, was entertained by some very sensible people—that Heaven had wrought an absolute miracle by transporting an eminent Doctor of Physic from a German university bodily through the air and setting him down at the door of Mr. Dimmesdale's study! Individuals of wiser faith, indeed, who knew that Heaven promotes its purposes without aiming at the stage effect of what is called miraculous interposition, were inclined to see a providential hand in Roger Chillingworth's so opportune arrival.

This idea was countenanced by the strong interest which the physician ever manifested in the young clergyman; he attached himself to him as a parishioner, and sought to win a friendly regard and confidence from his naturally reserved sensibility. He expressed great alarm at his pastor's state of health, but was anxious to attempt the cure, and, if early undertaken, seemed not despondent of a favorable result. The elders, the deacons, the motherly dames, and the young and fair maidens of Mr. Dimmesdale's flock were alike importunate that he should make trial of the physician's frankly offered skill. Mr. Dimmesdale gently repelled their entreaties.

"I need no medicine," said he.

But how could the young minister say so, when, with every successive Sabbath, his cheek was paler and thinner, and his voice more tremulous than before—when it had now become a constant habit, rather than a casual gesture, to press his hand over his heart? Was he weary of his labors? Did he wish to die? These questions were solemnly propounded to Mr. Dimmesdale by the elder ministers of Boston and the deacons of his church, who, to use their own phrase, "dealt with him" on the sin of rejecting the aid which Providence so manifestly held out. He listened in silence, and finally promised to confer with the physician.

"Were it God's will," said the Reverend Mr. Dimmesdale, when, in fulfilment of this pledge, he requested old Roger Chillingworth's professional advice, "I could be well content that my labors, and my sorrows, and my sins, and my pains, should shortly end with me, and what is earthly of them be buried in my grave, and the spiritual go with me to my eternal state, rather than that you should put your skill to the proof in my behalf."

"Ah," replied Roger Chillingworth, with that quietness which, whether imposed or natural, marked all his deportment, "it is thus that a young clergyman is apt to speak. Youthful men, not having taken a deep root, give up their hold of life so easily! And saintly men, who walk with God on earth, would fain be away, to walk with him on the golden pavements of the New Jerusalem."

"Nay," rejoined the young minister, putting his hand to his heart, with a flush of pain flitting over his brow, "were I worthier to walk there, I could be better content to toil here."

"Good men ever interpret themselves too meanly," said the physician.

In this manner, the mysterious old Roger Chillingworth became the medical adviser of the Reverend Mr. Dimmesdale. As not only the disease interested the physician, but he was strongly moved to look into the character and qualities of the patient, these two men, so different in age, came gradually to spend much time together. For the sake of the minister's health, and to enable the leech to gather plants with healing balm in them, they took long walks on the seashore or in the forest; mingling various talk with the plash and murmur of the waves, and the solemn wind anthem among the treetops. Often, likewise, one was the guest of the other in his place of study and retirement. There was a fascination for the minister in the company of the man of science, in whom he recognized an intellectual cultivation of no moderate depth or scope, together with a range and freedom of ideas that he would have vainly looked for among the members of his own profession. In truth, he was startled, if not shocked, to find this attribute in the physician. Mr. Dimmesdale was a true priest, a true religionist, with the reverential sentiment largely developed, and an order of mind that impelled itself powerfully along the track of a creed and wore its passage continually deeper with the lapse of time. In no state of society would he have been what is called a man of liberal views; it would always be essential to his peace to feel the pressure of a faith upon him, supporting, while it confined him within its iron framework. Not the less, however, though with a tremulous enjoyment, did he feel the occasional relief of looking at the universe through the medium of another kind of intellect than those with which he habitually held converse. It was as if a window were thrown open, admitting a freer atmosphere into the close and stifled study where his life was wasting itself away, amid lamplight, or obstructed day-beams, and the musty fragrance, be it sensual or moral, that exhales from books. But the air was too fresh and chill to be long breathed with comfort. So the minister, and the physician with him, withdrew again within the limits of what their church defined as orthodox.

Thus Roger Chillingworth scrutinized his patient carefully, both as he saw him in his ordinary life, keeping an accustomed pathway in the range of thoughts familiar to him, and as he appeared when thrown amidst other moral scenery, the novelty of which might call out something new to the surface of his character. He deemed it essential, it would seem, to know the man before attempting to do him good. Wherever there is a heart and an intellect, the diseases of the physical frame are tinged with the peculiarities of these. In Arthur Dimmesdale, thought and imagination were so active, and sensibility so intense, that the bodily infirmity would be likely to have its groundwork there. So Roger Chillingworth—the man of skill, the kind and friendly physician—strove to go deep into his patient's bosom, delving among his principles, prying into his recollections, and probing everything with a cautious touch, like a treasure-seeker in a dark cavern. Few secrets can escape an investigator who has opportunity and license to undertake such a quest and skill to follow it up. A man burdened with a secret should especially avoid the intimacy of his physician. If the latter possess native sagacity, and a nameless something more—let us call it intuition; if he show no intrusive egotism, nor disagreeably prominent characteristics of his own; if he have the power, which must be born with him, to bring his mind into such affinity with his patient's that this last shall unawares have spoken what he imagines himself only to have thought; if such revelations be received without tumult, and acknowledged not so often by an uttered sympathy as by silence, an inarticulate breath, and here and there a word, to indicate that all is understood; if to these qualifications of a confidant be joined the advantages afforded by his recognized character as a physician—then, at some inevitable moment will the soul of the sufferer be dissolved, and flow forth in a dark but transparent stream, bringing all its mysteries into the daylight.

Roger Chillingworth possessed all, or most, of the attributes above enumerated. Nevertheless, time went on; a kind of intimacy, as we have said, grew up between these two cultivated minds, which had as wide a field as the whole sphere of human thought and study to meet upon; they discussed every topic of ethics and religion, of public affairs, and private character; they talked much, on both sides, of matters that seemed personal to themselves; and yet no secret, such as the physician fancied must exist there, ever stole out of the minister's consciousness into his companion's ear. The latter had his suspicions, indeed, that even the nature of Mr. Dimmesdale's bodily disease had never fairly been revealed to him. It was a strange reserve!

After a time, at a hint from Roger Chillingworth, the friends of Mr. Dimmesdale effected an arrangement by which the two were lodged in the same house; so that every ebb and flow of the minister's life-tide might pass under the eye of his anxious and attached physician. There was much joy throughout the town when this greatly desirable object was attained. It was held to be the best possible measure for the young clergyman's welfare; unless, indeed, as often urged by such as felt authorized to do so, he had selected some one of the many blooming damsels, spiritually devoted to him, to become his devoted wife. This latter step, however, there was no present prospect that Arthur Dimmesdale would be prevailed upon to take; he rejected all suggestions of the kind, as if priestly celibacy were one of his articles of church discipline. Doomed by his own choice, therefore, as Mr. Dimmesdale so evidently was, to eat his unsavory morsel always at another's board and endure the lifelong chill which must be his lot who seeks to warm himself only at another's fireplace, it truly seemed that this sagacious, experienced, benevolent old physician, with his concord of paternal and reverential love for the young pastor, was the very man, of all mankind, to be constantly within reach of his voice.

The new abode of the two friends was with a pious widow, of good social rank, who dwelt in a house covering pretty nearly the site on which the venerable structure of King's Chapel has since been built. It had the graveyard, originally Isaac Johnson's home-field, on one side, and so was well adapted to call up serious reflections, suited to their respective employments, in both minister and man of physic. The motherly care of the good widow assigned to Mr. Dimmesdale a front apartment with a sunny exposure, and heavy window curtains to create a noontide shadow when desirable. The walls were hung round with tapestry, said to be from the Gobelin looms, and, at all events, representing the Scriptural story of David and Bathsheba, and Nathan the Prophet, in colors still unfaded, but which made the fair woman of the scene almost as grimly picturesque as the woe-denouncing seer. Here, the pale clergyman piled up his library, rich with parchment-bound folios of the Fathers and the lore of Rabbis and monkish erudition, of which the Protestant divines, even while they vilified and decried that class of writers, were yet constrained often to avail themselves. On the other side of the house, old Roger Chillingworth arranged his study and laboratory; not such as a modern man of science would reckon even tolerably complete, but provided with a distilling apparatus and the means of compounding drugs and chemicals, which the practised alchemist knew well how to turn to purpose. With such commodiousness of situation, these two learned persons sat themselves down, each in his own domain, yet familiarly passing from one apartment to the other, and bestowing a mutual and not incurious inspection into one another's business.

And the Reverend Arthur Dimmesdale's best discerning friends, as we have intimated, very reasonably imagined that the hand of Providence had done all this for the purpose—besought in so many public, and domestic, and secret prayers—of restoring the young minister to health. But—it must now be said—another portion of the community had latterly begun to take its own view of the relation betwixt Mr. Dimmesdale and the mysterious old physician. When an uninstructed multitude attempts to see with its eyes, it is exceedingly apt to be deceived. When, however, it forms its judgment, as it usually does, on the intuitions of its great and warm heart, the conclusions thus attained are often so profound and so unerring, as to possess the character of truths supernaturally revealed. The people, in the case of which we speak, could justify its prejudice against Roger Chillingworth by no fact or argument worthy of serious refutation. There was an aged handicraftsman, it is true, who had been a citizen of London at the period of Sir Thomas Overbury's murder, now some thirty years agone; he testified to having seen the physician, under some other name which the narrator of the story had now forgotten, in company with Doctor Forman, the famous old conjurer, who was implicated in the affair of Overbury. Two or three individuals hinted that the man of skill, during his Indian captivity, had enlarged his medical attainments by joining in the incantations of the savage priests, who were universally acknowledged to be powerful enchanters, often performing seemingly miraculous cures by their skill in the black art. A large number—and many of these were persons of such sober sense and practical observation that their opinions would have been valuable in other matters—affirmed that Roger Chillingworth's aspect had undergone a remarkable change while he had dwelt in town, and especially since his abode with Mr. Dimmesdale. At first, his expression had been calm, meditative, scholar-like. Now, there was something ugly and evil in his face which they had not previously noticed, and which grew still the more obvious to sight, the oftener they looked upon him. According to the vulgar idea, the fire in his laboratory had been brought from the lower regions, and was fed with infernal fuel; and so, as might be expected, his visage was getting sooty with the smoke.

To sum up the matter, it grew to be a widely diffused opinion that the Reverend Arthur Dimmesdale, like many other personages of especial sanctity, in all ages of the Christian world, was haunted either by Satan himself, or Satan's emissary, in the guise of old Roger Chillingworth. This diabolical agent had the Divine permission, for a season, to burrow into the clergyman's intimacy and plot against his soul. No sensible man, it was confessed, could doubt on which side the victory would turn. The people looked, with an unshaken hope, to see the minister come forth out of the conflict, transfigured with the glory which he would unquestionably win. Meanwhile, nevertheless, it was sad to think of the perchance mortal agony through which he must struggle towards his triumph.

Alas! to judge from the gloom and terror in the depths of the poor minister's eyes, the battle was a sore one, and the victory anything but secure.

X

The Leech and His Patient

OLD Roger Chillingworth, throughout life, had been calm in temperament, kindly, though not of warm affections, but ever, and in all his relations with the world, a pure and upright man. He had begun an investigation, as he imagined, with the severe and equal integrity of a judge, desirous only of truth, even as if the question involved no more than the air-drawn lines and figures of a geometrical problem, instead of human passions and wrongs inflicted on himself. But, as he proceeded, a terrible fascination, a kind of fierce, though still calm, necessity seized the old man within its gripe and never set him free again, until he had done all its bidding. He now dug into the poor clergyman's heart like a miner searching for gold; or, rather, like a sexton delving into a grave, possibly in quest of a jewel that had been buried on the dead man's bosom, but likely to find nothing save mortality and corruption. Alas for his own soul, if these were what he sought!

Sometimes, a light glimmered out of the physician's eyes, burning blue and ominous, like the reflection of a furnace, or, let us say, like one of those gleams of ghastly fire that darted from Bunyan's awful doorway in the hillside and quivered on the pilgrim's face. The soil where this dark miner was working had perchance shown indications that encouraged him.

"This man," said he, at one such moment, to himself, "pure as they deem him—all spiritual as he seems—hath inherited a strong animal nature from his father or mother. Let us dig a little further in the direction of this vein!"

Then, after long search into the minister's dim interior, and turning over many precious materials in the shape of high aspirations for the welfare of his race, warm love of souls, pure sentiments, natural piety, strengthened by thought and study, and illuminated by revelation—all of which invaluable gold was perhaps no better than rubbish to the seeker—he would turn back, discouraged, and begin his quest towards another point. He groped along as stealthily, with as cautious a tread, and as wary an outlook, as a thief entering a chamber where a man lies only half asleep—or, it may be, broad awake—with purpose to steal the very treasure which this man guards as the apple of his eye. In spite of his premeditated carefulness, the floor would now and then creak; his garments would rustle; the shadow of his presence, in a forbidden proximity, would be thrown across his victim. In other words, Mr. Dimmesdale, whose sensibility of nerve often produced the effect of spiritual intuition, would become vaguely aware that something inimical to his peace had thrust itself into relation with him. But old Roger Chillingworth, too, had perceptions that were almost intuitive; and when the minister threw his startled eyes towards him, there the physician sat; his kind, watchful, sympathizing, but never intrusive friend.

Yet Mr. Dimmesdale would perhaps have seen this individual's character more perfectly if a certain morbidness, to which sick hearts are liable, had not rendered him suspicious of all mankind. Trusting no man as his friend, he could not recognize his enemy when the latter actually appeared. He therefore still kept up a familiar intercourse with him, daily receiving the old physician in his study, or visiting the laboratory, and, for recreation's sake, watching the processes by which weeds were converted into drugs of potency.

One day, leaning his forehead on his hand and his elbow on the sill of the open window that looked towards the graveyard, he talked with Roger Chillingworth while the old man was examining a bundle of unsightly plants.

"Where," asked he, with a look askance at them—for it was the clergyman's peculiarity that he seldom, nowadays, looked straightforth at any object, whether human or inanimate—"where, my kind doctor, did you gather those herbs, with such a dark, flabby leaf?"

"Even in the graveyard here at hand," answered the

physician, continuing his employment. "They are new to me. I found them growing on a grave which bore no tombstone, nor other memorial of the dead man, save these ugly weeds that have taken upon themselves to keep him in remembrance. They grew out of his heart, and typify, it may be, some hideous secret that was buried with him, and which he had done better to confess during his lifetime."

"Perchance," said Mr. Dimmesdale, "he earnestly desired it, but could not."

"And wherefore?" rejoined the physician. "Wherefore not; since all the powers of nature call so earnestly for the confession of sin, that these black weeds have sprung up out of a buried heart to make manifest an unspoken crime?"

"That, good Sir, is but a fantasy of yours," replied the minister. "There can be, if I forebode aright, no power, short of the Divine mercy, to disclose, whether by uttered words, or by type or emblem, the secrets that may be buried with a human heart. The heart, making itself guilty of such secrets, must perforce hold them, until the day when all hidden things shall be revealed. Nor have I so read or interpreted Holy Writ as to understand that the disclosure of human thoughts and deeds, then to be made, is intended as a part of the retribution. That, surely, were a shallow view of it. No; these revelations, unless I greatly err, are meant merely to promote the intellectual satisfaction of all intelligent beings, who will stand waiting, on that day, to see the dark problem of this life made plain. A knowledge of men's hearts will be needful to the completest solution of that problem. And I conceive, moreover, that the hearts holding such miserable secrets as you speak of will yield them up, at that last day, not with reluctance, but with a joy unutterable."

"Then why not reveal them here?" asked Roger Chillingworth, glancing quietly aside at the minister. "Why should not the guilty ones sooner avail themselves of this unutterable solace?"

"They mostly do," said the clergyman, griping hard at his breast, as if afflicted with an importunate throb of pain. "Many, many a poor soul hath given its confidence to me, not only on the deathbed, but while strong in life, and fair in reputation. And ever, after such an outpouring, O, what a relief have I witnessed in those sinful brethren! even as in one who at last draws free air, after long stifling with his own polluted breath. How can it be otherwise? Why should a wretched man, guilty, we will say, of murder, prefer to keep the dead corpse buried in his own heart, rather than fling it forth at once, and let the universe take care of it!"

"Yet some men bury their secrets thus," observed the calm physician.

"True; there are such men," answered Mr. Dimmesdale. "But, not to suggest more obvious reasons, it may be that they are kept silent by the very constitution of their nature. Or—can we not suppose it?—guilty as they may be, retaining, nevertheless, a zeal for God's glory and man's welfare, they shrink from displaying themselves black and filthy in the view of men; because, thenceforward, no good can be achieved by them; no evil of the past be redeemed by better service. So, to their own unutterable torment, they go about among their fellow-creatures looking pure as new-fallen snow; while their hearts are all speckled and spotted with iniquity of which they cannot rid themselves."

"These men deceive themselves," said Roger Chillingworth, with somewhat more emphasis than usual, and making a slight gesture with his forefinger. "They fear to take up the shame that rightfully belongs to them. Their love for man, their zeal for God's service—these holy impulses may or may not coexist in their hearts with the evil inmates to which their guilt has unbarred the door, and which must needs propagate a hellish breed within them. But, if they seek to glorify God, let them not lift heavenward their unclean hands! If they would serve their fellow-men, let them do it by making manifest the power and reality of conscience, in constraining them to penitential self-abasement! Wouldst thou have me to believe, O wise and pious friend, that a false show can be better—can be more for God's glory, or man's welfare—than God's own truth? Trust me, such men deceive themselves!"

"It may be so," said the young clergyman, indifferently, as waiving a discussion that he considered irrelevant or unreasonable. He had a ready faculty, indeed, of escaping from any topic that agitated his too sensitive and nervous temperament.—"But, now, I would ask of my well-skilled physician whether, in good sooth, he deems me to have profited by his kindly care of this weak frame of mine?"

Before Roger Chillingworth could answer, they heard the clear, wild laughter of a young child's voice proceeding from the adjacent burial ground. Looking instinctively from the open window—for it was summertime—the minister beheld Hester Prynne and little Pearl passing along the footpath that traversed the enclosure. Pearl looked as beautiful as the day, but was in one of those moods of perverse merriment which, whenever they occurred, seemed to remove her entirely out of the sphere of sympathy or human contact. She now skipped irreverently from one grave to another; until, coming to the broad, flat, armorial tombstone of a departed worthy—perhaps of Isaac Johnson himself—she began to dance upon it. In reply to her mother's command and entreaty that she would behave more decorously, little Pearl paused to gather the prickly burrs from a tall burdock which grew beside the tomb. Taking a handful of these, she arranged them along the lines of the scarlet letter that decorated the maternal bosom, to which the burrs, as their nature was, tenaciously adhered. Hester did not pluck them off.

Roger Chillingworth had by this time approached the window, and smiled grimly down.

"There is no law, nor reverence for authority, no regard for human ordinances or opinions, right or wrong, mixed up with that child's composition," remarked he, as much to himself as to his companion. "I saw her, the other day, bespatter the Governor himself with water, at the cattle trough in Spring Lane. What, in Heaven's name, is she? Is the imp altogether evil? Hath she affections? Hath she any discoverable principle of being?"

"None—save the freedom of a broken law," answered Mr. Dimmesdale, in a quiet way, as if he had been discussing the point within himself. "Whether capable of good, I know not."

The child probably overheard their voices; for, looking up to the window with a bright but naughty smile of mirth and intelligence, she threw one of the prickly burrs at the Reverend Mr. Dimmesdale. The sensitive clergyman shrunk with nervous dread from the light missile. Detecting his emotion, Pearl clapped her little hands in the most extravagant ecstasy. Hester Prynne, likewise, had involuntarily looked up; and all these four persons, old and young, regarded one another in silence, till the child laughed aloud, and shouted,

"Come away, Mother! Come away, or yonder old Black Man will catch you! He hath got hold of the minister already. Come away, Mother, or he will catch you! But he cannot catch little Pearl!"

So she drew her mother away, skipping, dancing, and frisking fantastically among the hillocks of the dead people, like a creature that had nothing in common with a bygone and buried generation, nor owned herself akin to it. It was as if she had been made afresh out of new elements, and must perforce be permitted to live her own life, and be a law unto herself without her eccentricities being reckoned to her for a crime.

"There goes a woman," resumed Roger Chillingworth, after a pause, "who, be her demerits what they may, hath none of that mystery of hidden sinfulness which you deem so grievous to be borne. Is Hester Prynne the less miserable, think you, for that scarlet letter on her breast?"

"I do verily believe it," answer the clergyman. "Nevertheless, I cannot answer for her. There was a look of pain in her face which I would gladly have been spared the sight of. But still, methinks, it must needs be better for the sufferer to be free to show his pain, as this poor woman Hester is, than to cover it all up in his heart."

There was another pause; and the physician began anew to examine and arrange the plants which he had gathered.

"You inquired of me, a little time agone," said he, at length, "my judgment as touching your health."

"I did," answered the clergyman, "and would gladly learn it. Speak frankly, I pray you, be it for life or death."

"Freely then and plainly," said the physician, still busy with his plants, but keeping a wary eye on Mr. Dimmesdale, "the disorder is a strange one; not so much in itself, nor as outwardly manifested—in so far, at least, as the symptoms have been laid open to my observation. Looking daily at you, my good Sir, and watching the tokens of your aspect now for months gone by, I should deem you a man sore sick, it may be, yet not so sick but that an instructed and watchful physician might well hope to cure you. But—I know not what to say—the disease is what I seem to know, yet know it not."

"You speak in riddles, learned Sir," said the pale minister, glancing aside out of the window.

"Then, to speak more plainly," continued the physician, "and I crave pardon, Sir—should it seem to require pardon—for this needful plainness of my speech. Let me ask—as your friend, as one having charge, under Providence, of your life and physical well-being—hath all the operation of this disorder been fairly laid open and recounted to me?"

"How can you question it?" asked the minister. "Surely, it were child's play to call in a physician and then hide the sore!"

"You would tell me, then, that I know all?" said Roger Chillingworth deliberately and fixing an eye, bright with intense and concentrated intelligence, on the minister's face. "Be it so! But again! He to whom only the outward and physical evil is laid open, knoweth, oftentimes, but half the evil which he is called upon to cure. A bodily disease, which we look upon as whole and entire within itself, may, after all, be but a symptom of some ailment in the spiritual part. Your pardon, once again, good Sir, if my speech give the shadow of offence. You, Sir, of all men whom I have known, are he whose body is the closest conjoined, and imbued, and identified, so to speak, with the spirit whereof it is the instrument."

"Then I need ask no further," said the clergyman, somewhat hastily rising from his chair. "You deal not, I take it, in medicine for the soul!"

"Thus, a sickness," continued Roger Chillingworth, going on, in an unaltered tone, without heeding the interruption—but standing up and confronting the emaciated and white-cheeked minister with his low, dark and misshapen figure—"a sickness, a sore place, if we may so call it in your spirit hath immediately its appropriate manifestation in your bodily frame. Would you, therefore, that your physician heal the bodily evil? How may this be, unless you first lay open to him the wound or trouble in your soul?"

"No—not to thee!—not to an earthly physician!" cried Mr. Dimmesdale passionately and turning his eyes, full and bright and with a kind of fierceness, on old Roger Chillingworth. "Not to thee! But if it be the soul's disease, then do I commit myself to the one Physician of the soul! He, if it stand with his good pleasure, can cure; or he can kill! Let him do with me as, in his justice and wisdom, he shall see good. But who art thou, that meddlest in this matter?—that darest thrust himself between the sufferer and his God?"

With a frantic gesture, he rushed out of the room.

"It is as well to have made this step," said Roger Chillingworth to himself, looking after the minister with a grave smile. "There is nothing lost. We shall be friends again anon. But see, now, how passion takes hold upon this man, and hurrieth him out of himself! As with one passion, so with another! He hath done a wild thing ere now, this pious Master Dimmesdale, in the hot passion of his heart!"

It proved not difficult to re-establish the intimacy of the two companions, on the same footing and in the same degree as heretofore. The young clergyman, after a few hours of privacy, was sensible that the disorder of his nerves had hurried him into an unseemly outbreak of temper which there had been nothing in the physician's words to excuse or palliate. He marvelled, indeed, at the violence with which he had thrust back the kind old man, when merely proffering the advice which it was his duty to bestow, and which the minister himself had expressly sought. With these remorseful feelings, he lost no time in making the amplest apologies, and besought his friend still to continue the care, which, if not successful in restoring him to health, had, in all probability, been the means of prolonging his feeble existence to that hour. Roger Chillingworth readily assented, and went on with his medical supervision of the minister, doing his best for him, in all good faith, but always quitting the patient's apartment at the close of a professional interview with a mysterious and puzzled smile upon his lips. This expression was invisible in Mr. Dimmesdale's presence, but grew strongly evident as the physician crossed the threshold.

"A rare case!" he muttered. "I must needs look deeper into it. A strange sympathy betwixt soul and body! Were it only for the art's sake, I must search this matter to the bottom!"

It came to pass, not long after the scene above recorded, that the Reverend Mr. Dimmesdale, at noonday, and entirely unawares, fell into a deep, deep slumber, sitting in his chair, with a large black-letter volume open before him on the table. It must have been a work of vast ability in the somniferous school of literature. The profound depth of the minister's repose was the more remarkable, inasmuch as he was one of those persons whose sleep, ordinarily, is as light, as fitful, and as easily scared away, as a small bird hopping on a twig. To such an unwonted remoteness, however, had his spirit now withdrawn into itself, that he stirred not in his chair, when old Roger Chillingworth, without any extraordinary precaution, came into the room. The physician advanced directly in front of his patient, laid his hand upon his bosom, and thrust aside the vestment, that, hitherto, had always covered it even from the professional eye.

Then, indeed, Mr. Dimmesdale shuddered, and slightly stirred.

After a brief pause, the physician turned away.

But, with what a wild look of wonder, joy, and horror! With what a ghastly rapture, as it were, too mighty to be expressed only by the eye and features, and therefore bursting forth through the whole ugliness of his figure, and making itself even riotously manifest by the extravagant gestures with which he threw up his arms towards the ceiling, and stamped his foot upon the floor! Had a man seen old Roger Chillingworth, at that moment of his ecstasy, he would have had no need to ask how Satan comports himself when a precious human soul is lost to heaven and won into his kingdom.

But what distinguished the physician's ecstasy from Satan's was the trait of wonder in it!

XI

The Interior of a Heart

AFTER the incident last described, the intercourse between the clergyman and the physician, though externally the same, was really of another character than it had previously been. The intellect of Roger Chillingworth had now a sufficiently plain path before it. It was not, indeed, precisely that which he had laid out for himself to tread. Calm, gentle, passionless as he appeared, there was yet, we fear, a quiet depth of malice, hitherto latent, but active now, in this unfortunate old man, which led him to imagine a more intimate revenge than any mortal had ever wreaked upon an enemy. To make himself the one trusted friend to whom should be confided all the fear, the remorse, the agony, the ineffectual repentance, the backward rush of sinful thoughts, expelled in vain! All that guilty sorrow, hidden from the world, whose great heart would have pitied and forgiven, to be revealed to him, the Pitiless, to him, the Unforgiving! All that dark treasure to be lavished on the very man to whom nothing else could so adequately pay the debt of vengeance!

The clergyman's shy and sensitive reserve had balked this scheme. Roger Chillingworth, however, was inclined to be hardly, if at all, less satisfied with the aspect of affairs which Providence—using the avenger and his victim for its own purposes, and, perchance, pardoning where it seemed most to punish—had substituted for his black devices. A revelation, he could almost say, had been granted to him. It mattered little, for his object, whether celestial, or from what other region. By its aid, in all the subsequent relations betwixt him and Mr. Dimmesdale, not merely the external

presence, but the very inmost soul of the latter seemed to be
brought out before his eyes, so that he could see and comprehend its every movement. He became, thenceforth, not a
spectator only, but a chief actor in the poor minister's interior world. He could play upon him as he chose. Would he
arouse him with a throb of agony? The victim was forever
on the rack; it needed only to know the spring that controlled the engine—and the physician knew it well! Would
he startle him with sudden fear? As at the waving of a
magician's wand, uprose a grisly phantom—uprose a thousand phantoms—in many shapes, of death, or more awful
shame, all flocking round about the clergyman, and pointing
with their fingers at his breast!

All this was accomplished with a subtlety so perfect, that
the minister, though he had constantly a dim perception of
some evil influence watching over him, could never gain a
knowledge of its actual nature. True, he looked doubtfully,
fearfully—even, at times, with horror and the bitterness of
hatred—at the deformed figure of the old physician. His
gestures, his gait, his grizzled beard, his slightest and most
indifferent acts, the very fashion of his garments, were odious in the clergyman's sight; a token implicitly to be relied
on of a deeper antipathy in the breast of the latter than he
was willing to acknowledge to himself. For, as it was impossible to assign a reason for such distrust and abhorrence, so
Mr. Dimmesdale, conscious that the poison of one morbid
spot was infecting his heart's entire substance, attributed all
his presentiments to no other cause. He took himself to task
for his bad sympathies in reference to Roger Chillingworth,
disregarded the lesson that he should have drawn from
them, and did his best to root them out. Unable to accomplish this, he nevertheless, as a matter of principle, continued his habits of social familiarity with the old man, and
thus gave him constant opportunities for perfecting the purpose to which—poor, forlorn creature that he was, and
more wretched than his victim—the avenger had devoted
himself.

While thus suffering under bodily disease, and gnawed
and tortured by some black trouble of the soul, and given
over to the machinations of his deadliest enemy, the Reverend Mr. Dimmesdale had achieved a brilliant popularity in
his sacred office. He won it, indeed, in great part, by his

sorrows. His intellectual gifts, his moral perceptions, his power of experiencing and communicating emotion, were kept in a state of preternatural activity by the prick and anguish of his daily life. His fame, though still on its upward slope, already overshadowed the soberer reputations of his fellow-clergymen, eminent as several of them were. There were scholars among them who had spent more years in acquiring abstruse lore connected with the divine profession than Mr. Dimmesdale had lived; and who might well, therefore, be more profoundly versed in such solid and valuable attainments than their youthful brother. There were men, too, of a sturdier texture of mind than his, and endowed with a far greater share of shrewd, hard, iron, or granite understanding; which, duly mingled with a fair proportion of doctrinal ingredient, constitutes a highly respectable, efficacious, and unamiable variety of the clerical species. There were others, again, true saintly fathers, whose faculties had been elaborated by weary toil among their books, and by patient thought, and etherealized, moreover, by spiritual communications with the better world, into which their purity of life had almost introduced these holy personages with their garments of mortality still clinging to them. All that they lacked was the gift that descended upon the chosen disciples at Pentecost, in tongues of flame; symbolizing, it would seem, not the power of speech in foreign and unknown languages, but that of addressing the whole human brotherhood in the heart's native language. These fathers, otherwise so apostolic, lacked Heaven's last and rarest attestation of their office, the Tongue of Flame. They would have vainly sought—had they ever dreamed of seeking—to express the highest truths through the humblest medium of familiar words and images. Their voices came down, afar and indistinctly, from the upper heights where they habitually dwelt.

Not improbably, it was to this latter class of men that Mr. Dimmesdale, by many of his traits of character, naturally belonged. To the high mountain peaks of faith and sanctity he would have climbed, had not the tendency been thwarted by the burden, whatever it might be, of crime or anguish, beneath which it was his doom to totter. It kept him down, on a level with the lowest; him, the man of ethereal attributes, whose voice the angels might else have listened to and answered! But this very burden it was that gave him sympathies so intimate with the sinful brotherhood of mankind; so that his heart vibrated in unison with theirs, and received their pain into itself, and sent its own throb of pain through a thousand other hearts, in gushes of sad, persuasive eloquence. Oftenest persuasive, but sometimes terrible! The people knew not the power that moved them thus. They deemed the young clergyman a miracle of holiness. They fancied him the mouthpiece of Heaven's messages of wisdom and rebuke and love. In their eyes, the very ground on which he trod was sanctified. The virgins of his church grew pale around him, victims of a passion so imbued with religious sentiment that they imagined it to be all religion, and brought it openly, in their white bosoms, as their most acceptable sacrifice before the altar. The aged members of his flock, beholding Mr. Dimmesdale's frame so feeble while they were themselves so rugged in their infirmity, believed that he would go heavenward before them, and enjoined it upon their children that their old bones should be buried close to their young pastor's holy grave. And, all this time, perchance, when poor Mr. Dimmesdale was thinking of his grave, he questioned with himself whether the grass would ever grow on it, because an accursed thing must there be buried!

It is inconceivable, the agony with which this public veneration tortured him! It was his genuine impulse to adore the truth, and to reckon all things shadowlike, and utterly devoid of weight or value, that had not its divine essence as the life within their life. Then, what was he?—a substance? —or the dimmest of all shadows? He longed to speak out from his own pulpit at the full height of his voice, and tell the people what he was. "I, whom you behold in these black garments of the priesthood—I, who ascend the sacred desk, and turn my pale face heavenward, taking upon myself to hold communion, in your behalf, with the Most High Omniscience—I, in whose daily life you discern the sanctity of Enoch—I, whose footsteps, as you suppose, leave a gleam along my earthly track, whereby the pilgrims that shall come after me may be guided to the regions of the blest—I, who have laid the hand of baptism upon your children—I, who have breathed the parting prayer over your dying friends, to whom the Amen sounded faintly from a world which they had quitted—I, your pastor, whom you so reverence and trust am utterly a pollution and a lie!"

More than once, Mr. Dimmesdale had gone into the pulpit, with a purpose never to come down its steps until he should have spoken words like the above. More than once, he had cleared his throat and drawn in the long, deep, and tremulous breath, which, when sent forth again, would come burdened with the black secret of his soul. More than once—nay, more than a hundred times—he had actually spoken! Spoken! But how? He had told his hearers that he was altogether vile, a viler companion of the vilest, the worst of sinners, an abomination, a thing of unimaginable iniquity; and that the only wonder was that they did not see his wretched body shrivelled up before their eyes by the burning wrath of the Almighty! Could there be plainer speech than this? Would not the people start up in their seats by a simultaneous impulse, and tear him down out of the pulpit which he defiled? Not so, indeed! They heard it all, and did but reverence him the more. They little guessed what deadly purport lurked in those self-condemning words. "The godly youth!" said they among themselves. "The saint on earth! Alas, if he discern such sinfulness in his own white soul, what horrid spectacle would he behold in thine or mine!" The minister well knew—subtile, but remorseful hypocrite that he was!—the light in which his vague confession would be viewed. He had striven to put a cheat upon himself by making the avowal of guilty conscience, but had gained only one other sin, and a self-acknowledged shame, without the momentary relief of being self-deceived. He had spoken the very truth, and transformed it into the veriest falsehood. And yet, by the constitution of his nature, he loved the truth and loathed the lie, as few men ever did. Therefore, above all things else, he loathed his miserable self!

His inward trouble drove him to practices more in accordance with the old, corrupted faith of Rome than with the better light of the church in which he had been born and bred. In Mr. Dimmesdale's secret closet, under lock and key, there was a bloody scourge. Oftentimes, this Protestant and Puritan divine had plied it on his own shoulders, laughing bitterly at himself the while, and smiting so much the more pitilessly because of that bitter laugh. It was his custom, too, as it has been that of many other pious Puritans, to fast—not however, like them, in order to purify the body and render it the fitter medium of celestial illumination, but rigorously, and until his knees trembled beneath him, as an act of penance. He kept vigils, likewise, night after night, sometimes in utter darkness; sometimes with a glimmering lamp; and sometimes, viewing his own face in a looking glass, by the most powerful light which he could throw upon it. He thus typified the constant introspection wherewith he tortured, but could not purify, himself. In these lengthened vigils, his brain often reeled and visions seemed to flit before him; perhaps seen doubtfully, and by a faint light of their own, in the remote dimness of the chamber, or more vividly, and close beside him, within the looking glass. Now it was a herd of diabolic shapes that grinned and mocked at the pale minister, and beckoned him away with them; now a group of shining angels, who flew upward heavily, as sorrow-laden, but grew more ethereal as they rose. Now came the dead friends of his youth, and his whitebearded father, with a saintlike frown, and his mother, turning her face away as she passed by. Ghost of a mother—thinnest fantasy of a mother—methinks she might yet have thrown a pitying glance towards her son! And now, through the chamber which these spectral thoughts had made so ghastly, glided Hester Prynne, leading along little Pearl in her scarlet garb, and pointing her forefinger, first at the scarlet letter on her bosom, and then at the clergyman's own breast.

None of these visions ever quite deluded him. At any moment, by an effort of his will, he could discern substances through their misty lack of substance, and convince himself that they were not solid in their nature, like yonder table of carved oak, or that big, square, leathern-bound and brazen-clasped volume of divinity. But, for all that, they were, in one sense, the truest and most substantial things which the poor minister now dealt with. It is the unspeakable misery of a life so false as his, that it steals the pith and substance out of whatever realities there are around us, and which were meant by Heaven to be the spirit's joy and nutriment. To the untrue man, the whole universe is false—it is impalpable—it shrinks to nothing within his grasp. And he himself, in so far as he shows himself in a false light, becomes a shadow, or, indeed, ceases to exist. The only truth that continued to give Mr. Dimmesdale a real existence on

this earth was the anguish in his inmost soul, and the
undissembled expression of it in his aspect. Had he once
found power to smile, and wear a face of gayety, there
would have been no such man!

On one of those ugly nights, which we have faintly hinted
at but forborne to picture forth, the minister started from
his chair. A new thought had struck him. There might be a
moment's peace in it. Attiring himself with as much care as
if it had been for public worship, and precisely in the same
manner, he stole softly down the staircase, undid the door,
and issued forth.

XII

The Minister's Vigil

WALKING in the shadow of a dream, as it were, and perhaps actually under the influence of a species of somnambulism, Mr. Dimmesdale reached the spot where, now so long since, Hester Prynne had lived through her first hours of public ignominy. The same platform or scaffold, black and weather-stained with the storm or sunshine of seven long years, and foot-worn, too, with the tread of many culprits who had since ascended it, remained standing beneath the balcony of the meeting house. The minister went up the steps.

It was an obscure night of early May. An unvaried pall of cloud muffled the whole expanse of sky from zenith to horizon. If the same multitude which had stood as eyewitnesses while Hester Prynne sustained her punishment could now have been summoned forth, they would have discerned no face above the platform, nor hardly the outline of a human shape, in the dark gray of the midnight. But the town was all asleep. There was no peril of discovery. The minister might stand there, if it so pleased him, until morning should redden in the east, without other risk than that the dank and chill night air would creep into his frame and stiffen his joints with rheumatism and clog his throat with catarrh and cough, thereby defrauding the expectant audience of tomorrow's prayer and sermon. No eye could see him, save that ever-wakeful one which had seen him in his closet wielding the bloody scourge. Why, then, had he come hither? Was it but the mockery of penitence? A mockery, indeed, but one which his soul trifled with itself! A mockery at which angels blushed and wept, while fiends rejoiced with jeering laughter! He had been driven hither by the impulse of that Remorse which dogged him everywhere, and whose own sister and closely linked companion was that Cowardice which invariably drew him back with her tremulous gripe, just when the other impulse had hurried him to the verge of a disclosure. Poor, miserable man! what right had infirmity like his to burden itself with crime? Crime is for the iron-nerved, who have their choice either to endure it, or, if it press too hard, to exert their fierce and savage strength for a good purpose, and fling it off at once! This feeble and most sensitive of spirits could do neither, yet continually did one thing or another, which intertwined, in the same inextricable knot, the agony of heaven-defying guilt and vain repentance.

And thus, while standing on the scaffold, in this vain show of expiation, Mr. Dimmesdale was overcome with a great horror of mind, as if the universe were gazing at a scarlet token on his naked breast, right over his heart. On that spot, in very truth, there was, and there had long been, the gnawing and poisonous tooth of bodily pain. Without any effort of his will or power to restrain himself, he shrieked aloud; an outcry that went pealing through the night, and was beaten back from one house to another, and reverberated from the hills in the background as if a company of devils, detecting so much misery and terror in it, had made a plaything of the sound, and were bandying it to and fro.

"It is done!" muttered the minister, covering his face with his hands. "The whole town will awake, and hurry forth, and find me here!"

But it was not so. The shriek had perhaps sounded with a far greater power to his own startled ears than it actually possessed. The town did not awake; or, if it did, the drowsy slumberers mistook the cry either for something frightful in a dream, or for the noise of witches, whose voices, at that period, were often heard to pass over the settlements or lonely cottages, as they rode with Satan through the air. The clergyman, therefore, hearing no symptoms of disturbance, uncovered his eyes and looked about him. At one of the chamber windows of Governor Bellingham's mansion, which stood at some distance on the line of another street, he beheld the appearance of the old magistrate himself, with a lamp in his hand, a white nightcap on his head, and a long white gown enveloping his figure. He looked like a ghost, evoked unseasonably from the grave. The cry had evidently startled him. At another window of the same house, moreover, appeared old Mistress Hibbins, the Governor's sister, also with a lamp, which, even thus far off, revealed the expression of her sour and discontented face. She thrust forth her head from the lattice, and looked anxiously upward. Beyond the shadow of a doubt, this venerable witchlady had heard Mr. Dimmesdale's outcry, and interpreted it, with its multitudinous echoes and reverberations, as the clamor of the fiends and night-hags, with whom she was well known to make excursions into the forest.

Detecting the gleam of Governor Bellingham's lamp, the old lady quickly extinguished her own, and vanished. Possibly, she went up among the clouds. The minister saw nothing further of her motions. The magistrate, after a wary observation of the darkness—into which, nevertheless, he could see but little further than he might into a millstone—retired from the window.

The minister grew comparatively calm. His eyes, however, were soon greeted by a little, glimmering light, which, at first a long way off, was approaching up the street. It threw a gleam of recognition on here a post, and there a garden fence, and here a latticed windowpane, and there a pump with its full trough of water, and here, again, an arched door of oak, with an iron knocker, and a rough log for the doorstep. The Reverend Mr. Dimmesdale noted all these minute particulars, even while firmly convinced that the doom of his existence was stealing onward in the footsteps which he now heard; and that the gleam of the lantern would fall upon him, in a few moments more, and reveal his long-hidden secret. As the light drew nearer, he beheld, within its illuminated circle, his brother clergyman—or, to speak more accurately, his professional father, as well as highly valued friend—the Reverend Mr. Wilson; who, as Mr. Dimmesdale now conjectured, had been praying at the bedside of some dying man. And so he had. The good old minister came freshly from the death chamber of Governor Winthrop, who had passed from earth to heaven within that very hour. And now, surrounded, like the saintlike personages of olden times, with a radiant halo that glorified him amid this gloomy night of sin—as if the departed Governor had left him an inheritance of his glory, or as if he had caught upon himself the distant shine of the celestial city while looking thitherward to see the triumphant pilgrim pass within its gates—now, in short, good Father Wilson was moving homeward, aiding his footsteps with a lighted lantern! The glimmer of this luminary suggested the above conceits to Mr. Dimmesdale, who smiled—nay, almost laughed at them—and then wondered if he were going mad.

As the Reverend Mr. Wilson passed beside the scaffold, closely muffling his Geneva cloak about him with one arm and holding the lantern before his breast with the other, the minister could hardly restrain himself from speaking.

"A good evening to you, venerable Father Wilson! Come up hither, I pray you, and pass a pleasant hour with me!"

Good heavens! Had Mr. Dimmesdale actually spoken? For one instant, he believed that these words had passed his lips. But they were uttered only within his imagination. The venerable Father Wilson continued to step slowly onward, looking carefully at the muddy pathway before his feet, and never once turning his head towards the guilty platform. When the light of the glimmering lantern had faded quite away, the minister discovered, by the faintness which came over him, that the last few moments had been a crisis of terrible anxiety, although his mind had made an involuntary effort to relieve itself by a kind of lurid playfulness.

Shortly afterwards, the like grisly sense of the humorous again stole in among the solemn phantoms of his thought. He felt his limbs growing stiff with the unaccustomed chilliness of the night, and doubted whether he should be able to descend the steps of the scaffold. Morning would break, and find him there. The neighborhood would begin to rouse itself. The earliest riser, coming forth in the dim twilight, would perceive a vaguely defined figure aloft on the place of shame; and, half crazed betwixt alarm and curiosity, would go, knocking from door to door, summoning all the people to behold the ghost—as he needs must think it—of some defunct transgressor. A dusky tumult would flap its wings from one house to another. Then—the morning light still waxing stronger—old patriarchs would rise up in great haste, each in his flannel gown, and matronly dames, without pausing to put off their night-gear. The whole tribe of decorous personages, who had never heretofore been seen with a single hair of their heads awry, would start into public view with the disorder of a nightmare in their aspects. Old Governor Bellingham would come grimly forth with his King James' ruff fastened askew; and Mistress Hibbins, with some twigs of the forest clinging to her skirts, and looking sourer than ever, as having hardly got a wink of sleep after her night ride; and good Father Wilson, too, after spending half the night at a deathbed and liking ill to be disturbed, thus early, out of his dreams about the glorified saints. Hither, likewise, would come the elders and deacons of Mr. Dimmesdale's church, and the young virgins who so idolized their minister, and had made a shrine for him in their white bosoms; which now, by the by, in their hurry and confusion, they would scantly have given themselves time to cover with their kerchiefs. All people, in a word, would come stumbling over their thresholds, and turning up their amazed and horror-stricken visages around the scaffold. Whom would they discern there, with the red eastern light upon his brow? Whom, but the Reverend Arthur Dimmesdale, half frozen to death, overwhelmed with shame, and standing where Hester Prynne had stood!

Carried away by the grotesque horror of this picture, the minister, unawares, and to his own infinite alarm, burst into a great peal of laughter. It was immediately responded to by a light, airy, childish laugh, in which with a thrill of the heart—but he knew not whether of exquisite pain, or pleasure as acute—he recognized the tones of little Pearl.

"Pearl! Little Pearl!" cried he, after a moment's pause; then, suppressing his voice, "Hester! Hester Prynne! Are you there?"

"Yes; it is Hester Prynne!" she replied, in a tone of surprise; and the minister heard her footsteps approaching from the sidewalk, along which she had been passing. "It is I, and my little Pearl."

"Whence come you, Hester?" asked the minister. "What sent you hither?"

"I have been watching at a deathbed," answered Hester Prynne—"at Governor Winthrop's deathbed, and have taken his measure for a robe, and am now going homeward to my dwelling."

"Come up hither, Hester, thou and little Pearl," said the Reverend Mr. Dimmesdale. "Ye have both been here before, but I was not with you. Come up hither once again, and we will stand all three together!"

She silently ascended the steps, and stood on the platform, holding little Pearl by the hand. The minister felt for the child's other hand, and took it. The moment that he did so, there came what seemed a tumultuous rush of new life, other life than his own, pouring like a torrent into his heart and hurrying through all his veins, as if the mother and the child were communicating their vital warmth to his half-torpid system. The three formed an electric chain.

"Minister!" whispered little Pearl.

"What wouldst thou say, child?" asked Mr. Dimmesdale.

"Wilt thou stand here with Mother and me, tomorrow noontide?" inquired Pearl.

"Nay; not so, my little Pearl," answered the minister; for, with the new energy of the moment, all the dread of public exposure that had so long been the anguish of his life had returned upon him; and he was already trembling at the conjunction in which—with a strange joy, nevertheless—he now found himself. "Not so, my child. I shall, indeed, stand with thy mother and thee one other day, but not tomorrow."

Pearl laughed, and attempted to pull away her hand. But the minister held it fast.

"A moment longer, my child!" said he.

"But wilt thou promise," asked Pearl, "to take my hand, and Mother's hand, tomorrow noontide?"

"Not then, Pearl," said the minister, "but another time."

"And what other time?" persisted the child.

"At the great judgment day," whispered the minister —and, strangely enough, the sense that he was a professional teacher of the truth impelled him to answer the child so. "Then, and there, before the judgment seat, thy mother, and thou, and I, must stand together. But the daylight of this world shall not see our meeting!"

Pearl laughed again.

But, before Mr. Dimmesdale had done speaking, a light gleamed far and wide over all the muffled sky. It was doubtless caused by one of those meteors which the night-watcher may so often observe burning out to waste in the vacant regions of the atmosphere. So powerful was its radiance, that it thoroughly illuminated the dense medium of cloud betwixt the sky and earth. The great vault brightened,

like the dome of an immense lamp. It showed the fa........
scene of the street, with the distinctness of midday, but also
with the awfulness that is always imparted to familiar objects by an unaccustomed light. The wooden houses, with
their jutting stories and quaint gable peaks; the doorsteps
and thresholds, with the early grass springing up about
them; the garden plots, black with freshly turned earth; the
wheeltrack, little worn, and, even in the market place, mar-
gined with green on either side—all were visible, but with a
singularity of aspect that seemed to give another moral
interpretation to the things of this world than they had ever
borne before. And there stood the minister, with his hand
over his heart; and Hester Prynne, with the embroidered
letter glimmering on her bosom; and little Pearl, herself a
symbol, and the connecting link between those two. They
stood in the noon of that strange and solemn splendor as if
it were the light that is to reveal all secrets and the daybreak
that shall unite all who belong to one another.

There was witchcraft in little Pearl's eyes, and her face, as
she glanced upward at the minister, wore that naughty smile
which made its expression frequently so elvish. She withdrew her hand from Mr. Dimmesdale's and pointed across
the street. But he clasped both his hands over his breast,
and cast his eyes towards the zenith.

Nothing was more common in those days than to interpret
all meteoric appearances, and other natural phenomena that
occurred with less regularity than the rise and set of sun and
moon, as so many revelations from a supernatural source.
Thus, a blazing spear, a sword of flame, a bow, or a sheaf of
arrows, seen in the midnight sky, prefigured Indian warfare.
Pestilence was known to have been foreboded by a shower
of crimson light. We doubt whether any marked event, for
good or evil, ever befell New England, from its settlement
down to Revolutionary times, of which the inhabitants had
not been previously warned by some spectacle of this nature. Not seldom, it had been seen by multitudes. Oftener,
however, its credibility rested on the faith of some lonely
eyewitness, who beheld the wonder through the colored,
magnifying, and distorting medium of his imagination, and
shaped it more distinctly in his afterthought. It was, indeed,
a majestic idea that the destiny of nations should be revealed, in these awful hieroglyphics, on the cope of heaven.

A scroll so wide might not be deemed too expansive for Providence to write a people's doom upon. The belief was a favorite one with our forefathers, as betokening that their infant commonwealth was under a celestial guardianship of peculiar intimacy and strictness. But what shall we say when an individual discovers a revelation, addressed to himself alone, on the same vast sheet of record! In such a case, it could only be the symptom of a highly disordered mental state, when a man, rendered morbidly self-contemplative by long, intense, and secret pain, had extended his egotism over the whole expanse of nature, until the firmament itself should appear no more than a fitting page for his soul's history and fate!

We impute it, therefore, solely to the disease in his own eye and heart, that the minister, looking upward to the zenith, beheld there the appearance of an immense letter— the letter "A"—marked out in lines of dull red light. Not but the meteor may have shown itself at that point, burning duskily through a veil of cloud; but with no such shape as his guilty imagination gave it; or, at least, with so little definiteness, that another's guilt might have seen another symbol in it.

There was a singular circumstance that characterized Mr. Dimmesdale's psychological state at this moment. All the time that he gazed upward to the zenith, he was, nevertheless, perfectly aware that little Pearl was pointing her finger towards old Roger Chillingworth, who stood at no great distance from the scaffold. The minister appeared to see him with the same glance that discerned the miraculous letter. To his features, as to all other objects, the meteoric light imparted a new expression; or it might well be that the physician was not careful then, as at all other times, to hide the malevolence with which he looked upon his victim. Certainly, if the meteor kindled up the sky and disclosed the earth with an awfulness that admonished Hester Prynne and the clergyman of the day of judgment, then might Roger Chillingworth have passed with them for the archfiend, standing there with a smile and scowl, to claim his own. So vivid was the expression, or so intense the minister's perception of it, that it seemed still to remain painted on the darkness after the meteor had vanished, with an effect as if the street and all things else were at once annihilated.

"Who is that man, Hester?" gasped Mr. Dimmesdale, overcome with terror. "I shiver at him! Dost thou know the man? I hate him, Hester!"

She remembered her oath, and was silent.

"I tell thee, my soul shivers at him!" muttered the minister again. "Who is he? Who is he? Canst thou do nothing for me? I have a nameless horror of the man!"

"Minister," said little Pearl, "I can tell thee who he is!"

"Quickly, then, child!" said the minister, bending his ear close to her lips. "Quickly!—and as low as thou canst whisper."

Pearl mumbled something into his ear that sounded, indeed, like human language, but was only such gibberish as children may be heard amusing themselves with by the hour together. At all events, if it involved any secret information in regard to old Roger Chillingworth, it was in a tongue unknown to the erudite clergyman, and did but increase the bewilderment of his mind. The elvish child then laughed aloud.

"Dost thou mock me now?" said the minister.

"Thou wast not bold!—thou wast not true!" answered the child. "Thou wouldst not promise to take my hand, and Mother's hand, tomorrow noontide!"

"Worthy Sir," answered the physician, who had now advanced to the foot of the platform. "Pious Master Dimmesdale! can this be you? Well, well, indeed! We men of study, whose heads are in our books, have need to be straitly looked after! We dream in our waking moments, and walk in our sleep. Come, good Sir, and my dear friend, I pray you, let me lead you home!"

"How knewest thou that I was here?" asked the minister, fearfully.

"Verily, and in good faith," answered Roger Chillingworth, "I knew nothing of the matter. I had spent the better part of the night at the bedside of the worshipful Governor Winthrop, doing what my poor skill might to give him ease. He going home to a better world, I, likewise, was on my way homeward, when this strange light shone out. Come with me, I beseech you, Reverend Sir; else you will be poorly able to do Sabbath duty tomorrow. Aha! see now, how they trouble the brain—these books!—these books! You should study less, good Sir, and take a little pastime; or these night-whimseys will grow upon you."

"I will go home with you," said Mr. Dimmesdale.

With a chill despondency, like one awaking all nerveless from an ugly dream, he yielded himself to the physician, and was led away.

The next day, however, being the Sabbath, he preached a discourse which was held to be the richest and most powerful, and the most replete with heavenly influences, that had ever proceeded from his lips. Souls, it is said, more souls than one, were brought to the truth by the efficacy of that sermon, and vowed within themselves to cherish a holy gratitude towards Mr. Dimmesdale throughout the long hereafter. But, as he came down the pulpit steps, the graybearded sexton met him, holding up a black glove, which the minister recognized as his own.

"It was found," said the sexton, "this morning, on the scaffold where evil-doers are set up to public shame. Satan dropped it there, I take it, intending a scurrilous jest against your reverence. But, indeed, he was blind and foolish, as he ever and always is. A pure hand needs no glove to cover it!"

"Thank you, my good friend," said the minister, gravely, but startled at heart; for, so confused was his remembrance, that he had almost brought himself to look at the events of the past night as visionary. "Yes, it seems to be my glove, indeed!"

"And, since Satan saw fit to steal it your reverence must needs handle him without gloves, henceforward," remarked the old sexton, grimly smiling. "But did your reverence hear of the portent that was seen last night?—a great red letter in the sky—the letter 'A' which we interpret to stand for 'Angel.' For, as our good Governor Winthrop was made an angel this past night, it was doubtless held fit that there should be some notice thereof!"

"No," answered the minister, "I had not heard of it."

XIII

Another View of Hester

In her late singular interview with Mr. Dimmesdale, Hester Prynne was shocked at the condition to which she found the clergyman reduced. His nerve seemed absolutely destroyed. His moral force was abased into more than childish weakness. It grovelled helpless on the ground, even while his intellectual faculties retained their pristine strength, or had perhaps acquired a morbid energy, which disease only could have given them. With her knowledge of a train of circumstances hidden from all others, she could readily infer that besides the legitimate action of his own conscience, a terrible machinery had been brought to bear, and was still operating, on Mr. Dimmesdale's well-being and repose. Knowing what this poor, fallen man had once been, her whole soul was moved by the shuddering terror with which he had appealed to her—the outcast woman—for support against his instinctively discovered enemy. She decided, moreover, that he had a right to her utmost aid. Little accustomed, in her long seclusion from society, to measure her ideas of right and wrong by any standard external to herself, Hester saw—or seemed to see—that there lay a responsibility upon her in reference to the clergyman which she owed to no other, nor to the whole world besides. The links that united her to the rest of human kind—links of flowers, or silk, or gold, or whatever the material—had all been broken. Here was the iron link of mutual crime, which neither he nor she could break. Like all other ties, it brought along with it its obligations.

Hester Prynne did not now occupy precisely the same

position in which we beheld her during the earlier periods of her ignominy. Years had come and gone. Pearl was now seven years old. Her mother, with the scarlet letter on her breast, glittering in its fantastic embroidery, had long been a familiar object to the townspeople. As is apt to be the case when a person stands out in any prominence before the community, and, at the same time, interferes neither with public nor individual interests and convenience, a species of general regard had ultimately grown up in reference to Hester Prynne. It is to the credit of human nature, that, except where its selfishness is brought into play, it loves more readily than it hates. Hatred, by a gradual and quiet process, will even be transformed to love, unless the change be impeded by a continually new irritation of the original feeling of hostility. In this matter of Hester Prynne, there was neither irritation nor irksomeness. She never battled with the public, but submitted uncomplainingly to its worst usage; she made no claim upon it in requital for what she suffered; she did not weigh upon its sympathies. Then, also, the blameless purity of her life during all these years in which she had been set apart to infamy was reckoned largely in her favor. With nothing now to lose in the sight of mankind, and with no hope, and seemingly no wish, of gaining anything, it could only be a genuine regard for virtue that had brought back the poor wanderer to its paths.

It was perceived, too, that while Hester never put forward even the humblest title to share in the world's privileges—further than to breathe the common air, and earn daily bread for little Pearl and herself by the faithful labor of her hands—she was quick to acknowledge her sisterhood with the race of man, whenever benefits were to be conferred. None so ready as she to give of her little substance to every demand of poverty; even though the bitter-hearted pauper threw back a gibe in requital of the food brought regularly to his door, or the garments wrought for him by the fingers that could have embroidered a monarch's robe. None so self-devoted as Hester, when pestilence stalked through the town. In all seasons of calamity, indeed, whether general or of individuals, the outcast of society at once found her place. She came, not as a guest, but as a rightful inmate, into the household that was darkened by trouble, as if its gloomy twilight were a medium in which she was entitled to hold intercourse with her fellow-creatures. There glimmered the embroidered letter, with comfort in its unearthly ray. Elsewhere the token of sin, it was the taper of the sick-chamber. It had even thrown its gleam, in the sufferer's hard extremity, across the verge of time. It had shown him where to set his foot, while the light of earth was fast becoming dim, and ere the light of futurity could reach him. In such emergencies, Hester's nature showed itself warm and rich; a wellspring of human tenderness, unfailing to every real demand, and inexhaustible by the largest. Her breast, with its badge of shame, was but the softer pillow for the head that needed one. She was self-ordained a Sister of Mercy; or, we may rather say, the world's heavy hand had so ordained her, when neither the world nor she looked forward to this result. The letter was the symbol of her calling. Such helpfulness was found in her—so much power to do and power to sympathize—that many people refused to interpret the scarlet "A" by its original signification. They said that it meant "Able"; so strong was Hester Prynne, with a woman's strength.

It was only the darkened house that could contain her. When sunshine came again, she was not there. Her shadow had faded across the threshold. The helpful inmate had departed, without one backward glance to gather up the meed of gratitude, if any were in the hearts of those whom she had served so zealously. Meeting them in the street, she never raised her head to receive their greeting. If they were resolute to accost her, she laid her finger on the scarlet letter, and passed on. This might be pride, but was so like humility, that it produced all the softening influence of the latter quality on the public mind. The public is despotic in its temper; it is capable of denying common justice when too strenuously demanded as a right; but quite as frequently it awards more than justice when the appeal is made, as despots love to have it made, entirely to its generosity. Interpreting Hester Prynne's deportment as an appeal of this nature, society was inclined to show its former victim a more benign countenance than she cared to be favored with, or, perchance, than she deserved.

The rulers, and the wise and learned men of the community, were longer in acknowledging the influence of Hester's good qualities than the people. The prejudices which they

shared in common with the latter were fortified in themselves by an iron framework of reasoning, that made it a far
tougher labor to expel them. Day by day, nevertheless, their
sour and rigid wrinkles were relaxing into something which,
in the due course of years, might grow to be an expression
of almost benevolence. Thus it was with the men of rank, on
whom their eminent position imposed the guardianship of
the public morals. Individuals in private life, meanwhile,
had quite forgiven Hester Prynne for her frailty; nay, more,
they had begun to look upon the scarlet letter as the token,
not of that one sin, for which she had borne so long and
dreary a penance, but of her many good deeds since. "Do
you see that woman with the embroidered badge?" they
would say to strangers. "It is our Hester—the town's own
Hester—who is so kind to the poor, so helpful to the sick,
so comforting to the afflicted!" Then, it is true, the propensity of human nature to tell the very worst of itself, when
embodied in the person of another, would constrain them to
whisper the black scandal of bygone years. It was
none the less a fact, however, that, in the eyes of the very
men who spoke thus, the scarlet letter had the effect of the
cross on a nun's bosom. It imparted to the wearer a kind of
sacredness which enabled her to walk securely amid all peril.
Had she fallen among thieves, it would have kept her safe.
It was reported, and believed by many, that an Indian had
drawn his arrow against the badge, and that the missile
struck it, but fell harmless to the ground.

The effect of the symbol—or, rather, of the position in
respect to society that was indicated by it—on the mind of
Hester Prynne herself was powerful and peculiar. All the
light and graceful foliage of her character had been withered
up by this red-hot brand, and had long ago fallen away,
leaving a bare and harsh outline which might have been
repulsive, had she possessed friends or companions to be
repelled by it. Even the attractiveness of her person had
undergone a similar change. It might be partly owing to the
studied austerity of her dress, and partly to the lack of
demonstration in her manners. It was a sad transformation,
too, that her rich and luxuriant hair had either been cut off,
or was so completely hidden by a cap, that not a shining
lock of it ever once gushed into the sunshine. It was due in
part to all these causes, but still more to something else,

that there seemed to be no longer anything in Hester's face for Love to dwell upon; nothing in Hester's form, though majestic and statue-like, that Passion would ever dream of clasping in its embrace; nothing in Hester's bosom to make it ever again the pillow of Affection. Some attribute had departed from her, the permanence of which had been essential to keep her a woman. Such is frequently the fate, and such the stern development, of the feminine character and person, when the woman has encountered, and lived through, an experience of peculiar severity. If she be all tenderness, she will die. If she survive, the tenderness will either be crushed out of her, or—and the outward semblance is the same—crushed so deeply into her heart that it can never show itself more. The latter is perhaps the truest theory. She who has once been woman, and ceased to be so, might at any moment become a woman again, if there were only the magic touch to effect the transfiguration. We shall see whether Hester Prynne were ever afterwards so touched, and transfigured.

Much of the marble coldness of Hester's impression was to be attributed to the circumstance that her life had turned, in a great measure, from passion and feeling to thought. Standing alone in the world—alone, as to any dependence on society, and with little Pearl to be guided and protected—alone, and hopeless of retrieving her position, even had she not scorned to consider it desirable—she cast away the fragments of a broken chain. The world's law was no law for her mind. It was an age in which the human intellect, newly emancipated, had taken a more active and a wider range than for many centuries before. Men of the sword had overthrown nobles and kings. Men bolder than these had overthrown and rearranged—not actually, but within the sphere of theory, which was their most real abode—the whole system of ancient prejudice, wherewith was linked much of ancient principle. Hester Prynne imbibed this spirit. She assumed a freedom of speculation, then common enough on the other side of the Atlantic, but which our forefathers, had they known it, would have held to be a deadlier crime than that stigmatized by the scarlet letter. In her lonesome cottage by the seashore, thoughts visited her, such as dared to enter no other dwelling in New England; shadowy guests that would have been as perilous as demons to their entertainer, could they have been seen so much as knocking at her door.

It is remarkable that persons who speculate the most boldly often conform with the most perfect quietude to the external regulations of society. The thought suffices them, without investing itself in the flesh and blood of action. So it seemed to be with Hester. Yet, had little Pearl never come to her from the spiritual world, it might have been far otherwise. Then, she might have come down to us in history, hand in hand with Ann Hutchinson, as the foundress of a religious sect. She might, in one of her phases, have been a prophetess. She might, and not improbably would, have suffered death from the stern tribunals of the period for attempting to undermine the foundations of the Puritan establishment. But, in the education of her child, the mother's enthusiasm of thought had something to wreak itself upon. Providence, in the person of this little girl, had assigned to Hester's charge the germ and blossom of womanhood, to be cherished and developed amid a host of difficulties. Everything was against her. The world was hostile. The child's own nature had something wrong in it which continually betokened that she had been born amiss—the effluence of her mother's lawless passion—and often impelled Hester to ask, in bitterness of heart, whether it were for ill or good that the poor little creature had been born at all.

Indeed, the same dark question often rose into her mind with reference to the whole race of womanhood. Was existence worth accepting, even to the happiest among them? As concerned her own individual existence, she had long ago decided in the negative, and dismissed the point as settled. A tendency to speculation, though it may keep woman quiet, as it does man, yet makes her sad. She discerns, it may be, such a hopeless task before her. As a first step, the whole system of society is to be torn down and built up anew. Then, the very nature of the opposite sex, or its long hereditary habit which has become like nature, is to be essentially modified before woman can be allowed to assume what seems a fair and suitable position. Finally, all other difficulties being obviated, woman cannot take advantage of these preliminary reforms until she herself shall have undergone a still mightier change; in which, perhaps, the ethereal essence, wherein she has her truest life, will be found to have evaporated. A woman never overcomes these problems by any exercise of thought. They are not to be solved, or only in one way. If her heart chance to come uppermost, they vanish. Thus, Hester Prynne, whose heart had lost its regular and healthy throb, wandered without a clew in the dark labyrinth of mind; now turned aside by an insurmountable precipice; now starting back from a deep chasm. There was wild and ghastly scenery all around her, and a home and comfort nowhere. At times, a fearful doubt strove to possess her soul, whether it were not better to send Pearl at once to heaven, and go herself to such futurity as Eternal Justice should provide.

The scarlet letter had not done its office.

Now, however, her interview with the Reverend Mr. Dimmesdale on the night of his vigil had given her a new theme of reflection, and held up to her an object that appeared worthy of any exertion and sacrifice for its attainment. She had witnessed the intense misery beneath which the minister struggled, or, to speak more accurately, had ceased to struggle. She saw that he stood on the verge of lunacy, if he had not already stepped across it. It was impossible to doubt, that, whatever painful efficacy there might be in the secret sting of remorse, a deadlier venom had been infused into it by the hand that proffered relief. A secret enemy had been continually by his side, under the semblance of a friend and helper, and had availed himself of the opportunities thus afforded for tampering with the delicate springs of Mr. Dimmesdale's nature. Hester could not but ask herself whether there had not originally been a defect of truth, courage and loyalty on her own part in allowing the minister to be thrown into a position where so much evil was to be foreboded, and nothing auspicious to be hoped. Her only justification lay in the fact that she had been able to discern no method of rescuing him from the blacker ruin than had overwhelmed herself, except by ac-quiescing in Roger Chillingworth's scheme of disguise. Un-der that impulse, she had made her choice, and had chosen, as it now appeared, the more wretched alternative of the two. She determined to redeem her error, so far as it might yet be possible. Strengthened by years of hard and solemn trial, she felt herself no longer so inadequate to cope with

Roger Chillingworth as on that night, abased by sin, and half maddened by the ignominy that was still new, when they had talked together in the prison chamber. She had climbed her way, since then, to a higher point. The old man, on the other hand, had brought himself nearer to her level, or perhaps below it, by the revenge which he had stooped for.

In fine, Hester Prynne resolved to meet her former husband, and do what might be in her power for the rescue of the victim on whom he had so evidently set his gripe. The occasion was not long to seek. One afternoon, walking with Pearl in a retired part of the peninsula, she beheld the old physician, with a basket on one arm and a staff in the other hand, stooping along the ground, in quest of roots and herbs to concoct his medicines withal.

XIV

Hester and the Physician

HESTER bade little Pearl run down to the margin of the water and play with the shells and tangled seaweed, until she should have talked awhile with yonder gatherer of herbs. So the child flew away like a bird, and, making bare her small white feet, went pattering along the moist margin of the sea. Here and there she came to a full stop, and peeped curiously into a pool, left by the retiring tide as a mirror for Pearl to see her face in. Forth peeped at her, out of the pool, with dark, glistening curls around her head and an elf-smile in her eyes, the image of a little maid, whom Pearl, having no other playmate, invited to take her hand and run a race with her. But the visionary little maid, on her part, beckoned likewise, as if to say—"This is a better place! Come thou into the pool!" And Pearl, stepping in, mid-leg deep, beheld her own white feet at the bottom, while, out of a still lower depth, came the gleam of a kind of fragmentary smile, floating to and fro in the agitated water.

Meanwhile, her mother had accosted the physician.

"I would speak a word with you," said she, "a word that concerns us much."

"Aha! and is it Mistress Hester that has a word for old Roger Chillingworth?" answered he, raising himself from his stooping posture. "With all my heart! Why, Mistress, I hear good tidings of you, on all hands! No longer ago than yester-eve, a magistrate, a wise and godly man, was discoursing of your affairs, Mistress Hester, and whispered me that there had been question concerning you in the council. It was debated whether or no, with safety to the common weal, yonder scarlet letter might be taken off your bosom. On my life, Hester, I made my entreaty to the worshipful magistrate that it might be done forthwith!"

"It lies not in the pleasure of the magistrates to take off this badge," calmly replied Hester. "Were I worthy to be quit of it, it would fall away of its own nature, or be transformed into something that should speak a different purport."

"Nay, then, wear it, if it suit you better," rejoined he. "A woman must needs follow her own fancy, touching the adornment of her person. The letter is gayly embroidered, and shows right bravely on your bosom!"

All this while, Hester had been looking steadily at the old man, and was shocked, as well as wonder-smitten, to discern what a change had been wrought upon him within the past seven years. It was not so much that he had grown older; for though the traces of advancing life were visible, he bore his age well and seemed to retain a wiry vigor and alertness. But the former aspect of an intellectual and studious man, calm and quiet, which was what she best remembered in him, had altogether vanished and been succeeded by an eager, searching, almost fierce, yet carefully guarded look. It seemed to be his wish and purpose to mask this expression with a smile; but the latter played him false, and flickered over his visage so derisively, that the spectator could see his blackness all the better for it. Ever and anon, too, there came a glare of red light out of his eyes; as if the old man's soul were on fire, and kept on smouldering duskily within his breast, until, by some casual puff of passion, it was blown into a momentary flame. This he repressed, as speedily as possible, and strove to look as if nothing of the kind had happened.

In a word, old Roger Chillingworth was a striking evidence of man's faculty of transforming himself into a devil, if he will only, for a reasonable space of time, undertake a devil's office. This unhappy person had effected such a transformation by devoting himself, for seven years, to the constant analysis of a heart full of torture, and deriving his enjoyment thence, and adding fuel to those fiery tortures which he analyzed and gloated over.

The scarlet letter burned on Hester Prynne's bosom. Here

was another ruin, the responsibility of which came partly home to her.

"What see you in my face," asked the physician, "that you look at it so earnestly?"

"Something that would make me weep, if there were any tears bitter enough for it," answered she. "But let it pass! It is of yonder miserable man that I would speak."

"And what of him?" cried Roger Chillingworth, eagerly, as if he loved the topic, and were glad of an opportunity to discuss it with the only person of whom he could make a confidant. "Not to hide the truth, Mistress Hester, my thoughts happen just now to be busy with the gentleman. So speak freely; and I will make answer."

"When we last spake together," said Hester, "now seven years ago, it was your pleasure to extort a promise of secrecy, as touching the former relation betwixt yourself and me. As the life and good fame of yonder man were in your hands, there seemed no choice to me save to be silent, in accordance with your behest. Yet it was not without heavy misgivings that I thus bound myself; for, having cast off all duty towards other human beings, there remained a duty towards him; and something whispered me that I was betraying it in pledging myself to keep your counsel. Since that day, no man is so near to him as you. You tread behind his every footstep. You are beside him, sleeping and waking. You search his thoughts. You burrow and rankle in his heart! Your clutch is on his life, and you cause him to die daily a living death; and still he knows you not. In permitting this, I have surely acted a false part by the only man to whom the power was left me to be true!"

"What choice had you?" asked Roger Chillingworth. "My finger, pointed at this man, would have hurled him from his pulpit into a dungeon—thence, peradventure, to the gallows!"

"It had been better so!" said Hester Prynne.

"What evil have I done the man?" asked Roger Chillingworth again. "I tell thee, Hester Prynne, the richest fee that ever physician earned from monarch could not have bought such care as I have wasted on this miserable priest! But for my aid, his life would have burned away in torments within the first two years after the perpetration of his crime and thine. For, Hester, his spirit lacked the strength that could have borne up, as thine has, beneath a burden like thy scarlet letter. O, I could reveal a goodly secret! But enough! What art can do, I have exhausted on him. That he now breathes, and creeps about on earth, is owing all to me!"

"Better he had died at once!" said Hester Prynne.

"Yea, woman, thou sayest truly!" cried old Roger Chillingworth, letting the lurid fire of his heart blaze out before her eyes. "Better had he died at once! Never did mortal suffer what this man has suffered. And all, all, in the sight of his worst enemy! He has been conscious of me. He has felt an influence dwelling always upon him like a curse. He knew, by some spiritual sense—for the Creator never made another being so sensitive as this—he knew that no friendly hand was pulling at his heart-strings, and that an eye was looking curiously into him, which sought only evil, and found it. But he knew not that the eye and hand were mine! With the superstition common to his brotherhood, he fancied himself given over to a fiend, to be tortured with frightful dreams, and desperate thoughts, the sting of remorse, and despair of pardon, as a foretaste of what awaits him beyond the grave. But it was the constant shadow of my presence! —the closest propinquity of the man whom he had most vilely wronged!—and who had grown to exist only by this perpetual poison of the direst revenge! Yea, indeed!—he did not err!— here was a fiend at his elbow! A mortal man, with once a human heart, has become a fiend for his especial torment!"

The unfortunate physician, while uttering these words, lifted his hands with a look of horror, as if he had beheld some frightful shape, which he could not recognize, usurping the place of his own image in a glass. It was one of those moments—which sometimes occur only at the interval of years—when a man's moral aspect is faithfully revealed to his mind's eye. Not improbably, he had never before viewed himself as he did now.

"Hast thou not tortured him enough?" said Hester, noticing the old man's look. "Has he not paid thee all?"

"No!—no!—He has but increased the debt!" answered the physician; and as he proceeded, his manner lost its fiercer characteristics and subsided into gloom. "Dost thou remember me, Hester, as I was nine years agone? Even then, I was in the autumn of my days, nor was it the early autumn. But all my life had been made up of earnest, studious, thoughtful, quiet years, bestowed faithfully for the increase of mine own knowledge, and faithfully, too, though this latter object was but casual to the other—faithfully for the advancement of human welfare. No life had been more peaceful and innocent than mine; few lives so rich with benefits conferred. Dost thou remember me? Was I not, though you might deem me cold, nevertheless a man thoughtful for others, craving little for himself—kind, true, just, and of constant if not warm affections? Was I not all this?"

"All this, and more," said Hester.

"And what am I now?" demanded he, looking into her face, and permitting the whole evil within him to be written on his features. "I have already told thee what I am! A fiend! Who made me so?"

"It was myself!" cried Hester, shuddering. "It was I, not less than he. Why hast thou not avenged thyself on me?"

"I have left thee to the scarlet letter," replied Roger Chillingworth. "If that have not avenged me, I can do no more!"

He laid his finger on it, with a smile.

"It has avenged thee!" answered Hester Prynne.

"I judged no less," said the physician. "And now, what wouldst thou with me touching this man?"

"I must reveal the secret," answered Hester, firmly. "He must discern thee in thy true character. What may be the result, I know not. But this long debt of confidence, due from me to him, whose bane and ruin I have been, shall at length be paid. So far as concerns the overthrow or preservation of his fair fame and his earthly state, and perchance his life, he is in thy hands. Nor do I—whom the scarlet letter has disciplined to truth, though it be the truth of red-hot iron, entering into the soul—nor do I perceive such advantages in his living any longer a life of ghastly emptiness, that I shall stoop to implore thy mercy. Do with him as thou wilt! There is no good for him—no good for me—no good for thee! There is no good for little Pearl! There is no path to guide us out of this dismal maze!"

"Woman, I could well-nigh pity thee!" said Roger Chillingworth, unable to restrain a thrill of admiration too; for there was a quality almost majestic in the despair which she expressed. "Thou hadst great elements. Peradventure, hadst thou met earlier with a better love than mine, this evil had not been. I pity thee, for the good that has been wasted in thy nature!"

"And I thee," answered Hester Prynne, "for the hatred that has transformed a wise and just man to a fiend! Wilt thou yet purge it out of thee, and be once more human? If not for his sake, then doubly for thine own! Forgive, and leave his further retribution to the Power that claims it! I said, but now, that there could be no good event for him, or thee, or me, who are here wandering together in this gloomy maze of evil, and stumbling at every step over the guilt wherewith we have strewn our path. It is not so! There might be good for thee, and thee alone, since thou hast been deeply wronged, and hast it at thy will to pardon. Wilt thou give up that only privilege? Wilt thou reject that priceless benefit?"

"Peace, Hester, peace!" replied the old man, with gloomy sternness. "It is not granted me to pardon. I have no such power as thou tellest me of. My old faith, long forgotten, comes back to me, and explains all that we do, and all we suffer. By thy first step awry, thou didst plant the germ of evil; but since that moment, it has all been a dark necessity. Ye that have wronged me are not sinful, save in a kind of typical illusion; neither am I fiendlike, who have snatched a fiend's office from his hands. It is our fate. Let the black flower blossom as it may. Now go thy ways, and deal as thou wilt with yonder man."

He waved his hand, and betook himself again to his employment of gathering herbs.

XV

Hester and Pearl

So Roger Chillingworth—a deformed old figure, with a face that haunted men's memories longer than they liked—took leave of Hester Prynne, and went stooping away along the earth. He gathered here and there an herb, or grubbed up a root, and put it into the basket on his arm. His gray beard almost touched the ground, as he crept onward. Hester gazed after him a little while, looking with a half-fantastic curiosity to see whether the tender grass of early spring would not be blighted beneath him and show the wavering track of his footsteps, sere and brown, across its cheerful verdure. She wondered what sort of herbs they were, which the old man was so sedulous to gather. Would not the earth, quickened to an evil purpose by the sympathy of his eye, greet him with poisonous shrubs, of species hitherto unknown, that would start up under his fingers? Or might it suffice him, that every wholesome growth should be converted into something deleterious and malignant at his touch? Did the sun, which shone so brightly everywhere else, really fall upon him? Or was there, as it rather seemed, a circle of ominous shadow moving along with his deformity, whichever way he turned himself? And whither was he now going? Would he not suddenly sink into the earth, leaving a barren and blasted spot, where, in due course of time, would be seen deadly nightshade, dogwood, henbane, and whatever else of vegetable wickedness the climate could produce, all flourishing with hideous luxuriance? Or would he spread bat's wings and flee away, looking so much the uglier, the higher he rose towards heaven?

"Be it sin or no," said Hester Prynne, bitterly, as she still gazed after him, "I hate the man!"

She upbraided herself for the sentiment, but could not overcome or lessen it. Attempting to do so, she thought of those long-past days in a distant land, when he used to emerge at eventide from the seclusion of his study and sit down in the firelight of their home, and in the light of her nuptial smile. He needed to bask himself in that smile, he said, in order that the chill of so many lonely hours among his books might be taken off the scholar's heart. Such scenes had once appeared not otherwise than happy, but now, as viewed through the dismal medium of her subsequent life, they classed themselves among her ugliest remembrances. She marvelled how such scenes could have been! She marvelled how she could ever have been wrought upon to marry him! She deemed it her crime most to be repented of, that she had ever endured, and reciprocated, the lukewarm grasp of his hand, and had suffered the smile of her lips and eyes to mingle and melt into his own. And it seemed a fouler offence committed by Roger Chillingworth than any which had since been done him, that, in the time when her heart knew no better, he had persuaded her to fancy herself happy by his side.

"Yes, I hate him!" repeated Hester, more bitterly than before. "He betrayed me! He has done me worse wrong than I did him!"

Let men tremble to win the hand of woman, unless they win along with it the utmost passion of her heart! Else it may be their miserable fortune, as it was Roger Chillingworth's, when some mightier touch than their own may have awakened all her sensibilities, to be reproached even for the calm content, the marble image of happiness, which they will have imposed upon her as the warm reality. But Hester ought long ago to have done with this injustice. What did it betoken? Had seven long years, under the torture of the scarlet letter, inflicted so much of misery and wrought out no repentance?

The emotions of that brief space, while she stood gazing after the crooked figure of old Roger Chillingworth, threw a dark light on Hester's state of mind, revealing much that she might not otherwise have acknowledged to herself.

He being gone, she summoned back her child.

"Pearl! Little Pearl! Where are you?"

Pearl, whose activity of spirit never flagged, had been at no loss for amusement while her mother talked with the old gatherer of herbs. At first, as already told, she had flirted fancifully with her own image in a pool of water, beckoning the phantom forth, and—as it declined to venture—seeking a passage for herself into its sphere of impalpable earth and unattainable sky. Soon finding, however, that either she or the image was unreal, she turned elsewhere for better pastime. She made little boats out of birch-bark, and freighted them with snail shells, and sent out more ventures on the mighty deep than any merchant in New England; but the larger part of them foundered near the shore. She seized a live horseshoe by the tail, and made prize of several five-fingers, and laid out a jellyfish to melt in the warm sun. Then she took up the white foam that streaked the line of the advancing tide, and threw it upon the breeze, scampering after it with winged footsteps to catch the great snowflakes ere they fell. Perceiving a flock of beach birds that fed and fluttered along the shore, the naughty child picked up her apron full of pebbles, and, creeping from rock to rock after these small seafowl, displayed remarkable dexterity in pelting them. One little gray bird with a white breast, Pearl was almost sure, had been hit by a pebble, and fluttered away with a broken wing. But then the elf-child sighed, and gave up her sport; because it grieved her to have done harm to a little being that was as wild as the sea breeze, or as wild as Pearl herself.

Her final employment was to gather seaweed of various kinds and make herself a scarf, or mantle, and a headdress, and thus assume the aspect of a little mermaid. She inherited her mother's gift for devising drapery and costume. As the last touch to her mermaid's garb, Pearl took some eelgrass, and imitated, as best she could, on her own bosom, the decoration with which she was so familiar on her mother's. A letter—the letter "A"—but freshly green, instead of scarlet! The child bent her chin upon her breast, and contemplated this device with strange interest; even as if the one only thing for which she had been sent into the world was to make out its hidden import.

"I wonder if Mother will ask me what it means?" thought Pearl.

Just then she heard her mother's voice, and flitting along as lightly as one of the little sea birds, appeared before Hester Prynne, dancing, laughing, and pointing her finger to the ornament upon her bosom.

"My little Pearl!" said Hester, after a moment's silence, "the green letter, and on thy childish bosom, has no purport. But dost thou know, my child, what this letter means which thy mother is doomed to wear?"

"Yes, Mother," said the child. "It is the great letter 'A.' Thou hast taught me in the hornbook."

Hester looked steadily into her little face; but, though there was that singular expression which she had so often remarked in her black eyes, she could not satisfy herself whether Pearl really attached any meaning to the symbol. She felt a morbid desire to ascertain the point.

"Dost thou know, child, wherefore thy mother wears this letter?"

"Truly do I!" answered Pearl, looking brightly into her mother's face. "It is for the same reason that the minister keeps his hand over his heart!"

"And what reason is that?" asked Hester, half smiling at the absurd incongruity of the child's observation; but, on second thoughts, turning pale. "What has the letter to do with any heart, save mine?"

"Nay, Mother, I have told all I know," said Pearl more seriously than she was wont to speak. "Ask yonder old man whom thou hast been talking with! It may be he can tell. But in good earnest now, Mother dear, what does this scarlet letter mean?—and why dost thou wear it on thy bosom?—and why does the minister keep his hand over his heart?"

She took her mother's hand in both her own, and gazed into her eyes with an earnestness that was seldom seen in her wild and capricious character. The thought occurred to Hester that the child might really be seeking to approach her with childlike confidence, and doing what she could, and as intelligently as she knew how, to establish a meeting point of sympathy. It showed Pearl in an unwonted aspect. Heretofore, the mother, while loving her child with the intensity of a sole affection, had schooled herself to hope for little other return than the waywardness of an April breeze, which spends its time in airy sport, and has its gusts of inexplicable passion, and is petulant in its best of moods, and chills oftener than caresses you, when you take it to your bosom; in requital of which misdemeanors, it will sometimes, of its own vague purpose, kiss your cheek with a kind of doubtful tenderness, and play gently with your hair, and then be gone about its other idle business, leaving a dreamy pleasure at your heart. And this, moreover, was a mother's estimate of the child's disposition. Any other observer might have seen few but unamiable traits, and have given them a far darker coloring. But now the idea came strongly into Hester's mind that Pearl, with her remarkable precocity and acuteness, might already have approached the age when she could be made a friend, and intrusted with as much of a mother's sorrow as could be imparted, without irreverence either to the parent or the child. In the little chaos of Pearl's character, there might be seen emerging— and could have been, from the very first—the steadfast principles of an unflinching courage—an uncontrollable will—a sturdy pride, which might be disciplined into self-respect— and a bitter scorn of many things, which, when examined, might be found to have the taint of falsehood in them.

She possessed affections, too, though hitherto acrid and disagreeable as are the richest flavors of unripe fruit. With all these sterling attributes, thought Hester, the evil which she inherited from her mother must be great indeed, if a noble woman do not grow out of this elfish child.

Pearl's inevitable tendency to hover about the enigma of the scarlet letter seemed an innate quality of her being. From the earliest epoch of her conscious life, she had entered upon this as her appointed mission. Hester had often fancied that Providence had a design of justice and retribution, in endowing the child with this marked propensity; but never, until now, had she bethought herself to ask, whether, linked with that design, there might not likewise be a purpose of mercy and beneficence. If little Pearl were entertained with faith and trust, as a spirit messenger no less than an earthly child, might it not be her errand to soothe away the sorrow that lay cold in her mother's heart, and converted it into a tomb?—and to help her to overcome the passion, once so wild, and even yet neither dead nor asleep, but only imprisoned within the same tomb-like heart?

Such were some of the thoughts that now stirred in Hester's mind, with as much vivacity of impression as if they had actually been whispered into her ear. And there was little Pearl, all this while, holding her mother's hand in both her own, and turning her face upward, while she put these searching questions, once, and again, and still a third time.

"What does the letter mean, Mother?—and why dost thou wear it?—and why does the minister keep his hand over his heart?"

"What shall I say?" thought Hester to herself. "No! If this be the price of the child's sympathy, I cannot pay it."

Then she spoke aloud.

"Silly Pearl," said she, "what questions are these? There are many things in this world that a child must not ask about. What know I of the minister's heart? And as for the scarlet letter, I wear it for the sake of its gold thread."

In all the seven bygone years, Hester Prynne had never before been false to the symbol on her bosom. It may be that it was the talisman of a stern and severe, but yet a guardian spirit, who now forsook her, as recognizing that, in spite of his strict watch over her heart, some new evil had crept into it, or some old one had never been expelled. As for little Pearl, the earnestness soon passed out of her face.

But the child did not see fit to let the matter drop. Two or three times, as her mother and she went homeward, and as often at suppertime, and while Hester was putting her to bed, and once after she seemed to be fairly asleep, Pearl looked up, with mischief gleaming in her black eyes.

"Mother," said she, "what does the scarlet letter mean?"

And the next morning, the first indication the child gave of being awake was by popping up her head from the pillow and making that other inquiry, which she had so unaccountably connected with her investigations about the scarlet letter:

"Mother!—Mother!—Why does the minister keep his hand over his heart?"

"Hold thy tongue, naughty child!" answered her mother, with an asperity that she had never permitted to herself before. "Do not tease me; else I shall shut thee into the dark closet!"

XVI

A Forest Walk

HESTER Prynne remained constant in her resolve to make known to Mr. Dimmesdale, at whatever risk of present pain or ulterior consequences, the true character of the man who had crept into his intimacy. For several days, however, she vainly sought an opportunity of addressing him in some of the meditative walks which she knew him to be in the habit of taking, along the shores of the peninsula, or on the wooded hills of the neighboring country. There would have been no scandal, indeed, nor peril to the holy whiteness of the clergyman's good fame, had she visited him in his own study, where many a penitent, ere now, had confessed sins of perhaps as deep a dye as the one betokened by the scarlet letter. But, partly that she dreaded the secret or undisguised interference of old Roger Chillingworth, and partly that her conscious heart imputed suspicion where none could have been felt, and partly that both the minister and she would need the whole wide world to breathe in while they talked together—for all these reasons, Hester never thought of meeting him in any narrower privacy than beneath the open sky.

At last, while attending in a sick chamber, whither the Reverend Mr. Dimmesdale had been summoned to make a prayer, she learnt that he had gone the day before to visit the Apostle Eliot, among his Indian converts. He would probably return by a certain hour in the afternoon of the morrow. Betimes, therefore, the next day, Hester took little Pearl—who was necessarily the companion of all her mother's expeditions, however inconvenient her presence—and set forth.

The road, after the two wayfarers had crossed from the peninsula to the mainland, was no other than a footpath. It straggled onward into the mystery of the primeval forest. This hemmed it in so narrowly, and stood so black and dense on either side, and disclosed such imperfect glimpses of the sky above, that, to Hester's mind, it imaged not amiss the moral wilderness in which she had so long been wandering. The day was chill and sombre. Overhead was a gray expanse of cloud, slightly stirred, however, by a breeze, so that a gleam of flickering sunshine might now and then be seen at its solitary play along the path. This flitting cheerfulness was always at the further extremity of some long vista through the forest. The sportive sunlight—feebly sportive, at best, in the predominant pensiveness of the day and scene—withdrew itself as they came nigh, and left the spots where it had danced the drearier, because they had hoped to find them bright. "Mother," said little Pearl, "the sunshine does not love you. It runs away and hides itself, because it is afraid of something on your bosom. Now, see! There it is, playing, a good way off. Stand you here, and let me run and catch it. I am but a child. It will not flee from me; for I wear nothing on my bosom yet!"

"Nor ever will, my child, I hope," said Hester.

"And why not, Mother?" asked Pearl, stopping short, just at the beginning of her race. "Will not it come of its own accord, when I am a woman grown?"

"Run away, child," answered her mother, "and catch the sunshine! It will soon be gone."

Pearl set forth at a great pace, and, as Hester smiled to perceive, did actually catch the sunshine, and stood laughing in the midst of it, all brightened by its splendor, and scintillating with the vivacity excited by rapid motion. The light lingered about the lonely child, as if glad of such a playmate, until her mother had drawn almost nigh enough to step into the magic circle too.

"It will go now," said Pearl, shaking her head.

"See!" answered Hester, smiling. "Now I can stretch out my hand, and grasp some of it."

As she attempted to do so, the sunshine vanished; or, to judge from the bright expression that was dancing in Pearl's features, her mother could have fancied that the child had absorbed it into herself, and would give it forth again, with a gleam about her path, as they should plunge into some gloomier shade. There was no other attribute that so much impressed her with a sense of new and untransmitted vigor in Pearl's nature, as this never-failing vivacity of spirits; she had not the disease of sadness, which almost all children, in these latter days, inherit, with the scrofula, from the troubles of their ancestors. Perhaps this too was a disease, and but the reflex of the wild energy with which Hester had fought against her sorrows, before Pearl's birth. It was certainly a doubtful charm, imparting a hard, metallic lustre to the child's character. She wanted—what some people want throughout life—a grief that should deeply touch her, and thus humanize and make her capable of sympathy. But there was time enough yet for little Pearl.

"Come, my child!" said Hester, looking about her from the spot where Pearl stood still in the sunshine. "We will sit down a little way within the wood, and rest ourselves."

"I am not aweary, Mother," replied the little girl. "But you may sit down, if you will tell me a story meanwhile."

"A story, child!" said Hester. "And about what?"

"O, a story about the Black Man," answered Pearl, taking hold of her mother's gown, and looking up, half earnestly, half mischievously, into her face. "How he haunts this forest, and carries a book with him—a big, heavy book, with iron clasps; and how this ugly Black Man offers his book and an iron pen to everybody that meets him here among the trees; and they are to write their names with their own blood. And then he sets his mark on their bosoms! Didst thou ever meet the Black Man, Mother?"

"And who told you this story, Pearl?" asked her mother, recognizing a common superstition of the period.

"It was the old dame in the chimney-corner, at the house where you watched last night," said the child. "But she fancied me asleep while she was talking of it. She said that a thousand and a thousand people had met him here, and had written in his book, and have his mark on them. And that ugly-tempered lady, old Mistress Hibbins, was one. And, Mother, the old dame said that this scarlet letter was the Black Man's mark on thee, and that it glows like a red flame when thou meetest him at midnight, here in the dark wood.

Is it true, Mother? And dost thou go to meet him in the nighttime?"

"Didst thou ever awake, and find thy mother gone?" asked Hester.

"Not that I remember," said the child. "If thou fearest to leave me in our cottage, thou mightest take me along with thee. I would very gladly go! But, Mother, tell me now! Is there such a Black Man? And didst thou ever meet him? And is this his mark?"

"Wilt thou let me be at peace, if I once tell thee?" asked her mother.

"Yes, if thou tellest me all," answered Pearl.

"Once in my life I met the Black Man!" said her mother. "This scarlet letter is his mark!"

Thus conversing, they entered sufficiently deep into the wood to secure themselves from the observation of any casual passenger along the forest track. Here they sat down on a luxuriant heap of moss, which, at some epoch of the preceding century, had been a gigantic pine, with its root and trunk in the darksome shade, and its head aloft in the upper atmosphere. It was a little dell where they had seated themselves, with a leaf-strewn bank rising gently on either side, and a brook flowing through the midst over a bed of fallen and drowned leaves. The trees impending over it had flung down great branches from time to time, which choked up the current and compelled it to form eddies and black depths at some points, while, in its swifter and livelier passages, there appeared a channel-way of pebbles, and brown, sparkling sand. Letting the eyes follow along the course of the stream, they could catch the reflected light from its water at some short distance within the forest, but soon lost all traces of it amid the bewilderment of tree-trunks and underbrush, and here and there a huge rock covered over with gray lichens. All these giant trees and boulders of granite seemed intent on making a mystery of the course of this small brook; fearing, perhaps, that, with its never-ceasing loquacity, it should whisper tales out of the heart of the old forest whence it flowed, or mirror its revelations on the smooth surface of a pool. Continually, indeed, as it stole onward, the streamlet kept up a babble, kind, quiet, soothing, but melancholy, like the voice of a young child that was spending its infancy without playfulness, and knew not how to be merry among sad acquaintance and events of sombre hue.

"O brook! O foolish and tiresome little brook!" cried Pearl, after listening awhile to its talk. "Why art thou so sad? Pluck up a spirit, and do not be all the time sighing and murmuring!"

But the brook, in the course of its little lifetime among the forest trees, had gone through so solemn an experience that it could not help talking about it and seemed to have nothing else to say. Pearl resembled the brook, inasmuch as the current of her life gushed from a wellspring as mysterious, and had flowed through scenes shadowed as heavily with gloom. But, unlike the little stream, she danced and sparkled, and prattled airily along her course.

"What does this sad little brook say, Mother?" inquired she.

"If thou hadst a sorrow of thine own, the brook might tell thee of it," answered her mother, "even as it is telling me of mine! But now, Pearl, I hear a footstep along the path, and the noise of one putting aside the branches. I would have thee betake thyself to play, and leave me to speak with him that comes yonder."

"Is it the Black Man?" asked Pearl.

"Wilt thou go and play, child?" repeated her mother. "But do not stray far into the wood. And take heed that thou come at my first call."

"Yes, Mother," answered Pearl. "But if it be the Black Man, wilt thou not let me stay a moment, and look at him, with his big book under his arm?"

"Go, silly child!" said her mother, impatiently. "It is no Black Man! Thou canst see him now, through the trees. It is the minister!"

"And so it is!" said the child. "And, Mother, he has his hand over his heart! Is it because, when the minister wrote his name in the book, the Black Man set his mark in that place? But why does he not wear it outside his bosom, as thou dost, Mother?"

"Go now, child, and thou shalt tease me as thou wilt another time," cried Hester Prynne. "But do not stray far. Keep where thou canst hear the babble of the brook."

The child went singing away, following up the current of the brook and striving to mingle a more lightsome cadence with its melancholy voice. But the little stream would not be comforted, and still kept telling its unintelligible secret of some very mournful mystery that had happened—or making a prophetic lamentation about something that was yet to happen—within the verge of the dismal forest. So Pearl, who had enough of shadow in her own little life, chose to break off all acquaintance with this repining brook. She set herself, therefore, to gathering violets and wood anemones, and some scarlet columbines that she found growing in the crevices of a high rock.

When her elf-child had departed, Hester Prynne made a step or two towards the track that led through the forest, but still remained under the deep shadow of the trees. She beheld the minister advancing along the path, entirely alone, and leaning on a staff which he had cut by the wayside. He looked haggard and feeble, and betrayed a nerveless despondency in his air which had never so remarkably characterized him in his walks about the settlement, nor in any other situation where he deemed himself liable to notice. Here it was woefully visible, in this intense seclusion of the forest, which of itself would have been a heavy trial to the spirits. There was a listlessness in his gait, as if he saw no reason for taking one step further, nor felt any desire to do so, but would have been glad, could he be glad of anything, to fling himself down at the root of the nearest tree, and lie there passive, forevermore. The leaves might bestrew him and the soil gradually accumulate and form a little hillock over his frame, no matter whether there were life in it or no. Death was too definite an object to be wished for, or avoided.

To Hester's eye, the Reverend Mr. Dimmesdale exhibited no symptom of positive and vivacious suffering, except that, as little Pearl had remarked, he kept his hand over his heart.

XVII

The Pastor and His Parishioner

SLOWLY as the minister walked, he had almost gone by before Hester Prynne could gather voice enough to attract his observation. At length, she succeeded.

"Arthur Dimmesdale!" she said, faintly at first; then louder, but hoarsely. "Arthur Dimmesdale!"

"Who speaks?" answered the minister.

Gathering himself quickly up, he stood more erect, like a man taken by surprise in a mood to which he was reluctant to have witnesses. Throwing his eyes anxiously in the direction of the voice, he indistinctly beheld a form under the trees, clad in garments so sombre, and so little relieved from the gray twilight into which the clouded sky and the heavy foliage had darkened the noontide, that he knew not whether it were a woman or a shadow. It may be that his pathway through life was haunted thus, by a spectre that had stolen out from among his thoughts.

He made a step nigher, and discovered the scarlet letter.

"Hester! Hester Prynne!" said he. "Is it thou? Art thou in life?"

"Even so!" she answered. "In such life as has been mine these seven years past! And thou, Arthur Dimmesdale, dost thou yet live?"

It was no wonder that they thus questioned one another's actual and bodily existence, and even doubted of their own. So strangely did they meet in the dim wood, that it was like the first encounter, in the world beyond the grave, of two spirits who had been intimately connected in their former life, but now stood coldly shuddering, in mutual dread, as not yet familiar with their state, nor wonted to the companionship of disembodied beings. Each a ghost, and awestricken at the other ghost! They were awe-stricken likewise at themselves; because the crisis flung back to them their consciousness, and revealed to each heart its history and experience, as life never does, except at such breathless epochs. The soul beheld its features in the mirror of the passing moment. It was with fear, and tremulously, and, as it were, by a slow, reluctant necessity, that Arthur Dimmesdale put forth his hand, chill as death, and touched the chill hand of Hester Prynne. The grasp, cold as it was, took away what was dreariest in the interview. They now felt themselves, at least, inhabitants of the same sphere.

Without a word more spoken—neither he nor she assuming the guidance, but with an unexpressed consent—they glided back into the shadow of the woods whence Hester had emerged, and sat down on the heap of moss where she and Pearl had before been sitting. When they found voice to speak, it was at first only to utter remarks and inquiries such as any two acquaintances might have made, about the gloomy sky, the threatening storm, and, next, the health of each. Thus they went onward, not boldly, but step by step, into the themes that were brooding deepest in their hearts. So long estranged by fate and circumstances, they needed something slight and casual to run before, and throw open the doors of intercourse, so that their real thoughts might be led across the threshold.

After a while, the minister fixed his eyes on Hester Prynne's.

"Hester," said he, "hast thou found peace?"

She smiled drearily, looking down upon her bosom.

"Hast thou?" she asked.

"None!—nothing but despair!" he answered. "What else could I look for being what I am, and leading such a life as mine? Were I an atheist—a man devoid of conscience—a wretch with coarse and brutal instincts—I might have found peace, long ere now. Nay, I never should have lost it! But, as matters stand with my soul, whatever of good capacity there originally was in me, all of God's gifts that were the choicest have become the ministers of spiritual torment. Hester, I am most miserable!"

"The people reverence thee," said Hester. "And surely

thou workest good among them! Doth this bring thee no comfort?"

"More misery, Hester!—only the more misery!" answered the clergyman, with a bitter smile. "As concerns the good which I may appear to do, I have no faith in it. It must needs be a delusion. What can a ruined soul like mine effect towards the redemption of other souls?—or a polluted soul, towards their purification? And as for the people's reverence, would that it were turned to scorn and hatred! Canst thou deem it, Hester, a consolation, that I must stand up in my pulpit and meet so many eyes turned upward to my face, as if the light of heaven were beaming from it!—must see my flock hungry for the truth, and listening to my words as if a tongue of Pentecost were speaking!—and then look inward, and discern the black reality of what they idolize? I have laughed, in bitterness and agony of heart, at the contrast between what I seem and what I am! And Satan laughs at it!"

"You wrong yourself in this," said Hester, gently. "You have deeply and sorely repented. Your sin is left behind you, in the days long past. Your present life is no less holy, in very truth, than it seems in people's eyes. Is there no reality in the penitence thus sealed and witnessed by good works? And wherefore should it not bring you peace?"

"No, Hester, no!" replied the clergyman. "There is no substance in it! It is cold and dead, and can do nothing for me! Of penance, I have had enough! Of penitence, there has been none! Else, I should long ago have thrown off these garments of mock holiness and have shown myself to mankind as they will see me at the judgment seat. Happy are you, Hester, that wear the scarlet letter openly upon your bosom! Mine burns in secret! Thou little knowest what a relief it is, after the torment of a seven years' cheat, to look into an eye that recognizes me for what I am! Had I one friend—or were it my worst enemy!—to whom, when sickened with the praises of all other men, I could daily betake myself and be known as the vilest of all sinners, methinks my soul might keep itself alive thereby. Even thus much of truth would save me! But now, it is all falsehood! —all emptiness!—all death!"

Hester Prynne looked into his face, but hesitated to speak. Yet, uttering his long-restrained emotions so vehemently as he did, his words here offered her the very point of circumstances in which to interpose what she came to say. She conquered her fears, and spoke.

"Such a friend as thou hast even now wished for," said she, "with whom to weep over thy sin, thou hast in me, the partner of it!"—Again she hesitated, but brought out the words with an effort. "Thou hast long had such an enemy, and dwellest with him, under the same roof!"

The minister started to his feet gasping for breath and clutching at his heart, as if he would have torn it out of his bosom.

"Ha! What sayest thou!" cried he. "An enemy! And under mine own roof! What mean you?"

Hester Prynne was now fully sensible of the deep injury for which she was responsible to this unhappy man, in permitting him to lie for so many years, or, indeed, for a single moment, at the mercy of one whose purposes could not be other than malevolent. The very contiguity of his enemy, beneath whatever mask the latter might conceal himself, was enough to disturb the magnetic sphere of a being so sensitive as Arthur Dimmesdale. There had been a period when Hester was less alive to this consideration; or, perhaps, in the misanthropy of her own trouble, she left the minister to bear what she might picture to herself as a more tolerable doom. But of late, since the night of his vigil, all her sympathies towards him had been both softened and invigorated. She now read his heart more accurately. She doubted not that the continual presence of Roger Chillingworth—the secret poison of his malignity, infecting all the air about him, and his authorized interference, as a physician, with the minister's physical and spiritual infirmities—that these bad opportunities had been turned to a cruel purpose. By means of them, the sufferer's conscience had been kept in an irritated state, the tendency of which was, not to cure by wholesome pain, but to disorganize and corrupt his spiritual being. Its result, on earth, could hardly fail to be insanity, and hereafter, that eternal alienation from the Good and True, of which madness is perhaps the earthly type.

Such was the ruin to which she had brought the man, once—nay, why should we not speak it?—still so passionately loved! Hester felt that the sacrifice of the clergyman's good name, and death itself, as she had already told Roger

Chillingworth, would have been infinitely preferable to the alternative which she had taken upon herself to choose. And now, rather than have had this grievous wrong to confess, she would gladly have lain down on the forest leaves and died there, at Arthur Dimmesdale's feet.

"O Arthur," cried she, "forgive me! In all things else, I have striven to be true! Truth was the one virtue which I might have held fast, and did hold fast, through all extremity; save when thy good—thy life—thy fame—were put in question! Then I consented to a deception. But a lie is never good, even though death threaten on the other side! Dost thou not see what I would say? That old man!—the physician!—he whom they call Roger Chillingworth!—he was my husband!"

The minister looked at her, for an instant, with all that violence of passion, which—intermixed, in more shapes than one, with his higher, purer, softer qualities—was, in fact, the portion of him which the Devil claimed, and through which he sought to win the rest. Never was there a blacker or a fiercer frown than Hester now encountered. For the brief space that it lasted, it was a dark transfiguration. But his character had been so much enfeebled by suffering, that even its lower energies were incapable of more than a temporary struggle. He sank down on the ground, and buried his face in his hands.

"I might have known it," murmured he. "I did know it! Was not the secret told me, in the natural recoil of my heart, at the first sight of him, and as often as I have seen him since? Why did I not understand? O Hester Prynne, thou little, little knowest all the horror of this thing! And the shame!—the indelicacy!—the horrible ugliness of this exposure of a sick and guilty heart to the very eye that would gloat over it! Woman, woman, thou art accountable for this! I cannot forgive thee!"

"Thou shalt forgive me!" cried Hester, flinging herself on the fallen leaves beside him. "Let God punish! Thou shalt forgive!"

With sudden and desperate tenderness, she threw her arms around him, and pressed his head against her bosom; little caring though his cheek rested on the scarlet letter. He would have released himself, but strove in vain to do so. Hester would not set him free, lest he should look her sternly in the face. All the world had frowned on her—for seven long years had it frowned upon this lonely woman—and still she bore it all, nor ever once turned away her firm, sad eyes. Heaven, likewise, had frowned upon her, and she had not died. But the frown of this pale, weak, sinful, and sorrow-stricken man was what Hester could not bear, and live!

"Wilt thou yet forgive me?" she repeated over and over again. "Wilt thou not frown? Wilt thou forgive?"

"I do forgive you, Hester," replied the minister, at length, with a deep utterance out of an abyss of sadness, but no anger. "I freely forgive you now. May God forgive us both! We are not, Hester, the worst sinners in the world. There is one worse than even the polluted priest! That old man's revenge has been blacker than my sin. He has violated, in cold blood, the sanctity of a human heart. Thou and I, Hester, never did so!"

"Never, never!" whispered she. "What we did had a consecration of its own. We felt it so! We said so to each other! Hast thou forgotten it?"

"Hush, Hester!" said Arthur Dimmesdale, rising from the ground. "No! I have not forgotten!"

They sat down again, side by side, and hand clasped in hand, on the mossy trunk of the fallen tree. Life had never brought them a gloomier hour; it was the point whither their pathway had so long been tending, and darkening ever as it stole along—and yet it enclosed a charm that made them linger upon it and claim another, and another, and, after all, another moment. The forest was obscure around them, and creaked with a blast that was passing through it. The boughs were tossing heavily above their heads; while one solemn old tree groaned dolefully to another, as if telling the sad story of the pair that sat beneath, or constrained to forebode evil to come.

And yet they lingered. How dreary looked the forest track that led backwards to the settlement, where Hester Prynne must take up again the burden of her ignominy, and the minister the hollow mockery of his good name! So they lingered an instant longer. No golden light had ever been so precious as the gloom of this dark forest. Here, seen only by his eyes, the scarlet letter need not burn into the bosom of the fallen woman! Here, seen only by her eyes, Arthur

Dimmesdale, false to God and man, might be, for one moment, true!

He started at a thought that suddenly occurred to him.

"Hester," cried he, "here is a new horror! Roger Chillingworth knows your purpose to reveal his true character. Will he continue, then, to keep our secret? What will now be the course of his revenge?"

"There is a strange secrecy in his nature," replied Hester thoughtfully, "and it has grown upon him by the hidden practices of his revenge. I deem it not likely that he will betray the secret. He will doubtless seek other means of satiating his dark passions."

"And I!—how am I to live longer, breathing the same air with this deadly enemy?" exclaimed Arthur Dimmesdale, shrinking within himself, and pressing his hand nervously against his heart—a gesture that had grown involuntary with him. "Think for me, Hester! Thou art strong. Resolve for me!"

"Thou must dwell no longer with this man," said Hester, slowly and firmly. "Thy heart must be no longer under his evil eye!"

"It were far worse than death!" replied the minister. "But how to avoid it? What choice remains to me? Shall I lie down again on these withered leaves, where I cast myself when thou didst tell me what he was? Must I sink down here, and die at once?"

"Alas, what a ruin has befallen thee!" said Hester, with the tears gushing into her eyes. "Wilt thou die for very weakness? There is no other cause!"

"The judgment of God is on me," answered the conscience-stricken priest. "It is too mighty for me to struggle with!"

"Heaven would show mercy," rejoined Hester, "hadst thou but the strength to take advantage of it."

"Be thou strong for me!" answered he. "Advise me what to do."

"Is the world, then, so narrow?" exclaimed Hester Prynne, fixing her deep eyes on the minister's and instinctively exercising a magnetic power over a spirit so shattered and subdued that it could hardly hold itself erect. "Doth the universe lie within the compass of yonder town, which only a little time ago was but a leaf-strewn desert, as lonely as this around us? Whither leads yonder forest track? Backwards to the settlement, thou sayest! Yes; but onward, too! Deeper it goes, and deeper, into the wilderness, less plainly to be seen at every step! until, some few miles hence, the yellow leaves will show no vestige of the white man's tread. There thou art free! So brief a journey would bring thee from a world where thou hast been most wretched, to one where thou mayest still be happy! Is there not shade enough in all this boundless forest to hide thy heart from the gaze of Roger Chillingworth?"

"Yes, Hester; but only under the fallen leaves!" replied the minister, with a sad smile.

"Then there is the broad pathway of the sea!" continued Hester. "It brought thee hither. If thou so choose, it will bear thee back again. In our native land, whether in some remote rural village or in vast London—or surely, in Germany, in France, in pleasant Italy—thou wouldst be beyond his power and knowledge! And what hast thou to do with all these iron men, and their opinions? They have kept thy better part in bondage too long already!"

"It cannot be!" answered the minister, listening as if he were called upon to realize a dream. "I am powerless to go! Wretched and sinful as I am, I have had no other thought than to drag on my earthly existence in the sphere where Providence hath placed me. Lost as my own soul is, I would still do what I may for other human souls! I dare not quit my post, though an unfaithful sentinel, whose sure reward is death and dishonor, when his dreary watch shall come to an end!"

"Thou art crushed under this seven years' weight of misery," replied Hester, fervently resolved to buoy him up with her own energy. "But thou shalt leave it all behind thee! It shall not cumber thy steps as thou treadest along the forest path; neither shalt thou freight the ship with it, if thou prefer to cross the sea. Leave this wreck and ruin here where it happened. Meddle no more with it! Begin all anew! Hast thou exhausted possibility in the failure of this one trial? Not so! The future is yet full of trial and success. There is happiness to be enjoyed! There is good to be done! Exchange this false life of thine for a true one. Be, if thy spirit summon thee to such a mission, the teacher and apostle of the red men. Or—as is more thy nature—be a scholar and a sage among the wisest and the most renowned of the cultivated world. Preach! Write! Act! Do anything, save to lie down and die! Give up this name of Arthur Dimmesdale and make thyself another, and a high one, such as thou canst wear without fear or shame. Why shouldst thou tarry so much as one other day in the torments that have gnawed into thy life!—that have made thee feeble to will and to do!—that will leave thee powerless even to repent! Up, and away!"

"O Hester!" cried Arthur Dimmesdale, in whose eyes a fitful light, kindled by her enthusiasm, flashed up and died away, "thou tellest of running a race to a man whose knees are tottering beneath him! I must die here! There is not the strength or courage left me to venture into the wide, strange, difficult world, alone!"

It was the last expression of the despondency of a broken spirit. He lacked energy to grasp the better fortune that seemed within his reach.

He repeated the word.

"Alone, Hester!"

"Thou shalt not go alone!" answered she, in a deep whisper.

Then, all was spoken!

XVIII
A Flood of Sunshine

ARTHUR Dimmesdale gazed into Hester's face with a look in which hope and joy shone out, indeed, but with fear betwixt them, and a kind of horror at her boldness, who had spoken what he vaguely hinted at, but dared not speak.

But Hester Prynne, with a mind of native courage and activity, and for so long a period not merely estranged, but outlawed, from society, had habituated herself to such latitude of speculation as was altogether foreign to the clergyman. She had wandered, without rule or guidance, in a moral wilderness; as vast, as intricate and shadowy, as the untamed forest, amid the gloom of which they were now holding a colloquy that was to decide their fate. Her intellect and heart had their home, as it were, in desert places, where she roamed as freely as the wild Indian in his woods. For years past she had looked from the estranged point of view at human institutions, and whatever priests or legislators had established; criticizing all with hardly more reverence than the Indian would feel for the clerical band, the judicial robe, the pillory, the gallows, the fireside, or the church. The tendency of her fate and fortunes had been to set her free. The scarlet letter was her passport into regions where other women dared not tread. Shame, Despair, Solitude! These had been her teachers—stern and wild ones— and they had made her strong, but taught her much amiss.

The minister, on the other hand had never gone through an experience calculated to lead him beyond the scope of generally received laws, although, in a single instance, he had so fearfully transgressed one of the most sacred of them. But this had been a sin of passion, not of principle, nor even purpose. Since that wretched epoch, he had watched, with morbid zeal and minuteness, not his acts—for those it was easy to arrange—but each breath of emotion, and his every thought. At the head of the social system, as the clergymen of that day stood, he was only the more trammelled by its regulations, its principles, and even its prejudices. As a priest, the framework of his order inevitably hemmed him in. As a man who had once sinned, but who kept his conscience all alive and painfully sensitive by the fretting of an unhealed wound, he might have been supposed safer within the line of virtue than if he had never sinned at all.

Thus, we seem to see that, as regarded Hester Prynne, the whole seven years of outlaw and ignominy had been little other than a preparation for this very hour. But Arthur Dimmesdale! Were such a man once more to fall, what plea could be urged in extenuation of his crime? None; unless it avail him somewhat, that he was broken down by long and exquisite suffering; that his mind was darkened and confused by the very remorse which harrowed it; that, between fleeing as an avowed criminal, and remaining as a hypocrite, conscience might find it hard to strike the balance; that it was human to avoid the peril of death and infamy, and the inscrutable machinations of an enemy; that finally, to this poor pilgrim on his dreary and desert path, faint, sick, miserable, there appeared a glimpse of human affection and sympathy, a new life, and a true one, in exchange for the heavy doom which he was now expiating. And be the stern and sad truth spoken, that the breach which guilt has once made into the human soul is never, in this mortal state, repaired. It may be watched and guarded, so that the enemy shall not force his way again into the citadel and might even, in his subsequent assaults, select some other avenue, in preference to that where he had formerly succeeded. But there is still the ruined wall, and, near it, the stealthy tread of the foe that would win over again his unforgotten triumph.

The struggle, if there were one, need not be described. Let it suffice, that the clergyman resolved to flee, and not alone.

"If, in all these past seven years," thought he, "I could recall one instant of peace or hope, I would yet endure, for the sake of that earnest of Heaven's mercy. But now—since

I am irrevocably doomed—wherefore should I not snatch the solace allowed to the condemned culprit before his execution? Or, if this be the path to a better life, as Hester would persuade me, I surely give up no fairer prospect by pursuing it! Neither can I any longer live without her companionship; so powerful is she to sustain—so tender to soothe! O Thou to whom I dare not lift mine eyes, wilt Thou yet pardon me!"

"Thou wilt go!" said Hester, calmly, as he met her glance.

The decision once made, a glow of strange enjoyment threw its flickering brightness over the trouble of his breast. It was the exhilarating effect—upon a prisoner just escaped from the dungeon of his own heart—of breathing the wild, free atmosphere of an unredeemed, unchristianized, lawless region. His spirit rose, as it were, with a bound, and attained a nearer prospect of the sky than throughout all the misery which had kept him grovelling on the earth. Of a deeply religious temperament there was inevitably a tinge of the devotional in his mood.

"Do I feel joy again!" cried he, wondering at himself. "Methought the germ of it was dead in me! O Hester, thou art my better angel! I seem to have flung myself—sick, sin-stained, and sorrow-blackened—down upon these forest leaves, and to have risen up all made anew, and with new powers to glorify Him that hath been merciful! This is already the better life! Why did we not find it sooner?"

"Let us not look back," answered Hester Prynne. "The past is gone! Wherefore should we linger upon it now? See! With this symbol, I undo it all, and make it as it had never been!"

So speaking, she undid the clasp that fastened the scarlet letter, and, taking it from her bosom, threw it to a distance among the withered leaves. The mystic token alighted on the hither verge of the stream. With a hand's breadth further flight it would have fallen into the water, and have given the little brook another woe to carry onward, besides the unintelligible tale which it still kept murmuring about. But there lay the embroidered letter, glittering like a lost jewel, which some ill-fated wanderer might pick up, and thenceforth be haunted by strange phantoms of guilt, sinkings of the heart, and unaccountable misfortune.

The stigma gone, Hester heaved a long, deep sigh, in

which the burden of shame and anguish departed from her spirit. O exquisite relief! She had not known the weight until she felt the freedom! By another impulse, she took off the formal cap that confined her hair; and down it fell upon her shoulders, dark and rich, with at once a shadow and a light in its abundance, and imparting the charm of softness to her features. There played around her mouth and beamed out of her eyes a radiant and tender smile, that seemed gushing from the very heart of womanhood. A crimson flush was glowing on her cheek, that had been long so pale. Her sex, her youth, and the whole richness of her beauty, came back from what men call the irrevocable past, and clustered themselves, with her maiden hope and a happiness before unknown, within the magic circle of this hour. And, as if the gloom of the earth and sky had been but the effluence of these two mortal hearts, it vanished with their sorrow. All at once, as with a sudden smile of heaven, forth burst the sunshine, pouring a very flood into the obscure forest, gladdening each green leaf, transmitting the yellow fallen ones to gold, and gleaning adown the gray trunks of the solemn trees. The objects that had made a shadow hitherto embodied the brightness now. The course of the little brook might be traced by its merry gleam afar into the wood's heart of mystery, which had become a mystery of joy.

Such was the sympathy of Nature—that wild, heathen Nature of the forest, never subjugated by human law, nor illumined by higher truth—with the bliss of these two spirits! Love, whether newly born, or aroused from a deathlike slumber, must always create a sunshine, filling the heart so full of radiance that it overflows upon the outward world. Had the forest still kept its gloom, it would have been bright in Hester's eyes, and bright in Arthur Dimmesdale's!

Hester looked at him with the thrill of another joy.

"Thou must know Pearl!" said she. "Our little Pearl! Thou hast seen her—yes, I know it!—but thou wilt see her now with other eyes. She is a strange child! I hardly comprehend her! But thou wilt love her dearly, as I do, and wilt advise me how to deal with her."

"Dost thou think the child will be glad to know me?" asked the minister, somewhat uneasily. "I have long shrunk from children, because they often show a distrust—a backwardness to be familiar with me. I have even been afraid of little Pearl!"

"Ah, that was sad!" answered the mother. "But she will love thee dearly, and thou her. She is not far off. I will call her! Pearl! Pearl!"

"I see the child," observed the minister. "Yonder she is, standing in a streak of sunshine, a good way off, on the other side of the brook. So thou thinkest the child will love me?"

Hester smiled, and again called to Pearl, who was visible at some distance, as the minister had described her, like a bright-apparelled vision in a sunbeam, which fell down upon her through an arch of boughs. The ray quivered to and fro, making her figure dim or distinct—now like a real child, now like a child's spirit—as the splendor went and came again. She heard her mother's voice, and approached slowly through the forest.

Pearl had not found the hour pass wearisomely while her mother sat talking with the clergyman. The great black forest—stern as it showed itself to those who brought the guilt and troubles of the world into its bosom—became the playmate of the lonely infant, as well as it knew how. Sombre as it was, it put on the kindest of its moods to welcome her. It offered her the partridge berries, the growth of the preceding autumn, but ripening only in the spring, and now red as drops of blood upon the withered leaves. These Pearl gathered, and was pleased with their wild flavor. The small denizens of the wilderness hardly took pains to move out of her path. A partridge, indeed, with a brood of ten behind her, ran forward threateningly, but soon repented of her fierceness, and clucked to her young ones not to be afraid. A pigeon, alone on a low branch, allowed Pearl to come beneath, and uttered a sound as much of greeting as alarm. A squirrel, from the lofty depths of his domestic tree, chattered either in anger or merriment—for a squirrel is such a choleric and humorous little personage, that it is hard to distinguish between his moods—so he chattered at the child, and flung down a nut upon her head. It was a last year's nut, and already gnawed by his sharp tooth. A fox, startled from his sleep by her light footstep on the leaves, looked inquisitively at Pearl, as doubting whether it were better to steal off, or renew his nap on the same spot. A wolf, it is said—

but here the tale has surely lapsed into the improbable—came up, and smelt of Pearl's robe, and offered his savage head to be patted by her hand. The truth seems to be, however, that the mother-forest and these wild things which it nourished, all recognized a kindred wildness in the human child.

And she was gentler here than in the grassy-margined streets of the settlement, or in her mother's cottage. The flowers appeared to know it; and one and another whispered as she passed, "Adorn thyself with me, thou beautiful child, adorn thyself with me!"—and, to please them, Pearl gathered the violets, and anemones, and columbines, and some twigs of the freshest green which the old trees held down before her eyes. With these she decorated her hair, and her young waist, and became a nymph-child, or an infant dryad, or whatever else was in closest sympathy with the antique wood. In such guise had Pearl adorned herself, when she heard her mother's voice, and came slowly back.

Slowly; for she saw the clergyman!

XIX

The Child at the Brookside

"THOU wilt love her dearly," repeated Hester Prynne, as she and the minister sat watching little Pearl. "Dost thou not think her beautiful? And see with what natural skill she has made those simple flowers adorn her! Had she gathered pearls, and diamonds, and rubies, in the wood, they could not have become her better. She is a splendid child! But I know whose brow she has!"

"Dost thou know, Hester," said Arthur Dimmesdale, with an unquiet smile, "that this dear child, tripping about always at thy side, hath caused me many an alarm? Methought—O Hester, what a thought is that, and how terrible to dread it!—that my own features were partly repeated in her face, and so strikingly that the world might see them! But she is mostly thine!"

"No, no! Not mostly!" answered the mother, with a tender smile. "A little longer, and thou needest not to be afraid to trace whose child she is. But how strangely beautiful she looks, with those wild flowers in her hair! It is as if one of the fairies, whom we left in our dear old England, had decked her out to meet us."

It was with a feeling which neither of them had ever before experienced, that they sat and watched Pearl's slow advance. In her was visible the tie that united them. She had been offered to the world, these seven years past, as the living hieroglyphic, in which was revealed the secret they so darkly sought to hide—all written in this symbol, all plainly manifest had there been a prophet or magician skilled to read the character of flame! And Pearl was the oneness of their being. Be the foregone evil what it might, how could they doubt that their earthly lives and future destinies were conjoined, when they beheld at once the material union, and the spiritual idea, in whom they met, and were to dwell immortally together? Thoughts like these—and perhaps other thoughts, which they did not acknowledge or define—threw an awe about the child, as she came onward.

"Let her see nothing strange—no passion nor eagerness—in thy way of accosting her," whispered Hester. "Our Pearl is a fitful and fantastic little elf sometimes. Especially, she is seldom tolerant of emotion when she does not fully comprehend the why and wherefore. But the child hath strong affections! She loves me, and will love thee!"

"Thou canst not think," said the minister, glancing aside at Hester Prynne, "how my heart dreads this interview, and yearns for it! But, in truth, as I already told thee, children are not readily won to be familiar with me. They will not climb my knee, nor prattle in my ear, nor answer to my smile; but stand apart, and eye me strangely. Even little babies, when I take them in my arms, weep bitterly. Yet Pearl, twice in her little lifetime, hath been kind to me! The first time—thou knowest it well! The last was when thou ledst her with thee to the house of yonder stern old Governor."

"And thou didst plead so bravely in her behalf and mine!" answered the mother. "I remember it; and so shall little Pearl. Fear nothing! She may be strange and shy at first, but will soon learn to love thee!"

By this time Pearl had reached the margin of the brook and stood on the further side, gazing silently at Hester and the clergyman, who still sat together on the mossy tree-trunk, waiting to receive her. Just where she had paused, the brook chanced to form a pool, so smooth and quiet that it reflected a perfect image of her little figure, with all the brilliant picturesqueness of her beauty, in its adornment of flowers and wreathed foliage, but more refined and spiritualized than the reality. This image, so nearly identical with the living Pearl, seemed to communicate somewhat of its own shadowy and intangible quality to the child herself. It was strange the way in which Pearl stood, looking so steadfastly at them through the dim medium of the forest gloom; herself, meanwhile, all glorified with a ray of sunshine that was attracted thitherward as by a certain sympathy. In the brook beneath stood another child—another and the same—with likewise its ray of golden light. Hester felt herself, in some indistinct and tantalizing manner, estranged from Pearl; as if the child in her lonely ramble through the forest had strayed out of the sphere in which she and her mother dwelt together, and was now vainly seeking to return to it.

There was both truth and error in the impression; the child and mother were estranged, but through Hester's fault, not Pearl's. Since the latter rambled from her side, another inmate had been admitted within the circle of the mother's feelings, and so modified the aspect of them all, that Pearl, the returning wanderer, could not find her wonted place, and hardly knew where she was.

"I have a strange fancy," observed the sensitive minister, "that this brook is the boundary between two worlds, and that thou canst never meet thy Pearl again. Or is she an elfish spirit, who, as the legends of our childhood taught us, is forbidden to cross a running stream? Pray hasten her; for this delay has already imparted a tremor to my nerves."

"Come, dearest child!" said Hester encouragingly, and stretching out both her arms. "How slow thou art! When hast thou been so sluggish before now? Here is a friend of mine, who must be thy friend also. Thou wilt have twice as much love, henceforward, as thy mother alone could give thee! Leap across the brook and come to us. Thou canst leap like a young deer!"

Pearl, without responding in any manner to these honey-sweet expressions, remained on the other side of the brook. Now she fixed her bright, wild eyes on her mother, now on the minister, and now included them both in the same glance, as if to detect and explain to herself the relation which they bore to one another. For some unaccountable reason, as Arthur Dimmesdale felt the child's eyes upon himself, his hand—with that gesture so habitual as to have become involuntary—stole over his heart. At length, assuming a singular air of authority, Pearl stretched out her hand, with the small forefinger extended, and pointing evidently towards her mother's breast. And beneath, in the mirror of the brook, there was the flower-girdled and sunny image of little Pearl, pointing her small forefinger too.

"Thou strange child, why dost thou not come to me?" exclaimed Hester.

Pearl still pointed with her forefinger; and a frown gathered on her brow, the more impressive from the childish, the almost baby-like aspect of the features that conveyed it. As her mother still kept beckoning to her and arraying her face in a holiday suit of unaccustomed smiles, the child stamped her foot with a yet more imperious look and gesture. In the brook, again, was the fantastic beauty of the image, with its reflected frown, its pointed finger, and imperious gesture, giving emphasis to the aspect of little Pearl.

"Hasten, Pearl, or I shall be angry with thee!" cried Hester Prynne, who, however inured to such behavior on the elf-child's part at other seasons, was naturally anxious for a more seemly deportment now. "Leap across the brook, naughty child, and run hither! Else I must come to thee!"

But Pearl, not a whit startled at her mother's threats any more than mollified by her entreaties, now suddenly burst into a fit of passion, gesticulating violently, and throwing her small figure into the most extravagant contortions. She accompanied this wild outbreak with piercing shrieks, which the woods reverberated on all sides; so that, alone as she was in her childish and unreasonable wrath, it seemed as if a hidden multitude were lending her their sympathy and encouragement. Seen in the brook, once more, was the shadowy wrath of Pearl's image, crowned and girdled with flowers, but stamping its foot, wildly gesticulating, and, in the midst of all, still pointing its small forefinger at Hester's bosom!

"I see what ails the child," whispered Hester to the clergyman, and turning pale in spite of a strong effort to conceal her trouble and annoyance. "Children will not abide any, the slightest, change in the accustomed aspect of things that are daily before their eyes. Pearl misses something which she has always seen me wear!"

"I pray you," answered the minister, "if thou hast any means of pacifying the child, do it forthwith! Save it were the cankered wrath of an old witch, like Mistress Hibbins," added he, attempting to smile, "I know nothing that I would not sooner encounter than this passion in a child. In Pearl's young beauty, as in the wrinkled witch, it has a preternatural effect. Pacify her, if thou lovest me!"

Hester turned again towards Pearl with a crimson blush

upon her cheek, a conscious glance aside at the clergyman, and then a heavy sigh; while, even before she had time to speak, the blush yielded to a deadly pallor.

"Pearl," said she, sadly, "look down at thy feet! There! —before thee!—on the hither side of the brook!"

The child turned her eyes to the point indicated; and there lay the scarlet letter, so close upon the margin of the stream that the gold embroidery was reflected in it.

"Bring it hither!" said Hester.

"Come thou and take it up!" answered Pearl.

"Was ever such a child!" observed Hester, aside to the minister. "Oh, I have much to tell thee about her! But, in very truth, she is right as regards this hateful token. I must bear its torture yet a little longer—only a few days longer— until we shall have left this region and look back hither as to a land which we have dreamed of. The forest cannot hide it! The mid-ocean shall take it from my hand and swallow it up forever!"

With these words, she advanced to the margin of the brook, took up the scarlet letter, and fastened it again into her bosom. Hopefully, but a moment ago, as Hester had spoken of drowning it in the deep sea, there was a sense of inevitable doom upon her, as she thus received back this deadly symbol from the hand of fate. She had flung it into infinite space!—she had drawn an hour's free breath!—and here again was the scarlet misery, glittering on the old spot! So it ever is, whether thus typified or no, that an evil deed invests itself with the character of doom. Hester next gathered up the heavy tresses of her hair, and confined them beneath her cap. As if there were a withering spell in the sad letter, her beauty, the warmth and richness of her womanhood, departed, like fading sunshine; and a gray shadow seemed to fall across her.

When the dreary change was wrought, she extended her hand to Pearl.

"Dost thou know thy mother now, child?" asked she, reproachfully, but with a subdued tone. "Wilt thou come across the brook and own thy mother, now that she has her shame upon her—now that she is sad?"

"Yes; now I will!" answered the child, bounding across the brook, and clasping Hester in her arms. "Now thou art my mother indeed! And I am thy little Pearl!"

In a mood of tenderness that was not usual with her, she drew down her mother's head, and kissed her brow and both her cheeks. But then—by a kind of necessity that always impelled this child to alloy whatever comfort she might chance to give with a throb of anguish—Pearl put up her mouth, and kissed the scarlet letter too!

"That was not kind!" said Hester. "When thou hast shown me a little love, thou mockest me!"

"Why doth the minister sit yonder?" asked Pearl.

"He waits to welcome thee," replied her mother. "Come thou, and entreat his blessing! He loves thee, my little Pearl, and loves thy mother too. Wilt thou not love him? Come! he longs to greet thee!"

"Doth he love us?" said Pearl, looking up with acute intelligence into her mother's face. "Will he go back with us, hand in hand, we three together, into the town?"

"Not now, dear child," answered Hester. "But in days to come he will walk hand in hand with us. We will have a home and fireside of our own; and thou shalt sit upon his knee; and he will teach thee many things, and love thee dearly. Thou wilt love him; wilt thou not?"

"And will he always keep his hand over his heart?" inquired Pearl.

"Foolish child, what a question is that!" exclaimed her mother. "Come and ask his blessing!"

But, whether influenced by the jealousy that seems instinctive with every petted child towards a dangerous rival, or from whatever caprice of her freakish nature, Pearl would show no favor to the clergyman. It was only by an exertion of force that her mother brought her up to him, hanging back and manifesting her reluctance by odd grimaces; of which, ever since her babyhood, she had possessed a singular variety, and transform her mobile physiognomy into a series of different aspects, with a new mischief in them, each and all. The minister—painfully embarrassed, but hoping that a kiss might prove a talisman to admit him into the child's kindlier regards—bent forward, and impressed one on her brow. Hereupon, Pearl broke away from her mother, and, running to the brook, stooped over it and bathed her forehead, until the unwelcome kiss was quite washed off and diffused through a long lapse of the gliding water. She then remained apart, silently watching Hester and the clergy-

man, while they talked together, and made such arrangements as were suggested by their new position, and the
purposes soon to be fulfilled.

And now this fateful interview had come to a close. The
dell was to be left a solitude among its dark, old trees,
which, with their multitudinous tongues, would whisper long
of what had passed there, and no mortal be the wiser. And
the melancholy brook would add this other tale to the
mystery with which its little heart was already overburdened, and whereof it still kept up a murmuring babble,
with not a whit more cheerfulness of tone than for ages
heretofore.

XX

The Minister in a Maze

As the minister departed, in advance of Hester Prynne and little Pearl, he threw a backward glance, half expecting that he should discover only some faintly traced features or outline of the mother and the child, slowly fading into the twilight of the woods. So great a vicissitude in his life could not at once be received as real. But there was Hester, clad in her gray robe, still standing beside the tree-trunk which some blast had overthrown a long antiquity ago, and which time had ever since been covering with moss, so that these two fated ones, with earth's heaviest burden on them, might there sit down together and find a single hour's rest and solace. And there was Pearl, too, lightly dancing from the margin of the brook—now that the intrusive third person was gone—and taking her old place by her mother's side. So the minister had not fallen asleep, and dreamed!

In order to free his mind from this indistinctness and duplicity of impression which vexed it with a strange disquietude, he recalled and more thoroughly defined the plans which Hester and himself had sketched for their departure. It had been determined between them that the Old World, with its crowds and cities, offered them a more eligible shelter and concealment than the wilds of New England, or all America, with its alternatives of an Indian wigwam or the few settlements of Europeans, scattered thinly along the seaboard. Not to speak of the clergyman's health, so inadequate to sustain the hardships of a forest life, his native gifts, his culture, and his entire development would secure him a home only in the midst of civilization and refinement;

the higher the state, the more delicately adapted to it the man. In furtherance of his choice, it so happened that a ship lay in the harbor; one of those questionable cruisers, frequent at that day, which, without being absolutely outlaws of the deep, yet roamed over its surface with a remarkable irresponsibility of character. This vessel had recently arrived from the Spanish Main, and within three days' time would sail for Bristol. Hester Prynne—whose vocation as a self-enlisted Sister of Charity had brought her acquainted with the captain and crew—could take upon herself to secure the passage of two individuals and a child with all the secrecy which circumstances rendered more than desirable.

The minister had inquired of Hester, with no little interest, the precise time at which the vessel might be expected to depart. It would probably be on the fourth day from the present. "That is most fortunate!" he had then said to himself. Now, why the Reverend Mr. Dimmesdale considered it so very fortunate, we hesitate to reveal. Nevertheless —to hold nothing back from the reader—it was because on the third day from the present he was to preach the Election Sermon; and, as such an occasion formed an honorable epoch in the life of a New England clergyman, he could not have chanced upon a more suitable mode and time of terminating his professional career. "At least they shall say of me," thought this exemplary man, "that I leave no public duty unperformed, nor ill performed!" Sad, indeed, that an introspection so profound and acute as this poor minister's should be so miserably deceived! We have had, and may still have, worse things to tell of him; but none, we apprehend, so pitiably weak; no evidence, at once so slight and irrefragable, of a subtile disease that had long since begun to eat into the real substance of his character. No man for any considerable period can wear one face to himself and another to the multitude, without finally getting bewildered as to which may be the true.

The excitement of Mr. Dimmesdale's feelings as he returned from his interview with Hester lent him unaccustomed physical energy, and hurried him townward at a rapid pace. The pathway among the woods seemed wilder, more uncouth with its rude natural obstacles, and less trodden by the foot of man, than he remembered it on his outward journey. But he leaped across the plashy places, thrust himself through the clinging underbrush, climbed the ascent, plunged into the hollow, and overcame, in short, all the difficulties of the track with an unweariable activity that astonished him. He could not but recall how feebly, and with what frequent pauses for breath, he had toiled over the same ground only two days before. As he drew near the town, he took an impression of change from the series of familiar objects that presented themselves. It seemed not yesterday, not one, nor two, but many days, or even years ago, since he had quitted them. There, indeed, was each former trace of the street, as he remembered it, and all the peculiarities of the houses, with the due multitude of gable peaks, and a weathercock at every point where his memory suggested one. Not the less, however, came this importunately obtrusive sense of change. The same was true as regarded the acquaintances whom he met and all the well-known shapes of human life about the little town. They looked neither older nor younger now; the beards of the aged were no whiter, nor could the creeping babe of yesterday walk on his feet today; it was impossible to describe in what respect they differed from the individuals on whom he had so recently bestowed a parting glance; and yet the minister's deepest sense seemed to inform him of their mutability. A similar impression struck him most remarkably as he passed under the walls of his own church. The edifice had so very strange, and yet so familiar, an aspect, that Mr. Dimmesdale's mind vibrated between two ideas; either that he had seen it only in a dream hitherto, or that he was merely dreaming about it now.

This phenomenon, in the various shapes which it assumed, indicated no external change, but so sudden and important a change in the spectator of the familiar scene, that the intervening space of a single day had operated on his consciousness like the lapse of years. The minister's own will, and Hester's will, and the fate that grew between them, had wrought this transformation. It was the same town as heretofore; but the same minister returned not from the forest. He might have said to the friends who greeted him, "I am not the man for whom you take me! I left him yonder in the forest, withdrawn into a secret dell, by a mossy tree-trunk, and near a melancholy brook! Go, seek your minister, and see if his emaciated figure, his thin cheek, his white, heavy, pain-wrinkled brow, be not flung down there, like a cast-off garment!" His friends, no doubt, would still have insisted with him, "Thou art thyself the man!" but the error would have been their own, not his.

Before Mr. Dimmesdale reached home, his inner man gave him other evidences of a revolution in the sphere of thought and feeling. In truth, nothing short of a total change of dynasty and moral code in that interior kingdom was adequate to account for the impulses now communicated to the unfortunate and startled minister. At every step he was incited to do some strange, wild, wicked thing or other, with a sense that it would be at once involuntary and intentional; in spite of himself, yet growing out of a profounder self than that which opposed the impulse. For instance, he met one of his own deacons. The good old man addressed him with the paternal affection and patriarchal privilege, which his venerable age, his upright and holy character, and his station in the Church entitled him to use, and, conjoined with this, the deep, almost worshipping respect which the minister's professional and private claims alike demanded. Never was there a more beautiful example of how the majesty of age and wisdom may comport with the obeisance and respect enjoined upon it, as from a lower social rank and inferior order of endowment, towards a higher. Now, during a conversation of some two or three moments between the Reverend Mr. Dimmesdale and this excellent and hoary-bearded deacon, it was only by the most careful self-control that the former could refrain from uttering certain blasphemous suggestions that rose into his mind, respecting the communion supper. He absolutely trembled and turned pale as ashes, lest his tongue should wag itself, in utterance of these horrible matters, and plead his own consent for so doing without his having fairly given it. And, even with this terror in his heart, he could hardly avoid laughing, to imagine how the sanctified old patriarchal deacon would have been petrified by his minister's impiety!

Again, another incident of the same nature. Hurrying along the street, the Reverend Mr. Dimmesdale encountered the eldest female member of his church, a most pious and exemplary old dame; poor, widowed, lonely, and with a heart as full of reminiscences about her dead husband and children and her dead friends of long ago as a burial ground is full of storied gravestones. Yet all this, which would else have been such heavy sorrow, was made almost a solemn joy to her devout old soul by religious consolations and the truths of Scripture, wherewith she had fed herself continually for more than thirty years. And, since Mr. Dimmesdale had taken her in charge, the good grandam's chief earthly comfort—which, unless it had been likewise a heavenly comfort, could have been none at all—was to meet her pastor, whether casually, or of set purpose, and be refreshed with a word of warm, fragrant heaven-breathing Gospel truth, from his beloved lips into her dulled but rapturously attentive ear. But on this occasion, up to the moment of putting his lips to the old woman's ear, Mr. Dimmesdale, as the great enemy of souls would have it, could recall no text of Scripture, nor aught else, except a brief, pithy, and, as it then appeared to him, unanswerable argument against the immortality of the human soul. The instilment thereof into her mind would probably have caused this aged sister to drop down dead at once, as by the effect of an intensely poisonous infusion. What he really did whisper, the minister could never afterwards recollect. There was, perhaps, a fortunate disorder in his utterance, which failed to impart any distinct idea to the good widow's comprehension, or which Providence interpreted after a method of its own. Assuredly, as the minister looked back, he beheld an expression of divine gratitude and ecstasy that seemed like the shine of the celestial city on her face, so wrinkled and ashy pale.

Again, a third instance. After parting from the old church member, he met the youngest sister of them all. It was a maiden newly won—and won by the Reverend Mr. Dimmesdale's own sermon, on the Sabbath after his vigil—to barter the transitory pleasures of the world for the heavenly hope that was to assume brighter substance as life grew dark around her, and which would gild the utter gloom with final glory. She was fair and pure as a lily that had bloomed in Paradise. The minister knew well that he was himself enshrined within the stainless sanctity of her heart, which hung its snowy curtains about his image, imparting to religion the warmth of love, and to love a religious purity. Satan, that afternoon, had surely led the poor young girl away from her mother's side, and thrown her into the pathway of this sorely tempted, or—shall we not rather say?—this lost and desperate man. As she drew nigh, the archfiend whispered him to condense into small compass and drop into her tender bosom a germ of evil that would be sure to blossom darkly soon, and bear black fruit betimes. Such was his sense of power over this virgin soul, trusting him as she did, that the minister felt potent to blight all the field of innocence with but one wicked look, and develop all its opposite with but a word. So—with a mightier struggle than he had yet sustained—he held his Geneva cloak before his face, and hurried onward, making no sign of recognition, and leaving the young sister to digest his rudeness as she might. She ransacked her conscience—which was full of harmless little matters, like her pocket or her workbag—and took herself to task, poor thing! for a thousand imaginary faults; and went about her household duties with swollen eyelids the next morning.

Before the minister had time to celebrate his victory over this last temptation, he was conscious of another impulse, more ludicrous and almost as horrible. It was—we blush to tell it—it was to stop short in the road, and teach some very wicked words to a knot of little Puritan children who were playing there, and had but just begun to talk. Denying himself this freak as unworthy of his cloth, he met a drunken seaman, one of the ship's crew from the Spanish Main. And, here, since he had so valiantly forborne all other wickedness, poor Mr. Dimmesdale longed, at least, to shake hands with the tarry blackguard, and recreate himself with a few improper jests, such as dissolute sailors so abound with, and a volley of good, round, solid, satisfactory, and heaven-defying oaths! It was not so much a better principle, as partly his natural good taste, and still more his buckramed habit of clerical decorum, that carried him safely through the latter crisis.

"What is it that haunts and tempts me thus?" cried the minister to himself, at length, pausing in the street, and striking his hand against his forehead. "Am I mad? or am I given over utterly to the fiend? Did I make a contract with him in the forest, and sign it with my blood? And does he now summon me to its fulfilment, by suggesting the performance of every wickedness which his most foul imagination can conceive?"

At the moment when the Reverend Mr. Dimmesdale thus

communed with himself, and struck his forehead with his hand, old Mistress Hibbins, the reputed witch-lady, is said to have been passing by. She made a very grand appearance; having on a high headdress, a rich gown of velvet, and a ruff done up with the famous yellow starch, of which Ann Turner, her especial friend, had taught her the secret, before this last good lady had been hanged for Sir Thomas Overbury's murder. Whether the witch had read the minister's thoughts or no, she came to a full stop, looked shrewdly into his face, smiled craftily, and—though little given to converse with clergymen—began a conversation.

"So, reverend Sir, you have made a visit into the forest," observed the witch-lady, nodding her high headdress at him. "The next time, I pray you to allow me only a fair warning, and I shall be proud to bear you company. Without taking overmuch upon myself, my good word will go far towards gaining any strange gentleman a fair reception from yonder potentate you wot of!"

"I profess, Madam," answered the clergyman, with a grave obeisance, such as the lady's rank demanded and his own good-breeding made imperative—"I profess, on my conscience and character, that I am utterly bewildered as touching the purport of your words! I went not into the forest to seek a potentate; neither do I, at any future time, design a visit thither, with a view to gaining the favor of such personage. My one sufficient object was to greet that pious friend of mine, the Apostle Eliot, and rejoice with him over the many precious souls he hath won from heathendom!"

"Ha, ha, ha!" cackled the old witch-lady, still nodding her high headdress at the minister. "Well, well, we must needs talk thus in the daytime! You carry it off like an old hand! But at midnight, and in the forest, we shall have other talk together!"

She passed on with her aged stateliness, but often turning back her head and smiling at him, like one willing to recognize a secret intimacy of connection.

"Have I then sold myself," thought the minister, "to the fiend whom, if men say true, this yellow-starched and velveted old hag has chosen for her prince and master!"

The wretched minister! He had made a bargain very like it! Tempted by a dream of happiness, he had yielded himself with deliberate choice, as he had never done before, to what

he knew was deadly sin. And the infectious poison of that
sin had been thus rapidly diffused throughout his moral
system. It had stupefied all blessed impulses, and awakened
into vivid life the whole brotherhood of bad ones. Scorn,
bitterness, unprovoked malignity, gratuitous desire of ill,
ridicule of whatever was good and holy, all awoke, to tempt,
even while they frightened him. And his encounter with old
Mistress Hibbins, if it were a real incident, did but show his
sympathy and fellowship with wicked mortals, and the world
of perverted spirits.

He had by this time reached his dwelling on the edge of
the burial ground, and, hastening up the stairs, took refuge
in his study. The minister was glad to have reached this
shelter without first betraying himself to the world by any of
those strange and wicked eccentricities to which he had
been continually impelled while passing through the streets.
He entered the accustomed room and looked around him on
its books, its windows, its fireplace, and the tapestried comfort of the walls, with the same perception of strangeness
that had haunted him throughout his walk from the forest
dell into the town, and thitherward. Here he had studied
and written; here gone through fast and vigil, and come
forth half alive; here, striven to pray; here, borne a hundred
thousand agonies! There was the Bible, in its rich old Hebrew, with Moses and the Prophets speaking to him, and
God's voice through all! There, on the table, with the inky
pen beside it, was an unfinished sermon, with a sentence
broken in the midst, where his thoughts had ceased to gush
out upon the page, two days before. He knew that it was
himself, the thin and white-cheeked minister, who had done
and suffered these things, and written thus far into the
Election Sermon! But he seemed to stand apart and eye this
former self with scornful, pitying, but half-envious curiosity.
That self was gone. Another man had returned out of the
forest; a wiser one, with a knowledge of hidden mysteries
which the simplicity of the former never could have reached.
A bitter kind of knowledge that!

While occupied with these reflections, a knock came at
the door of the study, and the minister said, "Come in!"
—not wholly devoid of an idea that he might behold an evil
spirit. And so he did! It was old Roger Chillingworth that
entered. The minister stood, white and speechless, with one

hand on the Hebrew Scriptures, and the other spread upon his breast.

"Welcome home, reverend Sir," said the physician. "And how found you that godly man, the Apostle Eliot? But methinks, dear Sir, you look pale; as if the travel through the wilderness had been too sore for you. Will not my aid be requisite to put you in heart and strength to preach your Election Sermon?"

"Nay, I think not so," rejoined the Reverend Mr. Dimmesdale. "My journey, and the sight of the holy Apostle yonder, and the free air which I have breathed, have done me good, after so long confinement in my study. I think to need no more of your drugs, my kind physician, good though they be, and administered by a friendly hand."

All this time, Roger Chillingworth was looking at the minister with the grave and intent regard of a physician towards his patient. But, in spite of this outward show, the latter was almost convinced of the old man's knowledge, or, at least, his confident suspicion, with respect to his own interview with Hester Prynne. The physician knew then, that, in the minister's regard, he was no longer a trusted friend, but his bitterest enemy. So much being known, it would appear natural that a part of it should be expressed. It is singular, however, how long a time often passes before words embody things; and with what security two persons, who choose to avoid a certain subject, may approach its very verge, and retire without disturbing it. Thus, the minister felt no apprehension that Roger Chillingworth would touch, in express words, upon the real position which they sustained towards one another. Yet did the physician, in his dark way, creep frightfully near the secret.

"Were it not better," said he, "that you use my poor skill tonight? Verily, dear Sir, we must take pains to make you strong and vigorous for this occasion of the Election discourse. The people look for great things from you, apprehending that another year may come about and find their pastor gone."

"Yea, to another world," replied the minister, with pious resignation. "Heaven grant it be a better one; for, in good sooth, I hardly think to tarry with my flock through the flitting seasons of another year! But, touching your medicine, kind Sir, in my present frame of body, I need it not."

"I joy to hear it," answered the physician. "It may be that my remedies, so long administered in vain, begin now to take due effect. Happy man were I, and well deserving of New England's gratitude, could I achieve this cure!"

"I thank you from my heart, most watchful friend," said the Reverend Mr. Dimmesdale, with a solemn smile. "I thank you, and can but requite your good deeds with my prayers."

"A good man's prayers are golden recompense!" rejoined old Roger Chillingworth, as he took his leave. "Yea, they are the current gold coin of the New Jerusalem, with the King's own mint-mark on them!"

Left alone, the minister summoned a servant of the house and requested food, which, being set before him, he ate with ravenous appetite. Then, flinging the already written pages of the Election Sermon into the fire, he forthwith began another, which he wrote with such an impulsive flow of thought and emotion, that he fancied himself inspired; and only wondered that Heaven should see fit to transmit the grand and solemn music of its oracles through so foul an organ-pipe as he. However, leaving that mystery to solve itself or go unsolved forever, he drove his task onward, with earnest haste and ecstasy. Thus the night fled away, as if it were a winged steed and he careering on it; morning came and peeped, blushing, through the curtains; and at last sunrise threw a golden beam into the study, and laid it right across the minister's bedazzled eyes. There he was, with the pen still between his fingers, and a vast, immeasurable tract of written space behind him!

XXI

The New England Holiday

BETIMES in the morning of the day on which the new Governor was to receive his office at the hands of the people, Hester Prynne and little Pearl came into the market place. It was already thronged with the craftsmen and other plebeian inhabitants of the town, in considerable numbers; among whom, likewise, were many rough figures, whose attire of deerskins marked them as belonging to some of the forest settlements which surrounded the little metropolis of the colony.

On this public holiday, as on all other occasions, for seven years past, Hester was clad in a garment of coarse gray cloth. Not more by its hue than by some indescribable peculiarity in its fashion, it had the effect of making her fade personally out of sight and outline; while, again, the scarlet letter brought her back from this twilight indistinctness and revealed her under the moral aspect of its own illumination. Her face, so long familiar to the townspeople, showed the marble quietude which they were accustomed to behold there. It was like a mask; or, rather, like the frozen calmness of a dead woman's features, owing this dreary resemblance to the fact that Hester was actually dead, in respect to any claim of sympathy, and had departed out of the world with which she still seemed to mingle.

It might be, on this one day, that there was an expression unseen before, nor, indeed, vivid enough to be detected now; unless some preternaturally gifted observer should have first read the heart, and have afterwards sought a corresponding development in the countenance and mien. Such a spiritual seer might have conceived that, after sustaining the gaze of the multitude through seven miserable years as a necessity, a penance, and something which it was a stern religion to endure, she now, for one last time more, encountered it freely and voluntarily, in order to convert what had so long been agony into a kind of triumph. "Look your last on the scarlet letter and its wearer!"—the people's victim and lifelong bond-slave, as they fancied her, might say to them. "Yet a little while, and she will be beyond your reach! A few hours longer, and the deep, mysterious ocean will quench and hide forever the symbol which ye have caused to burn upon her bosom!" Nor were it an inconsistency too improbable to be assigned to human nature, should we suppose a feeling of regret in Hester's mind, at the moment when she was about to win her freedom from the pain which had been thus deeply incorporated with her being. Might there not be an irresistible desire to quaff a last, long, breathless draught of the cup of wormwood and aloes, with which nearly all her years of womanhood had been perpetually flavored? The wine of life, henceforth to be presented to her lips, must be indeed rich, delicious, and exhilarating, in its chased and golden beaker; or else leave an inevitable and weary languor, after the lees of bitterness wherewith she had been drugged, as with a cordial of intensest potency.

Pearl was decked out with airy gayety. It would have been impossible to guess that this bright and sunny apparition owed its existence to the shape of gloomy gray; or that a fancy, at once so gorgeous and so delicate as must have been requisite to contrive the child's apparel, was the same that had achieved a task perhaps more difficult, in imparting so distinct a peculiarity to Hester's simple robe. The dress, so proper was it to little Pearl, seemed an effluence, or inevitable development and outward manifestation of her character, no more to be separated from her than the many-hued brilliancy from a butterfly's wing or the painted glory from the leaf of a bright flower. As with these, so with the child; her garb was all of one idea with her nature. On this eventful day, moreover, there was a certain singular inquietude and excitement in her mood, resembling nothing so much as the shimmer of a diamond, that sparkles and flashes with the varied throbbings of the breast on which it is displayed. Children have always a sympathy in the agitations of those connected with them; always, especially, a sense of any trouble or impending revolution, of whatever kind, in domestic circumstances; and therefore Pearl, who was the gem on her mother's unquiet bosom, betrayed, by the very dance of her spirits, the emotions which none could detect in the marble passiveness of Hester's brow.

This effervescence made her flit with a birdlike movement, rather than walk by her mother's side. She broke continually into shouts of a wild, inarticulate, and sometimes piercing music. When they reached the market place, she became still more restless on perceiving the stir and bustle that enlivened the spot; for it was usually more like the broad and lonesome green before a village meeting house than the centre of a town's business.

"Why, what is this, Mother?" cried she. "Wherefore have all the people left their work today? Is it a playday for the whole world? See, there is the blacksmith! He has washed his sooty face and put on his Sabbath-day clothes and looks as if he would gladly be merry, if any kind body would only teach him how! And there is Master Brackett, the old jailer, nodding and smiling at me. Why does he do so, Mother?"

"He remembers thee a little babe, my child," answered Hester.

"He should not nod and smile at me, for all that—the black, grim, ugly-eyed old man!" said Pearl. "He may nod at thee, if he will; for thou art clad in gray, and wearest the scarlet letter. But see, Mother, how many faces of strange people, and Indians among them, and sailors! What have they all come to do, here in the market place?"

"They wait to see the procession pass," said Hester. "For the Governor and the magistrates are to go by, and the ministers, and all the great people and good people, with the music and the soldiers marching before them."

"And will the minister be there?" asked Pearl. "And will he hold out both his hands to me, as when thou ledst me to him from the brookside?"

"He will be there, child," answered her mother. "But he will not greet thee today; nor must thou greet him."

"What a strange, sad man is he!" said the child, as if speaking partly to herself. "In the dark nighttime he calls us to him, and holds thy hand and mine, as when we stood with him on the scaffold yonder! And in the deep forest, where only the old trees can hear and the strip of sky see it, he talks with thee, sitting on a heap of moss! And he kisses my forehead, too, so that the little brook would hardly wash it off! But here, in the sunny day, and among all the people, he knows us not; nor must we know him! A strange, sad man is he, with his hand always over his heart!"

"Be quiet, Pearl! Thou understandest not these things," said her mother. "Think not now of the minister, but look about thee, and see how cheery is everybody's face today. The children have come from their schools, and the grown people from their workshops and their fields, on purpose to be happy. For today a new man is beginning to rule over them; and so—as has been the custom of mankind ever since a nation was first gathered—they make merry and rejoice; as if a good and golden year were at length to pass over the poor old world!"

It was as Hester said, in regard to the unwonted jollity that brightened the faces of the people. Into this festal season of the year—as it already was, and continued to be during the greater part of two centuries—the Puritans compressed whatever mirth and public joy they deemed allowable to human infirmity, thereby so far dispelling the customary cloud, that, for the space of a single holiday, they appeared scarcely more grave than most other communities at a period of general affliction.

But we perhaps exaggerate the gray or sable tinge which undoubtedly characterized the mood and manners of the age. The persons now in the market place of Boston had not been born to an inheritance of Puritanic gloom. They were native Englishmen whose fathers had lived in the sunny richness of the Elizabethan epoch, a time when the life of England, viewed as one great mass, would appear to have been as stately, magnificent, and joyous as the world has ever witnessed. Had they followed their hereditary taste, the New England settlers would have illustrated all events of public importance by bonfires, banquets, pageantries, and processions. Nor would it have been impracticable, in the observance of majestic ceremonies, to combine mirthful recreation with solemnity, and give, as it were, a grotesque and brilliant embroidery to the great robe of state which a nation, at such festivals, puts on. There was some shadow of

an attempt of this kind in the mode of celebrating the day
on which the political year of the colony commenced. The
dim reflection of a remembered splendor, a colorless and
manifold diluted repetition of what they had beheld in proud
old London—we will not say at a royal coronation, but at a
Lord Mayor's show—might be traced in the customs which
our forefathers instituted with reference to the annual installation of magistrates. The fathers and founders of the
commonwealth—the statesman, the priest, and the soldier—
deemed it a duty then to assume the outward state and
majesty, which in accordance with antique style, was looked
upon as the proper garb of public or social eminence. All
came forth, to move in procession before the people's eye,
and thus impart a needed dignity to the simple framework
of a government so newly constructed.

Then, too, the people were countenanced, if not encouraged, in relaxing the severe and close application to
their various modes of rugged industry, which, at all other
times, seemed of the same piece and material with their
religion. Here, it is true, were none of the appliances which
popular merriment would so readily have found in the England of Elizabeth's time, or that of James—no rude shows
of a theatrical kind; no minstrel, with his harp and legendary ballad, nor gleeman, with an ape dancing to his music;
no juggler, with his tricks of mimic witchcraft, no Merry
Andrew, to stir up the multitude with jests, perhaps hundreds of years old, but still effective, by their appeals to the
very broadest sources of mirthful sympathy. All such professors of the several branches of jocularity would have been
sternly repressed, not only by the rigid discipline of law, but
by the general sentiment which gives law its vitality. Not the
less, however, the great, honest face of the people smiled,
grimly, perhaps, but widely too. Nor were sports wanting,
such as the colonists had witnessed and shared in long ago,
at the country fairs and on the village greens of England;
and which it was thought well to keep alive on this new soil,
for the sake of the courage and manliness that were essential in them. Wrestling matches, in the different fashions of
Cornwall and Devonshire, were seen here and there about
the market place; in one corner, there was a friendly bout at
quarterstaff; and—what attracted most interest of all—on
the platform of the pillory, already so noted in our pages,

two masters of defence were commencing an exhibition with the buckler and broadsword. But, much to the disappointment of the crowd, this latter business was broken off by the interposition of the town beadle, who had no idea of permitting the majesty of the law to be violated by such an abuse of one of its consecrated places.

It may not be too much to affirm, on the whole (the people being then in the first stages of joyless deportment, and the offspring of sires who had known how to be merry, in their day), that they would compare favorably, in point of holiday keeping, with their descendants, even at so long an interval as ourselves. Their immediate posterity, the generation next to the early emigrants, wore the blackest shade of Puritanism, and so darkened the national visage with it, that all the subsequent years have not sufficed to clear it up. We have yet to learn again the forgotten art of gayety.

The picture of human life in the market place, though its general tint was the sad gray, brown, or black of the English emigrants, was yet enlivened by some diversity of hue. A party of Indians—in their savage finery of curiously embroidered deerskin robes, wampum belts, red and yellow ochre, and feathers, and armed with the bow and arrow and stone-headed spear—stood apart with countenances of inflexible gravity, beyond what even the Puritan aspect could attain. Nor, wild as were these painted barbarians, were they the wildest feature of the scene. This distinction could more justly be claimed by some mariners—a part of the crew of the vessel from the Spanish Main—who had come ashore to see the humors of Election Day. They were rough-looking desperadoes with sun-blackened faces and an immensity of beard; their wide, short trousers were confined about the waist by belts, often clasped with a rough plate of gold, and sustaining always a long knife, and, in some instances, a sword. From beneath their broad-brimmed hats of palm-leaf gleamed eyes which, even in good nature and merriment, had a kind of animal ferocity. They transgressed, without fear or scruple, the rules of behavior that were binding on all others; smoking tobacco under the beadle's very nose, although each whiff would have cost a townsman a shilling; and quaffing, at their pleasure, draughts of wine or aquavitæ from pocket flasks, which they freely tendered to the gaping crowd around them. It remarkably characterized the incomplete morality of the age, rigid as we call it, that a license was allowed the seafaring class, not merely for their freaks on shore, but for far more desperate deeds on their proper element. The sailor of that day would go near to be arraigned as a pirate in our own. There could be little doubt, for instance, that this very ship's crew, though no unfavorable specimens of the nautical brotherhood, had been guilty, as we should phrase it, of depredations of the Spanish commerce such as would have perilled all their necks in a modern court of justice.

But the sea in those old times heaved, swelled and foamed, very much at its own will, or subject only to the tempestuous wind, with hardly any attempts at regulation by human law. The buccaneer on the wave might relinquish his calling, and become at once, if he chose, a man of probity and piety on land; nor even in the full career of his reckless life was he regarded as a personage with whom it was disreputable to traffic or casually associate. Thus, the Puritan elders, in their black cloaks, starched bands, and steeple-crowned hats, smiled not unbenignantly at the clamor and rude deportment of these jolly seafaring men; and it excited neither surprise nor animadversion when so reputable a citizen as old Roger Chillingworth, the physician, was seen to enter the market place in close and familiar talk with the commander of the questionable vessel.

The latter was by far the most showy and gallant figure, so far as apparel went, anywhere to be seen among the multitude. He wore a profusion of ribbons on his garment, and gold lace on his hat, which was also encircled by a gold chain and surmounted with a feather. There was a sword at his side, and a sword cut on his forehead, which, by the arrangement of his hair, he seemed anxious rather to display than hide. A landsman could hardly have worn this garb and shown this face, and worn and shown them both with such a galliard air, without undergoing stern question, before a magistrate, and probably incurring fine or imprisonment, or perhaps an exhibition in the stocks. As regarded the shipmaster, however, all was looked upon as pertaining to the character, as to a fish his glistening scales.

After parting from the physician, the commander of the Bristol ship strolled idly through the market place; until, happening to approach the spot where Hester Prynne was standing, he appeared to recognize, and did not hesitate to address her. As was usually the case wherever Hester stood, a small vacant area—a sort of magic circle—had formed itself about her, into which, though the people were elbowing one another at a little distance, none ventured, or felt disposed to intrude. It was a forcible type of the moral solitude in which the scarlet letter enveloped its fated wearer; partly by her own reserve, and partly by the instinctive, though no longer so unkindly, withdrawal of her fellow-creatures. Now, if never before, it answered a good purpose by enabling Hester and the seaman to speak together without risk of being overheard; and so changed was Hester Prynne's repute before the public, that the matron in town most eminent for rigid morality could not have held such intercourse with less result of scandal than herself.

"So, mistress," said the mariner, "I must bid the steward make ready one more berth than you bargained for! No fear of scurvy or ship-fever, this voyage! What with the ship's surgeon and this other doctor, our only danger will be from drug or pill; more by token, as there is a lot of apothecary's stuff aboard, which I traded for with a Spanish vessel."

"What mean you?" inquired Hester, startled more than she permitted to appear. "Have you another passenger?"

"Why, know you not," cried the shipmaster, "that this physician here—Chillingworth, he calls himself—is minded to try my cabin-fare with you? Ay, ay, you must have known it; for he tells me he is of your party, and a close friend to the gentleman you spoke of—he that is in peril from these sour old Puritan rulers!"

"They know each other well indeed," replied Hester, with a mien of calmness, though in the utmost consternation. "They have long dwelt together."

Nothing further passed between the mariner and Hester Prynne. But, at that instant, she beheld old Roger Chillingworth himself, standing in the remotest corner of the market place and smiling on her; a smile which—across the wide and bustling square, and through all the talk and laughter, and various thoughts, moods, and interests of the crowd—conveyed secret and fearful meaning.

XXII

The Procession

BEFORE Hester Prynne could call together her thoughts and consider what was practicable to be done in this new and startling aspect of affairs, the sound of military music was heard approaching along a contiguous street. It denoted the advance of the procession of magistrates and citizens on its way towards the meeting house, where, in compliance with a custom thus early established, and ever since observed, the Reverend Mr. Dimmesdale was to deliver an Election Sermon.

Soon the head of the procession showed itself, with a slow and stately march, turning a corner, and making its way across the market place. First came the music. It comprised a variety of instruments, perhaps imperfectly adapted to one another and played with no great skill, but yet attaining the great object for which the harmony of drum and clarion addresses itself to the multitude—that of imparting a higher and more heroic air to the scene of life that passes before the eye. Little Pearl at first clapped her hands, but then lost, for an instant, the restless agitation that had kept her in a continual effervescence throughout the morning; she gazed silently, and seemed to be borne upward, like a floating sea bird, on the long heaves and swells of sound. But she was brought back to her former mood by the shimmer of the sunshine on the weapons and bright armor of the military company, which followed after the music and formed the honorary escort of the procession. This body of soldiery—which still sustains a corporate existence and marches down from past ages with an ancient and honorable fame—was

composed of no mercenary materials. Its ranks were filled
with gentlemen who felt the stirrings of martial impulse and
sought to establish a kind of College of Arms, where, as in
an association of Knights Templar, they might learn the
science, and, so far as peaceful exercise would teach them,
the practices of war. The high estimation then placed upon
the military character might be seen in the lofty port of each
individual member of the company. Some of them, indeed,
by their services in the Low Countries and on other fields of
European warfare, had fairly won their title to assume the
name and pomp of soldiership. The entire array, moreover,
clad in burnished steel, and with plumage nodding over
their bright morions, had a brilliancy of effect which no
modern display can aspire to equal.

And yet the men of civil eminence, who came immediately
behind the military escort, were better worth a thoughtful
observer's eye. Even in outward demeanor, they showed a
stamp of majesty that made the warriors' haughty stride
look vulgar, if not absurd. It was an age when what we call
talent had far less consideration than now, but the massive
materials which produce stability and dignity of character a
great deal more. The people possessed, by hereditary right,
the quality of reverence, which, in their descendants, if it
survive at all, exists in smaller proportion, and with a vastly
diminished force, in the selection and estimate of public
men. The change may be for good or ill, and is partly,
perhaps, for both. In that old day, the English settler on
these rude shores—having left king, nobles, and all degrees
of awful rank behind, while still the faculty and necessity of
reverence were strong in him—bestowed it on the white hair
and venerable brow of age; on long-tried integrity; on solid
wisdom and sad-colored experience; on endowments of that
grave and weighty order which gives the idea of permanence
and comes under the general definition of respectability.
These primitive statesmen, therefore—Bradstreet, Endicott,
Dudley, Bellingham, and their compeers—who were elevated to power by the early choice of the people, seem to
have been not often brilliant, but distinguished by a ponderous sobriety rather than activity of intellect. They had forti-
tude and self-reliance, and, in time of difficulty or peril,
stood up for the welfare of the state like a line of cliffs
against a tempestuous tide. The traits of character here

indicated were well represented in the square cast of countenance and large physical development of the new colonial magistrates. So far as a demeanor of natural authority was concerned, the mother country need not have been ashamed to see these foremost men of an actual democracy adopted into the House of Peers, or made the Privy Council of the sovereign.

Next in order to the magistrates came the young and eminently distinguished divine, from whose lips the religious discourse of the anniversary was expected. His was the profession, at that era, in which intellectual ability displayed itself far more than in political life; for—leaving a higher motive out of the question—it offered inducements powerful enough, in the almost worshipping respect of the community, to win the most aspiring ambition into its service. Even political power—as in the case of Increase Mather—was within the grasp of a successful priest.

It was the observation of those who beheld him now, that never, since Mr. Dimmesdale first set his foot on the New England shore, had he exhibited such energy as was seen in the gait and air with which he kept his pace in the procession. There was no feebleness of step, as at other times; his frame was not bent; nor did his hand rest ominously upon his heart. Yet, if the clergyman were rightly viewed, his strength seemed not of the body. It might be spiritual, and imparted to him by angelic ministrations. It might be the exhilaration of that potent cordial, which is distilled only in the furnace-glow of earnest and long-continued thought. Or, perchance, his sensitive temperament was invigorated by the loud and piercing music that swelled heavenward and uplifted him on its ascending wave. Nevertheless, so abstracted was his look, it might be questioned whether Mr. Dimmesdale even heard the music. There was his body, moving onward, and with an unaccustomed force. But where was his mind? Far and deep in its own region, busying itself, with preternatural activity, to marshal a procession of stately thoughts that were soon to issue thence; and so he saw nothing, heard nothing, knew nothing, of what was around him; but the spiritual element took up the feeble frame, and carried it along, unconscious of the burden, and converting it to spirit like itself. Men of uncommon intellect, who have grown morbid, possess this occasional power of mighty effort, into which they throw the life of many days, and then are lifeless for as many more.

Hester Prynne, gazing steadfastly at the clergyman, felt a dreary influence come over her, but wherefore or whence she knew not; unless that he seemed so remote from her own sphere, and utterly beyond her reach. One glance of recognition, she had imagined, must needs pass between them. She thought of the dim forest, with its little dell of solitude, and love, and anguish, and the mossy tree-trunk, where, sitting hand in hand, they had mingled their sad and passionate talk with the melancholy murmur of the brook. How deeply had they known each other then! And was this the man? She hardly knew him now! He, moving proudly past, enveloped, as it were, in the rich music, with the procession of majestic and venerable fathers; he, so un-attainable in his worldly position, and still more so in that far vista of his unsympathizing thoughts, through which she now beheld him! Her spirit sank with the idea that all must have been a delusion, and that, vividly as she had dreamed it, there could be no real bond betwixt the clergyman and herself. And thus much of woman was there in Hester, that she could scarcely forgive him—least of all now, when the heavy footstep of their approaching Fate might be heard, nearer, nearer, nearer!—for being able so completely to withdraw himself from their mutual world, while she groped darkly, and stretched forth her cold hands, and found him not.

Pearl either saw and responded to her mother's feelings, or herself felt the remoteness and intangibility that had fallen around the minister. While the procession passed, the child was uneasy, fluttering up and down like a bird on the point of taking flight. When the whole had gone by, she looked up into Hester's face.

"Mother," said she, "was that the same minister that kissed me by the brook?"

"Hold thy peace, dear little Pearl!" whispered her mother. "We must not always talk in the market place of what happens to us in the forest."

"I could not be sure that it was he; so strange he looked," continued the child. "Else I would have run to him, and bid him kiss me now, before all the people; even as he did yonder among the dark old trees. What would the minister have said, Mother? Would he have clapped his hand over his heart, and scowled on me, and bid me begone?"

"What should he say, Pearl," answered Hester, "save that it was no time to kiss, and that kisses are not to be given in the market place? Well for thee, foolish child, that thou didst not speak to him!"

Another shade of the same sentiment in reference to Mr. Dimmesdale was expressed by a person whose eccentricities —or insanity, as we should term it—led her to do what few of the townspeople would have ventured on; to begin a conversation with the wearer of the scarlet letter in public. It was Mistress Hibbins, who, arrayed in great magnificence, with a triple ruff, a broidered stomacher, a gown of rich velvet, and a gold-headed cane, had come forth to see the procession. As this ancient lady had the renown (which subsequently cost her no less a price than her life) of being a principal actor in all the works of necromancy that were continually going forward, the crowd gave way before her, and seemed to fear the touch of her garment, as if it carried the plague among its gorgeous folds. Seen in conjunction with Hester Prynne—kindly as so many now felt towards the latter—the dread inspired by Mistress Hibbins was doubled, and caused a general movement from that part of the market place in which the two women stood.

"Now, what mortal imagination could conceive it!" whispered the old lady confidentially to Hester. "Yonder divine man! That saint on earth, as the people uphold him to be, and as—I must needs say—he really looks! Who, now, that saw him pass in the procession, would think how little while it is since he went forth out of his study—chewing a Hebrew text of Scripture in his mouth, I warrant—to take an airing in the forest! Aha! we know what that means, Hester Prynne! But, truly, forsooth, I find it hard to believe him the same man. Many a church member saw I, walking behind the music, that has danced in the same measure with me, when Somebody was fiddler, and, it might be, an Indian powwow or a Lapland wizard changing hands with us! That is but a trifle, when a woman knows the world. But this minister! Couldst thou surely tell, Hester, whether he was the same man that encountered thee on the forest path?"

"Madam, I know not of what you speak," answered Hester Prynne, feeling Mistress Hibbins to be of infirm mind;

yet strangely startled and awe-stricken by the confidence
with which she affirmed a personal connection between so
many persons (herself among them) and the Evil One. "It is
not for me to talk lightly of a learned and pious minister of
the Word, like the Reverend Mr. Dimmesdale!"

"Fie, woman, fie!" cried the old lady, shaking her finger
at Hester. "Dost thou think I have been to the forest so
many times, and have yet no skill to judge who else has
been there? Yea; though no leaf of the wild garlands, which
they wore while they danced, be left in their hair! I know
thee, Hester; for I behold the token. We may all see it in
the sunshine; and it glows like a red flame in the dark. Thou
wearest it openly; so there need be no question about that.
But this minister! Let me tell thee, in thine ear! When the
Black Man sees one of his own servants, signed and sealed,
so shy of owning to the bond as is the Reverend Mr.
Dimmesdale, he hath a way of ordering matters so that the
mark shall be disclosed in open daylight to the eyes of all
the world! What is it that the minister seeks to hide, with his
hand always over his heart? Ha, Hester Prynne!"

"What is it, good Mistress Hibbins?" eagerly asked little
Pearl. "Hast thou seen it?"

"No matter, darling!" responded Mistress Hibbins, making Pearl a profound reverence. "Thou thyself wilt see it,
one time or another. They say, child, thou art of the lineage
of the Prince of the Air! Wilt thou ride with me, some fine
night, to see thy father? Then thou shalt know wherefore the
minister keeps his hand over his heart!"

Laughing so shrilly that all the market place could hear
her, the weird old gentlewoman took her departure.

By this time the preliminary prayer had been offered in
the meeting house, and the accents of the Reverend Mr.
Dimmesdale were heard commencing his discourse. An irresistible feeling kept Hester near the spot. As the sacred
edifice was too much thronged to admit another auditor, she
took up her position close beside the scaffold of the pillory.
It was in sufficient proximity to bring the whole sermon to
her ears, in the shape of an indistinct, but varied, murmur
and flow of the minister's very peculiar voice.

This vocal organ was in itself a rich endowment; insomuch
that a listener, comprehending nothing of the language in
which the preacher spoke, might still have been swayed to

and fro by the mere tone and cadence. Like all other music, it breathed passion and pathos, and emotions high or tender, in a tongue native to the human heart, wherever educated. Muffled as the sound was by its passage through the church walls, Hester Prynne listened with such intentness, and sympathized so intimately, that the sermon had throughout a meaning for her entirely apart from its indistinguishable words. These, perhaps, if more distinctly heard, might have been only a grosser medium and have clogged the spiritual sense. Now she caught the low undertone, as of the wind sinking down to repose itself; then ascended with it, as it rose through progressive gradations of sweetness and power, until its volume seemed to envelop her with an atmosphere of awe and solemn grandeur. And yet, majestic as the voice sometimes became, there was forever in it an essential character of plaintiveness. A loud or low expression of anguish—the whisper, or the shriek, as it might be conceived, of suffering humanity, that touched a sensibility in every bosom! At times this deep strain of pathos was all that could be heard, and scarcely heard, sighing amid a desolate silence. But even when the minister's voice grew high and commanding—when it gushed irrepressibly upward—when it assumed its utmost breadth and power, so overfilling the church as to burst its way through the solid walls and diffuse itself in the open air—still, if the auditor listened intently, and for the purpose, he could detect the same cry of pain. What was it? The complaint of a human heart, sorrow-laden, perchance guilty, telling its secret, whether of guilt or sorrow, to the great heart of mankind; beseeching its sympathy or forgiveness—at every moment—in each accent—and never in vain! It was this profound and continual undertone that gave the clergyman his most appropriate power.

During all this time, Hester stood, statue-like, at the foot of the scaffold. If the minister's voice had not kept her there, there would nevertheless have been an inevitable magnetism in that spot, whence she dated the first hour of her life of ignomy. There was a sense within her—too ill-defined to be made a thought, but weighing heavily on her mind—that her whole orb of life, both before and after, was connected with this spot, as with the one point that gave it unity.

Little Pearl, meanwhile, had quitted her mother's side,

and was playing at her own will about the market place. She made the sombre crowd cheerful by her erratic and glistening ray, even as a bird of bright plumage illuminates a whole tree of dusky foliage, by darting to and fro, half seen and half concealed amid the twilight of the clustering leaves. She had an undulating, but oftentimes, a sharp and irregular movement. It indicated the restless vivacity of her spirit, which today was doubly indefatigable in its tiptoe dance, because it was played upon and vibrated with her mother's disquietude. Whenever Pearl saw anything to excite her ever-active and wandering curiosity, she flew thitherward, and, as we might say, seized upon that man or thing as her own property, so far as she desired it; but without yielding the minutest degree of control over her motions in requital. The Puritans looked on, and, if they smiled, were none the less inclined to pronounce the child a demon offspring, from the indescribable charm of beauty and eccentricity that shone through her little figure, and sparkled with its activity. She ran and looked the wild Indian in the face; and he grew conscious of a nature wilder than his own. Thence, with native audacity, but still with a reserve as characteristic, she flew into the midst of a group of mariners, the swarthy-cheeked wild men of the ocean, as the Indians were of the land; and they gazed wonderingly and admiringly at Pearl, as if a flake on the sea-foam had taken the shape of a little maid, and were gifted with a soul of the sea-fire that flashes beneath the prow in the nighttime.

One of these seafaring men—the shipmaster, indeed, who had spoken to Hester Prynne—was so smitten with Pearl's aspect, that he attempted to lay hands upon her, with purpose to snatch a kiss. Finding it as impossible to touch her as to catch a hummingbird in the air, he took from his hat the gold chain that was twisted about it, and threw it to the child. Pearl immediately twined it around her neck and waist with such happy skill that, once seen there, it became a part of her, and it was difficult to imagine her without it.

"Thy mother is yonder woman with the scarlet letter," said the seaman. "Wilt thou carry her a message from me?"

"If the message pleases me, I will," answered Pearl.

"Then tell her," rejoined he, "that I spake again with the black-a-visaged hump-shouldered old doctor, and he engages to bring his friend, the gentleman she wots of, aboard with him. So let thy mother take no thought, save for herself and thee. Wilt thou tell her this, thou witch-baby?"

"Mistress Hibbins says my father is the Prince of the Air!" cried Pearl, with a naughty smile. "If thou callest me that ill name, I shall tell him of thee, and he will chase thy ship with a tempest!"

Pursuing a zigzag course across the market place, the child returned to her mother and communicated what the mariner had said. Hester's strong, calm, steadfastly enduring spirit almost sank, at last, on beholding this dark and grim countenance of an inevitable doom, which—at the moment when a passage seemed to open for the minister and herself out of their labyrinth of misery—showed itself, with an unrelenting smile, right in the midst of their path.

With her mind harassed by the terrible perplexity in which the shipmaster's intelligence involved her, she was also subjected to another trial. There were many people present from the country round about who had often heard of the scarlet letter, and to whom it had been made terrific by a hundred false or exaggerated rumors, but who had never beheld it with their own bodily eyes. These, after exhausting other modes of amusement, now thronged about Hester Prynne with rude and boorish intrusiveness. Unscrupulous as it was, however, it could not bring them nearer than a circuit of several yards. At that distance they accordingly stood, fixed there by the centrifugal force of the repugnance which the mystic symbol inspired. The whole gang of sailors, likewise, observing the press of spectators, and learning the purport of the scarlet letter, came and thrust their sunburnt and desperado-looking faces into the ring. Even the Indians were affected by a sort of cold shadow of the white man's curiosity, and, gliding through the crowd, fastened their snakelike black eyes on Hester's bosom, conceiving, perhaps, that the wearer of this brilliantly embroidered badge must needs be a personage of high dignity among her people. Lastly the inhabitants of the town (their own interest in this worn-out subject languidly reviving itself by sympathy with what they saw others feel) lounged idly to the same quarter, and tormented Hester Prynne, perhaps more than all the rest, with their cool, well-acquainted gaze at her familiar shame. Hester saw and recognized the selfsame faces of that group of matrons who had awaited her forthcoming from the prison door seven years ago; all save one, the youngest and only compassionate among them, whose burial robe she had since made. At the final hour, when she was so soon to fling aside the burning letter, it had strangely become the centre of more remark and excitement, and was thus made to sear her breast more painfully, than at any time since the first day she put it on.

While Hester stood in that magic circle of ignominy where the cunning cruelty of her sentence seemed to have fixed her forever, the admirable preacher was looking down from the sacred pulpit upon an audience whose very inmost spirits had yielded to his control. The sainted minister in the church! The woman of the scarlet letter in the market place! What imagination would have been irreverent enough to surmise that the same scorching stigma was on them both!

XXIII

The Revelation of the Scarlet Letter

THE eloquent voice, on which the souls of the listening audience had been borne aloft as on the swelling waves of the sea, at length came to a pause. There was a momentary silence, profound as what should follow the utterance of oracles. Then ensued a murmur and half-hushed tumult, as if the auditors, released from the high spell that had transported them into the region of another's mind, were returning into themselves, with all their awe and wonder still heavy on them. In a moment more, the crowd began to gush forth from the doors of the church. Now that there was an end, they needed other breath, more fit to support the gross and earthly life into which they relapsed than that atmosphere which the preacher had converted into words of flame and had burdened with the rich fragrance of his thought.

In the open air their rapture broke into speech. The street and the market place absolutely babbled, from side to side, with applauses of the minister. His hearers could not rest until they had told one another of what each knew better than he could tell or hear. According to their united testimony, never had man spoken in so wise, so high, and so holy a spirit as he that spake this day; nor had inspiration ever breathed through mortal lips more evidently than it did through his. Its influence could be seen, as it were, descending upon him, and possessing him, and continually lifting him out of the written discourse that lay before him, and filling him with ideas that must have been as marvellous to himself as to his audience. His subject it appeared, had been the relation between the Deity and the communities of mankind, with a special reference to the New England which they were here planting in the wilderness. And as he drew towards the close, a spirit as of prophecy had come upon him, constraining him to its purpose as mightily as the old prophets of Israel were constrained; only with this difference, that whereas the Jewish seers had denounced judgments and ruin on their country, it was his mission to foretell a high and glorious destiny for the newly gathered people of the Lord. But, throughout it all, and through the whole discourse, there had been a certain deep, sad undertone of pathos, which could not be interpreted otherwise than as the natural regret of one soon to pass away. Yes; their minister whom they so loved—and who so loved them all, that he could not depart heavenward without a sigh—had the foreboding of untimely death upon him, and would soon leave them in their tears! This idea of his transitory stay on earth gave the last emphasis to the effect which the preacher had produced; it was as if an angel, in his passage to the skies, had shaken his bright wings over the people for an instant—at once a shadow and a splendor—and had shed down a shower of golden truths upon them.

Thus, there had come to the Reverend Mr. Dimmesdale—as to most men, in their various spheres, though seldom recognized until they see it far behind them—an epoch of life more brilliant and full of triumph than any previous one, or than any which could hereafter be. He stood, at this moment, on the very proudest eminence of superiority to which the gifts of intellect, rich lore, prevailing eloquence, and a reputation of whitest sanctity, could exalt a clergyman in New England's earliest days, when the professional character was of itself a lofty pedestal. Such was the position which the minister occupied, as he bowed his head forward on the cushions of the pulpit, at the close of his Election Sermon. Meanwhile Hester Prynne was standing beside the scaffold of the pillory, with the scarlet letter still burning on her breast!

Now was heard again the clangor of the music, and the measured tramp of the military escort, issuing from the church door. The procession was to be marshalled thence to the town hall, where a solemn banquet would complete the ceremonies of the day.

Once more, therefore, the train of venerable and majestic

fathers was seen moving through a broad pathway of the people, who drew back reverently on either side as the Governor and magistrates, the old and wise men, the holy ministers, and all that were eminent and renowned, advanced into the midst of them. When they were fairly in the market place, their presence was greeted by a shout. This—though doubtless it might acquire additional force and volume from the childlike loyalty which the age awarded to its rulers—was felt to be an irrepressible outburst of enthusiasm kindled in the auditors by that high strain of eloquence which was yet reverberating in their ears. Each felt the impulse in himself, and, in the same breath, caught it from his neighbor. Within the church, it had hardly been kept down; beneath the sky, it pealed upward to the zenith. There were human beings enough, and enough of highly wrought and symphonious feeling, to produce that more impressive sound than the organ tones of the blast, or the thunder, or the roar of the sea; even that mighty swell of many voices, blended into one great voice by the universal impulse which makes likewise one vast heart of the many. Never, from the soil of New England, had gone up such a shout! Never, on New England soil, had stood the man so honored by his mortal brethren as the preacher!

How fared it with him then? Were there not the brilliant particles of a halo in the air about his head? So etherealized by spirit as he was, and so apotheosized by worshipping admirers, did his footsteps, in the procession, really tread upon the dust of earth?

As the ranks of military men and civil fathers moved onward, all eyes were turned towards the point where the minister was seen to approach among them. The shout died into a murmur, as one portion of the crowd after another obtained a glimpse of him. How feeble and pale he looked, amid all his triumph! The energy—or say, rather, the inspiration which had held him up, until he should have delivered the sacred message that brought its own strength along with it from heaven—was withdrawn, now that it had so faithfully performed its office. The glow, which they had just before beheld burning on his cheek, was extinguished, like a flame that sinks down hopelessly among the late-decaying embers. It seemed hardly the face of a man alive, with such a deathlike hue; it was hardly a man with life in him, that tottered on his path so nervelessly, yet tottered, and did not fall!

One of his clerical brethren—it was the venerable John Wilson—observing the state in which Mr. Dimmesdale was left by the retiring wave of intellect and sensibility, stepped forward hastily to offer him his support. The minister tremulously, but decidedly, repelled the old man's arm. He still walked onward, if that movement could be so described, which rather resembled the wavering effort of an infant, with its mother's arms in view, outstretched to tempt him forward. And now, almost imperceptible as were the latter steps of his progress, he had come opposite the well-remembered and weather-darkened scaffold, where, long since, with all that dreary lapse of time between, Hester Prynne had encountered the world's ignominious stare. There stood Hester, holding little Pearl by the hand! And there was the scarlet letter on her breast! The minister here made a pause, although the music still played the stately and rejoicing march to which the procession moved. It summoned him onward—onward to the festival!—but here he made a pause.

Bellingham, for the last few moments, had kept an anxious eye upon him. He now left his own place in the procession, and advanced to give assistance, judging, from Mr. Dimmesdale's aspect, that he must otherwise inevitably fall. But there was something in the latter's expression that warned back the magistrate, although a man not readily obeying the vague intimations that pass from one spirit to another. The crowd, meanwhile, looked on with awe and wonder. This earthly faintness was, in their view, only another phase of the minister's celestial strength; nor would it have seemed a miracle too high to be wrought for one so holy, had he ascended before their eyes, waxing dimmer and brighter, and fading at last into the light of heaven.

He turned towards the scaffold, and stretched forth his arms.

"Hester," said he, "come hither! Come, my little Pearl!"

It was a ghastly look with which he regarded them; but there was something at once tender and strangely triumphant in it. The child, with the birdlike motion which was one of her characteristics, flew to him, and clasped her arms about his knees. Hester Prynne—slowly, as if impelled by inevitable fate, and against her strongest will—likewise drew near, but paused before she reached him. At this instant, old Roger Chillingworth thrust himself through the crowd—or, perhaps so dark, disturbed and evil, was his look, he rose up out of some nether region—to snatch back his victim from what he sought to do! Be that as it might, the old man rushed forward, and caught the minister by the arm.

"Madman, hold! what is your purpose?" whispered he. "Wave back that woman! Cast off this child! All shall be well! Do not blacken your fame and perish in dishonor! I can yet save you! Would you bring infamy on your sacred profession?"

"Ha, tempter! Methinks thou art too late!" answered the minister, encountering his eye, fearfully but firmly. "Thy power is not what it was! With God's help, I shall escape thee now!"

He again extended his hand to the woman of the scarlet letter.

"Hester Prynne," cried he, with a piercing earnestness, "in the name of Him, so terrible and so merciful, who gives me grace, at this last moment, to do what—for my own heavy sin and miserable agony—I withheld myself from doing seven years ago, come hither now, and twine thy strength about me! Thy strength, Hester; but let it be guided by the will which God hath granted me! This wretched and wronged old man is opposing it with all his might!—with all his own might, and the fiend's! Come, Hester, come! Support me up yonder scaffold!"

The crowd was in a tumult. The men of rank and dignity, who stood more immediately around the clergyman, were so taken by surprise and so perplexed as to the purport of what they saw—unable to receive the explanation which most readily presented itself, or to imagine any other—that they remained silent and inactive spectators of the judgment which Providence seemed about to work. They beheld the minister, leaning on Hester's shoulder and supported by her arm around him, approach the scaffold and ascend its steps; while still the little hand of the sin-born child was clasped in his. Old Roger Chillingworth followed, as one intimately connected with the drama of guilt and sorrow in which they had all been actors, and well entitled, therefore, to be present, at its closing scene.

"Hadst thou sought the whole earth over," said he, looking darkly at the clergyman, "there was no one place so secret—no high place nor lowly place where thou couldst have escaped me—save on this very scaffold!"

"Thanks be to Him who hath led me hither!" answered the minister.

Yet he trembled, and turned to Hester with an expression of doubt and anxiety in his eyes, not the less evidently betrayed that there was a feeble smile upon his lips.

"Is not this better," murmured he, "than what we dreamed of in the forest?"

"I know not! I know not!" she hurriedly replied. "Better? Yea; so we may both die, and little Pearl die with us!"

"For thee and Pearl, be it as God shall order," said the minister; "and God is merciful! Let me now do the will which he hath made plain before my sight. For, Hester, I am a dying man. So let me make haste to take my shame upon me!"

Partly supported by Hester Prynne and holding one hand of little Pearl, the Reverend Mr. Dimmesdale turned to the dignified and venerable rulers; to the holy ministers, who were his brethren; to the people, whose great heart was thoroughly appalled, yet overflowing with tearful sympathy, as knowing that some deep life-matter—which, if full of sin, was full of anguish and repentance likewise—was now to be laid open to them. The sun, but little past its meridian, shone down upon the clergyman, and gave a distinctness to his figure, as he stood out from all the earth to put in his plea of guilty at the bar of Eternal Justice.

"People of New England!" cried he, with a voice that rose over them, high, solemn, and majestic—yet had always a tremor through it, and sometimes a shriek, struggling up out of a fathomless depth of remorse and woe—"ye, that have loved me!—ye, that have deemed me holy!—behold me here, the one sinner of the world! At last!—at last!—I stand upon the spot where, seven years since, I should have stood; here, with this woman, whose arm, more than the little strength wherewith I have crept hitherward, sustains me, at this dreadful moment, from grovelling down upon my face! Lo, the scarlet letter which Hester wears! Ye have all shuddered at it! Wherever her walk hath been—wherever, so miserably burdened, she may have hoped to find repose—

it hath cast a lurid gleam of awe and horrible repugnance round about her. But there stood one in the midst of you, at whose brand of sin and infamy ye have not shuddered!"

It seemed, at this point, as if the minister must leave the remainder of his secret undisclosed. But he fought back the bodily weakness—and, still more, the faintness of heart—that was striving for the mastery with him. He threw off all assistance, and stepped passionately forward a pace before the woman and the child.

"It was on him!" he continued, with a kind of fierceness, so determined was he to speak out the whole. "God's eye beheld it! The angels were forever pointing at it! The Devil knew it well, and fretted it continually with the touch of his burning finger! But he hid it cunningly from men, and walked among you with the mien of a spirit, mournful, because so pure in a sinful world!—and sad, because he missed his heavenly kindred! Now, at the death-hour, he stands up before you! He bids you look again at Hester's scarlet letter! He tells you that, with all its mysterious horror, it is but the shadow of what he bears on his own breast, and that even this, his own red stigma, is no more than the type of what has seared his inmost heart! Stand any here that question God's judgment on a sinner? Behold! Behold a dreadful witness of it!"

With a convulsive motion, he tore away the ministerial band from before his breast. It was revealed! But it were irreverent to describe that revelation. For an instant, the gaze of the horror-stricken multitude was concentred on the ghastly miracle; while the minister stood, with a flush of triumph in his face, as one who, in the crisis of acutest pain, had won a victory. Then, down he sank upon the scaffold! Hester partly raised him, and supported his head against her bosom. Old Roger Chillingworth knelt down beside him, with a blank, dull countenance, out of which the life seemed to have departed.

"Thou hast escaped me!" he repeated more than once. "Thou hast escaped me!"

"May God forgive thee!" said the minister. "Thou, too, hast deeply sinned!"

He withdrew his dying eyes from the old man, and fixed them on the woman and the child.

"My little Pearl," said he, feebly—and there was a sweet

and gentle smile over his face, as of a spirit sinking into deep repose; nay, now that the burden was removed, it seemed almost as if he would be sportive with the child— "dear little Pearl, wilt thou kiss me now? Thou wouldst not, yonder, in the forest! But now thou wilt!"

Pearl kissed his lips. A spell was broken. The great scene of grief, in which the wild infant bore a part, had developed all her sympathies; and as her tears fell upon her father's cheek, they were the pledge that she would grow up amid human joy and sorrow, nor forever do battle with the world, but be a woman in it. Towards her mother, too, Pearl's errand as a messenger of anguish was all fulfilled.

"Hester," said the clergyman, "farewell!"

"Shall we not meet again?" whispered she, bending her face down close to his. "Shall we not spend our immortal life together? Surely, surely, we have ransomed one another, with all this woe! Thou lookest far into eternity, with those bright dying eyes! Then tell me what thou seest?"

"Hush, Hester, hush!" said he, with tremulous solemnity. "The law we broke!—the sin here so awfully revealed!—let these alone be in thy thoughts! I fear! I fear! It may be, that, when we forgot our God—when we violated our reverence each for the other's soul—it was thenceforth vain to hope that we could meet hereafter, in an everlasting and pure reunion. God knows; and he is merciful! He hath proved his mercy, most of all, in my afflictions. By giving me this burning torture to bear upon my breast! By sending yonder dark and terrible old man to keep the torture always at red-heat! By bringing me hither, to die this death of triumphant ignominy before the people! Had either of these agonies been wanting, I had been lost forever! Praised be his name! His will be done! Farewell!"

That final word came forth with the minister's expiring breath. The multitude, silent till then, broke out in a strange, deep voice of awe and wonder, which could not as yet find utterance, save in this murmur that rolled so heavily after the departed spirit.

XXIV

Conclusion

AFTER many days, when time sufficed for the people to arrange their thoughts in reference to the foregoing scene, there was more than one account of what had been witnessed on the scaffold.

Most of the spectators testified to having seen, on the breast of the unhappy minister, a *scarlet letter*—the very semblance of that worn by Hester Prynne—imprinted in the flesh. As regarded its origin, there were various explanations, all of which must necessarily have been conjectural. Some affirmed that the Reverend Mr. Dimmesdale, on the very day when Hester Prynne first wore her ignominious badge, had begun a course of penance—which he afterwards, in so many futile methods, followed out—by inflicting a hideous torture on himself. Others contended that the stigma had not been produced until a long time subsequent, when old Roger Chillingworth, being a potent necromancer, had caused it to appear through the agency of magic and poisonous drugs. Others, again—and those best able to appreciate the minister's peculiar sensibility and the wonderful operation of his spirit upon the body—whispered their belief that the awful symbol was the effect of the ever active tooth of remorse, gnawing from the inmost heart outwardly, and at last manifesting Heaven's dreadful judgment by the visible presence of the letter. The reader may choose among these theories. We have thrown all the light we could acquire upon the portent, and would gladly, now that it has done its office, erase its deep print out of our own brain, where long meditation has fixed it in very undesirable distinctness.

It is singular, nevertheless, that certain persons, who were spectators of the whole scene and professed never once to have removed their eyes from the Reverend Mr. Dimmesdale, denied that there was any mark whatever on his breast, more than on a newborn infant's. Neither, by their report, had his dying words acknowledged, nor even remotely implied, any, the slightest connection, on his part, with the guilt for which Hester Prynne had so long worn the scarlet letter. According to these highly respectable witnesses, the minister, conscious that he was dying—conscious, also, that the reverence of the multitude placed him already among saints and angels—had desired, by yielding up his breath in the arms of that fallen woman, to express to the world how utterly nugatory is the choicest of man's own righteousness. After exhausting life in his efforts for mankind's spiritual good, he had made the manner of his death a parable, in order to impress on his admirers the mighty and mournful lesson that, in the view of Infinite Purity, we are sinners all alike. It was to teach them that the holiest among us has but attained so far above his fellows as to discern more clearly the Mercy which looks down, and repudiate more utterly the phantom of human merit which would look aspiringly upward. Without disputing a truth so momentous, we must be allowed to consider this version of Mr. Dimmesdale's story as only an instance of that stubborn fidelity with which a man's friends—and especially a clergyman's—will sometimes uphold his character, when proofs, clear as the mid-day sunshine on the scarlet letter, establish him a false and sin-stained creature of the dust.

The authority which we have chiefly followed—a manuscript of old date, drawn up from the verbal testimony of individuals, some of whom had known Hester Prynne, while others had heard the tale from contemporary witnesses—fully confirms the view taken in the foregoing pages. Among many morals which press upon us from the poor minister's miserable experience, we put only this into a sentence:—"Be true! Be true! Be true! Show freely to the world, if not your worst, yet some trait whereby the worst may be inferred!"

Nothing was more remarkable than the change which took place, almost immediately after Mr. Dimmesdale's death, in the appearance and demeanor of the old man known as Roger Chillingworth. All his strength and energy—all his vital and intellectual force—seemed at once to desert him; insomuch that he positively withered up, shrivelled away, and almost vanished from mortal sight, like an uprooted weed that lies wilting in the sun. This unhappy man had made the very principle of his life to consist in the pursuit and systematic exercise of revenge; and when, by its completest triumph and consummation, that evil principle was left with no further material to support it, when, in short, there was no more Devil's work on earth for him to do, it only remained for the unhumanized mortal to betake himself whither his Master would find him tasks enough, and pay him his wages duly. But, to all these shadowy beings, so long our near acquaintances—as well Roger Chillingworth as his companions—we would fain be merciful. It is a curious subject of observation and inquiry, whether hatred and love be not the same thing at bottom. Each, in its utmost development, supposes a high degree of intimacy and heart-knowledge; each renders one individual dependent for the food of his affections and spiritual life upon another; each leaves the passionate lover, or the no less passionate hater, forlorn and desolate by the withdrawal of his object. Philosophically considered, therefore, the two passions seem essentially the same, except that one happens to be seen in a celestial radiance and the other in a dusky and lurid glow. In the spiritual world, the old physician and the minister—mutual victims as they have been—may, unawares, have found their earthly stock of hatred and antipathy transmuted into golden love.

Leaving this discussion apart, we have a matter of business to communicate to the reader. At old Roger Chillingworth's decease (which took place within the year), and by his last will and testament, of which Governor Bellingham and the Reverend Mr. Wilson were executors, he bequeathed a very considerable amount of property, both here and in England, to little Pearl, the daughter of Hester Prynne.

So Pearl—the elf-child—the demon offspring, as some people, up to that epoch, persisted in considering her —became the richest heiress of her day, in the New World. Not improbably, this circumstance wrought a very material change in the public estimation, and, had the mother and child remained here, little Pearl, at a marriageable period of life, might have mingled her wild blood with the lineage of the devoutest Puritan among them all. But, in no long time after the physician's death, the wearer of the scarlet letter disappeared, and Pearl along with her. For many years, though a vague report would now and then find its way across the sea—like a shapeless piece of driftwood tossed ashore, with the initials of a name upon it—yet no tidings of them unquestionably authentic were received. The story of the scarlet letter grew into a legend. Its spell, however, was still potent, and kept the scaffold awful where the poor minister had died, and likewise the cottage by the seashore, where Hester Prynne had dwelt. Near this latter spot, one afternoon, some children were at play, when they beheld a tall woman, in a gray robe, approach the cottage door. In all those years it had never once been opened; but either she unlocked it, or the decaying wood and iron yielded to her hand, or she glided shadowlike through these impediments—and, at all events, went in.

On the threshold she paused—turned partly round—for, perchance, the idea of entering all alone, and all so changed, the home of so intense a former life, was more dreary and desolate than even she could bear. But her hesitation was only for an instant, though long enough to display a scarlet letter on her breast.

And Hester Prynne had returned, and taken up her long-forsaken shame! But where was little Pearl? If still alive, she must now have been in the flush and bloom of early womanhood. None knew—nor ever learned, with the fulness of perfect certainty—whether the elf-child had gone thus untimely to a maiden grave; or whether her wild, rich nature had been softened and subdued, and made capable of a woman's gentle happiness. But, through the remainder of Hester's life, there were indications that the recluse of the scarlet letter was the object of love and interest with some inhabitant of another land. Letters came, with armorial seals upon them, though of bearing unknown to English heraldry. In the cottage there were articles of comfort and luxury, such as Hester never cared to use, but which only wealth could have purchased, and affection have imagined for her. There were trifles, too, little ornaments, beautiful tokens of a continual remembrance, that must have been wrought by delicate fingers at the impulse of a fond heart. And, once, Hester was seen embroidering a baby garment, with such a lavish richness of golden fancy as would have raised a public tumult had any infant, thus apparelled, been shown to our sober-hued community.

In fine, the gossips of that day believed—and Mr. Surveyor Pue, who made investigations a century later, believed—and one of his recent successors in office, moreover, faithfully believes—that Pearl was not only alive, but married, and happy, and mindful of her mother; and that she would most joyfully have entertained that sad and lonely mother at her fireside.

But there was a more real life for Hester Prynne here in New England than in that unknown region where Pearl had found a home. Here had been her sin; here, her sorrow; and here was yet to be her penitence. She had returned, therefore, and resumed—of her own free will, for not the sternest magistrate of that iron period would have imposed it— resumed the symbol of which we have related so dark a tale. Never afterwards did it quit her bosom. But, in the lapse of the toilsome, thoughtful, and self-devoted years that made up Hester's life, the scarlet letter ceased to be a stigma which attracted the world's scorn and bitterness, and became a type of something to be sorrowed over, and looked upon with awe, yet with reverence too. And, as Hester Prynne had no selfish ends, nor lived in any measure for her own profit and enjoyment, people brought all their sorrows and perplexities and besought her counsel, as one who had herself gone through a mighty trouble. Women, more especially—in the continually recurring trials of wounded, wasted, wronged, misplaced, or erring and sinful passion—or with the dreary burden of a heart unyielded, because unvalued and unsought—came to Hester's cottage, demanding why they were so wretched, and what the remedy! Hester comforted and counselled them, as best she might. She assured them, too, of her firm belief, that, at some brighter period, when the world should have grown ripe for it, in Heaven's own time, a new truth would be revealed, in order to establish the whole relation between man and woman on a surer ground of mutual happiness. Earlier in life, Hester had vainly imagined that she herself might be the destined prophetess, but had long since recognized the impossibility that any mission of divine and mysterious truth should be confided to a woman stained with sin, bowed down with shame, or even burdened with a lifelong sorrow. The angel and apostle of the coming revelation must be a woman, indeed, but lofty, pure, and beautiful; and wise, moreover, not through dusky grief, but the ethereal medium of joy; and showing how sacred love should make us happy, by the truest test of a life successful to such an end!

So said Hester Prynne, and glanced her sad eyes downward at the scarlet letter. And, after many, many years, a new grave was delved, near an old and sunken one, in that burial ground beside which King's Chapel has since been built. It was near that old and sunken grave, yet with a space between, as if the dust of the two sleepers had no right to mingle. Yet one tombstone served for both. All around, there were monuments carved with armorial bearings; and on this simple slab of slate—as the curious investigator may still discern, and perplex himself with the purport—there appeared the semblance of an engraved escutcheon. It bore a device, a herald's wording of which might serve for a motto and brief description of our now concluded legend; so sombre is it, and relieved only by one ever glowing point of light gloomier than the shadow:

"On a field, sable, the letter A, gules."

The House of the
Seven Gables

CONTENTS

Preface by the Author

WHEN a writer calls his work a Romance, it need hardly be observed that he wishes to claim a certain latitude, both as to its fashion and material, which he would not have felt himself entitled to assume had he professed to be writing a Novel. The latter form of composition is presumed to aim at a very minute fidelity, not merely to the possible, but to the probable and ordinary course of man's experience. The former—while, as a work of art, it must rigidly subject itself to laws, and while it sins unpardonably so far as it may swerve aside from the truth of the human heart—has fairly a right to present that truth under circumstances, to a great extent, of the writer's own choosing or creation. If he think fit, also, he may so manage his atmospherical medium as to bring out or mellow the lights and deepen and enrich the shadows of the picture. He will be wise, no doubt, to make a very moderate use of the privileges here stated, and, especially, to mingle the Marvelous rather as a slight, delicate, and evanescent flavor than as any portion of the actual substance of the dish offered to the public. He can hardly be said, however, to commit a literary crime even if he disregard this caution.

In the present work, the author has proposed to himself—but with what success, fortunately, it is not for him to judge—to keep undeviatingly within his immunities. The point of view in which this tale comes under the Romantic definition lies in the attempt to connect a bygone time with the very present that is flitting away from us. It is a legend prolonging itself, from an epoch now gray in the distance, down into our own broad daylight, and bringing along with it some of its legendary mist, which the reader, according to his pleasure, may either disregard, or allow it to float almost imperceptibly about the characters and events for the sake of a picturesque effect. The narrative, it may be, is woven of so humble a texture as to require this advantage, and, at the same time, to render it the more difficult of attainment.

Many writers lay very great stress upon some definite moral purpose, at which they profess to aim their works. Not to be deficient in this particular, the author has provided himself with a moral—the truth, namely, that the wrongdoing of one generation lives into the successive ones, and, divesting itself of every temporary advantage, becomes a pure and uncontrollable mischief; and he would feel it a singular gratification if this romance might effectually convince mankind—or, indeed, any one man—of the folly of tumbling down an avalanche of ill-gotten gold, or real estate, on the heads of an unfortunate posterity, thereby to maim and crush them, until the accumulated mass shall be scattered abroad in its original atoms. In good faith, however, he is not sufficiently imaginative to flatter himself with the slightest hope of this kind. When romances do really teach anything, or produce any effective operation, it is usually through a far more subtle process than the ostensible one. The author has considered it hardly worth his while, therefore, relentlessly to impale the story with its moral as with an iron rod—or, rather, as by sticking a pin through a butterfly—thus at once depriving it of life, and causing it to stiffen in an ungainly and unnatural attitude. A high truth, indeed, fairly, finely, and skillfully wrought out, brightening at every step, and crowning the final development of a work of fiction, may add an artistic glory, but is never any truer, and seldom any more evident, at the last page than at the first.

The reader may perhaps choose to assign an actual locality to the imaginary events of this narrative. If permitted by the historical connection—which, though slight, was essential to his plan—the author would very willingly have avoided anything of this nature. Not to speak of other objections, it exposes the romance to an inflexible and exceedingly dangerous species of criticism, by bringing his fancy pictures almost into positive contact with the realities of the moment. It has been no part of his object, however, to describe local manners, nor in any way to meddle with the characteristics of a community for whom he cherishes a proper respect and a natural regard. He trusts not to be considered as unpardonably offending by laying out a street that infringes upon nobody's private rights, and appropriating a lot of land which had no visible owner, and building a house of materials long in use for constructing castles in the air. The personages of the tale—though they give themselves out to be of ancient stability and considerable prominence—are really of the author's own making, or, at all events, of his own mixing; their virtues can shed no luster, nor their defects redound, in the remotest degree, to the discredit of the venerable town of which they profess to be inhabitants. He would be glad, therefore, if—especially in the quarter to which he alludes—the book may be read strictly as a Romance, having a great deal more to do with the clouds overhead than with any portion of the actual soil of the County of Essex.

LENOX, January 27, 1851

I

The Old Pyncheon Family

HALFWAY down a bystreet of one of our New England towns stands a rusty wooden house, with seven acutely peaked gables, facing towards various points of the compass, and a huge, clustered chimney in the midst. The street is Pyncheon Street; the house is the old Pyncheon House; and an elm tree, of wide circumference, rooted before the door, is familiar to every town-born child by the title of the Pyncheon Elm. On my occasional visits to the town aforesaid, I seldom failed to turn down Pyncheon Street, for the sake of passing through the shadow of these two antiquities—the great elm tree and the weather-beaten edifice.

The aspect of the venerable mansion has always affected me like a human countenance, bearing the traces not merely of outward storm and sunshine, but expressive, also, of the long lapse of mortal life, and accompanying vicissitudes that have passed within. Were these to be worthily recounted, they would form a narrative of no small interest and instruction, and possessing, moreover, a certain remarkable unity, which might almost seem the result of artistic arrangement. But the story would include a chain of events extending over the better part of two centuries, and, written out with reasonable amplitude, would fill a bigger folio volume, or a longer series of duodecimos, than could prudently be appropriated to the annals of all New England during a similar period. It consequently becomes imperative to make short work with most of the traditionary lore of which the old Pyncheon House, otherwise known as the House of the Seven Gables, has been the theme. With a brief sketch, therefore, of the circumstances amid which the foundation of the house was laid, and a rapid glimpse at its quaint exterior, as it grew black in the prevalent east wind—pointing, too, here and there, at some spot of more verdant mossiness on its roof and walls—we shall commence the real action of our tale at an epoch not very remote from the present day. Still, there will be a connection with the long past—a reference to forgotten events and personages, and to manners, feelings, and opinions, almost or wholly obsolete—which, if adequately translated to the reader, would serve to illustrate how much of old material goes to make up the freshest novelty of human life. Hence, too, might be drawn a weighty lesson from the little-regarded truth that the act of the passing generation is the germ which may and must produce good or evil fruit in a far-distant time; that together with the seed of the merely temporary crop, which mortals term expediency, they inevitably sow the acorns of a more enduring growth, which may darkly overshadow their posterity.

The House of the Seven Gables, antique as it now looks, was not the first habitation erected by civilized man on precisely the same spot of ground. Pyncheon Street formerly bore the humbler appellation of Maule's Lane, from the name of the original occupant of the soil, before whose cottage door it was a cowpath. A natural spring of soft and pleasant water—a rare treasure on the sea-girt peninsula, where the Puritan settlement was made—had early induced Matthew Maule to build a hut, shaggy with thatch, at this point, although somewhat too remote from what was then the center of the village. In the growth of the town, however, after some thirty or forty years, the site covered by this rude hovel had become exceedingly desirable in the eyes of a prominent and powerful personage, who asserted plausible claims to the proprietorship of this, and a large adjacent tract of land, on the strength of a grant from the legislature. Colonel Pyncheon, the claimant, as we gather from whatever traits of him are preserved, was characterized by an iron energy of purpose. Matthew Maule, on the other hand, though an obscure man, was stubborn in the defense of what he considered his right; and, for several years, he succeeded in protecting the acre or two of earth which, with his own toil, he had hewn out of the primeval forest, to be his garden ground and homestead. No written

record of this dispute is known to be in existence. Our
acquaintance with the whole subject is derived chiefly from
tradition. It would be bold, therefore, and possibly unjust,
to venture a decisive opinion as to its merits; although it
appears to have been at least a matter of doubt whether
Colonel Pyncheon's claim were not unduly stretched, in
order to make it cover the small metes and bounds of
Matthew Maule. What greatly strengthens such a suspicion
is the fact that this controversy between two ill-matched
antagonists—at a period, moreover, laud it as we may,
when personal influence had far more weight than now—
remained for years undecided, and came to a close only with
the death of the party occupying the disputed soil. The
mode of his death, too, affects the mind differently, in our
day, from what it did a century and a half ago. It was a
death that blasted with strange horror the humble name of
the dweller in the cottage, and made it seem almost a
religious act to drive the plow over the little area of his
habitation, and obliterate his place and memory from among
men.

Old Matthew Maule, in a word, was executed for the
crime of witchcraft. He was one of the martyrs to that
terrible delusion, which should teach us, among its other
morals, that the influential classes, and those who take upon
themselves to be leaders of the people, are fully liable to all
the passionate error that has ever characterized the maddest
mob. Clergymen, judges, statesmen—the wisest, calmest,
holiest persons of their day—stood in the inner circle round
about the gallows, loudest to applaud the work of blood,
latest to confess themselves miserably deceived. If any one
part of their proceedings can be said to deserve less blame
than another, it was the singular indiscrimination with which
they persecuted not merely the poor and aged, as in former
judicial massacres, but people of all ranks; their own equals,
brethren, and wives. Amid the disorder of such various
ruin, it is not strange that a man of inconsiderable note, like
Maule, should have trodden the martyr's path to the hill of
execution almost unremarked in the throng of his fellow
sufferers. But, in after days, when the frenzy of that hideous
epoch had subsided, it was remembered how loudly Colonel
Pyncheon had joined in the general cry, to purge the land
from witchcraft; nor did it fail to be whispered that there

was an invidious acrimony in the zeal with which he had sought the condemnation of Matthew Maule. It was well known that the victim had recognized the bitterness of personal enmity in his prosecutor's conduct towards him, and that he declared himself hunted to death for his spoil. At the moment of execution—with the halter about his neck, and while Colonel Pyncheon sat on horseback, grimly gazing at the scene—Maule had addressed him from the scaffold, and uttered a prophecy, of which history, as well as fireside tradition, has preserved the very words. "God," said the dying man, pointing his finger, with a ghastly look, at the undismayed countenance of his enemy, "God will give him blood to drink!"

After the reputed wizard's death, his humble homestead had fallen an easy spoil into Colonel Pyncheon's grasp. When it was understood, however, that the Colonel intended to erect a family mansion—spacious, ponderously framed of oaken timber, and calculated to endure for many generations of his posterity—over the spot first covered by the log-built hut of Matthew Maule, there was much shaking of the head among the village gossips. Without absolutely expressing a doubt whether the stalwart Puritan had acted as a man of conscience and integrity throughout the proceedings which have been sketched, they, nevertheless, hinted that he was about to build his house over an unquiet grave. His home would include the home of the dead and buried wizard, and would thus afford the ghost of the latter a kind of privilege to haunt its new apartments, and the chambers into which future bridegrooms were to lead their brides, and where children of the Pyncheon blood were to be born. The terror and ugliness of Maule's crime, and the wretchedness of his punishment, would darken the freshly plastered walls, and infect them early with the scent of an old and melancholy house. Why, then—while so much of the soil around him was bestrewn with the virgin forest leaves—why should Colonal Pyncheon prefer a site that had already been accursed?

But the Puritan soldier and magistrate was not a man to be turned aside from his well-considered scheme, either by dread of the wizard's ghost or by flimsy sentimentalities of any kind, however specious. Had he been told of a bad air, it might have moved him somewhat; but he was ready to encounter an evil spirit on his own ground. Endowed with common sense, as massive and hard as blocks of granite, fastened together by stern rigidity of purpose, as with iron clamps, he followed out his original design, probably without so much as imagining an objection to it. On the score of delicacy, or any scrupulousness which a finer sensibility might have taught him, the Colonel, like most of his breed and generation, was impenetrable. He, therefore, dug his cellar, and laid the deep foundations of his mansion, on the square of earth whence Matthew Maule, forty years before, had first swept away the fallen leaves. It was a curious and, as some people thought, an ominous fact that, very soon after the workmen began their operations, the spring of water, above mentioned, entirely lost the deliciousness of its pristine quality. Whether its sources were disturbed by the depth of the new cellar, or whatever subtler cause might lurk at the bottom, it is certain that the water of Maule's Well, as it continued to be called, grew hard and brackish. Even such we find it now; and any old woman of the neighborhood will certify that it is productive of intestinal mischief to those who quench their thirst there.

The reader may deem it singular that the head carpenter of the new edifice was no other than the son of the very man from whose dead gripe the property of the soil had been wrested. Not improbably he was the best workman of his time; or, perhaps, the Colonel thought it expedient, or was impelled by some better feeling, thus openly to cast aside all animosity against the race of his fallen antagonist. Nor was it out of keeping with the general coarseness and matter-of-fact character of the age that the son should be willing to earn an honest penny, or, rather, a weighty amount of sterling pounds, from the purse of his father's deadly enemy. At all events, Thomas Maule became the architect of the House of the Seven Gables, and performed his duty so faithfully that the timber framework fastened by his hands still holds together.

Thus the great house was built. Familiar as it stands in the writer's recollection—for it has been an object of curiosity with him from boyhood, both as a specimen of the best and stateliest architecture of a long-past epoch, and as the scene of events more full of human interest, perhaps, than those of a gray feudal castle—familiar as it stands, in its rusty old age, it is therefore only the more difficult to imagine the bright novelty with which it first caught the sunshine. The impression of its actual state, at this distance of a hundred and sixty years, darkens inevitably through the picture which we would fain give of its appearance on the morning when the Puritan magnate bade all the town to be his guests. A ceremony of consecration, festive as well as religious, was now to be performed. A prayer and discourse from the Rev. Mr. Higginson, and the outpouring of a psalm from the general throat of the community, was to be made acceptable to the grosser sense by ale, cider, wine, and brandy, in copious effusion, and, as some authorities aver, by an ox, roasted whole, or, at least, by the weight and substance of an ox, in more manageable joints and sirloins. The carcass of a deer, shot within twenty miles, had supplied material for the vast circumference of a pasty. A codfish of sixty pounds, caught in the bay, had been dissolved into the rich liquid of a chowder. The chimney of the new house, in short, belching forth its kitchen smoke, impregnated the whole air with the scent of meats, fowls, and fishes, spicily concocted with odoriferous herbs, and onions in abundance. The mere smell of such festivity, making its way to everybody's nostrils, was at once an invitation and an appetite.

Maule's Lane, or Pyncheon Street, as it were now more decorous to call it, was thronged, at the appointed hour, as with a congregation on its way to church. All, as they approached, looked upward at the imposing edifice, which was henceforth to assume its rank among the habitations of mankind. There it rose, a little withdrawn from the line of the street, but in pride, not modesty. Its whole visible exterior was ornamented with quaint figures, conceived in the grotesqueness of a Gothic fancy, and drawn or stamped in the glittering plaster, composed of lime, pebbles, and bits of glass, with which the woodwork of the walls was overspread. On every side the seven gables pointed sharply towards the sky, and presented the aspect of a whole sisterhood of edifices, breathing through the spiracles of one great chimney. The many lattices, with their small, diamond-shaped panes, admitted the sunlight into hall and chamber, while, nevertheless, the second story, projecting far over the base, and itself retiring beneath the third, threw a shadowy and thoughtful gloom into the lower rooms. Carved globes of wood were affixed under the jutting stories. Little spiral rods of iron beautified each of the seven peaks. On the triangular portion of the gable that fronted next the street was a dial, put up that very morning, and on which the sun was still marking the passage of the first bright hour in a history that was not destined to be all so bright. All around were scattered shavings, chips, shingles, and broken halves of bricks; these, together with the lately turned earth, on which the grass had not begun to grow, contributed to the impression of strangeness and novelty proper to a house that had yet its place to make among men's daily interests.

The principal entrance, which had almost the breadth of a church door, was in the angle between the two front gables, and was covered by an open porch, with benches beneath its shelter. Under this arched doorway, scraping their feet on the unworn threshold, now trod the clergymen, the elders, the magistrates, the deacons, and whatever of aristocracy there was in town or county. Thither, too, thronged the plebeian classes as freely as their betters, and in larger number. Just within the entrance, however, stood two servingmen, pointing some of the guests to the neighborhood of the kitchen, and ushering others into the statelier rooms—hospitable alike to all, but still with a scrutinizing regard to the high or low degree of each. Velvet garments, somber but rich, stiffly plaited ruffs and bands, embroidered gloves, venerable beards, the mien and countenance of authority, made it easy to distinguish the gentleman of worship, at that period, from the tradesman, with his plodding air, or the laborer, in his leathern jerkin, stealing awe-stricken into the house which he had perhaps helped to build.

One inauspicious circumstance there was, which awakened a hardly concealed displeasure in the breasts of a few of the more punctilious visitors. The founder of this stately mansion—a gentleman noted for the square and ponderous courtesy of his demeanor—ought surely to have stood in his own hall, and to have offered the first welcome to so many eminent personages as here presented themselves in honor of his solemn festival. He was as yet invisible; the most favored of the guests had not beheld him. This sluggishness on Colonel Pyncheon's part became still more unaccountable when the second dignitary of the province made his appearance, and found no more ceremonious a reception. The lieutenant governor, although his visit was one of the anticipated glories of the day, had alighted from his horse, and assisted his lady from her sidesaddle, and crossed the Colonel's threshold, without other greeting than that of the principal domestic.

This person—a grayheaded man, of quiet and most respectful deportment—found it necessary to explain that his master still remained in his study, or private apartment; on entering which, an hour before, he had expressed a wish on no account to be disturbed.

"Do not you see, fellow," said the high sheriff of the county, taking the servant aside, "that this is no less a man than the lieutenant governor? Summon Colonel Pyncheon at once! I know that he received letters from England this morning; and, in the perusal and consideration of them, an hour may have passed away without his noticing it. But he will be ill pleased, I judge, if you suffer him to neglect the courtesy due to one of our chief rulers, and who may be said to represent King William, in the absence of the governor himself. Call your master instantly!"

"Nay, please your worship," answered the man, in much perplexity, but with a backwardness that strikingly indicated the hard and severe character of Colonel Pyncheon's domestic rule. "My master's orders were exceeding strict; and, as your worship knows, he permits of no discretion in the obedience of those who owe him service. Let who list open yonder door; I dare not, though the governor's own voice should bid me do it!"

"Pooh, pooh, master high sheriff!" cried the lieutenant governor, who had overheard the foregoing discussion, and felt himself high enough in station to play a little with his dignity. "I will take the matter into my own hands. It is time that the good Colonel came forth to greet his friends; else we shall be apt to suspect that he has taken a sip too much of his Canary wine, in his extreme deliberation which cask it were best to broach in honor of the day! But since he is so much behindhand, I will give him a remembrancer myself!"

Accordingly, with such a tramp of his ponderous riding boots as might of itself have been audible in the remotest of the seven gables, he advanced to the door, which the servant pointed out, and made its new panels re-echo with a loud, free knock. Then, looking round, with a smile, to the spectators, he awaited a response. As none came, however, he knocked again, but with the same unsatisfactory result as at first. And now, being a trifle choleric in his temperament, the lieutenant governor uplifted the heavy hilt of his sword, wherewith he so beat and banged upon the door that, as some of the bystanders whispered, the racket might have disturbed the dead. Be that as it might, it seemed to produce no awakening effect on Colonel Pyncheon. When the sound subsided, the silence through the house was deep, dreary, and oppressive, notwithstanding that the tongues of many of the guests had already been loosened by a surreptitious cup or two of wine or spirits.

"Strange, forsooth—very strange!" cried the lieutenant governor, whose smile was changed to a frown. "But seeing that our host sets us the good example of forgetting ceremony, I shall likewise throw it aside, and make free to intrude on his privacy!"

He tried the door, which yielded to his hand, and was flung wide open by a sudden gust of wind that passed, as with a loud sigh, from the outermost portal through all the passages and apartments of the new house. It rustled the silken garments of the ladies, and waved the long curls of the gentlemen's wigs, and shook the window hangings and the curtains of the bedchambers; causing everywhere a singular stir, which yet was more like a hush. A shadow of awe and half-fearful anticipation—nobody knew wherefore, nor of what—had all at once fallen over the company.

They thronged, however, to the now open door, pressing the lieutenant governor, in the eagerness of their curiosity, into the room in advance of them. At the first glimpse they beheld nothing extraordinary: a handsomely furnished room, of moderate size, somewhat darkened by curtains; books arranged on shelves; a large map on the wall, and likewise a portrait of Colonel Pyncheon, beneath which sat the original Colonel himself, in an oaken elbow-chair, with a pen in his hand. Letters, parchments, and blank sheets of paper were on the table before him. He appeared to gaze at the curious crowd, in front of which stood the lieutenant governor; and there was a frown on his dark and massive countenance, as if sternly resentful of the boldness that had impelled them into his private retirement.

A little boy—the Colonel's grandchild, and the only human being that ever dared to be familiar with him—now made his way among the guests, and ran towards the seated figure; then pausing halfway, he began to shriek with terror. The company, tremulous as the leaves of a tree, when all are shaking together, drew nearer, and perceived that there was an unnatural distortion in the fixedness of Colonel Pyncheon's stare; that there was blood on his ruff, and that his hoary beard was saturated with it. It was too late to give assistance. The ironhearted Puritan, the relentless persecutor, the grasping and strong-willed man, was dead! Dead, in his new house! There is a tradition, only worth alluding to as lending a tinge of superstitious awe to a scene perhaps gloomy enough without it, that a voice spoke loudly among the guests, the tones of which were like those of old Matthew Maule, the executed wizard—"God hath given him blood to drink!"

Thus early had that one guest—the only guest who is certain, at one time or another, to find his way into every human dwelling—thus early had Death stepped across the threshold of the House of the Seven Gables!

Colonel Pyncheon's sudden and mysterious end made a vast deal of noise in its day. There were many rumors, some of which have vaguely drifted down to the present time, how that appearances indicated violence; that there were the marks of fingers on his throat, and the print of a bloody hand on his plaited ruff; and that his peaked beard was disheveled, as if it had been fiercely clutched and pulled. It was averred, likewise, that the lattice window, near the Colonel's chair, was open; and that, only a few minutes before the fatal occurrence, the figure of a man had been seen clambering over the garden fence, in the rear of the house. But it were folly to lay any stress on stories of this kind, which are sure to spring up around such an event as that now related, and which, as in the present case, sometimes prolong themselves for ages afterwards, like the toadstools that indicate where the fallen and buried trunk of a tree has long since moldered into the earth. For our own part, we allow them just as little credence as to that other fable of the skeleton hand which the lieutenant governor was said to have seen at the Colonel's throat, but which vanished away as he advanced farther into the room. Certain it is, however, that there was a great consultation and dispute of doctors over the dead body. One—John Swinnerton by name—who appears to have been a man of eminence, upheld it, if we have rightly understood his terms of art, to be a case of apoplexy. His professional brethren, each for himself, adopted various hypotheses, more or less plausible, but all dressed out in a perplexing mystery of phrase, which, if it do not show a bewilderment of mind in these erudite physicians, certainly causes it in the unlearned peruser of their opinions. The coroner's jury sat upon the corpse, and, like sensible men, returned an unassailable verdict of "Sudden Death!"

It is indeed difficult to imagine that there could have been a serious suspicion of murder, or the slightest grounds for implicating any particular individual as the perpetrator. The rank, wealth, and eminent character of the deceased must have insured the strictest scrutiny into every ambiguous circumstance. As none such is on record, it is safe to assume that none existed. Tradition—which sometimes brings down truth that history has let slip, but is oftener the wild babble of the time, such as was formerly spoken at the fireside and now congeals in newspapers—tradition is responsible for all contrary averments. In Colonel Pyncheon's funeral sermon, which was printed, and is still extant, the Rev. Mr. Higginson enumerates, among the many felicities of his distinguished parishioner's earthly career, the happy seasonableness of his death. His duties all performed, the highest prosperity attained, his race and future generations fixed on a stable basis, and with a stately roof to shelter them, for centuries to come—what other upward step remained for this good man to take, save the final step from earth to the golden gate of heaven! The pious clergyman surely would not have uttered words like these had he in the least suspected that the Colonel had been thrust into the other world with the clutch of violence upon his throat.

The family of Colonel Pyncheon, at the epoch of his death, seemed destined to as fortunate a permanence as can anywise consist with the inherent instability of human affairs. It might fairly be anticipated that the progress of time would rather increase and ripen their prosperity than wear away and destroy it. For, not only had his son and heir come into immediate enjoyment of a rich estate, but there was a claim through an Indian deed, confirmed by a subsequent grant of the General Court, to a vast and as yet unexplored and unmeasured tract of Eastern lands. These possessions—for as such they might almost certainly be reckoned—comprised the greater part of what is now known as Waldo County, in the State of Maine, and were more extensive than many a dukedom, or even a reigning prince's territory, on European soil. When the pathless forest that still covered this wild principality should give place—as it inevitably must, though perhaps not till ages hence—to the golden fertility of human culture, it would be the source of incalculable wealth to the Pyncheon blood. Had the Colonel survived only a few weeks longer, it is probable that his great political influence, and powerful connections at home and abroad, would have consummated all that was necessary to render the claim available. But, in spite of good Mr. Higginson's congratulatory eloquence, this appeared to be the one thing which Colonel Pyncheon, provident and sagacious as he was, had allowed to go at loose ends. So far as the prospective territory was concerned, he unquestionably died too soon. His son lacked not merely the father's eminent position, but the talent and force of character to achieve it: he could, therefore, effect nothing by dint of political interest; and the bare justice or legality of the claim was not so apparent, after the Colonel's decease, as it had been pronounced in his lifetime. Some connecting link had slipped out of the evidence, and could not anywhere be found.

Efforts, it is true, were made by the Pyncheons, not only then, but at various periods for nearly a hundred years afterwards, to obtain what they stubbornly persisted in deeming their right. But, in course of time, the territory was partly regranted to more favored individuals, and partly cleared and occupied by actual settlers. These last, if they ever heard of the Pyncheon title, would have laughed at the idea of any man's asserting a right—on the strength of moldy parchments, signed with the faded autographs of governors and legislators long dead and forgotten—to the lands which they or their fathers had wrested from the wild hand of nature by their own sturdy toil. This impalpable claim, therefore, resulted in nothing more solid than to cherish, from generation to generation, an absurd delusion of family importance, which all along characterized the Pyncheons. It caused the poorest member of the race to feel as if he inherited a kind of nobility, and might yet come into the possession of princely wealth to support it. In the better specimens of the breed, this peculiarity threw an ideal grace over the hard material of human life, without stealing away any truly valuable quality. In the baser sort, its effect was to increase the liability to sluggishness and dependence, and induce the victim of a shadowy hope to remit all self-effort, while awaiting the realization of his dreams. Years and years after their claim had passed out of the public memory, the Pyncheons were accustomed to consult the Colonel's ancient map, which had been projected while Waldo County was still an unbroken wilderness. Where the old land-surveyor had put down woods, lakes, and rivers, they marked out the cleared spaces, and dotted the villages and towns, and calculated the progressively increasing value of the territory, as if there were yet a prospect of its ultimately forming a principality for themselves.

In almost every generation, nevertheless, there happened to be some one descendant of the family gifted with a portion of the hard, keen sense, and practical energy, that had so remarkably distinguished the original founder. His character, indeed, might be traced all the way down, as distinctly as if the Colonel himself, a little diluted, had been gifted with a sort of intermittent immortality on earth. At two or three epochs, when the fortunes of the family were low, this representative of hereditary qualities had made his appearance, and caused the traditionary gossips of the town to whisper among themselves, "Here is the old Pyncheon come again! Now the Seven Gables will be new-shingled!" From father to son, they clung to the ancestral house with singular tenacity of home attachment. For various reasons, however, and from impressions often too vaguely founded to be put on paper, the writer cherishes the belief that many, if not most, of the successive proprietors of this estate were troubled with doubts as to their moral right to hold it. Of their legal tenure there could be no question; but old Matthew Maule, it is to be feared, trode downward from his own age to a far later one, planting a heavy footstep, all the way, on the conscience of a Pyncheon. If so, we are left to dispose of the awful query, whether each inheritor of the property—conscious of wrong, and failing to rectify it—did not commit anew the great guilt of his ancestor, and incur all its original responsibilities. And supposing such to be the case, would it not be a far truer mode of expression to say of the Pyncheon family that they inherited a great misfortune, than the reverse?

We have already hinted that it is not our purpose to trace down the history of the Pyncheon family, in its unbroken connection with the House of the Seven Gables; nor to show, as in a magic picture, how the rustiness and infirmity of age gathered over the venerable house itself. As regards its interior life, a large, dim looking glass used to hang in one of the rooms, and was fabled to contain within its depths all the shapes that had ever been reflected there—the old Colonel himself, and his many descendants, some in the garb of antique babyhood, and others in the bloom of feminine beauty or manly prime, or saddened with the wrinkles of frosty age. Had we the secret of that mirror, we would gladly sit down before it, and transfer its revelations to our page. But there was a story, for which it is difficult to conceive any foundation, that the posterity of Matthew Maule had some connection with the mystery of the looking glass, and that, by what appears to have been a sort of mesmeric process, they could make its inner region all alive with the departed Pyncheons; not as they had shown themselves to the world nor in their better and happier hours, but as doing over again some deed of sin, or in the crisis of life's bitterest sorrow. The popular imagination, indeed, long kept itself busy with the affair of the old Puritan Pyncheon and the wizard Maule; the curse, which the latter flung from his scaffold, was remembered, with the very important addition that it had become a part of the Pyncheon inheritance. If one of the family did but gurgle in his throat, a bystander would be likely enough to whisper, between jest and earnest, "He has Maule's blood to drink!" The sudden death of a Pyncheon, about a hundred years ago, with circumstances very similar to what have been related of the Colonel's exit, was held as giving additional probability to the received opinion on this topic. It was considered, moreover, an ugly and ominous circumstance that Colonel Pyncheon's picture

—in obedience,. it was said, to a provision of his will—
remained affixed to the wall of the room in which he.died.
Those stern, immitigable features seemed to symbolize an
evil influence, and so darkly to mingle the shadow of their
presence with the sunshine of the passing hour that no good
thoughts or purposes could ever spring up and blossom
there. To the thoughtful mind there will be no tinge of
superstition in what we figuratively express, by affirming
that the ghost of a dead progenitor—perhaps as a portion of
his own punishment—is often doomed to become the Evil
Genius of his family.

The Pyncheons, in brief, lived along, for the better part of
two centuries, with perhaps less of outward vicissitude than
has attended most other New England families during the
same period of time. Possessing very distinctive traits of
their own, they nevertheless took the general characteristics
of the little community in which they dwelt; a town noted
for its frugal, discreet, well-ordered, and home-loving inhabitants, as well as for the somewhat confined scope of its
sympathies; but in which, be it said, there are odder individuals, and, now and then, stranger occurrences, than one
meets with almost anywhere else. During the Revolution,
the Pyncheon of that epoch, adopting the royal side, became a refugee; but repented, and made his reappearance,
just at the point of time to preserve the House of the Seven
Gables from confiscation. For the last seventy years, the
most noted event in the Pyncheon annals had been likewise
the heaviest calamity that ever befell the race; no less than
the violent death—for so it was adjudged—of one member
of the family by the criminal act of another. Certain circumstances attending this fatal occurrence had brought the deed
irresistibly home to a nephew of the deceased Pyncheon.
The young man was tried and convicted of the crime; but
either the circumstantial nature of the evidence, and possibly some lurking doubt in the breast of the executive, or,
lastly—an argument of greater weight in a republic than it
could have been under a monarchy—the high respectability
and political influence of the criminal's connections, had
availed to mitigate his doom from death to perpetual imprisonment. This sad affair had chanced about thirty years
before the action of our story commences. Latterly, there
were rumors (which few believed, and only one or two felt

greatly interested in) that this long-buried man was likely, for some reason or other, to be summoned forth from his living tomb.

It is essential to say a few words respecting the victim of this now almost forgotten murder. He was an old bachelor, and possessed of great wealth, in addition to the house and real estate which constituted what remained of the ancient Pyncheon property. Being of an eccentric and melancholy turn of mind, and greatly given to rummaging old records and hearkening to old traditions, he had brought himself, it is averred, to the conclusion that Matthew Maule, the wizard, had been foully wronged out of his homestead, if not out of his life. Such being the case, and he, the old bachelor, in possession of the ill-gotten spoil—with the black stain of blood sunken deep into it, and still to be scented by conscientious nostrils—the question occurred whether it were not imperative upon him, even at this late hour, to make restitution to Maule's posterity. To a man living so much in the past, and so little in the present, as the secluded and antiquarian old bachelor, a century and a half seemed not so vast a period as to obviate the propriety of substituting right for wrong. It was the belief of those who knew him best that he would positively have taken the very singular step of giving up the House of the Seven Gables to the representative of Matthew Maule, but for the unspeakable tumult which a suspicion of the old gentleman's project awakened among his Pyncheon relatives. Their exertions had the effect of suspending his purpose; but it was feared that he would perform, after death, by the operation of his last will, what he had so hardly been prevented from doing in his proper lifetime. But there is no one thing which men so rarely do, whatever the provocation or inducement, as to bequeath patrimonial property away from their own blood. They may love other individuals far better than their relatives—they may even cherish dislike, or positive hatred, to the latter— but yet, in view of death, the strong prejudice of propinquity revives, and impels the testator to send down his estate in the line marked out by custom so immemorial that it looks like nature. In all the Pyncheons, this feeling had the energy of disease. It was too powerful for the conscientious scruples of the old bachelor; at whose death, accordingly, the mansion house, together with most of his other riches, passed into the possession of his next legal representative.

This was a nephew, the cousin of the miserable young man who had been convicted of the uncle's murder. The new heir, up to the period of his accession, was reckoned rather a dissipated youth, but had at once reformed, and made himself an exceedingly respectable member of society. In fact, he showed more of the Pyncheon quality, and had won higher eminence in the world, than any of his race since the time of the original Puritan. Applying himself in earlier manhood to the study of the law, and having a natural tendency towards office, he had attained, many years ago, to a judicial situation in some inferior court, which gave him for life the very desirable and imposing title of judge. Later, he had engaged in politics, and served a part of two terms in Congress, besides making a considerable figure in both branches of the State legislature. Judge Pyncheon was unquestionably an honor to his race. He had built himself a country seat within a few miles of his native town, and there spent such portions of his time as could be spared from public service in the display of every grace and virtue—as a newspaper phrased it, on the eve of an election—befitting the Christian, the good citizen, the horticulturist, and the gentleman.

There were few of the Pyncheons left to sun themselves in the glow of the Judge's prosperity. In respect to natural increase, the breed had not thriven; it appeared rather to be dying out. The only members of the family known to be extant were, first, the Judge himself, and a single surviving son, who was now traveling in Europe; next, the thirty years' prisoner, already alluded to, and a sister of the latter, who occupied, in an extremely retired manner, the House of the Seven Gables, in which she had a life estate by the will of the old bachelor. She was understood to be wretchedly poor, and seemed to make it her choice to remain so, inasmuch as her affluent cousin, the Judge, had repeatedly offered her all the comforts of life, either in the old mansion or his own modern residence. The last and youngest Pyncheon was a little country girl of seventeen, the daughter of another of the Judge's cousins, who had married a young woman of no family or property, and died early and in poor circumstances. His widow had recently taken another husband.

As for Matthew Maule's posterity, it was supposed now to be extinct. For a very long period after the witchcraft delusion, however, the Maules had continued to inhabit the town where their progenitor had suffered so unjust a death. To all appearance, they were a quiet, honest, well-meaning race of people, cherishing no malice against individuals or the public for the wrong which had been done them; or if, at their own fireside, they transmitted, from father to child, any hostile recollection of the wizard's fate and their lost patrimony, it was never acted upon, nor openly expressed. Nor would it have been singular had they ceased to remember that the House of the Seven Gables was resting its heavy framework on a foundation that was rightfully their own. There is something so massive, stable, and almost irresistibly imposing in the exterior presentment of established rank and great possessions that their very existence seems to give them a right to exist; at least, so excellent a counterfeit of right, that few poor and humble men have moral force enough to question it, even in their secret minds. Such is the case now, after so many ancient prejudices have been overthrown; and it was far more so in ante-Revolutionary days, when the aristocracy could venture to be proud, and the low were content to be abased. Thus the Maules, at all events, kept their resentments within their own breasts. They were generally poverty-stricken; always plebeian and obscure; working with unsuccessful diligence at handicrafts; laboring on the wharves, or following the sea, as sailors before the mast; living here and there about the town, in hired tenements, and coming finally to the almshouse as the natural home of their old age. At last, after creeping, as it were, for such a length of time, along the utmost verge of the opaque puddle of obscurity, they had taken that downright plunge which, sooner or later, is the destiny of all families, whether princely or plebeian. For thirty years past, neither town record, nor gravestone, nor the directory, nor the knowledge or memory of man, bore any trace of Matthew Maule's descendants. His blood might possibly exist elsewhere; here, where its lowly current could be traced so far back, it had ceased to keep an onward course.

So long as any of the race were to be found, they had

been marked out from other men—not strikingly, nor as with a sharp line, but with an effect that was felt rather than spoken of—by an hereditary character of reserve. Their companions, or those who endeavored to become such, grew conscious of a circle round about the Maules, within the sanctity or the spell of which, in spite of an exterior of sufficient frankness and good-fellowship, it was impossible for any man to step. It was this indefinable peculiarity, perhaps, that, by insulating them from human aid, kept them always so unfortunate in life. It certainly operated to prolong in their case, and to confirm to them as their only inheritance, those feelings of repugnance and superstitious terror with which the people of the town, even after awakening from their frenzy, continued to regard the memory of the reputed witches. The mantle, or rather the ragged cloak, of old Matthew Maule had fallen upon his children. They were half believed to inherit mysterious attributes; the family eye was said to possess strange power. Among other good-for-nothing properties and privileges, one was especially assigned them—that of exercising an influence over people's dreams. The Pyncheons, if all stories were true, haughtily as they bore themselves in the noonday streets of their native town, were no better than bond servants to these plebeian Maules, on entering the topsy-turvy commonwealth of sleep. Modern psychology, it may be, will endeavor to reduce these alleged necromancies within a system, instead of rejecting them as altogether fabulous.

A descriptive paragraph or two, treating of the seven-gabled mansion in its more recent aspect, will bring this preliminary chapter to a close. The street in which it up-reared its venerable peaks has long ceased to be a fashionable quarter of the town; so that, though the old edifice was surrounded by habitations of modern date, they were mostly small, built entirely of wood, and typical of the most plodding uniformity of common life. Doubtless, however, the whole story of human existence may be latent in each of them, but with no picturesqueness, externally, that can attract the imagination or sympathy to seek it there. But as for the old structure of our story, its white-oak frame, and its boards, shingles, and crumbling plaster, and even the huge, clustered chimney in the midst, seemed to constitute only the least and meanest part of its reality. So much of mankind's varied experience had passed there—so much had been suffered, and something, too, enjoyed—that the very timbers were oozy, as with the moisture of a heart. It was itself like a great human heart, with a life of its own, and full of rich and somber reminiscences.

The deep projection of the second story gave the house such a meditative look that you could not pass it without the idea that it had secrets to keep, and an eventful history to moralize upon. In front, just on the edge of the unpaved sidewalk, grew the Pyncheon Elm, which, in reference to such trees as one usually meets with, might well be termed gigantic. It had been planted by a great-grandson of the first Pyncheon, and, though now four-score years of age, or perhaps nearer a hundred, was still in its strong and broad maturity, throwing its shadow from side to side of the street, overtopping the seven gables, and sweeping the whole black roof with its pendent foliage. It gave beauty to the old edifice, and seemed to make it a part of nature. The street having been widened about forty years ago, the front gable was now precisely on a line with it. On either side extended a ruinous wooden fence of open latticework, through which could be seen a grassy yard, and, especially in the angles of the building, an enormous fertility of burdocks, with leaves, it is hardly an exaggeration to say, two or three feet long. Behind the house there appeared to be a garden, which undoubtedly had once been extensive, but was now infringed upon by other enclosures, or shut in by habitations and outbuildings that stood on another street. It would be an omission, trifling, indeed, but unpardonable, were we to forget the green moss that had long since gathered over the projections of the windows, and on the slopes of the roof; nor must we fail to direct the reader's eye to a crop, not of weeds, but flower shrubs, which were growing aloft in the air, not a great way from the chimney, in the nook between two of the gables. They were called Alice's Posies. The tradition was that a certain Alice Pyncheon had flung up the seeds, in sport, and that the dust of the street and the decay of the roof gradually formed a kind of soil for them, out of which they grew, when Alice had long been in her grave. However the flowers might have come there, it was both sad and sweet to observe how Nature adopted to herself this desolate, decaying, gusty, rusty old house of the Pyncheon family; and how the ever-returning summer did her best to gladden it with tender beauty, and grew melancholy in the effort.

There is one other feature, very essential to be noticed, but which, we greatly fear, may damage any picturesque and romantic impression which we have been willing to throw over our sketch of this respectable edifice. In the front gable, under the impending brow of the second story, and contiguous to the street, was a shop door, divided horizontally in the midst, and with a window for its upper segment, such as is often seen in dwellings of a somewhat ancient date. This same shop door had been a subject of no slight mortification to the present occupant of the august Pyncheon House, as well as to some of her predecessors. The matter is disagreeably delicate to handle; but, since the reader must needs be let into the secret, he will please to understand that, about a century ago, the head of the Pyncheons found himself involved in serious financial difficulties. The fellow (gentleman, as he styled himself) can hardly have been other than a spurious interloper; for, instead of seeking office from the king or the royal governor, or urging his hereditary claim to Eastern lands, he bethought himself of no better avenue to wealth than by cutting a shop door through the side of his ancestral residence. It was the custom of the time, indeed, for merchants to store their goods and transact business in their own dwellings. But there was something pitifully small in this old Pyncheon's mode of setting about his commercial operations; it was whispered that, with his own hands, all beruffled as they were, he used to give change for a shilling, and would turn a halfpenny twice over, to make sure that it was a good one. Beyond all question, he had the blood of a petty huckster in his veins, through whatever channel it may have found its way there.

Immediately on his death, the shop door had been locked, bolted, and barred, and, down to the period of our story, had probably never once been opened. The old counter, shelves, and other fixtures of the little shop remained just as he had left them. It used to be affirmed that the dead shopkeeper, in a white wig, a faded velvet coat, an apron at his waist, and his ruffles carefully turned back from his wrists, might be seen through the chinks of the shutters, any night of the year, ransacking his till, or poring over the dingy pages of his daybook. From the look of unutterable woe upon his face, it appeared to be his doom to spend eternity in a vain effort to make his accounts balance.

And now—in a very humble way, as will be seen—we proceed to open our narrative.

II

The Little Shopwindow

It still lacked half an hour of sunrise, when Miss Hepzibah Pyncheon—we will not say awoke, it being doubtful whether the poor lady had so much as closed her eyes during the brief night of midsummer—but, at all events, arose from her solitary pillow, and began what it would be mockery to term the adornment of her person. Far from us be the indecorum of assisting, even in imagination, at a maiden lady's toilet! Our story must therefore await Miss Hepzibah at the threshold of her chamber; only presuming, meanwhile, to note some of the heavy sighs that labored from her bosom, with little restraint as to their lugubrious depth and volume of sound, inasmuch as they could be audible to nobody save a disembodied listener like ourself. The Old Maid was alone in the old house. Alone, except for a certain respectable and orderly young man, an artist in the daguerreotype line, who, for about three months back, had been a lodger in a remote gable—quite a house by itself, indeed—with locks, bolts, and oaken bars on all the intervening doors. Inaudible, consequently, were poor Miss Hepzibah's gusty sighs. Inaudible the creaking joints of her stiffened knees, as she knelt down by the bedside. And inaudible, too, by mortal ear, but heard with all-comprehending love and pity in the farthest heaven, that almost agony of prayer—now whispered, now a groan, now a struggling silence—wherewith she besought the Divine assistance through the day! Evidently, this is to be a day of more than ordinary trial to Miss Hepzibah, who, for above a quarter of a century gone by, has dwelt in strict seclusion, taking no part in the business of life, and just as little in its intercourse and pleasures. Not with such fervor prays the torpid recluse, looking forward to the cold, sunless, stagnant calm of a day that is to be like innumerable yesterdays!

The maiden lady's devotions are concluded. Will she now issue forth over the threshold of our story? Not yet, by many moments. First, every drawer in the tall, old-fashioned bureau is to be opened, with difficulty, and with a succession of spasmodic jerks; then, all must close again, with the same fidgety reluctance. There is a rustling of stiff silks; a tread of backward and forward footsteps to and fro across the chamber. We suspect Miss Hepzibah, moreover, of taking a step upward into a chair, in order to give heedful regard to her appearance on all sides, and at full length, in the oval, dingy-framed toilet glass that hangs above her table. Truly! well, indeed! who would have thought it! Is all this precious time to be lavished on the matutinal repair and beautifying of an elderly person, who never goes abroad, whom nobody ever visits, and from whom, when she shall have done her utmost, it were the best charity to turn one's eyes another way?

Now she is almost ready. Let us pardon her one other pause; for it is given to the sole sentiment, or, we might better say—heightened and rendered intense, as it has been, by sorrow and seclusion—to the strong passion of her life. We heard the turning of a key in a small lock; she has opened a secret drawer of an escritoire, and is probably looking at a certain miniature, done in Malbone's most perfect style, and representing a face worthy of no less delicate a pencil. It was once our good fortune to see this picture. It is a likeness of a young man, in a silken dressing gown of an old fashion, the soft richness of which is well adapted to the countenance of reverie, with its full, tender lips, and beautiful eyes, that seem to indicate not so much capacity of thought as gentle and voluptuous emotion. Of the possessor of such features we shall have a right to ask nothing, except that he would take the rude world easily, and make himself happy in it. Can it have been an early lover of Miss Hepzibah? No; she never had a lover—poor thing, how could she?—nor ever knew, by her own experience, what love technically means. And yet, her undying

faith and trust, her fresh remembrance, and continual devotedness towards the original of that miniature, have been
the only substance for her heart to feed upon.

She seems to have put aside the miniature, and is standing
again before the toilet glass. There are tears to be wiped off.
A few more footsteps to and fro; and here, at last—with
another pitiful sigh, like a gust of chill, damp wind out of a
long-closed vault, the door of which has accidentally been
set ajar—here comes Miss Hepzibah Pyncheon! Forth she
steps into the dusky, time-darkened passage; a tall figure,
clad in black silk, with a long and shrunken waist, feeling
her way towards the stairs like a nearsighted person, as in
truth she is.

The sun, meanwhile, if not already above the horizon,
was ascending nearer and nearer to its verge. A few clouds,
floating high upward, caught some of the earliest light, and
threw down its golden gleam on the windows of all the
houses in the street, not forgetting the House of the Seven
Gables, which—many such sunrises as it had witnessed—
looked cheerfully at the present one. The reflected radiance
served to show, pretty distinctly, the aspect and arrangement of the room which Hepzibah entered, after descending
the stair, It was a low-studded room, with a beam across the
ceiling, paneled with dark wood, and having a large chimney piece, set round with pictured tiles, but now closed by
an iron fireboard, through which ran the funnel of a modern
stove. There was a carpet on the floor, originally of rich
texture, but so worn and faded in these latter years that its
once brilliant figure had quite vanished into one indistinguishable hue. In the way of furniture, there were two
tables: one, constructed with perplexing intricacy and exhib-
iting as many feet as a centipede; the other, most delicately
wrought, with four long and slender legs, so apparently frail
that it was almost incredible what a length of time the
ancient tea table had stood upon them. Half a dozen chairs
stood about the room, straight and stiff, and so ingeniously
contrived for the discomfort of the human person that they
were irksome even to sight, and conveyed the ugliest possible idea of the state of society to which they could have
been adapted. One exception there was, however, in a very
antique elbow-chair, with a high back, carved elaborately in
oak, and a roomy depth within its arms, that made up, by its

spacious comprehensiveness, for the lack of any of those
artistic curves which abound in a modern chair.

As for ornamental articles of furniture, we recollect but
two, if such they may be called. One was a map of the
Pyncheon territory at the eastward, not engraved, but the
handiwork of some skillful old draftsman, and grotesquely
illuminated with pictures of Indians and wild beasts, among
which was seen a lion; the natural history of the region
being as little known as its geography, which was put down
most fantastically awry. The other adornment was the portrait of old Colonel Pyncheon, at two-thirds length, representing the stern features of a Puritanic-looking personage,
in a skullcap, with a laced band and a grizzly beard; holding
a Bible with one hand, and in the other uplifting an iron
sword hilt. The latter object, being more successfully depicted by the artist, stood out in far greater prominence
than the sacred volume. Face to face with this picture, on
entering the apartment, Miss Hepzibah Pyncheon came to a
pause; regarding it with a singular scowl, a strange contortion of the brow which, by people who did not know her,
would probably have been interpreted as an expression of
bitter anger and ill will. But it was no such thing. She, in
fact, felt a reverence for the pictured visage, of which only a
far-descended and time-stricken virgin could be susceptible;
and this forbidding scowl was the innocent result of her
nearsightedness, and an effort so to concentrate her powers
of vision as to substitute a firm outline of the object
instead of a vague one.

We must linger a moment on this unfortunate expression
of poor Hepzibah's brow. Her scowl—as the world, or such
part of it as sometimes caught a transitory glimpse of her at
the window, wickedly persisted in calling it—her scowl had
done Miss Hepzibah a very ill office, in establishing her
character as an ill-tempered old maid; nor does it appear
improbable that, by often gazing at herself in a dim looking
glass, and perpetually encountering her own frown within its
ghostly sphere, she had been led to interpret the expression
almost as unjustly as the world did. "How miserably cross I
look!" she must often have whispered to herself; and ultimately have fancied herself so, by a sense of inevitable
doom. But her heart never frowned. It was naturally tender,

sensitive, and full of little tremors and palpitations; all of which weaknesses it retained, while her visage was growing so perversely stern, and even fierce. Nor had Hepzibah ever any hardihood, except what came from the very warmest nook in her affections.

All this time, however, we are loitering faintheartedly on the threshold of our story. In very truth, we have an invincible reluctance to disclose what Miss Hepzibah Pyncheon was about to do.

It has already been observed that, in the basement story of the gable fronting on the street, an unworthy ancestor, nearly a century ago, had fitted up a shop. Ever since the old gentleman retired from trade, and fell asleep under his coffin lid, not only the shop door, but the inner arrangements, had been suffered to remain unchanged; while the dust of ages gathered inch-deep over the shelves and counter, and partly filled an old pair of scales, as if it were of value enough to be weighed. It treasured itself up, too, in the half-open till, where there still lingered a base sixpence, worth neither more nor less than the hereditary pride which had here been put to shame. Such had been the state and condition of the little shop in old Hepzibah's childhood, when she and her brother used to play at hide-and-seek in its forsaken precincts. So it had remained, until within a few days past.

But now, though the shopwindow was still closely curtained from the public gaze, a remarkable change had taken place in its interior. The rich and heavy festoons of cobweb, which it had cost a long ancestral succession of spiders their life's labor to spin and weave, had been carefully brushed away from the ceiling. The counter, shelves, floor had all been scoured, and the latter was overstrewn with fresh blue sand. The brown scales, too, had evidently undergone rigid discipline, in an unavailing effort to rub off the rust, which, alas! had eaten through and through their substance. Neither was the little old shop any longer empty of merchantable goods. A curious eye, privileged to take an account of stock, and investigate behind the counter, would have discovered a barrel—yea, two or three barrels and half ditto—one containing flour, another apples, and a third, perhaps, Indian meal. There was likewise a square box of pinewood, full of soap in bars; also, another of the same size, in which were tallow candles, ten to the pound. A small stock of brown sugar, some white beans and split peas, and a few other commodities of low price, and such as are constantly in demand, made up the bulkier portion of the merchandise. It might have been taken for a ghostly or phantasmagoric reflection of the old shopkeeper Pyncheon's shabbily provided shelves, save that some of the articles were of a description and outward form which could hardly have been known in his day. For instance, there was a glass pickle jar, filled with fragments of Gibraltar rock; not, indeed, splinters of the veritable stone foundation of the famous fortress, but bits of delectable candy, neatly done up in white paper. Jim Crow, moreover, was seen executing his world-renowned dance, in gingerbread. A party of leaden dragoons were galloping along one of the shelves, in equipments and uniform of modern cut; and there were some sugar figures, with no strong resemblance to the humanity of any epoch, but less unsatisfactorily representing our own fashions than those of a hundred years ago. Another phenomenon, still more strikingly modern, was a package of lucifer matches, which, in old times, would have been thought actually to borrow their instantaneous flame from the nether fires of Tophet.

In short, to bring the matter at once to a point, it was incontrovertibly evident that somebody had taken the shop and fixtures of the long-retired and forgotten Mr. Pyncheon, and was about to renew the enterprise of that departed worthy, with a different set of customers. Who could this bold adventurer be? And, of all places in the world, why had he chosen the House of the Seven Gables as the scene of his commercial speculations?

We return to the elderly maiden. She at length withdrew her eyes from the dark countenance of the Colonel's portrait, heaved a sigh—indeed, her breast was a very cave of Aeolus that morning—and stepped across the room on tiptoe, as is the customary gait of elderly women. Passing through an intervening passage, she opened a door that communicated with the shop, just now so elaborately described. Owing to the projection of the upper story—and still more to the thick shadow of the Pyncheon Elm, which stood almost directly in front of the gable—the twilight, here, was still as much akin to night as morning. Another heavy sigh from Miss Hepzibah! After a moment's pause on the threshold, peering towards the window with her near-sighted scowl, as if frowning down some bitter enemy, she suddenly projected herself into the shop. The haste, and, as it were, the galvanic impulse of the movement, were really quite startling.

Nervously—in a sort of frenzy, we might almost say—she began to busy herself in arranging some children's play-things, and other little wares, on the shelves and at the shopwindow. In the aspect of this dark-arrayed, pale-faced, ladylike old figure there was a deeply tragic character that contrasted irreconcilably with the ludicrous pettiness of her employment. It seemed a queer anomaly that so gaunt and dismal a personage should take a toy in hand; a miracle that the toy did not vanish in her grasp; a miserably absurd idea that she should go on perplexing her stiff and somber intellect with the question how to tempt little boys into her premises! Yet such is undoubtedly her object. Now she places a gingerbread elephant against the window, but with so tremulous a touch that it tumbles upon the floor, with the dismemberment of three legs and its trunk; it has ceased to be an elephant, and has become a few bits of musty ginger-bread. There, again, she has upset a tumbler of marbles, all of which roll different ways, and each individual marble, devil-directed, into the most difficult obscurity that it can find. Heaven help our poor old Hepzibah, and forgive us for taking a ludicrous view of her position! As her rigid and rusty frame goes down upon its hands and knees, in quest of the absconding marbles, we positively feel so much the more inclined to shed tears of sympathy, from the very fact that we must needs turn aside and laugh at her. For here— and if we fail to impress it suitably upon the reader, it is our own fault, not that of the theme—here is one of the truest points of melancholy interest that occur in ordinary life. It was the final throe of what called itself old gentility. A lady—who had fed herself from childhood with the shadowy food of aristocratic reminiscences, and whose religion it was that a lady's hand soils itself irremediably by doing aught for bread—this born lady, after sixty years of narrowing means, is fain to step down from her pedestal of imaginary rank. Poverty, treading closely at her heels for a lifetime, has come up with her at last. She must earn her own food, or starve! And we have stolen upon Miss Hepzibah Pyncheon, too irreverently, at the instant of time when the patrician lady is to be transformed into the plebeian woman.

In this republican country, amid the fluctuating waves of our social life, somebody is always at the drowning point. The tragedy is enacted with as continual a repetition as that of a popular drama on a holiday; and, nevertheless, is felt as deeply, perhaps, as when an hereditary noble sinks below his order. More deeply; since, with us, rank is the grosser substance of wealth and a splendid establishment, and has no spiritual existence after the death of these, but dies hopelessly along with them. And, therefore, since we have been unfortunate enough to introduce our heroine at so inauspicious a juncture, we would entreat for a mood of due solemnity in the spectators of her fate. Let us behold, in poor Hepzibah, the immemorial lady—two hundred years old, on this side of the water, and thrice as many on the other—with her antique portraits, pedigrees, coats of arms, records and traditions, and her claim, as joint heiress, to that princely territory at the eastward, no longer a wilderness, but a populous fertility—born, too, in Pyncheon Street, under the Pyncheon Elm, and in the Pyncheon House, where she has spent all her days—reduced now, in that very house, to be the hucksteress of a cent shop.

This business of setting up a petty shop is almost the only resource of women in circumstances at all similar to those of our unfortunate recluse. With her nearsightedness, and those tremulous fingers of hers, at once inflexible and delicate, she could not be a seamstress; although her sampler, of fifty years gone by, exhibited some of the most recondite specimens of ornamental needlework. A school for little children had been often in her thoughts; and, at one time, she had begun a review of her early studies in the New England Primer, with a view to prepare herself for the office of instructress. But the love of children had never been quickened in Hepzibah's heart, and was now torpid, if not extinct; she watched the little people of the neighborhood from her chamber window, and doubted whether she could tolerate a more intimate acquaintance with them. Besides, in our day, the very A B C has become a science greatly too

abstruse to be any longer taught by pointing a pin from
letter to letter. A modern child could teach old Hepzibah
more than old Hepzibah could teach the child. So—with
many a cold, deep heartquake at the idea of at last coming
into sordid contact with the world, from which she had so
long kept aloof, while every added day of seclusion had
rolled another stone against the cavern door of her hermitage—the poor thing bethought herself of the ancient .
shopwindow, the rusty scales, and dusty till. She might have
held back a little longer; but another circumstance, not yet
hinted at, had somewhat hastened her decision. Her humble
preparations, therefore, were duly made, and the enterprise
was now to be commenced. Nor was she entitled to complain of any remarkable singularity in her fate; for, in the
town of her nativity, we might point to several little shops of
a similar description, some of them in houses as ancient as
that of the Seven Gables; and one or two, it may be, where
a decayed gentlewoman stands behind the counter, as grim
an image of family pride as Miss Hepzibah Pyncheon herself.

It was overpoweringly ridiculous—we must honestly confess it—the deportment of the maiden lady while setting her
shop in order for the public eye. She stole on tiptoe to the
window, as cautiously as if she conceived some bloody-
minded villain to be watching behind the elm tree, with
intent to take her life. Stretching out her long, lank arm, she
put a paper of pearl buttons, a jew's-harp, or whatever the
small article might be, in its destined place, and straightway
vanished back into the dusk, as if the world need never
hope for another glimpse of her. It might have been fancied,
indeed, that she expected to minister to the wants of the
community unseen, like a disembodied divinity or enchant-
ress, holding forth her bargains to the reverential and awe-
stricken purchaser in an invisible hand. But Hepzibah had
no such flattering dream. She was well aware that she must
ultimately come forward, and stand revealed in her proper
individuality; but, like other sensitive persons, she could not
bear to be observed in the gradual process, and chose rather
to flash forth on the world's astonished gaze at once.

The inevitable moment was not much longer to be de-
layed. The sunshine might now be seen stealing down the
front of the opposite house, from the windows of which
came a reflected gleam, struggling through the boughs of

the elm tree, and enlightening the interior of the shop more distinctly than heretofore. The town appeared to be waking up. A baker's cart had already rattled through the street, chasing away the latest vestige of night's sanctity with the jingle-jangle of its dissonant bells. A milkman was distributing the contents of his cans from door to door; and the harsh peal of a fisherman's conch shell was heard far off, around the corner. None of these tokens escaped Hepzibah's notice. The moment had arrived. To delay longer would be only to lengthen out her misery. Nothing remained, except to take down the bar from the shop door, leaving the entrance free—more than free: welcome, as if all were household friends—to every passer-by, whose eyes might be attracted by the commodities at the window. This last act Hepzibah now performed, letting the bar fall with what smote upon her excited nerves as a most astounding clatter. Then—as if the only barrier betwixt herself and the world had been thrown down, and a flood of evil consequences would come tumbling through the gap—she fled into the inner parlor, threw herself into the ancestral elbow-chair, and wept.

Our miserable old Hepzibah! It is a heavy annoyance to a writer, who endeavors to represent nature, its various attitudes and circumstances, in a reasonably correct outline and true coloring, that so much of the mean and ludicrous should be hopelessly mixed up with the purest pathos which life anywhere supplies to him. What tragic dignity, for example, can be wrought into a scene like this! How can we elevate our history of retribution for the sin of long ago, when, as one of our most prominent figures, we are compelled to introduce—not a young and lovely woman, nor even the stately remains of beauty, storm-shattered by affliction—but a gaunt, sallow, rusty-jointed maiden, in a long-waisted silk gown, and with the strange horror of a turban on her head! Her visage is not even ugly. It is redeemed from insignificance only by the contraction of her eyebrows into a near-sighted scowl. And, finally, her great life trial seems to be that, after sixty years of idleness, she finds it convenient to earn comfortable bread by setting up a shop in a small way. Nevertheless, if we look through all the heroic fortunes of mankind, we shall find this same entanglement of something mean and trivial with whatever is noblest in joy or sorrow.

Life is made up of marble and mud. And, without all the deeper trust in a comprehensive sympathy above us, we might hence be led to suspect the insult of a sneer, as well as an immitigable frown, on the iron countenance of fate. What is called poetic insight is the gift of discerning, in this sphere of strangely mingled elements, the beauty and the majesty which are compelled to assume a garb so sordid.

III

The First Customer

Miss Hepzibah Pyncheon sat in the oaken elbow-chair, with her hands over her face, giving way to that heavy down-sinking of the heart which most persons have experienced, when the image of hope itself seems ponderously molded of lead, on the eve of an enterprise at once doubtful and momentous. She was suddenly startled by the tinkling alarum—high, sharp, and irregular—of a little bell. The maiden lady arose upon her feet, as pale as a ghost at cockcrow; for she was an enslaved spirit, and this the talisman to which she owed obedience. This little bell—to speak in plainer terms—being fastened over the shop door, was so contrived as to vibrate by means of a steel spring, and thus convey notice to the inner regions of the house when any customer should cross the threshold. Its ugly and spiteful little din (heard now for the first time, perhaps, since Hepzibah's periwigged predecessor had retired from trade) at once set every nerve of her body in responsive and tumultuous vibration. The crisis was upon her! Her first customer was at the door!

Without giving herself time for a second thought, she rushed into the shop, pale, wild, desperate in gesture and expression, scowling portentously, and looking far better qualified to do fierce battle with a housebreaker than to stand smiling behind the counter, bartering small wares for a copper recompense. Any ordinary customer, indeed, would have turned his back and fled. And yet there was nothing fierce in Hepzibah's poor old heart; nor had she, at the moment, a single bitter thought against the world at large, or one individual man or woman. She wished them all well, but wished, too, that she herself were done with them, and in her quiet grave.

The applicant, by this time, stood within the doorway. Coming freshly, as he did, out of the morning light, he appeared to have brought some of its cheery influences into the shop along with him. It was a slender young man, not more than one or two and twenty years old, with rather a grave and thoughtful expression for his years, but likewise a springy alacrity and vigor. These qualities were not only perceptible, physically, in his make and motions, but made themselves felt almost immediately in his character. A brown beard, not too silken in its texture, fringed his chin, but as yet without completely hiding it; he wore a short mustache, too, and his dark, high-featured countenance looked all the better for these natural ornaments. As for his dress, it was of the simplest kind; a summer sack of cheap and ordinary material, thin checkered pantaloons, and a straw hat, by no means of the finest braid. Oak Hall might have supplied his entire equipment. He was chiefly marked as a gentleman—if such, indeed, he made any claim to be—by the rather remarkable whiteness and nicety of his clean linen.

He met the scowl of old Hepzibah without apparent alarm, as having heretofore encountered it and found it harmless.

"So, my dear Miss Pyncheon," said the daguerreotypist —for it was that sole other occupant of the seven-gabled mansion, "I am glad to see that you have not shrunk from your good purpose. I merely look in to offer my best wishes, and to ask if I can assist you any further in your preparations."

People in difficulty and distress, or in any manner at odds with the world, can endure a vast amount of harsh treatment, and perhaps be only the stronger for it; whereas they give way at once before the simplest expression of what they perceive to be genuine sympathy. So it proved with poor Hepzibah; for, when she saw the young man's smile—looking so much the brighter on a thoughtful face—and heard his kindly tone, she broke first into a hysteric giggle and then began to sob.

"Ah, Mr. Holgrave," cried she, as soon as she could speak, "I never can go through with it! Never, never, never! I wish I were dead, and in the old family tomb, with all my forefathers! With my father, and my mother, and my sister!

Yes, and with my brother, who had far better find me there than here! The world is too chill and hard—and I am too old, and too feeble, and too hopeless!"

"Oh, believe me, Miss Hepzibah," said the young man, quietly, "these feelings will not trouble you any longer, after you are once fairly in the midst of your enterprise. They are unavoidable at this moment, standing, as you do, on the outer verge of your long seclusion, and peopling the world with ugly shapes, which you will soon find to be as unreal as the giants and ogres of a child's storybook. I find nothing so singular in life as that everything appears to lose its substance the instant one actually grapples with it. So it will be with what you think so terrible."

"But I am a woman!" said Hepzibah, piteously. "I was going to say a lady, but I consider that as past."

"Well, no matter if it be past!" answered the artist, a strange gleam of half-hidden sarcasm flashing through the kindliness of his manner. "Let it go! You are the better without it. I speak frankly, my dear Miss Pyncheon, for are we not friends? I look upon this as one of the fortunate days of your life. It ends an epoch and begins one. Hitherto, the lifeblood has been gradually chilling in your veins as you sat aloof, within your circle of gentility, while the rest of the world was fighting out its battle with one kind of necessity or another. Henceforth, you will at least have the sense of healthy and natural effort for a purpose, and of lending your strength—be it great or small—to the united struggle of mankind. This is success—all the success that anybody meets with!"

"It is natural enough, Mr. Holgrave, that you should have ideas like these," rejoined Hepzibah, drawing up her gaunt figure, with slightly offended dignity. "You are a man, a young man, and brought up, I suppose, as almost everybody is nowadays, with a view to seeking your fortune. But I was born a lady, and have always lived one; no matter in what narrowness of means, always a lady!"

"But I was not born a gentleman; neither have I lived like one," said Holgrave, slightly smiling. "So, my dear madam, you will hardly expect me to sympathize with sensibilities of this kind; though, unless I deceive myself, I have some imperfect comprehension of them. These names of gentleman and lady had a meaning, in the past history of the world, and conferred privileges, desirable or otherwise, on those entitled to bear them. In the present—and still more in the future condition of society—they imply not privilege, but restriction!"

"These are new notions," said the old gentlewoman, shaking her head. "I shall never understand them; neither do I wish it."

"We will cease to speak of them, then," replied the artist, with a friendlier smile than his last one, "and I will leave you to feel whether it is not better to be a true woman than a lady. Do you really think, Miss Hepzibah, that any lady of your family has ever done a more heroic thing, since this house was built, than you are performing in it today? Never; and if the Pyncheons had always acted so nobly, I doubt whether an old wizard Maule's anathema, of which you told me once, would have had much weight with Providence against them."

"Ah! No, no!" said Hepzibah, not displeased at this allusion to the somber dignity of an inherited curse. "If old Maule's ghost, or a descendant of his, could see me behind the counter today, he would call it the fulfillment of his worst wishes. But I thank you for your kindness, Mr. Holgrave, and will do my utmost to be a good shopkeeper."

"Pray do," said Holgrave, "and let me have the pleasure of being your first customer. I am about taking a walk to the seashore, before going to my rooms, where I misuse heaven's blessed sunshine by tracing out human features through its agency. A few of those biscuits, dipped in sea water, will be just what I need for breakfast. What is the price of half a dozen?"

"Let me be a lady a moment longer," replied Hepzibah, with a manner of antique stateliness to which a melancholy smile lent a kind of grace. She put the biscuits into his hand, but rejected the compensation. "A Pyncheon must not, at all events under her forefathers' roof, receive money for a morsel of bread from her only friend!"

Holgrave took his departure, leaving her, for the moment, with spirits not quite so much depressed. Soon, however, they had subsided nearly to their former dead level. With a beating heart, she listened to the footsteps of early passengers, which now began to be frequent along the street. Once or twice they seemed to linger; these strangers, or neighbors, as the case might be, were looking at the display of toys and petty commodities in Hepzibah's shopwindow. She was doubly tortured; in part, with a sense of overwhelming shame that strange and unloving eyes should have the privilege of gazing, and partly because the idea occurred to her, with ridiculous importunity, that the window was not arranged so skillfully, nor nearly to so much advantage, as it might have been. It seemed as if the whole fortune or failure of her shop might depend on the display of a different set of articles, or substituting a fairer apple for one which appeared to be specked. So she made the change, and straightway fancied that everything was spoiled by it; not recognizing that it was the nervousness of the juncture, and her own native squeamishness as an old maid, that wrought all the seeming mischief.

Anon, there was an encounter, just at the doorstep, betwixt two laboring men, as their rough voices denoted them to be. After some slight talk about their own affairs, one of them chanced to notice the shopwindow, and directed the other's attention to it.

"See here!" cried he. "What do you think of this? Trade seems to be looking up in Pyncheon Street!"

"Well, well, this is a sight, to be sure!" exclaimed the other. "In the old Pyncheon House, and underneath the Pyncheon Elm! Who would have thought it? Old Maid Pyncheon is setting up a cent shop!"

"Will she make it go, think you, Dixey?" said his friend. "I don't call it a very good stand. There's another shop just round the corner."

"Make it go!" cried Dixey, with a most contemptuous expression, as if the very idea were impossible to be conceived. "Not a bit of it! Why, her face—I've seen it, for I dug her garden for her one year—her face is enough to frighten the Old Nick himself, if he had ever so great a mind to trade with her. People can't stand it, I tell you! She scowls dreadfully, reason or none, out of pure ugliness of temper!"

"Well, that's not so much matter," remarked the other man. "These sour-tempered folks are mostly handy at business, and know pretty well what they are about. But, as you say, I don't think she'll do much. This business of keeping cent shops is overdone, like all other kinds of trade, handicraft, and bodily labor. I know it, to my cost! My wife kept a cent shop three months, and lost five dollars on her outlay!"

"Poor business!" responded Dixey, in a tone as if he were shaking his head. "Poor business!"

For some reason or other, not very easy to analyze, there had hardly been so bitter a pang in all her previous misery about the matter as what thrilled Hepzibah's heart on over-hearing the above conversation. The testimony in regard to her scowl was frightfully important; it seemed to hold up her image wholly relieved from the false light of her self-partialities, and so hideous that she dared not look at it. She was absurdly hurt, moreover, by the slight and idle effect that her setting up shop—an event of such breathless inter-est to herself—appeared to have upon the public, of which these two men were the nearest representatives. A glance; a passing word or two; a coarse laugh; and she was doubtless forgotten before they turned the corner! They cared nothing for her dignity, and just as little for her degradation. Then, also, the augury of ill success, uttered from the sure wisdom of experience, fell upon her half-dead hope like a clod into a grave. The man's wife had already tried the same experi-ment, and failed! How could the born lady—the recluse of half a lifetime, utterly unpracticed in the world, at sixty years of age—how could she ever dream of succeeding, when the hard, vulgar, keen, busy, hackneyed New England woman had lost five dollars on her little outlay! Success presented itself as an impossibility, and the hope of it as a wild hallucination.

Some malevolent spirit, doing his utmost to drive Hepzibah mad, unrolled before her imagination a kind of panorama, representing the great thoroughfare of a city all astir with customers. So many and so magnificent shops as there were! Groceries, toyshops, dry goods stores, with their immense panes of plate glass, their gorgeous fixtures, their vast and complete assortments of merchandise, in which fortunes had been invested; and those noble mirrors at the farther end of each establishment, doubling all this wealth by a brightly burnished vista of unrealities! On one side of the street this splendid bazaar, with a multitude of perfumed and glossy salesmen, smirking, smiling, bowing, and measuring out the goods. On the other, the dusky old House of the Seven

Gables, with the antiquated shopwindow under its projecting story, and Hepzibah herself, in a gown of rusty black
silk, behind the counter, scowling at the world as it went by!
This mighty contrast thrust itself forward as a fair expression
of the odds against which she was to begin her struggle for a
subsistence. Success? Preposterous! She would never think
of it again! The house might just as well be buried in an
eternal fog while all other houses had the sunshine on them;
for not a foot would ever cross the threshold, nor a hand so
much as try the door!

But, at this instant, the shop bell, right over her head,
tinkled as if it were bewitched. The old gentlewoman's heart
seemed to be attached to the same steel spring, for it went
through a series of sharp jerks, in unison with the sound.
The door was thrust open, although no human form was
perceptible on the other side of the half window. Hepzibah,
nevertheless, stood at a gaze, with her hands clasped, looking very much as if she had summoned up an evil spirit, and
were afraid, yet resolved, to hazard the encounter.

"Heaven help me!" she groaned, mentally. "Now is my
hour of need!"—

The door, which moved with difficulty on its creaking and
rusty hinges, being forced quite open, a square and sturdy
little urchin became apparent, with cheeks as red as an
apple. He was clad rather shabbily (but, as it seemed, more
owing to his mother's carelessness than his father's poverty),
in a blue apron, very wide and short trousers, shoes somewhat out at the toes, and a chip hat, with the frizzles of his
curly hair sticking through its crevices. A book and a small
slate, under his arm, indicated that he was on his way to
school. He stared at Hepzibah a moment, as an elder customer than himself would have been likely enough to do,
not knowing what to make of the tragic attitude and queer
scowl wherewith she regarded him.

"Well, child," said she, taking heart at sight of a personage so little formidable, "well, my child, what did you
wish for?"

"That Jim Crow there in the window," answered the
urchin, holding out a cent, and pointing to the gingerbread
figure that had attracted his notice, as he loitered along to
school. "The one that has not a broken foot."

So Hepzibah put forth her lank arm, and, taking the effigy from the shopwindow, delivered it to her first customer.

"No matter for the money," said she, giving him a little push towards the door; for her old gentility was contumaciously squeamish at sight of the copper coin, and, besides, it seemed such pitiful meanness to take the child's pocket money in exchange for a bit of stale gingerbread. "No matter for the cent. You are welcome to Jim Crow."

The child, staring with round eyes at this instance of liberality, wholly unprecedented in his large experience of cent shops, took the man of gingerbread, and quitted the premises. No sooner had he reached the sidewalk (little cannibal that he was!) than Jim Crow's head was in his mouth. As he had not been careful to shut the door, Hepzibah was at the pains of closing it after him, with a pettish ejaculation or two about the troublesomeness of young people, and particularly of small boys. She had just placed another representative of the renowned Jim Crow at the window, when again the shop bell tinkled clamorously, and again the door being thrust open, with its characteristic jerk and jar, disclosed the same sturdy little urchin who, precisely two minutes ago, had made his exit. The crumbs and discoloration of the cannibal feast, as yet hardly consummated, were exceedingly visible about his mouth.

"What is it now, child?" asked the maiden lady rather impatiently. "Did you come back to shut the door?"

"No," answered the urchin, pointing to the figure that had just been put up. "I want that other Jim Crow."

"Well, here it is for you," said Hepzibah, reaching it down; but recognizing that this pertinacious customer would not quit her on any other terms, so long as she had a gingerbread figure in her shop, she partly drew back her extended hand. "Where is the cent?"

The little boy had the cent ready, but, like a trueborn Yankee, would have preferred the better bargain to the worse. Looking somewhat chagrined, he put the coin into Hepzibah's hand, and departed, sending the second Jim Crow in quest of the former one. The new shopkeeper dropped the first solid result of her commercial enterprise into the till. It was done! The sordid stain of that copper coin could never be washed away from her palm. The little schoolboy, aided by the impish figure of the Negro dancer, had wrought an irreparable ruin. The structure of ancient aristocracy had been demolished by him, even as if his childish gripe had torn down the seven-gabled mansion. Now let Hepzibah turn the old Pyncheon portraits with their faces to the wall, and take the map of her Eastern territory to kindle the kitchen fire, and blow up the flame with the empty breath of her ancestral traditions! What had she to do with ancestry? Nothing; no more than with posterity! No lady, now, but simply Hepzibah Pyncheon, a forlorn old maid, and keeper of a cent shop!

Nevertheless, even while she paraded these ideas somewhat ostentatiously through her mind, it is altogether surprising what a calmness had come over her. The anxiety and misgivings which had tormented her, whether asleep or in melancholy daydreams, ever since her project began to take an aspect of solidity, had now vanished quite away. She felt the novelty of her position, indeed, but no longer with disturbance or affright. Now and then, there came a thrill of almost youthful enjoyment. It was the invigorating breath of a fresh outward atmosphere, after the long torpor and monotonous seclusion of her life. So wholesome is effort! So miraculous the strength that we do not know of! The healthiest glow that Hepzibah had known for years had come now in the dreaded crisis, when, for the first time, she had put forth her hand to help herself. The little circlet of the schoolboy's copper coin—dim and lusterless though it was, with the small services which it had been doing here and there about the world—had proved a talisman, fragrant with good, and deserving to be set in gold and worn next her heart. It was as potent, and perhaps endowed with the same kind of efficacy, as a galvanic ring! Hepzibah, at all events, was indebted to its subtle operation both in body and spirit; so much the more, as it inspired her with energy to get some breakfast, at which, still the better to keep up her courage, she allowed herself an extra spoonful in her infusion of black tea.

Her introductory day of shopkeeping did not run on, however, without many and serious interruptions of this mood of cheerful vigor. As a general rule, Providence seldom vouchsafes to mortals any more than just that degree of encouragement which suffices to keep them at a reasonably full exertion of their powers. In the case of our old

gentlewoman, after the excitement of new effort had subsided, the despondency of her whole life threatened, ever
and anon, to return. It was like the heavy mass of clouds
which we may often see obscuring the sky, and making a
gray twilight everywhere, until, towards nightfall, it yields
temporarily to a glimpse of sunshine. But, always, the envious cloud strives to gather again across the streak of celestial azure.

Customers came in, as the forenoon advanced, but rather
slowly; in some cases, too, it must be owned, with little
satisfaction either to themselves or Miss Hepzibah; nor, on
the whole, with an aggregate of very rich emolument to the
till. A little girl, sent by her mother to match a skein of
cotton thread, of a peculiar hue, took one that the near-
sighted old lady pronounced extremely like, but soon came
running back, with a blunt and cross message that it would
not do, and, besides, was very rotten! Then there was a
pale, care-wrinkled woman, not old but haggard, and already with streaks of gray among her hair, like silver ribbons; one of those women, naturally delicate, whom you at
once recognize as worn to death by a brute—probably a
drunken brute—of a husband, and at least nine children.
She wanted a few pounds of flour, and offered the money,
which the decayed gentlewoman silently rejected, and gave
the poor soul better measure than if she had taken it.
Shortly afterwards, a man in a blue cotton frock, much
soiled, came in and bought a pipe, filling the whole shop,
meanwhile, with the hot odor of strong drink, not only
exhaled in the torrid atmosphere of his breath, but oozing
out of his entire system, like an inflammable gas. It was
impressed on Hepzibah's mind that this was the husband of
the care-wrinkled woman. He asked for a paper of tobacco;
and as she had neglected to provide herself with the article,
her brutal customer dashed down his newly bought pipe and
left the shop, muttering some unintelligible words, which
had the tone and bitterness of a curse. Hereupon Hepzibah
threw up her eyes, unintentionally scowling in the face of
Providence!

No less than five persons, during the forenoon, inquired
for ginger beer, or root beer, or any drink of a similar
brewage, and, obtaining nothing of the kind, went off in an
exceedingly bad humor. Three of them left the door open,

and the other two pulled it so spitefully in going out that the little bell played the very deuce with Hepzibah's nerves. A round, bustling, fire-ruddy housewife of the neighborhood burst breathless into the shop, fiercely demanding yeast; and when the poor gentlewoman, with her cold shyness of manner, gave her hot customer to understand that she did not keep the article, this very capable housewife took upon herself to administer a regular rebuke.

"A cent shop, and no yeast!" quoth she. "That will never do! Who ever heard of such a thing? Your loaf will never rise, no more than mine will today. You had better shut up shop at once."

"Well," said Hepzibah, heaving a deep sigh, "perhaps I had!"

Several times, moreover, besides the above instance, her ladylike sensibilities were seriously infringed upon by the familiar, if not rude, tone with which people addressed her. They evidently considered themselves not merely her equals, but her patrons and superiors. Now, Hepzibah had unconsciously flattered herself with the idea that there would be a gleam or halo, of some kind or other, about her person, which would insure an obeisance to her sterling gentility, or, at least, a tacit recognition of it. On the other hand, nothing tortured her more intolerably than when this recognition was too prominently expressed. To one or two rather officious offers of sympathy, her responses were little short of acrimonious; and, we regret to say, Hepzibah was thrown into a positively unchristian state of mind by the suspicion that one of her customers was drawn to the shop not by any real need of the article which she pretended to seek, but by a wicked wish to stare at her. The vulgar creature was determined to see for herself what sort of a figure a mildewed piece of aristocracy, after wasting all the bloom and much of the decline of her life apart from the world, would cut behind a counter. In this particular case, however mechanical and innocuous it might be at other times, Hepzibah's contortion of brow served her in good stead.

"I never was so frightened in my life!" said the curious customer, in describing the incident to one of her acquaintances. "She's a real old vixen, take my word of it! She says little, to be sure; but if you could only see the mischief in her eye!"

On the whole, therefore, her new experience led our decayed gentlewoman to very disagreeable conclusions as to the temper and manners of what she termed the lower classes, whom heretofore she had looked down upon with a gentle and pitying complaisance, as herself occupying a sphere of unquestionable superiority. But, unfortunately, she had likewise to struggle against a bitter emotion of a directly opposite kind: a sentiment of virulence, we mean, towards the idle aristocracy to which it had so recently been her pride to belong. When a lady, in a delicate and costly summer garb, with a floating veil and gracefully swaying gown, and, altogether, an ethereal lightness that made you look at her beautifully slippered feet, to see whether she trod on the dust or floated in the air—when such a vision happened to pass through this retired street, leaving it tenderly and delusively fragrant with her passage, as if a bouquet of tea roses had been borne along—then again, it is to be feared, old Hepzibah's scowl could no longer vindicate itself entirely on the plea of nearsightedness.

"For what end," thought she, giving vent to that feeling of hostility which is the only real abasement of the poor in the presence of the rich, "for what good end, in the wisdom of Providence, does that woman live? Must the whole world toil, that the palms of her hands may be kept white and delicate?"

Then, ashamed and penitent, she hid her face.

"May God forgive me!" said she.

Doubtless, God did forgive her. But, taking the inward and outward history of the first half day into consideration, Hepzibah began to fear that the shop would prove her ruin in a moral and religious point of view, without contributing very essentially towards even her temporal welfare.

IV

A Day Behind the Counter

TOWARDS noon, Hepzibah saw an elderly gentleman, large and portly, and of remarkably dignified demeanor, passing slowly along on the opposite side of the white and dusty street. On coming within the shadow of the Pyncheon Elm, he stopped, and (taking off his hat, meanwhile, to wipe the perspiration from his brow) seemed to scrutinize, with especial interest, the dilapidated and rusty-visaged House of the Seven Gables. He himself, in a very 'different style, was as well worth looking at as the house. No better model need be sought, nor could have been found, of a very high order of respectability, which, by some indescribable magic, not merely expressed itself in his looks and gestures, but even governed the fashion of his garments, and rendered them all proper and essential to the man. Without appearing to differ, in any tangible way, from other people's clothes, there was yet a wide and rich gravity about them that must have been a characteristic of the wearer, since it could not be defined as pertaining either to the cut or material. His gold-headed cane, too—a serviceable staff, of dark polished wood—had similar traits, and, had it chosen to take a walk by itself, would have been recognized anywhere as a tolerably adequate representative of its master. This character—which showed itself so strikingly in everything about him, and the effect of which we seek to convey to the reader—went no deeper than his station, habits of life, and external circumstances. One perceived him to be a personage of marked influence and authority; and, especially, you could feel just as certain that he was opulent as if he had exhibited his

bank account, or as if you had seen him touching the twigs
of the Pyncheon Elm, and Midas-like, transmuting them to
gold.

In his youth, he had probably been considered a handsome man; at his present age, his brow was too heavy, his
temples too bare, his remaining hair too gray, his eye too
cold, his lips too closely compressed, to bear any relation to
mere personal beauty. He would have made a good and
massive portrait; better now, perhaps, than at any previous
period of his life, although his look might grow positively
harsh in the process of being fixed upon the canvas. The
artist would have found it desirable to study his face, and
prove its capacity for varied expression; to darken it with a
frown, to kindle it up with a smile.

While the elderly gentleman stood looking at the Pyncheon House, both the frown and the smile passed suc-
cessively over his countenance. His eye rested on the
shopwindow, and putting up a pair of gold-bowed spectacles, which he held in his hand, he minutely surveyed
Hepzibah's little arrangement of toys and commodities. At
first it seemed not to please him—nay, to cause him exceeding displeasure—and yet, the very next moment, he smiled.
While the latter expression was yet on his lips, he caught a
glimpse of Hepzibah, who had involuntarily bent forward to
the window; and then the smile changed from acrid and
disagreeable to the sunniest complacency and benevolence.
He bowed, with a happy mixture of dignity and courteous
kindliness, and pursued his way.

"There he is!" said Hepzibah to herself, gulping down a
very bitter emotion, and, since she could not rid herself of
it, trying to drive it back into her heart. "What does he
think of it, I wonder? Does it please him? Ah! He is looking
back!"

The gentleman had paused in the street, and turned himself half about, still with his eyes fixed on the shopwindow.
In fact, he wheeled wholly round, and commenced a step or
two, as if designing to enter the shop; but, as it chanced, his
purpose was anticipated by Hepzibah's first customer, the
little cannibal of Jim Crow, who, staring up at the window,
was irresistibly attracted by an elephant of gingerbread.
What a grand appetite had this small urchin! Two Jim Crows
immediately after breakfast—and now an elephant, as a

preliminary whet before dinner! By the time this latter purchase was completed, the elderly gentleman had resumed
his way, and turned the street corner.

"Take it as you like, Cousin Jaffrey!" muttered the maiden
lady, as she drew back, after cautiously thrusting out her
head, and looking up and down the street. "Take it as you
like! You have seen my little shopwindow! Well! What have
you to say? Is not the Pyncheon House my own, while I'm
alive?"

After this incident, Hepzibah retreated to the back parlor, where she at first caught up a half-finished stocking, and
began knitting at it with nervous and irregular jerks; but
quickly finding herself at odds with the stitches, she threw it
aside, and walked hurriedly about the room. At length, she
paused before the portrait of the stern old Puritan, her
ancestor, and the founder of the house. In one sense, this
picture had almost faded into the canvas, and hidden itself
behind the duskiness of age; in another, she could not but
fancy that it had been growing more prominent, and strikingly expressive, ever since her earliest familiarity with it as
a child. For, while the physical outline and substance were
darkening away from the beholder's eye, the bold, hard,
and, at the same time, indirect character of the man seemed
to be brought out in a kind of spiritual relief. Such an effect
may occasionally be observed in pictures of antique date.
They acquire a look which an artist (if he have anything like
the complacency of artists nowadays) would never dream of
presenting to a patron as his own characteristic expression,
but which, nevertheless, we at once recognize as reflecting
the unlovely truth of a human soul. In such cases, the
painter's deep conception of his subject's inward traits has
wrought itself into the essence of the picture, and is seen
after the superficial coloring has been rubbed off by time.

While gazing at the portrait, Hepzibah trembled under its
eye. Her hereditary reverence made her afraid to judge
the character of the original so harshly as a perception of the
truth compelled her to do. But still she gazed, because the
face of the picture enabled her—at least, she fancied so—to
read more accurately, and to a greater depth, the face which
she had just seen in the street.

"This is the very man!" murmured she to herself. "Let
Jaffrey Pyncheon smile as he will, there is that look be-

neath! Put on him a skullcap, and a band, and a black coat, and a Bible in one hand and a sword in the other—then let Jaffrey smile as he might; nobody would doubt that it was the old Pyncheon come again! He has proved himself the very man to build up a new house! Perhaps, too, to draw down a new curse!"

Thus did Hepzibah bewilder herself with these fantasies of the old time. She had dwelt too much alone—too long in the Pyncheon House—until her very brain was impregnated with the dry rot of its timbers. She needed a walk along the noonday street to keep her sane.

By the spell of contrast, another portrait rose up before her, painted with more daring flattery than any artist would have ventured upon, but yet so delicately touched that the likeness remained perfect. Malbone's miniature, though from the same original, was far inferior to Hepzibah's air-drawn picture, at which affection and sorrowful remembrance wrought together. Soft, mildly, and cheerfully contempla- tive, with full, red lips, just on the verge of a smile, which the eyes seemed to herald by a gentle kindling-up of their orbs! Feminine traits, molded inseparably with those of the other sex! The miniature, likewise, had this last peculiarity; so that you inevitably thought of the original as resembling his mother, and she a lovely and lovable woman, with perhaps some beautiful infirmity of character, that made it all the pleasanter to know and easier to love her.

"Yes," thought Hepzibah, with grief of which it was only the more tolerable portion that welled up from her heart to her eyelids, "they persecuted his mother in him! He never was a Pyncheon!"

But here the shop bell rang; it was like a sound from a remote distance, so far had Hepzibah descended into the sepulchral depths of her reminiscences. On entering the shop, she found an old man there, a humble resident of Pyncheon Street, and whom, for a great many years past, she had suffered to be a kind of familiar of the house. He was an immemorial personage, who seemed always to have had a white head and wrinkles, and never to have possessed but a single tooth, and that a half-decayed one, in the front of the upper jaw. Well advanced as Hepzibah was, she could not remember when Uncle Venner, as the neighbor- hood called him, had not gone up and down the street, stooping a little and drawing his feet heavily over the gravel or pavement. But still there was something tough and vigorous about him, that not only kept him in daily breath, but enabled him to fill a place which would else have been vacant in the apparently crowded world. To go of errands with his slow and shuffling gait, which made you doubt how he ever was to arrive anywhere; to saw a small household's foot or two of firewood, or knock to pieces an old barrel, or split up a pine board for kindling stuff; in summer, to dig the few yards of garden ground appertaining to a low-rented tenement, and share the produce of his labor at the halves; in winter, to shovel away the snow from the sidewalk, or open paths to the woodshed, or along the clothesline; such were some of the essential offices which Uncle Venner performed among at least a score of families. Within that circle, he claimed the same sort of privilege, and probably felt as much warmth of interest, as a clergyman does in the range of his parishioners. Not that he laid claim to the tithe pig; but, as an analogous mode of reverence, he went his rounds, every morning, to gather up the crumbs of the table and overflowings of the dinner pot, as food for a pig of his own.

In his younger days—for, after all, there was a dim tradition that he had been, not young, but younger—Uncle Venner was commonly regarded as rather deficient, than otherwise, in his wits. In truth, he had virtually pleaded guilty to the charge, by scarcely aiming at such success as other men seek, and by taking only that humble and modest part in the intercourse of life which belongs to the alleged deficiency. But now, in his extreme old age—whether it were that his long and hard experience had actually brightened him, or that his decaying judgment rendered him less capable of fairly measuring himself—the venerable man made pretensions to no little wisdom, and really enjoyed the credit of it. There was likewise, at times, a vein of something like poetry in him; it was the moss or wallflower of his mind in its small dilapidation, and gave a charm to what might have been vulgar and commonplace in his earlier and middle life. Hepzibah had a regard for him, because his name was ancient in the town and had formerly been respectable. It was a still better reason for awarding him a species of familiar reverence that Uncle Venner was himself the most ancient existence, whether of man or thing, in Pyncheon Street, except the House of the Seven Gables, and perhaps the elm that overshadowed it.

This patriarch now presented himself before Hepzibah, clad in an old blue coat, which had a fashionable air, and must have accrued to him from the cast-off wardrobe of some dashing clerk. As for his trousers, they were of tow cloth, very short in the legs, and bagging down strangely in the rear, but yet having a suitableness to his figure which his other garment entirely lacked. His hat had relation to no other part of his dress, and but very little to the head that wore it. Thus Uncle Venner was a miscellaneous old gentleman, partly himself, but, in good measure, somebody else; patched together, too, of different epochs; an epitome of times and fashions.

"So, you have really begun trade," said he, "really begun trade! Well, I'm glad to see it. Young people should never live idle in the world, nor old ones neither, unless when the rheumatize gets hold of them. It has given me warning already; and in two or three years longer, I shall think of putting aside business and retiring to my farm. That's yonder— the great brick house, you know—the workhouse, most folks call it; but I mean to do my work first, and go there to be idle and enjoy myself. And I'm glad to see you beginning to do your work, Miss Hepzibah!"

"Thank you, Uncle Venner," said Hepzibah, smiling; for she always felt kindly towards the simple and talkative old man. Had he been an old woman, she might probably have repelled the freedom, which she now took in good part. "It is time for me to begin work, indeed! Or, to speak the truth, I have just begun when I ought to be giving it up."

"Oh, never say that, Miss Hepzibah!" answered the old man. "You are a young woman yet. Why, I hardly thought myself younger than I am now, it seems so little while ago since I used to see you playing about the door of the old house, quite a small child! Oftener, though, you used to be sitting at the threshold, and looking gravely into the street; for you had always a grave kind of way with you—a grown-up air, when you were only the height of my knee. It seems as if I saw you now; and your grandfather with his red cloak, and his white wig, and his cocked hat, and his cane, coming out of the house, and stepping so grandly up the street!

Those old gentlemen that grew up before the Revolution used to put on grand airs. In my young days, the great man of the town was commonly called King; and his wife, not Queen to be sure, but Lady. Nowadays, a man would not dare to be called King; and if he feels himself a little above common folks, he only stoops so much the lower to them. I met your cousin, the Judge, ten minutes ago; and, in my old tow-cloth trousers, as you see, the Judge raised his hat to me, I do believe! At any rate, the Judge bowed and smiled!"

"Yes," said Hepzibah, with something bitter stealing unawares into her tone. "My cousin Jaffrey is thought to have a very pleasant smile!"

"And so he has!" replied Uncle Venner. "And that's rather remarkable in a Pyncheon; for, begging your pardon, Miss Hepzibah, they never had the name of being an easy and agreeable set of folks. There was no getting close to them. But now, Miss Hepzibah, if an old man may be bold to ask, why don't Judge Pyncheon, with his great means, step forward, and tell his cousin to shut up her little shop at once? It's for your credit to be doing something, but it's not for the Judge's credit to let you!"

"We won't talk of this, if you please, Uncle Venner," said Hepzibah, coldly. "I ought to say, however, that, if I choose to earn bread for myself, it is not Judge Pyncheon's fault. Neither will he deserve the blame," added she, more kindly, remembering Uncle Venner's privileges of age and humble familiarity, "if I should, by and by, find it convenient to retire with you to your farm."

"And it's no bad place, either, that farm of mine!" cried the old man, cheerily, as if there were something positively delightful in the prospect. "No bad place is the great brick farmhouse, especially for them that will find a good many old cronies there, as will be my case. I quite long to be among them, sometimes, of the winter evenings; for it is but dull business for a lonesome elderly man, like me, to be nodding, by the hour together, with no company but his airtight stove. Summer or winter, there's a great deal to be said in favor of my farm! And, take it in the autumn, what can be pleasanter than to spend a whole day on the sunny side of a barn or a woodpile, chatting with somebody as old as one's self; or, perhaps, idling away the time with a natural-born simpleton, who knows how to be idle, because

even our busy Yankees never have found out how to put
him to any use? Upon my word, Miss Hepzibah, I doubt
whether I've ever been so comfortable as I mean to be at
my farm, which most folks call the workhouse. But you,
you're a young woman yet; you never need go there! Something still better will turn up for you. I'm sure of it!"

Hepzibah fancied that there was something peculiar in her
venerable friend's look and tone; insomuch, that she gazed
into his face with considerable earnestness, endeavoring to
discover what secret meaning, if any, might be lurking there.
Individuals whose affairs have reached an utterly desperate
crisis almost invariably keep themselves alive with hopes, so
much the more airily magnificent as they have the less of
solid matter within their grasp whereof to mold any judi-
cious and moderate expectation of good. Thus, all the while
Hepzibah was perfecting the scheme of her little shop, she
had cherished an unacknowledged idea that some harlequin
trick of fortune would intervene in her favor. For example,
an uncle—who had sailed for India fifty years before, and
never been heard of since—might yet return, and adopt her
to be the comfort of his very extreme and decrepit age, and
adorn her with pearls, diamonds, and Oriental shawls and
turbans, and make her the ultimate heiress of his unreckonable
riches. Or the member of Parliament, now at the head of
the English branch of the family—with which the elder
stock, on this side of the Atlantic, had held little or no
intercourse for the last two centuries—this eminent gentleman might invite Hepzibah to quit the ruinous House of the
Seven Gables, and come over to dwell with her kindred at
Pyncheon Hall. But, for reasons the most imperative, she
could not yield to his request. It was more probable, therefore, that the descendants of a Pyncheon who had emigrated
to Virginia, in some past generation, and became a great
planter there, hearing of Hepzibah's destitution, and impelled by the splendid generosity of character with which
their Virginian mixture must have enriched the New England blood, would send her a remittance of a thousand
dollars, with a hint of repeating the favor annually. Or—
and, surely, anything so undeniably just could not be beyond
the limits of reasonable anticipation—the great claim to the
heritage of Waldo County might finally be decided in favor
of the Pyncheons; so that, instead of keeping a cent shop,

Hepzibah would build a palace, and look down from its highest tower on hill, dale, forest, field, and town, as her own share of the ancestral territory.

These were some of the fantasies which she had long dreamed about; and, aided by these, Uncle Venner's casual attempt at encouragement kindled a strange festal glory in the poor, bare, melancholy chambers of her brain, as if that inner world were suddenly lighted up with gas. But either he knew nothing of her castles in the air—as how should he?—or else her earnest scowl disturbed his recollection, as it might a more courageous man's. Instead of pursuing any weightier topic, Uncle Venner was pleased to favor Hepzibah with some sage counsel in her shopkeeping capacity.

"Give no credit!"—these were some of his golden maxims—"Never take paper money! Look well to your change! Ring the silver on the four-pound weight! Shove back all English halfpence and base copper tokens, such as are very plenty about town! At your leisure hours, knit children's woolen socks and mittens! Brew your own yeast, and make your own ginger beer!"

And while Hepzibah was doing her utmost to digest the hard little pellets of his already uttered wisdom, he gave vent to his final, and what he declared to be his all-important advice, as follows:

"Put on a bright face for your customers, and smile pleasantly as you hand them what they ask for! A stale article, if you dip it in a good, warm, sunny smile, will go off better than a fresh one that you've scowled upon."

To this last apothegm poor Hepzibah responded with a sigh so deep and heavy that it almost rustled Uncle Venner quite away, like a withered leaf—as he was—before an autumnal gale. Recovering himself, however, he bent forward and with a good deal of feeling in his ancient visage, beckoned her nearer to him.

"When do you expect him home?" whispered he.

"Whom do you mean?" asked Hepzibah, turning pale.

"Ah? You don't love to talk about it," said Uncle Venner. "Well, well! We'll say no more, though there's word of it all over town. I remember him, Miss Hepzibah, before he could run alone!"

During the remainder of the day, poor Hepzibah acquitted herself even less creditably, as a shopkeeper, than in her earlier efforts. She appeared to be walking in a dream; or, more truly, the vivid life and reality assumed by her emotions made all outward occurrences unsubstantial, like the teasing phantasms of a half-conscious slumber. She still responded, mechanically, to the frequent summons of the shop bell, and, at the demand of her customers, went prying with vague eyes about the shop, proffering them one article after another, and thrusting aside—perversely, as most of them supposed—the identical thing they asked for. There is sad confusion, indeed, when the spirit thus flits away into the past, or into the more awful future, or, in any manner, steps across the spaceless boundary betwixt its own region and the actual world; where the body remains to guide itself as best it may, with little more than the mechanism of animal life. It is like death, without death's quiet privilege— its freedom from mortal care. Worst of all, when the actual duties are comprised in such petty details as now vexed the brooding soul of the old gentlewoman. As the animosity of fate would have it, there was a great influx of custom in the course of the afternoon. Hepzibah blundered to and fro about her small place of business, committing the most unheard-of errors: now stringing up twelve, and now seven, tallow candles, instead of ten to the pound; selling ginger for Scotch snuff, pins for needles, and needles for pins; misreckoning her change, sometimes to the public detriment, and much oftener to her own; and thus she went on, doing her utmost to bring chaos back again, until, at the close of the day's labor, to her inexplicable astonishment, she found the money drawer almost destitute of coin. After all her painful traffic, the whole proceeds were perhaps half a dozen coppers, and a questionable ninepence which ultimately proved to be copper likewise.

At this price, or at whatever price, she rejoiced that the day had reached its end. Never before had she had such a sense of the intolerable length of time that creeps between dawn and sunset, and of the miserable irksomeness of having aught to do, and of the better wisdom that it would be to lie down at once, in sullen resignation, and let life, and its toils and vexations, trample over one's prostrate body as they may! Hepzibah's final operation was with the little devourer of Jim Crow and the elephant, who now proposed to eat a camel. In her bewilderment, she offered him first a wooden dragoon, and next a handful of marbles; neither of which being adapted to his else omnivorous appetite, she hastily held out her whole remaining stock of natural history in gingerbread, and huddled the small customer out of the shop. She then muffled the bell in an unfinished stocking, and put up the oaken bar across the door.

During the latter process, an omnibus came to a standstill under the branches of the elm tree. Hepzibah's heart was in her mouth. Remote and dusky, and with no sunshine on all the intervening space, was that region of the Past whence her only guest might be expected to arrive! Was she to meet him now?

Somebody, at all events, was passing from the farthest interior of the omnibus towards its entrance. A gentleman alighted; but it was only to offer his hand to a young girl, whose slender figure, nowise needing such assistance, now lightly descended the steps, and made an airy little jump from the final one to the sidewalk. She rewarded her cavalier with a smile, the cheery glow of which was seen reflected on his own face as he re-entered the vehicle. The girl then turned towards the House of the Seven Gables, to the door of which, meanwhile—not the shop door, but the antique portal—the omnibusman had carried a light trunk and a bandbox. First giving a sharp rap of the old iron knocker, he left his passenger and her luggage at the doorstep, and departed.

"Who can it be?" thought Hepzibah, who had been screwing her visual organs into the acutest focus of which they were capable. "The girl must have mistaken the house!"

She stole softly into the hall, and, herself invisible, gazed through the dusty side lights of the portal at the young, blooming, and very cheerful face, which presented itself for admittance into the gloomy old mansion. It was a face to which almost any door would have opened of its own accord.

The young girl, so fresh, so unconventional, and yet so orderly and obedient to common rules, as you at once recognized her to be, was widely in contrast, at that moment, with everything about her. The sordid and ugly luxuriance of gigantic weeds that grew in the angle of the house, and the heavy projection that overshadowed her, and the timeworn framework of the door—none of these things belonged to her sphere. But, even as a ray of sunshine, fall into what dismal place it may, instantaneously creates for itself a propriety in being there, so did it seem altogether fit that the girl should be standing at the threshold. It was no less evidently proper that the door should swing open to admit her. The maiden lady herself, sternly inhospitable in her first purposes, soon began to feel that the door ought to be shoved back, and the rusty key be turned in the reluctant lock.

"Can it be Phoebe?" questioned she within herself. "It must be little Phoebe, for it can be nobody else—and there is a look of her father about her, too! But what does she want here? And how like a country cousin, to come down upon a poor body in this way, without so much as a day's notice, or asking whether she would be welcome! Well; she must have a night's lodging, I suppose; and tomorrow the child shall go back to her mother!"

Phoebe, it must be understood, was that one little off-shoot of the Pyncheon race to whom we have already referred, as a native of a rural part of New England, where the old fashions and feelings of relationship are still partially kept up. In her own circle, it was regarded as by no means improper for kinsfolk to visit one another without invitation, or preliminary and ceremonious warning. Yet, in consideration of Miss Hepzibah's recluse way of life, a letter had actually been written and despatched, conveying information of Phoebe's projected visit. This epistle, for three or four days past, had been in the pocket of the penny-postman, who, happening to have no other business in Pyncheon Street, had not yet made it convenient to call at the House of the Seven Gables.

"No! She can stay only one night," said Hepzibah, unbolting the door. "If Clifford were to find her here, it might disturb him!"

V

May and November

PHOEBE Pyncheon slept, on the night of her arrival, in a chamber that looked down on the garden of the old house. It fronted towards the east, so that at a very seasonable hour, a glow of crimson light came flooding through the window, and bathed the dingy ceiling and paper hangings in its own hue. There were curtains to Phoebe's bed; a dark, antique canopy, and ponderous festoons of a stuff which had been rich, and even magnificent, in its time; but which now brooded over the girl like a cloud, making a night in that one corner, while elsewhere it was beginning to be day. The morning light, however, soon stole into the aperture at the foot of the bed, betwixt those faded curtains. Finding the new guest there—with a bloom on her cheeks like the morning's own, and a gentle stir of departing slumber in her limbs, as when an early breeze moves the foliage—the dawn kissed her brow. It was the caress which a dewy maiden—such as the Dawn is, immortally—gives to her sleeping sister, partly from the impulse of irresistible fondness, and partly as a pretty hint that it is time now to unclose her eyes.

At the touch of those lips of light, Phoebe quietly awoke, and, for a moment, did not recognize where she was, nor how those heavy curtains chanced to be festooned around her. Nothing, indeed, was absolutely plain to her, except that it was now early morning, and that, whatever might happen next, it was proper, first of all, to get up and say her prayers. She was the more inclined to devotion from the grim aspect of the chamber and its furniture, especially the tall, stiff chairs; one of which stood close by her bedside, and looked as if some old-fashioned personage had been sitting there all night, and had vanished only just in season to escape discovery.

When Phoebe was quite dressed, she peeped out of the window, and saw a rosebush in the garden. Being a very tall one, and of luxuriant growth, it had been propped up against the side of the house, and was literally covered with a rare and very beautiful species of white rose. A large portion of them, as the girl afterwards discovered, had blight or mildew at their hearts; but, viewed at a fair distance, the whole rosebush looked as if it had been brought from Eden that very summer, together with the mold in which it grew. The truth was, nevertheless, that it had been planted by Alice Pyncheon—she was Phoebe's great-great-grand-aunt—in soil which, reckoning only its cultivation as a garden plat, was now unctuous with nearly two hundred years of vegetable decay. Growing as they did, however, out of the old earth, the flowers still sent a fresh and sweet incense up to their Creator; nor could it have been the less pure and acceptable because Phoebe's young breath mingled with it, as the fragrance floated past the window. Hastening down the creaking and carpetless staircase, she found her way into the garden, gathered some of the most perfect of the roses, and brought them to her chamber.

Little Phoebe was one of those persons who possess, as their exclusive patrimony, the gift of practical arrangement. It is a kind of natural magic that enables these favored ones to bring out the hidden capabilities of things around them; and particularly to give a look of comfort and habitableness to any place which, for however brief a period, may happen to be their home. A wild hut of underbrush, tossed together by wayfarers through the primitive forest, would acquire the home aspect by one night's lodging of such a woman, and would retain it long after her quiet figure had disappeared into the surrounding shade. No less a portion of such homely witchcraft was requisite to reclaim, as it were, Phoebe's waste, cheerless, and dusky chamber, which had been untenanted so long—except by spiders, and mice, and rats, and ghosts—that it was all overgrown with the desolation which watches to obliterate every trace of man's happier hours. What was precisely Phoebe's process we find it impossible to say. She appeared to have no preliminary design, but gave a touch here and another there; brought some articles of furniture to light and dragged others into the shadow; looped up or let down a window curtain; and, in the course of half an hour, had fully succeeded in throwing a kindly and hospitable smile over the apartment. No longer ago than the night before, it had resembled nothing so much as the old maid's heart; for there was neither sunshine nor household fire in one nor the other, and, save for ghosts and ghostly reminiscences, not a guest, for many years gone by, had entered the heart or the chamber.

There was still another peculiarity of this inscrutable charm. The bedchamber, no doubt, was a chamber of very great and varied experience, as a scene of human life: the joy of bridal nights had throbbed itself away here; new immortals had first drawn earthly breath here; and here old people had died. But—whether it were the white roses, or whatever the subtle influence might be—a person of delicate instinct would have known at once that it was now a maiden's bedchamber, and had been purified of all former evil and sorrow by her sweet breath and happy thoughts. Her dreams of the past night, being such cheerful ones, had exorcised the gloom, and now haunted the chamber in its stead.

After arranging matters to her satisfaction, Phoebe emerged from her chamber, with a purpose to descend again into the garden. Besides the rosebush, she had observed several other species of flowers growing there in a wilderness of neglect, and obstructing one another's development (as is often the parallel case in human society) by their uneducated entanglement and confusion. At the head of the stairs, however, she met Hepzibah, who, it being still early, invited her into a room which she would probably have called her boudoir, had her education embraced any such French phrase. It was strewn about with a few old books, and a workbasket, and a dusty writing desk; and had, on one side, a large, black article of furniture, of very strange appearance, which the old gentlewoman told Phoebe was a harpsichord. It looked more like a coffin than anything else; and, indeed— not having been played upon, or opened, for years—there must have been a vast deal of dead music in it, stifled for want of air. Human finger was hardly known to have touched its chords since the days of Alice Pyncheon, who had learned the sweet accomplishment of melody in Europe.

Hepzibah bade her young guest sit down, and, herself taking a chair nearby, looked as earnestly at Phoebe's trim little figure as if she expected to see right into its springs and motive secrets.

"Cousin Phoebe," said she, at last, "I really can't see my way clear to keep you with me."

These words, however, had not the inhospitable bluntness with which they may strike the reader; for the two relatives, in a talk before bedtime, had arrived at a certain degree of mutual understanding. Hepzibah knew enough to enable her to appreciate the circumstances (resulting from the second marriage of the girl's mother) which made it desirable for Phoebe to establish herself in another home. Nor did she misinterpret Phoebe's character, and the genial activity pervading it—one of the most valuable traits of the true New England woman—which had impelled her forth, as might be said, to seek her fortune, but with a self-respecting purpose to confer as much benefit as she could anywise receive. As one of her nearest kindred, she had naturally betaken herself to Hepzibah, with no idea of forcing herself on her cousin's protection, but only for a visit of a week or two, which might be indefinitely extended, should it prove for the happiness of both.

To Hepzibah's blunt observation, therefore, Phoebe replied, as frankly, and more cheerfully.

"Dear cousin, I cannot tell how it will be," said she. "But I really think we may suit one another much better than you suppose."

"You are a nice girl, I see it plainly," continued Hepzibah, "and it is not any question as to that point which makes me hesitate. But, Phoebe, this house of mine is but a melancholy place for a young person to be in. It lets in the wind and rain, and the snow, too, in the garret and upper chambers, in wintertime, but it never lets in the sunshine! And as for myself, you see what I am—a dismal and lonesome old woman (for I begin to call myself old, Phoebe), whose temper, I am afraid, is none of the best, and whose spirits are as bad as can be. I cannot make your life pleasant, Cousin Phoebe, neither can I so much as give you bread to eat."

"You will find me a cheerful little body," answered Phoebe, smiling, and yet with a kind of gentle dignity, "and I mean to earn my bread. You know I have not been brought up a Pyncheon. A girl learns many things in a New England village."

"Ah! Phoebe," said Hepzibah, sighing, "your knowledge would do but little for you here! And then it is a wretched thought that you should fling away your young days in a place like this. Those cheeks would not be so rosy after a month or two. Look at my face!"—and, indeed, the contrast was very striking. "You see how pale I am! It is my idea that the dust and continual decay of these old houses are unwholesome for the lungs."

"There is the garden, the flowers to be taken care of," observed Phoebe. "I should keep myself healthy with exercise in the open air."

"And, after all, child," exclaimed Hepzibah, suddenly rising, as if to dismiss the subject, "it is not for me to say who shall be a guest or inhabitant of the old Pyncheon House. Its master is coming."

"Do you mean Judge Pyncheon?" asked Phoebe, in surprise.

"Judge Pyncheon!" answered her cousin, angrily. "He will hardly cross the threshold while I live! No, no! But, Phoebe, you shall see the face of him I speak of."

She went in quest of the miniature already described, and returned with it in her hand. Giving it to Phoebe, she watched her features narrowly, and with a certain jealousy as to the mode in which the girl would show herself affected by the picture.

"How do you like the face?" asked Hepzibah.

"It is handsome—it is very beautiful!" said Phoebe, admiringly. "It is as sweet a face as a man's can be, or ought to be. It has something of a child's expression—and yet not childish—only one feels so very kindly towards him! He ought never to suffer anything. One would bear much for the sake of sparing him toil or sorrow. Who is it, Cousin Hepzibah?"

"Did you never hear," whispered her cousin, bending towards her, "of Clifford Pyncheon?"

"Never! I thought there were no Pyncheons left, except yourself and our cousin Jaffrey," answered Phoebe. "And yet I seem to have heard the name of Clifford Pyncheon.

Yes—from my father or my mother; but has he not been a long while dead?"

"Well, well, child, perhaps he has!" said Hepzibah, with a sad, hollow laugh, "but, in old houses like this, you know, dead people are very apt to come back again! We shall see. And, Cousin Phoebe, since, after all that I have said, your courage does not fail you, we will not part so soon. You are welcome, my child, for the present, to such a home as your kinswoman can offer you."

With this measured, but not exactly cold assurance of a hospitable purpose, Hepzibah kissed her cheek.

They now went belowstairs, where Phoebe—not so much assuming the office as attracting it to herself, by the magnetism of innate fitness—took the most active part in preparing breakfast. The mistress of the house, meanwhile, as is usual with persons of her stiff and unmalleable cast, stood mostly aside; willing to lend her aid, yet conscious that her natural inaptitude would be likely to impede the business in hand. Phoebe, and the fire that boiled the teakettle, were equally bright, cheerful, and efficient, in their respective offices. Hepzibah gazed forth from her habitual sluggishness, the necessary result of long solitude, as from another sphere. She could not help being interested, however, and even amused, at the readiness with which her new inmate adapted herself to the circumstances, and brought the house, moreover, and all its rusty old appliances, into a suitableness for her purposes. Whatever she did, too, was done without conscious effort, and with frequent outbreaks of song, which were exceedingly pleasant to the ear. This natural tunefulness made Phoebe seem like a bird in a shadowy tree; or conveyed the idea that the stream of life warbled through her heart as a brook sometimes warbles through a pleasant little dell. It betokened the cheeriness of an active temperament, finding joy in its activity, and, therefore, rendering it beautiful; it was a New England trait—the stern old stuff of Puritanism with a gold thread in the web.

Hepzibah brought out some old silver spoons with the family crest upon them, and a china tea set painted over with grotesque figures of man, bird, and beast, in as grotesque a landscape. These pictured people were odd humorists, in a world of their own—a world of vivid brilliancy, so far as color went, and still unfaded, although the teapot and small cups were as ancient as the custom itself of tea-drinking.

"Your great-great-great-great-grandmother had these cups, when she was married," said Hepzibah to Phoebe. "She was a Davenport, of a good family. They were almost the first teacups ever seen in the colony; and if one of them were to be broken, my heart would break with it. But it is nonsense to speak so about a brittle teacup, when I remember what my heart has gone through without breaking."

The cups—not having been used, perhaps, since Hepzibah's youth—had contracted no small burden of dust, which Phoebe washed away with so much care and delicacy as to satisfy even the proprietor of this invaluable china.

"What a nice little housewife you are!" exclaimed the latter, smiling, and, at the same time, frowning so prodigiously that the smile was sunshine under a thundercloud. "Do you do other things as well? Are you as good at your book as you are at washing teacups?"

"Not quite, I am afraid," said Phoebe, laughing at the form of Hepzibah's question. "But I was schoolmistress for the little children in our district last summer, and might have been so still."

"Ah! 'tis all very well!" observed the maiden lady, drawing herself up. "But these things must have come to you with your mother's blood. I never knew a Pyncheon that had any turn for them."

It is very queer, but not the less true, that people are generally quite as vain, or even more so, of their deficiencies than of their available gifts; as was Hepzibah of this native inapplicability, so to speak, of the Pyncheons to any useful purpose. She regarded it as an hereditary trait; and so, perhaps, it was, but, unfortunately, a morbid one, such as is often generated in families that remain long above the surface of society.

Before they left the breakfast table, the shop bell rang sharply, and Hepzibah set down the remnant of her final cup of tea, with a look of sallow despair that was truly piteous to behold. In cases of distasteful occupation, the second day is generally worse than the first; we return to the rack with all the soreness of the preceding torture in our limbs. At all events, Hepzibah had fully satisfied herself of the impossibility of ever becoming wonted to this peevishly obstreperous little bell. Ring as often as it might, the sound always smote upon her nervous system rudely and suddenly. And especially now, while, with her crested teaspoons and antique china, she was flattering herself with ideas of gentility, she felt an unspeakable disinclination to confront a customer.

"Do not trouble yourself, dear cousin!" cried Phoebe, starting lightly up. "I am shopkeeper today."

"You, child!" exclaimed Hepzibah. "What can a little country girl know of such matters?"

"Oh, I have done all the shopping for the family at our village store," said Phoebe. "And I have had a table at a fancy fair, and made better sales than anybody. These things are not to be learnt; they depend upon a knack that comes, I suppose," added she, smiling, "with one's mother's blood. You shall see that I am as nice a little saleswoman as I am a housewife!"

The old gentlewoman stole behind Phoebe, and peeped from the passageway into the shop, to note how she would manage her undertaking. It was a case of some intricacy. A very ancient woman, in a white short gown and a green petticoat, with a string of gold beads about her neck, and what looked like a nightcap on her head, had brought a quantity of yarn to barter for the commodities of the shop. She was probably the very last person in town who still kept the time-honored spinning wheel in constant revolution. It was worth while to hear the croaking and hollow tones of the old lady, and the pleasant voice of Phoebe, mingling in one twisted thread of talk; and still better to contrast their figures—so light and bloomy, so decrepit and dusky—with only the counter betwixt them, in one sense, but more than threescore years, in another. As for the bargain, it was wrinkled slyness and craft pitted against native truth and sagacity.

"Was not that well done? asked Phoebe, laughing, when the customer was gone.

"Nicely done, indeed, child!" answered Hepzibah. "I could not have gone through with it nearly so well. As you say, it must be a knack that belongs to you on the mother's side."

It is a very genuine admiration, that with which persons too shy or too awkward to take a due part in the bustling world regard the real actors in life's stirring scenes; so genuine, in fact, that the former are usually fain to make it palatable to their self-love, by assuming that these active and forcible qualities are incompatible with others, which they choose to deem higher and more important. Thus, Hepzibah was well content to acknowledge Phoebe's vastly superior gifts as a shopkeeper; she listened, with compliant ear, to her suggestion of various methods whereby the influx of trade might be increased, and rendered profitable, without a hazardous outlay of capital. She consented that the village maiden should manufacture yeast, both liquid and in cakes; and should brew a certain kind of beer, nectareous to the palate, and of rare stomachic virtues; and, moreover, should bake and exhibit for sale some little spice cakes, which whosoever tasted would longingly desire to taste again. All such proofs of a ready mind and skillful handiwork were highly acceptable to the aristocratic hucksteress, so long as she could murmur to herself with a grim smile, and a half-natural sigh, and a sentiment of mixed wonder, pity, and growing affection:

"What a nice little body she is! If she could only be a lady, too—but that's impossible! Phoebe is no Pyncheon. She takes everything from her mother."

As to Phoebe's not being a lady, or whether she were a lady or no, it was a point, perhaps, difficult to decide, but which could hardly have come up for judgment at all in any fair and healthy mind. Out of New England, it would be impossible to meet with a person combining so many lady-like attributes with so many others that form no necessary (if compatible) part of the character. She shocked no canon of taste; she was admirably in keeping with herself, and never jarred against surrounding circumstances. Her figure, to be sure—so small as to be almost childlike, and so elastic that motion seemed as easy or easier to it than rest—would hardly have suited one's idea of a countess. Neither did her face—with the brown ringlets on either side, and the slightly piquant nose, and the wholesome bloom, and the clear shade of tan, and the half a dozen freckles, friendly remembrancers of the April sun and breeze—precisely give us a right to call her beautiful. But there was both luster and depth in her eyes. She was very pretty; as graceful as a bird, and graceful much in the same way; as pleasant about the house as a gleam of sunshine falling on the floor through a shadow of twinkling leaves, or as a ray of firelight that dances on the wall while evening is drawing nigh. Instead of discussing her claim to rank among ladies, it would be preferable to regard Phoebe as the example of feminine grace and availability combined, in a state of society, if there were any such, where ladies did not exist. There it should be woman's office to move in the midst of practical affairs, and to gild them all, the very homeliest—were it even the scouring of pots and kettles—with an atmosphere of loveliness and joy.

Such was the sphere of Phoebe. To find the born and educated lady, on the other hand, we need look no farther than Hepzibah, our forlorn old maid, in her rustling and rusty silks, with her deeply cherished and ridiculous consciousness of long descent, her shadowy claims to princely territory, and, in the way of accomplishment, her recollections, it may be, of having formerly thrummed on a harpsichord, and walked a minuet, and worked an antique tapestry stitch on her sampler. It was a fair parallel between new Plebeianism and old Gentility.

It really seemed as if the battered visage of the House of the Seven Gables, black and heavy-browed as it still certainly looked, must have shown a kind of cheerfulness glimmering through its dusky windows as Phoebe passed to and fro in the interior. Otherwise, it is impossible to explain how the people of the neighborhood so soon became aware of the girl's presence. There was a great run of custom, setting steadily in, from about ten o'clock until towards noon; relaxing, somewhat, at dinnertime, but recommencing in the afternoon, and, finally, dying away a half an hour or so before the long day's sunset. One of the stanchest patrons was little Ned Higgins, the devourer of Jim Crow and the elephant, who today had signalized his omnivorous prowess by swallowing two dromedaries and a locomotive. Phoebe laughed, as she summed up her aggregate of sales upon the slate; while Hepzibah, first drawing on a pair of silk gloves, reckoned over the sordid accumulation of copper coin, not without silver intermixed, that had jingled into the till.

"We must renew our stock, Cousin Hepzibah!" cried the little saleswoman. "The gingerbread figures are all gone, and so are those Dutch wooden milkmaids, and most of our other playthings. There has been constant inquiry for cheap raisins, and a great cry for whistles, and trumpets, and jew's-harps; and at least a dozen little boys have asked for molasses candy. And we must contrive to get a peck of russet apples, late in the season as it is. But, dear cousin, what an enormous heap of copper! Positively a copper mountain!"

"Well done! well done! well done!" quoth Uncle Venner, who had taken occasion to shuffle in and out of the shop several times in the course of the day. "Here's a girl that will never end her days at my farm! Bless my eyes, what a brisk little soul!"

"Yes, Phoebe is a nice girl!" said Hepzibah, with a scowl of austere approbation. "But, Uncle Venner, you have known the family a great many years. Can you tell me whether there ever was a Pyncheon whom she takes after?"

"I don't believe there ever was," answered the venerable man. "At any rate, it never was my luck to see her like among them, nor, for that matter, anywhere else. I've seen a great deal of the world, not only in people's kitchens and back yards, but at the street corners, and on the wharves, and in other places where my business calls me; and I'm free to say, Miss Hepzibah, that I never knew a human creature do her work so much like one of God's angels as this child Phoebe does!"

Uncle Venner's eulogium, if it appear rather too high-strained for the person and occasion, had, nevertheless, a sense in which it was both subtile and true. There was a spiritual quality in Phoebe's activity. The life of the long and busy day—spent in occupations that might so easily have taken a squalid and ugly aspect—had been made pleasant, and even lovely, by the spontaneous grace with which these homely duties seemed to bloom out of her character; so that labor, while she dealt with it, had the easy and flexible charm of play. Angels do not toil, but let their good works grow out of them; and so did Phoebe.

The two relatives—the young maid and the old one—found time before nightfall, in the intervals of trade, to make rapid advances towards affection and confidence. A recluse, like Hepzibah, usually displays remarkable frankness, and at least temporary affability, on being absolutely cornered, and brought to the point of personal intercourse; like the angel whom Jacob wrestled with, she is ready to bless you when once overcome.

The old gentlewoman took a dreary and proud satisfaction in leading Phoebe from room to room of the house, and recounting the traditions with which, as we may say, the walls were lugubriously frescoed. She showed the indentations made by the lieutenant governor's sword hilt in the door panels of the apartment where old Colonel Pyncheon, a dead host, had received his affrighted visitors with an awful frown. The dusky terror of that frown, Hepzibah observed, was thought to be lingering ever since in the passageway. She bade Phoebe step into one of the tall chairs, and inspect the ancient map of the Pyncheon territory at the eastward. In a tract of land on which she laid her finger, there existed a silver mine, the locality of which was precisely pointed out in some memoranda of Colonel Pyncheon himself, but only to be made known when the family claim should be recognized by government. Thus it was for the interest of all New England that the Pyncheons should have justice done them. She told, too, how that there was undoubtedly an immense treasure of English guineas hidden somewhere about the house, or in the cellar, or possibly in the garden.

"If you should happen to find it, Phoebe," said Hepzibah, glancing aside at her with a grim yet kindly smile, "we will tie up the shop bell for good and all!"

"Yes, dear cousin," answered Phoebe, "but, in the meantime, I hear somebody ringing it!"

When the customer was gone, Hepzibah talked rather vaguely, and at great length about a certain Alice Pyncheon, who had been exceedingly beautiful and accomplished in her lifetime, a hundred years ago. The fragrance of her rich and delightful character still lingered about the place where she had lived, as a dried rosebud scents the drawer where it has withered and perished. This lovely Alice had met with some great and mysterious calamity, and had grown thin and white, and gradually faded out of the world. But, even now, she was supposed to haunt the House of the Seven Gables, and, a great many times—especially when one of the Pyncheons was to die—she had been heard playing sadly and beautifully on the harpsichord. One of these tunes, just as it had sounded from her spiritual touch, had been written down by an amateur of music; it was so exquisitely mournful that nobody, to this day, could bear to hear it played, unless when a great sorrow had made them know the still profounder sweetness of it.

"Was it the same harpsichord that you showed me?" inquired Phoebe.

"The very same," said Hepzibah. "It was Alice Pyncheon's harpsichord. When I was learning music, my father would never let me open it. So, as I could only play on my teacher's instrument, I have forgotten all my music long ago."

Leaving these antique themes, the old lady began to talk about the daguerreotypist, whom, as he seemed to be a well-meaning and orderly young man, and in narrow circumstances, she had permitted to take up his residence in one of the seven gables. But, on seeing more of Mr. Holgrave, she hardly knew what to make of him. He had the strangest companions imaginable; men with long beards, and dressed in linen blouses, and other such newfangled and ill-fitting garments; reformers, temperance lecturers, and all manner of cross-looking philanthropists; community men, and come-outers, as Hepzibah believed, who acknowledged no law, and ate no solid food, but lived on the scent of other people's cookery, and turned up their noses at the fare. As for the daguerreotypist, she had read a paragraph in a penny paper, the other day, accusing him of making a speech full of wild and disorganizing matter, at a meeting of his banditti-like associates. For her own part, she had reason to believe that he practiced animal magnetism, and, if such things were in fashion nowadays, should be apt to suspect him of studying the Black Art up there in his lonesome chamber.

"But, dear cousin," said Phoebe, "if the young man is so dangerous, why do you let him stay? If he does nothing worse, he may set the house on fire!"

"Why, sometimes," answered Hepzibah, "I have seriously made it a question, whether I ought not to send him away. But, with all his oddities, he is a quiet kind of a person, and has such a way of taking hold of one's mind that, without exactly liking him (for I don't know enough of the young man), I should be sorry to lose sight of him entirely. A woman clings to slight acquaintances when she lives so much alone as I do."

"But if Mr. Holgrave is a lawless person!" remonstrated Phoebe, a part of whose essence it was to keep within the limits of law.

"Oh!" said Hepzibah, carelessly—for, formal as she was, still, in her life's experience, she had gnashed her teeth against human law, "I suppose he has a law of his own!"

VI

Maule's Well

AFTER an early tea, the little country girl strayed into the garden. The enclosure had formerly been very extensive, but was now contracted within small compass, and hemmed about, partly by high wooden fences, and partly by the outbuildings of houses that stood on another street. In its center was a grass plat, surrounding a ruinous little structure, which showed just enough of its original design to indicate that it had once been a summerhouse. A hopvine, springing from last year's root, was beginning to clamber over it, but would be long in covering the roof with its green mantle. Three of the seven gables either fronted or looked sideways, with a dark solemnity of aspect, down into the garden.

The black, rich soil had fed itself with the decay of a long period of time; such as fallen leaves, the petals of flowers, and the stalks and seed vessels of vagrant and lawless plants, more useful after their death than ever while flaunting in the sun. The evil of these departed years would naturally have sprung up again, in such rank weeds (symbolic of the transmitted vices of society) as are always prone to root themselves about human dwellings. Phoebe saw, however, that their growth must have been checked by a degree of careful labor, bestowed daily and systematically on the garden. The white double rosebush had evidently been propped up anew against the house since the commencement of the season; and a pear tree and three damson trees, which, except a row of currant bushes, constituted the only varieties of fruit, bore marks of the recent amputation of several superfluous or defective limbs. There were also a few species of antique and hereditary flowers, in no very flourishing condition, but scrupulously weeded; as if some person, either out of love or curiosity, had been anxious to bring them to such perfection as they were capable of attaining. The remainder of the garden presented a well-selected assortment of esculent vegetables, in a praiseworthy state of advancement. Summer squashes, almost in their golden blossom; cucumbers, now evincing a tendency to spread away from the main stock, and ramble far and wide; two or three rows of string beans, and as many more that were about to festoon themselves on poles; tomatoes, occupying a site so sheltered and sunny that the plants were already gigantic, and promised an early and abundant harvest.

Phoebe wondered whose care and toil it could have been that had planted these vegetables, and kept the soil so clean and orderly. Not surely her cousin Hepzibah's, who had no taste nor spirits for the ladylike employment of cultivating flowers, and—with her recluse habits, and tendency to shelter herself within the dismal shadow of the house—would hardly have come forth under the speck of open sky to weed and hoe among the fraternity of beans and squashes.

It being her first day of complete estrangement from rural objects, Phoebe found an unexpected charm in this little nook of grass, and foliage, and aristocratic flowers, and plebeian vegetables. The eye of heaven seemed to look down into it pleasantly, and with a peculiar smile, as if glad to perceive that nature, elsewhere overwhelmed, and driven out of the dusty town, had here been able to retain a breathing place. The spot acquired a somewhat wilder grace, and yet a very gentle one, from the fact that a pair of robins had built their nest in the pear tree, and were making themselves exceedingly busy and happy in the dark intricacy of its boughs. Bees, too—strange to say—had thought it worth their while to come hither, possibly from the range of hives beside some farmhouse miles away. How many aerial voyages might they have made, in quest of honey, or honey-laden, betwixt dawn and sunset! Yet, late as it now was, there still arose a pleasant hum out of one or two of the squash blossoms, in the depths of which these bees were plying their golden labor. There was one other object in the garden which Nature might fairly claim as her inalienable property, in spite of whatever man could do to render it his own. This was a fountain, set round with a rim of old mossy stones, and paved, in its bed, with what appeared to be a sort of mosaic work of variously colored pebbles. The play and slight agitation of the water, in its upward gush, wrought magically with these variegated pebbles, and made a continually shifting apparition of quaint figures, vanishing too suddenly to be definable. Thence, swelling over the rim of moss-grown stones, the water stole away under the fence, through what we regret to call a gutter, rather than a channel.

Nor must we forget to mention a hen coop of very reverend antiquity that stood in the farther corner of the garden, not a great way from the fountain. It now contained only Chanticleer, his two wives, and a solitary chicken. All of them were pure specimens of a breed which had been transmitted down as an heirloom in the Pyncheon family, and were said, while in their prime, to have attained almost the size of turkeys, and, on the score of delicate flesh, to be fit for a prince's table. In proof of the authenticity of this legendary renown, Hepzibah could have exhibited the shell of a great egg, which an ostrich need hardly have been ashamed of. Be that as it might, the hens were now scarcely larger than pigeons, and had a queer, rusty, withered aspect, and a gouty kind of movement, and a sleepy and melancholy tone throughout all the variations of their clucking and cackling. It was evident that the race had degenerated, like many a noble race besides, in consequence of too strict a watchfulness to keep it pure. These feathered people had existed too long in their distinct variety; a fact of which the present representatives, judging by their lugubrious deportment, seemed to be aware. They kept themselves alive, unquestionably, and laid now and then an egg, and hatched a chicken; not for any pleasure of their own, but that the world might not absolutely lose what had once been so admirable a breed of fowls. The distinguishing mark of the hens was a crest of lamentably scanty growth, in these latter days, but so oddly and wickedly analogous to Hepzibah's turban, that Phoebe—to the poignant distress of her conscience, but inevitably—was led to fancy a general resemblance betwixt these forlorn bipeds and her respectable relative.

The girl ran into the house to get some crumbs of bread,

cold potatoes, and other such scraps as were suitable to the
accommodating appetite of fowls. Returning, she gave a
peculiar call, which they seemed to recognize. The chicken
crept through the pales of the coop and ran, with some show
of liveliness, to her feet, while Chanticleer and the ladies of
his household regarded her with queer, sidelong glances,
and then croaked one to another, as if communicating their
sage opinions of her character. So wise, as well as antique,
was their aspect, as to give color to the idea not merely that
they were the descendants of a time-honored race, but that
they had existed, in their individual capacity, ever since the
House of the Seven Gables was founded, and were somehow mixed up with its destiny. They were a species of
tutelary sprite, or Banshee; although winged and feathered
differently from most other guardian angels.

"Here, you odd little chicken!" said Phoebe. "Here are
some nice crumbs for you!"

The chicken, hereupon, though almost as venerable in
appearance as its mother—possessing, indeed, the whole
antiquity of its progenitors in miniature—mustered vivacity
enough to flutter upward and alight on Phoebe's shoulder.

"That little fowl pays you a high compliment!" said a
voice behind Phoebe.

Turning quickly, she was surprised at sight of a young
man, who had found access into the garden by a door
opening out of another gable than that whence she had
emerged. He held a hoe in his hand, and, while Phoebe was
gone in quest of the crumbs, had begun to busy himself with
drawing up fresh earth about the roots of the tomatoes.

"The chicken really treats you like an old acquaintance,"
continued he, in a quiet way, while a smile made his face
pleasanter than Phoebe at first fancied it. "Those venerable
personages in the coop, too, seem very affably disposed.
You are lucky to be in their good graces so soon! They have
known me much longer, but never honor me with any
familiarity, though hardly a day passes without my bringing
them food. Miss Hepzibah, I suppose, will interweave the
fact with her other traditions, and set it down that the fowls
know you to be a Pyncheon!"

"The secret is," said Phoebe, smiling, "that I have learned
how to talk with hens and chickens."

"Ah, but these hens," answered the young man, "these

hens of aristocratic lineage would scorn to understand the vulgar language of a barnyard fowl. I prefer to think—and so would Miss Hepzibah—that they recognize the family tone. For you are a Pyncheon?"

"My name is Phoebe Pyncheon," said the girl, with a manner of some reserve; for she was aware that her new acquaintance could be no other than the daguerreotypist, of whose lawless propensities the old maid had given her a disagreeable idea. "I did not know that my cousin Hepzibah's garden was under another person's care."

"Yes," said Holgrave. "I dig, and hoe, and weed, in this black old earth, for the sake of refreshing myself with what little nature and simplicity may be left in it, after men have so long sown and reaped here. I turn up the earth by way of pastime. My sober occupation, so far as I have any, is with a lighter material. In short, I make pictures out of sunshine; and, not to be too much dazzled with my own trade, I have prevailed with Miss Hepzibah to let me lodge in one of these dusky gables. It is like a bandage over one's eyes, to come into it. But would you like to see a specimen of my productions?"

"A daguerreotype likeness, do you mean?" asked Phoebe, with less reserve; for, in spite of prejudice, her own youthfulness sprang forward to meet his. "I don't much like pictures of that sort—they are so hard and stern; besides dodging away from the eye, and trying to escape altogether. They are conscious of looking very unamiable, I suppose, and therefore hate to be seen."

"If you would permit me," said the artist, looking at Phoebe, "I should like to try whether the daguerreotype can bring out disagreeable traits on a perfectly amiable face. But there certainly is truth in what you have said. Most of my likenesses do look unamiable; but the very sufficient reason, I fancy, is because the originals are so. There is a wonderful insight in heaven's broad and simple sunshine. While we give it credit only for depicting the merest surface, it actually brings out the secret character with a truth that no painter would ever venture upon, even could he detect it. There is, at least, no flattery in my humble line of art. Now, here is a likeness which I have taken over and over again, and still with no better result. Yet the original wears, to common eyes, a very different expression. It would gratify me to have your judgment on this character."

He exhibited a daguerreotype miniature in a morocco case. Phoebe merely glanced at it, and gave it back.

"I know the face," she replied, "for its stern eye has been following me about all day. It is my Puritan ancestor, who hangs yonder in the parlor. To be sure, you have found some way of copying the portrait without its black velvet cap and gray beard, and have given him a modern coat and satin cravat, instead of his cloak and band. I don't think him improved by your alterations."

"You would have seen other differences had you looked a little longer," said Holgrave, laughing, yet apparently much struck. "I can assure you that this is a modern face, and one which you will very probably meet. Now, the remarkable point is, that the original wears, to the world's eye—and, for aught I know, to his most intimate friends—an exceedingly pleasant countenance, indicative of benevolence, openness of heart, sunny good humor, and other praiseworthy qualities of that cast. The sun, as you see, tells quite another story, and will not be coaxed out of it, after half a dozen patient attempts on my part. Here we have the man, sly, subtle, hard, imperious, and, withal, cold as ice. Look at that eye! Would you like to be at its mercy? At that mouth! Could it ever smile? And yet, if you could only see the benign smile of the original! It is so much the more unfortunate, as he is a public character of some eminence, and the likeness was intended to be engraved."

"Well, I don't wish to see it any more," observed Phoebe, turning away her eyes. "It is certainly very like the old portrait. But my cousin Hepzibah has another picture, a miniature. If the original is still in the world, I think he might defy the sun to make him look stern and hard."

"You have seen that picture, then!" exclaimed the artist, with an expression of much interest. "I never did, but have a great curiosity to do so. And you judge favorably of the face?"

"There never was a sweeter one," said Phoebe. "It is almost too soft and gentle for a man's."

"Is there nothing wild in the eye?" continued Holgrave, so earnestly that it embarrassed Phoebe, as did also the quiet freedom with which he presumed on their so recent acquaintance. "Is there nothing dark or sinister anywhere? Could you not conceive the original to have been guilty of a great crime?"

"It is nonsense," said Phoebe, a little impatiently, "for us to talk about a picture which you have never seen. You mistake it for some other. A crime, indeed! Since you are a friend of my cousin Hepzibah's, you should ask her to show you the picture."

"It will suit my purpose still better to see the original," replied the daguerreotypist coolly. "As to his character, we need not discuss its points; they have already been settled by a competent tribunal, or one which called itself competent. But, stay! Do not go yet, if you please! I have a proposition to make you."

Phoebe was on the point of retreating, but turned back, with some hesitation; for she did not exactly comprehend his manner, although, on better observation, its feature seemed rather to be lack of ceremony than any approach to offensive rudeness. There was an odd kind of authority, too, in what he now proceeded to say, rather as if the garden were his own than a place to which he was admitted merely by Hepzibah's courtesy.

"If agreeable to you," he observed, "it would give me pleasure to turn over these flowers, and those ancient and respectable fowls, to your care. Coming fresh from country air and occupations, you will soon feel the need of some such out-of-door employment. My own sphere does not so much lie among flowers. You can trim and tend them, therefore, as you please; and I will ask only the least trifle of a blossom, now and then, in exchange for all the good, honest kitchen vegetables with which I propose to enrich Miss Hepzibah's table. So we will be fellow laborers, somewhat on the community system."

Silently, and rather surprised at her own compliance, Phoebe accordingly betook herself to weeding a flower bed, but busied herself still more with cogitations respecting this young man, with whom she so unexpectedly found herself on terms approaching to familiarity. She did not altogether like him. His character perplexed the little country girl, as it might a more practiced observer; for, while the tone of his conversation had generally been playful, the impression left on her mind was that of gravity, and, except as his youth modified it, almost sternness. She rebelled, as it were, against a certain magnetic element in the artist's nature, which he exercised towards her, possibly without being conscious of it.

After a little while, the twilight, deepened by the shadows of the fruit trees and the surrounding buildings, threw an obscurity over the garden.

"There," said Holgrave. "It is time to give over work! That last stroke of the hoe has cut off a bean stalk. Good night, Miss Phoebe Pyncheon! Any bright day, if you will put one of those rosebuds in your hair, and come to my rooms in Central street, I will seize the purest ray of sunshine, and make a picture of the flower and its wearer."

He retired towards his own solitary gable, but turned his head, on reaching the door, and called to Phoebe, with a tone which certainly had laughter in it, yet which seemed to be more than half in earnest.

"Be careful not to drink at Maule's well!" said he. "Neither drink nor bathe your face in it!"

"Maule's well!" answered Phoebe. "Is that it with the rim of mossy stones? I have no thought of drinking there—but why not?"

"Oh," rejoined the daguerreotypist, "because, like an old lady's cup of tea, it is water bewitched!"

He vanished; and Phoebe, lingering a moment, saw a glimmering light, and then the steady beam of a lamp, in a chamber of the gable. On returning into Hepzibah's apartment of the house, she found the low-studded parlor so dim and dusky that her eyes could not penetrate the interior. She was indistinctly aware, however, that the gaunt figure of the old gentlewoman was sitting in one of the straight-backed chairs, a little withdrawn from the window, the faint gleam of which showed the blanched paleness of her cheek, turned sideway towards a corner.

"Shall I light a lamp, Cousin Hepzibah?" she asked.

"Do, if you please, my dear child," answered Hepzibah. "But put it on the table in the corner of the passage. My eyes are weak; and I can seldom bear the lamplight on them."

What an instrument is the human voice! How wonderfully responsive to every emotion of the human soul! In Hepzibah's tone, at that moment, there was a certain rich depth and moisture, as if the words, commonplace as they were, had been steeped in the warmth of her heart. Again, while lighting the lamp in the kitchen, Phoebe fancied that her cousin spoke to her.

"In a moment, cousin!" answered the girl. "These matches just glimmer, and go out."

But, instead of a response from Hepzibah, she seemed to hear the murmur of an unknown voice. It was strangely indistinct, however, and less like articulate words than an unshaped sound, such as would be the utterance of feeling and sympathy, rather than of the intellect. So vague was it, that its impression or echo in Phoebe's mind was that of unreality. She concluded that she must have mistaken some other sound for that of the human voice; or else that it was altogether in her fancy.

She set the lighted lamp in the passage, and again entered the parlor. Hepzibah's form, though its sable outline mingled with the dusk, was now less imperfectly visible. In the remoter parts of the room, however, its walls being so ill adapted to reflect light, there was nearly the same obscurity as before.

"Cousin," said Phoebe, "did you speak to me just now?"

"No, child!" replied Hepzibah.

Fewer words than before, but with the same mysterious music in them! Mellow, melancholy, yet not mournful, the tone seemed to gush up out of the deep well of Hepzibah's heart, all steeped in its profoundest emotion. There was a tremor in it, too, that—as all strong feeling is electric—partly communicated itself to Phoebe. The girl sat silently for a moment. But soon, her senses being very acute, she became conscious of an irregular respiration in an obscure corner of the room. Her physical organization, moreover, being at once delicate and healthy, gave her a perception, operating with almost the effect of a spiritual medium, that somebody was near at hand.

"My dear cousin," asked she, overcoming an indefinable reluctance, "is there not someone in the room with us?"

"Phoebe, my dear little girl," said Hepzibah, after a moment's pause, "you were up betimes, and have been busy all day. Pray go to bed; for I am sure you must need rest. I will sit in the parlor awhile, and collect my thoughts. It has been my custom for more years, child, than you have lived!"

While thus dismissing her, the maiden lady stepped forward, kissed Phoebe, and pressed her to her heart, which beat against the girl's bosom with a strong, high, and tumultuous swell. How came there to be so much love in this desolate old heart, that it could afford to well over thus abundantly?

"Good night, cousin," said Phoebe, strangely affected by Hepzibah's manner. "If you begin to love me, I am glad!"

She retired to her chamber, but did not soon fall asleep, nor then very profoundly. At some uncertain period in the depths of night, and, as it were, through the thin veil of a dream, she was conscious of a footstep mounting the stairs heavily, but not with force and decision. The voice of Hepzibah, with a hush through it, was going up along with the footsteps; and, again, responsive to her cousin's voice, Phoebe heard that strange, vague murmur, which might be likened to an indistinct shadow of human utterance.

VII

The Guest

WHEN Phoebe awoke—which she did with the early twittering of the conjugal couple of robins in the pear tree—she
heard movements belowstairs, and, hastening down, found
Hepzibah already in the kitchen. She stood by a window,
holding a book in close contiguity to her nose, as if with the
hope of gaining an olfactory acquaintance with its contents,
since her imperfect vision made it not very easy to read
them. If any volume could have manifested its essential
wisdom in the mode suggested, it would certainly have been
the one now in Hepzibah's hand; and the kitchen, in such an
event, would forthwith have steamed with the fragrance of
venison, turkeys, capons, larded partridges, puddings, cakes,
and Christmas pies, in all manner of elaborate mixture and
concoction. It was a cookery book, full of innumerable old
fashions of English dishes, and illustrated with engravings,
which represented the arrangements of the table at such
banquets as it might have befitted a nobleman to give in the
great hall of his castle. And, amid these rich and potent
devices of the culinary art (not one of which, probably, had
been tested, within the memory of any man's grandfather),
poor Hepzibah was seeking for some nimble little titbit,
which, with what skill she had, and such materials as were at
hand, she might toss up for breakfast.

Soon, with a deep sigh, she put aside the savory volume,
and inquired of Phoebe whether old Speckle, as she called
one of the hens, had laid an egg the preceding day. Phoebe
ran to see, but returned without the expected treasure in her
hand. At that instant, however, the blast of a fish-dealer's

conch was heard, announcing his approach along the street. With energetic raps at the shopwindow, Hepzibah summoned the man in, and made purchase of what he warranted as the finest mackerel in his cart, and as fat a one as ever he felt with his finger so early in the season. Requesting Phoebe to roast some coffee—which she casually observed was the real Mocha, and so long kept that each of the small berries ought to be worth its weight in gold—the maiden lady heaped fuel into the vast receptacle of the ancient fireplace in such quantity as soon to drive the lingering dusk out of the kitchen. The country girl, willing to give her utmost assistance, proposed to make an Indian cake, after her mother's peculiar method, of easy manufacture, and which she could vouch for as possessing a richness, and, if rightly prepared, a delicacy, unequaled by any other mode of breakfast cake. Hepzibah gladly assenting, the kitchen was soon the scene of savory preparation. Perchance, amid their proper element of smoke, which eddied forth from the ill-constructed chimney, the ghosts of departed cookmaids looked wonderingly on, or peeped down the great breadth of the flue, despising the simplicity of the projected meal, yet ineffectually pining to thrust their shadowy hands into each inchoate dish. The half-starved rats, at any rate, stole visibly out of their hiding places, and sat on their hind legs, snuffing the fumy atmosphere, and wistfully awaiting an opportunity to nibble.

Hepzibah had no natural turn for cookery, and, to say the truth, had fairly incurred her present meagerness by often choosing to go without her dinner rather than be attendant on the rotation of the spit, or ebullition of the pot. Her zeal over the fire, therefore, was quite an heroic test of sentiment. It was touching, and positively worthy of tears (if Phoebe, the only spectator, except the rats and ghosts aforesaid, had not been better employed than in shedding them), to see her rake out a bed of fresh and glowing coals, and proceed to broil the mackerel. Her usually pale cheeks were all ablaze with heat and hurry. She watched the fish with as much tender care and minuteness of attention as if—we know not how to express it otherwise—as if her own heart were on the gridiron, and her immortal happiness were involved in its being done precisely to a turn!

Life, within doors, has few pleasanter prospects than a

neatly arranged and well-provisioned breakfast table. We come to it freshly, in the dewy youth of the day, and when our spiritual and sensual elements are in better accord than at a later period; so that the material delights of the morning meal are capable of being fully enjoyed, without any very grievous reproaches, whether gastric or conscientious, for yielding even a trifle overmuch to the animal department of our nature. The thoughts, too, that run around the ring of familiar guests have a piquancy and mirthfulness, and oftentimes a vivid truth, which more rarely find their way into the elaborate intercourse of dinner. Hepzibah's small and ancient table, supported on its slender and graceful legs, and covered with a cloth of the richest damask, looked worthy to be the scene and center of one of the cheerfulest of parties. The vapor of the broiled fish arose like incense from the shrine of a barbarian idol, while the fragrance of the Mocha might have gratified the nostrils of a tutelary Lar, or whatever power has scope over a modern breakfast table. Phoebe's Indian cakes were the sweetest offering of all—in their hue befitting the rustic altars of the innocent and golden age—or, so brightly yellow were they, resembling some of the bread which was changed to glistening gold when Midas tried to eat it. The butter must not be forgotten—butter which Phoebe herself had churned, in her own rural home, and brought it to her cousin as a propitiatory gift—smelling of clover blossoms, and diffusing the charm of pastoral scenery through the dark-paneled parlor. All this, with the quaint gorgeousness of the old china cups and saucers, and the crested spoons, and a silver cream jug (Hepzibah's only other article of plate, and shaped like the rudest porringer), set out a board at which the stateliest of old Colonel Pyncheon's guests need not have scorned to take his place. But the Puritan's face scowled down out of the picture, as if nothing on the table pleased his appetite.

By way of contributing what grace she could, Phoebe gathered some roses and a few other flowers, possessing either scent or beauty, and arranged them in a glass pitcher, which, having long ago lost its handle, was so much the fitter for a flower vase. The early sunshine—as fresh as that which peeped into Eve's bower while she and Adam sat at breakfast there—came twinkling through the branches of the pear tree, and fell quite across the table. All was now ready. There were chairs and plates for three. A chair and plate for Hepzibah, the same for Phoebe—but what other guest did her cousin look for?

Throughout this preparation, there had been a constant tremor in Hepzibah's frame; an agitation so powerful that Phoebe could see the quivering of her gaunt shadow, as thrown by the firelight on the kitchen wall, or by the sunshine on the parlor floor. Its manifestations were so various, and agreed so little with one another, that the girl knew not what to make of it. Sometimes it seemed an ecstasy of delight and happiness. At such moments, Hepzibah would fling out her arms, and infold Phoebe in them, and kiss her cheek as tenderly as ever her mother had; she appeared to do so by an inevitable impulse, and as if her bosom were oppressed with tenderness, of which she must needs pour out a little, in order to gain breathing room. The next moment, without any visible cause for the change, her unwonted joy shrank back, appalled, as it were, and clothed itself in mourning; or it ran and hid itself, so to speak, in the dungeon of her heart, where it had long lain chained, while a cold, spectral sorrow took the place of the imprisoned joy, that was afraid to be enfranchised—a sorrow as black as that was bright. She often broke into a little, nervous, hysteric laugh, more touching than any tears could be; and forthwith, as if to try which was the most touching, a gush of tears would follow; or perhaps the laughter and tears came both at once, and surrounded our poor Hepzibah, in a moral sense, with a kind of pale, dim rainbow. Towards Phoebe, as we have said, she was affectionate—far tenderer than ever before, in their brief acquaintance, except for that one kiss on the preceding night—yet with a continually recurring pettishness and irritability. She would speak sharply to her; then, throwing aside all the starched reserve of her ordinary manner, ask pardon, and the next instant renew the just-forgiven injury.

At last, when their mutual labor was all finished, she took Phoebe's hand in her own trembling one.

"Bear with me, my dear child," she cried, "for truly my heart is full to the brim! Bear with me; for I love you, Phoebe, though I speak so roughly! Think nothing of it, dearest child! By and by, I shall be kind, and only kind!"

"My dearest cousin, cannot you tell me what has happened?" asked Phoebe, with a sunny and tearful sympathy. "What is it that moves you so?"

"Hush! hush! He is coming!" whispered Hepzibah, hastily wiping her eyes. "Let him see you first, Phoebe; for you are young and rosy, and cannot help letting a smile break out whether or no. He always liked bright faces! And mine is old now, and the tears are hardly dry on it. He never could abide tears. There; draw the curtain a little, so that the shadow may fall across his side of the table! But let there be a good deal of sunshine, too; for he never was fond of gloom, as some people are. He has had but little sunshine in his life—poor Clifford—and, oh, what a black shadow! Poor, poor Clifford!"

Thus murmuring in an undertone, as if speaking rather to her own heart than to Phoebe, the old gentlewoman stepped on tiptoe about the room, making such arrangements as suggested themselves at the crisis.

Meanwhile, there was a step in the passageway above-stairs. Phoebe recognized it as the same which had passed upward, as through her dream, in the nighttime. The approaching guest, whoever it might be, appeared to pause at the head of the staircase; he paused twice or thrice in the descent; he paused again at the foot. Each time, the delay seemed to be without purpose, but rather from a forgetfulness of the purpose which had set him in motion, or as if the person's feet came involuntarily to a standstill because the motive power was too feeble to sustain his progress. Finally, he made a long pause at the threshold of the parlor. He took hold of the knob of the door; then loosened his grasp without opening it. Hepzibah, her hands convulsively clasped, stood gazing at the entrance.

"Dear Cousin Hepzibah, pray don't look so!" said Phoebe, trembling; for her cousin's emotion, and this mysteriously reluctant step, made her feel as if a ghost were coming into the room. "You really frighten me! Is something awful going to happen?"

"Hush!" whispered Hepzibah. "Be cheerful! Whatever may happen, be nothing but cheerful!"

The final pause at the threshold proved so long that Hepzibah, unable to endure the suspense, rushed forward, threw open the door, and led in the stranger by the hand. At the first glance, Phoebe saw an elderly personage, in an old-fashioned dressing gown of faded damask, and wearing his gray or almost white hair of an unusual length. It quite overshadowed his forehead, except when he thrust it back, and stared vaguely about the room. After a very brief inspection of his face, it was easy to conceive that his footstep must necessarily be such an one as that which, slowly, and with as indefinite an aim as a child's first journey across a floor, had just brought him hitherward. Yet there were no tokens that his physical strength might not have sufficed for a free and determined gait. It was the spirit of the man that could not walk. The expression of his countenance—while, notwithstanding, it had the light of reason in it—seemed to waver, and glimmer, and nearly to die away, and feebly to recover itself again. It was like a flame which we see twinkling among half-extinguished embers; we gaze at it more intently than if it were a positive blaze, gushing vividly upward—more intently, but with a certain impatience, as if it ought either to kindle itself into satisfactory splendor, or be at once extinguished.

For an instant after entering the room, the guest stood still, retaining Hepzibah's hand, instinctively, as a child does that of the grown person who guides it. He saw Phoebe, however, and caught an illumination from her youthful and pleasant aspect, which, indeed, threw a cheerfulness about the parlor, like the circle of reflected brilliancy around the glass vase of flowers that was standing in the sunshine. He made a salutation, or, to speak nearer the truth, an ill-defined, abortive attempt at courtesy. Imperfect as it was, however, it conveyed an idea, or, at least, gave a hint, of indescribable grace, such as no practiced art of external manners could have attained. It was too slight to seize upon at the instant; yet, as recollected afterwards, seemed to transfigure the whole man.

"Dear Clifford," said Hepzibah, in the tone with which one soothes a wayward infant, "this is our cousin Phoebe— little Phoebe Pyncheon—Arthur's only child, you know. She has come from the country to stay with us awhile; for our old house has grown to be very lonely now."

"Phoebe? Phoebe Pyncheon? Phoebe?" repeated the guest, with a strange, sluggish, ill-defined utterance. "Arthur's child! Ah, I forget! No matter! She is very welcome!"

"Come, dear Clifford, take this chair," said Hepzibah,

leading him to his place. "Pray, Phoebe, lower the curtain a very little more. Now let us begin breakfast."

The guest seated himself in the place assigned him, and looked strangely around. He was evidently trying to grapple with the present scene, and bring it home to his mind with a more satisfactory distinctness. He desired to be certain, at least, that he was here, in the low-studded, cross-beamed, oaken-paneled parlor, and not in some other spot, which had stereotyped itself into his senses. But the effort was too great to be sustained with more than a fragmentary success. Continually, as we may express it, he faded away out of his place; or, in other words, his mind and consciousness took their departure, leaving his wasted, gray, and melancholy figure—a substantial emptiness, a material ghost—to occupy his seat at table. Again, after a blank moment, there would be a flickering taper-gleam in his eyeballs. It betokened that his spiritual part had returned, and was doing its best to kindle the heart's household fire, and light up intellectual lamps in the dark and ruinous mansion, where it was doomed to be a forlorn inhabitant.

At one of these moments of less torpid, yet still imperfect animation, Phoebe became convinced of what she had at first rejected as too extravagant and startling an idea. She saw that the person before her must have been the original of the beautiful miniature in her cousin Hepzibah's possession. Indeed, with a feminine eye for costume, she had at once identified the damask dressing gown, which enveloped him, as the same, in figure, material, and fashion, with that so elaborately represented in the picture. This old, faded garment, with all its pristine brilliancy extinct, seemed, in some indescribable way, to translate the wearer's untold misfortune, and make it perceptible to the beholder's eye. It was the better to be discerned, by this exterior type, how worn and old were the soul's more immediate garments; that form and countenance, the beauty and grace of which had almost transcended the skill of the most exquisite of artists. It could the more adequately be known that the soul of the man must have suffered some miserable wrong, from its earthly experience. There he seemed to sit, with a dim veil of decay and ruin betwixt him and the world, but through which, at flitting intervals, might be caught the same expression, so refined, so softly imaginative, which

Malbone—venturing a happy touch, with suspended breath—
had imparted to the miniature! There had been something
so innately characteristic in this look, that all the dusky
years, and the burden of unfit calamity which had fallen
upon him, did not suffice utterly to destroy it.

Hepzibah had now poured out a cup of deliciously fragrant coffee, and presented it to her guest. As his eyes met
hers, he seemed bewildered and disquieted.

"Is this you, Hepzibah?" he murmured, sadly; then, more
apart, and perhaps unconscious that he was overheard, "How
changed! how changed! And is she angry with me? Why
does she bend her brow so?"

Poor Hepzibah! It was that wretched scowl, which time
and her nearsightedness, and the fret of inward discomfort,
had rendered so habitual that any vehemence of mood invariably evoked it. But at the indistinct murmur of his
words, her whole face grew tender, and even lovely, with
sorrowful affection; the harshness of her features disappeared, as it were, behind the warm and misty glow.

"Angry!" she repeated. "Angry with you, Clifford!"

Her tone, as she uttered the exclamation, had a plaintive
and really exquisite melody thrilling through it, yet without
subduing a certain something which an obtuse auditor might
still have mistaken for asperity. It was as if some transcen-
dent musician should draw a soul-thrilling sweetness out of a
cracked instrument, which makes its physical imperfection
heard in the midst of ethereal harmony—so deep was the
sensibility that found an organ in Hepzibah's voice!

"There is nothing but love here, Clifford," she added,
"nothing but love! You are at home!"

The guest responded to her tone by a smile, which did not
half light up his face. Feeble as it was, however, and gone in
a moment, it had a charm of wonderful beauty. It was
followed by a coarser expression; or one that had the effect
of coarseness on the fine mold and outline of his countenance, because there was nothing intellectual to temper it.
It was a look of appetite. He ate food with what might
almost be termed voracity; and seemed to forget himself,
Hepzibah, the young girl, and everything else around him,
in the sensual enjoyment which the bountifully spread table
afforded. In his natural system, though high-wrought and
delicately refined, a sensibility to the delights of the palate

was probably inherent. It would have been kept in check, however, and even converted into an accomplishment, and one of the thousand modes of intellectual culture, had his more ethereal characteristics retained their vigor. But as it existed now, the effect was painful and made Phoebe droop her eyes.

In a little while, the guest became sensible of the fragrance of the yet untasted coffee. He quaffed it eagerly. The subtle essence acted on him like a charmed draught, and caused the opaque substance of his animal being to grow transparent, or, at least, translucent; so that a spiritual gleam was transmitted through it, with a clearer luster than hitherto.

"More, more!" he cried, with nervous haste in his utterance, as if anxious to retain his grasp of what sought to escape him. "This is what I need! Give me more!"

Under this delicate and powerful influence, he sat more erect, and looked out from his eyes with a glance that took note of what it rested on. It was not so much that his expression grew more intellectual; this, though it had its share, was not the most peculiar effect. Neither was what we call the moral nature so forcibly awakened as to present itself in remarkable prominence. But a certain fine temper of being was now not brought out in full relief, but changeably and imperfectly betrayed, of which it was the function to deal with all beautiful and enjoyable things. In a character where it should exist as the chief attribute, it would bestow on its possessor an exquisite taste, and an enviable susceptibility of happiness. Beauty would be his life; his aspirations would all tend towards it; and, allowing his frame and physical organs to be in consonance, his own developments would likewise be beautiful. Such a man should have nothing to do with sorrow; nothing with strife; nothing with the martyrdom which, in an infinite variety of shapes, awaits those who have the heart, and will, and conscience, to fight a battle with the world. To these heroic tempers, such martyrdom is the richest meed in the world's gift. To the individual before us, it could only be a grief, intense in due proportion with the severity of the infliction. He had no right to be a martyr; and, beholding him so fit to be happy and so feeble for all other purposes, a generous, strong, and noble spirit would, methinks, have been ready to sacrifice what little enjoyment it might have planned for itself—it would have flung down the hopes, so paltry in its regard—if thereby the wintry blasts of our rude sphere might come tempered to such a man.

Not to speak it harshly or scornfully, it seemed Clifford's nature to be a sybarite. It was perceptible, even there, in the dark old parlor, in the inevitable polarity with which his eyes were attracted towards the quivering play of sunbeams through the shadowy foliage. It was seen in his appreciating notice of the vase of flowers, the scent of which he inhaled with a zest almost peculiar to a physical organization so refined that spiritual ingredients are molded in with it. It was betrayed in the unconscious smile with which he regarded Phoebe, whose fresh and maidenly figure was both sunshine and flowers—their essence, in a prettier and more agreeable mode of manifestation. Not less evident was this love and necessity for the Beautiful, in the instinctive caution with which, even so soon, his eyes turned away from his hostess, and wandered to any quarter rather than come back. It was Hepzibah's misfortune, not Clifford's fault. How could he—so yellow as she was, so wrinkled, so sad of mien, with that odd uncouthness of a turban on her head, and that most perverse of scowls contorting her brow—how could he love to gaze at her? But did he owe her no affection for so much as she had silently given? He owed her nothing. A nature like Clifford's can contract no debts of that kind. It is—we say it without censure, nor in diminution of the claim which it indefeasibly possesses on beings of another mold—it is always selfish in its essence; and we must give it leave to be so, and heap up our heroic and disinterested love upon it so much the more, without a recompense. Poor Hepzibah knew this truth, or, at least, acted on the instinct of it. So long estranged from what was lovely as Clifford had been, she rejoiced—rejoiced, though with a present sigh, and a secret purpose to shed tears in her own chamber—that he had brighter objects now before his eyes than her aged and uncomely features. They never possessed a charm; and if they had, the canker of her grief for him would long since have destroyed it.

The guest leaned back in his chair. Mingled in his countenance with a dreamy delight, there was a troubled look of effort and unrest. He was seeking to make himself more fully sensible of the scene around him; or, perhaps, dreading it to be a dream, or a play of imagination, was vexing the fair moment with a struggle for some added brilliancy and more durable illusion.

"How pleasant! How delightful!" he murmured, but not as if addressing anyone. "Will it last? How balmy the atmosphere through that open window! An open window! How beautiful that play of sunshine! Those flowers, how very fragrant! That young girl's face, how cheerful, how blooming —a flower with the dew on it, and sunbeams in the dewdrops! Ah! This must be all a dream! A dream! A dream! But it has quite hidden the four stone walls!"

Then his face darkened, as if the shadow of a cavern or a dungeon had come over it; there was no more light in its expression than might have come through the iron grates of a prison window—still lessening, too, as if he were sinking farther into the depths. Phoebe (being of that quickness and activity of temperament that she seldom long refrained from taking a part, and generally a good one, in what was going forward) now felt herself moved to address the stranger.

"Here is a new kind of rose, which I found this morning in the garden," said she, choosing a small crimson one from among the flowers in the vase. "There will be but five or six on the bush this season. This is the most perfect of them all; not a speck of blight or mildew in it. And how sweet it is—sweet like no other rose! One can never forget that scent!"

"Ah! Let me see—let me hold it!" cried the guest, eagerly seizing the flower, which, by the spell peculiar to remembered odors, brought innumerable associations along with the fragrance that it exhaled. "Thank you! This has done me good. I remember how I used to prize this flower—long ago, I suppose, very long ago!—or was it only yesterday? It makes me feel young again! Am I young? Either this remembrance is singularly distinct, or this consciousness strangely dim! But how kind of the fair young girl! Thank you! Thank you!"

The favorable excitement derived from this little crimson rose afforded Clifford the brightest moment which he enjoyed at the breakfast table. It might have lasted longer, but that his eyes happened, soon afterwards, to rest on the face of the old Puritan, who, out of his dingy frame and lusterless canvas, was looking down on the scene like a ghost, and a most ill-tempered and ungenial one. The guest made an impatient gesture of the hand, and addressed Hepzibah with what might easily be recognized as the licensed irritability of a petted member of the family.

"Hepzibah! Hepzibah!" cried he with no little force and distinctness. "Why do you keep that odious picture on the wall? Yes, yes! That is precisely your taste! I have told you, a thousand times, that it was the evil genius of the house—my evil genius particularly! Take it down, at once!"

"Dear Clifford," said Hepzibah, sadly, "you know it cannot be!"

"Then, at all events," continued he, still speaking with some energy, "pray cover it with a crimson curtain, broad enough to hang in folds, and with a golden border and tassels. I cannot bear it! It must not stare me in the face!"

"Yes, dear Clifford, the picture shall be covered," said Hepzibah, soothingly. "There is a crimson curtain in a trunk abovestairs, a little faded and moth-eaten, I'm afraid, but Phoebe and I will do wonders with it."

"This very day, remember!" said he; and then added, in a low, self-communing voice, "Why should we live in this dismal house at all? Why not go to the South of France—to Italy—Paris, Naples, Venice, Rome? Hepzibah will say we have not the means. A droll idea that!"

He smiled to himself, and threw a glance of fine sarcastic meaning towards Hepzibah.

But the several moods of feeling, faintly as they were marked, through which he had passed, occurring in so brief an interval of time, had evidently wearied the stranger. He was probably accustomed to a sad monotony of life, not so much flowing in a stream, however sluggish, as stagnating in a pool around his feet. A slumberous veil diffused itself over his countenance, and had an effect, morally speaking, on its naturally delicate and elegant outline, like that which a brooding mist, with no sunshine in it, throws over the features of a landscape. He appeared to become grosser—almost cloddish. If aught of interest or beauty—even ruined beauty— had heretofore been visible in this man, the beholder might now begin to doubt it, and to accuse his own imagination of deluding him with whatever grace had flickered over that visage, and whatever exquisite luster had gleamed in those filmy eyes.

Before he had quite sunken away, however, the sharp and peevish tinkle of the shop bell made itself audible. Striking most disagreeably on Clifford's auditory organs and the characteristic sensibility of his nerves, it caused him to start upright out of his chair.

"Good heavens, Hepzibah! What horrible disturbance have we now in the house?" cried he, wreaking his resentful impatience—as a matter of course, and a custom of old—on the one person in the world that loved him. "I have never heard such a hateful clamor! Why do you permit it? In the name of all dissonance, what can it be?"

It was very remarkable into what prominent relief—even as if a dim picture should leap suddenly from its canvas— Clifford's character was thrown by this apparently trifling annoyance. The secret was that an individual of his temper can always be pricked more acutely through his sense of the beautiful and harmonious than through his heart. It is even possible—for similar cases have often happened—that if Clifford, in his foregoing life, had enjoyed the means of cultivating his taste to its utmost perfectibility, that subtile attribute might, before this period, have completely eaten out or filed away his affections. Shall we venture to pronounce, therefore, that his long and black calamity may not have had a redeeming drop of mercy at the bottom?

"Dear Clifford, I wish I could keep the sound from your ears," said Hepzibah, patiently, but reddening with a painful suffusion of shame. "It is very disagreeable even to me. But, do you know, Clifford, I have something to tell you? This ugly noise—pray run, Phoebe, and see who is there! —this naughty little tinkle is nothing but our shop bell!"

"Shop bell!" repeated Clifford, with a bewildered stare.

"Yes, our shop bell," said Hepzibah, a certain natural dignity, mingled with deep emotion, now asserting itself in her manner. "For you must know, dearest Clifford, that we are very poor. And there was no other resource but either to accept assistance from a hand that I would push aside (and so would you!) were it to offer bread when we were dying for it—no help, save from him, or else to earn our subsistence with my own hands! Alone, I might have been content to starve. But you were to be given back to me! Do you think, then, dear Clifford," added she, with a wretched smile, "that I have brought an irretrievable disgrace on the old house, by opening a little shop in the front gable? Our great-great-grandfather did the same, when there was far less need! Are you ashamed of me?"

"Shame! Disgrace! Do you speak these words to me, Hepzibah?" said Clifford, not angrily, however; for when a man's spirit has been thoroughly crushed, he may be peevish at small offenses, but never resentful of great ones. So he spoke with only a grieved emotion. "It was not kind to say so, Hepzibah! What shame can befall me now?"

And then the unnerved man—he that had been born for enjoyment, but had met a doom so very wretched—burst into a woman's passion of tears. It was but of brief continuance, however; soon leaving him in a quiescent, and, to judge by his countenance, not an uncomfortable state. From this mood, too, he partially rallied for an instant, and looked at Hepzibah with a smile, the keen, half-derisory purport of which was a puzzle to her.

"Are we so very poor, Hepzibah?" said he.

Finally, his chair being deep and softly cushioned, Clifford fell asleep. Hearing the more regular rise and fall of his breath (which, however, even then, instead of being strong and full, had a feeble kind of tremor, corresponding with the lack of vigor in his character)—hearing these tokens of settled slumber, Hepzibah seized the opportunity to peruse his face more attentively than she had yet dared to do. Her heart melted away in tears; her profoundest spirit sent forth a moaning voice, low, gentle, but inexpressibly sad. In this depth of grief and pity, she felt that there was no irreverence in gazing at his altered, aged, faded, ruined face. But no sooner was she a little relieved than her conscience smote her for gazing curiously at him, now that he was so changed; and, turning hastily away, Hepzibah let down the curtain over the sunny window, and left Clifford to slumber there.

VIII

The Pyncheon of Today

PHOEBE, on entering the shop, beheld there the already familiar face of the little devourer—if we can reckon his mighty deeds aright—of Jim Crow, the elephant, the camel, the dromedaries, and the locomotive. Having expended his private fortune, on the two preceding days, in the purchase of the above unheard-of luxuries, the young gentleman's present errand was on the part of his mother, in quest of three eggs and half a pound of raisins. These articles Phoebe accordingly supplied, and, as a mark of gratitude for his previous patronage, and a slight superadded morsel after breakfast, put likewise into his hand a whale! The great fish, reversing his experience with the prophet of Nineveh, immediately began his progress down the same red pathway of fate whither so varied a caravan had preceded him. This remarkable urchin, in truth, was the very emblem of old Father Time, both in respect of his all-devouring appetite for men and things, and because he, as well as Time, after ingulfing thus much of creation, looked almost as youthful as if he had been just that moment made.

After partly closing the door, the child turned back, and mumbled something to Phoebe, which, as the whale was but half disposed of, she could not perfectly understand.

"What did you say, my little fellow?" asked she.

"Mother wants to know," repeated Ned Higgins, more distinctly, "how Old Maid Pyncheon's brother does? Folks say he has got home."

"My cousin Hepzibah's brother!" exclaimed Phoebe, surprised at this sudden explanation of the relationship be-

348

tween Hepzibah and her guest. "Her brother! And where can he have been?"

The little boy only put his thumb to his broad snub nose, with that look of shrewdness which a child, spending much of his time in the street, so soon learns to throw over his features, however unintelligent in themselves. Then, as Phoebe continued to gaze at him, without answering his mother's message, he took his departure.

As the child went down the steps, a gentleman ascended them, and made his entrance into the shop. It was the portly, and, had it possessed the advantage of a little more height, would have been the stately figure of a man considerably in the decline of life, dressed in a black suit of some thin stuff, resembling broadcloth as closely as possible. A gold-headed cane, of rare Oriental wood, added materially to the high respectability of his aspect, as did also a neck cloth of the utmost snowy purity, and the conscientious polish of his boots. His dark, square countenance, with its almost shaggy depth of eyebrows, was naturally impressive, and would, perhaps, have been rather stern, had not the gentleman considerately taken upon himself to mitigate the harsh effect by a look of exceeding good humor and benevolence. Owing, however, to a somewhat massive accumulation of animal substance about the lower region of his face, the look was, perhaps, unctuous, rather than spiritual, and had, so to speak, a kind of fleshly effulgence, not altogether so satisfactory as he doubtless intended it to be. A susceptible observer, at any rate, might have regarded it as affording very little evidence of the general benignity of soul whereof it purported to be the outward reflection. And if the observer chanced to be ill-natured, as well as acute and susceptible, he would probably suspect that the smile on the gentleman's face was a good deal akin to the shine on his boots, and that each must have cost him and his bootblack, respectively, a good deal of hard labor to bring out and preserve them.

As the stranger entered the little shop, where the projection of the second story and the thick foliage of the elm tree, as well as the commodities at the window, created a sort of gray medium, his smile grew as intense as if he had set his heart on counteracting the whole gloom of the atmosphere (besides any moral gloom pertaining to Hepzibah and her inmates) by the unassisted light of his countenance. On perceiving a young rosebud of a girl, instead of the gaunt presence of the old maid, a look of surprise was manifest. He at first knit his brows; then smiled with more unctuous benignity than ever.

"Ah, I see how it is!" said he, in a deep voice—a voice which, had it come from the throat of an uncultivated man, would have been gruff, but, by dint of careful training, was now sufficiently agreeable. "I was not aware that Miss Hepzibah Pyncheon had commenced business under such favorable auspices. You are her assistant, I suppose?"

"I certainly am," answered Phoebe, and added, with a little air of ladylike assumption (for, civil as the gentleman was, he evidently took her to be a young person serving for wages), "I am a cousin of Miss Hepzibah, on a visit to her."

"Her cousin—and from the country? Pray pardon me, then," said the gentleman, bowing and smiling, as Phoebe never had been bowed to nor smiled on before. "In that case, we must be better acquainted; for, unless I am sadly mistaken, you are my own little kinswoman likewise! Let me see—Mary? Dolly? Phoebe? Yes, Phoebe is the name! Is it possible that you are Phoebe Pyncheon, only child of my dear cousin and classmate, Arthur? Ah, I see your father now, about your mouth! Yes, yes! We must be better acquainted! I am your kinsman, my dear. Surely you must have heard of Judge Pyncheon?"

As Phoebe courtesied in reply, the Judge bent forward, with the pardonable and even praiseworthy purpose—considering the nearness of blood, and the difference of age—of bestowing on his young relative a kiss of acknowledged kindred and natural affection. Unfortunately (without design, or only with such instinctive design as gives no account of itself to the intellect) Phoebe, just at the critical moment, drew back; so that her highly respectable kinsman, with his body bent over the counter, and his lips protruded, was betrayed into the rather absurd predicament of kissing the empty air. It was a modern parallel to the case of Ixion embracing a cloud, and was so much the more ridiculous, as the Judge prided himself on eschewing all airy matter, and never mistaking a shadow for a substance. The truth was—and it is Phoebe's only excuse—that, although Judge Pyncheon's glowing benignity might not be absolutely unpleasant to the feminine beholder, with the width of a street, or even an ordinary-sized room, interposed between, yet it became quite too intense, when this dark, full-fed physiognomy (so roughly bearded, too, that no razor could ever make it smooth) sought to bring itself into actual contact with the object of its regards. The man, the sex, somehow or other, was entirely too prominent in the Judge's demonstrations of that sort. Phoebe's eyes sank, and, without knowing why, she felt herself blushing deeply under his look. Yet she had been kissed before, and without any particular squeamishness, by perhaps half a dozen different cousins, younger as well as older than this dark-browed, grisly-bearded, white-neck-clothed, and unctuously benevolent Judge! Then, why not by him?

On raising her eyes, Phoebe was startled by the change in Judge Pyncheon's face. It was quite as striking, allowing for the difference of scale, as that betwixt a landscape under a broad sunshine and just before a thunderstorm; not that it had the passionate intensity of the latter aspect, but was cold, hard, immitigable, like a day-long brooding cloud.

"Dear me! What is to be done now?" thought the country girl to herself. "He looks as if there were nothing softer in him than a rock, nor milder than the east wind! I meant no harm! Since he is really my cousin, I would have let him kiss me, if I could!"

Then, all at once, it struck Phoebe that this very Judge Pyncheon was the original of the miniature which the daguerreotypist had shown her in the garden, and that the hard, stern, relentless look now on his face was the same that the sun had so inflexibly persisted in bringing out. Was it, therefore, no momentary mood, but, however skillfully concealed, the settled temper of his life? And not merely so, but was it hereditary in him, and transmitted down, as a precious heirloom, from that bearded ancestor in whose picture both the expression, and, to a singular degree, the features of the modern Judge were shown as by a kind of prophecy? A deeper philosopher than Phoebe might have found something very terrible in this idea. It implied that the weaknesses and defects, the bad passions, the mean tendencies, and the moral diseases which lead to crime are handed down from one generation to another, by a far surer process of transmission than human law has been able to establish in respect to the riches and honors which it seeks to entail upon posterity.

But, as it happened, scarcely had Phoebe's eyes rested again on the Judge's countenance than all its ugly sternness vanished; and she found herself quite overpowered by the sultry, dog-day heat, as it were, of benevolence, which this excellent man diffused out of his great heart into the surrounding atmosphere—very much like a serpent, which, as a preliminary to fascination, is said to fill the air with his peculiar odor.

"I like that, Cousin Phoebe!" cried he, with an emphatic nod of approbation. "I like it much, my little cousin! You are a good child, and know how to take care of yourself. A young girl—especially if she be a very pretty one—can never be too chary of her lips."

"Indeed, sir," said Phoebe, trying to laugh the matter off, "I did not mean to be unkind."

Nevertheless, whether or no it were entirely owing to the inauspicious commencement of their acquaintance, she still acted under a certain reserve, which was by no means customary to her frank and genial nature. The fantasy would not quit her, that the original Puritan, of whom she had heard so many somber traditions—the progenitor of the whole race of New England Pyncheons, the founder of the House of the Seven Gables, and who had died so strangely in it—had now stepped into the shop. In these days of offhand equipment, the matter was easily enough arranged. On his arrival from the other world, he had merely found it necessary to spend a quarter of an hour at a barber's, who had trimmed down the Puritan's full beard into a pair of grizzled whiskers, then, patronizing a ready-made clothing establishment, he had exchanged his velvet doublet and sable cloak, with the richly worked band under his chin, for a white collar and cravat, coat, vest, and pantaloons; and lastly, putting aside his steel-hilted broadsword to take up a gold-headed cane, the Colonel Pyncheon of two centuries ago steps forward as the Judge of the passing moment!

Of course, Phoebe was far too sensible a girl to entertain this idea in any other way than as matter for a smile. Possibly, also, could the two personages have stood together before her eye, many points of difference would have been perceptible, and perhaps only a general resemblance. The long lapse of intervening years, in a climate so unlike that which had fostered the ancestral Englishman, must inevitably have wrought important changes in the physical system of his descendant. The Judge's volume of muscle could hardly be the same as the Colonel's; there was undoubtedly less beef in him. Though looked upon as a weighty man among his contemporaries in respect of animal substance, and as favored with a remarkable degree of fundamental development, well adapting him for the judicial bench, we conceive that the modern Judge Pyncheon, if weighed in the same balance with his ancestor, would have required at least an old-fashioned fifty-six to keep the scale in *equilibrio*. Then, the Judge's face had lost the ruddy English hue that showed its warmth through all the duskiness of the Colonel's weather-beaten cheek, and had taken a sallow shade, the established complexion of his countrymen. If we mistake not, moreover, a certain quality of nervousness had become more or less manifest, even in so solid a specimen of Puritan descent as the gentleman now under discussion. As one of its effects, it bestowed on his countenance a quicker mobility than the old Englishman's had possessed, and keener vivacity, but at the expense of a sturdier something, on which these acute endowments seemed to act like dissolving acids. This process, for aught we know, may belong to the great system of human progress, which, with every ascending footstep, as it diminishes the necessity for animal force, may be destined gradually to spiritualize us, by refining away our grosser attributes of body. If so, Judge Pyncheon could endure a century or two more of such refinement as well as most other men.

The similarity, intellectual and moral, between the Judge and his ancestor appears to have been at least as strong as the resemblance of mien and feature would afford reason to anticipate. In old Colonel Pyncheon's funeral discourse, the clergyman absolutely canonized his deceased parishioner, and opening, as it were, a vista through the roof of the church, and thence through the firmament above, showed him seated, harp in hand, among the crowned choristers of the spiritual world. On his tombstone, too, the record is highly eulogistic; nor does history, so far as he holds a place upon its page, assail the consistency and uprightness of his character. So also, as regards the Judge Pyncheon of today, neither clergyman, nor legal critic, nor inscriber of tomb-stones, nor historian of general or local politics, would venture a word against this eminent person's sincerity as a Christian, or respectability as a man, or integrity as a judge, or courage and faithfulness as the often-tried representative of his political party. But, besides these cold, formal, and empty words of the chisel that inscribes, the voice that speaks, and the pen that writes, for the public eye and for distant time—and which inevitably lose much of their truth and freedom by the fatal consciousness of so doing—there were traditions about the ancestor, and private diurnal gossip about the Judge, remarkably accordant in their testimony. It is often instructive to take the woman's, the private and domestic, view of a public man; nor can anything be more curious than the vast discrepancy between portraits intended for engraving and the pencil sketches that pass from hand to hand behind the original's back.

For example: tradition affirmed that the Puritan had been greedy of wealth; the Judge, too, with all the show of liberal expenditure, was said to be as close-fisted as if his gripe were of iron. The ancestor had clothed himself in a grim assumption of kindliness, a rough heartiness of word and manner, which most people took to be the genuine warmth of nature, making its way through the thick and inflexible hide of a manly character. His descendant, in compliance with the requirements of a nicer age, had etherealized this rude benevolence into that broad benignity of smile wherewith he shone like a noonday sun along the streets, or glowed like a household fire in the drawing rooms of his private acquaintance. The Puritan—if not belied by some singular stories, murmured, even at this day, under the narrator's breath—had fallen into certain transgressions to which men of his great animal development, whatever their faith or principles, must continue liable, until they put off impurity, along with the gross earthly substance that involves it. We must not stain our page with any contemporary scandal, to a similar purport, that may have been whispered against the Judge. The Puritan, again, an autocrat in his own household, had worn out three wives, and, merely by the remorseless weight and hardness of his character in the conjugal relation, had sent them, one after another, broken-hearted, to their graves. Here the parallel, in some sort, fails. The Judge had wedded but a single wife, and lost her in the third or fourth year of their marriage. There was a fable, however—for such we choose to consider it, though not impossibly typical of Judge Pyncheon's marital deportment—that the lady got her death blow in the honeymoon, and never smiled again, because her husband compelled her to serve him with coffee every morning at his bedside, in token of fealty to her liege lord and master.

But it is too fruitful a subject, this of hereditary resemblances, the frequent recurrence of which, in a direct line, is truly unaccountable, when we consider how large an accumulation of ancestry lies behind every man at the distance of one or two centuries. We shall only add, therefore, that the Puritan—so, at least, says chimney-corner tradition, which often preserves traits of character with marvelous fidelity—was bold, imperious, relentless, crafty; laying his purposes deep, and following them out with an inveteracy of pursuit that knew neither rest nor conscience; trampling on the weak, and, when essential to his ends, doing his utmost to beat down the strong. Whether the Judge in any degree resembled him, the further progress of our narrative may show.

Scarcely any of the items in the above-drawn parallel occurred to Phoebe, whose country birth and residence, in truth, had left her pitifully ignorant of most of the family traditions, which lingered, like cobwebs and incrustations of smoke, about the rooms and chimney corners of the House of the Seven Gables. Yet there was a circumstance, very trifling in itself, which impressed her with an odd degree of horror. She had heard of the anathema flung by Maule, the executed wizard, against Colonel Pyncheon and his posterity—that God would give them blood to drink—and likewise of the popular notion that this miraculous blood might now and then be heard gurgling in their throats. The latter scandal—as became a person of sense, and, more especially, a member of the Pyncheon family—Phoebe had set down for the absurdity which it unquestionably was. But ancient superstitions, after being steeped in human hearts and embodied in human breath, and passing from lip to ear in manifold repetition, through a series of generations, become imbued with an effect of homely truth. The smoke of the domestic hearth has scented them through and through. By long transmission among household facts, they grow to look like them, and have such a familiar way of making themselves at home that their influence is usually greater than we suspect. Thus it happened that when Phoebe heard a certain noise in Judge Pyncheon's throat—rather habitual with him, not altogether voluntary, yet indicative of nothing, unless it were a slight bronchial complaint, or, as some people hinted, an apoplectic symptom—when the girl heard this queer and awkward ingurgitation (which the writer never did hear, and therefore cannot describe), she, very foolishly started, and clasped her hands.

Of course, it was exceedingly ridiculous in Phoebe to be discomposed by such a trifle, and still more unpardonable to show her discomposure to the individual most concerned in it. But the incident chimed in so oddly with her previous fancies about the Colonel and the Judge that, for the moment, it seemed quite to mingle their identity.

"What is the matter with you, young woman?" said Judge Pyncheon, giving her one of his harsh looks. "Are you afraid of anything?"

"Oh, nothing, sir—nothing in the world!" answered Phoebe, with a little laugh of vexation at herself. "But perhaps you wish to speak with my cousin Hepzibah. Shall I call her?"

"Stay a moment, if you please," said the Judge, again beaming sunshine out of his face. "You seem to be a little nervous this morning. The town air, Cousin Phoebe, does not agree with your good, wholesome country habits. Or has anything happened to disturb you—anything remarkable in Cousin Hepzibah's family? An arrival, eh? I thought so! No wonder you are out of sorts, my little cousin. To be an inmate with such a guest may well startle an innocent young girl!"

"You quite puzzle me, sir," replied Phoebe, gazing inquiringly at the Judge. "There is no frightful guest in the house, but only a poor, gentle, childlike man, whom I believe to be Cousin Hepzibah's brother. I am afraid (but you, sir, will know better than I) that he is not quite in his sound senses; but so mild and quiet he seems to be, that a mother might trust her baby with him; and I think he would play with the baby as if he were only a few years older than itself. He startle me! Oh, no indeed!"

"I rejoice to hear so favorable and so ingenuous an account of my cousin Clifford," said the benevolent Judge. "Many years ago, when we were boys and young men together, I had a great affection for him, and still feel a tender interest in all his concerns. You say, Cousin Phoebe, he appears to be weak-minded. Heaven grant him at least enough of intellect to repent of his past sins!"

"Nobody, I fancy," observed Phoebe, "can have fewer to repent of."

"And is it possible, my dear," rejoined the Judge, with a commiserating look, "that you have never heard of Clifford Pyncheon—that you know nothing of his history? Well, it is all right; and your mother has shown a very proper regard for the good name of the family with which she connected herself. Believe the best you can of this unfortunate person, and hope the best! It is a rule which Christians should always follow, in their judgments of one another; and especially is it right and wise among near relatives, whose characters have necessarily a degree of mutual dependence. But is Clifford in the parlor? I will just step in and see."

"Perhaps, sir, I had better call my cousin Hepzibah," said Phoebe; hardly knowing, however, whether she ought to obstruct the entrance of so affectionate a kinsman into the private regions of the house. "Her brother seemed to be just falling asleep after breakfast; and I am sure she would not like him to be disturbed. Pray sir, let me give her notice!"

But the Judge showed a singular determination to enter unannounced; and as Phoebe, with the vivacity of a person whose movements unconsciously answer to her thoughts, had stepped towards the door, he used little or no ceremony in putting her aside.

"No, no, Miss Phoebe!" said Judge Pyncheon, in a voice as deep as a thunder growl, and with a frown as black as the cloud whence it issues. "Stay you here! I know the house, and know my cousin Hepzibah, and know her brother Clifford likewise! Nor need my little country cousin put herself to the trouble of announcing me!" In these latter words, by the by, there were symptoms of a change from his sudden harshness into his previous benignity of manner. "I am at home here, Phoebe, you must recollect, and you are the stranger. I will just step in, therefore, and see for myself how Clifford is, and assure him and Hepzibah of my kindly feelings and best wishes. It is right, at this juncture, that they should both hear from my own lips how much I desire to serve them. Ha! Here is Hepzibah herself!''

Such was the case. The vibrations of the Judge's voice had reached the old gentlewoman in the parlor, where she sat, with face averted, waiting on her brother's slumber. She now issued forth, as would appear, to defend the entrance, looking, we must needs say, amazingly like the dragon which, in fairy tales, is wont to be the guardian over an enchanted beauty. The habitual scowl of her brow was, undeniably, too fierce, at this moment, to pass itself off on the innocent score of nearsightedness; and it was bent on Judge Pyncheon in a way that seemed to confound, if not alarm him, so inadequately had he estimated the moral force of a deeply grounded antipathy. She made a repelling gesture with her hand, and stood a perfect picture of prohibition, at full length, in the dark frame of the doorway. But we must betray Hepzibah's secret, and confess that the native timorousness of her character even now developed itself in a quick tremor, which, to her own perception, set each of her joints at variance with its fellows.

Possibly, the Judge was aware how little true hardihood lay behind Hepzibah's formidable front. At any rate, being a gentleman of steady nerves, he soon recovered himself, and failed not to approach his cousin with outstretched hand; adopting the sensible precaution, however, to cover his advance with a smile so broad and sultry that, had it been only half as warm as it looked, a trellis of grapes might at once have turned purple under its summer-like exposure. It may have been his purpose, indeed, to melt poor Hepzibah on the spot, as if she were a figure of yellow wax.

"Hepzibah, my beloved cousin, I am rejoiced!" exclaimed the Judge, most emphatically. "Now, at length, you have something to live for. Yes, and all of us, let me say, your friends and kindred, have more to live for than we had yesterday. I have lost no time in hastening to offer any assistance in my power towards making Clifford comfortable. He belongs to us all. I know how much he requires—how much he used to require—with his delicate taste, and his love of the beautiful. Anything in my house—pictures, books, wine, luxuries of the table—he may command them all! It would afford me most heartfelt gratification to see him! Shall I step in, this moment?"

"No," replied Hepzibah, her voice quivering too painfully to allow of many words. "He cannot see visitors!"

"A visitor, my dear cousin! Do you call me so?" cried the Judge, whose sensibility, it seems, was hurt by the coldness of the phrase. "Nay, then, let me be Clifford's host, and your own likewise. Come at once to my house. The country air, and all the conveniences—I may say luxuries—that I have gathered about me, will do wonders for him. And you and I, dear Hepzibah, will consult together, and watch together, and labor together, to make our dear Clifford happy. Come! Why should we make more words about what is both a duty and a pleasure on my part? Come to me at once!"

On hearing these so hospitable offers, and such generous recognition of the claims of kindred, Phoebe felt very much in the mood of running up to Judge Pyncheon, and giving him, of her own accord, the kiss from which she had so recently shrunk away. It was quite otherwise with Hepzibah; the Judge's smile seemed to operate on her acerbity of heart like sunshine upon vinegar, making it ten times sourer than ever.

"Clifford," said she, still too agitated to utter more than an abrupt sentence, "Clifford has a home here!"

"May heaven forgive you, Hepzibah," said Judge Pyncheon, reverently lifting his eyes towards that high court of equity to which he appealed, "if you suffer any ancient prejudice or animosity to weigh with you in this matter! I stand here with an open heart, willing and anxious to receive yourself and Clifford into it. Do not refuse my good offices, my earnest propositions for your welfare! They are such, in all respects, as it behooves your nearest kinsman to make. It will be a heavy responsibility, cousin, if you confine your brother to this dismal house and stifled air, when the delightful freedom of my country seat is at his command."

"It would never suit Clifford," said Hepzibah, as briefly as before.

"Woman!" broke forth the Judge, giving way to his resentment. "What is the meaning of all this? Have you other resources? Nay, I suspected as much! Take care, Hepzibah, take care! Clifford is on the brink of as black a ruin as ever befell him yet! But why do I talk with you, woman as you · are? Make way! I must see Clifford!"

Hepzibah spread out her gaunt figure across the door, and seemed really to increase in bulk; looking the more terrible, also, because there was so much terror and agitation in her heart. But Judge Pyncheon's evident purpose of forcing a passage was interrupted by a voice from the inner room; a weak, tremulous, wailing voice, indicating helpless alarm, with no more energy for self-defense than belongs to a frightened infant.

"Hepzibah, Hepzibah!" cried the voice. "Go down on your knees to him! Kiss his feet! Entreat him not to come in! Oh, let him have mercy on me! Mercy! Mercy!"

For the instant, it appeared doubtful whether it were not the Judge's resolute purpose to set Hepzibah aside, and step across the threshold into the parlor, whence issued that broken and miserable murmur of entreaty. It was not pity that restrained him, for, at the first sound of the enfeebled voice, a red fire kindled in his eyes, and he made a quick pace forward, with something inexpressibly fierce and grim darkening forth, as it were, out of the whole man. To know Judge Pyncheon was to see him at that moment. After such a revelation, let him smile with what sultriness he would, he could much sooner turn grapes purple, or pumpkins yellow, than melt the iron-branded impression out of the beholder's memory. And it rendered his aspect not the less, but more frightful, that it seemed not to express wrath or hatred, but a certain hot fellness of purpose, which annihilated everything but itself.

Yet, after all, are we not slandering an excellent and amiable man? Look at the Judge now! He is apparently conscious of having erred, in too energetically pressing his deeds of loving-kindness on persons unable to appreciate them. He will await their better mood, and hold himself as ready to assist them then as at this moment. As he draws back from the door, an all-comprehensive benignity blazes from his visage, indicating that he gathers Hepzibah, little Phoebe, and the invisible Clifford, all three, together with the whole world besides, into his immense heart, and gives them a warm bath in its flood of affection.

"You do me great wrong, dear Cousin Hepzibah!" said he, first kindly offering her his hand, and then drawing on his glove preparatory to departure. "Very great wrong! But I forgive it, and will study to make you think better of me. Of course, our poor Clifford being in so unhappy a state of mind, I cannot think of urging an interview at present. But I shall watch over his welfare as if he were my own beloved brother; nor do I at all despair, my dear cousin, of constraining both him and you to acknowledge your injustice. When that shall happen, I desire no other revenge than your acceptance of the best offices in my power to do you."

With a bow to Hepzibah, and a degree of paternal benevolence in his parting nod to Phoebe, the Judge left the shop, and went smiling along the street. As is customary with the rich, when they aim at the honors of a republic, he apologized, as it were, to the people, for his wealth, prosperity, and elevated station, by a free and hearty manner towards those who knew him; putting off the more of his dignity in due proportion with the humbleness of the man whom he saluted, and thereby proving a haughty consciousness of his advantages as irrefragably as if he had marched forth preceded by a troop of lackeys to clear the way. On this particular forenoon, so excessive was the warmth of Judge Pyncheon's kindly aspect that (such, at least, was the rumor about town) an extra passage of the water carts was found essential, in order to lay the dust occasioned by so much extra sunshine!

No sooner had he disappeared than Hepzibah grew deadly white, and, staggering towards Phoebe, let her head fall on the young girl's shoulder.

"Oh, Phoebe!" murmured she. "That man has been the horror of my life! Shall I never, never have the courage, will my voice never cease from trembling long enough to let me tell him what he is?"

"Is he so very wicked?" asked Phoebe. "Yet his offers were surely kind!"

"Do not speak of them; he has a heart of iron!" rejoined Hepzibah. "Go now, and talk to Clifford! Amuse and keep him quiet! It would disturb him wretchedly to see me so agitated as I am. There, go, dear child, and I will try to look after the shop."

Phoebe went, accordingly, but perplexed herself, meanwhile, with queries as to the purport of the scene which she had just witnessed, and also whether judges, clergymen, and other characters of that eminent stamp and respectability could really, in any single instance, be otherwise than just and upright men. A doubt of this nature has a most disturbing influence, and, if shown to be a fact, comes with fearful and startling effect on minds of the trim, orderly, and limit-loving class, in which we find our little country girl. Dispositions more boldly speculative may derive a stern enjoyment from the discovery, since there must be evil in the world, that a high man is as likely to grasp his share of it as a low one. A wider scope of view, and a deeper insight, may see rank, dignity, and station all proved illusory, so far as regards their claim to human reverence, and yet not feel as if the universe were thereby tumbled headlong into chaos. But Phoebe, in order to keep the universe in its old place, was fain to smother, in some degree, her own intuitions as to Judge Pyncheon's character. And as for her cousin's testimony in disparagement of it, she concluded that Hepzibah's judgment was imbittered by one of those family feuds which render hatred the more deadly by the dead and corrupted love that they intermingle with its native poison.

IX

Clifford and Phoebe

TRULY was there something high, generous, and noble in the native composition of our poor old Hepzibah! Or else— and it was quite as probably the case—she had been en- riched by poverty, developed by sorrow, elevated by the strong and solitary affection of her life, and thus endowed with heroism, which never could have characterized her in what are called happier circumstances. Through dreary years, Hepzibah had looked forward—for the most part despair- ingly, never with any confidence of hope, but always with the feeling that it was her brightest possibility—to the very position in which she now found herself. In her own behalf, she had asked nothing of Providence but the opportunity of devoting herself to this brother, whom she had so loved—so admired for what he was, or might have been—and to whom she had kept her faith, alone of all the world, wholly, unfalteringly, at every instant, and throughout life. And here, in his late decline, the lost one had come back out of his long and strange misfortune, and was thrown on her sympathy, as it seemed, not merely for the bread of his physical existence, but for everything that should keep him morally alive. She had responded to the call. She had come forward—our poor, gaunt Hepzibah, in her rusty silks, with her rigid joints, and the sad perversity of her scowl—ready to do her utmost; and with affection enough, if that were all, to do a hundred times as much! There could be few more tearful sights—and heaven forgive us if a smile insist on mingling with our conception of it!—few sights with truer pathos in them than Hepzibah presented on that first afternoon.

How patiently did she endeavor to wrap Clifford up in her great, warm love, and make it all the world to him, so that he should retain no torturing sense of the coldness and dreariness without! Her little efforts to amuse him! How pitiful, yet magnanimous, they were!

Remembering his early love of poetry and fiction, she unlocked a bookcase, and took down several books that had been excellent reading in their day. There was a volume of Pope, with *The Rape of the Lock* in it, and another of *The Tatler,* and an odd one of Dryden's *Miscellanies,* all with tarnished gilding on their covers, and thoughts of tarnished brilliancy inside. They had no success with Clifford. These, and all such writers of society, whose new works glow like the rich texture of a just-woven carpet, must be content to relinquish their charm, for every reader, after an age or two, and could hardly be supposed to retain any portion of it for a mind that had utterly lost its estimate of modes and manners. Hepzibah then took up *Rasselas,* and began to read of the Happy Valley, with a vague idea that some secret of a contented life had there been elaborated which might at least serve Clifford and herself for this one day. But the Happy Valley had a cloud over it. Hepzibah troubled her auditor, moreover, by innumerable sins of emphasis, which he seemed to detect, without any reference to the meaning; nor, in fact, did he appear to take much note of the sense of what she read, but evidently felt the tedium of the lecture, without harvesting its profit. His sister's voice, too, naturally harsh, had, in the course of her sorrowful lifetime, contracted a kind of croak, which, when it once gets into the human throat, is as ineradicable as sin. In both sexes, occasionally, this lifelong croak, accompanying each word of joy or sorrow, is one of the symptoms of a settled melancholy; and wherever it occurs, the whole history of misfortune is conveyed in its slightest accent. The effect is as if the voice had been dyed black; or—if we must use a more moderate simile—this miserable croak, running through all the variations of the voice, is like a black silken thread, on which the crystal beads of speech are strung, and whence they take their hue. Such voices have put on mourning for dead hopes; and they ought to die and be buried along with them!

Discerning that Clifford was not gladdened by her efforts, Hepzibah searched about the house for the means of more exhilarating pastime. At one time, her eyes chanced to rest on Alice Pyncheon's harpsichord. It was a moment of great peril; for—despite the traditionary awe that had gathered over this instrument of music, and the dirges which spiritual fingers were said to play on it—the devoted sister had solemn thoughts of thrumming on its chords for Clifford's benefit, and acompanying the performance with her voice. Poor Clifford! Poor Hepzibah! Poor harpsichord! All three would have been miserable together. By some good agency— possibly, by the unrecognized interposition of the long-buried Alice herself—the threatening calamity was averted.

But the worst of all—the hardest stroke of fate for Hepzibah to endure, and perhaps for Clifford, too—was his invincible distaste for her appearance. Her features, never the most agreeable, and now harsh with age and grief, and resentment against the world for his sake; her dress, and especially her turban; the queer and quaint manners, which had unconsciously grown upon her in solitude—such being the poor gentlewoman's outward characteristics, it is no great marvel, although the mournfulest of pities, that the instinctive lover of the Beautiful was fain to turn away his eyes. There was no help for it. It would be the latest impulse to die within him. In his last extremity, the expiring breath stealing faintly through Clifford's lips, he would doubtless press Hepzibah's hand, in fervent recognition of all her lavished love, and close his eyes—but not so much to die as to be constrained to look no longer on her face! Poor Hepzibah! She took counsel with herself what might be done, and thought of putting ribbons on her turban; but, by the instant rush of several guardian angels, was withheld from an experiment that could hardly have proved less than fatal to the beloved object of her anxiety.

To be brief, besides Hepzibah's disadvantages of person, there was an uncouthness pervading all her deeds; a clumsy something that could but ill adapt itself for use, and not at all for ornament. She was a grief to Clifford, and she knew it. In this extremity, the antiquated virgin turned to Phoebe.

No groveling jealousy was in her heart. Had it pleased heaven to crown the heroic fidelity of her life by making her personally the medium of Clifford's happiness, it would have rewarded her for all the past, by a joy with no bright tints, indeed, but deep and true, and worth a thousand gayer ecstasies. This could not be. She therefore turned to Phoebe, and resigned the task into the young girl's hands. The latter took it up cheerfully, as she did everything, but with no sense of a mission to perform, and succeeding all the better for that same simplicity.

By the involuntary effect of a genial temperament, Phoebe soon grew to be absolutely essential to the daily comfort, if not the daily life, of her two forlorn companions. The grime and sordidness of the House of the Seven Gables seemed to have vanished since her appearance there; the gnawing tooth of the dry rot was stayed among the old timbers of its skeleton frame; the dust had ceased to settle down so densely, from the antique ceilings, upon the floors and furniture of the rooms below—or, at any rate, there was a little house-wife, as light-footed as the breeze that sweeps a garden walk, gliding hither and thither to brush it all away. The shadows of gloomy events that haunted the else lonely and desolate apartments; the heavy, breathless scent which death had left in more than one of the bedchambers, ever since his visits of long ago—these were less powerful than the purifying influence scattered throughout the atmosphere of the household by the presence of one youthful, fresh, and thoroughly wholesome heart. There was no morbidness in Phoebe; if there had been, the old Pyncheon House was the very locality to ripen it into incurable disease. But now her spirit resembled, in its potency, a minute quantity of attar of rose in one of Hepzibah's huge, iron-bound trunks, diffusing its fragrance through the various articles of linen and wrought lace, kerchiefs, caps, stockings, folded dresses, gloves, and whatever else was treasured there. As every article in the great trunk was the sweeter for the rose scent, so did all the thoughts and emotions of Hepzibah and Clifford, somber as they might seem, acquire a subtle attribute of happiness from Phoebe's intermixture with them. Her activity of body, intellect, and heart impelled her continually to perform the ordinary little toils that offered themselves around her, and to think the thought proper for the moment, and to sym-

pathize—now with the twittering gaiety of the robins in the
pear tree, and now to such a depth as she could—with
Hepzibah's dark anxiety, or the vague moan of her brother.
This facile adaptation was at once the symptom of perfect
health and its best preservative.

A nature like Phoebe's has invariably its due influence,
but is seldom regarded with due honor. Its spiritual force,
however, may be partially estimated by the fact of her
having found a place for herself, amid circumstances so
stern as those which surrounded the mistress of the house;
and also by the effect which she produced on a character of
so much more mass than her own. For the gaunt, bony
frame and limbs of Hepzibah, as compared with the tiny
lightsomeness of Phoebe's figure, were perhaps in some fit
proportion with the moral weight and substance, respectively, of the woman and the girl.

To the guest, to Hepzibah's brother—or Cousin Clifford,
as Phoebe now began to call him—she was especially necessary. Not that he could ever be said to converse with her, or
often manifest, in any other very definite mode, his sense of
a charm in her society. But if she were a long while absent,
he became pettish and nervously restless, pacing the room
to and fro with the uncertainty that characterized all his
movements; or else would sit broodingly in his great chair,
resting his head on his hands, and evincing life only by an
electric sparkle of ill humor, whenever Hepzibah endeavored to arouse him. Phoebe's presence, and the contiguity
of her fresh life to his blighted one, was usually all that he
required. Indeed, such was the native gush and play of her
spirit that she was seldom perfectly quiet and undemonstra-
tive, any more than a fountain ever ceases to dimple and
warble with its flow. She possessed the gift of song, and
that, too, so naturally that you would as little think of
inquiring whence she had caught it, or what master had
taught her, as of asking the same questions about a bird, in
whose small strain of music we recognize the voice of the
Creator as distinctly as in the loudest acents of His thunder.
So long as Phoebe sang, she might stray at her own will
about the house. Clifford was content, whether the sweet,
airy homeliness of her tones came down from the upper
chambers, or along the passageway from the shop, or was
sprinkled through the foliage of the pear tree, inward from

the garden, with the twinkling sunbeams. He would sit
quietly, with a gentle pleasure gleaming over his face, brighter
now, and now a little dimmer, as the song happened to float
near him, or was more remotely heard. It pleased him best,
however, when she sat on a low footstool at his knee.

It is perhaps remarkable, considering her temperament,
that Phoebe oftener chose a strain of pathos than of gaiety.
But the young and happy are not ill pleased to temper their
life with a transparent shadow. The deepest pathos of Phoebe's voice and song, moreover, came sifted through the
golden texture of a cheery spirit, and was somehow so
interfused with the quality thence acquired that one's heart
felt all the lighter for having wept at it. Broad mirth, in the
sacred presence of dark misfortune, would have jarred harshly
and irreverently with the solemn symphony that rolled its
undertone through Hepzibah's and her brother's life. Therefore, it was well that Phoebe so often chose sad themes, and
not amiss that they ceased to be so sad while she was singing
them.

Becoming habituated to her companionship, Clifford readily showed how capable of imbibing pleasant tints and gleams
of cheerful light from all quarters his nature must originally
have been. He grew youthful while she sat by him. A
beauty—not precisely real, even in its utmost manifestation,
and which a painter would have watched long to seize and
fix upon his canvas, and, after all, in vain—beauty, nevertheless, that was not a mere dream would sometimes play
upon and illuminate his face. It did more than to illuminate;
it transfigured him with an expression that could only be
interpreted as the glow of an exquisite and happy spirit.
That gray hair, and those furrows—with their record of
infinite sorrow so deeply written across his brow, and so
compressed, as with a futile effort to crowd in all the tale,
that the whole inscription was made illegible—these, for the
moment, vanished. An eye, at once tender and acute, might
have beheld in the man some shadow of what he was meant
to be. Anon, as age came stealing, like a sad twilight, back
over his figure, you would have felt tempted to hold an
argument with Destiny, and affirm that either this being
should not have been made mortal, or mortal existence
should have been tempered to his qualities. There seemed

no necessity for his having drawn breath at all; the world
never wanted him; but, as he had breathed, it ought always
to have been the balmiest of summer air. The same perplexity will invariably haunt us with regard to natures that tend
to feed exclusively upon the Beautiful, let their earthly fate
be as lenient as it may.

Phoebe, it is probable, had but a very imperfect comprehension of the character over which she had thrown so
beneficent a spell. Nor was it necessary. The fire upon the
hearth can gladden a whole semicircle of faces round about
it, but need not know the individuality of one among them
all. Indeed, there was something too fine and delicate in
Clifford's traits to be perfectly appreciated by one whose
sphere lay so much in the Actual as Phoebe's did. For
Clifford, however, the reality, and simplicity, and thorough
homeliness of the girl's nature were as powerful a charm as
any that she possessed. Beauty, it is true, and beauty almost
perfect in its own style, was indispensable. Had Phoebe
been coarse in feature, shaped clumsily, of a harsh voice,
and uncouthly mannered, she might have been rich with all
good gifts, beneath this unfortunate exterior, and still, so
long as she wore the guise of woman, she would have
shocked Clifford, and depressed him by her lack of beauty.
But nothing more beautiful—nothing prettier, at least—was
ever made than Phoebe. And, therefore, to this man—whose
whole poor and impalpable enjoyment of existence heretofore, and until both his heart and fancy died within him, had
been a dream; whose images of women had more and more
lost their warmth and substance, and been frozen, like the
pictures of secluded artists, into the chillest ideality—to
him, this little figure of the cheeriest household life was just
what he required to bring him back into the breathing
world. Persons who have wandered, or been expelled, out
of the common track of things, even were it for a better
system, desire nothing so much as to be led back. They
shiver in their loneliness, be it on a mountaintop or in a
dungeon. Now, Phoebe's presence made a home about her—
that very sphere which the outcast, the prisoner, the potentate; the wretch beneath mankind, the wretch aside from it,
or the wretch above it instinctively pines after—a home! She
was real! Holding her hand, you felt something; a tender
something; a substance, and a warm one—and so long as

you should feel its grasp, soft as it was, you might be certain that your place was good in the whole sympathetic chain of human nature. The world was no longer a delusion.

By looking a little further in this direction, we might suggest an explanation of an often-suggested mystery. Why are poets so apt to choose their mates not for any similarity of poetic endowment, but for qualities which might make the happiness of the rudest handicraftsman as well as that of the ideal craftsman of the spirit? Because, probably, at his highest elevation, the poet needs no human intercourse; but he finds it dreary to descend, and be a stranger.

There was something very beautiful in the relation that grew up between this pair, so closely and constantly linked together, yet with such a waste of gloomy and mysterious years from his birthday to hers. On Clifford's part it was the feeling of a man naturally endowed with the liveliest sensibility to feminine influence, but who had never quaffed the cup of passionate love, and knew that it was now too late. He knew it, with the instinctive delicacy that had survived his intellectual decay. Thus, his sentiment for Phoebe, without being paternal, was not less chaste than if she had been his daughter. He was a man, it is true, and recognized her as a woman. She was his only representative of womankind. He took unfailing note of every charm that appertained to her sex, and saw the ripeness of her lips, and the virginal development of her bosom. All her little womanly ways, budding out of her like blossoms on a young fruit tree, had their effect on him, and sometimes caused his very heart to tingle with the keenest thrills of pleasure. At such moments—for the effect was seldom more than momentary—the half-torpid man would be full of harmonious life, just as a long-silent harp is full of sound, when the musician's fingers sweep across it. But, after all, it seemed rather a perception, or a sympathy, than a sentiment belonging to himself as an individual. He read Phoebe, as he would a sweet and simple story; he listened to her, as if she were a verse of household poetry, which God, in requital of his bleak and dismal lot, had permitted some angel, that most pitied him, to warble through the house. She was not an actual fact for him, but the interpretation of all that he had lacked on earth brought warmly home to his conception; so that this mere symbol, or lifelike picture, had almost the comfort of reality.

But we strive in vain to put the idea into words. No
adequate expression of the beauty and profound pathos with
which it impresses us is attainable. This being, made only
for happiness, and heretofore so miserably failing to be
happy—his tendencies so hideously thwarted that, some unknown time ago, the delicate springs of his character, never
morally or intellectually strong, had given way, and he was
now imbecile—this poor, forlorn voyager from the Islands
of the Blest, in a frail bark, on a tempestuous sea, had been
flung, by the last mountain wave of his shipwreck, into a
quiet harbor. There, as he lay more than half lifeless on the
strand, the fragrance of an earthly rosebud had come to his
nostrils, and, as odors will, had summoned up reminiscences
or visions of all the living and breathing beauty amid which
he should have had his home. With his native susceptibility
of happy influences, he inhales the slight, ethereal rapture
into his soul, and expires!

And how did Phoebe regard Clifford? The girl's was not
one of those natures which are most attracted by what is
strange and exceptional in human character. The path which
would best have suited her was the well-worn track of ordinary life; the companions in whom she would most have
delighted were such as one encounters at every turn. The
mystery which enveloped Clifford, so far as it affected her at
all, was an annoyance, rather than the piquant charm which
many women might have found in it. Still, her native kindliness was brought strongly into play, not by what was darkly
picturesque in his situation, nor so much, even, by the finer
graces of his character, as by the simple appeal of a heart so
forlorn as his to one so full of genuine sympathy as hers.
She gave him an affectionate regard, because he needed so
much love, and seemed to have received so little. With a
ready tact, the result of ever-active and wholesome sensibility, she discerned what was good for him, and did it. Whatever was morbid in his mind and experience she ignored;
and thereby kept their intercourse healthy, by the incau-
tious, but, as it were, heaven-directed freedom of her whole
conduct. The sick in mind, and, perhaps, in body, are rendered more darkly and hopelessly so by the manifold reflection of their disease, mirrored back from all quarters in the
deportment of those about them; they are compelled to
inhale the poison of their own breath, in infinite repetition.

But Phoebe afforded her poor patient a supply of purer air. She impregnated it, too, not with a wild-flower scent—for wildness was no trait of hers—but with the perfume of garden roses, pinks, and other blossoms of much sweetness, which nature and man have consented together in making grow from summer to summer, and from century to century. Such a flower was Phoebe, in her relation with Clifford, and such the delight that he inhaled from her.

Yet, it must be said, her petals sometimes drooped a little, in consequence of the heavy atmosphere about her. She grew more thoughtful than heretofore. Looking aside at Clifford's face, and seeing the dim, unsatisfactory elegance and the intellect almost quenched, she would try to inquire what had been his life. Was he always thus? Had this veil been over him from his birth—this veil under which far more of his spirit was hidden than revealed, and through which he so imperfectly discerned the actual world—or was its gray texture woven of some dark calamity? Phoebe loved no riddles, and would have been glad to escape the perplexity of this one. Nevertheless, there was so far a good result of her meditations on Clifford's character that, when her involuntary conjectures, together with the tendency of every strange circumstance to tell its own story, had gradually taught her the fact, it had no terrible effect upon her. Let the world have done him what vast wrong it might, she knew Cousin Clifford too well—or fancied so—ever to shudder at the touch of his thin, delicate fingers.

Within a few days after the appearance of this remarkable inmate, the routine of life had established itself with a good deal of uniformity in the old house of our narrative. In the morning, very shortly after breakfast, it was Clifford's custom to fall asleep in his chair; nor, unless accidentally disturbed, would he emerge from a dense cloud of slumber or the thinner mists that flitted to and fro, until well towards noonday. These hours of drowsihead were the season of the old gentlewoman's attendance on her brother, while Phoebe took charge of the shop; an arrangement which the public speedily understood, and evinced their decided preference of the younger shopwoman by the multiplicity of their calls during her administration of affairs. Dinner over, Hepzibah took her knitting work—a long stocking of gray yarn, for her brother's winter wear—and with a sigh, and a scowl of affectionate farewell to Clifford, and a gesture enjoining watchfulness on Phoebe, went to take her seat behind the counter. It was now the young girl's turn to be the nurse, the guardian, the playmate—or whatever is the fitter phrase—of the gray-haired man.

X

The Pyncheon Garden

CLIFFORD, except for Phoebe's more active instigation, would ordinarily have yielded to the torpor which had crept through all his modes of being, and which sluggishly counseled him to sit in his morning chair till eventide. But the girl seldom failed to propose a removal to the garden, where Uncle Venner and the daguerreotypist had made such repairs on the roof of the ruinous arbor, or summerhouse, that it was now a sufficient shelter from sunshine and casual showers. The hopvine, too, had begun to grow luxuriantly over the sides of the little edifice, and made an interior of verdant seclusion, with innumerable peeps and glimpses into the wider solitude of the garden.

Here, sometimes, in this green play place of flickering light, Phoebe read to Clifford. Her acquaintance, the artist, who appeared to have a literary turn, had supplied her with works of fiction, in pamphlet form, and a few volumes of poetry, in altogether a different style and taste from those which Hepzibah selected for his amusement. Small thanks were due to the books, however, if the girl's readings were in any degree more successful than her elderly cousin's. Phoebe's voice had always a pretty music in it, and could either enliven Clifford by its sparkle and gaiety of tone, or soothe him by a continued flow of pebbly and brooklike cadences. But the fictions—in which the country girl, un-used to works of that nature, often became deeply absorbed—interested her strange auditor very little, or not at all. Pictures of life, scenes of passion or sentiment, wit, humor, and pathos, were all thrown away, or worse than thrown away, on Clifford; either because he lacked an experience by which to test their truth, or because his own griefs were a touchstone of reality that few feigned emotions could withstand. When Phoebe broke into a peal of merry laughter at what she read, he would now and then laugh for sympathy, but oftener respond with a troubled, questioning look. If a tear—a maiden's sunshiny tear over imaginary woe—dropped upon some melancholy page, Clifford either took it as a token of actual calamity, or else grew peevish, and angrily motioned her to close the volume. And, wisely, too! Is not the world sad enough, in genuine earnest, without making a pastime of mock sorrows?

With poetry it was rather better. He delighted in the swell and subsidence of the rhythm, and the happily recurring rhyme. Nor was Clifford incapable of feeling the sentiment of poetry—not, perhaps, where it was highest or deepest, but where it was most flitting and ethereal. It was impossible to foretell in what exquisite verse the awakening spell might lurk; but, on raising her eyes from the page to Clifford's face, Phoebe would be made aware, by the light breaking through it, that a more delicate intelligence than her own had caught a lambent flame from what she read. One glow of this kind, however, was often the precursor of gloom for many hours afterward; because, when the glow left him, he seemed conscious of a missing sense and power, and groped about for them, as if a blind man should go seeking his lost eyesight.

It pleased him more, and was better for his inward welfare, that Phoebe should talk, and make passing occurrences vivid to his mind by her accompanying description and remarks. The life of the garden offered topics enough for such discourse as suited Clifford best. He never failed to inquire what flowers had bloomed since yesterday. His feeling for flowers was very exquisite, and seemed not so much a taste as an emotion; he was fond of sitting with one in his hand, intently observing it, and looking from its petals into Phoebe's face, as if the garden flower were the sister of the household maiden. Not merely was there a delight in the flower's perfume, or pleasure in its beautiful form, and the delicacy or brightness of its hue; but Clifford's enjoyment was accompanied with a perception of life, character, and individuality that made him love these blossoms of the garden, as if they were endowed with sentiment and intelligence. This affection and sympathy for flowers is almost exclusively a woman's trait. Men, if endowed with it by nature, soon lose, forget, and learn to despise it, in their contact with coarser things than flowers. Clifford, too, had long forgotten it; but found it again now, as he slowly revived from the chill torpor of his life.

It is wonderful how many pleasant incidents continually came to pass in that secluded garden spot when once Phoebe had set herself to look for them. She had seen or heard a bee there, on the first day of her acquaintance with the place. And often—almost continually, indeed—since then, the bees kept coming thither, heaven knows why, or by what pertinacious desire, for farfetched sweets, when, no doubt, there were broad clover fields, and all kinds of garden growth, much nearer home than this. Thither the bees came, however, and plunged into the squash blossoms, as if there were no other squash vines within a long day's flight, or as if the soil of Hepzibah's garden gave its productions just the very quality which these laborious little wizards wanted, in order to impart the Hymettus odor to their whole hive of New England honey. When Clifford heard their sunny, buzzing murmur, in the heart of the great yellow blossoms, he looked about him with a joyful sense of warmth, and blue sky, and green grass, and of God's free air in the whole height from earth to heaven. After all, there need be no question why the bees came to that one green nook in the dusty town. God sent them thither to gladden our poor Clifford. They brought the rich summer with them, in requital of a little honey.

When the bean vines began to flower on the poles, there was one particular variety which bore a vivid scarlet blossom. The daguerreotypist had found these beans in a garret, over one of the seven gables, treasured up in an old chest of drawers by some horticultural Pyncheon of days gone by, who, doubtless, meant to sow them the next summer, but was himself first sown in Death's garden ground. By way of testing whether there were still a living germ in such ancient seeds, Holgrave had planted some of them; and the result of his experiment was a splendid row of bean vines, clambering, early, to the full height of the poles, and arraying them, from top to bottom, in a spiral profusion of red blossoms.

And, ever since the unfolding of the first bud, a multitude of hummingbirds had been attracted thither. At times, it seemed as if for every one of the hundred blossoms, there was one of these tiniest fowls of the air—a thumb's bigness of burnished plumage, hovering and vibrating about the bean poles. It was with indescribable interest, and even more than childish delight, that Clifford watched the hummingbirds. He used to thrust his head softly out of the arbor to see them the better; all the while, too, motioning Phoebe to be quiet, and snatching glimpses of the smile upon her face, so as to heap his enjoyment up the higher with her sympathy. He had not merely grown young—he was a child again.

Hepzibah, whenever she happened to witness one of these fits of miniature enthusiasm, would shake her head, with a strange mingling of the mother and sister, and of pleasure and sadness, in her aspect. She said that it had always been thus with Clifford when the hummingbirds came—always, from his babyhood—and that his delight in them had been one of the earliest tokens by which he showed his love for beautiful things. And it was a wonderful coincidence, the good lady thought, that the artist should have planted these scarlet-flowering beans—which the hummingbirds sought far and wide, and which had not grown in the Pyncheon garden before for forty years—on the very summer of Clifford's return.

Then would the tears stand in poor Hepzibah's eyes, or overflow them with a too abundant gush, so that she was fain to betake herself into some corner lest Clifford should espy her agitation. Indeed, all the enjoyments of this period were provocative of tears. Coming so late as it did, it was a kind of Indian summer, with a mist in its balmiest sunshine, and decay and death in its gaudiest delight. The more Clifford seemed to taste the happiness of a child, the sadder was the difference to be recognized. With a mysterious and terrible Past, which had annihilated his memory, and a blank Future before him, he had only this visionary and impalpable Now, which, if you once look closely at it, is nothing. He himself, as was perceptible by many symptoms, lay darkly behind his pleasure, and knew it to be a baby play, which he was to toy and trifle with, instead of thoroughly believing. Clifford saw, it may be, in the mirror of his deeper consciousness, that he was an example and representative of that great class of people whom an inexplicable Providence is continually putting at cross-purposes with the world: breaking what seems its own promise in their nature; withholding their proper food, and setting poison before them for a banquet; and thus—when it might so easily, as one would think, have been adjusted otherwise—making their existence a strangeness, a solitude, and torment. All his life long, he had been learning how to be wretched, as one learns a foreign tongue; and now, with the lesson thoroughly by heart, he could with difficulty comprehend his little airy happiness. Frequently, there was a dim shadow of doubt in his eyes. "Take my hand, Phoebe," he would say, "and pinch it hard with your little fingers! Give me a rose, that I may press its thorns, and prove myself awake by the sharp touch of pain!" Evidently, he desired this prick of a trifling anguish, in order to assure himself, by that quality which he best knew to be real, that the garden, and the seven weather-beaten gables, and Hepzibah's scowl, and Phoebe's smile, were real likewise. Without this signet in his flesh, he could have attributed no more substance to them than to the empty confusion of imaginary scenes with which he had fed his spirit, until even that poor sustenance was exhausted.

The author needs great faith in his reader's sympathy; else he must hesitate to give details so minute, and incidents apparently so trifling, as are essential to make up the idea of this garden life. It was the Eden of a thundersmitten Adam, who had fled for refuge thither out of the same dreary and perilous wilderness into which the original Adam was expelled.

One of the available means of amusement, of which Phoebe made the most in Clifford's behalf, was that feathered society, the hens, a breed of whom, as we have already said, was an immemorial heirloom in the Pyncheon family. In compliance with a whim of Clifford, as it troubled him to see them in confinement, they had been set at liberty, and now roamed at will about the garden; doing some little mischief but hindered from escape by buildings on three sides, and the difficult peaks of a wooden fence on the other. They spent much of their abundant leisure on the margin of Maule's well, which was haunted by a kind of snail, evidently a titbit to their palates; and the brackish

water itself, however nauseous to the rest of the world, was
so greatly esteemed by these fowls that they might be seen
tasting, turning up their heads, and smacking their bills,
with precisely the air of wine-bibbers round a probationary
cask. Their generally quiet, yet often brisk, and constantly
diversified talk, one to another, or sometimes in soliloquy—as
they scratched worms out of the rich, black soil, or pecked
at such plants as suited their taste—had such a domestic
tone that it was almost a wonder why you could not establish a regular interchange of ideas about household matters,
human and gallinaceous. All hens are well worth studying
for the piquancy and rich variety of their manners; but by
no possibility can there have been other fowls of such odd
appearance and deportment as these ancestral ones. They
probably embodied the traditionary peculiarities of their
whole line of progenitors, derived through an unbroken
succession of eggs; or else this individual Chanticleer and his
two wives had grown to be humorists, and a little crack-
brained withal, on account of their solitary way of life, and
out of sympathy for Hepzibah, their lady patroness.

Queer, indeed, they looked! Chanticleer himself, though
stalking on two stiltlike legs, with the dignity of interminable descent in all his gestures, was hardly bigger than an
ordinary partridge; his two wives were about the size of
quails; and as for the one chicken, it looked small enough to
be still in the egg, and, at the same time, sufficiently old,
withered, wizened, and experienced, to have been the founder
of the antiquated race. Instead of being the youngest of the
family, it rather seemed to have aggregated into itself the
ages not only of these living specimens of the breed, but of
all its forefathers and foremothers, whose united excellences
and oddities were squeezed into its little body. Its mother
evidently regarded it as the one chicken of the world, and as
necessary, in fact, to the world's continuance, or, at any
rate, to the equilibrium of the present system of affairs,
whether in church or state. No lesser sense of the infant
fowl's importance could have justified, even in a mother's
eyes, the perseverance with which she watched over its
safety, ruffling her small person to twice its proper size, and
flying in everybody's face that so much as looked towards
her hopeful progeny. No lower estimate could have vindi-
cated the indefatigable zeal with which she scratched, and

her unscrupulousness in digging up the choicest flower or vegetable, for the sake of the fat earthworm at its root. Her nervous cluck, when the chicken happened to be hidden in the long grass or under the squash leaves; her gentle croak of satisfaction, while sure of it beneath her wing; her note of ill-concealed fear and obstreperous defiance, when she saw her arch-enemy, a neighbor's cat, on the top of the high fence—one or other of these sounds was to be heard at almost every moment of the day. By degrees, the observer came to feel nearly as much interest in this chicken of illustrious race as the mother hen did.

Phoebe, after getting well acquainted with the old hen, was sometimes permitted to take the chicken in her hand, which was quite capable of grasping its cubic inch or two of body. While she curiously examined its hereditary marks—the peculiar speckle of its plumage, the funny tuft on its head, and a knob on each of its legs—the little biped, as she insisted, kept giving her a sagacious wink. The daguerreotypist once whispered her that these marks betokened the oddities of the Pyncheon family, and that the chicken itself was a symbol of the life of the old house, embodying its interpretation, likewise, although an unintelligible one, as such clues generally are. It was a feathered riddle; a mystery hatched out of an egg, and just as mysterious as if the egg had been addle!

The second of Chanticleer's two wives, ever since Phoebe's arrival, had been in a state of heavy despondency, caused, as it afterwards appeared, by her inability to lay an egg. One day, however, by her self-important gait, the sideway turn of her head, and the cock of her eye, as she pried into one and another nook of the garden—croaking to herself, all the while, with inexpressible complacency—it was made evident that this identical hen, much as mankind undervalued her, carried something about her person the worth of which was not to be estimated either in gold or precious stones. Shortly after, there was a prodigious cackling and gratulation of Chanticleer and all his family, including the wizened chicken, who appeared to understand the matter quite as well as did his sire, his mother, or his aunt. That afternoon, Phoebe found a diminutive egg—not in the regular nest, it was far too precious to be trusted there—but cunningly hidden under the currant bushes, on some dry stalks of last year's grass. Hepzibah, on learning the fact, took possession of the egg and appropriated it to Clifford's breakfast, on account of a certain delicacy of flavor, for which, as she affirmed, these eggs had always been famous. Thus unscrupulously did the old gentlewoman sacrifice the continuance, perhaps, of an ancient feathered race, with no better end than to supply her brother with a dainty that hardly filled the bowl of a teaspoon! It must have been in reference to this outrage that Chanticleer, the next day, accompanied by the bereaved mother of the egg, took his post in front of Phoebe and Clifford, and delivered himself of a harangue that might have proved as long as his own pedigree, but for a fit of merriment on Phoebe's part. Hereupon, the offended fowl stalked away on his long stilts, and utterly withdrew his notice from Phoebe and the rest of human nature, until she made her peace with an offering of spice cake, which, next to snails, was the delicacy most in favor with his aristocratic taste.

We linger too long, no doubt, beside this paltry rivulet of life that flowed through the garden of the Pyncheon House. But we deem it pardonable to record these mean incidents and poor delights, because they proved so greatly to Clifford's benefit. They had the earth smell in them, and contributed to give him health and substance. Some of his occupations wrought less desirably upon him. He had a singular propensity, for example, to hang over Maule's well, and look at the constantly shifting phantasmagoria of figures produced by the agitation of the water over the mosaicwork of colored pebbles at the bottom. He said that faces looked upward to him there—beautiful faces, arrayed in bewitching smiles—each momentary face so fair and rosy, and every smile so sunny, that he felt wronged at its departure, until the same flitting witchcraft made a new one. But sometimes he would suddenly cry out, "The dark face gazes at me!" and be miserable the whole day afterwards. Phoebe, when she hung over the fountain by Clifford's side, could see nothing of all this—neither the beauty nor the ugliness—but only the colored pebbles, looking as if the gush of the waters shook and disarranged them. And the dark face, that so troubled Clifford, was no more than the shadow thrown from a branch of one of the damson trees, and breaking the inner light of Maule's well. The truth was, however, that his fancy—reviving faster than his will and judgment, and always stronger than they—created shapes of loveliness that were symbolic of his native character, and now and then a stern and dreadful shape that typified his fate.

On Sundays, after Phoebe had been at church—for the girl had a churchgoing conscience, and would hardly have been at ease had she missed either prayer, singing, sermon, or benediction—after churchtime, therefore, there was, ordinarily, a sober little festival in the garden. In addition to Clifford, Hepzibah, and Phoebe, two guests made up the company. One was the artist, Holgrave, who, in spite of his consociation with reformers, and his other queer and questionable traits, continued to hold an elevated place in Hepzibah's regard. The other, we are almost ashamed to say, was the venerable Uncle Venner, in a clean shirt, and a broadcloth coat, more respectable than his ordinary wear, inasmuch as it was neatly patched on each elbow, and might be called an entire garment, except for a slight inequality in the length of its skirts. Clifford, on several occasions, had seemed to enjoy the old man's intercourse, for the sake of his mellow, cheerful vein, which was like the sweet flavor of a frost-bitten apple, such as one picks up under the tree in December. A man at the very lowest point of the social scale was easier and more agreeable for the fallen gentleman to encounter than a person at any of the intermediate degrees; and, moreover, as Clifford's young manhood had been lost, he was fond of feeling himself comparatively youthful, now, in apposition with the patriarchal age of Uncle Venner. In fact, it was sometimes observable that Clifford half willfully hid from himself the consciousness of being stricken in years, and cherished visions of an earthly future still before him; visions, however, too indistinctly drawn to be followed by disappointment—though, doubtless, by depression—when any casual incident or recollection made him sensible of the withered leaf.

So this oddly composed little social party used to assemble under the ruinous arbor. Hepzibah—stately as ever at heart, and yielding not an inch of her old gentility, but resting upon it so much the more, as justifying a princess-like condescension—exhibited a not ungraceful hospitality. She talked kindly to the vagrant artist, and took sage counsel—lady as she was— with the woodsawyer, the mes-

senger of everybody's petty errands, the patched philosopher. And Uncle Venner, who had studied the world at
street corners, and other posts equally well adapted for just
observation, was as ready to give out his wisdom as a town
pump to give water.

"Miss Hepzibah, ma'am," said he once, after they had all
been cheerful together, "I really enjoy these quiet little
meetings of a Sabbath afternoon. They are very much like
what I expect to have after I retire to my farm!"

"Uncle Venner," observed Clifford, in a drowsy, inward
tone, "is always talking about his farm. But I have a better
scheme for him, by and by. We shall see!"

"Ah, Mr. Clifford Pyncheon!" said the man of patches.
"You may scheme for me as much as you please; but I'm
not going to give up this one scheme of my own, even if I
never bring it really to pass. It does seem to me that men
make a wonderful mistake in trying to heap up property
upon property. If I had done so, I should feel as if Providence was not bound to take care of me; and, at all events,
the city wouldn't be! I'm one of those people who think that
infinity is big enough for us all—and eternity long enough."

"Why, so they are, Uncle Venner," remarked Phoebe,
after a pause; for she had been trying to fathom the profun-
dity and appositeness of this concluding apothegm. "But for
this short life of ours, one would like a house and a moderate garden spot of one's own."

"It appears to me," said the daguerreotypist, smiling,
"that Uncle Venner has the principles of Fourier at the
bottom of his wisdom; only they have not quite so much
distinctness, in his mind, as in that of the systematizing
Frenchman."

"Come, Phoebe," said Hepzibah, "it is time to bring the
currants."

And then, while the yellow richness of the declining sunshine still fell into the open space of the garden, Phoebe
brought out a loaf of bread and a china bowl of currants,
freshly gathered from the bushes, and crushed with sugar.
These, with water—but not from the fountain of ill omen,
close at hand—constituted all the entertainment. Meanwhile,
Holgrave took some pains to establish an intercourse with
Clifford, actuated, it might seem, entirely by an impulse of
kindliness, in order that the present hour might be cheerfuler

than most which the poor recluse had spent, or was destined yet to spend. Nevertheless, in the artist's deep, thoughtful, all-observant eyes, there was, now and then, an expression not sinister, but questionable; as if he had some other interest in the scene than a stranger, a youthful and unconnected adventurer, might be supposed to have. With great mobility of outward mood, however, he applied himself to the task of enlivening the party; and with so much success that even dark-hued Hepzibah threw off one tint of melancholy, and made what shift she could with the remaining portion. Phoebe said to herself, "How pleasant he can be!" As for Uncle Venner, as a mark of friendship and approbation, he readily consented to afford the young man his countenance in the way of his profession—not metaphorically, be it understood, but literally, by allowing a daguerreotype of his face, so familiar to the town, to be exhibited at the entrance of Holgrave's studio.

Clifford, as the company partook of their little banquet, grew to be the gayest of them all. Either it was one of those upquivering flashes of the spirit, to which minds in an abnormal state àre liable, or else the artist had subtly touched some chord that made musical vibration. Indeed, what with the pleasant summer evening, and the sympathy of this little circle of not unkindly souls, it was perhaps natural that a character so susceptible as Clifford's should become animated, and show itself readily responsive to what was said around him. But he gave out his own thoughts, likewise, with an airy and fanciful glow; so that they glistened, as it were, through the arbor, and made their escape among the interstices of the foliage. He had been as cheerful, no doubt, while alone with Phoebe, but never with such tokens of acute, although partial, intelligence.

But, as the sunlight left the peaks of the Seven Gables, so did the excitement fade out of Clifford's eyes. He gazed vaguely and mournfully about him, as if he missed something precious, and missed it the more drearily for not knowing precisely what it was.

"I want my happiness!" at last he murmured, hoarsely and indistinctly, hardly shaping out the words. "Many, many years have I waited for it! It is late! It is late! I want my happiness!"

Alas, poor Clifford! You are old, and worn with troubles

that ought never to have befallen you. You are partly crazy and partly imbecile; a ruin, a failure, as almost everybody is—though some in less degree, or less perceptibly, than their fellows. Fate has no happiness in store for you; unless your quiet home in the old family residence with the faithful Hepzibah, and your long summer afternoons with Phoebe, and these Sabbath festivals with Uncle Venner and the daguerreotypist deserve to be called happiness! Why not? If not the thing itself, it is marvelously like it, and the more so for that ethereal and intangible quality which causes it all to vanish at too close an introspection. Take it, therefore, while you may! Murmur not—question not—but make the most of it!

XI

The Arched Window

FROM the inertness, or what we may term the vegetative character, of his ordinary mood, Clifford would perhaps have been content to spend one day after another, interminably—or, at least, throughout the summertime—in just the kind of life described in the preceding pages. Fancying, however, that it might be for his benefit occasionally to diversify the scene, Phoebe sometimes suggested that he should look out upon the life of the street. For this purpose, they used to mount the staircase together, to the second story of the house, where, at the termination of a wide entry, there was an arched window of uncommonly large dimensions, shaded by a pair of curtains. It opened above the porch, where there had formerly been a balcony, the balustrade of which had long since gone to decay, and been removed. At this arched window, throwing it open but keeping himself in comparative obscurity by means of the curtain, Clifford had an opportunity of witnessing such a portion of the great world's movement as might be supposed to roll through one of the retired streets of a not very populous city. But he and Phoebe made a sight as well worth seeing as any that the city could exhibit. The pale, gray, childish, aged, melancholy, yet often simply cheerful, and sometimes delicately intelligent aspect of Clifford, peering from behind the faded crimson of the curtain—watching the monotony of everyday occurrences with a kind of inconsequential interest and earnestness, and, at every petty throb of his sensibility, turning for sympathy to the eyes of the bright young girl!

If once he were fairly seated at the window, even Pyncheon Street would hardly be so dull and lonely but that, somewhere or other along its extent, Clifford might discover matter to occupy his eye, and titillate, if not engross, his observation. Things familiar to the youngest child that had begun its outlook at existence seemed strange to him. A cab; an omnibus, with its populous interior, dropping here and there a passenger, and picking up another, and thus typifying that vast rolling vehicle the world, the end of whose journey is everywhere and nowhere; these objects he followed eagerly with his eyes, but forgot them before the dust raised by the horses and wheels had settled along their track. As regarded novelties (among which cabs and omnibuses were to be reckoned), his mind appeared to have lost its proper gripe and retentiveness. Twice or thrice, for example, during the sunny hours of the day, a water cart went along by the Pyncheon House, leaving a broad wake of moistened earth, instead of the white dust that had risen at a lady's lightest footfall; it was like a summer shower, which the city authorities had caught and tamed, and compelled it into the commonest routine of their convenience. With the water cart Clifford could never grow familiar; it always affected him with just the same surprise as at first. His mind took an apparently sharp impression from it, but lost the recollection of this perambulatory shower, before its next reappearance, as completely as did the street itself, along which the heat so quickly strewed white dust again. It was the same with the railroad. Clifford could hear the obstreperous howl of the steam devil, and, by leaning a little way from the arched window, could catch a glimpse of the trains of cars, flashing a brief transit across the extremity of the street. The idea of terrible energy thus forced upon him was new at every recurrence, and seemed to affect him as disagreeably, and with almost as much surprise, the hundredth time as the first.

Nothing gives a sadder sense of decay than this loss or suspension of the power to deal with unaccustomed things, and to keep up with the swiftness of the passing moment. It can merely be a suspended animation; for, were the power actually to perish, there would be little use of immortality. We are less than ghosts, for the time being, whenever this calamity befalls us.

Clifford was indeed the most inveterate of conservatives. All the antique fashions of the street were dear to him; even such as were characterized by a rudeness that would naturally have annoyed his fastidious senses. He loved the old rumbling and jolting carts, the former track of which he still found in his long-buried remembrance, as the observer of today finds the wheel tracks of ancient vehicles in Herculaneum. The butcher's cart, with its snowy canopy, was an acceptable object; so was the fish cart, heralded by its horn; so, likewise, was the countryman's cart of vegetables, plodding from door to door, with long pauses of the patient horse, while his owner drove a trade in turnips, carrots, summer squashes, string beans, green peas, and new potatoes, with half the housewives of the neighborhood. The baker's cart, with the harsh music of its bells, had a pleasant effect on Clifford, because, as few things else did, it jingled the very dissonance of yore. One afternoon, a scissor-grinder chanced to set his wheel agoing under the Pyncheon Elm, and just in front of the arched window. Children came running with their mothers' scissors, or the carving knife, or the paternal razor, or anything else that lacked an edge (except, indeed, poor Clifford's wits), that the grinder might apply the article to his magic wheel, and give it back as good as new. Round went the busily revolving machinery, kept in motion by the scissor-grinder's foot, and wore away the hard steel against the hard stone, whence issued an intense and spiteful prolongation of a hiss as fierce as those emitted by Satan and his compeers in Pandemonium, though squeezed into smaller compass. It was an ugly, little, venomous serpent of a noise, as ever did petty violence to human ears. But Clifford listened with rapturous delight. The sound, however disagreeable, had very brisk life in it, and, together with the circle of curious children watching the revolutions of the wheel, appeared to give him a more vivid sense of active, bustling, and sunshiny existence than he had attained in almost any other way. Nevertheless, its charm lay chiefly in the past; for the scissor-grinder's wheel had hissed in his childish ears.

He sometimes made doleful complaint that there were no stagecoaches nowadays. And he asked in an injured tone what had become of all those old square-top chaises, with wings sticking out on either side, that used to be drawn by a plow horse, and driven by a farmer's wife and daughter, peddling whortleberries and blackberries about the town. Their disappearance made him doubt, he said, whether the berries had not left off growing in the broad pastures and along the shady country lanes.

But anything that appealed to the sense of beauty, in however humble a way, did not require to be recommended by these old associations. This was observable when one of those Italian boys (who are rather a modern feature of our streets) came along with his barrel organ, and stopped under the wide and cool shadows of the elm. With his quick professional eye, he took note of the two faces watching him from the arched window, and, opening his instrument, began to scatter its melodies abroad. He had a monkey on his shoulder, dressed in a Highland plaid; and, to complete the sum of splendid attractions wherewith he presented himself to the public, there was a company of little figures, whose sphere and habitation was in the mahogany case of his organ, and whose principle of life was the music which the Italian made it his business to grind out. In all their variety of occupation—the cobbler, the blacksmith, the soldier, the lady with her fan, the toper with his bottle, the milkmaid sitting by her cow—this fortunate little society might truly be said to enjoy a harmonious existence, and to make life literally a dance. The Italian turned a crank; and, behold! every one of these small individuals started into the most curious vivacity. The cobbler wrought upon a shoe; the blacksmith hammered his iron; the soldier waved his glittering blade; the lady raised a tiny breeze with her fan; the jolly toper swigged lustily at his bottle; a scholar opened his book with eager thirst for knowledge, and turned his head to and fro along the page; the milkmaid energetically drained her cow; and a miser counted gold into his strongbox—all at the same turning of a crank. Yes; and, moved by the selfsame impulse, a lover saluted his mistress on her lips! Possibly some cynic, at once merry and bitter, had desired to signify, in this pantomimic scene, that we mortals, whatever our business or amusement—however serious, however trifling—all dance to one identical tune, and, in spite of our ridiculous activity, bring nothing finally to pass. For the most remarkable aspect of the affair was that, at the cessation of the music, everybody was petrified, at once, from

the most extravagant life into a dead torpor. Neither was
the cobbler's shoe finished, nor the blacksmith's iron shaped
out; nor was there a drop less of brandy in the toper's
bottle, nor a drop more of milk in the milkmaid's pail, nor
one additional coin in the miser's strongbox, nor was the
scholar a page deeper in his book. All were precisely in the
same condition as before they made themselves so ridiculous by their haste to toil, to enjoy, to accumulate gold, and
to become wise. Saddest of all, moreover, the lover was
none the happier for the maiden's granted kiss! But, rather
than swallow this last too acrid ingredient, we reject the
whole moral of the show.

The monkey, meanwhile, with a thick tail curling out into
preposterous prolixity from beneath his tartans, took his
station at the Italian's feet. He turned a wrinkled and abominable little visage to every passer-by, and to the circle of
children that soon gathered round, and to Hepzibah's shop
door, and upward to the arched window, whence Phoebe
and Clifford were looking down. Every moment, also, he
took off his Highland bonnet, and performed a bow and
scrape. Sometimes, moreover, he made personal application
to individuals, holding out his small black palm, and otherwise plainly signifying his excessive desire for whatever filthy
lucre might happen to be in anybody's pocket. The mean
and low, yet strangely manlike expression of his wilted
countenance; the prying and crafty glance, that showed him
ready to gripe at every miserable advantage; his enormous
tail (too enormous to be decently concealed under his gab-
ardine), and the deviltry of nature which it betokened—take
this monkey just as he was, in short, and you could desire
no better image of the Mammon of copper coin, symbolizing the grossest form of the love of money. Neither was
there any possibility of satisfying the covetous little devil.
Phoebe threw down a whole handful of cents, which he
picked up with joyless eagerness, handed them over to the
Italian for safekeeping, and immediately recommenced a
series of pantomimic petitions for more.

Doubtless, more than one New Englander—or, let him be
of what country he might, it is as likely to be the case—
passed by, and threw a look at the monkey, and went on,
without imagining how nearly his own moral condition was
here exemplified. Clifford, however, was a being of another

order. He had taken childish delight in the music, and
smiled, too, at the figures which it set in motion. But, after
looking a while at the long-tailed imp, he was so shocked by
his horrible ugliness, spiritual as well as physical, that he
actually began to shed tears; a weakness which men of
merely delicate endowments, and destitute of the fiercer,
deeper, and more tragic power of laughter, can hardly avoid,
when the worst and meanest aspect of life happens to be
presented to them.

Pyncheon Street was sometimes enlivened by spectacles
of more imposing pretensions than the above, and which
brought the multitude along with them. With a shivering
repugnance at the idea of personal contact with the world, a
powerful impulse still seized on Clifford, whenever the rush
and roar of the human tide grew strongly audible to him.
This was made evident, one day, when a political procession, with hundreds of flaunting banners, and drums, fifes,
clarions, and cymbals, reverberating between the rows of
buildings, marched all through town, and trailed its length
of trampling footsteps, and most infrequent uproar, past the
ordinarily quiet House of the Seven Gables. As a mere
object of sight, nothing is more deficient in picturesque
features than a procession seen in its passage through narrow streets. The spectator feels it to be fool's play, when he
can distinguish the tedious commonplace of each man's visage, with the perspiration and weary self-importance on it,
and the very cut of his pantaloons, and the stiffness or laxity
of his shirt collar, and the dust on the back of his black coat.
In order to become majestic, it should be viewed from some
vantage point, as it rolls its slow and long array through the
center of a wide plain, or the stateliest public square of a
city; for then, by its remoteness, it melts all the petty per-
sonalities, of which it is made up, into one broad mass of
existence—one great life—one collected body of mankind,
with a vast, homogeneous spirit animating it. But, on the
other hand, if an impressible person, standing alone over
the brink of one of these processions, should behold it, not
in its atoms, but in its aggregate—as a mighty river of life,
massive in its tide, and black with mystery, and, out of its
depths, calling to the kindred depth within him—then the
contiguity would add to the effect. It might so fascinate him

that he would hardly be restrained from plunging into the surging stream of human sympathies.

So it proved with Clifford. He shuddered; he grew pale; he threw an appealing look at Hepzibah and Phoebe, who were with him at the window. They comprehended nothing of his emotions, and supposed him merely disturbed by the unaccustomed tumult. At last, with tremulous limbs, he started up, set his foot on the window sill, and in an instant more would have been in the unguarded balcony. As it was, the whole procession might have seen him, a wild, haggard figure, his gray locks floating in the wind that waved their banners; a lonely being, estranged from his race, but now feeling himself man again, by virtue of the irrepressible instinct that possessed him. Had Clifford attained the balcony, he would probably have leaped into the street; but whether impelled by the species of terror that sometimes urges its victim over the very precipice which he shrinks from, or by a natural magnetism, tending towards the great center of humanity, it were not easy to decide. Both impulses might have wrought on him at once.

But his companions, affrighted by his gesture—which was that of a man hurried away in spite of himself—seized Clifford's garment and held him back. Hepzibah shrieked. Phoebe, to whom all extravagance was a horror, burst into sobs and tears.

"Clifford, Clifford! Are you crazy?" cried his sister.

"I hardly know, Hepzibah," said Clifford, drawing a long breath. "Fear nothing—it is over now—but had I taken that plunge, and survived it, methinks it would have made me another man!"

Possibly, in some sense, Clifford may have been right. He needed a shock; or perhaps he required to take a deep, deep plunge into the ocean of human life, and to sink down and be covered by its profoundness, and then to emerge, sobered, invigorated, restored to the world and himself. Perhaps, again, he required nothing less than the great final remedy—death!

A similar yearning to renew the broken links of brotherhood with his kind sometimes showed itself in a milder form; and once it was made beautiful by the religion that lay even deeper than itself. In the incident now to be sketched, there was a touching recognition, on Clifford's part, of

God's care and love towards him—towards this poor, forsaken man, who, if any mortal could, might have been
pardoned for regarding himself as thrown aside, forgotten,
and left to be the sport of some fiend, whose playfulness
was an ecstasy of mischief.

It was the Sabbath morning; one of those bright, calm
Sabbaths, with its own hallowed atmosphere, when heaven
seems to diffuse itself over the earth's face in a solemn
smile, no less sweet than solemn. On such a Sabbath morn,
were we pure enough to be its medium, we should be
conscious of the earth's natural worship ascending through
our frames, on whatever spot of ground we stood. The
church bells, with various tones, but all in harmony, were
calling out, and responding to one another—"It is the
Sabbath!—The Sabbath!—Yea; the Sabbath!"—and over the
whole city the bells scattered the blessed sounds, now slowly,
now with livelier joy, now one bell alone, now all the bells
together, crying earnestly, "It is the Sabbath!" and flinging
their accents afar off, to melt into the air, and pervade it
with the holy word. The air, with God's sweetest and tenderest
sunshine in it, was meet for mankind to breathe into their
hearts, and send it forth again as the utterance of prayer.

Clifford sat at the window with Hepzibah, watching the
neighbors as they stepped into the street. All of them,
however unspiritual on other days, were transfigured by the
Sabbath influence; so that their very garments—whether it
were an old man's decent coat, well brushed for the thousandth time, or a little boy's first sack and trousers, finished
yesterday by his mother's needle—had somewhat of the
quality of ascension robes. Forth, likewise, from the portal
of the old house stepped Phoebe, putting up her small green
sunshade, and throwing upward a glance and smile of parting kindness to the faces at the arched window. In her
aspect there was a familiar gladness, and a holiness that you
could play with, and yet reverence it as much as ever. She
was like a prayer, offered up in the homeliest beauty of
one's mother tongue. Fresh was Phoebe, moreover, and airy
and sweet in her apparel; as if nothing that she wore—
neither her gown, nor her small straw bonnet, nor her little
kerchief, any more than her snowy stockings—had ever
been put on before; or, if worn, were all the fresher for it,
and with a fragrance as if they had lain among the rosebuds.

The girl waved her hand to Hepzibah and Clifford, and went up the street; a religion in herself, warm, simple, true, with a substance that could walk on earth, and a spirit that was capable of heaven.

"Hepzibah," asked Clifford, after watching Phoebe to the corner, "do you never go to church?"

"No, Clifford!" she replied. "Not these many, many years!"

"Were I to be there," he rejoined, "it seems to me that I could pray once more, when so many human souls were praying all around me!"

She looked into Clifford's face, and beheld there a soft natural effusion; for his heart gushed out, as it were, and ran over at his eyes, in delightful reverence for God, and kindly affection for his human brethren. The emotion communicated itself to Hepzibah. She yearned to take him by the hand, and go and kneel down, they two together—both so long separate from the world, and, as she now recognized, scarcely friends with Him above—to kneel down among the people, and be reconciled to God and man at once.

"Dear brother," said she, earnestly, "let us go! We belong nowhere. We have not a foot of space in any church to kneel upon; but let us go to some place of worship, even if we stand in the broad aisle. Poor and forsaken as we are, some pew door will be opened to us!"

So Hepzibah and her brother made themselves ready—as ready as they could in the best of their old-fashioned garments, which had hung on pegs, or been laid away in trunks, so long that the dampness and moldy smell of the past was on them—made themselves ready, in their faded bettermost, to go to church. They descended the staircase together—gaunt, sallow Hepzibah, and pale, emaciated, age-stricken Clifford! They pulled open the front door, and stepped across the threshold, and felt, both of them, as if they were standing in the presence of the whole world, and with mankind's great and terrible eye on them alone. The eye of their Father seemed to be withdrawn, and gave them no encouragement. The warm, sunny air of the street made them shiver. Their hearts quaked within them at the idea of taking one step farther.

"It cannot be, Hepzibah! It is too late," said Clifford, with deep sadness. "We are ghosts! We have no right among human beings—no right anywhere but in this old house, which has a curse on it, and which, therefore, we are doomed to haunt! And, besides," he continued, with a fastidious sensibility, inalienably characteristic of the man, "it would not be fit nor beautiful to go! It is an ugly thought that I should be frightful to my fellow beings, and that children would cling to their mothers' gowns at sight of me!"

They shrank back into the dusky passageway, and closed the door. But, going up the staircase again, they found the whole interior of the house tenfold more dismal, and the air closer and heavier, for the glimpse and breath of freedom which they had just snatched. They could not flee; their jailer had but left the door ajar in mockery, and stood behind it to watch them stealing out. At the threshold, they felt his pitiless gripe upon them. For, what other dungeon is so dark as one's own heart! What jailer so inexorable as one's self!

But it would be no fair picture of Clifford's state of mind were we to represent him as continually or prevailingly wretched. On the contrary, there was no other man in the city, we are bold to affirm, of so much as half his years, who enjoyed so many lightsome and griefless moments as himself. He had no burden of care upon him; there were none of those questions and contingencies with the future to be settled which wear away all other lives, and render them not worth having by the very process of providing for their support. In this respect he was a child—a child for the whole term of his existence, be it long or short. Indeed, his life seemed to be standing still at a period little in advance of childhood, and to cluster all his reminiscences about that epoch; just as, after the torpor of a heavy blow, the sufferer's reviving consciousness goes back to a moment considerably behind the accident that stupefied him. He sometimes told Phoebe and Hepzibah his dreams, in which he invariably played the part of a child, or a very young man. So vivid were they, in his relation of them, that he once held a dispute with his sister as to the particular figure or print of a chintz morning dress, which he had seen their mother wear, in the dream of the preceding night. Hepzibah, piquing herself on a woman's accuracy in such matters, held it to be slightly different from what Clifford described; but, producing the very gown from an old trunk, it proved to be identical with his remembrance of it. Had Clifford, every time that he emerged out of dreams so lifelike, undergone the torture of transformation from a boy into an old and broken man, the daily recurrence of the shock would have been too much to bear. It would have caused an acute agony to thrill from the morning twilight, all the day through, until bedtime; and even then would have mingled a dull, inscrutable pain, and pallid hue of misfortune, with the visionary bloom and adolescence of his slumber. But the nightly moonshine interwove itself with the morning mist, and enveloped him as in a robe, which he hugged about his person, and seldom let realities pierce through; he was not often quite awake, but slept open-eyed, and perhaps fancied himself most dreaming then.

Thus, lingering always so near his childhood, he had sympathies with children, and kept his heart the fresher thereby, like a reservoir into which rivulets were pouring not far from the fountainhead. Though prevented, by a subtile sense of propriety, from desiring to associate with them, he loved few things better than to look out of the arched window, and see a little girl driving her hoop along the sidewalk, or schoolboys at a game of ball. Their voices, also, were very pleasant to him, heard at a distance, all swarming and intermingling together as flies do in a sunny room.

Clifford would, doubtless, have been glad to share their sports. One afternoon, he was seized with an irresistible desire to blow soap bubbles; an amusement, as Hepzibah told Phoebe apart, that had been a favorite one with her brother when they were both children. Behold him, therefore, at the arched window, with an earthen pipe in his mouth! Behold him, with his gray hair, and a wan, unreal smile over his countenance, where still hovered a beautiful grace, which his worst enemy must have acknowledged to be spiritual and immortal, since it had survived so long! Behold him, scattering airy spheres abroad, from the window into the street! Little impalpable worlds were those soap bubbles, with the big world depicted, in hues bright as imagination, on the nothing of their surface. It was curious to see how the passers-by regarded these brilliant fantasies, as they came floating down, and made the dull atmosphere imaginative about them. Some stopped to gaze, and, perhaps, carried a pleasant recollection of the bubbles onward as far as the street corner; some looked angrily upward, as if poor Clifford wronged them by setting an image of beauty afloat so near their dusty pathway. A great many put out their fingers or their walking sticks to touch, withal; and were perversely gratified, no doubt, when the bubble, with all its pictured earth and sky scene, vanished as if it had never been.

At length, just as an elderly gentleman of very dignified presence happened to be passing, a large bubble sailed majestically down, and burst right against his nose! He looked up, at first with a stern, keen glance, which penetrated at once into the obscurity behind the arched window, then with a smile, which might be conceived as diffusing a dog-day sultriness for the space of several yards about him.

"Aha, Cousin Clifford!" cried Judge Pyncheon. "What! Still blowing soap bubbles!"

The tone seemed as if meant to be kind and soothing, but yet had a bitterness of sarcasm in it. As for Clifford, an absolute palsy of fear came over him. Apart from any definite cause of dread which his past experience might have given him, he felt that native and original horror of the excellent Judge which is proper to a weak, delicate, and apprehensive character in the presence of massive strength. Strength is incomprehensible by weakness, and, therefore, the more terrible. There is no greater bugbear than a strong-willed relative in the circle of his own connections.

XII

The Daguerreotypist

It must not be supposed that the life of a personage naturally so active as Phoebe could be wholly confined within the precincts of the old Pyncheon House. Clifford's demands upon her time were usually satisfied, in those long days, considerably earlier than sunset. Quiet as his daily existence seemed, it nevertheless drained all the resources by which he lived. It was not physical exercise that overwearied him—for except that he sometimes wrought a little with a hoe, or paced the garden walk, or, in rainy weather, traversed a large, unoccupied room—it was his tendency to remain only too quiescent, as regarded any toil of the limbs and muscles. But, either there was a smoldering fire within him that consumed his vital energy, or the monotony that would have dragged itself with benumbing effect over a mind differently situated was no monotony to Clifford. Possibly, he was in a state of second growth and recovery, and was constantly assimilating nutriment for his spirit and intellect from sights, sounds, and events which passed as a perfect void to persons more practiced with the world. As all is activity and vicissitude to the new mind of a child, so might it be, likewise, to a mind that had undergone a kind of new creation, after its long-suspended life.

Be the cause what it might, Clifford commonly retired to rest, thoroughly exhausted, while the sunbeams were still melting through his window curtains, or were thrown with late luster on the chamber wall. And while he thus slept early, as other children do, and dreamed of childhood,

Phoebe was free to follow her own tastes for the remainder of the day and evening.

This was a freedom essential to the health even of a character so little susceptible of morbid influences as that of Phoebe. The old house, as we have already said, had both the dry rot and the damp rot in its walls; it was not good to breathe no other atmosphere than that. Hepzibah, though she had her valuable and redeeming traits, had grown to be a kind of lunatic, by imprisoning herself so long in one place, with no other company than a single series of ideas, and but one affection, and one bitter sense of wrong. Clifford, the reader may perhaps imagine, was too inert to operate morally on his fellow creatures, however intimate and exclusive their relations with him. But the sympathy or magnetism among human beings is more subtile and universal than we think; it exists, indeed, among different classes of organized life, and vibrates from one to another. A flower, for instance, as Phoebe herself observed, always began to droop sooner in Clifford's hand, or Hepzibah's, than in her own; and by the same law, converting her whole daily life into a flower fragrance for these two sickly spirits, the blooming girl must inevitably droop and fade much sooner than if worn on a younger and happier breast. Unless she had now and then indulged her brisk impulses, and breathed rural air in a suburban walk, or ocean breezes along the shore; had occasionally obeyed the impulse of Nature, in New England girls, by attending a metaphysical or philosophical lecture, or viewing a seven-mile panorama, or listening to a concert; had gone shopping about the city, ransacking entire depots of splendid merchandise, and bringing home a ribbon; had employed, likewise, a little time to read the Bible in her chamber, and had stolen a little more to think of her mother and her native place—unless for such moral medicines as the above, we should soon have beheld our poor Phoebe grow thin and put on a bleached, unwholesome aspect, and assume strange, shy ways, prophetic of old-maidenhood and a cheerless future.

Even as it was, a change grew visible; a change partly to be regretted, although whatever charm it infringed upon was repaired by another, perhaps more precious. She was not so constantly gay, but had her moods of thought, which Clifford, on the whole, liked better than her former phase of unmingled cheerfulness; because now she understood him better and more delicately, and sometimes even interpreted him to himself. Her eyes looked larger, and darker, and deeper; so deep, at some silent moments, that they seemed like Artesian wells, down, down, into the infinite. She was less girlish than when we first beheld her alighting from the omnibus; less girlish, but more a woman.

The only youthful mind with which Phoebe had an opportunity of frequent intercourse was that of the daguerreotypist. Inevitably, by the pressure of the seclusion about them, they had been brought into habits of some familiarity. Had they met under different circumstances, neither of these young persons would have been likely to bestow much thought upon the other, unless, indeed, their extreme dissimilarity should have proved a principle of mutual attraction. Both, it is true, were characters proper to New England life, and possessing a common ground, therefore, in their more external developments; but as unlike, in their respective interiors, as if their native climes had been at worldwide distance. During the early part of their acquaintance, Phoebe had held back rather more than was customary with her frank and simple manners from Holgrave's not very marked advances. Nor was she yet satisfied that she knew him well, although they almost daily met and talked together, in a kind, friendly, and what seemed to be a familiar way.

The artist, in a desultory manner, had imparted to Phoebe something of his history. Young as he was, and had his career terminated at the point already attained, there had been enough of incident to fill, very creditably, an autobiographic volume. A romance on the plan of Gil Blas, adapted to American society and manners, would cease to be a romance. The experience of many individuals among us, who think it hardly worth the telling, would equal the vicissitudes of the Spaniard's earlier life; while their ultimate success, or the point whither they tend, may be incomparably higher than any that a novelist would imagine for his hero. Holgrave, as he told Phoebe somewhat proudly, could not boast of his origin, unless as being exceedingly humble, nor of his education, except that it had been the scantiest possible, and obtained by a few winter months' attendance at a district school. Left early to his own guidance, he had begun to be self-dependent while yet a boy; and it was a

condition aptly suited to his natural force of will. Though
now but twenty-two years old (lacking some months, which
are years in such a life), he had already been, first, a
country schoolmaster; next, a salesman in a country store;
and either at the same time or afterwards, the political
editor of a country newspaper. He had subsequently traveled New England and the Middle States, as a peddler, in
the employment of a Connecticut manufactory of cologne
water and other essences. In an episodical way, he had
studied and practiced dentistry, and with very flattering
success, especially in many of the factory towns along our
inland streams. As a supernumerary official, of some kind
or other, aboard a packet ship, he had visited Europe, and
found means, before his return, to see Italy, and part of
France and Germany. At a later period, he had spent some
months in a community of Fourierists. Still more recently,
he had been a public lecturer on Mesmerism, for which
science (as he assured Phoebe, and, indeed, satisfactorily
proved, by putting Chanticleer, who happened to be scratching nearby, to sleep) he had very remarkable endowments.

His present phase, as a daguerreotypist, was of no more
importance in his own view, nor likely to be more permanent, than any of the preceding ones. It had been taken up
with the careless alacrity of an adventurer, who had his
bread to earn. It would be thrown aside as carelessly, whenever he should choose to earn his bread by some other
equally digressive means. But what was most remarkable,
and, perhaps, showed a more than common poise in the
young man, was the fact that, amid all these personal vicissitudes, he had never lost his identity. Homeless as he had
been—continually changing his whereabout, and, therefore,
responsible neither to public opinion nor to individuals;
putting off one exterior, and snatching up another, to be
soon shifted for a third—he had never violated the innermost man, but had carried his conscience along with him. It
was impossible to know Holgrave without recognizing this
to be the fact. Hepzibah had seen it. Phoebe soon saw it,
likewise, and gave him the sort of confidence which such a
certainty inspires. She was startled, however, and sometimes repelled, not by any doubt of his integrity to whatever
law he acknowledged, but by a sense that his law differed
from her own. He made her uneasy, and seemed to unsettle

everything around her, by his lack of reverence for what was fixed, unless, at a moment's warning, it could establish its right to hold its ground.

Then, moreover, she scarcely thought him affectionate in his nature. He was too calm and cool an observer. Phoebe felt his eye often; his heart, seldom or never. He took a certain kind of interest in Hepzibah and her brother, and Phoebe herself. He studied them attentively, and allowed no slightest circumstance of their individualities to escape him. He was ready to do them whatever good he might; but, after all, he never exactly made common cause with them, nor gave any reliable evidence that he loved them better in proportion as he knew them more. In his relations with them, he seemed to be in quest of mental food, not heart sustenance. Phoebe could not conceive what interested him so much in her friends and herself, intellectually, since he cared nothing for them, or, comparatively, so little, as objects of human affection.

Always, in his interviews with Phoebe, the artist made especial inquiry as to the welfare of Clifford, whom, except at the Sunday festival, he seldom saw.

"Does he still seem happy?" he asked one day.

"As happy as a child," answered Phoebe, "but—like a child, too—very easily disturbed."

"How disturbed?" inquired Holgrave. "By things without, or by thoughts within?"

"I cannot see his thoughts! How should I?" replied Phoebe, with simple piquancy. "Very often, his humor changes without any reason that can be guessed at, just as a cloud comes over the sun. Latterly, since I have begun to know him better, I feel it to be not quite right to look closely into his moods. He has had such a great sorrow that his heart is made all solemn and sacred by it. When he is cheerful—when the sun shines into his mind—then I venture to peep in, just as far as the light reaches, but no further. It is holy ground where the shadow falls!"

"How prettily you express this sentiment!" said the artist. "I can understand the feeling, without possessing it. Had I your opportunities, no scruples would prevent me from fathoming Clifford to the full depth of my plummet line!"

"How strange that you should wish it!" remarked Phoebe, involuntarily. "What is Cousin Clifford to you?"

"Oh, nothing—of course, nothing!" answered Holgrave, with a smile. "Only this is such an odd and incomprehensible world! The more I look at it, the more it puzzles me, and I begin to suspect that a man's bewilderment is the measure of his wisdom. Men and women, and children, too, are such strange creatures that one never can be certain that he really knows them; nor ever guess what they have been, from what he sees them to be now. Judge Pyncheon! Clifford! What a complex riddle—a complexity of complexities—do they present! It requires intuitive sympathy, like a young girl's, to solve it. A mere observer, like myself (who never have any intuitions, and am, at best, only subtle and acute), is pretty certain to go astray."

The artist now turned the conversation to themes less dark than that which they had touched upon. Phoebe and he were young together; nor had Holgrave, in his premature experience of life, wasted entirely that beautiful spirit of youth, which, gushing forth from one small heart and fancy, may diffuse itself over the universe, making it all as bright as on the first day of creation. Man's own youth is the world's youth; at least, he feels as if it were, and imagines that the earth's granite substance is something not yet hardened, and which he can mold into whatever shape he likes. So it was with Holgrave. He could talk sagely about the world's old age, but never actually believed what he said; he was a young man still, and therefore looked upon the world—that gray-bearded and wrinkled profligate, decrepit without being venerable—as a tender stripling, capable of being improved into all that it ought to be, but scarcely yet had shown the remotest promise of becoming. He had that sense, or inward prophecy—which a young man had better never have been born than not to have, and a mature man had better die at once than utterly to relinquish—that we are not doomed to creep on forever in the old bad way, but that, this very now, there are the harbingers abroad of a golden era, to be accomplished in his own lifetime. It seemed to Holgrave—as doubtless it has seemed to the hopeful of every century since the epoch of Adam's grandchildren—that in this age, more than ever before, the moss-grown and rotten Past is to be torn down, and lifeless institutions to be thrust out of the way, and their dead corpses buried, and everything to begin anew.

As to the main point—may we never live to doubt it!—as to the better centuries that are coming, the artist was surely right. His error lay in supposing that this age, more than any past or future one, is destined to see the tattered garments of Antiquity exchanged for a new suit, instead of gradually renewing themselves by patchwork; in applying his own little life span as the measure of an interminable achievement; and, more than all, in fancying that it mattered anything to the great end in view whether he himself should contend for it or against it. Yet it was well for him to think so. This enthusiasm, infusing itself through the calmness of his character, and thus taking an aspect of settled thought and wisdom, would serve to keep his youth pure, and make his aspirations high. And when, with the years settling down more weightily upon him, his early faith should be modified by inevitable experience, it would be with no harsh and sudden revolution of his sentiments. He would still have faith in man's brightening destiny, and perhaps love him all the better, as he should recognize his helplessness in his own behalf; and the haughty faith, with which he began life, would be well bartered for a far humbler one at its close, in discerning that man's best-directed effort accomplishes a kind of dream, while God is the sole worker of realities.

Holgrave had read very little, and that little in passing through the thoroughfare of life, where the mystic language of his books was necessarily mixed up with the babble of the multitude, so that both one and the other were apt to lose any sense that might have been properly their own. He considered himself a thinker, and was certainly of a thoughtful turn, but, with his own path to discover, had perhaps hardly yet reached the point where an educated man begins to think. The true value of his character lay in that deep consciousness of inward strength, which made all his past vicissitudes seem merely like a change of garments; in that enthusiasm, so quiet that he scarcely knew of its existence, but which gave a warmth to everything that he laid his hand on; in that personal ambition, hidden—from his own as well as other eyes—among his more generous impulses, but in which lurked a certain efficacy, that might solidify him from a theorist into the champion of some practicable cause. Altogether, in his culture and want of culture—in his crude, wild, and misty philosophy, and the practical experience that counteracted some of its tendencies; in his magnanimous zeal for man's welfare, and his recklessness of whatever the ages had established in man's behalf; in his faith, and in his infidelity; in what he had, and in what he lacked—the artist might fitly enough stand forth as the representative of many compeers in his native land.

His career it would be difficult to prefigure. There appeared to be qualities in Holgrave such as, in a country where everything is free to the hand that can grasp it, could hardly fail to put some of the world's prizes within his reach. But these matters are delightfully uncertain. At almost every step in life, we meet with young men of just about Holgrave's age, for whom we anticipate wonderful things, but of whom, even after much and careful inquiry, we never happen to hear another word. The effervescence of youth and passion, and the fresh gloss of the intellect and imagination, endow them with a false brilliancy, which makes fools of themselves and other people. Like certain chintzes, calicoes, and ginghams, they show finely in their first newness, but cannot stand the sun and rain, and assume a very sober aspect after washing day.

But our business is with Holgrave as we find him on this particular afternoon, and in the arbor of the Pyncheon garden. In that point of view, it was a pleasant sight to behold this young man, with so much faith in himself, and so fair an appearance of admirable powers—so little harmed, too, by the many tests that had tried his mettle—it was pleasant to see him in his kindly intercourse with Phoebe. Her thought had scarcely done him justice when it pronounced him cold; or, if so, he had grown warmer now. Without such purpose on her part, and unconsciously on his, she made the House of the Seven Gables like a home to him, and the garden a familiar precinct. With the insight on which he prided himself, he fancied that he could look through Phoebe, and all around her, and could read her off like a page of a child's story book. But these transparent natures are often deceptive in their depth; those pebbles at the bottom of the fountain are farther from us than we think. Thus the artist, what ever he might judge of Phoebe's capacity, was beguiled, by some silent charm of hers, to talk freely of what he dreamed of doing in the world. He poured himself out as to another self. Very possibly, he forgot Phoebe while he talked to her, and was moved only by the inevitable tendency of thought, when rendered sympathetic by enthusiasm and emotion, to flow into the first safe reservoir which it finds. But, had you peeped at them through the chinks of the garden fence, the young man's earnestness and heightened color might have led you to suppose that he was making love to the young girl!

At length, something was said by Holgrave that made it apposite for Phoebe to inquire what had first brought him acquainted with her cousin Hepzibah, and why he now chose to lodge in the desolate old Pyncheon House. Without directly answering her, he turned from the Future, which had heretofore been the theme of his discourse, and began to speak of the influences of the Past. One subject, indeed, is but the reverberation of the other.

"Shall we never, never get rid of this Past?" cried he, keeping up the earnest tone of his preceding conversation. "It lies upon the Present like a giant's dead body! In fact, the case is just as if a young giant were compelled to waste all his strength in carrying about the corpse of the old giant, his grandfather, who died a long while ago, and only needs to be decently buried. Just think a moment, and it will startle you to see what slaves we are to bygone times—to Death, if we give the matter the right word!"

"But I do not see it," observed Phoebe.

"For example, then," continued Holgrave. "A dead man, if he happen to have made a will, disposes of wealth no longer his own; or, if he die intestate, it is distributed in accordance with the notions of men much longer dead than he. A dead man sits on all our judgment seats; and living judges do but search out and repeat his decisions. We read in dead men's books! We laugh at dead men's jokes, and cry at dead men's pathos! We are sick of dead men's diseases, physical and moral, and die of the same remedies with which dead doctors killed their patients! We worship the living Deity according to dead men's forms and creeds. Whatever we seek to do, of our own free motion, a dead man's icy hand obstructs us! Turn our eyes to what point we may, a dead man's white, immitigable face encounters them, and freezes our very heart! And we must be dead ourselves before we can begin to have our proper influence on our own world, which will then be no longer our world, but the world of another generation, with which we shall have no shadow of a right to interfere. I ought to have said, too, that we live in dead men's houses; as, for instance, in this of the Seven Gables!"

"And why not," said Phoebe, "so long as we can be comfortable in them?"

"But we shall live to see the day, I trust," went on the artist, "when no man shall build his house for posterity. Why should he? He might just as reasonably order a durable suit of clothes—leather, or gutta-percha, or whatever else lasts longest—so that his great-grandchildren should have the benefit of them, and cut precisely the same figure in the world that he himself does. If each generation were allowed and expected to build its own houses, that single change, comparatively unimportant in itself, would imply almost every reform which society is now suffering for. I doubt whether even our public edifices—our capitols, state houses, courthouses, city hall, and churches—ought to be built of such permanent materials as stone or brick. It were better that they should crumble to ruin once in twenty years, or thereabouts, as a hint to the people to examine into and reform the institutions which they symbolize."

"How you hate everything old!" said Phoebe, in dismay. "It makes me dizzy to think of such a shifting world!"

"I certainly love nothing moldy," answered Holgrave. "Now, this old Pyncheon House! Is it a wholesome place to live in, with its black shingles, and the green moss that shows how damp they are; its dark, low-studded rooms; its grime and sordidness, which are the crystallization on its walls of the human breath that has been drawn and exhaled here in discontent and anguish? The house ought to be purified with fire—purified till only its ashes remain!"

"Then why do you live in it?" asked Phoebe, a little piqued.

"Oh, I am pursuing my studies here; not in books, however," replied Holgrave. "The house, in my view, is expressive of that odious and abominable Past, with all its bad influences, against which I have just been declaiming. I dwell in it for a while, that I may know the better how to hate it. By the by, did you ever hear the story of Maule, the wizard, and what happened between him and your immeasurably great-grandfather?"

"Yes, indeed!" said Phoebe. "I heard it long ago, from my father, and two or three times from my cousin Hepzibah, in the month that I have been here. She seems to think that all the calamities of the Pyncheons began from that quarrel with the wizard, as you call him. And you, Mr. Holgrave, look as if you thought so, too! How singular that you should believe what is so very absurd, when you reject many things that are a great deal worthier of credit!"

"I do believe it," said the artist, seriously, "not as a superstition, however, but as proved by unquestionable facts, and as exemplifying a theory. Now, see: under those seven gables, at which we now look up—and which old Colonel Pyncheon meant to be the house of his descendants, in prosperity and happiness, down to an epoch far beyond the present—under that roof, through a portion of three centuries, there has been perpetual remorse of conscience, a constantly defeated hope, strife amongst kindred, various misery, a strange form of death, dark suspicion, unspeakable disgrace—all or most of which calamity I have the means of tracing to the old Puritan's inordinate desire to plant and endow a family. To plant a family! This idea is at the bottom of most of the wrong and mischief which men do. The truth is, that, once in every half century, at longest, a family should be merged into the great, obscure mass of humanity, and forget all about its ancestors. Human blood, in order to keep its freshness, should run in hidden streams, as the water of an aqueduct is conveyed in subterranean pipes. In the family existence of these Pyncheons, for instance—forgive me, Phoebe; but I cannot think of you as one of them—in their brief New England pedigree, there has been time enough to infect them all with one kind of lunacy or another!"

"You speak very unceremoniously of my kindred," said Phoebe, debating with herself whether she ought to take offense.

"I speak true thoughts to a true mind!" answered Holgrave, with a vehemence which Phoebe had not before witnessed in him. "The truth is as I say! Furthermore, the original perpetrator and father of this mischief appears to have perpetuated himself, and still walks the street—at least, his very image, in mind and body—with the fairest prospect of transmitting to posterity as rich and as wretched an inheritance as he has received! Do you remember the daguerreotype, and its resemblance to the old portrait?"

"How strangely in earnest you are!" exclaimed Phoebe, looking at him with surprise and perplexity; half alarmed and partly inclined to laugh. "You talk of the lunacy of the Pyncheons; is it contagious?"

"I understand you!" said the artist, coloring and laughing. "I believe I am a little mad. This subject has taken hold of my mind with the strangest tenacity of clutch since I have lodged in yonder old gable. As one method of throwing it off, I have put an incident of the Pyncheon family history, with which I happen to be acquainted, into the form of a legend, and mean to publish it in a magazine."

"Do you write for the magazines?" inquired Phoebe.

"Is it possible you did not know it?" cried Holgrave. "Well, such is literary fame! Yes, Miss Phoebe Pyncheon, among the multitude of my marvelous gifts I have that of writing stories; and my name has figured, I can assure you, on the covers of *Graham* and *Godey,* making as respectable an appearance, for aught I could see, as any of the canonized beadroll with which it was associated. In the humorous line, I am thought to have a very pretty way with me; and as for pathos, I am as provocative of tears as an onion. But shall I read you my story?"

"Yes, if it is not very long," said Phoebe, and added laughingly, "nor very dull."

As this latter point was one which the daguerreotypist could not decide for himself, he forthwith produced his roll of manuscript, and, while the late sunbeams gilded the seven gables, began to read.

XIII

Alice Pyncheon

THERE was a message brought, one day, from the worshipful Gervayse Pyncheon to young Matthew Maule, the carpenter, desiring his immediate presence at the House of the Seven Gables.

"And what does your master want with me?" said the carpenter to Mr. Pyncheon's black servant. "Does the house need any repair? Well it may, by this time; and no blame to my father who built it, neither! I was reading the old Colonel's tombstone, no longer ago than last Sabbath; and, reckoning from that date, the house has stood seven and thirty years. No wonder if there should be a job to do on the roof."

"Don't know what massa wants," answered Scipio. "The house is a berry good house, and old Colonel Pyncheon think so, too, I reckon; else why the old man haunt it so, and frighten a poor nigga, as he does?"

"Well, well, friend Scipio; let your master know that I'm coming," said the carpenter, with a laugh. "For a fair, workmanlike job, he'll find me his man. And so the house is haunted, is it? It will take a tighter workman than I am to keep the spirits out of the Seven Gables. Even if the Colonel would be quiet," he added, muttering to himself, "my old grandfather, the wizard, will be pretty sure to stick to the Pyncheons as long as their walls hold together."

"What's that you mutter to yourself, Matthew Maule?" asked Scipio. "And what for do you look so black at me?"

"No matter, darky!" said the carpenter. "Do you think nobody is to look black but yourself? Go tell your master

I'm coming; and if you happen to see Mistress Alice, his daughter, give Matthew Maule's humble respects to her. She has brought a fair face from Italy—fair, and gentle, and proud—has that same Alice Pyncheon!"

"He talk of Mistress Alice!" cried Scipio, as he returned from his errand. "The low carpenter man! He no business so much as to look at her a great way off!"

This young Matthew Maule, the carpenter, it must be observed, was a person little understood, and not very generally liked, in the town where he resided; not that anything could be alleged against his integrity, or his skill and diligence in the handicraft which he exercised. The aversion (as it might justly be called) with which many persons regarded him was partly the result of his own character and deportment, and partly an inheritance.

He was the grandson of a former Matthew Maule, one of the early settlers of the town, and who had been a famous and terrible wizard in his day. This old reprobate was one of the sufferers when Cotton Mather, and his brother ministers, and the learned judges, and other wise men, and Sir William Phipps, the sagacious governor, made such laudable efforts to weaken the great enemy of souls, by sending a multitude of his adherents up the rocky pathway of Gallows Hill. Since those days, no doubt, it had grown to be suspected that, in consequence of an unfortunate overdoing of a work praiseworthy in itself, the proceedings against the witches had proved far less acceptable to the Beneficent Father than to that very Archenemy whom they were intended to distress and utterly overwhelm. It is not the less certain, however, that awe and terror brooded over the memories of those who died for this horrible crime of witchcraft. Their graves, in the crevices of the rocks, were supposed to be incapable of retaining the occupants who had been so hastily thrust into them. Old Matthew Maule, especially, was known to have as little hesitation or difficulty in rising out of his grave as an ordinary man in getting out of bed, and was as often seen at midnight as living people at noonday. This pestilent wizard (in whom his just punishment seemed to have wrought no manner of amendment) had an inveterate habit of haunting a certain mansion, styled the House of the Seven Gables, against the owner of which he pretended to hold an unsettled claim for ground rent. The ghost, it appears—with the pertinacity which was one of his distinguishing characteristics while alive—insisted that he was the rightful proprietor of the site upon which the house stood. His terms were that either the aforesaid ground rent, from the day when the cellar began to be dug, should be paid down, or the mansion itself given up; else he, the ghostly creditor, would have his finger in all the affairs of the Pyncheons, and make everything go wrong with them, though it should be a thousand years after his death. It was a wild story, perhaps, but seemed not altogether so incredible to those who could remember what an inflexibly obstinate old fellow this wizard Maule had been.

Now, the wizard's grandson, the young Matthew Maule of our story, was popularly supposed to have inherited some of his ancestor's questionable traits. It is wonderful how many absurdities were promulgated in reference to the young man. He was fabled, for example, to have a strange power of getting into people's dreams, and regulating matters there according to his own fancy, pretty much like the stage manager of a theatre. There was a great deal of talk among the neighbors, particularly the petticoated ones, about what they called the witchcraft of Maule's eye. Some said that he could look into people's minds; others, that, by the marvelous power of this eye, he could draw people into his own mind, or send them, if he pleased, to do errands to his grandfather, in the spiritual world; others, again, that it was what is termed an Evil Eye, and possessed the valuable faculty of blighting corn, and drying children into mummies with the heartburn. But, after all, what worked most to the young carpenter's disadvantage was, first, the reserve and sternness of his natural disposition, and next, the fact of his not being a church communicant, and the suspicion of his holding heretical tenets in matters of religion and polity.

After receiving Mr. Pyncheon's message, the carpenter merely tarried to finish a small job, which he happened to have in hand, and then took his way towards the House of the Seven Gables. This noted edifice, though its style might be getting a little out of fashion, was still as respectable a family residence as that of any gentleman in town. The present owner, Gervayse Pyncheon, was said to have con-

tracted a dislike to the house, in consequence of a shock to
his sensibility, in early childhood, from the sudden death of
his grandfather. In the very act of running to climb Colonel
Pyncheon's knee, the boy had discovered the old Puritan to
be a corpse! On arriving at manhood, Mr. Pyncheon had
visited England, where he married a lady of fortune, and
had subsequently spent many years, partly in the mother
country, and partly in various cities on the continent of
Europe. During this period, the family mansion had been
consigned to the charge of a kinsman, who was allowed to
make it his home for the time being, in consideration of
keeping the premises in thorough repair. So faithfully had
this contract been fulfilled, that now, as the carpenter approached the house, his practiced eye could detect nothing
to criticize in its condition. The peaks of the seven gables
rose up sharply; the shingled roof looked thoroughly water-
tight; and the glittering plasterwork entirely covered the
exterior walls, and sparkled in the October sun, as if it had
been new only a week ago.

The house had that pleasant aspect of life which is like the
cheery expression of comfortable activity in the human countenance. You could see, at once, that there was the stir of a
large family within it. A huge load of oak wood was passing
through the gateway, towards the outbuildings in the rear;
the fat cook—or probably it might be the housekeeper—
stood at the side door, bargaining for some turkeys and
poultry, which a countryman had brought for sale. Now and
then a maidservant, neatly dressed, and now the shining
sable face of a slave, might be seen bustling across the
windows, in the lower part of the house. At an open window of a room in the second story, hanging over some pots
of beautiful and delicate flowers—exotics, but which had
never known a more genial sunshine than that of the New
England autumn—was the figure of a young lady, an exotic,
like the flowers, and beautiful and delicate as they. Her
presence imparted an indescribable grace and faint witchery
to the whole edifice. In other respects, it was a substantial,
jolly-looking mansion, and seemed fit to be the residence of
a patriarch, who might establish his own headquarters in the
front gable and assign one of the remainder to each of his
six children, while the great chimney in the center should

symbolize the old fellow's hospitable heart, which kept them all warm, and made a great whole of the seven smaller ones.

There was a vertical sundial on the front gable; and as the carpenter passed beneath it, he looked up and noted the hour.

"Three o'clock!" said he to himself. "My father told me that dial was put up only an hour before the old Colonel's death. How truly it has kept time these seven and thirty years past! The shadow creeps and creeps, and is always looking over the shoulder of the sunshine!"

It might have befitted a craftsman, like Matthew Maule, on being sent for to a gentleman's house, to go to the back door, where servants and workpeople were usually admitted; or at least to the side entrance, where the better class of tradesmen made application. But the carpenter had a great deal of pride and stiffness in his nature; and, at this moment, moreover, his heart was bitter with the sense of hereditary wrong, because he considered the great Pyncheon House to be standing on soil which should have been his own. On this very site, beside a spring of delicious water, his grandfather had felled the pine trees and built a cottage, in which children had been born to him; and it was only from a dead man's stiffened fingers that Colonel Pyncheon had wrested away the title deeds. So young Maule went straight to the principal entrance, beneath a portal of carved oak, and gave such a peal of the iron knocker that you would have imagined the stern old wizard himself to be standing at the threshold.

Black Scipio answered the summons in a prodigious hurry; but showed the whites of his eyes, in amazement on beholding only the carpenter.

"Lord-a-mercy! what a great man he be, this carpenter fellow!" mumbled Scipio, down in his throat. "Anybody think he beat on the door with his biggest hammer!"

"Here I am!" said Maule, sternly. "Show me the way to your master's parlor!"

As he stepped into the house, a note of sweet and melancholy music thrilled and vibrated along the passageway, proceeding from one of the rooms abovestairs. It was the harpsichord which Alice Pyncheon had brought with her from beyond the sea. The fair Alice bestowed most of her maiden leisure between flowers and music, although the former were apt to droop, and the melodies were often sad. She was of foreign education, and could not take kindly to the New England modes of life, in which nothing beautiful had ever been developed.

As Mr. Pyncheon had been impatiently awaiting Maule's arrival, black Scipio, of course, lost no time in ushering the carpenter into his master's presence. The room in which this gentleman sat was a parlor of moderate size, looking out upon the garden of the house, and having its windows partly shadowed by the foliage of fruit trees. It was Mr. Pyncheon's peculiar apartment, and was provided with furniture, in an elegant and costly style, principally from Paris; the floor (which was unusual at that day) being covered with a carpet, so skillfully and richly wrought that it seemed to glow as with living flowers. In one corner stood a marble woman, to whom her own beauty was the sole and sufficient garment. Some pictures—that looked old, and had a mellow tinge diffused through all their artful splendor—hung on the walls. Near the fireplace was a large and very beautiful cabinet of ebony, inlaid with ivory—a piece of antique furniture, which Mr. Pyncheon had bought in Venice, and which he used as the treasure place for medals, ancient coins, and whatever small and valuable curiosities he had picked up on his travels. Through all this variety of decoration, however, the room showed its original characteristics—its low stud, its crossbeam, its chimney piece, with the old-fashioned Dutch tiles—so that it was the emblem of a mind industriously stored with foreign ideas, and elaborated into artificial refinement, but neither larger, nor, in its proper self, more elegant than before.

There were two objects that appeared rather out of place in this very handsomely furnished room. One was a large map, or surveyor's plan, of a tract of land, which looked as if it had been drawn a good many years ago, and was now dingy with smoke, and soiled, here and there, with the touch of fingers. The other was a portrait of a stern old man, in a Puritan garb, painted roughly, but with a bold effect, and a remarkably strong expression of character.

At a small table, before a fire of English sea coal, sat Mr. Pyncheon, sipping coffee, which had grown to be a very favorite beverage with him in France. He was a middle-aged and really handsome man, with a wig flowing down upon his shoulders; his coat was of blue velvet, with lace on the borders and at the buttonholes; and the firelight glistened on the spacious breadth of his waistcoat, which was flowered all over with gold. On the entrance of Scipio, ushering in the carpenter, Mr. Pyncheon turned partly round, but resumed his former position, and proceeded deliberately to finish his cup of coffee, without immediate notice of the guest whom he had summoned to his presence. It was not that he intended any rudeness or improper neglect—which, indeed, he would have blushed to be guilty of—but it never occurred to him that a person in Maule's station had a claim on his courtesy, or would trouble himself about it one way or the other.

The carpenter, however, stepped at once to the hearth, and turned himself about, so as to look Mr. Pyncheon in the face.

"You sent for me," said he. "Be pleased to explain your business, that I may go back to my own affairs."

"Ah! Excuse me," said Mr. Pyncheon, quietly. "I did not mean to tax your time without a recompense. Your name, I think, is Maule—Thomas or Matthew Maule—a son or grandson of the builder of this house?"

"Matthew Maule," replied the carpenter, "son of him who built the house, grandson of the rightful proprietor of the soil."

"I know the dispute to which you allude," observed Mr. Pyncheon, with undisturbed equanimity. "I am well aware that my grandfather was compelled to resort to a suit at law, in order to establish his claim to the foundation site of this edifice. We will not, if you please, renew the discussion. The matter was settled at the time, and by the competent authorities—equitably, it is to be presumed, and, at all events, irrevocably. Yet, singularly enough, there is an incidental reference to this very subject in what I am now about to say to you. And this same inveterate grudge—excuse me, I mean no offense—this irritability, which you have just shown, is not entirely aside from the matter."

"If you can find anything for your purpose, Mr. Pyncheon," said the carpenter, "in a man's natural resentment for the wrongs done to his blood, you are welcome to it!"

"I take you at your word, Goodman Maule," said the

owner of the Seven Gables, with a smile, "and will proceed to suggest a mode in which your hereditary resentments—justifiable, or otherwise—may have had a bearing on my affairs. You have heard, I suppose, that the Pyncheon family, ever since my grandfather's days, have been prosecuting a still unsettled claim to a very large extent of territory at the eastward?"

"Often," replied Maule, and it is said that a smile came over his face, "very often—from my father!"

"This claim," continued Mr. Pyncheon, after pausing a moment, as if to consider what the carpenter's smile might mean, "appeared to be on the very verge of a settlement and full allowance, at the period of my grandfather's decease. It was well known, to those in his confidence, that he anticipated neither difficulty nor delay. Now, Colonel Pyncheon, I need hardly say, was a practical man, well acquainted with public and private business, and not at all the person to cherish ill-founded hopes, or to attempt the following out of an impracticable scheme. It is obvious to conclude, therefore, that he had grounds, not apparent to his heirs, for his confident anticipation of success in the matter of this Eastern claim. In a word, I believe—and my legal advisers coincide in the belief, which, moreover, is authorized, to a certain extent, by the family traditions—that my grandfather was in possession of some deed, or other document, essential to this claim, but which has since disappeared."

"Very likely," said Matthew Maule, and again, it is said, there was a dark smile on his face, "but what can a poor carpenter have to do with the grand affairs of the Pyncheon family?"

"Perhaps nothing," returned Mr. Pyncheon, "possibly much!"

Here ensued a great many words between Matthew Maule and the proprietor of the Seven Gables, on the subject which the latter had thus broached. It seems (although Mr. Pyncheon had some hesitation in referring to stories so exceedingly absurd in their aspect) that the popular belief pointed to some mysterious connection and dependence, existing between the family of the Maules and these vast unrealized possessions of the Pyncheons. It was an ordinary saying that the old wizard, hanged though he was, had

obtained the best end of the bargain in his contest with
Colonel Pyncheon; inasmuch as he had got possession of the
great Eastern claim, in exchange for an acre or two of
garden ground. A very aged woman, recently dead, had
often used the metaphorical expression, in her fireside talk,
that miles and miles of the Pyncheon lands had been shov-
eled into Maule's grave; which, by the by, was but a very
shallow nook, between two rocks, near the summit of Gallows Hill. Again, when the lawyers were making inquiry for
the missing document, it was a byword that it would never
be found, unless in the wizard's skeleton hand. So much
weight had the shrewd lawyers assigned to these fables, that
(but Mr. Pyncheon did not see fit to inform the carpenter of
the fact) they had secretly caused the wizard's grave to be
searched. Nothing was discovered, however, except that,
unaccountably, the right hand of the skeleton was gone.

Now, what was unquestionably important, a portion of
these popular rumors could be traced, though rather doubtfully and indistinctly, to chance words and obscure hints of
the executed wizard's son, and the father of this present
Matthew Maule. And here Mr. Pyncheon could bring an
item of his own personal evidence into play. Though but a
child at the time, he either remembered or fancied that
Matthew's father had had some job to perform, on the day
before, or possibly the very morning of the Colonel's decease, in the private room where he and the carpenter were
at this moment talking. Certain papers belonging to Colonel
Pyncheon, as his grandson distinctly recollected, had been
spread out on the table.

Matthew Maule understood the insinuated suspicion.

"My father," he said, but still there was that dark smile,
making a riddle of his countenance, "my father was an
honester man than the bloody old Colonel! Not to get his
rights back again would he have carried off one of those
papers!"

"I shall not bandy words with you," observed the foreign-
bred Mr. Pyncheon, with haughty composure. "Nor will it
become me to resent any rudeness towards either my grandfather or myself. A gentleman, before seeking intercourse
with a person of your station and habits, will first consider
whether the urgency of the end may compensate for the

disagreeableness of the means. It does so in the present instance."

He then renewed the conversation, and made great pecuniary offers to the carpenter, in case the latter should give information leading to the discovery of the lost document, and the consequent success of the Eastern claim. For a long time, Matthew Maule is said to have turned a cold ear to these propositions. At last, however, with a strange kind of laugh, he inquired whether Mr. Pyncheon would make over to him the old wizard's homestead ground, together with the House of the Seven Gables, now standing on it, in requital of the documentary evidence so urgently required.

The wild, chimney-corner legend (which, without copying all its extravagances, my narrative essentially follows) here gives an account of some very strange behavior on the part of Colonel Pyncheon's portrait. This picture, it must be understood, was supposed to be so intimately connected with the fate of the house, and so magically built into its walls, that, if once it should be removed, that very instant the whole edifice would come thundering down in a heap of dusty ruin. All through the foregoing conversation between Mr. Pyncheon and the carpenter, the portrait had been frowning, clenching its fist, and giving many such proofs of excessive discomposure, but without attracting the notice of either of the two colloquists. And finally, at Matthew Maule's audacious suggestion of a transfer of the seven-gabled structure, the ghostly portrait is averred to have lost all patience, and to have shown itself on the point of descending bodily from its frame. But such incredible incidents are merely to be mentioned aside.

"Give up this house!" exclaimed Mr. Pyncheon, in amazement at the proposal. "Were I to do so, my grandfather would not rest quiet in his grave!"

"He never has, if all stories are true," remarked the carpenter, composedly. "But that matter concerns his grandson more than it does Matthew Maule. I have no other terms to propose."

Impossible as he at first thought it to comply with Maule's conditions, still, on a second glance, Mr. Pyncheon was of opinion that they might at least be made matter of discussion. He himself had no personal attachment for the house, nor any pleasant associations connected with his childish

residence in it. On the contrary, after seven and thirty
years, the presence of his dead grandfather seemed still to
pervade it, as on that morning when the affrighted boy had
beheld him, with so ghastly an aspect, stiffening in his chair.
His long abode in foreign parts, moreover, and familiarity
with many of the castles and ancestral halls of England, and
the marble palaces of Italy, had caused him to look con-
temptuously at the House of the Seven Gables, whether in
point of splendor or convenience. It was a mansion exceedingly inadequate to the style of living which it would be
incumbent on Mr. Pyncheon to support, after realizing his
territorial rights. His steward might deign to occupy it, but
never, certainly, the great landed proprietor himself. In the
event of success, indeed, it was his purpose to return to
England; nor, to say the truth, would he recently have
quitted that more congenial home, had not his own fortune,
as well as his deceased wife's, begun to give symptoms of
exhaustion. The Eastern claim once fairly settled, and put
upon the firm basis of actual possession, Mr. Pyncheon's
property—to be measured by miles, not acres—would be
worth an earldom, and would reasonably entitle him to
solicit, or enable him to purchase, that elevated dignity from
the British monarch. Lord Pyncheon! Or the Earl of Waldo!
How could such a magnate be expected to contract his
grandeur within the pitiful compass of seven shingled gables?

In short, on an enlarged view of the business, the carpenter's terms appeared so ridiculously easy that Mr. Pyncheon
could scarcely forbear laughing in his face. He was quite
ashamed, after the foregoing reflections, to propose any
diminution of so moderate a recompense for the immense
service to be rendered.

"I consent to your proposition, Maule," cried he. "Put
me in possession of the document essential to establish my
rights, and the House of the Seven Gables is your own!"

According to some versions of the story, a regular contract to the above effect was drawn up by a lawyer, and
signed and sealed in the presence of witnesses. Others say
that Matthew Maule was contented with a private written
agreement, in which Mr. Pyncheon pledged his honor and
integrity to the fulfillment of the terms concluded upon. The
gentleman then ordered wine, which he and the carpenter

drank together, in confirmation of their bargain. During the whole preceding discussion and subsequent formalities, the old Puritan's portrait seems to have persisted in its shadowy gestures of disapproval; but without effect, except that, as Mr. Pyncheon set down the emptied glass, he thought he beheld his grandfather frown.

"This sherry is too potent a wine for me; it has affected my brain already," he observed, after a somewhat startled look at the picture. "On returning to Europe, I shall confine myself to the more delicate vintages of Italy and France, the best of which will not bear transportation."

"My Lord Pyncheon may drink what wine he will, and wherever he pleases," replied the carpenter, as if he had been privy to Mr. Pyncheon's ambitious projects. "But first, sir, if you desire tidings of this lost document, I must crave the favor of a little talk with your fair daughter Alice."

"You are mad, Maule!" exclaimed Mr. Pyncheon, haughtily; and now, at last, there was anger mixed up with his pride. "What can my daughter have to do with a business like this?"

Indeed, at this new demand on the carpenter's part, the proprietor of the Seven Gables was even more thunderstruck than at the cool proposition to surrender his house. There was, at least, an assignable motive for the first stipulation; there appeared to be none whatever for the last. Nevertheless, Matthew Maule sturdily insisted on the young lady being summoned, and even gave her father to understand, in a mysterious kind of explanation—which made the matter considerably darker than it looked before—that the only chance of acquiring the requisite knowledge was through the clear, crystal medium of a pure and virgin intelligence, like that of the fair Alice. Not to encumber our story with Mr. Pyncheon's scruples, whether of conscience, pride, or fatherly affection, he at length ordered his daughter to be called. He well knew that she was in her chamber, and engaged in no occupation that could not readily be laid aside; for, as it happened, ever since Alice's name had been spoken, both her father and the carpenter had heard the sad and sweet music of her harpsichord, and the airier melancholy of her accompanying voice.

So Alice Pyncheon was summoned and appeared. A portrait of this young lady, painted by a Venetian artist, and left by her father in England, is said to have fallen into the hands of the present Duke of Devonshire, and to be now preserved at Chatsworth; not on account of any associations with the original, but for its value as a picture, and the high character of beauty in the countenance. If ever there was a lady born, and set apart from the world's vulgar mass by a certain gentle and cold stateliness, it was this very Alice Pyncheon. Yet there was the womanly mixture in her; the tenderness, or, at least, the tender capabilities. For the sake of that redeeming quality, a man of generous nature would have forgiven all her pride, and have been content, almost, to lie down in her path, and let Alice set her slender foot upon his heart. All that he would have required was simply the acknowledgment that he was indeed a man, and a fellow being, molded of the same elements as she.

As Alice came into the room, her eyes fell upon the carpenter, who was standing near its center, clad in a green woolen jacket, a pair of loose breeches, open at the knees, and with a long pocket for his rule, the end of which protruded; it was as proper a mark of the artisan's calling as Mr. Pyncheon's full-dress sword of that gentleman's aristocratic pretensions. A glow of artistic approval brightened over Alice Pyncheon's face; she was struck with admiration—which she made no attempt to conceal—of the remarkable comeliness, strength, and energy of Maule's figure. But that admiring glance (which most other men, perhaps, would have cherished as a sweet recollection, all through life) the carpenter never forgave. It must have been the devil himself that made Maule so subtle in his perception.

"Does the girl look at me as if I were a brute beast?" thought he, setting his teeth. "She shall know whether I have a human spirit; and the worse for her, if it prove stronger than her own!"

"My father, you sent for me," said Alice, in her sweet and harplike voice. "But, if you have business with this young man, pray let me go again. You know I do not love this room, in spite of that Claude, with which you try to bring back sunny recollections."

"Stay a moment, young lady, if you please!" said Matthew Maule. "My business with your father is over. With yourself, it is now to begin!"

Alice looked towards her father in surprise and inquiry.

Alice Pyncheon

"Yes, Alice," said Mr. Pyncheon, with some distu____ and confusion. "This young man—his name is M_____ Maule—professes, so far as I can understand him, to be able to discover, through your means, a certain paper or parchment, which was missing long before your birth. The importance of the document in question renders it advisable to neglect no possible, even if improbable, method of regaining it. You will therefore oblige me, my dear Alice, by answering this person's inquiries, and complying with his lawful and reasonable requests, so far as they may appear to have the aforesaid object in view. As I shall remain in the room, you need apprehend no rude nor unbecoming deportment, on the young man's part; and, at your slightest wish, of course, the investigation, or whatever we may call it, shall immediately be broken off."

"Mistress Alice Pyncheon," remarked Matthew Maule, with the utmost deference, but yet a half-hidden sarcasm in his look and tone, "will no doubt feel herself quite safe in her father's presence, and under his all-sufficient protection."

"I certainly shall entertain no manner of apprehension, with my father at hand," said Alice, with maidenly dignity. "Neither do I conceive that a lady, while true to herself, can have aught to fear from whomsoever, or in any circumstances!"

Poor Alice! By what unhappy impulse did she thus put herself at once on terms of defiance against a strength which she could not estimate?

"Then, Mistress Alice," said Matthew Maule, handing a chair—gracefully enough, for a craftsman, "will it please you only to sit down, and do me the favor (though altogether beyond a poor carpenter's deserts) to fix your eyes on mine!"

Alice complied. She was very proud. Setting aside all advantages of rank, this fair girl deemed herself conscious of a power—combined of beauty, high, unsullied purity, and the preservative force of womanhood—that could make her sphere impenetrable, unless betrayed by treachery within. She instinctively knew, it may be, that some sinister or evil potency was now striving to pass her barriers; nor would she decline the contest. So Alice put woman's might against man's might; a match not often equal on the part of woman.

Her father meanwhile had turned away, and seemed absorbed in the contemplation of a landscape by Claude, where a shadowy and sun-streaked vista penetrated so remotely into an ancient wood that it would have been no wonder if his fancy had lost itself in the picture's bewildering depths. But, in truth, the picture was no more to him at that moment than the blank wall against which it hung. His mind was haunted with the many and strange tales which he had heard, attributing mysterious if not supernatural endowments to these Maules, as well the grandson here present as his two immediate ancestors. Mr. Pyncheon's long residence abroad, and intercourse with men of wit and fashion—courtiers, worldlings, and free-thinkers—had done much towards obliterating the grim Puritan superstitions which no man of New England birth at that early period could entirely escape. But, on the other hand, had not a whole community believed Maule's grandfather to be a wizard? Had not the crime been proved? Had not the wizard died for it? Had he not bequeathed a legacy of hatred against the Pyncheons to this only grandson, who, as it appeared, was now about to exercise a subtle influence over the daughter of his enemy's house? Might not this influence be the same that was called witchcraft?

Turning half around, he caught a glimpse of Maule's figure in the looking glass. At some paces from Alice, with his arms uplifted in the air, the carpenter made a gesture as if directing downward a slow, ponderous, and invisible weight upon the maiden.

"Stay, Maule!" exclaimed Mr. Pyncheon, stepping forward. "I forbid your proceeding further!"

"Pray, my dear father, do not interrupt the young man," said Alice, without changing her position. "His efforts, I assure you, will prove very harmless."

Again Mr. Pyncheon turned his eyes towards the Claude. It was then his daughter's will, in opposition to his own, that the experiment should be fully tried. Henceforth, therefore, he did but consent, not urge it. And was it not for her sake far more than for his own that he desired its success? That lost parchment once restored, the beautiful Alice Pyncheon, with the rich dowry which he could then bestow, might wed an English duke or a German reigning prince, instead of some New England clergyman or lawyer! At the thought, the ambitious father almost consented, in his heart, that, if the devil's power were needed to the accomplishment of this great object, Maule might evoke him. Alice's own purity would be her safeguard.

With his mind full of imaginary magnificence, Mr. Pyncheon heard a half-uttered exclamation from his daughter. It was very faint and low; so indistinct that there seemed but half a will to shape out the words, and too undefined a purport to be intelligible. Yet it was a call for help—his conscience never doubted it—and, little more than a whisper to his ear, it was a dismal shriek, and long re-echoed so, in the region round his heart! But this time the father did not turn.

After a further interval, Maule spoke.

"Behold your daughter!" said he.

Mr. Pyncheon came hastily forward. The carpenter was standing erect in front of Alice's chair, and pointing his finger towards the maiden with an expression of triumphant power the limits of which could not be defined, as, indeed, its scope stretched vaguely towards the unseen and the infinite. Alice sat in an attitude of profound repose, with the long brown lashes drooping over her eyes.

"There she is!" said the carpenter. "Speak to her!"

"Alice! My daughter!" exclaimed Mr. Pyncheon. "My own Alice!"

She did not stir.

"Louder!" said Maule, smiling.

"Alice! Awake!" cried her father. "It troubles me to see you thus! Awake!"

He spoke loudly, with terror in his voice, and close to that delicate ear which had always been so sensitive to every discord. But the sound evidently reached her not. It is indescribable what a sense of remote, dim, unattainable distance, betwixt himself and Alice, was impressed on the father by this impossibility of reaching her with his voice.

"Best touch her!" said Matthew Maule. "Shake the girl, and roughly, too! My hands are hardened with too much use of ax, saw, and plane—else I might help you!"

Mr. Pyncheon took her hand, and pressed it with the

earnestness of startled emotion. He kissed her, with so great a heartthrob in the kiss that he thought she must needs feel it. Then, in a gust of anger at her insensibility, he shook her maiden form with a violence which, the next moment, it affrighted him to remember. He withdrew his encircling arms, and Alice—whose figure, though flexible, had been wholly impassive—relapsed into the same attitude as before these attempts to arouse her. Maule having shifted his position, her face was turned towards him slightly, but with what seemed to be a reference of her very slumber to his guidance.

Then it was a strange sight to behold how the man of conventionalities shook the powder out of his periwig; how the reserved and stately gentleman forgot his dignity; how the gold-embroidered waistcoat flickered and glistened in the firelight with the convulsion of rage, terror, and sorrow in the human heart that was beating under it.

"Villain!" cried Mr. Pyncheon, shaking his clenched fist at Maule. "You and the fiend together have robbed me of my daughter! Give her back, spawn of the old wizard, or you shall climb Gallows Hill in your grandfather's footsteps!"

"Softly, Mr. Pyncheon!" said the carpenter, with scornful composure. "Softly, an it please your worship, else you will spoil those rich lace ruffles at your wrists! Is it my crime if you have sold your daughter for the mere hope of getting a sheet of yellow parchment into your clutch? There sits Mistress Alice quietly asleep! Now let Matthew Maule try whether she be as proud as the carpenter found her awhile since."

He spoke, and Alice responded, with a soft, subdued, inward acquiescence, and a bending of her form towards him, like the flame of a torch when it indicates a gentle draught of air. He beckoned with his hand, and, rising from her chair—blindly, but undoubtingly, as tending to her sure and inevitable center—the proud Alice approached him. He waved her back, and, retreating, Alice sank again into her seat.

"She is mine!" said Matthew Maule. "Mine, by the right of the strongest spirit!"

In the further progress of the legend, there is a long, grotesque, and occasionally awe-striking account of the carpenter's incantations (if so they are to be called), with a

view of discovering the lost document. It appears to have
been his object to convert the mind of Alice into a kind of
telescopic medium, through which Mr. Pyncheon and himself might obtain a glimpse into the spiritual world. He
succeeded, accordingly, in holding an imperfect sort of intercourse, at one remove, with the departed personages in
whose custody the so much valued secret had been carried
beyond the precincts of earth. During her trance, Alice
described three figures as being present to her spiritualized
perception. One was an aged, dignified, stern-looking gentleman, clad as for a solemn festival in grave and costly
attire, but with a great bloodstain on his richly wrought
band; the second, an aged man, meanly dressed, with a dark
and malign countenance, and a broken halter about his
neck; the third, a person not so advanced in life as the
former two, but beyond the middle age, wearing a coarse
woolen tunic and leather breeches, and with a carpenter's
rule sticking out of his side pocket. These three visionary
characters possessed a mutual knowledge of the missing
document. One of them, in truth—it was he with the bloodstain on his hand—seemed, unless his gestures were misun-
derstood, to hold the parchment in his immediate keeping,
but was prevented, by his two partners in the mystery, from
disburdening himself of the trust. Finally, when he showed a
purpose of shouting forth the secret, loudly enough to be
heard from his own sphere into that of mortals, his companions struggled with him, and pressed their hands over his
mouth; and forthwith—whether that he were choked by it,
or that the secret itself was of a crimson hue—there was a
fresh flow of blood upon his band. Upon this, the two
meanly dressed figures mocked and jeered at the much-
abashed old dignitary, and pointed their fingers at the
stain.

At this juncture, Maule turned to Mr. Pyncheon.

"It will never be allowed," said he. "The custody of this
secret, that would so enrich his heirs, makes part of your
grandfather's retribution. He must choke with it until it is
no longer of any value. And keep you the House of the
Seven Gables! It is too dear bought an inheritance, and too
heavy with the curse upon it, to be shifted yet awhile from
the Colonel's posterity!"

Mr. Pyncheon tried to speak, but—what with fear and

passion—could make only a gurgling murmur in his throat. The carpenter smiled.

"Aha, worshipful sir! So, you have old Maule's blood to drink!" said he, jeeringly.

"Fiend in man's shape! Why dost thou keep dominion over my child?" cried Mr. Pyncheon, when his choked utterance could make way. "Give me back my daughter! Then go thy ways; and may we never meet again!"

"Your daughter!" said Matthew Maule. "Why, she is fairly mine! Nevertheless, not to be too hard with fair Mistress Alice, I will leave her in your keeping: but I do not warrant you that she shall never have occasion to remember Maule, the carpenter."

He waved his hands with an upward motion; and, after a few repetitions of similar gestures, the beautiful Alice Pyncheon awoke from her strange trance. She awoke, without the slightest recollection of her visionary experience; but as one losing herself in a momentary reverie, and returning to the consciousness of actual life, in almost as brief an interval as the down-sinking flame of the hearth should quiver again up the chimney. On recognizing Matthew Maule, she assumed an air of somewhat cold but gentle dignity, the rather as there was a certain peculiar smile on the carpenter's visage that stirred the native pride of the fair Alice. So ended, for that time, the quest for the lost title deed of the Pyncheon territory at the eastward; nor, though often subsequently renewed, has it ever yet befallen a Pyncheon to set his eye upon that parchment.

But, alas for the beautiful, the gentle, yet too haughty Alice! A power that she little dreamed of had laid its grasp upon her maiden soul. A will, most unlike her own, constrained her to do its grotesque and fantastic bidding. Her father, as it proved, had martyred his poor child to an inordinate desire for measuring his land by miles instead of acres. And, therefore, while Alice Pyncheon lived, she was Maule's slave, in a bondage more humiliating, a thousandfold, than that which binds its chain around the body. Seated by his humble fireside, Maule had but to wave his hand; and, wherever the proud lady chanced to be—whether in her chamber, or entertaining her father's stately guests, or worshiping at church—whatever her place or occupation, her spirit passed from beneath her own control, and bowed itself to Maule. "Alice, laugh!" the carpenter, beside his hearth, would say; or perhaps intensely will it, without a spoken word. And, even were it prayer time, or at a funeral, Alice must break into wild laughter. "Alice, be sad!" and, at the instant, down would come her tears, quenching all the mirth of those around her like sudden rain upon a bonfire. "Alice, dance!" and dance she would, not in such courtlike measures as she had learned abroad, but some high-paced jig, or hop-skip rigadoon, befitting the brisk lasses at a rustic merrymaking. It seemed to be Maule's impulse not to ruin Alice, nor to visit her with any black or gigantic mischief, which would have crowned her sorrows with the grace of tragedy, but to wreak a low, ungenerous scorn upon her. Thus all the dignity of life was lost. She felt herself too much abased, and longed to change natures with some worm!

One evening, at a bridal party (but not her own; for, so lost from self-control, she would have deemed it sin to marry), poor Alice was beckoned forth by her unseen despot, and constrained, in her gossamer white dress and satin slippers, to hasten along the street to the mean dwelling of a laboring man. There was laughter and good cheer within; for Matthew Maule, that night, was to wed the laborer's daughter, and had summoned proud Alice Pyncheon to wait upon his bride. And so she did; and when the twain were one, Alice awoke out of her enchanted sleep. Yet, no longer proud—humbly, and with a smile all steeped in sadness— she kissed Maule's wife, and went her way. It was an inclement night; the southeast wind drove the mingled snow and rain into her thinly sheltered bosom; her satin slippers were wet through and through, as she trod the muddy sidewalks. The next day, a cold; soon, a settled cough; anon, a hectic cheek, a wasted form, that sat beside the harpsichord, and filled the house with music! Music, in which a strain of the heavenly choristers was echoed! Oh, joy! For Alice had borne her last humiliation! Oh, greater joy! For Alice was penitent of her one earthly sin, and proud no more!

The Pyncheons made a great funeral for Alice. The kith and kin were there, and the whole respectability of the town besides. But, last in the procession, came Matthew Maule, gnashing his teeth, as if he would have bitten his own heart in twain—the darkest and woefulest man that ever walked behind a corpse! He meant to humble Alice, not to kill her; but he had taken a woman's delicate soul into his rude gripe, to play with—and she was dead!

XIV
Phoebe's Good-by

HOLGRAVE, plunging into his tale with the energy and absorption natural to a young author, had given a good deal of action to the parts capable of being developed and exemplified in that manner. He now observed that a certain remarkable drowsiness (wholly unlike that with which the reader possibly feels himself affected) had been flung over the senses of his auditress. It was the effect, unquestionably, of the mystic gesticulations by which he had sought to bring bodily before Phoebe's perception the figure of the mesmerizing carpenter. With the lids drooping over her eyes—now lifted for an instant, and drawn down again as with leaden weights—she leaned slightly towards him, and seemed almost to regulate her breath by his. Holgrave gazed at her, as he rolled up his manuscript, and recognized an incipient stage of that curious psychological condition which, as he had himself told Phoebe, he possessed more than an ordinary faculty of producing. A veil was beginning to be muffled about her, in which she could behold only him, and live only in his thoughts and emotions. His glance, as he fastened it on the young girl, grew involuntarily more concentrated; in his attitude there was the consciousness of power, investing his hardly mature figure with a dignity that did not belong to its physical manifestation. It was evident, that, with but one wave of his hand and a corresponding effort of his will, he could complete his mastery over Phoebe's yet free and virgin spirit: he could establish an influence over this good, pure, and simple child as dangerous, and perhaps as disastrous, as that which the carpenter of his legend had acquired and exercised over the ill-fated Alice.

To a disposition like Holgrave's, at once speculative and active, there is no temptation so great as the opportunity of acquiring empire over the human spirit; nor any idea more seductive to a young man than to become the arbiter of a young girl's destiny. Let us, therefore—whatever his defects of nature and education, and in spite of his scorn for creeds and institutions—concede to the daguerreotypist the rare and high quality of reverence for another's individuality. Let us allow him integrity, also, forever after to be confided in; since he forbade himself to twine that one link more which might have rendered his spell over Phoebe indissoluble.

He made a slight gesture upward with his hand.

"You really mortify me, my dear Miss Phoebe!" he exclaimed, smiling half-sarcastically at her. "My poor story, it is but too evident, will never do for *Godey* or *Graham*! Only think of your falling asleep at what I hoped the newspaper critics would pronounce a most brilliant, powerful, imaginative, pathetic, and original winding up! Well, the manuscript must serve to light lamps with—if, indeed, being so imbued with my gentle dullness, it is any longer capable of flame!"

"Me asleep! How can you say so?" answered Phoebe, as unconscious of the crisis through which she had passed as an infant of the precipice to the verge of which it has rolled. "No, no! I consider myself as having been very attentive; and, though I don't remember the incidents quite distinctly, yet I have an impression of a vast deal of trouble and calamity—so, no doubt, the story will prove exceedingly attractive."

By this time, the sun had gone down, and was tinting the clouds towards the zenith with those bright hues which are not seen there until some time after sunset, and when the horizon has quite lost its richer brilliancy. The moon, too, which had long been climbing overhead, and unobtrusively melting its disk into the azure—like an ambitious demagogue, who hides his aspiring purpose by assuming the prevalent hue of popular sentiment—now began to shine out, broad and oval, in its middle pathway. These silvery beams were already powerful enough to change the character of the lingering daylight. They softened and embellished the aspect of the old house; although the shadows fell deeper

into the angles of its many gables, and lay brooding under
the projecting story, and within the half-open door. With
the lapse of every moment, the garden grew more picturesque; the fruit trees, shrubbery, and flower bushes had a
dark obscurity among them. The commonplace characteristics—which, at noontide, it seemed to have taken a century of sordid life to accumulate—were now transfigured by
a charm of romance. A hundred mysterious years were
whispering among the leaves, whenever the slight sea breeze
found its way thither and stirred them. Through the foliage
that roofed the little summerhouse, the moonlight flickered
to and fro, and fell silvery white on the dark floor, the table,
and the circular bench, with a continual shift and play,
according as the chinks and wayward crevices among the
twigs admitted or shut out the glimmer.

So sweetly cool was the atmosphere, after all the feverish
day, that the summer eve might be fancied as sprinkling
dews and liquid moonlight, with a dash of icy temper in
them, out of a silver vase. Here and there, a few drops of
this freshness were scattered on a human heart, and gave it
youth again, and sympathy with the eternal youth of nature.
The artist chanced to be one on whom the reviving influence
fell. It made him feel—what he sometimes almost forgot,
thrust so early as he had been into the rude struggle of man
with man—how youthful he still was.

"It seems to me," he observed, "that I never watched the
coming of so beautiful an eve, and never felt anything so
very much like happiness as at this moment. After all, what
a good world we live in! How good, and beautiful! How
young it is, too, with nothing really rotten or ageworn in it!
This old house, for example, which sometimes has positively
oppressed my breath with its smell of decaying timber! And
this garden, where the black mold always clings to my
spade, as if I were a sexton delving in a graveyard! Could I
keep the feeling that now possesses me, the garden would
every day be virgin soil, with the earth's first freshness in
the flavor of its beans and squashes; and the house! It would
be like a bower in Eden, blossoming with the earliest roses
that God ever made. Moonlight, and the sentiment in man's
heart responsive to it, are the greatest of renovators and
reformers. And all other reform and renovation, I suppose,
will prove to be no better than moonshine!"

"I have been happier than I am now; at least, much gayer," said Phoebe, thoughtfully. "Yet I am sensible of a great charm in this brightening moonlight; and I love to watch how the day, tired as it is, lags away reluctantly, and hates to be called yesterday so soon. I never cared much about moonlight before. What is there, I wonder, so beautiful in it tonight?"

"And you have never felt it before?" inquired the artist, looking earnestly at the girl through the twilight.

"Never," answered Phoebe. "And life does not look the same, now that I have felt it so. It seems as if I had looked at everything, hitherto, in broad daylight, or else in the ruddy light of a cheerful fire, glimmering and dancing through a room. Ah, poor me!" she added, with a half-melancholy laugh. "I shall never be so merry as before I knew Cousin Hepzibah and poor Cousin Clifford. I have grown a great deal older, in this little time. Older, and, I hope, wiser, and—not exactly sadder, but, certainly, with not half so much lightness in my spirits! I have given them my sunshine, and have been glad to give it; but, of course, I cannot both give and keep it. They are welcome, notwithstanding!"

"You have lost nothing, Phoebe, worth keeping, nor which it was possible to keep," said Holgrave, after a pause. "Our first youth is of no value; for we are never conscious of it until after it is gone. But sometimes—always, I suspect, unless one is exceedingly unfortunate—there comes a sense of second youth, gushing out of the heart's joy at being in love; or, possibly, it may come to crown some other grand festival in life, if any other such there be. This bemoaning of one's self (as you do now) over the first careless, shallow gaiety of youth departed, and this profound happiness at youth regained—so much deeper and richer than that we lost—are essential to the soul's development. In some cases, the two states come almost simultaneously, and mingle the sadness and the rapture in one mysterious emotion."

"I hardly think I understand you," said Phoebe.

"No wonder," replied Holgrave, smiling. "For I have told you a secret which I hardly began to know before I found myself giving it utterance. Remember it, however; and when the truth becomes clear to you, then think of this moonlight scene!"

"It is entirely moonlight now, except only a little flush of faint crimson, upward from the west, between those buildings," remarked Phoebe. "I must go in. Cousin Hepzibah is not quick at figures, and will give herself a headache over the day's accounts, unless I help her."

But Holgrave detained her a little longer.

"Miss Hepzibah tells me," observed he, "that you return to the country in a few days."

"Yes, but only for a little while," answered Phoebe, "for I look upon this as my present home. I go to make a few arrangements, and to take a more deliberate leave of my mother and friends. It is pleasant to live where one is much desired and very useful; and I think I may have the satisfaction of feeling myself so here."

"You surely may, and more than you imagine," said the artist. "Whatever health, comfort, and natural life exists in the house is embodied in your person. These blessings came along with you, and will vanish when you leave the threshold. Miss Hepzibah, by secluding herself from society, has lost all true relation with it, and is, in fact, dead; although she galvanizes herself into a semblance of life, and stands behind her counter, afflicting the world with a greatly-to-be-deprecated scowl. Your poor cousin Clifford is another dead and long-buried person, on whom the governor and council have wrought a necromantic miracle. I should not wonder if he were to crumble away, some morning, after you are gone, and nothing be seen of him more, except a heap of dust. Miss Hepzibah, at any rate, will lose what little flexibility she has. They both exist by you."

"I should be very sorry to think so," answered Phoebe, gravely. "But it is true that my small abilities were precisely what they needed; and I have a real interest in their welfare—an odd kind of motherly sentiment—which I wish you would not laugh at! And let me tell you frankly, Mr. Holgrave, I am sometimes puzzled to know whether you wish them well or ill."

"Undoubtedly," said the daguerreotypist, "I do feel an interest in this antiquated, poverty-stricken old maiden lady, and this degraded and shattered gentleman—this abortive lover of the beautiful. A kindly interest, too, helpless old children that they are! But you have no conception what a different kind of heart mine is from your own. It is not my impulse, as regards these two individuals, either to help or hinder; but to look on, to analyze, to explain matters to myself, and to comprehend the drama which, for almost two hundred years, has been dragging its slow length over the ground where you and I now tread. If permitted to witness the close, I doubt not to derive a moral satisfaction from it, go matters how they may. There is a conviction within me that the end draws nigh. But, though Providence sent you hither to help, and sends me only as a privileged and meet spectator, I pledge myself to lend these unfortunate beings whatever aid I can!"

"I wish you would speak more plainly," cried Phoebe, perplexed and displeased, "and, above all, that you would feel more like a Christian and a human being! How is it possible to see people in distress, without desiring, more than anything else, to help and comfort them? You talk as if this old house were a theater; and you seem to look at Hepzibah's and Clifford's misfortunes, and those of generations before them, as a tragedy, such as I have seen acted in the hall of a country hotel, only the present one appears to be played exclusively for your amusement. I do not like this. The play costs the performers too much, and the audience is too coldhearted."

"You are severe," said Holgrave, compelled to recognize a degree of truth in this piquant sketch of his own mood.

"And then," continued Phoebe, "what can you mean by your conviction, which you tell me of, that the end is drawing near? Do you know of any new trouble hanging over my poor relatives? If so, tell me at once, and I will not leave them!"

"Forgive me, Phoebe!" said the daguerreotypist, holding out his hand, to which the girl was constrained to yield her own. "I am somewhat of a mystic, it must be confessed. The tendency is in my blood, together with the faculty of mesmerism, which might have brought me to Gallows Hill, in the good old times of witchcraft. Believe me, if I were really aware of any secret the disclosure of which would benefit your friends—who are my own friends, likewise—you should learn it before we part. But I have no such knowledge."

"You hold something back!" said Phoebe.

"Nothing—no secrets but my own," answered Holgrave. "I can perceive, indeed, that Judge Pyncheon still keeps his eye on Clifford, in whose ruin he had so large a share. His motives and intentions, however, are a mystery to me. He is a determined and relentless man, with the genuine character of an inquisitor; and had he any object to gain by putting Clifford to the rack, I verily believe that he would wrench his joints from their sockets, in order to accomplish it. But, so wealthy and eminent as he is—so powerful in his own strength, and in the support of society on all sides—what can Judge Pyncheon have to hope or fear from the imbecile, branded, half-torpid Clifford?"

"Yet," urged Phoebe, "you did speak as if misfortune were impending!"

"Oh, that was because I am morbid!" replied the artist. "My mind has a twist aside, like almost everybody's mind, except your own. Moreover, it is so strange to find myself an inmate of this old Pyncheon House, and sitting in this old garden (hark, how Maule's well is murmuring!) that, were it only for this one circumstance, I cannot help fancying that Destiny is arranging its fifth act for a catastrophe."

"There!" cried Phoebe with renewed vexation; for she was by nature as hostile to mystery as the sunshine to a dark corner. "You puzzle me more than ever!"

"Then let us part friends!" said Holgrave, pressing her hand. "Or, if not friends, let us part before you entirely hate me. You, who love everybody else in the world!"

"Good-by, then," said Phoebe, frankly. "I do not mean to be angry a great while, and should be sorry to have you think so. There has Cousin Hepzibah been standing in the shadow of the doorway, this quarter of an hour past! She thinks I stay too long in the damp garden. So, good night, and good-by!"

On the second morning thereafter, Phoebe might have been seen, in her straw bonnet, with a shawl on one arm and a little carpet bag on the other, bidding adieu to Hepzibah and Cousin Clifford. She was to take a seat in the next train of cars, which would transport her to within half a dozen miles of her country village.

The tears were in Phoebe's eyes; a smile, dewy with affectionate regret, was glimmering around her pleasant mouth. She wondered how it came to pass that her life of a few weeks, here in this heavyhearted old mansion, had taken such hold of her, and so melted into her associations, as now to seem a more important center point of remembrance than all which had gone before. How had Hepzibah—grim, silent, and irresponsive to her overflow of cordial sentiment—contrived to win so much love? And Clifford—in his abortive decay, with the mystery of fearful crime upon him, and the close prison atmosphere yet lurking in his breath—how had he transformed himself into the simplest child, whom Phoebe felt bound to watch over, and be, as it were, the providence of his unconsidered hours! Everything, at that instant of farewell, stood out prominently to her view. Look where she would, lay her hand on what she might, the object responded to her consciousness, as if a moist human heart were in it.

She peeped from the window into the garden, and felt herself more regretful at leaving this spot of black earth, vitiated with such an agelong growth of weeds, than joyful at the idea of again scenting her pine forests and fresh clover fields. She called Chanticleer, his two wives, and the venerable chicken, and threw them some crumbs of bread from the breakfast table. These being hastily gobbled up, the chicken spread its wings, and alighted close by Phoebe on the windowsill, where it looked gravely into her face and vented its emotions in a croak. Phoebe bade it be a good old chicken during her absence, and promised to bring it a little bag of buckwheat.

"Ah, Phoebe!" remarked Hepzibah. "You do not smile so naturally as when you came to us! Then, the smile chose to shine out; now, you choose it should. It is well that you are going back, for a little while, into your native air. There has been too much weight on your spirits. The house is too gloomy and lonesome; the shop is full of vexations; and as for me, I have no faculty of making things look brighter than they are. Dear Clifford has been your only comfort!"

"Come hither, Phoebe," suddenly cried her cousin Clifford, who had said very little all the morning. "Close—closer—and look me in the face!"

Phoebe put one of her small hands on each elbow of his chair, and leaned her face towards him, so that he might peruse it as carefully as he would. It is probable that the latent emotions of this parting hour had revived, in some degree, his bedimmed and enfeebled faculties. At any rate, Phoebe soon felt that, if not the profound insight of a seer, yet a more than feminine delicacy of appreciation was making her heart the subject of its regard. A moment before, she had known nothing which she would have sought to hide. Now, as if some secret were hinted to her own consciousness through the medium of another's perception, she was fain to let her eyelids droop beneath Clifford's gaze. A blush, too—the redder because she strove hard to keep it down—ascended higher and higher, in a tide of fitful progress, until even her brow was all suffused with it.

"It is enough, Phoebe," said Clifford, with a melancholy smile. "When I first saw you, you were the prettiest little maiden in the world; and now you have deepened into beauty! Girlhood has passed into womanhood; the bud is a bloom! Go, now! I feel lonelier than I did."

Phoebe took leave of the desolate couple, and passed through the shop, twinkling her eyelids to shake off a dewdrop; for—considering how brief her absence was to be, and therefore the folly of being cast down about it—she would not so far acknowledge her tears as to dry them with her handkerchief. On the doorstep, she met the little urchin whose marvelous feats of gastronomy have been recorded in the earlier pages of our narrative. She took from the window some specimen or other of natural history—her eyes being too dim with moisture to inform her accurately whether it was a rabbit or a hippopotamus—put it into the child's hand, as a parting gift, and went her way. Old Uncle Venner was just coming out of his door, with a wood horse and saw on his shoulder; and, trudging along the street, he scrupled not to keep company with Phoebe so far as their paths lay together; nor, in spite of his patched coat and rusty beaver, and the curious fashion of his tow-cloth trousers, could she find it in her heart to outwalk him.

"We shall miss you, next Sabbath afternoon," observed the street philosopher. "It is unaccountable how little while it takes some folks to grow just as natural to a man as his own breath; and, begging your pardon, Miss Phoebe (though there can be no offense in an old man's saying it), that's just what you've grown to me! My years have been a great many, and your life is but just beginning; and yet, you are somehow as familiar to me as if I had found you at my mother's door, and you had blossomed, like a running vine, all along my pathway since. Come back soon, or I shall be gone to my farm; for I begin to find these wood-sawing jobs a little too tough for my backache."

"Very soon, Uncle Venner," replied Phoebe.

"And let it be all the sooner, Phoebe, for the sake of those poor souls yonder," continued her companion. "They can never do without you now—never, Phoebe, never!—no more than if one of God's angels had been living with them, and making their dismal house pleasant and comfortable! Don't it seem to you they'd be in a sad case, if, some pleasant summer morning like this, the angel should spread his wings, and fly to the place he came from? Well, just so they feel, now that you're going home by the railroad! They can't bear it, Miss Phoebe; so be sure to come back!"

"I am no angel, Uncle Venner," said Phoebe, smiling, as she offered him her hand at the street corner. "But, I suppose, people never feel so much like angels as when they are doing what little good they may. So I shall certainly come back!"

Thus parted the old man and the rosy girl; and Phoebe took the wings of the morning, and was soon flitting almost as rapidly away as if endowed with the aerial locomotion of the angels to whom Uncle Venner had so graciously compared her.

XV

The Scowl and Smile

SEVERAL days passed over the Seven Gables, heavily and drearily enough. In fact (not to attribute the whole gloom of sky and earth to the one inauspicious circumstance of Phoebe's departure), an easterly storm had set in, and indefatigably applied itself to the task of making the black roof and walls of the old house look more cheerless than ever before. Yet was the outside not half so cheerless as the interior. Poor Clifford was cut off, at once, from all his scanty resources of enjoyment. Phoebe was not there; nor did the sunshine fall upon the floor. The garden, with its muddy walks, and the chill, dripping foliage of its summerhouse, was an image to be shuddered at. Nothing flourished in the cold, moist, pitiless atmosphere, drifting with the brackish scud of sea breezes, except the moss along the joints of the shingle roof, and the great bunch of weeds, that had lately been suffering from drought, in the angle between the two front gables.

As for Hepzibah, she seemed not merely possessed with the east wind, but to be, in her very person, only another phase of this gray and sullen spell of weather—the east wind itself, grim and disconsolate, in a rusty black silk gown, and with a turban of cloud wreaths on its head. The custom of the shop fell off, because a story got abroad that she soured her small beer and other damageable commodities, by scowling on them. It is, perhaps, true that the public had something reasonably to complain of in her deportment; but towards Clifford she was neither ill-tempered nor unkind, nor felt less warmth of heart than always, had it been possible to make it reach him. The inutility of her best efforts, however, palsied the poor old gentlewoman. She could do little else than sit silently in a corner of the room, when the wet pear-tree branches, sweeping across the small windows, created a noonday dusk, which Hepzibah unconsciously darkened with her woebegone aspect. It was no fault of Hepzibah's. Everything—even the old chairs and tables, that had known what weather was for three or four such lifetimes as her own—looked as damp and chill as if the present were their worst experience. The picture of the Puritan Colonel shivered on the wall. The house itself shivered, from every attic of its seven gables, down to the great kitchen fireplace, which served all the better as an emblem of the mansion's heart, because, though built for warmth, it was now so comfortless and empty.

Hepzibah attempted to enliven matters by a fire in the parlor. But the storm demon kept watch above, and, whenever a flame was kindled, drove the smoke back again, choking the chimney's sooty throat with its own breath. Nevertheless, during four days of this miserable storm, Clifford wrapped himself in an old cloak, and occupied his customary chair. On the morning of the fifth, when summoned to breakfast, he responded only by a brokenhearted murmur, expressive of a determination not to leave his bed. His sister made no attempt to change his purpose. In fact, entirely as she loved him, Hepzibah could hardly have borne any longer the wretched duty—so impracticable by her few and rigid faculties—of seeking pastime for a still sensitive but ruined mind, critical and fastidious, without force or volition. It was, at least, something short of positive despair that, today, she might sit shivering alone, and not suffer continually a new grief, and unreasonable pang of remorse, at every fitful sigh of her fellow sufferer.

But Clifford, it seemed, though he did not make his appearance belowstairs, had, after all, bestirred himself in quest of amusement. In the course of the forenoon, Hepzibah heard a note of music, which (there being no other tuneful contrivance in the House of the Seven Gables) she knew must proceed from Alice Pyncheon's harpsichord. She was aware that Clifford, in his youth, had possessed a cultivated taste for music, and a considerable degree of skill in its practice. It was difficult, however, to conceive of his retain-

ing an accomplishment to which daily exercise is so essential, in the measure indicated by the sweet, airy, and delicate,
though most melancholy strain that now stole upon her ear.
Nor was it less marvelous that the long-silent instrument
should be capable of so much melody. Hepzibah involuntarily thought of the ghostly harmonies, prelusive of death in
the family, which were attributed to the legendary Alice.
But it was, perhaps, proof of the agency of other than
spiritual fingers that, after a few touches, the chords seemed
to snap asunder with their own vibrations, and the music
ceased.

But a harsher sound succeeded to the mysterious notes;
nor was the easterly day fated to pass without an event
sufficient in itself to poison, for Hepzibah and Clifford, the
balmiest air that ever brought the hummingbirds along with
it. The final echoes of Alice Pyncheon's performance (or
Clifford's, if his we must consider it) were driven away by
no less vulgar a dissonance than the ringing of the shop bell.
A foot was heard scraping itself on the threshold, and thence
somewhat ponderously stepping on the floor. Hepzibah de-
layed a moment, while muffling herself in a faded shawl
which had been her defensive armor in a forty years' warfare against the east wind. A characteristic sound, however—
neither a cough nor a hem, but a kind of rumbling and
reverberating spasm in somebody's capacious depth of chest—
impelled her to hurry forward, with that aspect of fierce
faintheartedness so common to women in cases of perilous
emergency. Few of her sex, on such occasions, have ever
looked so terrible as our poor scowling Hepzibah. But the
visitor quietly closed the shop door behind him, stood up his
umbrella against the counter, and turned a visage of composed benignity, to meet the alarm and anger which his
appearance had excited.

Hepzibah's presentiment had not deceived her. It was no
other than Judge Pyncheon, who, after in vain trying the
front door, had now effected his entrance into the shop.

"How do you do, Cousin Hepzibah? And how does this
most inclement weather affect our poor Clifford?" began
the Judge; and wonderful it seemed, indeed, that the easterly storm was not put to shame, or, at any rate, a little
mollified, by the genial benevolence of his smile. "I could

not rest without calling to ask, once more, whether I can in any manner promote his comfort, or your own."

"You can do nothing," said Hepzibah, controlling her agitation as well as she could. "I devote myself to Clifford. He has every comfort which his situation admits of."

"But allow me to suggest, dear cousin," rejoined the Judge, "you err—in all affection and kindness, no doubt, and with the very best intentions—but you do err, nevertheless, in keeping your brother so secluded. Why insulate him thus from all sympathy and kindness? Clifford, alas, has had too much of solitude. Now let him try society—the society, that is to say, of kindred and old friends. Let me, for instance, but see Clifford, and I will answer for the good effect of the interview."

"You cannot see him," answered Hepzibah. "Clifford has kept his bed since yesterday."

"What! How! Is he ill?" exclaimed Judge Pyncheon, starting with what seemed to be angry alarm; for the very frown of the old Puritan darkened through the room as he spoke. "Nay, then, I must and will see him! What if he should die?"

"He is in no danger of death," said Hepzibah, and added, with bitterness that she could repress no longer, "none; unless he shall be persecuted to death, now, by the same man who long ago attempted it!"

"Cousin Hepzibah," said the Judge, with an impressive earnestness of manner, which grew even to tearful pathos as he proceeded, "is it possible that you do not perceive how unjust, how unkind, how unchristian, is this constant, this long-continued bitterness against me, for a part which I was constrained by duty and conscience, by the force of law, and at my own peril, to act? What did I do, in detriment to Clifford, which it was possible to leave undone? How could you, his sister—if, for your never-ending sorrow, as it has been for mine, you had known what I did—have shown greater tenderness? And do you think, cousin, that it has cost me no pang? That it has left no anguish in my bosom, from that day to this, amidst all the prosperity with which heaven has blessed me? Or that I do not now rejoice, when it is deemed consistent with the dues of public justice and the welfare of society that this dear kinsman, this early friend, this nature so delicately and beautifully constituted—so unfortunate, let us pronounce him, and forbear to say, so guilty—that our own Cllfford, in fine, should be given back to life, and its possibilities of enjoyment? Ah, you little know me, Cousin Hepzibah! You little know this heart! It now throbs at the thought of meeting him! There lives not the human being (except yourself—and you not more than I) who has shed so many tears for Clifford's calamity! You behold some of them now. There is none who would so delight to promote his happiness! Try me, Hepzibah—try me, cousin—try the man whom you have treated as your enemy and Clifford's—try Jaffrey Pyncheon, and you shall find him true, to the heart's core!"

"In the name of heaven," cried Hepzibah, provoked only to intenser indignation by this outgush of the inestimable tenderness of a stern nature, "in God's name, whom you insult—and whose power I could almost question, since he hears you utter so many false words without palsying your tongue—give over, I beseech you, this loathsome pretense of affection for your victim! You hate him! Say so, like a man! You cherish, at this moment, some black purpose against him in your heart! Speak it out, at once! Or, if you hope so to promote it better, hide it till you can triumph in its success! But never speak again of your love for my poor brother! I cannot bear it! It will drive me beyond a woman's decency! It will drive me mad! Forbear! Not another word! It will make me spurn you!"

For once, Hepzibah's wrath had given her courage. She had spoken. But, after all, was this unconquerable distrust of Judge Pyncheon's integrity, and this utter denial, apparently, of his claim to stand in the ring of human sympathies—were they founded in any just perception of his character, or merely the offspring of a woman's unreasonable prejudice, deduced from nothing?

The Judge, beyond all question, was a man of eminent respectability. The church acknowledged it; the state acknowledged it. It was denied by nobody. In all the very extensive sphere of those who knew him, whether in his public or private capacities, there was not an individual—except Hepzibah, and some lawless mystic, like the daguerreotypist, and, possibly, a few political opponents—who would have dreamed of seriously disputing his claim to a high and honorable place in the world's regard. Nor (we must do him the further justice to say) did Judge Pyncheon himself, probably, entertain many or very frequent doubts that his enviable reputation accorded with his deserts. His conscience, therefore, usually considered the surest witness to a man's integrity—his conscience, unless it might be for the little space of five minutes in the twenty-four hours, or, now and then, some black day in the whole year's circle— his conscience bore an accordant testimony with the world's laudatory voice. And yet, strong as this evidence may seem to be, we should hesitate to peril our own conscience on the assertion that the Judge and the consenting world were right, and that poor Hepzibah, with her solitary prejudice, was wrong. Hidden from mankind—forgotten by himself, or buried so deeply under a sculptured and ornamented pile of ostentatious deeds that his daily life could take no note of it—there may have lurked some evil and unsightly thing. Nay, we could almost venture to say, further, that a daily guilt might have been acted by him, continually renewed, and reddening forth afresh, like the miraculous bloodstain of a murder, without his necessarily and at every moment being aware of it.

Men of strong minds, great force of character, and a hard texture of the sensibilities are very capable of falling into mistakes of this kind. They are ordinarily men to whom forms are of paramount importance. Their field of action lies among the external phenomena of life. They possess vast ability in grasping, and arranging, and appropriating to themselves the big, heavy, solid unrealities, such as gold, landed estate, offices of trust and emolument, and public honors. With these materials, and with deeds of goodly aspect, done in the public eye, an individual of this class builds up, as it were, a tall and stately edifice, which, in the view of other people, and ultimately in his own view, is no other than the man's character, or the man himself. Behold, therefore, a palace! Its splendid halls, and suites of spacious apartments, are floored with a mosaicwork of costly marbles; its windows, the whole height of each room, admit the sunshine through the most transparent of plate glass; its high cornices are gilded, and its ceilings gorgeously painted; and a lofty dome—through which, from the central pavement, you may gaze up to the sky, as with no obstructing medium between—surmounts the whole. With what fairer

and nobler emblem could any man desire to shadow forth
his character? Ah, but in some low and obscure nook—
some narrow closet on the ground floor, shut, locked and
bolted, and the key flung away; or beneath the marble
pavement, in a stagnant water puddle, with the richest pattern of mosaicwork above—may lie a corpse, half decayed,
and still decaying, and diffusing its death scent all through
the palace! The inhabitant will not be conscious of it, for it
has long been his daily breath! Neither will the visitors, for
they smell only the rich odors which the master sedulously
scatters through the palace, and the incense which they
bring, and delight to burn before him! Now and then, perchance, comes in a seer, before whose sadly gifted eye the
whole structure melts into thin air, leaving only the hidden
nook, the bolted closet, with the cobwebs festooned over its
forgotten door, or the deadly hole under the pavement, and
the decaying corpse within. Here, then, we are to seek the
true emblem of the man's character, and of the deed that
gives whatever reality it possesses to his life. And, beneath
the show of a marble palace, that pool of stagnant water,
foul with many impurities, and, perhaps, tinged with blood—
that secret abomination, above which, possibly, he may say
his prayers, without remembering it—is this man's miserable
soul!

To apply this train of remark somewhat more closely to
Judge Pyncheon: We might say (without in the least imput-
ing crime to a personage of his eminent respectability) that
there was enough of splendid rubbish in his life to cover up
and paralyze a more active and subtile conscience than the
Judge was ever troubled with. The purity of his judicial
character, while on the bench; the faithfulness of his public
service in subsequent capacities; his devotedness to his party,
and the rigid consistency with which he had adhered to its
principles, or, at all events, kept pace with its organized
movements; his remarkable zeal as president of a Bible
society; his unimpeachable integrity as treasurer of a widow's and orphan's fund; his benefits to horticulture, by
producing two much-esteemed varieties of the pear, and to
agriculture, through the agency of the famous Pyncheon
bull; the cleanliness of his moral deportment, for a great
many years past; the severity with which he had frowned
upon, and finally cast off, an expensive and dissipated son,

delaying forgiveness until within the final quarter of an hour of the young man's life; his prayers at morning and eventide, and graces at mealtime; his efforts in furtherance of the temperance cause; his confining himself, since the last attack of the gout, to five diurnal glasses of old sherry wine; the snowy whiteness of his linen, the polish of his boots, the handsomeness of his gold-headed cane, the square and roomy fashion of his coat, and the fineness of its material, and, in general, the studied propriety of his dress and equipment; the scrupulousness with which he paid public notice, in the street, by a bow, a lifting of the hat, a nod, or a motion of the hand, to all and sundry of his acquaintances, rich or poor; the smile of broad benevolence wherewith he made it a point to gladden the whole world—what room could possibly be found for darker traits in a portrait made up of lineaments like these? This proper face was what he beheld in the looking glass. This admirably arranged life was what he was conscious of in the progress of every day. Then, might not he claim to be its result and sum, and say to himself and the community, "Behold Judge Pyncheon there"?

And allowing that many, many years ago, in his early and reckless youth, he had committed some one wrong act—or that, even now, the inevitable force of circumstances should occasionally make him do one questionable deed among a thousand praiseworthy, or, at least, blameless ones—would you characterize the Judge by that one necessary deed, and that half-forgotten act, and let it overshadow the fair aspect of a lifetime? What is there so ponderous in evil that a thumb's bigness of it should outweigh the mass of things not evil which were heaped into the other scale! This scale-and-balance system is a favorite one with people of Judge Pyncheon's brotherhood. A hard, cold man, thus unfortunately situated, seldom or never looking inward, and resolutely taking his idea of himself from what purports to be his image as reflected in the mirror of public opinion, can scarcely arrive at true self-knowledge, except through loss of property and reputation. Sickness will not always help him do it; not always the death hour!

But our affair now is with Judge Pyncheon as he stood confronting the fierce outbreak of Hepzibah's wrath. Without premeditation, to her own surprise, and indeed terror, she had given vent, for once, to the inveteracy of her resentment, cherished against this kinsman for thirty years.

Thus far the Judge's countenance had expressed mild forbearance—grave and almost gentle deprecation of his cousin's unbecoming violence, free and Christian-like forgiveness of the wrong inflicted by her words. But when those words were irrevocably spoken, his look assumed sternness, the sense of power, and immitigable resolve; and this with so natural and imperceptible a change that it seemed as if the iron man had stood there from the first, and the meek man not at all. The effect was as when the light, vapory clouds, with their soft coloring, suddenly vanish from the stony brow of a precipitous mountain, and leave there the frown which you at once feel to be eternal. Hepzibah almost adopted the insane belief that it was her old Puritan ancestor, and not the modern Judge, on whom she had just been wreaking the bitterness of her heart. Never did a man show stronger proof of the lineage attributed to him than Judge Pyncheon, at this crisis, by his unmistakable resemblance to the picture in the inner room.

"Cousin Hepzibah," said he, very calmly, "it is time to have done with this."

"With all my heart!" answered she. "Then, why do you persecute us any longer? Leave poor Clifford and me in peace. Neither of us desires anything better!"

"It is my purpose to see Clifford before I leave this house," continued the Judge. "Do not act like a madwoman, Hepzibah! I am his only friend, and an all-powerful one. Has it never occurred to you—are you so blind as not to have seen—that, without not merely my consent, but my efforts, my representations, the exertion of my whole influence, political, official, personal, Clifford would never have been what you call free? Did you think his release a triumph over me? Not so, my good cousin; not so, by any means! The furthest possible from that! No; but it was the accomplishment of a purpose long entertained on my part. I set him free!"

"You!" answered Hepzibah. "I never will believe it! He owed his dungeon to you; his freedom to God's providence!"

"I set him free!" reaffirmed Judge Pyncheon, with the calmest composure. "And I came hither now to decide whether he shall retain his freedom. It will depend upon himself. For this purpose, I must see him."

"Never! It would drive him mad!" exclaimed Hepzibah, but with an irresoluteness sufficiently perceptible to the keen eye of the Judge; for, without the slightest faith in his good intentions, she knew not whether there was most to dread in yielding or resistance. "And why should you wish to see this wretched, broken man, who retains hardly a fraction of his intellect, and will hide even that from an eye which has no love in it?"

"He shall see love enough in mine, if that be all!" said the Judge, with well-grounded confidence in the benignity of his aspect. "But, Cousin Hepzibah, you confess a great deal, and very much to the purpose. Now, listen, and I will frankly explain my reasons for insisting on this interview. At the death, thirty years since, of our uncle Jaffrey, it was found—I know not whether the circumstance ever attracted much of your attention, among the sadder interests that clustered round that event—but it was found that his visible estate, of every kind, fell far short of any estimate ever made of it. He was supposed to be immensely rich. Nobody doubted that he stood among the weightiest men of his day. It was one of his eccentricities, however—and not altogether a folly, neither—to conceal the amount of his property by making distant and foreign investments, perhaps under other names than his own, and by various means familiar enough to capitalists, but unnecessary here to be specified. By Uncle Jaffrey's last will and testament, as you are aware, his entire property was bequeathed to me, with the single exception of a life interest to yourself in this old family mansion, and the strip of patrimonial estate remaining attached to it."

"And do you seek to deprive us of that?" asked Hepzibah, unable to restrain her bitter contempt. "Is this your price for ceasing to persecute poor Clifford?"

"Certainly not, my dear cousin!" answered the Judge, smiling benevolently. "On the contrary, as you must do me the justice to own, I have constantly expressed my readiness to double or treble your resources, whenever you should make up your mind to accept any kindness of that nature at the hands of your kinsman. No, no! But here lies the gist of the matter. Of my uncle's unquestionably great estate, as I

have said, not the half—no, not one third, as I am fully
convinced—was apparent after his death. Now, I have the
best possible reasons for believing that your brother Clifford
can give me a clue to the recovery of the remainder."

"Clifford! Clifford know of any hidden wealth? Clifford
have it in his power to make you rich?" cried the old
gentlewoman, affected with a sense of something like ridicule at the idea. "Impossible! You deceive yourself! It is
really a thing to laugh at!"

"It is as certain as that I stand here!" said Judge Pyncheon,
striking his gold-headed cane on the floor, and at the same
time stamping his foot, as if to express his conviction the
more forcibly by the whole emphasis of his substantial person. "Clifford told me so himself!"

"No, no!" exclaimed Hepzibah, incredulously. 'You are
dreaming, Cousin Jaffrey!"

"I do not belong to the dreaming class of men," said the
Judge, quietly. "Some months before my uncle's death,
Clifford boasted to me of the possession of the secret of
incalculable wealth. His purpose was to taunt me, and excite
my curiosity. I know it well. But, from a pretty distinct
recollection of the particulars of our conversation, I am
thoroughly convinced that there was truth in what he said.
Clifford, at this moment, if he chooses—and choose he
must!—can inform me where to find the schedule, the documents, the evidences, in whatever shape they exist, of the
vast amount of Uncle Jaffrey's missing property. He has the
secret. His boast was no idle word. It had a directness, an
emphasis, a particularity, that showed a backbone of solid
meaning within the mystery of his expression."

"But what could have been Clifford's object," asked
Hepzibah, "in concealing it so long?"

"It was one of the bad impulses of our fallen nature,"
replied the Judge, turning up his eyes. "He looked upon me
as his enemy. He considered me as the cause of his overwhelming disgrace, his imminent peril of death, his irretrievable ruin. There was no great probability, therefore, of his
volunteering information, out of his dungeon, that should
elevate me still higher on the ladder of prosperity. But the
moment has now come when he must give up his secret."

"And what if he should refuse?" inquired Hepzibah.

"Or—as I steadfastly believe—what if he has no knowledge of this wealth?"

"My dear cousin," said Judge Pyncheon, with a quietude which he had the power of making more formidable than any violence. "Since your brother's return, I have taken the precaution (a highly proper one in the near kinsman and natural guardian of an individual so situated) to have his deportment and habits constantly and carefully overlooked. Your neighbors have been eyewitnesses to whatever has passed in the garden. The butcher, the baker, the fishmonger, some of the customers of your shop, and many a prying old woman have told me several of the secrets of your interior. A still larger circle—I myself, among the rest—can testify to his extravagances at the arched window. Thousands beheld him, a week or two ago, on the point of flinging himself thence into the street. From all this testimony, I am led to apprehend—reluctantly, and with deep grief—that Clifford's misfortunes have so affected his intellect, never very strong, that he cannot safely remain at large. The alternative, you must be aware—and its adoption will depend entirely on the decision which I am now about to make—the alternative is his confinement, probably for the remainder of his life, in a public asylum for persons in his unfortunate state of mind."

"You cannot mean it!" shrieked Hepzibah.

"Should my cousin Clifford," continued Judge Pyncheon, wholly undisturbed, "from mere malice, and hatred of one whose interests ought naturally to be dear to him—a mode of passion that, as often as any other, indicates mental disease—should he refuse me the information so important to myself, and which he assuredly possesses, I shall consider it the one needed jot of evidence to satisfy my mind of his insanity. And, once sure of the course pointed out by conscience, you know me too well, Cousin Hepzibah, to entertain a doubt that I shall pursue it."

"Oh, Jaffrey, Cousin Jaffrey!' cried Hepzibah, mournfully, not passionately. "It is you that are diseased in mind, not Clifford! You have forgotten that a woman was your mother—that you have had sisters, brothers, children of your own—or that there ever was affection between man and man, or pity from one man to another, in this miserable world! Else, how could you have dreamed of this? You are not young, Cousin Jaffrey—no, nor middle-aged—but already an old man! The hair is white upon your head! How many years have you to live? Are you not rich enough for that little time? Shall you be hungry—shall you lack clothes, or a roof to shelter you—between this point and the grave? No! But, with the half of what you now possess, you could revel in costly food and wines, and build a house twice as splendid as you now inhabit, and make a far greater show to the world—and yet leave riches to your only son, to make him bless the hour of your death! Then, why should you do this cruel, cruel thing? So mad a thing, that I know not whether to call it wicked! Alas, Cousin Jaffrey, this hard and grasping spirit has run in our blood these two hundred years. You are but doing over again, in another shape, what your ancestor before you did, and sending down to your posterity the curse inherited from him!"

"Talk sense, Hepzibah, for heaven's sake!" exclaimed the Judge, with the impatience natural to a reasonable man, on hearing anything so utterly absurd as the above, in a discussion about matters of business. "I have told you my determination. I am not apt to change. Clifford must give up his secret or take the consequences. And let him decide quickly; for I have several affairs to attend to this morning, and an important dinner engagement with some political friends."

"Clifford has no secret!" answered Hepzibah. "And God will not let you do the thing you meditate!"

"We shall see," said the unmoved Judge. "Meanwhile, choose whether you will summon Clifford, and allow this business to be amicably settled by an interview between two kinsmen, or drive me to harsher measures, which I should be most happy to feel myself justified in avoiding. The responsibility is altogether on your part."

"You are stronger than I," said Hepzibah, after a brief consideration, "and you have no pity in your strength! Clifford is not now insane; but the interview which you insist upon may go far to make him so. Nevertheless, knowing you as I do, I believe it to be my best course to allow you to judge for yourself as to the improbability of his possessing any valuable secret. I will call Clifford. Be merciful in your dealings with him—be far more merciful than your heart bids you be—for God is looking at you, Jaffrey Pyncheon!"

The Judge followed his cousin from the shop, where the

foregoing conversation had passed, into the parlor, and flung himself heavily into the great ancestral chair. Many a former Pyncheon had found repose in its capacious arms: rosy children, after their sports; young men, dreamy with love; grown men, weary with cares; old men, burdened with winters—they had mused, and slumbered, and departed to a yet profounder sleep. It had been a long tradition, though a doubtful one, that this was the very chair, seated in which, the earliest of the Judge's New England forefathers—he whose picture still hung upon the wall—had given a dead man's silent and stern reception to the throng of distinguished guests. From that hour of evil omen until the present, it may be—though we know not the secret of his heart—but it may be that no wearier and sadder man had ever sunk into the chair than this same Judge Pyncheon, whom we have just beheld so immitigably hard and resolute. Surely, it must have been at no slight cost that he had thus fortified his soul with iron. Such calmness is a mightier effort than the violence of weaker men. And there was yet a heavy task for him to do. Was it a little matter—a trifle to be prepared for in a single moment, and to be rested from in another moment—that he must now, after thirty years, encounter a kinsman risen from a living tomb, and wrench a secret from him, or else consign him to a living tomb again?

"Did you speak?" asked Hepzibah, looking in from the threshold of the parlor; for she imagined that the Judge had uttered some sound which she was anxious to interpret as a relenting impulse. "I thought you called me back."

"No, no!" gruffly answered Judge Pyncheon, with a harsh frown, while his brow grew almost a black purple, in the shadow of the room. "Why should I call you back? Time flies! Bid Clifford come to me!"

The Judge had taken his watch from his vest pocket and now held it in his hand, measuring the interval which was to ensue before the appearance of Clifford.

XVI
Clifford's Chamber

NEVER had the old house appeared so dismal to poor Hepzibah as when she departed on that wretched errand. There was a strange aspect in it. As she trod along the footworn passages, and opened one crazy door after another, and ascended the creaking staircase, she gazed wistfully and fearfully around. It would have been no marvel, to her excited mind, if, behind or beside her, there had been the rustle of dead people's garments, or pale visages awaiting her on the landing place above. Her nerves were set all ajar by the scene of passion and terror through which she had just struggled. Her colloquy with Judge Pyncheon, who so perfectly represented the person and attributes of the founder of the family, had called back the dreary past. It weighed upon her heart. Whatever she had heard, from legendary aunts and grandmothers, concerning the good or evil fortunes of the Pyncheons—stories which had heretofore been kept warm in her remembrance by the chimney-corner glow that was associated with them—now recurred to her, somber, ghastly, cold, like most passages of family history, when brooded over in melancholy mood. The whole seemed little else but a series of calamity, reproducing itself in successive generations, with one general hue, and varying in little, save the outline. But Hepzibah now felt as if the Judge, and Clifford, and herself—they three together—were on the point of adding another incident to the annals of the house, with a bolder relief of wrong and sorrow, which would cause it to stand out from all the rest. Thus it is that the grief of the passing moment takes upon itself an individ-

uality, and a character of climax, which it is destined to lose
after a while, and to fade into the dark gray tissue common
to the grave or glad events of many years ago. It is but for a
moment, comparatively, that anything looks strange or
startling—a truth that has the bitter and the sweet in it.

But Hepzibah could not rid herself of the sense of something unprecedented at that instant passing and soon to be
accomplished. Her nerves were in a shake. Instinctively she
paused before the arched window, and looked out upon the
street, in order to seize its permanent objects with her
mental grasp, and thus to steady herself from the reel and
vibration which affected her more immediate sphere. It
brought her up, as we may say, with a kind of shock, when
she beheld everything under the same appearance as the day
before, and numberless preceding days, except for the difference between sunshine and sullen storm. Her eyes traveled along the street, from doorstep to doorstep, noting the
wet sidewalks, with here and there a puddle in hollows that
had been imperceptible until filled with water. She screwed
her dim optics to their acutest point, in the hope of making
out, with greater distinctness, a certain window, where she
half saw, half guessed, that a tailor's seamstress was sitting
at her work. Hepzibah flung herself upon that unknown
woman's companionship, even thus far off. Then she was
attracted by a chaise rapidly passing, and watched its moist
and glistening top, and its splashing wheels, until it had
turned the corner, and refused to carry any further her idly
trifling, because appalled and overburdened, mind. When
the vehicle had disappeared, she allowed herself still another loitering moment; for the patched figure of good
Uncle Venner was now visible, coming slowly from the head
of the street downward, with a rheumatic limp, because the
east wind had got into his joints. Hepzibah wished that he
would pass yet more slowly, and befriend her shivering
solitude a little longer. Anything that would take her out of
the grievous present, and interpose human beings betwixt
herself and what was nearest to her: Whatever would defer,
for an instant, the inevitable errand on which she was bound—
all such impediments were welcome. Next to the lightest
heart, the heaviest is apt to be most playful.

Hepzibah had little hardihood for her own proper pain
and far less for what she must inflict on Clifford. Of so slight

a nature, and so shattered by his previous calamities, it could not well be short of utter ruin to bring him face to face with the hard, relentless man who had been his evil destiny through life. Even had there been no bitter recollections, nor any hostile interest now at stake between them, the mere natural repugnance of the more sensitive system to the massive, weighty, and unimpressible one must, in itself, have been disastrous to the former. It would be like flinging a porcelain vase, with already a crack in it, against a granite column. Never before had Hepzibah so adequately estimated the powerful character of her cousin Jaffrey—powerful by intellect, energy of will, the long habit of acting among men, and, as she believed, by his unscrupulous pursuit of selfish ends through evil means. It did but increase the difficulty that Judge Pyncheon was under a delusion as to the secret which he supposed Clifford to possess. Men of his strength of purpose, and customary sagacity, if they chance to adopt a mistaken opinion in practical matters, so wedge it and fasten it among things known to be true, that to wrench it out of their minds is hardly less difficult than pulling up an oak. Thus, as the Judge required an impossibility of Clifford, the latter, as he could not perform it, must needs perish. For what, in the grasp of a man like this, was to become of Clifford's soft, poetic nature, that never should have had a task more stubborn than to set a life of beautiful enjoyment to the flow and rhythm of musical cadences! Indeed, what had become of it already? Broken! Blighted! All but annihilated! Soon to be wholly so!

For a moment, the thought crossed Hepzibah's mind whether Clifford might not really have such knowledge of their deceased uncle's vanished estate as the Judge imputed to him. She remembered some vague intimations, on her brother's part, which—if the supposition were not essentially preposterous—might have been so interpreted. There had been schemes of travel and residence abroad, daydreams of brilliant life at home, and splendid castles in the air, which it would have required boundless wealth to build and realize. Had this wealth been in her power, how gladly would Hepzibah have bestowed it all upon her ironhearted kinsman, to buy for Clifford the freedom and seclusion of the desolate old house! But she believed that her brother's schemes were as destitute of actual substance and purpose as a child's pictures of its future life, while sitting in a little chair by its mother's knee. Clifford had none but shadowy gold at his command; and it was not the stuff to satisfy Judge Pyncheon!

Was there no help, in their extremity? It seemed strange that there should be none, with a city round about her. It would be so easy to throw up the window, and send forth a shriek, at the strange agony of which everybody would come hastening to the rescue, well understanding it to be the cry of a human soul at some dreadful crisis! But how wild, how almost laughable, the fatality—and yet how continually it comes to pass, thought Hepzibah, in this dull delirium of a world—that whosoever, and with however kindly a purpose, should come to help, they would be sure to help the strongest side! Might and wrong combined, like iron magnetized, are endowed with irresistible attraction. There would be Judge Pyncheon—a person eminent in the public view, of high station and great wealth, a philanthropist, a member of Congress and of the church, and intimately associated with whatever else bestows good name—so imposing, in these advantageous lights, that Hepzibah herself could hardly help shrinking from her own conclusions as to his hollow integrity. The Judge, on one side! And who, on the other? The guilty Clifford! Once a byword! Now, an indistinctly remembered ignominy!

Nevertheless, in spite of this perception that the Judge would draw all human aid to his own behalf, Hepzibah was so unaccustomed to act for herself that the least word of counsel would have swayed her to any mode of action. Little Phoebe Pyncheon would at once have lighted up the whole scene, if not by any available suggestion, yet simply by the warm vivacity of her character. The idea of the artist occurred to Hepzibah. Young and unknown, mere vagrant adventurer as he was, she had been conscious of a force in Holgrave which might well adapt him to be the champion of a crisis. With this thought in her mind, she unbolted a door, cobwebbed and long disused, but which had served as a former medium of communication between her own part of the house and the gable where the wandering daguerreotypist had now established his temporary home. He was not there. A book, face downward, on the table, a roll of manuscript, a half-written sheet, a newspaper; some tools of his present

occupation, and several rejected daguerreotypes conveyed
an impression as if he were close at hand. But, at this period
of the day, as Hepzibah might have anticipated, the artist
was at his public rooms. With an impulse of idle curiosity,
that flickered among her heavy thoughts, she looked at one
of the daguerreotypes, and beheld Judge Pyncheon frowning at her. Fate stared her in the face. She turned back from
her fruitless quest, with a heart-sinking sense of disappointment. In all her years of seclusion, she had never felt, as
now, what it was to be alone. It seemed as if the house
stood in a desert, or, by some spell, was made invisible to
those who dwelt around, or passed beside it; so that any
mode of misfortune, miserable accident, or crime might
happen in it without the possibility of aid. In her grief and
wounded pride, Hepzibah had spent her life in divesting
herself of friends; she had willfully cast off the support
which God has ordained his creatures to need from one
another; and it was now her punishment that Clifford and
herself would fall the easier victims to their kindred enemy.

Returning to the arched window, she lifted her eyes—
scowling, poor, dim-sighted Hepzibah, in the face of heaven!
—and strove hard to send up a prayer through the dense
gray pavement of clouds. Those mists had gathered, as if to
symbolize a great, brooding mass of human trouble, doubt,
confusion, and chill indifference, between earth and the
better regions. Her faith was too weak; the prayer too heavy
to be thus uplifted. It fell back, a lump of lead, upon her
heart. It smote her with the wretched conviction that Providence intermeddled not in these petty wrongs of one individual to his fellow, nor had any balm for these little agonies
of a solitary soul; but shed its justice, and its mercy, in a
broad, sunlike sweep, over half the universe at once. Its
vastness made it nothing. But Hepzibah did not see that,
just as there comes a warm sunbeam into every cottage
window, so comes a lovebeam of God's care and pity for
every separate need.

At last, finding no other pretext for deferring the torture
that she was to inflict on Clifford—her reluctance to which
was the true cause of her loitering at the window, her search
for the artist, and even her abortive prayer—dreading, also,
to hear the stern voice of Judge Pyncheon from belowstairs,
chiding her delay, she crept slowly, a pale, grief-stricken

figure, a dismal shape of woman, with almost torpid limbs, slowly to her brother's door, and knocked!

There was no reply!

And how should there have been? Her hand, tremulous with the shrinking purpose which directed it, had smitten so feebly against the door that the sound could hardly have gone inward. She knocked again. Still, no response! Nor was it to be wondered at. She had struck with the entire force of her heart's vibration, communicating, by some subtile magnetism, her own terror to the summons. Clifford would turn his face to the pillow, and cover his head beneath the bedclothes, like a startled child at midnight. She knocked a third time, three regular strokes, gentle, but perfectly distinct, and with meaning in them; for, modulate it with what cautious art we will, the hand cannot help playing some tune of what we feel, upon the senseless wood.

Clifford returned no answer.

"Clifford! Dear brother!" said Hepzibah. "Shall I come in?"

A silence.

Two or three times, and more, Hepzibah repeated his name, without result; till, thinking her brother's sleep unwontedly profound, she undid the door, and entering, found the chamber vacant. How could he have come forth, and when, without her knowledge? Was it possible that, in spite of the stormy day, and worn out with the irksomeness within doors, he had betaken himself to his customary haunt in the garden, and was now shivering under the cheerless shelter of the summerhouse? She hastily threw up a window, thrust forth her turbaned head and the half of her gaunt figure, and searched the whole garden through, as completely as her dim vision would allow. She could see the interior of the summerhouse, and its circular seat, kept moist by the droppings of the roof. It had no occupant. Clifford was not thereabouts; unless, indeed, he had crept for concealment (as, for a moment, Hepzibah fancied might be the case) into a great, wet mass of tangled and broad-leaved shadow, where the squash vines were clambering tumultuously upon an old wooden framework, set casually aslant against the fence. This could not be, however; he was not there; for, while Hepzibah was looking, a strange grimalkin stole forth from the very spot, and picked his way across the garden. Twice he paused to snuff the air, and then anew directed his course towards the parlor window. Whether it was only on account of the stealthy, prying manner common to the race, or that this cat seemed to have more than ordinary mischief in his thoughts, the old gentlewoman, in spite of her much perplexity, felt an impulse to drive the animal away, and accordingly flung down a window stick. The cat stared up at her, like a detected thief or murderer, and, the next instant, took to flight. No other living creature was visible in the garden. Chanticleer and his family had either not left their roost, disheartened by the interminable rain, or had done the next wisest thing, by seasonably returning to it. Hepzibah closed the window.

But where was Clifford? Could it be that, aware of the presence of his Evil Destiny, he had crept silently down the staircase, while the Judge and Hepzibah stood talking in the shop, and had softly undone the fastenings of the outer door, and made his escape into the street? With that thought, she seemed to behold his gray, wrinkled, yet childlike aspect, in the old-fashioned garments which he wore about the house; a figure such as one sometimes imagines himself to be, with the world's eye upon him, in a troubled dream. This figure of her wretched brother would go wandering through the city, attracting all eyes, and everybody's wonder and repugnance, like a ghost, the more to be shuddered at because visible at noontide. To incur the ridicule of the younger crowd, that knew him not—the harsher scorn and indignation of a few old men, who might recall his once familiar features! To be the sport of boys, who, when old enough to run about the streets, have no more reverence for what is beautiful and holy, nor pity for what is sad—no more sense of sacred misery, sanctifying the human shape in which it embodies itself—than if Satan were the father of them all! Goaded by their taunts, their loud, shrill cries, and cruel laughter, insulted by the filth of the public ways, which they would fling upon him—or, as it might well be, distracted by the mere strangeness of his situation, though nobody should afflict him with so much as a thoughtless word—what wonder if Clifford were to break into some wild extravagance which was certain to be interpreted as lunacy?

Thus Judge Pyncheon's fiendish scheme would be ready accomplished to his hands!

Then Hepzibah reflected that the town was almost completely water-girdled. The wharves stretched out towards the center of the harbor, and, in this inclement weather, were deserted by the ordinary throng of merchants, laborers, and seafaring men; each wharf a solitude, with the vessels moored stem and stern, along its misty length. Should her brother's aimless footsteps stray thitherward, and he but bend, one moment, over the deep, black tide, would he not bethink himself that here was the sure refuge within his reach, and that, with a single step, or the slightest overbalance of his body, he might be forever beyond his kinsman's gripe? Oh, the temptation! To make of his ponderous sorrow a security! To sink, with its leaden weight upon him, and never rise again!

The horror of this last conception was too much for Hepzibah. Even Jaffrey Pyncheon must help her now! She hastened down the staircase, shrieking as she went.

"Clifford is gone!" she cried. "I cannot find my brother! Help, Jaffrey Pyncheon! Some harm will happen to him!"

She threw open the parlor door. But, what with the shade of branches across the windows, and the smoke-blackened ceiling, and the dark oak paneling of the walls, there was hardly so much daylight in the room that Hepzibah's imperfect sight could accurately distinguish the Judge's figure. She was certain, however, that she saw him sitting in the ancestral armchair, near the center of the floor, with his face somewhat averted, and looking towards a window. So firm and quiet is the nervous system of such men as Judge Pyncheon, that he had perhaps stirred not more than once since her departure, but, in the hard composure of his temperament, retained the position into which accident had thrown him.

"I tell you, Jaffrey," cried Hepzibah, impatiently, as she turned from the parlor door to search other rooms, "my brother is not in his chamber! You must help me seek him!"

But Judge Pyncheon was not the man to let himself be startled from an easy chair with haste ill-befitting either the dignity of his character or his broad personal basis, by the alarm of an hysteric woman. Yet, considering his own interest in the matter, he might have bestirred himself with a little more alacrity.

"Do you hear me, Jaffrey Pyncheon?" screamed Hepzibah, as she again approached the parlor door, after an ineffectual search elsewhere. "Clifford is gone!"

At this instant, on the threshold of the parlor, emerging from within, appeared Clifford himself! His face was preternaturally pale; so deadly white, indeed, that, through all the glimmering indistinctness of the passageway, Hepzibah could discern his features, as if a light fell on them alone. Their vivid and wild expression seemed likewise sufficient to illuminate them; it was an expression of scorn and mockery, coinciding with the emotions indicated by his gesture. As Clifford stood on the threshold, partly turning back, he pointed his finger within the parlor, and shook it slowly as though he would have summoned not Hepzibah alone, but the whole world, to gaze at some object inconceivably ridiculous. This action, so ill-timed and extravagant—accompanied, too, with a look that showed more like joy than any other kind of excitement—compelled Hepzibah to dread that her stern kinsman's ominous visit had driven her poor brother to absolute insanity. Nor could she otherwise account for the Judge's quiescent mood than by supposing him craftily on the watch, while Clifford developed these symptoms of a distracted mind.

"Be quiet, Clifford!" whispered his sister, raising her hand to impress caution. "Oh, for heaven's sake, be quiet!"

"Let him be quiet! What can he do better?" answered Clifford, with a still wilder gesture, pointing into the room which he had just quitted. "As for us, Hepzibah, we can dance now—we can sing, laugh, play, do what we will! The weight is gone, Hepzibah! It is gone off this weary old world, and we may be as lighthearted as little Phoebe herself!"

And, in accordance with his words, he began to laugh, still pointing his finger at the object, invisible to Hepzibah, within the parlor. She was seized with a sudden intuition of some horrible thing. She thrust herself past Clifford, and disappeared into the room; but almost immediately returned, with a cry choking in her throat. Gazing at her brother with an affrighted glance of inquiry, she beheld him all in a tremor and a quake, from head to foot, while, amid these

commoted elements of passion or alarm, still flickered his
gusty mirth.

"My God! What is to become of us?" gasped Hepzibah.

"Come!" said Clifford, in a tone of brief decision, most
unlike what was usual with him. "We stay here too long!
Let us leave the old house to our cousin Jaffrey! He will
take good care of it!"

Hepzibah now noticed that Clifford had on a cloak—a
garment of long ago—in which he had constantly muffled
himself during these days of easterly storm. He beckoned
with his hand, and intimated, so far as she could comprehend him, his purpose that they should go together from the
house. There are chaotic, blind, or drunken moments, in
the lives of persons who lack real force of character—moments
of test, in which courage would most assert itself—but where
these individuals, if left to themselves, stagger aimlessly
along, or follow implicitly whatever guidance may befall
them, even if it be a child's. No matter how preposterous or
insane, a purpose is a godsend to them. Hepzibah had
reached this point. Unaccustomed to action or responsibility—
full of horror at what she had seen, and afraid to inquire, or
almost to imagine, how it had come to pass—affrighted at
the fatality which seemed to pursue her brother—stupefied
by the dim, thick, stifling atmosphere of dread, which filled
the house as with a death smell, and obliterated all definiteness of thought—she yielded without a question, and on the
instant, to the will which Clifford expressed. For herself, she
was like a person in a dream, when the will always sleeps.
Clifford, ordinarily so destitute of this faculty, had found it
in the tension of the crisis.

"Why do you delay so?" cried he, sharply. "Put on your
cloak and hood, or whatever it pleases you to wear! No
matter what; you cannot look beautiful nor brilliant, my
poor Hepzibah! Take your purse, with money in it, and
come along!"

Hepzibah obeyed these instructions, as if nothing else
were to be done or thought of. She began to wonder, it is
true, why she did not wake up, and at what still more
intolerable pitch of dizzy trouble her spirit would struggle
out of the maze, and make her conscious that nothing of all
this had actually happened. Of course it was not real; no
such black, easterly day as this had yet begun to be; Judge

Pyncheon had not talked with her; Clifford had not laughed, pointed, beckoned her away with him; but she had merely been afflicted—as lonely sleepers often are—with a great deal of unreasonable misery, in a morning dream!

"Now—now—I shall certainly awake!" thought Hepzibah, as she went to and fro, making her little preparations. "I can bear it no longer! I must wake up now!"

But it came not, that awakening moment! It came not, even when, just before they left the house, Clifford stole to the parlor door, and made a parting obeisance to the sole occupant of the room.

"What an absurd figure the old fellow cuts now!" whispered he to Hepzibah. "Just when he fancied he had me completely under his thumb! Come, come; make haste, or he will start up, like Giant Despair in pursuit of Christian and Hopeful, and catch us yet!"

As they passed into the street, Clifford directed Hepzibah's attention to something on one of the posts of the front door. It was merely the initials of his own name, which, with somewhat of his characteristic grace about the forms of the letters, he had cut there when a boy. The brother and sister departed, and left Judge Pyncheon sitting in the old home of his forefathers, all by himself; so heavy and lumpish that we can liken him to nothing better than a defunct nightmare, which had perished in the midst of its wickedness, and left its flabby corpse on the breast of the tormented one, to be gotten rid of as it might!

XVII

The Flight of Two Owls

SUMMER as it was, the east wind set poor Hepzibah's few remaining teeth chattering in her head, as she and Clifford faced it, on their way up Pyncheon Street, and towards the center of the town. Not merely was it the shiver which this pitiless blast brought to her frame (although her feet and hands, especially, had never seemed so death-a-cold as now), but there was a moral sensation, mingling itself with the physical chill, and causing her to shake more in spirit than in body. The world's broad, bleak atmosphere was all so comfortless! Such, indeed, is the impression which it makes on every new adventurer, even if he plunge into it while the warmest tide of life is bubbling through his veins. What, then, must it have been to Hepzibah and Clifford—so time-stricken as they were, yet so like children in their inexperience—as they left the doorstep, and passed from beneath the wide shelter of the Pyncheon Elm! They were wandering all abroad, on precisely such a pilgrimage as a child often meditates, to the world's end, with perhaps a sixpence and a biscuit in his pocket. In Hepzibah's mind, there was the wretched consciousness of being adrift. She had lost the faculty of self-guidance; but, in view of the difficulties around her, felt it hardly worth an effort to regain it, and was, moreover, incapable of making one.

As they proceeded on their strange expedition, she now and then cast a look sidelong at Clifford, and could not but observe that he was possessed and swayed by a powerful excitement. It was this, indeed, that gave him the control

which he had at once, and so irresistibly, established over
his movements. It not a little resembled the exhilaration of
wine. Or, it might more fancifully be compared to a joyous
piece of music, played with wild vivacity, but upon a disordered instrument. As the cracked, jarring note might always
be heard, and as it jarred loudest amid the loftiest exulta-
tion of the melody, so was there a continual quake through
Clifford, causing him most to quiver while he wore a triumphant smile, and seemed almost under a necessity to skip in
his gait.

They met few people abroad, even on passing from the
retired neighborhood of the House of the Seven Gables into
what was ordinarily the more thronged and busier portion of
the town. Glistening sidewalks, with little pools of rain, here
and there, along their unequal surface; umbrellas displayed
ostentatiously in the shopwindows, as if the life of trade had
concentered itself in that one article; wet leaves of the horse
chestnut or elm trees, torn off untimely by the blast and
scattered along the public way; an unsightly accumulation of
mud in the middle of the street, which perversely grew the
more unclean for its long and laborious washing—these
were the more definable points of a very somber picture. In
the way of movement, and human life, there was the hasty
rattle of a cab or coach, its driver protected by a waterproof
cap over his head and shoulders; the forlorn figure of an old
man, who seemed to have crept out of some subterranean
sewer, and was stooping along the kennel, and poking the
wet rubbish with a stick, in quest of rusty nails; a merchant
or two, at the door of the post office, together with an
editor, and a miscellaneous politician, awaiting a dilatory
mail; a few visages of retired sea captains at the window of
an insurance office, looking out vacantly at the vacant street,
blaspheming at the weather, and fretting at the dearth as
well of public news as local gossip. What a treasure trove to
these venerable quidnuncs, could they have guessed the
secret which Hepzibah and Clifford were carrying along
with them! But their two figures attracted hardly so much
notice as that of a young girl, who passed at the same
instant, and happened to raise her skirt a trifle too high
above her ankles. Had it been a sunny and cheerful day,
they could hardly have gone through the streets without

making themselves obnoxious to remark. Now, probably, they were felt to be in keeping with the dismal and bitter weather, and therefore did not stand out in strong relief; as if the sun were shining on them, but melted into the gray gloom and were forgotten as soon as gone.

Poor Hepzibah! Could she have understood this fact, it would have brought her some little comfort; for, to all her other troubles—strange to say!—there was added the womanish and old-maiden-like misery arising from a sense of unseemliness in her attire. Thus, she was fain to shrink deeper into herself, as it were, as if in the hope of making people suppose that here was only a cloak and hood, threadbare and woefully faded, taking an airing in the midst of the storm, without any wearer!

As they went on, the feeling of indistinctness and unreality kept dimly hovering round about her, and so diffusing itself into her system that one of her hands was hardly palpable to the touch of the other. Any certainty would have been preferable to this. She whispered to herself, again and again, "Am I awake? Am I awake?" and sometimes exposed her face to the chill spatter of the wind, for the sake of its rude assurance that she was. Whether it was Clifford's purpose, or only chance, had led them thither, they now found themselves passing beneath the arched entrance of a large structure of gray stone. Within, there was a spacious breadth, and an airy height from floor to roof, now partially filled with smoke and steam, which eddied voluminously upward and formed a mimic cloud region over their heads. A train of cars was just ready for a start; the locomotive was fretting and fuming, like a steed impatient for a headlong rush; and the bell rang out its hasty peal, so well expressing the brief summons which life vouchsafes to us in its hurried career. Without question or delay—with the irresistible decision, if not rather to be called recklessness, which had so strangely taken possession of him, and through him of Hepzibah—Clifford impelled her towards the cars, and assisted her to enter. The signal was given; the engine puffed forth its short, quick breaths; the train began its movement; and, along with a hundred other passengers, these two unwonted travelers sped onward like the wind.

At last, therefore, and after so long estrangement from

everything that the world acted or enjoyed, they had been drawn into the great current of human life, and were swept away with it, as by the suction of fate itself.

Still haunted with the idea that not one of the past incidents, inclusive of Judge Pyncheon's visit, could be real, the recluse of the Seven Gables murmured in her brother's ear:

"Clifford! Clifford! Is not this a dream?"

"A dream, Hepzibah!" repeated he, almost laughing in her face. "On the contrary, I have never been awake before!"

Meanwhile, looking from the window, they could see the world racing past them. At one moment, they were rattling through a solitude; the next, a village had grown up around them; a few breaths more, and it had vanished, as if swallowed by an earthquake. The spires of meeting houses seemed set adrift from their foundations; the broad-based hills glided away. Everything was unfixed from its agelong rest, and moving at whirlwind speed in a direction opposite to their own.

Within the car, there was the usual interior life of the railroad, offering little to the observation of other passengers, but full of novelty for this pair of strangely enfranchised prisoners. It was novelty enough, indeed, that there were fifty human beings in close relation with them, under one long and narrow roof, and drawn onward by the same mighty influence that had taken their two selves into its grasp. It seemed marvelous how all these people could remain so quietly in their seats, while so much noisy strength was at work in their behalf. Some, with tickets in their hats (long travelers these, before whom lay a hundred miles of railroad), had plunged into the English scenery and adventures of pamphlet novels, and were keeping company with dukes and earls. Others, whose briefer span forbade their devoting themselves to studies so abstruse, beguiled the little tedium of the way with penny papers. A party of girls, and one young man, on opposite sides of the car, found huge amusement in a game of ball. They tossed it to and fro, with peals of laughter that might be measured by mile lengths; for, faster than the nimble ball could fly, the merry players fled unconsciously along, leaving the trail of their

mirth afar behind, and ending their game under another sky
than had witnessed its commencement. Boys, with apples,
cakes, candy, and rolls of variously tinctured lozenges—
merchandise that reminded Hepzibah of her deserted shop—
appeared at each momentary stopping place, doing up their
business in a hurry, or breaking it short off, lest the market
should ravish them away with it. New people continually
entered. Old acquaintances—for such they soon grew to be,
in this rapid current of affairs—continually departed. Here
and there, amid the rumble and the tumult, sat one asleep.
Sleep; sport; business; graver or lighter study; and the common and inevitable movement onward! It was life itself!

Clifford's naturally poignant sympathies were all aroused.
He caught the color of what was passing about him, and
threw it back more vividly than he received it, but mixed,
nevertheless, with a lurid and portentous hue. Hepzibah, on
the other hand, felt herself more apart from humankind
than even in the seclusion which she had just quitted.

"You are not happy, Hepzibah!" said Clifford, apart, in a
tone of reproach. "You are thinking of that dismal old
house, and of Cousin Jaffrey"—here came the quake through
him—"and of Cousin Jaffrey sitting there, all by himself!
Take my advice—follow my example—and let such things
slip aside. Here we are, in the world, Hepzibah—in the
midst of life—in the throng of our fellow beings! Let you
and I be happy! As happy as that youth, and those pretty
girls, at their game of ball!"

"Happy!" thought Hepzibah, bitterly conscious, at the
word, of her dull and heavy heart, with the frozen pain in it.
"Happy! He is mad already; and, if I could once feel myself
broad awake, I should go mad, too!"

If a fixed idea be madness, she was perhaps not remote
from it. Fast and far as they had rattled and clattered along
the iron track, they might just as well, as regarded Hepzibah's
mental images, have been passing up and down Pyncheon
Street. With miles and miles of varied scenery between,
there was no scene for her, save the seven old gable peaks,
with their moss, and the tuft of weeds in one of the angles,
and the shopwindow, and a customer shaking the door, and
compelling the little bell to jingle fiercely, but without disturbing Judge Pyncheon! This one old house was every-

where! It transported its great, lumbering bulk with more than railroad speed, and set itself phlegmatically down on whatever spot she glanced at. The quality of Hepzibah's mind was too unmalleable to take new impressions so readily as Clifford's. He had a winged nature; she was rather of the vegetable kind, and could hardly be kept long alive, if drawn up by the roots. Thus it happened that the relation heretofore existing between her brother and herself was changed. At home, she was his guardian; here, Clifford had become hers, and seemed to comprehend whatever belonged to their new position with a singular rapidity of intelligence. He had been startled into manhood and intellectual vigor; or, at least, into a condition that resembled them, though it might be both diseased and transitory.

The conductor now applied for their tickets; and Clifford, who had made himself the purse bearer, put a bank note into his hand, as he had observed others do.

"For the lady and yourself?" asked the conductor. "And how far?"

"As far as that will carry us," said Clifford. "It is no great matter. We are riding for pleasure merely!"

"You choose a strange day for it, sir!" remarked a gimlet-eyed old gentleman, on the other side of the car, looking at Clifford and his companion, as if curious to make them out. "The best chance of pleasure, in an easterly rain, I take it, is in a man's own house, with a nice little fire in the chimney."

"I cannot precisely agree with you," said Clifford, courteously bowing to the old gentleman, and at once taking up the clue of conversation which the latter had proffered. "It had just occurred to me, on the contrary, that this admirable invention of the railroad—with the vast and inevitable improvements to be looked for, both as to speed and convenience—is destined to do away with those stale ideas of home and fireside, and substitute something better."

"In the name of common sense," asked the old gentleman, rather testily, "what can be better for a man than his own parlor and chimney corner?"

"These things have not the merit which many good people attribute to them," replied Clifford. "They may be said, in few and pithy words, to have ill served a poor purpose. My impression is that our wonderfully increased and still

increasing facilities of locomotion are destined to bring us
round again to the nomadic state. You are aware, my dear
sir—you must have observed it in your own experience—
that all human progress is in a circle; or, to use a more
accurate and beautiful figure, in an ascending spiral curve.
While we fancy ourselves going straight forward, and attaining, at every step, an entirely new position of affairs, we do
actually return to something long ago tried and abandoned,
but which we now find etherealized, refined, and perfected
to its ideal. The past is but a coarse and sensual prophecy of
the present and the future. To apply this truth to the topic
now under discussion: In the early epochs of our race, men
dwelt in temporary huts, of bowers of branches, as easily
constructed as a bird's nest, and which they built—if it
should be called building, when such sweet homes of a
summer solstice rather grew than were made with hands—
which Nature, we will say, assisted them to rear where fruit
abounded, where fish and game were plentiful, or, most
especially, where the sense of beauty was to be gratified by
a lovelier shade than elsewhere, and a more exquisite arrangement of lake, wood, and hill. This life possessed a
charm, which, ever since man quitted it, has vanished from
existence. And it typified something better than itself. It
had its drawbacks; such as hunger and thirst, inclement
weather, hot sunshine, and weary and foot-blistering marches
over barren and ugly tracts, that lay between the sites desirable for their fertility and beauty. But in our ascending
spiral, we escape all this. These railroads—could but the
whistle be made musical, and the rumble and the jar got rid
of—are positively the greatest blessing that the ages have
wrought out for us. They give us wings; they annihilate the
toil and dust of pilgrimage; they spiritualize travel! Transition being so facile, what can be any man's inducement to
tarry in one spot? Why, therefore, should he build a more
cumbrous habitation than can readily be carried off with
him? Why should he make himself a prisoner for life in
brick, and stone, and old worm-eaten timber, when he may
just as easily dwell, in one sense, nowhere—in a better
sense, wherever the fit and beautiful shall offer him a
home?"

Clifford's countenance glowed, as he divulged this theory;

a youthful character shone out from within, converting the wrinkles and pallid duskiness of age into an almost transparent mask. The merry girls let their ball drop upon the floor, and gazed at him. They said to themselves, perhaps, that, before his hair was gray and the crow's feet tracked his temples, this now decaying man must have stamped the impress of his features on many a woman's heart. But, alas! No woman's eye had seen his face while it was beautiful.

"I should scarcely call it an improved state of things," observed Clifford's new acquaintance, "to live everywhere and nowhere!"

"Would you not?" exclaimed Clifford, with singular energy. "It is as clear to me as sunshine—were there any in the sky—that the greatest possible stumbling blocks in the path of human happiness and improvement are these heaps of bricks and stones, consolidated with mortar, or hewn timber, fastened together with spike nails, which men painfully contrive for their own torment, and call them house and home! The soul needs air; a wide sweep and frequent change of it. Morbid influences, in a thousandfold variety, gather about hearths, and pollute the life of households. There is no such unwholesome atmosphere as that of an old home, rendered poisonous by one's defunct forefathers and relatives. I speak of what I know. There is a certain house within my familiar recollection, one of those peaked-gable (there are seven of them), projecting-storied edifices, such as you occasionally see in our older towns—a rusty, crazy, creaky, dry-rotted, damp-rotted, dingy, dark, and miserable old dungeon, with an arched window over the porch, and a little shop door on one side, and a great, melancholy elm before it! Now sir, whenever my thoughts recur to this seven-gabled mansion (the fact is so very curious that I must needs mention it), immediately I have a vision or image of an elderly man, of remarkably stern countenance, sitting in an oaken elbow-chair, dead, stone dead, with an ugly flow of blood upon his shirt bosom! Dead, but with open eyes! He taints the whole house, as I remember it. I could never flourish there, nor be happy, nor do nor enjoy what God meant me to do and enjoy!"

His face darkened, and seemed to contract, and shrivel itself up, and wither into age.

"Never, sir!" he repeated. "I could never draw cheerful breath there!"

"I should think not," said the old gentleman, eying Clifford earnestly, and rather apprehensively. "I should conceive not, sir, with that notion in your head!"

"Surely not," continued Clifford, "and it were a relief to me if that house could be torn down, or burnt up, and so the earth be rid of it, and grass be sown abundantly over its foundation. Not that I should ever visit its site again! For, sir, the farther I get away from it, the more does the joy, the lightsome freshness, the heart leap, the intellectual dance, the youth, in short—yes, my youth, my youth!—the more does it come back to me. No longer ago than this morning, I was old. I remember looking in the glass, and wondering at my own gray hair, and the wrinkles, many and deep, right across my brow, and the furrows down my cheeks, and the prodigious trampling of crow's feet about my temples! It was too soon! I could not bear it! Age had no right to come! I had not lived! But now do I look old? If so, my aspect belies me strangely; for—a great weight being off my mind—I feel in the very heyday of my youth, with the world and my best days before me!"

"I trust you may find it so," said the old gentleman, who seemed rather embarrassed, and desirous of avoiding the observation which Clifford's wild talk drew on them both. "You have my best wishes for it."

"For heaven's sake, dear Clifford, be quiet!" whispered his sister. "They think you mad."

"Be quiet yourself, Hepzibah!" returned her brother. "No matter what they think! I am not mad. For the first time in thirty years, my thoughts gush up and find words ready for them. I must talk, and I will!"

He turned again towards the old gentleman, and renewed the conversation.

"Yes, my dear sir," said he, "it is my firm belief and hope that these terms of roof and hearthstone, which have so long been held to embody something sacred, are soon to pass out of men's daily use, and be forgotten. Just imagine, for a moment, how much of human evil will crumble away, with this one change! What we call real estate—the solid ground to build a house on—is the broad foundation on which nearly all the guilt of this world rests. A man will commit almost any wrong—he will heap up an immense pile of wickedness, as hard as granite, and which will weigh as heavily upon his soul, to eternal ages—only to build a great, gloomy, dark-chambered mansion, for himself to die in, and for his posterity to be miserable in. He lays his own dead corpse beneath the underpinning, as one may say, and hangs his frowning picture on the wall, and, after thus converting himself into an evil destiny, expects his remotest great-grandchildren to be happy there. I do not speak wildly! I have just such a house in my mind's eye!"

"Then, sir," said the old gentleman, getting anxious to drop the subject, "you are not to blame for leaving it."

"Within the lifetime of the child already born," Clifford went on, "all this will be done away. The world is growing too ethereal and spiritual to bear these enormities a great while longer. To me—though, for a considerable period of time, I have lived chiefly in retirement, and know less of such things than most men—even to me, the harbingers of a better era are unmistakable. Mesmerism, now! Will that effect nothing, think you, towards purging away the grossness out of human life?"

"All a humbug!" growled the old gentleman.

"These rapping spirits, that little Phoebe told us of, the other day," said Clifford, "what are these but the messengers of the spiritual world, knocking at the door of substance? And it shall be flung wide open!"

"A humbug, again!" cried the old gentleman, growing more and more testy, at these glimpses of Clifford's metaphysics. "I should like to rap with a good stick on the empty pates of the dolts who circulate such nonsense!"

"Then there is electricity—the demon, the angel, the mighty physical power, the all-pervading intelligence!" exclaimed Clifford. "Is that a humbug, too? Is it a fact—or have I dreamt it—that, by means of electricity, the world of matter has become a great nerve, vibrating thousands of miles in a breathless point of time? Rather, the round globe is a vast head, a brain, instinct with intelligence! Or, shall we say, it is itself a thought, nothing but thought, and no longer the substance which we deemed it!"

"If you mean the telegraph," said the old gentleman, glancing his eye toward its wire, alongside the rail track, "it is an excellent thing—that is, of course, if the speculators in cotton and politics don't get possession of it. A great thing, indeed, sir, particularly as regards the detection of bank robbers and murderers."

"I don't quite like it, in that point of view," replied Clifford. "A bank robber, and what you call a murderer, likewise, has his rights, which men of enlightened humanity and conscience should regard in so much the more liberal spirit, because the bulk of society is prone to controvert their existence. An almost spiritual medium, like the electric telegraph, should be consecrated to high, deep, joyful, and holy missions. Lovers, day by day—hour by hour, if so often moved to do it—might send their heartthrobs from Maine to Florida, with some such words as these: 'I love you forever!' 'My heart runs over with love!' 'I love you more than I can!' and, again, at the next message, 'I have lived an hour longer, and love you twice as much!' Or, when a good man has departed, his distant friend should be conscious of an electric thrill, as from the world of happy spirits, telling him, 'Your dear friend is in bliss!' Or, to an absent husband, should come tidings thus, 'An immortal being, of whom you are the father, has this moment come from God!' and immediately its little voice would seem to have reached so far, and to be echoing in his heart. But for these poor rogues, the bank robbers, who, after all, are about as honest as nine people in ten, except that they disregard certain formalities, and prefer to transact business at midnight rather than 'Change hours, and for these murderers, as you phrase it, who are often excusable in the motives of their deed, and deserve to be ranked among public benefactors, if we consider only its result—for unfortunate individuals like these, I really cannot applaud the enlistment of an immaterial and miraculous power in the universal world hunt at their heels!"

"You can't, hey?" cried the old gentleman, with a hard look.

"Positively, no!" answered Clifford. "It puts them too miserably at disadvantage. For example, sir, in a dark, low, cross-beamed, paneled room of an old house, let us suppose a dead man, sitting in an armchair, with a bloodstain on his shirt bosom; and let us add to our hypothesis another man, issuing from the house, which he feels to be overfilled with the dead man's presence; and let us lastly imagine him fleeing, heaven knows whither, at the speed of a hurricane, by railroad! Now, sir, if the fugitive alight in some distant town, and find all the people babbling about that selfsame dead man, whom he has fled so far to avoid the sight and thought of, will you not allow that his natural rights have been infringed? He has been deprived of his city of refuge, and, in my humble opinion, has suffered infinite wrong!"

"You are a strange man, sir!" said the old gentleman, bringing his gimlet eye to a point on Clifford, as if determined to bore right into him. "I can't see through you!"

"No, I'll be bound you can't!" cried Clifford, laughing. "And yet, my dear sir, I am as transparent as the water of Maule's well! But come, Hepzibah! We have flown far enough for once. Let us alight, as the birds do, and perch ourselves on the nearest twig, and consult whither we shall fly next!"

Just then, as it happened, the train reached a solitary way station. Taking advantage of the brief pause, Clifford left the car, and drew Hepzibah along with him. A moment afterwards, the train—with all the life of its interior, amid which Clifford had made himself so conspicuous an object— was gliding away in the distance, and rapidly lessening to a point, which, in another moment, vanished. The world had fled away from these two wanderers. They gazed drearily about them. At a little distance stood a wooden church, black with age, and in a dismal state of ruin and decay, with broken windows, a great rift through the main body of the edifice, and a rafter dangling from the top of the square tower. Farther off was a farmhouse, in the old style, as venerably black as the church, with a roof sloping downward from the three-story peak, to within a man's height of the ground. It seemed uninhabited. There were the relics of a woodpile, indeed, near the door, but with grass sprouting up among the chips and scattered logs. The small raindrops came down aslant; the wind was not turbulent, but sullen, and full of chilly moisture.

Clifford shivered from head to foot. The wild effervescence of his mood—which had so readily supplied thoughts, fantasies, and a strange aptitude of words, and impelled him to talk from the mere necessity of giving vent to this bubbling-up gush of ideas—had entirely subsided. A powerful excitement had given him energy and vivacity. Its operation over, he forthwith began to sink.

"You must take the lead now, Hepzibah!" murmured he,

with a torpid and reluctant utterance. "Do with me as you will!"

She knelt down upon the platform where they were standing and lifted her clasped hands to the sky. The dull, gray weight of clouds made it invisible; but it was no hour for disbelief—no juncture this to question that there was a sky above, and an Almighty Father looking from it!

"Oh God!" ejaculated poor, gaunt Hepzibah, then paused a moment, to consider what her prayer should be—"O God—our Father—are we not thy children? Have mercy on us!"

XVIII
Governor Pyncheon

JUDGE Pyncheon, while his two relatives have fled away with such ill-considered haste, still sits in the old parlor, keeping house, as the familiar phrase is, in the absence of its ordinary occupants. To him, and to the venerable House of the Seven Gables, does our story now betake itself, like an owl, bewildered in the daylight, and hastening back to his hollow tree.

The Judge has not shifted his position for a long while now. He has not stirred hand or foot, nor withdrawn his eyes so much as a hairbreadth from their fixed gaze towards the corner of the room, since the footsteps of Hepzibah and Clifford creaked along the passage, and the outer door was closed cautiously behind their exit. He holds his watch in his left hand, but clutched in such a manner that you cannot see the dial plate. How profound a fit of meditation! Or, supposing him asleep, how infantile a quietude of conscience, and what wholesome order in the gastric region, are betokened by slumber so entirely undisturbed with starts, cramp, twitches, muttered dream talk, trumpet blasts through the nasal organ, or any the slightest irregularity of breath! You must hold your own breath, to satisfy yourself whether he breathes at all. It is quite inaudible. You hear the ticking of his watch; his breath you do not hear. A most refreshing slumber, doubtless! And yet, the Judge cannot be asleep. His eyes are open! A veteran politician, such as he, would never fall asleep with wide-open eyes, lest some enemy or mischief-maker, taking him thus as unawares, should peep through these windows into his consciousness, and make strange discoveries among the reminiscences, projects, hopes, apprehensions, weaknesses, and strong points which he has heretofore shared with nobody. A cautious man is proverbially said to sleep with one eye open. That may be wisdom. But not with both; for this were heedlessness! No, no! Judge Pyncheon cannot be asleep.

It is odd, however, that a gentleman so burdened with engagements—and noted, too, for punctuality—should linger thus in an old, lonely mansion, which he has never seemed very fond of visiting. The oaken chair, to be sure, may tempt him with its roominess. It is, indeed, a spacious, and, allowing for the rude age that fashioned it, a moderately easy seat, with capacity enough, at all events, and offering no restraint to the Judge's breadth of beam. A bigger man might find ample accommodation in it. His ancestor, now pictured upon the wall, with all his English beef about him, used hardly to present a front extending from elbow to elbow of this chair, or a base that would cover its whole cushion. But there are better chairs than this—mahogany, black-walnut, rosewood, spring-seated and damask-cushioned, with varied slopes, and innumerable artifices to make them easy, and obviate the irksomeness of too tame an ease—a score of such might be at Judge Pyncheon's service. Yes! in a score of drawing rooms he would be more than welcome. Mama would advance to meet him, with outstretched hand; the virgin daughter, elderly as he has now got to be—an old widower, as he smilingly describes himself—would shake up the cushion for the Judge, and do her pretty little utmost to make him comfortable. For the Judge is a prosperous man. He cherishes his schemes, moreover, like other people, and reasonably brighter than most others; or did so, at least, as he lay abed this morning, in an agreeable half-drowse, planning the business of the day, and speculating on the probabilities of the next fifteen years. With his firm health, and the little inroad that age has made upon him, fifteen years or twenty—yes, or perhaps five and twenty!—are no more than he may fairly call his own. Five and twenty years for the enjoyment of his real estate in town and country, his railroad, bank, and insurance shares, his United States stock—his wealth, in short, however invested, now in possession, or soon to be acquired, together with the public honors that have fallen upon him, and the weightier ones that are yet to fall! It is good! It is excellent! It is enough!

Still lingering in the old chair! If the Judge has a little time to throw away, why does not he visit the insurance office, as is his frequent custom, and sit awhile in one of their leathern-cushioned armchairs, listening to the gossip of the day, and dropping some deeply designed chance word, which will be certain to become the gossip of tomorrow! And have not the bank directors a meeting at which it was the Judge's purpose to be present, and his office to preside? Indeed they have; and the hour is noted on a card, which is, or ought to be, in Judge Pyncheon's right vest pocket. Let him go thither, and loll at ease upon his moneybags! He has lounged long enough in the old chair!

This was to have been such a busy day! In the first place, the interview with Clifford. Half an hour, by the Judge's reckoning, was to suffice for that; it would probably be less, but—taking into consideration that Hepzibah was first to be dealt with, and that these women are apt to make many words where a few would do much better—it might be safest to allow half an hour. Half an hour? Why, Judge, it is already two hours, by your own undeviatingly accurate chronometer! Glance your eye down at it and see! Ah! He will not give himself the trouble either to bend his head, or elevate his hand, so as to bring the faithful timekeeper within his range of vision! Time, all at once, appears to have become a matter of no moment with the Judge!

And has he forgotten all the other items of his memoranda? Clifford's affair arranged, he was to meet a State Street broker, who has undertaken to procure a heavy percentage, and the best of paper, for a few loose thousands which the Judge happens to have by him, uninvested. The wrinkled note-shaver will have taken his railroad trip in vain. Half an hour later, in the street next to this, there was to be an auction of real estate, including a portion of the old Pyncheon property, originally belonging to Maule's garden ground. It has been alienated from the Pyncheons these fourscore years; but the Judge had kept it in his eye, and had set his heart on reannexing it to the small demesne still left around the Seven Gables; and now, during this odd fit of oblivion, the fatal hammer must have fallen, and transferred our ancient patrimony to some alien possessor! Possibly, indeed, the sale may have been postponed till fairer weather. If so, will the Judge make it convenient to be present, and favor the auctioneer with his bid, on the proximate occasion?

The next affair was to buy a horse for his own driving. The one heretofore his favorite stumbled, this very morning, on the road to town, and must be at once discarded. Judge Pyncheon's neck is too precious to be risked on such a contingency as a stumbling steed. Should all the above business be seasonably got through with, he might attend the meeting of a charitable society; the very name of which, however, in the multiplicity of his benevolence, is quite forgotten; so that this engagement may pass unfulfilled, and no great harm done. And if he have time, amid the press of more urgent matters, he must take measures for the renewal of Mrs. Pyncheon's tombstone, which, the sexton tells him, has fallen on its marble face, and is cracked quite in twain. She was a praiseworthy woman enough, thinks the Judge, in spite of her nervousness, and the tears that she was so oozy with, and her foolish behavior about the coffee; and as she took her departure so seasonably, he will not grudge the second tombstone. It is better, at least, than if she had never needed any! The next item on his list was to give orders for some fruit trees, of a rare variety, to be deliverable at his country-seat, in the ensuing autumn. Yes, buy them, by all means; and may the peaches be luscious in your mouth, Judge Pyncheon! After this comes something more important. A committee of his political party has besought him for a hundred or two of dollars, in addition to his previous disbursements, towards carrying on the fall campaign. The Judge is a patriot; the fate of the country is staked on the November election; and besides, as will be shadowed forth in another paragraph, he has no trifling stake of his own in the same great game. He will do what the committee asks; nay, he will be liberal beyond their expectations; they shall have a check for five hundred dollars, and more anon, if it be needed. What next? A decayed widow, whose husband was Judge Pyncheon's early friend, has laid her case of destitution before him, in a very moving letter. She and her fair daughter have scarcely bread to eat. He partly intends to call on her, today—perhaps so, perhaps not—accordingly as he may happen to have leisure, and a small bank note.

Another business, which, however, he puts no great weight on (it is well, you know, to be heedful, but not overanxious, as respects one's personal health)—another business, then, was to consult his family physician. About what, for heaven's sake? Why, it is rather difficult to describe the symptoms. A mere dimness of sight and dizziness of brain, was it—or a disagreeable choking, or stifling, or gurgling, or bubbling, in the region of the thorax, as the anatomists say—or was it a pretty severe throbbing and kicking of the heart, rather creditable to him than otherwise, as showing that the organ had not been left out of the Judge's physical contrivance? No matter what it was. The doctor, probably, would smile at the statement of such trifles to his professional ear; the Judge would smile in his turn; and meeting one another's eyes, they would enjoy a hearty laugh together! But a fig for medical advice! The Judge will never need it.

Pray, pray, Judge Pyncheon, look at your watch, now! What—not a glance! It is within ten minutes of the dinner hour! It surely cannot have slipped your memory that the dinner of today is to be the most important, in its consequences, of all the dinners you ever ate. Yes, precisely the most important; although, in the course of your somewhat eminent career, you have been placed high towards the head of the table, at splendid banquets, and have poured out your festive eloquence to ears yet echoing with Webster's mighty organ tones. No public dinner this, however. It is merely a gathering of some dozen or so of friends from several districts of the State; men of distinguished character and influence, assembling, almost casually, at the house of a common friend, likewise distinguished, who will make them welcome to a little better than his ordinary fare. Nothing in the way of French cookery, but an excellent dinner nevertheless. Real turtle, we understand, and salmon, tautog, canvasbacks, pig, English mutton, good roast beef, or dainties of that serious kind, fit for substantial country gentlemen, as these honorable persons mostly are. The delicacies of the season, in short, and flavored by a brand of old Madeira which has been the pride of many seasons. It is the Juno brand; a glorious wine, fragrant, and full of gentle might; a bottled-up happiness, put by for use; a golden liquid, worth more than liquid gold; so rare and admirable,

that veteran wine-bibbers count it among their epochs to
have tasted it! It drives away the heartache, and substitutes
no headache! Could the Judge but quaff a glass, it might
enable him to shake off the unaccountable lethargy which
(for the ten intervening minutes, and five to boot, are already past) has made him such a laggard at this momentous
dinner. It would all but revive a dead man! Would you like
to sip it now, Judge Pyncheon?

Alas, this dinner! Have you really forgotten its true object? Then let us whisper it, that you may start at once out
of the oaken chair, which really seems to be enchanted, like
the one in Comus, or that in which Moll Pitcher imprisoned
your own grandfather. But ambition is a talisman more
powerful than witchcraft. Start up, then, and, hurrying through
the streets, burst in upon the company, that they may begin
before the fish is spoiled! They wait for you; and it is little
for your interest that they should wait. These gentlemen—
need you be told it?—have assembled, not without purpose,
from every quarter of the State. They are practiced politicians, every man of them, and skilled to adjust those preliminary measures which steal from the people, without its
knowledge, the power of choosing its own rulers. The popular voice, at the next gubernatorial election, though loud as
thunder, will be really but an echo of what these gentlemen
shall speak, under their breath, at your friend's festive board.
They meet to decide upon their candidate. This little knot of
subtle schemers will control the convention, and, through it,
dictate to the party. And what worthier candidate—more
wise and learned, more noted for philanthropic liberality,
truer to safe principles, tried oftener by public trusts, more
spotless in private character, with a larger stake in the
common welfare, and deeper grounded, by hereditary descent, in the faith and practice of the Puritans—what man
can be presented by the suffrage of the people so eminently
combining all these claims to the chief-rulership as Judge
Pyncheon here before us?

Make haste, then! Do your part! The meed for which you
have toiled, and fought, and climbed, and crept, is ready for
your grasp! Be present at this dinner—drink a glass or two
of that noble wine—make your pledges in as low a whisper
as you will—and you rise up from table virtually governor of
the glorious old State! Governor Pyncheon of Massachusetts!

And is there no potent and exhilarating cordial in a certainty like this? It has been the grand purpose of half your lifetime to obtain it. Now, when there needs little more than to signify your acceptance, why do you sit so lumpishly in your great-great-grandfather's oaken chair, as if preferring it to the gubernatorial one? We have all heard of King Log; but, in these jostling times, one of that royal kindred will hardly win the race for an elective chief magistracy.

Well! It is absolutely too late for dinner! Turtle, salmon, tautog, woodcock, boiled turkey, Southdown mutton, pig, roast beef have vanished, or exist only in fragments, with lukewarm potatoes, and gravies crusted over with cold fat. The Judge, had he done nothing else, would have achieved wonders with his knife and fork. It was he, you know, of whom it used to be said, in reference to his ogre-like appetite, that his Creator made him a great animal, but that the dinner hour made him a great beast. Persons of his large sensual endowments must claim indulgence, at their feeding time. But, for once, the Judge is entirely too late for dinner! Too late, we fear, even to join the party at their wine! The guests are warm and merry; they have given up the Judge; and, concluding that the Free-Soilers have him, they will fix upon another candidate. Were our friend now to stalk in among them, with that wide-open stare, at once wild and stolid, his ungenial presence would be apt to change their cheer. Neither would it be seemly in Judge Pyncheon, generally so scrupulous in his attire, to show himself at a dinner table with that crimson stain upon his shirt bosom. By the by, how came it there? It is an ugly sight, at any rate; and the wisest way for the Judge is to button his coat closely over his breast, and, taking his horse and chaise from the livery stable, to make all speed to his own house. There, after a glass of brandy and water, and a mutton chop, a beefsteak, a broiled fowl, or some such hasty little dinner and supper all in one, he had better spend the evening by the fireside. He must toast his slippers a long while, in order to get rid of the chilliness which the air of this vile old house has sent curdling through his veins.

Up, therefore, Judge Pyncheon, up! You have lost a day. But tomorrow will be here anon. Will you rise, betimes, and make the most of it? Tomorrow! Tomorrow! Tomorrow! We, that are live, may rise betimes tomorrow. As for him that has died today, his morrow will be the resurrection morn.

Meanwhile, the twilight is glooming upward out of the corners of the room. The shadows of the tall furniture grow deeper, and at first become more definite; then, spreading wider, they lose their distinctness of outline in the dark gray tide of oblivion, as it were, that creeps slowly over the various objects, and the one human figure sitting in the midst of them. The gloom has not entered from without; it has brooded here all day, and now, taking its own inevitable time, will possess itself of everything. The Judge's face, indeed, rigid, and singularly white, refuses to melt into this universal solvent. Fainter and fainter grows the light. It is as if another double handful of darkness had been scattered through the air. Now it is no longer gray, but sable. There is still a faint appearance at the window; neither a glow, nor a gleam, nor a glimmer—any phrase of light would express something far brighter than this doubtful perception, or sense, rather, that there is a window there. Has it yet vanished? No! Yes! Not quite! And there is still the swarthy whiteness—we shall venture to marry these ill-agreeing words—the swarthy whiteness of Judge Pyncheon's face. The features are all gone: there is only the paleness of them left. And how looks it now? There is no window! There is no face! An infinite, inscrutable blackness has annihilated sight! Where is our universe? All crumbled away from us; and we, adrift in chaos, may hearken to the gusts of homeless wind, that go sighing and murmuring about, in quest of what was once a world!

Is there no other sound? One other, and a fearful one. It is the ticking of the Judge's watch, which, ever since Hepzibah left the room in search of Clifford, he has been holding in his hand. Be the cause what it may, this little, quiet, never-ceasing throb of Time's pulse, repeating its small strokes with such busy regularity, in Judge Pyncheon's motionless hand, has an effect of terror, which we do not find in any other accompaniment of the scene.

But, listen! That puff of the breeze was louder; it had a tone unlike the dreary and sullen one which has bemoaned itself, and afflicted all mankind with miserable sympathy, for five days past. The wind was veered about! It now comes boisterously from the northwest, and, taking hold of the aged framework of the Seven Gables, gives it a shake, like a wrestler that would try strength with his antagonist. Another and another sturdy tussle with the blast! The old house creaks again, and makes a vociferous but somewhat unintelligible bellowing in its sooty throat (the big flue, we mean, of its wide chimney), partly in complaint at the rude wind, but rather, as befits their century and a half of hostile intimacy, in tough defiance. A rumbling kind of a bluster roars behind the fireboard. A door has slammed abovestairs. A window, perhaps, has been left open, or else is driven in by an unruly gust. It is not to be conceived, beforehand, what wonderful wind instruments are these old timber mansions, and how haunted with the strangest noises, which immediately begin to sing, and sigh, and sob, and shriek— and to smite with sledge hammers, airy but ponderous, in some distant chamber—and to tread along the entries as with stately footsteps, and rustle up and down the staircase, as with silks miraculously stiff—whenever the gale catches the house with a window open, and gets fairly into it. Would that we were not an attendant spirit here! It is too awful! This clamor of the wind through the lonely house; the Judge's quietude, as he sits invisible; and that pertinacious ticking of his watch!

As regards Judge Pyncheon's invisibility, however, that matter will soon be remedied. The northwest wind has swept the sky clear. The window is distinctly seen. Through its panes, moreover, we dimly catch the sweep of the dark, clustering foliage, outside, fluttering with a constant irregularity of movement, and letting in a peep of starlight, now here, now there. Oftener than any other object, these glimpses illuminate the Judge's face. But here comes more effectual light. Observe that silvery dance upon the upper branches of the pear tree, and now a little lower, and now on the whole mass of boughs, while, through their shifting intricacies, the moonbeams fall aslant into the room. They play over the Judge's figure and show that he has not stirred throughout the hours of darkness. They follow the shadows, in changeful sport, across his unchanging features. They gleam upon his watch. His grasp conceals the dial plate; but we know that the faithful hands have met; for one of the city clocks tells midnight.

A man of sturdy understanding, like Judge Pyncheon,

cares no more for twelve o'clock at night than for the corresponding hour of noon. However just the parallel drawn, in some of the preceding pages, between his Puritan ancestor and himself, it fails in this point. The Pyncheon of two centuries ago, in common with most of his contemporaries, professed his full belief in spiritual ministrations, although reckoning them chiefly of a malignant character. The Pyncheon of tonight, who sits in yonder armchair, believes in no such nonsense. Such, at least, was his creed, some few hours since. His hair will not bristle, therefore, at the stories which—in times when chimney corners had benches in them, where old people sat poking into the ashes of the past, and raking out traditions like live coals—used to be told about this very room of his ancestral house. In fact, these tales are too absurd to bristle even childhood's hair. What sense, meaning, or moral, for example, such as even ghost stories should be susceptible of, can be traced in the ridiculous legend that, at midnight, all the dead Pyncheons are bound to assemble in this parlor? And, pray, for what? Why, to see whether the portrait of their ancestor still keeps its place upon the wall, in compliance with his testamentary directions! Is it worth while to come out of their graves for that?

We are tempted to make a little sport with the idea. Ghost stories are hardly to be treated seriously, any longer. The family party of the defunct Pyncheons, we presume, goes off in this wise.

First comes the ancestor himself, in his black cloak, steeple hat, and trunk breeches, girt about the waist with a leathern belt, in which hangs his steel-hilted sword; he has a long staff in his hand, such as gentlemen in advanced life used to carry, as much for the dignity of the thing as for the support to be derived from it. He looks up at the portrait; a thing of no substance, gazing at its own painted image! All is safe. The picture is still there. The purpose of his brain has been kept sacred thus long after the man himself has sprouted up in graveyard grass. See! He lifts his ineffectual hand, and tries the frame. All safe! But is that a smile? Is it not, rather, a frown of deadly import, that darkens over the shadow of his features? The stout Colonel is dissatisfied! So decided is his look of discontent as to impart additional distinctness to his features; through which, nevertheless, the moonlight passes, and flickers on the wall beyond. Something has strangely vexed the ancestor! With a grim shake of the head, he turns away. Here come other Pyncheons, the whole tribe, in their half a dozen generations, jostling and elbowing one another, to reach the picture. We behold aged men and grandames, a clergyman with the Puritanic stiffness still in his garb and mien, and a red-coated officer of the old French war; and there comes the shopkeeping Pyncheon of a century ago, with the ruffles turned back from his wrists; and there the periwigged and brocaded gentleman of the artist's legend, with the beautiful and pensive Alice, who brings no pride out of her virgin grave. All try the picture frame. What do these ghostly people seek? A mother lifts her child, that his little hands may touch it! There is evidently a mystery about the picture, that perplexes these poor Pyncheons when they ought to be at rest. In a corner, meanwhile, stands the figure of an elderly man, in a leather jerkin and breeches, with a carpenter's rule sticking out of his side pocket; he points his finger at the bearded Colonel and his descendants, nodding, jeering, mocking, and finally bursting into obstreperous though inaudible laughter.

Indulging our fancy in this freak, we have partly lost the power of restraint and guidance. We distinguish an unlooked-for figure in our visionary scene. Among those ancestral people there is a young man, dressed in the very fashion of today: he wears a dark frock coat, almost destitute of skirts, gray pantaloons, gaiter boots of patent leather, and has a finely wrought gold chain across his breast, and a little silver-headed whalebone stick in his hand. Were we to meet this figure at noonday, we should greet him as young Jaffrey Pyncheon, the Judge's only surviving child, who has been spending the last two years in foreign travel. If still in life, how comes his shadow hither? If dead, what a misfortune! The old Pyncheon property, together with the great estate acquired by the young man's father, would devolve on whom? On poor, foolish Clifford, gaunt Hepzibah, and rustic little Phoebe! But another and a greater marvel greets us! Can we believe our eyes? A stout, elderly gentleman has made his appearance; he has an aspect of eminent respectability, wears a black coat and pantaloons, of roomy width, and might be pronounced scrupulously neat in his attire, but for a broad crimson stain across his snowy neckcloth and down his shirt bosom. Is it the Judge, or no? How can it be Judge Pyncheon?

We discern his figure, as plainly as the flickering moon-beams can show us anything, still seated in the oaken chair! Be the apparition whose it may, it advances to the picture, seems to seize the frame, tries to peep behind it, and turns away, with a frown as black as the ancestral one.

The fantastic scene just hinted at must by no means be considered as forming an actual portion of our story. We were betrayed into this brief extravagance by the quiver of the moonbeams; they dance hand in hand with shadows, and are reflected in the looking glass, which, you are aware, is always a kind of window or doorway into the spiritual world. We needed relief, moreover, from our too long and exclusive contemplation of that figure in the chair. This wild wind, too, has tossed our thoughts into strange confusion, but without tearing them away from their one determined center. Yonder leaden Judge sits immovably upon our soul. Will he never stir again? We shall go mad unless he stirs! You may the better estimate his quietude by the fearlessness of a little mouse, which sits on its hind legs, in a streak of moonlight, close by Judge Pyncheon's foot, and seems to meditate a journey of exploration over this great black bulk. Ha! What has startled the nimble little mouse? It is the visage of grimalkin, outside of the window, where he appears to have posted himself for a deliberate watch. This grimalkin has a very ugly look. Is it a cat watching for a mouse, or the devil for a human soul? Would we could scare him from the window!

Thank heaven, the night is well-nigh past! The moon-beams have no longer so silvery a gleam, nor contrast so strongly with the blackness of the shadows among which they fall. They are paler now; the shadows look gray, not black. The boisterous wind is hushed. What is the hour? Ah! The watch has at last ceased to tick; for the Judge's forgetful fingers neglected to wind it up, as usual, at ten o'clock, being half an hour or so before his ordinary bed-time, and it has run down, for the first time in five years. But the great world clock of Time still keeps its beat. The dreary night—for, oh, how dreary seems its haunted waste, behind us!—gives place to a fresh, transparent, cloudless morn. Blessed, blessed radiance! The day beam—even what little of it finds its way into this always dusky parlor—seems part of the universal benediction, annulling evil, and rendering all goodness possible, and happiness attainable. Will Judge Pyncheon now rise up from his chair? Will he go forth, and receive the early sunbeams on his brow? Will he begin this new day—which God has smiled upon, and blessed, and given to mankind—will he begin it with better purposes than the many that have been spent amiss? Or are all the deep-laid schemes of yesterday as stubborn in his heart, and as busy in his brain, as ever?

In this latter case, there is much to do. Will the Judge still insist with Hepzibah on the interview with Clifford? Will he buy a safe, elderly gentleman's horse? Will he persuade the purchaser of the old Pyncheon property to relinquish the bargain, in his favor? Will he see his family physician, and obtain a medicine that shall preserve him, to be an honor and blessing to his race, until the utmost term of patriarchal longevity? Will Judge Pyncheon, above all, make due apologies to that company of honorable friends, and satisfy them that his absence from the festive board was unavoidable, and so fully retrieve himself in their good opinion that he shall yet be Governor of Massachusetts? And all these great purposes accomplished, will he walk the streets again, with that dog-day smile of elaborate benevolence, sultry enough to tempt flies to come and buzz in it? Or will he, after the tomblike seclusion of the past day and night, go forth a humbled and repentant man, sorrowful, gentle, seeking no profit, shrinking from worldly honor, hardly daring to love God, but bold to love his fellow man, and to do him what good he may? Will he bear about with him no odious grin of feigned benignity, insolent in its pretense, and loathsome in its falsehood, but the tender sadness of a contrite heart, broken, at last, beneath its own weight of sin? For it is our belief, whatever show of honor he may have piled upon it, that there was heavy sin at the base of this man's being.

Rise up, Judge Pyncheon! The morning sunshine glimmers through the foliage, and, beautiful and holy as it is, shuns not to kindle up your face. Rise up, thou subtle, worldly, selfish, ironhearted hypocrite, and make thy choice whether still to be subtle, worldly, selfish, ironhearted, and hypocritical, or to tear these sins out of thy nature, though they bring the lifeblood with them! The Avenger is upon thee! Rise up, before it be too late!

What! Thou art not stirred by this last appeal? No, not a

jot! And there we see a fly—one of your common house-flies, such as are always buzzing on the windowpane—which has smelt out Governor Pyncheon, and alights, now on his forehead, now on his chin, and now, heaven help us! is creeping over the bridge of his nose, towards the would-be chief magistrate's wide-open eyes! Canst thou not brush the fly away? Art thou too sluggish? Thou man, that hadst so many busy projects yesterday! Art thou too weak, that wast so powerful? Not brush away a fly? Nay, then, we give thee up!

And hark! The shop bell rings. After hours like these latter ones, through which we have borne our heavy tale, it is good to be made sensible that there is a living world, and that even this old, lonely mansion retains some manner of connection with it. We breathe more freely, emerging from Judge Pyncheon's presence into the street before the Seven Gables.

XIX

Alice's Posies

UNCLE Venner, trundling a wheelbarrow, was the earliest person stirring in the neighborhood the day after the storm.

Pyncheon Street, in front of the House of the Seven Gables, was a far pleasanter scene than a by-lane, confined by shabby fences, and bordered with wooden dwellings of the meaner class, could reasonably be expected to present. Nature made sweet amends, that morning, for the five unkindly days which had preceded it. It would have been enough to live for, merely to look up at the wide benediction of the sky, or as much of it as was visible between the houses, genial once more with sunshine. Every object was agreeable, whether to be gazed at in the breadth, or examined more minutely. Such, for example, were the well-washed pebbles and gravel of the sidewalk; even the sky-reflecting pools in the center of the street; and the grass, now freshly verdant, that crept along the base of the fences, on the other side of which, if one peeped over, was seen the multifarious growth of gardens. Vegetable productions, of whatever kind, seemed more than negatively happy, in the juicy warmth and abundance of their life. The Pyncheon Elm, throughout its great circumference, was all alive, and full of the morning sun and a sweet-tempered little breeze, which lingered within this verdant sphere, and set a thousand leafy tongues awhispering all at once. This aged tree appeared to have suffered nothing from the gale. It had kept its boughs unshattered, and its full complement of leaves; and the whole in perfect vendure, except a single branch, that, by the earlier change with which the elm tree

493

sometimes prophesies the autumn, had been transmuted to bright gold. It was like the golden branch that gained Aeneas and the Sibyl admittance into Hades.

This one mystic branch hung down before the main entrance of the Seven Gables, so nigh the ground that any passer-by might have stood on tiptoe and plucked it off. Presented at the door, it would have been a symbol of his right to enter, and be made acquainted with all the secrets of the house. So little faith is due to external appearance that there was really an inviting aspect over the venerable edifice, conveying an idea that its history must be a decorous and happy one, and such as would be delightful for a fireside tale. Its windows gleamed cheerfully in the slanting sunlight. The lines and tufts of green moss, here and there, seemed pledges of familiarity and sisterhood with Nature; as if this human dwelling place, being of such old date, had established its prescriptive title among primeval oaks and whatever other objects, by virtue of their long continuance, have acquired a gracious right to be. A person of imaginative temperament, while passing by the house, would turn, once and again, and peruse it well: its many peaks, consenting together in the clustered chimneys; the deep projection over its basement story; the arched window, imparting a look, if not of grandeur, yet of antique gentility, to the broken portal over which it opened; the luxuriance of gigantic burdocks, near the threshold; he would note all these characteristics, and be conscious of something deeper than he saw. He would conceive the mansion to have been the residence of the stubborn old Puritan, Integrity, who, dying in some forgotten generation, had left a blessing in all its rooms and chambers, the efficacy of which was to be seen in the religion, honesty, moderate competence, or upright poverty and solid happiness, of his descendants, to this day.

One object, above all others, would take root in the imaginative observer's memory. It was the great tuft of flowers—weeds you would have called them, only a week ago—the tuft of crimson-spotted flowers, in the angle between the two front gables. The old people used to give them the name of Alice's Posies, in remembrance of fair Alice Pyncheon, who was believed to have brought their seeds from Italy. They were flaunting in rich beauty and full bloom today, and seemed, as it were, a mystic expression that something within the house was consummated.

It was but little after sunrise, when Uncle Venner made his appearance, as aforesaid, impelling a wheelbarrow along the street. He was going his matutinal rounds to collect cabbage leaves, turnip tops, potato skins, and the miscellaneous refuse of the dinner pot, which the thrifty housewives of the neighborhood were accustomed to put aside, as fit only to feed a pig. Uncle Venner's pig was fed entirely, and kept in prime order, on these eleemosynary contributions; insomuch that the patched philosopher used to promise that, before retiring to his farm, he would make a feast of the portly grunter, and invite all his neighbors to partake of the joints and spare ribs which they had helped to fatten. Miss Hepzibah Pyncheon's housekeeping had so greatly improved, since Clifford became a member of the family, that her share of the banquet would have been no lean one; and Uncle Venner, accordingly, was a good deal disappointed not to find the large earthen pan, full of fragmentary eatables, that ordinarily awaited his coming at the back doorstep of the Seven Gables.

"I never knew Miss Hepzibah so forgetful before," said the patriarch to himself. "She must have had a dinner yesterday—no question of that! She always has one, nowadays. So where's the pot liquor and potato skins? I ask. Shall I knock, and see if she's stirring yet? No, no, 'twon't do! If little Phoebe was about the house, I should not mind knocking; but Miss Hepzibah, likely as not, would scowl down at me out of the window, and look cross, even if she felt pleasantly. So, I'll come back at noon."

With these reflections, the old man was shutting the gate of the little back yard. Creaking on its hinges, however, like every other gate and door about the premises, the sound reached the ears of the occupant of the northern gable, one of the windows of which had a side view towards the gate.

"Good morning, Uncle Venner!" said the daguerreotypist, leaning out of the window. "Do you hear nobody stirring?"

"Not a soul," said the man of patches. "But that's no wonder. 'Tis barely half an hour past sunrise, yet. But I'm really glad to see you, Mr. Holgrave! There's a strange, lonesome look about this side of the house; so that my heart misgave me, somehow or other, and I felt as if there was nobody alive in it. The front of the house looks a good deal cheerier; and Alice's posies are blooming there beautifully; and if I were a young man, Mr. Holgrave, my sweetheart should have one of those flowers in her bosom, though I risked my neck climbing for it! Well, and did the wind keep you awake last night?"

"It did, indeed!" answered the artist, smiling. "If I were a believer in ghosts—and I don't quite know whether I am or not—I should have concluded that all the old Pyncheons were running riot in the lower rooms, especially in Miss Hepzibah's part of the house. But it is very quiet now."

"Yes, Miss Hepzibah will be apt to oversleep herself, after being disturbed, all night, with the racket," said Uncle Venner. "But it would be odd, now, wouldn't it, if the Judge had taken both his cousins into the country along with him? I saw him go into the shop yesterday."

"At what hour?" inquired Holgrave.

"Oh, along in the forenoon," said the old man. "Well, well! I must go my rounds, and so must my wheelbarrow. But I'll be back here at dinnertime; for my pig likes a dinner as well as a breakfast. No mealtime, and no sort of victuals, ever seems to come amiss to my pig. Good morning to you! And, Mr. Holgrave, if I were a young man, like you, I'd get one of Alice's posies, and keep it in water till Phoebe comes back."

"I have heard," said the daguerreotypist, as he drew in his head, "that the water of Maule's well suits these flowers best."

Here the conversation ceased, and Uncle Venner went on his way. For half an hour longer, nothing disturbed the repose of the Seven Gables; nor was there any visitor, except a carrier boy, who, as he passed the front doorstep, threw down one of his newspapers; for Hepzibah, of late, had regularly taken it in. After a while, there came a fat woman, making prodigious speed, and stumbling as she ran up the steps of the shop door. Her face glowed with fire heat, and, it being a pretty warm morning, she bubbled and hissed, as it were, as if all afry with chimney warmth, and summer warmth, and the warmth of her own corpulent velocity. She tried the shop door; it was fast. She tried it again, with so angry a jar that the bell tinkled angrily back at her.

"The deuce take Old Maid Pyncheon!" muttered the irascible housewife. "Think of her pretending to set up a cent shop, and then lying abed til noon! These are what she calls gentlefolk's airs, I suppose! But I'll either start her ladyship, or break the door down!"

She shook it accordingly, and the bell, having a spiteful little temper of its own, rang obstreperously, making its remonstrances heard—not, indeed, by the ears for which they were intended—but by a good lady on the opposite side of the street. She opened her window, and addressed the impatient applicant.

"You'll find nobody there, Mrs. Gubbins."

"But I must and will find somebody here!" cried Mrs. Gubbins, inflicting another outrage on the bell. "I want a half pound of pork, to fry some first-rate flounders, for Mr. Gubbins's breakfast; and, lady or not, Old Maid Pyncheon shall get up and serve me with it!"

"But do hear reason, Mrs. Gubbins!" responded the lady opposite. "She, and her brother, too, have both gone to their cousin, Judge Pyncheon's, at his country seat. There's not a soul in the house, but that young daguerreotype man that sleeps in the north gable. I saw old Hepzibah and Clifford go away yesterday; and a queer couple of ducks they were, paddling through the mud puddles! They're gone, I'll assure you."

"And how do you know they're gone to the Judge's?" asked Mrs. Gubbins. "He's a rich man; and there's been a quarrel between him and Hepzibah, this many a day, because he won't give her a living. That's the main reason of her setting up a cent shop."

"I know that well enough," said the neighbor. "But they're gone—that's one thing certain. And who but a blood relation, that couldn't help himself, I ask you, would take in that awful-tempered old maid, and that dreadful Clifford? That's it, you may be sure."

Mrs. Gubbins took her departure, still brimming over with hot wrath against the absent Hepzibah. For another half hour, or, perhaps, considerably more, there was almost as much quiet on the outside of the house as within. The elm, however, made a pleasant, cheerful, sunny sigh, responsible to the breeze that was elsewhere imperceptible; a swarm of insects buzzed merrily under its drooping shadow, and became specks of light whenever they darted into the sunshine; a locust sang, once or twice, in some inscrutable seclusion of the tree; and a solitary little bird, with plumage of pale gold, came and hovered about Alice's Posies.

At last, our small acquaintance, Ned Higgins, trudged up the street, on his way to school; and happening, for the first time in a fortnight, to be the possessor of a cent, he could by no means get past the shop door of the Seven Gables. But it would not open. Again and again; however, and half a dozen other agains, with the inexorable pertinacity of a child intent upon some object important to itself, did he renew his efforts for admittance. He had, doubtless, set his heart upon an elephant; or, possibly, with Hamlet, he meant to eat a crocodile. In response to his more violent attacks, the bell gave, now and then, a moderate tinkle, but could not be stirred into clamor by any exertion of the little fellow's childish and tiptoe strength. Holding by the door handle, he peeped through a crevice of the curtain, and saw that the inner door, communicating with the passage towards the parlor, was closed.

"Miss Pyncheon!" screamed the child, rapping on the windowpane. "I want an elephant!"

There being no answer to several repetitions of the summons, Ned began to grow impatient; and his little pot of passion quickly boiling over, he picked up a stone, with a naughty purpose to fling it through the window; at the same time blubbering and sputtering with wrath. A man—one of two who happened to be passing by—caught the urchin's arm.

"What's the trouble, old gentleman?" he asked.

"I want old Hepzibah, or Phoebe, or any of them!" answered Ned, sobbing. "They won't open the door; and I can't get my elephant!"

"Go to school, you little scamp!" said the man. "There's another cent shop round the corner. 'Tis very strange, Dixey," added he to his companion, "what's become of all these Pyncheons! Smith, the livery-stable keeper, tells me Judge Pyncheon put his horse up yesterday, to stand till after dinner, and has not taken him away yet. And one of the Judge's hired men has been in, this morning, to make inquiry about him. He's a kind of person, they say, that seldom breaks his habits, or stays out o' nights."

"Oh, he'll turn up safe enough!" said Dixey. "And as for Old Maid Pyncheon, take my word for it, she has run in debt, and gone off from her creditors. I foretold, you remember, the first morning she set up shop, that her devilish scowl would frighten away customers. They couldn't stand it!"

"I never thought she'd make it go," remarked his friend. "This business of cent shops is overdone among the women-folks. My wife tried it, and lost five dollars on her outlay!"

"Poor business!" said Dixey, shaking his head. "Poor business!"

In the course of the morning, there were various other attempts to open a communication with the supposed inhabitants of this silent and impenetrable mansion. The man of root beer came, in his neatly painted wagon, with a couple of dozen full bottles, to be exchanged for empty ones; the baker, with a lot of crackers which Hepzibah had ordered for her retail custom; the butcher, with a nice titbit which he fancied she would be eager to secure for Clifford. Had any observer of these proceedings been aware of the fearful secret hidden within the house, it would have affected him with a singular shape and modification of horror, to see the current of human life making this small eddy hereabouts—whirling sticks, straws, and all such trifles, round and round, right over the black depth where a dead corpse lay unseen!

The butcher was so much in earnest with his sweetbread of lamb, or whatever the dainty might be, that he tried every accessible door of the Seven Gables, and at length came round again to the shop, where he ordinarily found admittance.

"It's a nice article, and I know the old lady would jump at it," said he to himself. "She can't be gone away! In fifteen years that I have driven my cart through Pyncheon Street, I've never known her to be away from home; though often enough, to be sure, a man might knock all day without bringing her to the door. But that was when she'd only herself to provide for."

Peeping through the same crevice of the curtain where, only a little while before, the urchin of elephantine appetite had peeped, the butcher beheld the inner door, not closed, as the child had seen it, but ajar, and almost wide open.

However it might have happened, it was the fact. Through the passageway there was a dark vista into the lighter but still obscure interior of the parlor. It appeared to the butcher that he could pretty clearly discern what seemed to be the stalwart legs, clad in black pantaloons, of a man sitting in a large oaken chair, the back of which concealed all the remainder of his figure. This contemptuous tranquillity on the part of an occupant of the house, in response to the butcher's indefatigable efforts to attract notice, so piqued the man of flesh that he determined to withdraw.

"So," thought he, "there sits Old Maid Pyncheon's bloody brother, while I've been giving myself all this trouble! Why, if a hog hadn't more manners, I'd stick him! I call it demeaning a man's business to trade with such people; and from this time forth, if they want a sausage or an ounce of liver, they shall run after the cart for it!"

He tossed the titbit angrily into his cart, and drove off in a pet.

Not a great while afterwards, there was a sound of music turning the corner, and approaching down the street, with several intervals of silence, and then a renewed and nearer outbreak of brisk melody. A mob of children was seen moving onward, or stopping, in unison with the sound, which appeared to proceed from the center of the throng; so that they were loosely bound together by slender strains of harmony, and drawn along captive; with ever and anon an accession of some little fellow in an apron and straw hat, capering forth from door or gateway. Arriving under the shadow of the Pyncheon Elm, it proved to be the Italian boy, who, with his monkey and show of puppets, had once before played his hurdy-gurdy beneath the arched window. The pleasant face of Phoebe—and doubtless, too, the liberal recompense which she had flung him—still dwelt in his remembrance. His expressive features kindled up, as he recognized the spot where this trifing incident of his erratc life had chanced. He entered the neglected yard (now wilder than ever, with its growth of hogweed and burdock), stationed himself on the doorstep of the main entrance, and, opening his show box, began to play. Each individual of the automatic community forthwith set to work, according to his or her proper vocation: the monkey, taking off his Highland bonnet, bowed and scraped to the bystanders most obsequiously, with ever an observant eye to pick up a stray cent; and the young foreigner himself, as he turned the crank of his machine, glanced upward to the arched window, expectant of a presence that would make his music the livelier and sweeter. The throng of children stood near; some on the sidewalk; some within the yard; two or three establishing themselves on the very doorsteps; and one squatting on the threshold. Meanwhile, the locust kept singing in the great old Pyncheon Elm.

"I don't hear anybody in the house," said one of the children to another. "The monkey won't pick up anything here."

"There is somebody at home," affirmed the urchin on the threshold. "I heard a step!"

Still the young Italian's eye turned sidelong upward; and it really seemed as if the touch of genuine, though slight and almost playful, emotion communicated a juicier sweetness to the dry, mechanical process of his minstrelsy. These wanderers are readily responsive to any natural kindness—be it no more than a smile, or a word itself not understood, but only a warmth in it—which befalls them on the roadside of life. They remember these things, because they are the little enchantments which, for the instant—for the space that reflects a landscape in a soap bubble—build up a home about them. Therefore, the Italian boy would not be discouraged by the heavy silence with which the old house seemed resolute to clog the vivacity of his instrument. He persisted in his melodious appeals; he still looked upward, trusting that his dark, alien countenance would soon be brightened by Phoebe's sunny aspect. Neither could he be willing to depart without again beholding Clifford, whose sensibility, like Phoebe's smile, had talked a kind of heart's language to the foreigner. He repeated all his music over and over again, until his auditors were getting weary. So were the little wooden people in his show box, and the monkey most of all. There was no response, save the singing of the locust.

"No children live in this house," said a schoolboy, at last. "Nobody lives here but an old maid and an old man. You'll get nothing here! Why don't you go along?"

"You fool, you, why do you tell him?" whispered a shrewd little Yankee, caring nothing for the music, but a good deal for the cheap rate at which it was had. "Let him play as long as he likes! If there's nobody to pay him, that's his own lookout!"

Once more, however, the Italian ran over his round of melodies. To the common observer—who could understand nothing of the case, except the music and the sunshine on the hither side of the door—it might have been amusing to watch the pertinacity of the street performer. Will he succeed at last? Will that stubborn door be suddenly flung open? Will a group of joyous children, the young ones of the house, come dancing, shouting, laughing, into the open air, and cluster round the show box, looking with eager merriment at the puppets, and tossing each a copper for long-tailed Mammon, the monkey, to pick up?

But to us, who know the inner heart of the Seven Gables as well as its exterior face, there is a ghastly effect in this repetition of light popular tunes at its doorstep. It would be an ugly business, indeed, if Judge Pyncheon (who would not have cared a fig for Paganini's fiddle in his most harmonious mood) should make his appearance at the door, with a bloody shirt bosom, and a grim frown on his swarthily white visage, and motion the foreign vagabond away! Was ever before such a grinding out of jigs and waltzes, where nobody was in the queue to dance? Yes, very often. This contrast, or intermingling of tragedy with mirth, happens daily, hourly, momently. The gloomy and desolate old house, deserted of life, and with awful Death sitting sternly in its solitude, was the emblem of many a human heart, which, nevertheless, is compelled to hear the thrill and echo of the world's gaiety around it.

Before the conclusion of the Italian's performance, a couple of men happened to be passing, on their way to dinner.

"I say, you young French fellow!" called out one of them. "Come away from that doorstep, and go somewhere else with your nonsense! The Pyncheon family live there; and they are in great trouble, just about this time. They don't feel musical today. It is reported all over town that Judge Pyncheon, who owns the house, has been murdered; and the city marshal is going to look into the matter. So be off with you, at once!"

As the Italian shouldered his hurdy-gurdy, he saw on the doorstep a card, which had been covered, all the morning, by the newspaper that the carrier had flung upon it, but was now shuffled into sight. He picked it up, and perceiving something written in pencil, gave it to the man to read. In fact, it was an engraved card of Judge Pyncheon's with certain penciled memoranda on the back, referring to various businesses which it had been his purpose to transact during the preceding day. It formed a prospective epitome of the day's history; only that affairs had not turned out altogether in accordance with the program. The card must have been lost from the Judge's vest pocket, in his preliminary attempt to gain access by the main entrance of the house. Though well soaked with rain, it was still partially legible.

"Look here, Dixey!" cried the man. "This has something to do with Judge Pyncheon. See! Here's his name printed on it; and here, I suppose, is some of his handwriting."

"Let's go to the city marshal with it!" said Dixey. "It may give him just the clue he wants. After all," whispered he in his companion's ear, "it would be no wonder if the Judge has gone into that door and never come out again! A certain cousin of his may have been at his old tricks. And Old Maid Pyncheon having got herself in debt by the cent shop—and the Judge's pocketbook being well filled—and bad blood amongst them already! Put all these things together and see what they make!"

"Hush, hush!" whispered the other. "It seems like a sin to be the first to speak of such a thing. But I think, with you, that we had better go to the city marshal."

"Yes, yes!" said Dixey. "Well! I always said there was something devilish in that woman's scowl!"

The men wheeled about, accordingly, and retraced their steps up the street. The Italian, also, made the best of his way off, with a parting glance up at the arched window. As for the children, they took to their heels, with one accord, and scampered as if some giant or ogre were in pursuit, until, at a good distance from the house, they stopped as suddenly and simultaneously as they had set out. Their susceptible nerves took an indefinite alarm from what they had overheard. Looking back at the grotesque peaks and shadowy angles of the old mansion, they fancied a gloom diffused about it which no brightness of the sunshine could dispel. An imaginary Hepzibah scowled and shook her finger at them, from several windows at the same moment. An imaginary Clifford—for (and it would have deeply wounded him to know it) he had always been a horror to these small people—stood behind the unreal Hepzibah, making awful gestures, in a faded dressing gown. Children are even more apt, if possible, than grown people to catch the contagion of a panic terror. For the rest of the day, the more timid went whole streets about, for the sake of avoiding the Seven Gables; while the bolder signalized their hardihood by challenging their comrades to race past the mansion at full speed.

It could not have been more than half an hour after the disappearance of the Italian boy, with his unseasonable melodies, when a cab drove down the street. It stopped beneath the Pyncheon Elm; the cabman took a trunk, a canvas bag, and a bandbox from the top of his vehicle, and deposited them on the doorstep of the old house; a straw bonnet, and then the pretty figure of a young girl came into view from the interior of the cab. It was Phoebe! Though not altogether so blooming as when she first tripped into our story—for, in the few intervening weeks, her experiences had made her graver, more womanly, and deeper-eyed, in token of a heart that had begun to suspect its depths—still there was the quiet glow of natural sunshine over her. Neither had she forfeited her proper gift of making things look real, rather than fantastic, within her sphere. Yet we feel it to be a questionable venture, even for Phoebe, at this juncture, to cross the threshold of the Seven Gables. Is her healthful presence potent enough to chase away the crowd of pale, hideous, and sinful phantoms that have gained admittance there since her departure? Or will she, likewise, fade, sicken, sadden, and grow into deformity, and be only another pallid phantom, to glide noiselessly up and down the stairs, and affright children as she pauses at the window?

At least, we would gladly forewarn the unsuspecting girl that there is nothing in human shape or substance to receive her, unless it be the figure of Judge Pyncheon, who—wretched spectacle that he is, and frightful in our remembrance, since our night-long vigil with him!—still keeps his place in the oaken chair.

Phoebe first tried the shop door. It did not yield to her hand; and the white curtain, drawn across the window which formed the upper section of the door, struck her quick perceptive faculty as something unusual. Without making another effort to enter here, she betook herself to the great portal, under the arched window. Finding it fastened, she knocked. A reverberation came from the emptiness within. She knocked again, and a third time; and, listening intently, fancied that the floor creaked, as if Hepzibah were coming, with her ordinary tiptoe movement, to admit her. But so dead a silence ensued upon this imaginary sound, that she began to question whether she might not have mistaken the house, familiar as she thought herself with its exterior.

Her notice was now attracted by a child's voice, at some distance. It appeared to call her name. Looking in the direction whence it proceeded, Phoebe saw little Ned Higgins, a good way down the street, stamping, shaking his head violently, making deprecatory gestures with both hands, and shouting to her at mouth-wide screech.

"No, no, Phoebe!" he screamed. "Don't you go in! There's something wicked there! Don't—don't—don't go in!"

But, as the little personage could not be induced to approach near enough to explain himself, Phoebe concluded that he had been frightened, on some of his visits to the shop, by her cousin Hepzibah; for the good lady's manifestations, in truth, ran about an equal chance of scaring children out of their wits, or compelling them to unseemly laughter. Still, she felt the more, for this incident, how unaccountably silent and impenetrable the house had become. As her next resort, Phoebe made her way into the garden, where on so warm and bright a day as the present, she had little doubt of finding Clifford, and perhaps Hepzibah also, idling away the noontide in the shadow of the arbor. Immediately on her entering the garden gate, the family of hens half ran, half flew, to meet her; while a strange grimalkin, which was prowling under the parlor window, took to his heels, clambered hastily over the fence, and vanished. The arbor was vacant and its floor, table, and circular bench were still damp, and bestrewn with twigs and the disarray of the past storm. The growth of the garden seemed to have got quite out of bounds; the weeds had taken advantage of Phoebe's absence, and the long-continued rain, to run rampant over the flowers and kitchen vegetables. Maule's well had overflowed its stone border, and made a pool of formidable breadth in that corner of the garden.

The impression of the whole scene was that of a spot where no human foot had left its print for many preceding days—probably not since Phoebe's departure—for she saw a side comb of her own under the table of the arbor, where it must have fallen on the last afternoon when she and Clifford sat there.

The girl knew that her two relatives were capable of far greater oddities than that of shutting themselves up in their old house, as they appeared now to have done. Nevertheless, with indistinct misgivings of something amiss, and apprehensions to which she couid not give shape, she approached the door that formed the customary communication between the house and garden. It was secured within, like the two which she had already tried. She knocked, however; and immediately, as if the application had been expected, the door was drawn open, by a considerable exertion of some unseen person's strength, not wide, but far enough to afford her a side-long entrance. As Hepzibah, in order not to expose herself to inspection from without, invariably opened a door in this manner, Phoebe necessarily concluded that it was her cousin who now admitted her.

Without hesitation, therefore, she stepped across the threshold, and had no sooner entered than the door closed behind her.

XX

The Flower of Eden

PHOEBE, coming so suddenly from the sunny daylight, was altogether bedimmed in such density of shadow as lurked in most of the passages of the old house. She was not at first aware by whom she had been admitted. Before her eyes had adapted themselves to the obscurity, a hand grasped her own, with a firm but gentle and warm pressure, thus imparting a welcome which caused her heart to leap and thrill with an indefinable shiver of enjoyment. She felt herself drawn along, not towards the parlor, but into a large and unoccupied apartment, which had formerly been the grand reception room of the Seven Gables. The sunshine came freely into all the uncurtained windows of this room, and fell upon the dusty floor; so that Phoebe now clearly saw—what, indeed, had been no secret, after the encounter of a warm hand with hers—that it was not Hepzibah nor Clifford, but Holgrave, to whom she owed her reception. The subtile, intuitive communication, or, rather, the vague and formless impression of something to be told, had made her yield unresistingly to his impulse. Without taking away her hand, she looked eagerly in his face, not quick to forebode evil, but unavoidably conscious that the state of the family had changed since her departure, and therefore anxious for an explanation.

The artist looked paler than ordinary; there was a thoughtful and severe contraction of his forehead, tracing a deep, vertical line between the eyebrows. His smile, however, was full of genuine warmth, and had in it a joy, by far the most vivid expression that Phoebe had ever witnessed, shining out of the New England reserve with which Holgrave habitually masked whatever lay near his heart. It was the look wherewith a man, brooding alone over some fearful object, in a dreary forest, or illimitable desert, would recognize the familiar aspect of his dearest friend, bringing up all the peaceful ideas that belong to home, and the gentle current of everyday affairs. And yet, as he felt the necessity of responding to her look of inquiry, the smile disappeared.

"I ought not to rejoice that you have come, Phoebe," said he. "We meet at a strange moment!"

"What has happened?" she exclaimed. "Why is the house so deserted? Where are Hepzibah and Clifford?"

"Gone! I cannot imagine where they are!" answered Holgrave. "We are alone in the house!"

"Hepzibah and Clifford gone?" cried Phoebe. "It is not possible! And why have you brought me into this room, instead of the parlor? Ah, something terrible has happened! I must run and see!"

"No, no, Phoebe!" said Holgrave, holding her back. "It is as I have told you. They are gone, and I know not whither. A terrible event has, indeed, happened, but not to them, nor, as I undoubtingly believe, through any agency of theirs. If I read your character rightly, Phoebe," he continued, fixing his eyes on hers, with stern anxiety, intermixed with tenderness, "gentle as you are, and seeming to have your sphere among common things, you yet possess remarkable strength. You have wonderful poise, and a faculty which, when tested, will prove itself capable of dealing with matters that fall far out of the ordinary rule."

"Oh, no, I am very weak!" replied Phoebe, trembling. "But tell me what has happened!"

"You are strong!" persisted Holgrave. "You must be both strong and wise; for I am all astray, and need your counsel. It may be you can suggest the one right thing to do!"

"Tell me—tell me!" said Phoebe, all in a tremble. "It oppresses—it terrifies me—this mystery! Anything else I can bear!"

The artist hesitated. Notwithstanding what he had just said, and most sincerely, in regard to the self-balancing power with which Phoebe impressed him, it still seemed almost wicked to bring the awful secret of yesterday to her knowledge. It was like dragging a hideous shape of death into the cleanly and cheerful space before a household fire, where it would present all the uglier aspect, amid the decorousness of everything about it. Yet it could not be concealed from her; she must needs know it.

"Phoebe," said he, "do you remember this?"

He put into her hand a daguerreotype; the same that he had shown her at their first interview in the garden, and which so strikingly brought out the hard and relentless traits of the original.

"What has this to do with Hepzibah and Clifford?" asked Phoebe, with impatient surprise that Holgrave should so trifle with her at such a moment. "It is Judge Pyncheon! You have shown it to me before!"

"But here is the same face, taken within this half hour," said the artist, presenting her with another miniature. "I had just finished it, when I heard you at the door."

"This is death!" shuddered Phoebe, turning very pale. "Judge Pyncheon dead!"

"Such as there represented," said Holgrave, "he sits in the next room. The Judge is dead, and Clifford and Hepzibah have vanished! I know no more. All beyond is conjecture. On returning to my solitary chamber, last evening, I noticed no light, either in the parlor, or Hepzibah's room, or Clifford's; no stir nor footstep about the house. This morning, there was the same deathlike quiet. From my window, I overheard the testimony of a neighbor that your relatives were seen leaving the house, in the midst of yesterday's storm. A rumor reached me, too, of Judge Pyncheon being missed. A feeling which I cannot describe—an indefinite sense of some catastrophe, or consummation—impelled me to make my way into this part of the house, where I discovered what you see. As a point of evidence that may be useful to Clifford, and also as a memorial valuable to myself— for, Phoebe, there are hereditary reasons that connect me strangely with that man's fate—I used the means at my disposal to preserve this pictorial record of Judge Pyncheon's death."

Even in her agitation, Phoebe could not help remarking the calmness of Holgrave's demeanor. He appeared, it is true, to feel the whole awfulness of the Judge's death, yet had received the fact into his mind without any mixture of surprise, but as an event preordained, happening inevitably, and so fitting itself into past occurences that it could almost have been prophesied.

"Why have you not thrown open the doors, and called in witnesses?" inquired she, with a painful shudder. "It is terrible to be here alone!"

"But Clifford!" suggested the artist. "Clifford and Hepzibah! We must consider what is best to be done in their behalf. It is a wretched fatality that they should have disappeared! Their flight will throw the worst coloring over this event of which it is susceptible. Yet how easy is the explanation, to those who know them! Bewildered and terror-stricken by the similarity of this death to a former one, which was attended with such disastrous consequences to Clifford, they have had no idea but of removing themselves from the scene. How miserably unfortunate! Had Hepzibah but shrieked aloud—had Clifford flung wide the door, and proclaimed Judge Pyncheon's death—it would have been, however awful in itself, an event fruitful of good consequences to them. As I view it, it would have gone far towards obliterating the black stain on Clifford's character."

"And how," asked Phoebe, "could any good come from what is so very dreadful?"

"Because," said the artist, "if the matter can be fairly considered and candidly interpreted, it must be evident that Judge Pyncheon could not have come unfairly to his end. This mode of death has been an idiosyncrasy with his family, for generations past; not often occurring, indeed, but, when it does occur, usually attacking individuals about the Judge's time of life, and generally in the tension of some mental crisis, or, perhaps, in an access of wrath. Old Maule's prophecy was probably founded on a knowledge of this physical predisposition in the Pyncheon race. Now, there is a minute and almost exact similarity in the appearances connected with the death that occurred yesterday and those recorded of the death of Clifford's uncle thirty years ago. It is true, there was a certain arrangement of circumstances, unnecessary to be recounted, which made it possible—nay, as men look at these things, probable, or even certain—that old Jaffrey Pyncheon came to a violent death, and by Clifford's hands."

"Whence came those circumstances?" exclaimed Phoebe, "he being innocent, as we know him to be!"

"They were arranged," said Holgrave, "at least, such has long been my conviction—they were arranged after the uncle's death, and before it was made public, by the man who sits in yonder parlor. His own death, so like that former one, yet attended by none of those suspicious once a punishment for his wickedness, and making plain the innocence of Clifford. But this flight—it distorts everything! He may be in concealment, near at hand. Could we but bring him back before the discovery of the Judge's death, the evil might be rectified."

"We must not hide this thing a moment longer!" said Phoebe. "It is dreadful to keep it so closely in our hearts. Clifford is innocent. God will make it manifest! Let us throw open the doors, and call all the neighborhood to see the truth!"

"You are right, Phoebe," rejoined Holgrave. "Doubtless you are right."

Yet the artist did not feel the horror, which was proper to Phoebe's sweet and order-loving character, at thus finding herself at issue with society, and brought in contact with an event that transcended ordinary rules. Neither was he in haste, like her, to betake himself within the precincts of common life. On the contrary, he gathered a wild enjoyment—as it were, a flower of strange beauty, growing in a desolate spot, and blossoming in the wind—such a flower of momentary happiness he gathered from his present position. It separated Phoebe and himself from the world, and bound them to each other, by their exclusive knowledge of Judge Pyncheon's mysterious death, and the counsel which they were forced to hold respecting it. The secret, so long as it should continue such, kept them within the circle of a spell, a solitude in the midst of men, a remoteness as entire as that of an island in midocean; once divulged, the ocean would flow betwixt them, standing on its widely sundered shores. Meanwhile, all the circumstances of their situation seemed to draw them together; they were like two children who go hand in hand, pressing closely to one another's side, through a shadow-haunted passage. The image of awful Death, which filled the house, held them united by his stiffened grasp.

These influences hastened the development of emotions

that might not otherwise have flowered so. Possibly, indeed, it had been Holgrave's purpose to let them die in their undeveloped germs.

"Why do we delay so?" asked Phoebe. "This secret takes away my breath! Let us throw open the doors!"

"In all our lives there can never come another moment like this!" said Holgrave. "Phoebe, is it all terror—nothing but terror? Are you conscious of no joy, as I am, that has made this the only point of life worth living for?"

"It seems a sin," replied Phoebe, trembling, "to think of joy at such a time!"

"Could you but know, Phoebe, how it was with me the hour before you came!" exclaimed the artist. "A dark, cold, miserable hour! The presence of yonder dead man threw a great black shadow over everything; he made the universe, so far as my perception could reach, a scene of guilt and retribution more dreadful than the guilt. The sense of it took away my youth. I never hoped to feel young again! The world looked strange, wild, evil, hostile; my past life, so lonesome and dreary; my future, a shapeless gloom, which I must mold into gloomy shapes! But, Phoebe, you crossed the threshold; and hope, warmth, and joy came in with you! The black moment became at once a blissful one. It must not pass without the spoken word. I love you!"

"How can you love a simple girl like me?" asked Phoebe, compelled by his earnestness to speak. "You have many, many thoughts, with which I should try in vain to sympathize. And I—I, too—I have tendencies with which you would sympathize as little. That is less matter. But I have not scope enough to make you happy."

"You are my only possibility of happiness!" answered Holgrave. "I have no faith in it, except as you bestow it on me!"

"And then—I am afraid!" continued Phoebe, shrinking towards Holgrave, even while she told him so frankly the doubts with which he affected her. "You will lead me out of my own quiet path. You will make me strive to follow you where it is pathless. I cannot do so. It is not my nature. I shall sink down and perish!"

"Ah, Phoebe!" exclaimed Holgrave, with almost a sigh, and a smile that was burdened with thought. "It will be far otherwise than as you forebode. The world owes all its onward impulses to men ill at ease. The happy man inevitably confines himself within ancient limits. I have a presentiment that, hereafter, it will be my lot to set out trees, to make fences—perhaps, even, in due time, to build a house for another generation—in a word, to conform myself to laws, and the peaceful practice of society. Your poise will be more powerful than any oscillating tendency of mine."

"I would not have it so!" said Phoebe, earnestly.

"Do you love me?" asked Holgrave. "If we love one another, the moment has room for nothing more. Let us pause upon it, and be satisfied. Do you love me, Phoebe?"

"You look into my heart," said she, letting her eyes drop. "You know I love you!"

And it was in this hour, so full of doubt and awe, that the one miracle was wrought without which every human existence is a blank. The bliss which makes all things true, beautiful, and holy shone around this youth and maiden. They were conscious of nothing sad nor old. They transfigured the earth, and made it Eden again, and themselves the two first dwellers in it. The dead man, so close beside them, was forgotten. At such a crisis, there is no death; for immortality is revealed anew, and embraces everything in its hallowed atmosphere.

But how soon the heavy earth dream settled down again!

"Hark!" whispered Phoebe. "Somebody is at the street door!"

"Now let us meet the world!" said Holgrave. "No doubt, the rumor of Judge Pyncheon's visit to this house, and the flight of Hepzibah and Clifford, is about to lead to the investigation of the premises. We have no way but to meet it. Let us open the door at once."

But, to their surprise, before they could reach the street door—even before they quitted the room in which the foregoing interview had passed—they heard footsteps in the farther passage. The door, therefore, which they supposed to be securely locked—which Holgrave, indeed, had seen to be so, and at which Phoebe had vainly tried to enter—must have been opened from without. The sound of footsteps was not harsh, bold, decided, and intrusive, as the gait of strangers would naturally be, making authoritative entrance into a dwelling where they knew themselves unwelcome. It was feeble, as of persons either weak or weary; there was the mingled murmur of two voices, familiar to both the listeners.

"Can it be?" whispered Holgrave.

"It is they!" answered Phoebe. "Thank God! Thank God!"

And then, as if in sympathy with Phoebe's whispered ejaculation, they heard Hepzibah's voice, more distinctly.

"Thank God, my brother, we are at home!"

"Well! Yes! Thank God!" responded Clifford. "A dreary home, Hepzibah! But you have done well to bring me hither! Stay! That parlor door is open. I cannot pass by it! Let me go and rest me in the arbor, where I used—oh, very long ago, it seems to me, after what has befallen us—where I used to be so happy with little Phoebe!"

But the house was not altogether so dreary as Clifford imagined it. They had not made many steps—in truth, they were lingering in the entry, with the listlessness of an accomplished purpose, uncertain what to do next—when Phoebe ran to meet them. On beholding her, Hepzibah burst into tears. With all her might, she had staggered onward beneath the burden of grief and responsibility, until now that it was safe to fling it down. Indeed, she had not energy to fling it down, but had ceased to uphold it, and suffered it to press her to the earth. Clifford appeared the stronger of the two.

"It is our own little Phoebe! Ah, and Holgrave with her," exclaimed he, with a glance of keen and delicate insight, and a smile, beautiful, kind, but melancholy. "I thought of you both, as we came down the street, and beheld Alice's Posies in full bloom. And so the flower of Eden has bloomed, likewise, in this old, darksome house today."

XXI

The Departure

THE sudden death of so prominent a member of the social world as the Honorable Judge Jaffrey Pyncheon created a sensation (at least, in the circles more immediately connected with the deceased), which had hardly quite subsided in a fortnight.

It may be remarked, however, that, of all the events which constitute a person's biography, there is scarcely one—none, certainly, of anything like a similar importance—to which the world so easily reconciles itself as to his death. In most other cases and contingencies, the individual is present among us, mixed up with the daily revolution of affairs, and affording a definite point for observation. At his decease, there is only a vacancy, and a momentary eddy—very small, as compared with the apparent magnitude of the ingurgitated object—and a bubble or two, ascending out of the black depth and bursting at the surface. As regarded Judge Pyncheon, it seemed probable, at first blush, that the mode of his final departure might give him a larger and longer posthumous vogue than ordinarily attends the memory of a distinguished man. But when it came to be understood, on the highest professional authority, that the event was a natural, and—except for some unimportant particulars, denoting a slight idiosyncrasy—by no means an unusual form of death, the public, with its customary alacrity, proceeded to forget that he had ever lived. In short, the honorable Judge was beginning to be a stale subject before half the county newspapers had found time to put their columns in mourning, and publish his exceedingly eulogistic obituary.

Nevertheless, creeping darkly through the places which this excellent person had haunted in his lifetime, there was a hidden stream of private talk, such as it would have shocked all decency to speak loudly at the street corners. It is very singular how the fact of a man's death often seems to give people a truer idea of his character, whether for good or evil, than they have ever possessed while he was living and acting among them. Death is so genuine a fact that it excludes falsehood, or betrays its emptiness; it is a touchstone that proves the gold, and dishonors the baser metal. Could the departed, whoever he may be, return in a week after his decease, he would almost invariably find himself at a higher or lower point than he had formerly occupied, on the scale of public appreciation. But the talk, or scandal, to which we now allude had reference to matters of no less old a date than the supposed murder, thirty or forty years ago, of the late Judge Pyncheon's uncle. The medical opinion, with regard to his own recent and regretted decease, had almost entirely obviated the idea that a murder was committed in the former case. Yet, as the record showed, there were circumstances irrefragably indicating that some person had gained access to old Jaffrey Pyncheon's private apartments, at or near the moment of his death. His desk and private drawers, in a room contiguous to his bedchamber, had been ransacked; money and valuable articles were missing; there was a bloody handprint on the old man's linen; and, by a powerfully welded chain of deductive evidence, the guilt of the robbery and apparent murder had been fixed on Clifford, then residing with his uncle in the House of the Seven Gables.

Whencesoever originating, there now arose a theory that undertook so to account for these circumstances as to exclude the idea of Clifford's agency. Many persons affirmed that the history and elucidation of the facts, long so mysterious, had been obtained by the daguerreotypist from one of those mesmerical seers, who, nowadays, so strangely perplex the aspect of human affairs, and put everybody's natural vision to the blush, by the marvels which they see with their eyes shut.

According to this version of the story, Judge Pyncheon, exemplary as we have portrayed him in our narrative, was, in his youth, an apparently irreclaimable scapegrace. The brutish, the animal instincts, as is often the case, had been developed earlier than the intellectual qualities and the force of character, for which he was afterwards remarkable. He had shown himself wild, dissipated, addicted to low pleasures, little short of ruffianly in his propensities, and recklessly expensive, with no other resources than the bounty of his uncle. This course of conduct had alienated the old bachelor's affection, once strongly fixed upon him. Now it is averred—but whether on authority available in a court of justice, we do not pretend to have investigated—that the young man was tempted by the devil, one night, to search his uncle's private drawers, to which he had unsuspected means of access. While thus criminally occupied, he was startled by the opening of the chamber door. There stood old Jaffrey Pyncheon, in his nightclothes! The surprise of such a discovery, his agitation, alarm, and horror, brought on the crisis of a disorder to which the old bachelor had an hereditary liability; he seemed to choke with blood, and fell upon the floor, striking his temple a heavy blow against the corner of a table. What was to be done? The old man was surely dead! Assistance would come too late! What a misfortune, indeed, should it come too soon, since his reviving consciousness would bring the recollection of the ignominious offense which he had beheld his nephew in the very act of committing!

But he never did revive. With the cool hardihood that always pertained to him, the young man continued his search of the drawers, and found a will, of recent date, in favor of Clifford, which he destroyed, and an older one, in his own favor, which he suffered to remain. But before retiring, Jaffrey bethought himself of the evidence, in these ransacked drawers, that someone had visited the chamber with sinister purposes. Suspicion, unless averted, might fix upon the real offender. In the very presence of the dead man, therefore, he laid a scheme that should free himself at the expense of Clifford, his rival, for whose character he had at once a contempt and a repugnance. It is not probable, be it said, that he acted with any set purpose of involving Clifford in a charge of murder. Knowing that his uncle did not die by violence, it may not have occurred to him, in the hurry of the crisis, that such an inference might be drawn. But, when the affair took this darker aspect, Jaffrey's previous steps had already pledged him to those which remained. So craftily had he arranged the circumstances that, at Clifford's trial, his cousin hardly found it necessary to swear to anything false, but only to withhold the one decisive explanation, by refraining to state what he had himself done and witnessed.

Thus Jaffrey Pyncheon's inward criminality, as regarded Clifford, was, indeed, black and damnable; while its mere outward show and positive commission was the smallest that could possibly consist with so great a sin. This is just the sort of guilt that a man of eminent respectability finds it easiest to dispose of. It was suffered to fade out of sight or be reckoned a venial matter, in the Honorable Judge Pyncheon's long subsequent survey of his own life. He shuffled it aside, among the forgotten and forgiven frailties of his youth, and seldom thought of it again.

We leave the Judge to his repose. He could not be styled fortunate at the hour of death. Unknowingly, he was a childless man, while striving to add more wealth to his only child's inheritance. Hardly a week after his decease, one of the Cunard steamers brought intelligence of the death, by cholera, of Judge Pyncheon's son, just at the point of embarkation for his native land. By this misfortune, Clifford became rich; so did Hepzibah; so did our little village maiden, and, through her, that sworn foe of wealth and all manner of conservatism, the wild reformer—Holgrave!

It was now far too late in Clifford's life for the good opinion of society to be worth the trouble and anguish of a formal vindication. What he needed was the love of a very few; not the admiration, or even the respect, of the unknown many. The latter might probably have been won for him, had those on whom the guardianship of his welfare had fallen deemed it advisable to expose Clifford to a miserable resuscitation of past ideas, when the condition of whatever comfort he might expect lay in the calm of forgetfulness. After such wrong as he had suffered, there is no reparation. The pitiable mockery of it, which the world might have been ready enough to offer, coming so long after the agony had done its utmost work, would have been fit only to provoke bitterer laughter than poor Clifford was ever capable of. It is a truth (and it would be a very sad one but for the higher hopes which it suggests) that no great mistake, whether acted or endured, in our mortal sphere, is ever really set right. Time, the continual vicissitude of circumstances, and the invariable inopportunity of death render it impossible. If, after long lapse of years, the right seems to be in our power, we find no niche to set it in. The better remedy is for the sufferer to pass on, and leave what he once thought his irreparable ruin far behind him.

The shock of Judge Pyncheon's death had a permanently invigorating and ultimately beneficial effect on Clifford. That strong and ponderous man had been Clifford's nightmare. There was no free breath to be drawn, within the sphere of so malevolent an influence. The first effect of freedom, as we have witnessed in Clifford's aimless flight, was a tremulous exhilaration. Subsiding from it, he did not sink into his former intellectual apathy. He never, it is true, attained to nearly the full measure of what might have been his faculties. But he recovered enough of them partially to light up his character, to display some outline of the marvelous grace that was abortive in it, and to make him the object of no less deep, although less melancholy interest than heretofore. He was evidently happy. Could we pause to give another picture of his daily life, with all the appliances now at command to gratify his instinct for the beautiful, the garden scenes, that seemed so sweet to him, would look mean and trivial in comparison.

Very soon after their change of fortune, Clifford, Hepzibah, and little Phoebe, with the approval of the artist, concluded to remove from the dismal old House of the Seven Gables, and take up their abode, for the present, at the elegant country seat of the late Judge Pyncheon. Chanticleer and his family had already been transported thither, where the two hens had forthwith begun an indefatigable process of egg-laying, with an evident design, as a matter of duty and conscience, to continue their illustrious breed under better auspices than for a century past. On the day set for their departure, the principal personages of our story, including good Uncle Venner, were assembled in the parlor.

"The country house is certainly a very fine one, so far as the plan goes," observed Holgrave, as the party were discussing their future arrangements. "But I wonder that the late Judge—being so opulent, and with a reasonable prospect of transmitting his wealth to descendants of his own—should not have felt the propriety of embodying so excellent a piece of domestic architecture in stone, rather than in wood. Then, every generation of the family might have altered the interior, to suit its own taste and convenience; while the exterior, through the lapse of years, might have been adding venerableness to permanence which I consider essential to the happiness of any one moment."

"Why," cried Phoebe, gazing into the artist's face with infinite amazement, "how wonderfully your ideas are changed! A house of stone, indeed! It is but two or three weeks ago that you seemed to wish people to live in something as fragile and temporary as a bird's nest!"

"Ah, Phoebe, I told you how it would be!" said the artist, with a half-melancholy laugh. "You find me a conservative already! Little did I think ever to become one. It is especially unpardonable in this dwelling of so much hereditary misfortune, and under the eye of yonder portrait of a model conservative, who, in that very character, rendered himself so long the evil destiny of his race."

"That picture!" said Clifford, seeming to shrink from its stern glance. "Whenever I look at it, there is an old dreamy recollection haunting me, but keeping just beyond the grasp of my mind. Wealth, it seems to say—boundless wealth—unimaginable wealth! I could fancy that, when I was a child, or a youth, that portrait had spoken, and told me a rich secret, or had held forth its hand, with the written record of hidden opulence. But those old matters are so dim with me, nowadays! What could this dream have been?"

"Perhaps I can recall it," answered Holgrave. "See! There are a hundred chances to one that no person, unacquainted with the secret, would ever touch this spring."

"A secret spring!" cried Clifford. "Ah, I remember now! I did discover it, one summer afternoon, when I was idling and dreaming about the house, long, long ago. But the mystery escapes me."

The artist put his finger on the contrivance to which he

had referred. In former days, the effect would probably have been to cause the picture to start forward. But, in so long a period of concealment, the machinery had been eaten through with rust; so that at Holgrave's pressure, the portrait, frame and all, tumbled suddenly from its position, and lay face downward on the floor. A recess in the wall was thus brought to light, in which lay an object so covered with a century's dust that it could not immediately be recognized as a folded sheet of parchment. Holgrave opened it, and displayed an ancient deed, signed with the hieroglyphics of several Indian sagamores, and conveying to Colonel Pyncheon and his heirs, forever, a vast extent of territory at the eastward.

"This is the very parchment the attempt to recover which cost the beautiful Alice Pyncheon her happiness and life," said the artist, alluding to his legend. "It is what the Pyncheons sought in vain, while it was valuable; and now that they find the treasure, it has long been worthless."

"Poor Cousin Jaffrey! This is what deceived him," exclaimed Hepzibah. "When they were young together, Clifford probably made a kind of fairy tale of this discovery. He was always dreaming hither and thither about the house, and lighting up its dark corners with beautiful stories. And poor Jaffrey, who took hold of everything as if it were real, thought my brother had found out his uncle's wealth. He died with this delusion in his mind!"

"But," said Phoebe, apart to Holgrave, "how came you to know the secret?"

"My dearest Phoebe," said Holgrave, "how will it please you to assume the name of Maule? As for the secret, it is the only inheritance that has come down to me from my ancestors. You should have known sooner (only that I was afraid of frightening you away) that, in this long drama of wrong and retribution, I represent the old wizard, and am probably as much a wizard as ever he was. The son of the executed Matthew Maule, while building this house, took the opportunity to construct that recess, and hide away the Indian deed, on which depended the immense land claim of the Pyncheons. Thus they bartered their Eastern territory for Maule's garden ground."

"And now," said Uncle Venner, "I suppose their whole claim is not worth one man's share in my farm yonder!"

"Uncle Venner," cried Phoebe, taking the patched philosopher's hand, "you must never talk any more about your farm! You shall never go there, as long as you live! There is a cottage in our new garden—the prettiest little yellowish-brown cottage you ever saw; and the sweetest-looking place, for it looks just as if it were made of gingerbread—and we are going to fit it up and furnish it, on purpose for you. And you shall do nothing but what you choose, and shall be as happy as the day is long, and shall keep Cousin Clifford in spirits with the wisdom and pleasantness which is always dropping from your lips!"

"Ah, my dear child," quoth good Uncle Venner, quite overcome, "if you were to speak to a young man as you do to an old one, his chance of keeping his heart another minute would not be worth one of the buttons on my waist-coat! And—soul alive!—that great sigh, which you made me heave, has burst off the very last of them! But, never mind! It was the happiest sigh I ever did heave; and it seems as if I must have drawn in a gulp of heavenly breath, to make it with. Well, well, Miss Phoebe! They'll miss me in the gardens hereabouts, and round by the back doors; and Pyncheon Street, I'm afraid, will hardly look the same without old Uncle Venner, who remembers it with a mowing field on one side, and the garden of the Seven Gables on the other. But either I must go to your country seat, or you must come to my farm—that's one of two things certain; and I leave you to choose which!"

"Oh, come with us, by all means, Uncle Venner!" said Clifford, who had a remarkable enjoyment of the old man's mellow, quiet, and simple spirit. "I want you always to be within five minutes' saunter of my chair. You are the only philosopher I ever knew of whose wisdom has not a drop of bitter essence at the bottom!"

"Dear me!" cried Uncle Venner, beginning partly to realize what manner of man he was. "And yet folks used to set me down among the simple ones, in my younger days! But I suppose I am like a Roxbury russet—a great deal the better, the longer I can be kept. Yes; and my words of wisdom, that you and Phoebe tell me of, are like the golden dandelions, which never grow in the hot months, but may be seen glistening among the withered grass, and under the dry

leaves, sometimes as late as December. And you are welcome, friends, to my mess of dandelions, if there were twice
as many!"

A plain, but handsome, dark-green barouche had now
drawn up in front of the ruinous portal of the old mansion
house. The party came forth, and (with the exception of
good Uncle Venner, who was to follow in a few days)
proceeded to take their places. They were chatting and
laughing very pleasantly together; and—as proves to be
often the case, at moments when we ought to palpitate with
sensibility—Clifford and Hepzibah bade a final farewell to
the abode of their forefathers with hardly more emotion
than if they had made it their arrangement to return thither
at tea time. Several children were drawn to the spot by so
unusual a spectacle as the barouche and pair of gray horses.
Recognizing little Ned Higgins among them, Hepzibah put
her hand into her pocket, and presented the urchin, her
earliest and staunchest customer, with silver enough to people the Domdaniel cavern of his interior with as various a
procession of quadrupeds as passed into the ark.

Two men were passing, just as the barouche drove off.

"Well, Dixey," said one of them, "what do you think of
this? My wife kept a cent shop three months, and lost five
dollars on her outlay. Old Maid Pyncheon has been in trade
just about as long, and rides off in her carriage with a
couple of hundred thousand—reckoning her share, and Clifford's, and Phoebe's—and some say twice as much! If you
choose to call it luck, it is all very well; but if we are to take
it as the will of Providence, why, I can't exactly fathom it!"

"Pretty good business!" quoth the sagacious Dixey. "Pretty
good business!"

Maule's well, all this time, though left in solitude, was
throwing up a succession of kaleidoscopic pictures in which
a gifted eye might have seen foreshadowed the coming
fortunes of Hepzibah and Clifford, and the descendant of
the legendary wizard, and the village maiden, over whom he
had thrown Love's web of sorcery. The Pyncheon Elm,
moreover, with what foliage the September gale had spared
to it, whispered unintelligible prophecies. And wise Uncle
Venner, passing slowly from the ruinous porch, seemed to
hear a strain of music, and fancied that sweet Alice

Pyncheon—after witnessing these deeds, this bygone woe and this present happiness, of her kindred mortals—had given one farewell touch of a spirit's joy upon her harpsichord, as she floated heavenward from the House of the Seven Gables!

O

SIGNET CLASSICS by American Authors

OUTSTANDING EUROPEAN WORKS

☐ **DUBLINERS by James Joyce.** With an Introduction by Edna O'Brien.
(525434—$3.99)

☐ **VICTORY by Joseph Conrad.** With an Introduction by Frederick Karl.
(525310—$3.95)

☐ **CANDIDE, ZADIG, and Selected Stories by Voltaire.** Translated and with an Introduction by Donald Frame. (524268—$2.95)

☐ **ANNA KARENINA by Leo Tolstoy.** Foreword by David Magarshack.
(524497—$4.50)

☐ **WAR AND PEACE by Leo Tolstoy.** Translated by Ann Dunnigan. Edited and with an Introduction by J. O. Bayley. (523261—$6.95)

☐ **THE SORROWS OF YOUNG WERTHER and SELECTED WRITINGS by Johann Wolfgang von Goethe.** Foreword by Hermann J. Weigand. Translated by Catherine Hutter. Glossary, Notes. (523032—$4.95)

☐ **SILAS MARNER by George Eliot.** Afterword by Walter Allen.
(524276—$2.50)

☐ **IVANHOE by Sir Walter Scott.** Afterword by Compton MacKenzie. Notes, Index and Glossary. (521943—$4.50)

Prices slightly higher in Canada.

SIGNET CLASSICS for Your Library